Deer Island in Autumn

VOLUME ONE

by
ROBERT J. BLACKWELL JR.

PAGE PUBLISHING, INC.
New York, NY

First originally published by Page Publishing, Inc. 2016

ISBN 978-1-68409-002-0 (pbk)
ISBN 978-1-68289-917-5 (digital)

Printed in the United States of America

Abstract

Deer Island is a real place! Though fictionalized, the characters accurately portray life in the lower Atchafalaya River basin (specific to Terrebonne Parish, Louisiana) and its tributaries from 1840–1921.

The Addison family legacy is expressed in the meticulously kept diaries of three generations of the family's matriarchs.

Each of the two volumes can stand on its own merits, but the story invites the reader to experience both.

The Author

Comments from a couple of readers:

"When I began reading *Deer Island in Autumn*, I just could not put the book down; it brought back many of my childhood memories. I could have been either of the two young girl characters. I believe this book is a cross between *Treasure Island* and *TheSwiss Family Robinson*; it has elements of both."

—*Alma C. Richard*

" For readers in like mood for a rare story of life in *Bayou Country*, *Deer Island in Autumn* is just the thing. Whether it's explicating, justifying, or celebrating life in Terrebonne Parish in the mid-nineteenth century, this story goes down quickly and easily, just like a glass of ice tea in the summer."

—*Alice R. Fields*

Deer Island in Autumn
Volume One
Building the Family Legacy
A novel by
Robert J. Blackwell Jr.

There is no intended resemblance between the characters of this novel and any people, living or dead.

Though the geographic areas are readily identified on any map of southeastern Louisiana, the characters of this story who settle these locations and who contribute to the establishment of the various communities never existed; the colors used to paint their portraits, however, are definitive and recognizable and true.

Robert J. Blackwell Jr.

Acknowledgments

This novel is dedicated to the memory of Alma C. Richard who was the first person to completely read and critique its contents. Her evaluation was inspirational, and it was she who farmed out the manuscript for other educators to review. She orchestrated an invitation for me to appear before the Terrebonne Parish Literary Society and to give a presentation of *Deer Island in Autumn*. Several of the society members had read my manuscript by this time with rave reviews. They received me well and encouraged me to pursue publication. Their confidence in the book's merits continued to influence the course of my efforts to publish, and I am sincerely grateful for their assistance.

I would also like to thank Tammy B. Daigle for her assistance in preparing the manuscript for final editing; I recognize the hard work she offered was a true blessing.

I would like to thank Hugh Paul St. Martin III for his encouragement and advice for getting this work into print for the general public to enjoy.

I would like to thank my son, Robert J. Blackwell III, for his contribution to this work. All signed pictures are examples of his hard work.

I would like to thank Stacey Lynn Liner for the use of her image in the daguerreotype of Pauline Longere. I would also like to thank Callie Rose Courteaux, a direct descendant of a Houmas Indian chieftain for the use of her image as inspiration for the sketch of Princess Kallie.

Preface

Most Americans know that Louisiana was settled and populated by Spanish and French colonists. There were peoples from many other areas of Europe who made their way to the vast untamed wilderness of the Louisiana Territory.

Though the colony was governed by France, then Spain, and then France again, before being sold to the United States by Napoleon, the kings of these two countries had a common allegiance, which played an important role in the development and history of Louisiana. Close ties to Rome, exemplified by aggressive determination to keep the colony exclusively Catholic, resulted in the repression of other forms of religious expression, which might otherwise have begun to take hold and flourish.

Further support demonstrating the powerful influence that these religious ideals spread can be readily seen in the lives of native Louisianans. The natives who live on the banks of the various bayous, later to become lower Terrebonne Parish, are descendants of the Chitimachas and Oumas (Houmas) Indians. They have long ago abandoned their languages and religious practices. Their native tongue was replaced by French and their religious culture was replaced by the ceremony and rituals of Roman Catholicism.

With French Catholicism firmly entrenched, English immigrants who came to "bayou country" found themselves floundering in the pursuit of their dreams for a fresh start in this new land. Treated with much disdain by the magisterial populace, religious and other social pressures forced many of *"les Americains"* to inhabit the most remote wetlands and ridges of extreme South Louisiana. Many early English immigrants lived in cabins affixed on wooden barges, moving their families from one bayou or lake to another, seeking to gain a foothold on "terra firma"; meanwhile, they carved out a meager existence by hunting, trapping and fishing. Having no land grants, many Anglicans were forced to occupy lands considered by most to be uninhabitable.

Early immigrants who came to the Louisiana Territory soon discovered that life was difficult for everyone. Those who inhabited the coastlines had to overcome many challenges, including violent storms (hurricanes),the fever, pestilence and mosquito-borne diseases, poisonous snakes, alligators, and every imaginable inconvenience. Staying alive was challenge enough for most.

In those early days, nearly everyone knew what it was like to be cold and hungry and hot and miserable. Over time, these common experiences began to slowly break down the stiff-necked cultural and spiritual separatism that existed when Joseph and Josephine Addison arrived in South Louisiana in 1840.

Unlike many other early English immigrants who came to bayou country, Joseph and Josephine would have a great advantage. A relative, a man of influence in Louisiana government, would provide them with the means for the realization of their dreams.

Though the characters in this story have been fictionalized, the essence of their lives and livelihoods is a genuine conception of life as it existed for one English couple who arrived in an American Louisiana when she was young and continuing to adapt from its long history of Spanish and French influence, especially in the Louisiana Territory.

Under a government "of the people, by the people, and for the people" Louisiana's multicultural heritage was simply relegated to

Louisiana living. This served to create the cultural mystique known throughout the world as unique to South Louisiana.

American politicians had begun to translate their power and influence into money and vast landholdings. A young Louisiana congressman, Patrick J. Adams, knew the privileges that were afforded to ambitious political devotees. A consistent rise in his means for living since his election to office some twenty years earlier prompted him to write a letter to his nephew in Southampton England.

The family legacy begins with the diary of Josephine Moore. She shares plans for her wedding to Joseph Addison, the congressman's nephew. Her first entry describes their nuptial arrangements and the events surrounding their upcoming marriage ceremony on January 5, 1836. She records events that led to their decision to leave England for an American Louisiana. She shares the experiences of the journey, which culminates in their arrival at the site that would become their home.

Establishing a family tradition, the Addisons celebrate Thanksgiving Day shortly after completing the construction of the "little house." God's hand in their destiny became increasingly evident as they arrived safely in New Orleans, having successfully sailed the vast expanses of the Atlantic Ocean and the Gulf of Mexico. Uncle Patrick's willingness to share his good fortune and his plans for the establishment of a settlement on a remote island in the lower Atchafalaya River Basin held great promise and a bright future for Joseph and Josephine Addison. Now, with a roof over their heads, it was time to give thanks.

The arrival of fall is being announced by brilliant colorful changes seen in the virgin forest poised atop ridges standing in the swamps along the river basin. A vast network of bayous and streams lends access to the high ground as they wind through endless miles of cypress and hardwood forest and vast tracts of open golden prairie undulating with each rise and fall of the tide. Northern breezes portend imminent cold as the approaching winter helps set the stage for the festive occasion that nature will host in the wilderness paradise.

Deer Island in Autumn

Prologue

There is a wilderness paradise where time is only significant when it welcomes or bids farewell to one of its consumers. Those who are bid adieu are preserved, for posterity's sake, by sharing their lives and experiences through the art of storytelling.

Deer Island is a place where the fabric of life is tightly woven; mutual interests are cultivated. Each shared expression of some heartfelt emotion, each account of some uncommon event, each expounded detail of some ideal or conviction, each celebration of life and living communicated unashamedly and in a forthright manner, produces a colored fiber. The hues of these threads may be brilliant and appealing, or they may be dim and dismal, but each is applied to the pattern of the weave for all to witness.

This "Garden of Eden" is a place where love drives the potter's wheel and guides the potter's hands. Each artist does his part in fashioning the ever changing masterpiece; as new pieces of clay are added and others removed, the essence of its character is enhanced—whose substance is the family legacy.

Autumn is a special time of the year on the densely forested ridge, a season when nature hosts and affords the means for the fulfillment of the wildest aspirations of its guests. Those who follow in the footsteps of the young couple, who left Southampton, England, seeking adventure and braving every uncertainty for the opportunity to begin anew in a distant land, in America when she was not yet assured of her sovereignty.

Deer Island in Autumn

Illustrations

Deer Island in Autumn
Volume One
Building A
Family Legacy

Introduction

Our story begins as twelve-year-old Nora Addison reviews the diary of her great-grandmother, Josephine Addison. Her most cherished possession, the written legend, was presented to her as a gift on her tenth birthday by her uncle, Justin Addison. Knowing that Nora was a brighʳ child and an avid reader, her uncle has hope that his little niece will be inspired to start her own diary, thus preserving the family history for future generations.

Chapter One

BUILDING A FAMILY LEGACY

THE WEDDING AND THE INVITATION

Twelve-year-old Nora Addison is reviewing one of her most cherished possessions. The following are excerpts from the diary of her great grand-mother, Josephine Moore Addison.

December 25, 1835

We are spending Christmas holiday with Joseph and his family. Final plans for our wedding ceremony have been completed. The matrimonial vows will be pronounced on the fifth of January, 1836. At that time, I will assume the name of my betrothed.

December 28, 1835

My maids of honor, Victoria Ramsey, Elizabeth Blackett, and Diana Eddington, were all fitted for their ceremonial gowns over a month ago. I just received notification that the dresses are ready to be picked up at any convenient time. The white, long flowing gowns have puffed sleeves and are decoratively trimmed in elegant lace. A lavender sash highlights the waist and matches the hats that are also that color. The hats are adorned with white lacing and will be garnished with pink and white carnations. Our flower girl will carry a lavender wickerwork basket, which will be filled with pink and white carnations.

Joseph has chosen three of his friends to be groomsmen. He will turn away from tradition, insisting that all three gentlemen will be his "best man." Edward Halley, Andrew Johnson, and Samuel Marlowe, will dress in three piece gray suits with brilliant white shirts and lavender bow ties. Each will have a white carnation pinned to his lapel.

My heart pounds excitedly with each passing moment. I find myself filled with wild anticipation as this wondrous occasion draws near. The joyous pleasantries surrounding this great event have overwhelmed me. I cannot imagine life as being any more fulfilling than what I have already been privileged to experience.

January 4, 1836

Victoria, Elizabeth, Diana, and me, are going to enjoy a picnic luncheon in the country today. Grandfather Moore's farm will host this outdoor affair. The serenity of his well-kept dairy will serve to allure, captivate, and delight those who sojourn with us there. The vast expanses of pasture land, the occasional groves of mature evergreens, the white-washed fences, which serve to divide and delineate the property boundaries, and the magnificent gazebo in the center of grandmother's rose garden will enhance our enjoyment.

The sunshine was refreshing on this moderately cold winter day. Deserving special mention is the delightful time we had listening to grandfather reminiscing about "life with grandmother Moore." His generous portrayal of their fifty-two years of marriage and his candid depiction of a three-year courtship, which was almost thwarted by a rival suitor, engaged us in a cavalcade of emotion prompted by accounts of suspense, unbridled love, and the challenges and rewards of an undying relationship.

Grandmother was noticeably moved by grandfather's self-described determination to make Marianne Becket his wife. "Nothing was going to keep me from having my dear Marianne's hand," he boasted, tenderly clasping his hand to hers.

Grandmother's tearing eyes revealed to me the depth of the love and affection she has for the man who won her heart so many years ago. Wanting desperately to identify with her experiences, I look forward with great expectation for my own romantic interludes with the man who won my heart, Joseph Addison.

January 5, 1836

At last, the day has come! I will be leaving for the church at 9:00 a.m this morning. I will meet my betrothed and finalize my promise to become Joseph's wife. Immediately following the ceremony, Joseph and I will be leaving for Plymouth where we will consummate the marriage and go on holiday. I sign my name here one last time as Josephine Moore.

–Josephine Moore

January 12, 1836

Joseph and I are enjoying an extended holiday just outside Plymouth. We will be spending ten glorious days at a cottage owned by Joseph's family. The weather has been splendid. We only had one gully-washer since our arrival here a week ago. We borrowed a horse and surrey from Grandfather Moore, and we have spent many hours touring the countryside. The marital bliss I am experiencing is beyond what I am capable of expressing. I am confident I have made the right choice for a life-long companion in Joseph. He is a real sweetheart. We are having great fun and wholesome fellowship as we relish in the splendor.

January 22, 1836

We returned to Southampton late this evening. I am completely exhausted from the trip home. I will be spending my first night in our newly rented home. It is not very large, but quite suitable for our needs. Tomorrow I will begin getting accustomed to the duties of keeping the home. I have been practicing signing my new name.

Josephine Moore Addison

January 31, 1836

Joseph received a letter today from America. His uncle, Patrick Adams, is a distinguished politician from New Orleans, Louisiana. He has served in the United States Congress for the past twenty years. Joseph informed me that his uncle has acquired vast land holdings through his astute political engineering. His Uncle Patrick, a bachelor with no nuptial aspiration, wrote the letter to invite us to move to Louisiana to share in his good fortune. I hereby reveal the entirety of his correspondence exactly as it appeared—I even traced his signature.

FROM THE CONGRESSIONAL DESK OF LOUISIANA STATESMAN AND REPRESENTATIVE

THE HONORABLE PATRICK J. ADAMS

October 1, 1835

Dear nephew,

I received correspondence announcing your plans to marry Josephine in early January of the coming year. I regret I will be unable to attend the ceremony to share in your happiness. Congratulations on the union, and I wish you and your wife all the best.

I am taking this opportunity to extend to you and Josephine an invitation to join me here in Louisiana for a breath of fresh air. Life here is genuinely splendid.

Recently, I acquired five square miles of beautiful wilderness located twenty miles south of a small settlement known as Brashear City. On a recent journey to the site, accompanied by a survey crew, I chose the location for a future homestead. The construction site is situated in the northernmost portion of this large tract of land. The section (one square mile) I have chosen for development is comprised of the most beautiful and breathtaking topography I have ever witnessed.

In the same transaction, I also acquired one section of land along the Bayou Du Large. This tract of land is about twenty miles downstream from the tiny village of Houma. Situated along the left descending bank of this watercourse the headland is shrouded by magnificent live oak trees; the rear of the property is marshland crowded with virgin cypress forest.

Both tracts of land are remote but easily accessible by small sailing vessel.

The site below Brashear City has an aquifer flowing through the clam shell deposits that are readily apparent throughout the region of the lower Atchafalaya River basin. The fountainhead of this underground spring feeds clear, cold, fresh water, down a ten-foot wide stream that flows about three-fourths mile before emptying into an unnamed bayou, which lends easy access to the construction site for the homestead. The bottom of the channel created by the stream is lined with clam shells, which stifle the erosion process that would normally occur with swift flowing water. At certain times of the day, the water can be seen sparkling like diamonds in the sunlight filtered by the massive trees that occupy the territory surrounding the stream's course.

Wildlife is abundant. In fact, there are so many deer in the vicinity of the proposed homestead I have decided to name the settlement "Deer Island." The previously unnamed bayou will become "Deer Island Bayou."

If you accept my invitation, you will be provided with everything that is necessary to get you established here. Your woodworking skills will be utilized to fashion various boats and houses, as well as utility buildings—a chicken house and a corn crib, for examples.

With the assistance I can provide, I am confident you and Josephine would find it easy to adapt to life in America. I trust I will hear from you soon. Send my love and best regards to your mother. Tell her she is sorely missed. Give my regards to your wife.

Sincerely,
Uncle Patrick

Indeed, Joseph is a master carpenter (a boat builder or ship-wright by trade). He has been excited! No! He has been overwhelmed by the invitation. Much to my chagrin, I was totally unprepared for such a risky and perilous venture. The notion of leaving civilization to pursue life in a wilderness region of a foreign land has left me pan-ic-stricken. I never before entertained such invalid reasoning; not in my entire life. It defies any logic with which I am familiar.

It is true that Joseph and I are young and healthy. I am confident we could survive any physical challenges, but wilderness! Wilderness! Now that is something I know nothing about. How can I evaluate possibilities for a good life when survival itself is in question?

Joseph is resourceful and industrious, but can he carve civiliza-tion from nothing? Can Joseph fulfill my need for communicating feelings void of the support normally provided by other loved ones and family members—friends, acquaintances, even strangers?

These are but a few of the myriad of questions that suddenly challenge my stability. What about Indians? Will we have to kill to stay alive? It will take some time for me to sort through it all.

Joseph says he understands my apprehension, and he will patiently await my decision. He appears confident that, at some point, I will agree with his ambitious plans to accept Uncle Patrick's offer. I suppose my hesitation to say "no!" has prompted his opti-mism. I certainly did not intend to convey that message. Time has a way of sorting things out. I will place the entire matter in God's hands. He knows what is best for us.

February 12, 1836
Joseph shared many interesting facts about his side of the family. I was delighted by his keen knowledge of his heritage and his aware-

ness of how it all somehow ties us in with the American experience. After his accounts of the various positions held and the achievements of some of his ancestors, I became suddenly aware of why the prospects for journeying to America did not frighten him as it did me. In fact, from Joseph's perspective of the world and how his family had been a part of things, it seemed quite rational for us to give Louisiana living a try.

Joseph's mother, Jennifer Adams, was born in New Orleans in 1788. She is four years older than her brother, Patrick Adams. Joseph's father, John Addison Jr., served as a captain in the Royal Navy during the War of 1812. When the Treaty of Ghent was signed, ending the war, he resigned his commission and settled in New Orleans in 1815. It was there and then that he met Jennifer Adams.

Shortly after they were married, John Addison convinced Jennifer to accompany him back to England. Their first child was born just two months after they arrived in Southampton. The fervency with which Joseph presented his family history was intriguing. For generations, his family has been directly involved in the evolution of America, the United States of America.

I asked Joseph to write the information on paper so I could transcribe it into my diary for posterity. He provided me with the following details: Joseph's immediate family: father, John Addison Jr., born March 4, 1780; mother, Jennifer Adams Addison, born May 5, 1788; brothers, James Addison, born March 5, 1816, Justin Addison, born June 12, 1817, and Joseph Addison, born September 28, 1818.

A brief family history: father's side, John Addison Jr., born March 4, 1780, served in the Royal Navy from 1800 to 1815, achieved rank of captain, resigned his commission after the signing of the Treaty of Ghent, settled in New Orleans for one year, met Jennifer Adams, married, and returned to England in 1816.

Grandfather: John Addison (1755–1815) father of John Addison Jr. served as a British soldier in the American Revolutionary War (1775–1783), and achieved rank of master sergeant.

Great-Grandfather: Samuel Addison Jr. (1725–1800) Father of John Addison served in the Royal Navy (1750–1760) he achieved the rank of captain; he fought in the French and Indian War.

Great-grandfather to Joseph's father: Samuel Addison Sr. (1705–1786), father of Samuel Addison Jr., British diplomat, served as an envoy during negotiations for peace (1762–1764) that brought about the signing of the Treaty of Paris in 1763, ending the war.

A brief history: mother's side, Jennifer Adams Addison, born May 5, 1788; married John Addison Jr. on March 15, 1815; Brother Patrick J. Adams, born July 4, 1791, and fought in the Battle of New Orleans 1815; congressman (1816–).

Richard Adams (1760–1825) father of Patrick and Jennifer Adams, fought in the American Revolution (1775–1783) served under American general, Andrew Jackson in the Battle of New Orleans 1815.

Stanford Adams (1742–1795) Father of Richard Adams, served as a soldier in the Continental Army under General George Washington in the American Revolution.

Buford Adams (1725–1782), father of Stanford Adams, early British settler in America, lived in Virginia and later moved to New Orleans in 1765, and distant cousin to the second president of the United States, John Adams.

March 1, 1836

Joseph wrote a letter of reply to Uncle Patrick last night. He informed him that his offer was a gracious one, but due to the gravity of any decision we would defer our answer until such a time that we could evaluate our choices further. He went on to say that consideration of the matter would be ever before us until a final decision is made. He closed the letter with a plea for patience as we deliberate further.

I was saddened by Joseph's apparent disappointment. I consoled him by offering to go for a visit with his mother to gain more insight into what life in America would be like. He said he would appreciate my efforts, and he would continue to honor my wishes.

March 5, 1836

Joseph came home from work, unable to quiet his enthusiasm any longer. He shared that it had always been a dream of his to one day move to America. The reason the idea was never mentioned in conversation before now was that it seemed to be impossible. Now, Uncle Patrick's offer has reawakened Joseph's previously subdued ambition. What once was a fantastic dream, has now become a burning desire waiting for its fulfillment. I pray I will not be the source of his disappointment should his plans falter.

September 5, 1836

I am worried about Joseph. He sits quietly for hours at a time. It's as though he is in a daze. He seems obsessed with the idea that we should just wake up one morning, pack our belongings and leave for America on the first ship heading west. The fact of the matter is that we lack the resources to make the journey.

Two years have passed…

September 28, 1838

We are celebrating Joseph's twentieth birthday today. We had a family reunion at Grandfather Moore's farm. We had a wonderful time with family and friends. Joseph blew out all the candles, and my grandmother insisted he reveal his wish.

I should not have been surprised to hear him ask God Almighty for the means for transport from Southampton to New Orleans; nevertheless, I was a bit astonished by his tenacity. This husband of mine refuses to give up on his dream for a new life in a new land.

Three and one half years have past since uncle Patrick's invitation.

July 17, 1839

England's vested interests abroad have made the shipbuilding artisans of Southampton the most valued craftsmen in all the land. Joseph has been so caught up in his work on a new ship design at the shipyard, that America is seldom mentioned in conversation any more.

Joseph seems to have acquiesced. I am sure the security provided by his profession has had some influence on his resolve. Recently, he mentioned that we were born here, married here, and there seems little doubt that we will die here on English soil.

January 5, 1840

We celebrated our fourth wedding anniversary today. The entire family turned out at Grandfather Moore's farm to join us in the festivities. Also attending the affair were my maids of honor and Joseph's best men.

Victoria Ramsey is now Victoria Ramsey Huxley. Her husband, Edward, is a blacksmith. They have two children: a boy named Edward Jr. and a girl named Julia. She has the same schoolgirl charm that she flaunted when we were buddies growing up.

Elizabeth Blackett is married to a butcher, Alexander Noyes. They have no children. Elizabeth is a joy to behold; she has a wit about her that is unmatched in my circle of friends. Beth told me that she and Alex are having so much fun together that children would just spoil things for them. I could not side with her point of view, but if that is what makes their union blissful, so be it.

Diana Eddington was escorted to our gathering by Edward Halley and Samuel Marlowe. All three of these single friends of ours say that the right marital partner has not become apparent to them.

Andrew Johnson, the third best man at our wedding four years ago, was already wed back then. His wife, Alice, has had three boys for him. Their names are Andrew Johnson Jr., George Johnson, and the youngest son is Michael. What a handsome family they make. All the boys are polite and well-behaved. Andy works with Joseph at the shipyard.

Over one hundred guests joined us on this festive occasion. Once again, the subject of our plans for going to America was resurrected by one of our curious friends. I sensed Joseph's disappointment as he tried in vain to offer a plausible response to the inquiry. He still longs for more in life than I can provide as his wife, or what a job can do for our living. I pray that one day he will find fulfillment.

AN OFFER WE COULD NOT REFUSE

January 27, 1840

Joseph received a letter from Uncle Patrick today. I transcribed it exactly as it was written.

FROM THE CONGRESSIONAL DESK OF LOUISIANA
STATESMAN AND REPRESENTATIVE

THE HONORABLE PATRICK J. ADAMS

November 7, 1839

Dear nephew,

I decided you needed a bit more encouragement. I have made all the necessary arrangements for your transport to New Orleans. You and Josephine are booked in the passenger's log of the sailing vessel *Island Mistress*, which will embark for America on February 10, 1840. Make haste and be on board when she sets sail.

Upon your arrival at the port of New Orleans, look for the produce vendor at the farmers market. His name is Salvadore Cortez. Mr. Cortez will instruct and care for you from that point. Barring unforeseen difficulty, you should arrive in New Orleans sometime in early June.

I look forward to meeting you and your wife, and godspeed! I have arranged for a line of credit with the owner of the *Island Mistress*. Feel free to use the money for incidental expenses. I trust you will have a safe passage. Give my love to your mother.

Sincerely,
Uncle Patrick

After reading the letter, Joseph gazed into my eyes inquisitively. At first I was spellbound, but I knew what he longed for me to say. In an enthusiastic outburst, I proclaimed, "Well, what are we waiting for? Let's pack our things and prepare for the journey to America!"

Joseph held me close in a tender embrace. Still holding me close in his arms, he looked into my eyes, searching for any hint of apprehension. Finding none, he kissed me gently on my lips and began to cry uncontrollably. "I am happy I chose Josephine Moore to be my lifelong companion. I will do everything in my power to insure you will not be disappointed in your choice for a husband," he announced with a sincere pledge.

Of course I was moved to tears by his noble promise, and I assured him that he was the right choice for my lifelong companion. I told him I welcomed the challenge to experience the adventure he so longed for me to share with him. I informed him that I would break the news to my family in the morning. He said he would do likewise.

January 28, 1840

I met with mother and father this morning. They were understandably surprised. I suspect they knew something was in the works for quite some time. Maybe they knew something but were not going to tell me. They were easily persuaded that I was confident my decision to follow Joseph to Louisiana was the right one. I pledged to write them often to keep them informed. I would let them know of any changes in our state of well-being.

Before I could complete my last sentence, Mama lost her composure and began to cry. Papa leaned over from where he was seated and consoled her with a tender embrace. "Everything is going to be just fine, Gracie Moore. You know that Joseph will take good care of Josephine. We will ask God to watch over them each night when we pray. Now dry those eyes before you have me crying with you," he said softly.

Suddenly, we discovered our time together was very precious. So often we fail to recognize that tomorrow is never guaranteed.

Sometimes it takes the unexpected, the separation of loved ones, to bring time into its proper perspective.

The intensity of the meeting is difficult to put into words. I was not in imminent danger! I was not sharing some fatal diagnosis from my family physician! I was, however, announcing my final departure from England! Is that similar to dying?

As I walked away from my childhood home, the pressure from the emotional upheaval unleashed its energy through my tear ducts. It was as though a mighty river had contemptuously broken a dam I had foolishly tried to build. I felt no shame as the constant flow began to wet my blouse. A few of the saline drops made my taste buds aware of what was happening outside of me. I was determined to withhold this display while in the presence of my family—I had to be a source of strength for them, I reasoned. Now that no one could witness my weakness, I was forced to abandon my resolve by the overpowering emotions from within me. There was a definite healing associated with this sudden outburst. The grieving process prompted by the reality of this sudden departure from England has now fled my presence. I sense, as the tears have stopped, I am now able to assume my usual composure.

This experience makes me wonder how Joseph is doing with his family. This is a good time to pray that things are going well at his father's home: "Dear Lord, you know how much this trip to America to begin a new life together means to both Joseph and I. I ask that you grant to all of us involved in making this decision, a sense of peace and the confidence that this choice to leave our homeland is the right one. Please let all go well with Joseph's family as it has gone so well with mine."

It's all in God's hands now!

Chapter Two

SETTING SAIL FOR AMERICA

February 10, 1840

Joseph and I boarded the sailing vessel *Island Mistress* early this morning. Joseph immediately sought and received permission from the ship's captain to have a look around the vessel. He soon disappeared from view below deck.

As I watched our trunks being loaded into the cargo hold, I struggled to fight off the growing sense of emptiness, the fearful uncertainty, compassion for my mother and father, and a sudden feeling of loneliness. I decided to be brave. Turning away from this attack on my emotions, I went ashore to administer final embraces to all of my well-wishers.

Just as I completed my cordial good-byes, Joseph showed up beside me. His eyes were sparkling. His adventurous spirit had been unleashed and his countenance was pleasant to behold. His wild enthusiasm strengthened me during this time of extreme vulnerability.

One of the ship's mates sounded a bell announcing that the gangway would be hoisted aboard in fifteen minutes. "All passengers setting sail for America should board this vessel immediately!" he authoritatively shouted.

Joseph grabbed my hand, and we hastily made our way through the crowd of onlookers. Once aboard, the gangway was taken up, the mooring lines cast off, and the crewmen climbed the three masts to unfurl the sails.

"The captain will begin the voyage under partial sail. Using only the three topsails and one jib sail we can be assured a safe passage through the crowded harbor. Once we reach the channel, we'll be under full sail, then we will experience what this mistress can do!" Joseph announced with childlike exuberance.

Joseph's affection for ships is unparalleled. His love for shipbuilding is second only to his love for me—I hope! I must admit the name *Island Mistress* is a trifle seductive, especially from a shipwright's point of view.

Numerous other passengers have chosen to remain on deck to witness, for the very first time, the open sea. Everyone is noticeably excited about the journey ahead. So much water!

It all happened so quickly that by the time I tried to wave a final good-bye, we were already under way. I was amazed by how quickly the partly rigged sails caught the wind and moved us from the dockside. "Good-bye, everyone! Good-bye, Mother and Father! Good-bye, Mr. and Mrs. Addison! Good-bye, Diana, Victoria, Elizabeth, Edward, Alexander, Samuel, Andrew, and Alice! Good-bye everyone! May God bless and keep you each and every one!" I shouted until my lungs seemed ready to collapse.

Joseph, in a tactical maneuver designed to draw my attention away from the scene of our departure, succeeded in engrossing me in his description of the vessel we had boarded just a few moments ago. "The *Island Mistress* is a sharp-bowed, sleek-lined, clipper ship with three masts. This newly designed vessel is built for speed. Its masts are tall and its beam is narrow. She is designed to catch the wind as a bird's wings and cut through the open sea with the ease of a knife through freshly churned butter. Under full sail, the *Island Mistress* is as fast as any ship afloat the captain boasted to me. My own personal inspection of this fine vessel revealed that she is a formidable craft. You can be assured of a safe passage my dear!" Joseph proclaimed.

As I gazed over the bulwarks for one last glance homeward, all that remained was the silhouette of the English coastline. As our seaworthy craft exercises total control of our destiny, each cresting wave steals away all I have known. I now train my thoughts on what lies ahead, trying desperately to adjust to the changes. Far from shore and heading west through the vast expanse of the English Channel, I cannot help wondering how our ship will manage the open seas of the North Atlantic.

Coming up behind us, Captain Todd Richardson introduced himself. He told us that he has been the captain of the *Island Mistress* since she was launched four years ago. He then proceeded to present his credentials.

"I was twelve years a crewman aboard packet ships before I became a captain. I was skipper aboard the packet *Marianna* for ten years before I accepted responsibility for sailing this vessel. After twenty-six years at sea, I guess you could say I have salt running through my veins!" he quipped with a pleasant smile.

It seems Captain Todd's love for the sea is as strong as Joseph's love of shipbuilding. They should get along rather well over the next few weeks of our voyage.

Knowing Joseph was a shipwright, the captain proudly began to describe his ship. "This vessel is 225 feet long. She's forty feet at the beam, with a displacement of thirteen hundred and twenty-five tons. She carries 175 passengers and has a crew of fifty-six men."

February 13, 1840

We have been at sea for three days. I have discovered that much of my anxiety about the safety of the voyage was unfounded. Aside from cramped quarters, the trip thus far has been exhilarating. The *Island Mistress* manages the huge ocean waves easily and with little discomfort. Once I grew accustomed to the motion of the ship, I gained confidence with each passing sea.

Though the ship has a multitude of passengers, all having amicable dispositions, Joseph and I have chosen not to mingle. It's not that we are unsociable, but there is no one on board with whom we are yet acquainted. No doubt, that will change with time. For now, I am content with things as they are.

February 14, 1840

My confidence was shaken today. About midmorning, a violent storm assaulted the ship. It caused no little stir! After a while when the storm persisted, the sky was darkened. Lightning flashes and deafening thunder added to the chaos. The hard-hitting rainfall and the pounding waves battered us incessantly. Fear gripped my heart!

Joseph tried to ease my fears by expressing that the ship would easily endure this ferocious weather and the experience of her crew would bring us safely through the ordeal. He held me tightly and dried my tears with his handkerchief. Once again, it was my husband's confidence that bolstered me when I needed reassurance the most.

I detected no hint of fear in Joseph's eyes during this bout with the sea, but when it was ended, I saw an expression of genuine relief. After all, he is mortal and subject to the same tests of emotion as I am. I am thankful for the obvious difference between husband and wife; Joseph and I are very compatible and sensitive to each other's needs. We make a good couple.

February 18, 1840

What started as a day of good breezes and fine weather was destined to change. Joseph had told me that breezes out of the northwest are frequent in the North Atlantic; there was nothing unusual about it.

As the day progressed, the moderate breezes out of the northwest had increased to strong winds, and then they rose to gale force. Joseph said that the towering rigging had become as tightly tuned as a violin.

Joseph kept me informed as conditions worsened. "Seas are growing ever larger as they march down on the hull, lifting her stern as they roll alongside. Giant combers are being toppled forward, the wind blowing off their crests and sweeping the decks with a salty spray."

Joseph continued, "It is taking two men to steady the helm. They are desperately trying to keep the massive hull from swinging about in each surging sea. The stress on the rigging is unimaginable. The crew is making a frantic effort to reduce sail. Once this has been accomplished, she should move more steadily."

February 19, 1840

The storm driven wind howled through the night; by late morning, the gale had somewhat abated. Joseph says our westward progress was greatly diminished by this latest trial at sea.

Joseph boasted, "The *Island Mistress* has proven herself seaworthy!"

I just thanked God for the captain being a good sailor.

For the record, Joseph and I were not the only ones showing concern during this latest ordeal; you should have seen the expressions I saw on the faces of some of our crewmen. Even the memory of that gives me the creeps!

February 27, 1840

There were sharks swimming along the sides of the ship this evening. I had never seen a shark before today. Those we observed from the deck were huge creatures. Spoils from the galley thrown overboard caused a violent display of their aggressiveness. They could easily eat anyone who fell over the side. When I got the notion that they might be following us, hoping for a human to eat, I immediately went back to my cabin berth. At least I would not have to look at the dreaded beasts from there.

Joseph stayed on deck watching the horizon in all directions, dreaming of what life on "Deer Island" will be like. He is constantly sharing his plans for living in the wilderness, some of which have given me great prospects for our future in remote south Louisiana.

One day, we will certainly have our own sailing vessel for traveling the bayous and rivers. I wonder about the house Joseph will build—will it have a fireplace? I try to imagine what it might look like. Will we be able to grow the vegetables that I like—cucumbers, squash, carrots, potatoes, green peas, chickpeas?

I still bemoan leaving England forever—my family, my friends, Joseph's family and friends. I am especially lonesome for my grandparents. They were not in attendance as we left Southampton's dockside. I knew, of course, that they would not be there. Joseph and I went for a final visit to the dairy farm before our departure. There was not the same degree of emotionalism displayed there as was the case with my family earlier. In fact, they were extremely supportive, encouraging us to "be brave and trust in God." Grandmother surprised me most of all. She actually seemed to envy me this opportunity for adventure in a foreign land. I wager that if she had been just a few years younger she would have tried to convince Grandfather to sell the farm and accompany us to America. I fear I will miss their wisdom, wit, and charm. At least I can cherish the fond memories of the wonderful times we shared at Grandfather Moore's farm.

March 5, 1840

Another bout with disappointment! The past two weeks were heralded by intermittent squalls and periods when the sea was as smooth as glass. The ship's progress, even under full sail, has been frustratingly meager.

Aboard ship there is little to occupy our time; days seem like weeks to me. We met quite a few people who are heading for what we all perceive as "the promised land"; all share the hope that our expectations will not be thwarted by disappointment. It is fun to have a dream, but it will be more fun if the dream is realized. I hope our dream will be proven true by the destiny we face, though for now, the fulfillment of that dream is clouded by uncertainty.

All I can do is trust in God!

March 9, 1840

Awakened this morning by squally weather! There was deafening thunder, and the lightning display was unlike any I have ever witnessed. I feared the towering masts might be struck!

By midafternoon the storm abated, and once again, we were enjoying gentle breezes and fine weather.

These unexpected challenges of the sea never cease to bewilder me; it's as though the ocean sees us as her enemy. The violence of each storm shows no mercy to intruders. The North Atlantic has demonstrated to me that she will not allow herself to be easily conquered; she has been a formidable adversary, one that still holds us in the palm of her hand.

March 16, 1840

A violent storm began its assault on our ship today. Captain Todd, having seen it approaching in the distance, had time to order skysails, royals and topgallants furled, and the topsails double-reefed. This action cut the exposed canvass surface area by at least one-third Joseph-related.

I believe this to be the worst of all the storms we faced since leaving the dock at Southampton. The windblown rain has been relentless in its intensity; outside, it looks like a sheet of white, impenetrable by the human eye. We are certainly traveling blind in this raging weather. "Lord, be merciful and guide us safely through this unnerving experience," I pleaded.

March 17, 1840

The great storm persisted all during the night; this morning came even stronger winds. It was a hard blowing gale! Joseph shared that the captain had ordered the topsails shortened to their last rows of reef points. Whatever those are!

I never cease to be amazed at the nautical acuity my husband has acquired. Not only does he understand the structural integrity of a vessel, but he also has a keen knowledge of rigging and sail configuration. He told me that each sail has a purpose, and each affects the maneuverability of the ship as conditions require. This all seems very complicated to me!

Describing the crew's actions during the storm, Joseph elaborated for the sake of my diary: "The rigging was reduced to close-reefed topsails and staysails; fore-and-aft triangles of canvas were rigged between the masts—these are intended to help steady the ship as she runs before the storm."

After a brief pause for me to rest my pen, he added, "The crew did a fantastic job. We had no structural damage, just a few torn and tattered sails—nothing that can't be quickly repaired or replaced."

March 18, 1840

All through this third night, our clipper ship was tested by this marathon tempest. The *Island Mistress* lurched and heaved amidst the huge waves as the phosphorescent surf exploded all around her.

This morning the atmosphere was gloomy—overcast with gray skies. By the time we finished the noon meal, the sun shone brightly at its apex overhead in the midst of a clear azure sky. How fickle the sea can be! Thank God the storm has ended!

Tomorrow the captain says we should see land, and once again, Joseph and I will experience what it's like to be on *terra firma*.

With my husband sound asleep, I thought it an appropriate time to make a few notes, reflecting on the magnitude of what he and

I had just experienced. This ocean crossing was a frightening yet an exhilarating experience.

The Lord knows I said many a heartfelt prayer since Joseph and I left England. Only my faith in God helped me manage the many bouts with fear that gripped my heart each time our ship's crew had to frantically rush to reduce sail. This afternoon, Joseph acknowledged that he too had to overcome the dreads of facing possible catastrophe. I am glad he waited until our voyage is nearly over to share his concerns with me. He has always remained stoic when facing adversity. Many times I fell on my knees beside my bed, praying earnestly for God's mercy.

I'll lay me down to sleep with one last request from God Almighty, "Lord, have mercy on us all! Amen."

ARRIVAL AT HALIFAX, NOVA SCOTIA

March 19, 1840

Storm petrels and seagulls announce that we are approaching land. The coastline of Nova Scotia!

"Halifax Harbor will soon be visible!" Captain Todd announced as we arrived on deck.

Anxious to survey the vessel, Joseph asked the skipper how long it would take to reach the dock and secure the mooring lines.

"That should take about an hour and a half if all goes well," Captain Todd estimated.

After getting permission, Joseph brought me on an inspection tour of the ship. He looked her over carefully from bow to stern above deck, below deck, even down in the bilge. When we finally came up for fresh air, the mooring lines were being cast. Seeing the captain nearby, Joseph approached him, tapping him on his shoulder: "Captain Todd, can I share a few words with you before my wife and I disembark?"

"Say on!" the captain answered emphatically.

Joseph began sharing his appreciation for the boat's durability and her excellent performance at sea. "Close inspection of the ship has revealed much to me. She's the most well-constructed vessel I have ever seen! I marvel that throughout our tempestuous journey across the sea, the integrity of the hull has remained sound; her system of ropes, chains, and other tackle used to support and control the masts, sails, and yards remain virtually unscathed even though they have been repeatedly tested with all an angry sea can throw at her. I am astonished, sir!"

Responding to Joseph's accolades, Captain Todd answered with a meek expression on his face, but with an assertive voice, "The *Island Mistress* is a well-built vessel, and she is manned by a competent crew. No captain of any other clipper can argue otherwise!" he lauded, taking no credit for his own ability as an experienced sailor.

Captain Todd Richardson has exceeded all Joseph's expectations. He has won our hearts, and he deserves our admiration and appreciation for bringing us safely to America.

"So this is America!" Joseph shouted. "Our journey to New Orleans has reached the halfway mark!" he added.

I could not restrain my feelings. Hugging my husband tightly to me, I cheerfully spouted, "Oh, happy day! Land at last! We have met all the challenges the sea threw at us! All those fearful episodes are now behind us! Glory be!"

As I loosened my grip on his torso, Joseph suggested we go ashore.

After enduring contrary winds and stormy seas for thirty-seven days, we finally arrived at the port of Halifax, Nova Scotia. Though it is the middle of March, the weather is bitterly cold. We will be in port for three or four days, exchanging cargo and accepting new passengers. Looks like we'll have plenty of free time!

The captain informed Joseph that three or four days are about the average stay at each port of call. Now I know why Uncle Patrick is not expecting us until late May or early June.

When I first disembarked from the boat, my legs seemed to wobble beneath me. No longer needing to compensate for the rolling and up-and-down motion of the boat between the waves and my knees, my body had to adjust somehow to correct my equilibrium. Before long, I was walking without the annoying sensation.

The exercise offered a welcome relief from the stuffy quarters and the cramped confines of the ship. The clipper ship seemed huge when I first laid eyes on her, but the long journey shrunk her down to a much smaller area as the days dragged along.

The sky being overcast did not diminish the beauty of the harbor and the surrounding countryside. The landscape, the buildings, the activity, the people doing their business, all these observations stimulate my perceptive senses which have been dulled by thirty-seven days of ocean and sky. The only variations at sea are color changes in the water and in the sky, which are both affected by the weather. The excitement of looking at the Atlantic Ocean quickly became a mundane experience.

Not far from where our ship was moored, there was a dockyard. Seeing three sizable vessels under construction heightened Joseph's curiosity. I told him I would stroll along the harbor and take in the view while he went over to examine the workmanship of the local shipwrights.

The village is situated on the eastern slope of a small peninsula in Halifax harbor. At the center of the peninsula stands the Citadel, the strongest fortress in British America. The mighty fortress crowns an eminence over two hundred feet high, and it commands a perfect view of the village and harbor.

There were countless vessels loading and unloading cargo. I saw wooden crates filled with apples, barrels of flour, live lobsters, containers holding dried fish, there was freshly milled lumber, huge piles of coal, and countless other items being transferred from boat to dock and from dock to boat. I saw bales of cotton, bundles of tobacco, and casks of gunpowder. There were also many dockside vendors peddling various goods and wares.

One merchant beckoned me to try a piece of dried fish, so I did. It was very tasty, but the salt used in the curing process forced me to ask for a glass of water. Instead, I was treated to a splendid cup of tea. Mr. Richard Cromwell and his wife Audrey had moved to Halifax from Dover, England, thirty years ago. He has been buying and selling apples and several other fresh fruit, and he also operates a dried fish market for export.

When Joseph returned from the dockyard, I introduced him to the hospitable couple, and we spent the remainder of the day discussing every imaginable subject with our new friends.

One interesting fact I learned is that Halifax Harbor is known by the local Indians as *Chebucto*, meaning "chief of the havens."

I intend to make the best of my stay here; the landscape is beautiful, and the people are cordial and friendly. I hope to gain a lasting perspective that will endure the test of time. Once we leave here, I am certain I'll never return again.

March 23, 1840

I must say the past few days spent ashore have been delightful. The opportunity to interact with new faces has been informative and soothing to my soul. I can't wait to see our next port of call!

We will be leaving Halifax at daybreak. Next stop: Boston, Massachusetts!

March 24, 1840

We are under sail. The captain says we are destined for Boston Harbor, where we will exchange more passengers and cargo.

Joseph informed me that there would soon be profound changes in the design of ocean-going vessels. If these design changes prove successful, it could mark the beginning of the end of sailing ships. The new ship he had started work on back at the Southampton shipyard was just such a vessel. The *Great Britain* will be an iron steamboat, powered by a steam engine that will drive a screw propeller. She is scheduled to be launched in 1845 and will be the vanguard for this revolutionary trend in boat building. Predecessors of this design incorporate both sail and steam-driven paddlewheels for locomotion. The paddles can only be used in calm seas, but the combination of the two power sources has reduced transoceanic travel time significantly. Joseph's awareness of new trends in boat design demonstrates the extent of the love affair he carries on with the vessels that dare to challenge the sea.

BOSTON HARBOR

March 25, 1840

We arrived in Boston harbor just after sunset this evening. The lamplights along the harbor road were the highlights of our arrival. We will remain aboard for the evening and disembark for a sightseeing tour as soon as we awake tomorrow.

I made friends with a young lady aboard ship. Mira Langley boarded ship at Halifax. She was born in Canada to English parents. She is traveling to New Orleans to meet her fiancé. Her charming wit and lively character will greatly assist me during the remainder of our long "prison term."

March 26, 1840

Joseph, Mira, and I took a stroll through the countryside. The harbor was very similar to the one at Halifax, as far as the daily activities are concerned. There are numerous ships and small fishing vessels loading and unloading passengers and cargo. Just out from the coastline are small sailing vessels Joseph calls "sharpies" (small fishing boats, long and slender, with one or two masts sporting triangular sails).

Walking away from the watery scenes and into the village of Boston, we happened upon many one-, two-, and three-storied wood-framed buildings. Most were constructed atop the hills that describe the topography of the land on the east side of the harbor where we had landed. Continuing down the country road, we entered the heart of the town where the building of prominence was the town house. Its ornate design reminded me of Grandfather Moore's gazebo, though this building far exceeds our family meeting place in stature. Attracting our attention to the center of an oblong circle formed by several stately buildings, the town house is a single-story structure built high above the ground and supported by massive timbers. There are two stairways from ground level, which lend access to the inside of the building; both are located beneath the first floor level. A brick chimney extends from the ground upward and follows the north side of the structure up to a point equal in height to a railing which surrounds a widow's walk, which crosses the hip and gabled rooftop. Pane glass windows sport decorative shutters, which can be closed in cold or violent weather. Looking like a bell tower, absent the bell, I am sure a clear view of the harbor can be accessed from that vantage point.

Horse-drawn carriages are ambling about in the streets. The occupants offer friendly gestures as they pass us by; men tip their hats with smiling faces and women nod their heads as a polite welcome is advanced. "Good day" was the common greeting.

THE TOWN HALL
BOSTON 1840

We decided to go upstairs into the town house to investigate the business that was being conducted inside. The proprietor informed us that most of the activity at the site occurs in the afternoon. That is when the farmers return from their fields bringing their fresh produce for sale or trade. Fresh fruit and vegetables attract the most attention.

Merchants display their furniture, leather products, clothing, quilts, and other goods in the breezeway beneath the building. The town house is a meeting hall, farmers' market, and general trading post.

Mira asked Mr. Roundtree, mayor of the town and manager of the town house, if we could go up on the rooftop to get a view of the village and the harbor. He was delighted to direct us to the staircase that led to the widow's walk, the highest point on the highest hill in Boston. Joseph pointed to the *Island Mistress* as soon as we looked toward the bay. We could see for many miles in every direction above the tree and housetops.

Returning to street level, Joseph asked Mr. Roundtree if there was a restaurant nearby. He suggested we go to Maude Carter's boarding house at the south end of the circle. Thanking him for his hospitality, we headed for the boarding house. We dined on chili and fresh corn bread and then we headed back to the dock site. Mira and I returned to the ship and Joseph headed for the boatyard to engage in conversation with the local shipwrights.

The captain informed us that we would be laid over a couple more days; we're waiting for important cargo. Joseph was delighted by the news and he straightway returned to the shipyard. Mira and I will spend the time together, walking the streets of Boston, engaging in playful antics, and enjoying women's talk; we may return to the boarding house for a spot of English tea. I would like to join the women making quilts to see how they are made; Lord knows it is a skill I will need to acquire.

VIRGINIA AND MARYLAND

March 31, 1840

The *Island Mistress* is traveling north in Chesapeake Bay. The captain says we are headed for Baltimore harbor at the upper end of the bay. After conducting business there, we will be sailing back toward the Atlantic, steering a course for Norfolk harbor at the mouth of the James River.

The captain of the *Island Mistress* told Joseph that we would be "coasting" for the rest of our journey south, taking advantage of the southern equatorial currents and avoiding the northerly currents of the Gulf Stream. Sailing will get a bit tricky off the coast of South Carolina, where sandbars extend into the Atlantic miles from shore. It's an area notorious for shipwrecks, sometimes referred to as "the graveyard of the Atlantic."

Joseph told me not to worry: "The skipper has traveled off the South Carolina coast hundreds of times. He knows what he is doing!"

That assertion was not enough to relieve me of the anxiety I was beginning to feel inside me. There are some things I would rather not know about. I believe the old saying that "Ignorance is bliss" definitely would be applicable for me and my sense of well-being. Lord, help me! I don't like the feeling of being afraid!

SOUTH CAROLINA

April 13, 1840

I must have misunderstood the captain's assertion that from here on, we would be "coasting south" on our voyage; I thought he meant shorter times at each port of call. After thirteen days, we are once again "coasting south."

We arrived at Charleston harbor about midmorning. Mira and I went on deck to watch the ship's crew load a large quantity of rice into the cargo hold. One of the crewmen told us that the rice was bound for New Orleans.

As is the usual practice, we are projected to be here at least four days. I have grown accustomed to the delays, trying my best to take in the beauty that is "America" along the way.

The general boredom of a long voyage has waned; our many stops have introduced me to interesting places. We have been hosted by a number of diverse individuals as we happened upon them during the course of our journey. Mira has been a source of comfort and joy for me; by sharing her personal feelings and concerns with me, the anxiety I was enduring has dissipated. It seems we have much in common; she reminds me of Victoria Ramsey, my girlfriend back home.

A CHANCE ENCOUNTER

April 18, 1840

As we exited the harbor and entered the Atlantic about mid-day, I knew the danger of the hidden shoals would soon be only a memory; I looked forward to an uneventful passage around the tip of Florida and into the Gulf of Mexico. "That body of water can't possibly be as intimidating as the vast expanse of the Atlantic," I nervously deduced.

About midafternoon, a call was made for passengers to come on deck to witness a marvelous sight. As soon as we arrived, a nearby crewman stood, pointing east and shouting, "That's the captain's former ship, the packet *Marianna!*"

There she was, some distance out from us off the Carolina coast, racing with the wind; a number of people were on her deck, waiving to attract our attention. We responded in kind. The crewman explained how she was taking advantage of the Gulf Stream, and with a brisk west wind filling her sails, she's moving along about eighteen knots.

When Joseph heard the crewman's observations, he marveled at the sight as she sliced through the choppy seas. "Look, Josephine, see how she handles!"

"Those dark, fast-moving clouds are indicative of a strong thunderstorm. She's heading straight into it! Good thing for us it's moving south, with the course we are on, we'll be running before the squall fair sea," Joseph calmly noted, as the seas began to grow bigger and bigger.

The captain says the packet's heading for her home port, New York Harbor—that's where she was built.

Coming alongside Joseph and me, Captain Todd began to share. "She's hauling cargo and passengers from New Orleans. The nonstop trip will only take fourteen to sixteen days. Those people you see on deck are some of my old crewmen. They must have remembered that I was aboard this ship. That's why they seem so excited."

MARIANNA
(A Chance Encounter)

Curious how Joseph felt about the *Marianna*, the captain asked him plainly, "What do you think?"

Joseph was quick to respond, "She's a fine ship! She's mighty fine!"

In less than an hour, the packet disappeared in the deluge, as the distance between us grew ever so quickly. The thrill diminished, and hard rain imminent, Joseph suggested we return to our cabin birth just as the heavy downpour began—we were the last to do so.

GEORGIA

April 19, 1840

We arrived at Savannah Harbor late this afternoon. Of the original passengers sailing from Southampton with us, only one couple remains. Arthur and Diana Kipling are bound for Atlanta. They will be disembarking shortly. Diana is happy their journey was ending; her husband, like Joseph, considered the voyage great fun. They appear to be a very loving couple, a good attribute for a husband and wife beginning a new life in a foreign land.

Located sixteen miles up the Savannah, the town is situated on top of a bluff overlooking the river. Just across the river from the town is a large island with cattle grazing on its lush grasses.

Joseph and I wished Arthur and Diana well, as we walked the gangway together. Sunlight turned to darkness as we shook hands and embraced for the last time. We will be setting sail in seven days, according to the skipper; meanwhile, we will enjoy the sites and stretch our legs for a while.

Joseph, Mira, and I were joined by several other passengers as we strolled through the lamp-lighted town. The wooden houses were a bit smaller than those we had seen during our previous layovers. There was a town hall, but not nearly as large or ornate as the one in Boston. Since our visit to Savannah started at night, we could not get the view of the town that daylight would have given to a wandering and curious eye. We'll have ample time to experience all this port city has to offer before we leave.

Joseph says the next leg of our journey will last for a few weeks. I hope that I will be able to persevere. We will be rounding the south-eastern tip of the continent of North America, entering the Gulf of Mexico, destined for Mobile Bay. That will mark the last stop before finally going to the port of New Orleans.

April 26, 1840

This was to be the day of our departure, but unfortunately, we will be here for a while longer; no one knows for sure how long. I believe we are waiting for a shipment of tobacco. In any case, the wait has been wearisome; there are only so many sites to see within walking distance of the dock. Mira and I are making the best of it; how could I endure without her?

Unlike the weather we encountered further north, the climate here is getting hot and sticky. If it were not for ocean breezes, life aboard ship would soon become almost unbearable. Joseph is growing a beard; he looks handsome that way. He is blending in with the American residents we have encountered along the way. I thought of asking him to shave it off, but now that he has worn it awhile, I think I like it.

Prayerfully, I ask God to bless and keep us safe during this last leg of our journey. I have also petitioned Him for help during the periods of loneliness that seem to persistently try to rob me of any joy. I thank God most of all for my husband, Joseph Addison; how I love my dear Joseph, a prince among men.

May 3, 1840

We have been patiently waiting for cargo for fourteen long days. Adding to the frustration is the turbulent weather. The winds have been very strong and the rain incessant. The captain promises we will be leaving for Mobile in just a couple of more days. Frankly, I believe he is using the weather as an excuse while awaiting some other unknown arrival.

Joseph, Mira, and I have exhausted ourselves trying to escape the extreme boredom of it all. We have been eating quite well, but that's not much consolation in light of this extreme disappointment.

May 7, 1840

Thank Almighty God for miracles; we are finally leaving Georgia for points south. Three days to Mobile, and then we will be bound for New Orleans. Words can't express the joy we all felt when we received word of our departure about midmorning.

A prayer for solace in this time of distress: "Dear Lord, keep us strong for the last leg of our journey. It's been more arduous than I could ever have imagined. I thank you for your many blessings—far too numerous to mention."

ALABAMA

May 10, 1840

We arrived just off the coast of Alabama around noon today. Due to moderately bad weather, we are slowly making our way past

Dauphine Island. Seas have been rough, but we are making steady progress. Captain says we will be in Mobile Bay before nightfall.

Having endured this inclement weather for three days now, I don't believe the sun has appeared once through the overcast skies. Though a bit shaky at times, the assault against the ship cannot compare with the challenges of the North Atlantic.

I sincerely hope we will not have an extended stay here at Mobile. The new sites will be refreshing, but my ultimate desire is to reach New Orleans as soon as possible.

May 11, 1840

Arriving later than expected, the captain dropped anchor in the middle of the bay last night. We docked in Mobile Harbor at nine o'clock this morning.

Joseph's excitement over meeting Uncle Patrick has been the source of many hours of conversation lately. Participating in our speculative comments, Mira offered her own personal perception of Louisiana living. Exchanging these ideas about our future has heightened our awareness that we are drawing near to our final destination. The excitement has been contagious. A few more days at sea, and I will be an old salty like our captain, I thought silently. I would not dare to say such a thing out loud.

Joseph has enjoyed every moment of this sea adventure. Aside from those anxious moments during the storm in the North Atlantic, I don't believe he has ever stopped smiling. Recently, he shared that he should have joined the Royal Navy as soon as he was of age. I told him such foolish notions were going a bit too far.

We went sightseeing to get some much needed exercise. One thing strikingly different about Mobile was the large number of black people—more than I saw at Savannah or Norfolk. I tried not to let it bother me, although I have heard the term "slave" used in reference to the dark people; I find that thought disheartening.

Later I was informed that the slave trade was a booming business in the South. Efforts to explain the need for such activity range from the high cost of labor to the plain old need for labor. Those making these comments about slavery seemed to be seedy characters, unlike people with whom I am familiar. I can only hope that we won't have to witness much of this harsh and unkind existence, not now or ever again. Joseph has remained silent on the subject, but I know slavery does not meet his approval.

While walking through the town, we happened upon a slave auction. It was a tragic sight to behold. There was fear in the eyes of the blacks who were about to be sold to the highest bidder. One woman began to scream, apparently due to the possibility of being separated from her brother. I later learned that the plantation owner purchased both of them.

Joseph led Mira and me away from the detestable scene. Shaken by what we had witnessed, we decided to make our way back to the ship.

May 17, 1840

After a six-day delay waiting on cargo, we were set to depart Mobile for Louisiana this morning. Now, we have another delay due to heavy thunderstorms. The captain says he will wait for improvement in the weather before we set sail for Louisiana. No doubt, he knows best!

May 20, 1840

Sunshine this morning made our departure from Mobile a pleasant event. Joseph, Mira, and I went on deck to watch our newest passengers say good-bye to well-wishers. I would like to say I was oblivious to it all, but my observance of the emotional exchanges struck a nerve. When I watched an elderly couple break into tears as their son waved his final good-bye from a position on deck very near to me, I began to cry.

Joseph and Mira, seeing my sorrowful expression, quickly began trying to amuse me in an effort to restore my spirits. Before long, they had me laughing at their wild and curious antics. Joseph's hand tightened its hold on mine. As I gazed into his smiling face, a final teardrop raced down the side of my cheek and onto my chin. He kissed me; first on my forehead, then on my lips. I yielded myself entirely to his tender embrace.

Mira, moved by this moment of tenderness between Joseph and me began to shed a few tears of her own. Joseph's display of love and caring made me suddenly oblivious toward anything that might otherwise have stolen away this time of marital bliss. I am certain that Mira understood.

MISSISSIPPI

May 21, 1840

Trouble aboard the *Island Mistress* has forced us to make an unexpected stop in the coastal Mississippi town of Biloxi.

After dropping anchor in Biloxi Bay, the captain had to dispatch a small company of passengers (Joseph was the first to volunteer) to disembark and row one of our lifeboats to shore to obtain medical supplies.

One of the crew members had purchased a feral hog (ready dressed) before we left the Mobile docks. Forty-two of our fifty-six man crew had succumbed to food poisoning. Though the captain had warned that the meat didn't appear to be fresh, the crew decided that the cook should prepare it anyway.

Plagued with stomach cramps, nausea, and bouts with the fever, our ship had lost its entire crew overnight. The *Island Mistress* was "dead in the water" so to speak. We were fortunate to make it into port with such a pathetic display of misery.

Near catastrophe! That's what it was! What if a storm had assaulted the ship before we came into safe harbor? We will have to wait several days for the men to recover. Woe is me!

Since leaving Virginia, we have had to endure countless delays; if it wasn't the weather, it was waiting for cargo to be loaded aboard. Now, this had to happen! We were almost there!

June 1, 1840

We sailed through Biloxi Bay this morning. The captain says that, barring unforeseen mishaps, we should arrive at the New Orleans docks in two days.

I sure hope he is right! This last leg of our journey has been quite dull and wearisome. It has taken all the strength within me to maintain my composure.

As usual, Joseph kept me from going completely mad with the incessant boredom of staying aboard our boat for long periods without being able to step out onto solid ground. What a sweet man he is!

As sunset came, looking out over the vast expanse of the Gulf of Mexico with my husband at my side, I found myself enthralled with entertaining good thoughts.

After all, Joseph and I are about to write the next chapter of our lives—one of adventure and filled with excitement. We have braved the Atlantic Ocean and, now, the Gulf of Mexico. I am confident we will meet any challenges that may lie before us. Life can only get better from here!

As I lay me down to sleep, I prayed this earnest and heartfelt prayer: "Dear Lord, thanks for your many blessings. Continue to see us safely through to our destination. Amen."

NEW ORLEANS, LOUISIANA

June 3, 1840

"So this is New Orleans!" Joseph heralded as we walked the gangway from the deck of the *Island Mistress* for the final time. The sun shone brilliantly for our jubilant exodus. As for myself, I celebrated our safe arrival; over at last was the arduous voyage. For Joseph, this departure marked the beginning of the second phase of his great adventure—though for him adventure has no bounds.

A dock worker standing near the base of the gangway hailed Joseph and I as we approached. "Do you happen to know Ms. Mira Langley?" He told us he had been requisitioned by Mira's fiancé to locate her as soon as the *Island Mistress* arrived.

No sooner had the inquiry been made when Mira appeared behind us, and we introduced her to the young man. He advised her that she was to board a coach that would take her to the Grand Hotel where her betrothed was registered and anxiously awaiting her arrival. We accompanied Mira to her transportation, all the while expressing our joy over making her acquaintance. Saddened by our abrupt separation, Joseph and I wished her love and happiness as she prepared to mount the awaiting carriage.

As the coach ambled away from our presence, we waived a solemn good-bye. Mira waved back frantically with half her body extending out of the window. "I'm going to miss that girl!" I lamented.

We asked the young envoy if he knew Mr. Salvadore Cortez. As he prepared to respond, another voice sounded nearby. "I know Mr. Salvadore Cortez!" a well-dressed man announced emphatically. "Just follow me!" he beckoned with a waving gesture. Mr. Cortez sells fruits and vegetables in the open-air market just over the levee from here; his store is part of what the locals call the "French Market."

As we walked along, the man identified himself. "My name is Joseph St. Romain. I own an import business not far from Ole Salvadore's produce market." As we continued walking, Mr. St. Romain continued, "Mr. Cortez is a short portly man, and he has a personality that can raise the dead! He is a man of character, and what a character he is!" he raved. After a few more paces, we found ourselves standing below a huge sign, which gave us a bit more insight into this jovial man's character. I believe Mr. Cortez will be one of the most interesting persons we have had the good fortune of meeting. The sign read as follows:

SALVADORE CORTEZ PRODUCE COMPANY

NEW ORLEANS FINEST FRUITS AND VEGETABLES

PRODUCE FRESHER THAN THE AIR YOU BREATHE

OR I WILL NOT SELL IT TO YOU

SATISFACTION IS GUARANTEED!

SALVADORE CORTEZ

Mr. St. Romain introduced Joseph and me to Mr. Cortez. It became immediately apparent that he had been expecting us. "I trust you had a pleasant journey. How was it?" Mr. Cortez cordially asked.

Joseph told him that our trip was exciting, adventurous, and pleasurable. He did not mention our terrible bout with a storm, which could have ended our lives, sending us and our ship to a watery grave somewhere in the deep and chilled waters of the North Atlantic.

I felt no urge to spoil things for the two men by interjecting my own thoughts about the voyage. Mr. Cortez smiled with hearty approval after Joseph painted his perfect picture of a wonderful experience. Sufficient for me is the assurance of having my two feet planted firmly on the ground. Voicing my passive reflection of the voyage is better left for some other time. There are more challenges before us that will warrant all of my attention, I reasoned within myself. Mr. Cortez shared Uncle Patrick's instructions. He is to escort us to the Grand Hotel Orleans. He advised that we only carry essentials; our trunks and personal belongings will be sent to us at the hotel. "No need to cumber yourselves over trifle things!" Mr. Cortez chuckled. "Congressman Adams is anxiously awaiting your arrival!" he added in humorous tones.

There was much activity surrounding the generous display of fresh fruits and vegetables. I had to stretch my hand through several crowded bodies to grasp a single exquisitely ripe plum, which I immediately began to consume. "Eat whatever you like! And from now on, call me Sal!" he insisted.

When I spotted Joseph, he was eating the last grape from a denuded cluster, which he had chosen from a heap of grapes on display before him. Walking over to the huge bin, filled with clusters of red, green, and purple-hulled grapes, I observed a sign overhead with the caption "sumptuous grapes." Above the cucumber bin was the phrase "pucker pickle prospects." There were "bonus beans," "crazy carrots," "hallmark garlic," "humdrum mushrooms," "luscious legumes," "calico squash," "merry melons," and how about this one: "sightless potatoes with eyes so tight you can hardly see them," "buttonhole berries," "velvet okra," "charming chilies," and the amusingly descriptive labels above each item would exhaust me to recall.

Mr. St. Romain's insight into Mr. Cortez's personality proved to be very concise. "Mr. Cortez is a character and what a character he is!" I could not have described him better: "a personality that can raise the dead!" What a fitting characterization for a convivial man who lends personality to each and every product he sells. Yes, Mr. St. Romain must know "Ole Sal" quite well.

Sal's pledge to his customers, insisting that everything is fresh, is indicative of the business ethic of a man who knows what his customers want. His name affixed to his store advertisement: "satisfaction is guaranteed" speaks loudly about the man and his merchandise.

Satisfaction is guaranteed! I wonder if Uncle Patrick will live up to the expectations I have of him. Mr. Cortez has been a cheerful host; what temperament will the congressman convey? I wonder.

Sal loaded us onto his delivery wagon and made his way along St. Peter's Street heading for the Grand Hotel Orleans. Turning on

Decatur Street, we soon found ourselves before a large open square. At the far side of the square stands a picturesque cathedral whose impressive towers reach for the sky. Continuing along the general course of the Mississippi River, we observed countless sailing vessels and steamboats traveling up and down the mighty waterway. Running perpendicular to our riverside road were streets with names like Toulouse, St. Louis, Conti, Bienville, and Iberville, which is where the hotel is located.

"Here we are!" Mr. Cortez proclaimed. "Time to meet the congressman!" he gleefully announced. Mr. Cortez informed us that Uncle Patrick has been vacationing in New Orleans for several weeks. I cannot imagine such a carefree lifestyle. He must be a very wealthy man. Who else could afford such extravagant behavior?

Sal ushered us into the hotel lobby where we were greeted by an attendant. We informed him that we were guests of Congressman Patrick Adams, and he scurried off to deliver the message. While waiting anxiously to meet for the first time, the most important man in our lives, Sal bid us adieu vowing to see us again before we leave the city. He hurried quickly out the doors to return to his business affairs.

Suddenly, a handsome, fashionably dressed gentleman appeared standing before us. He reached out to shake Joseph's hand with a warm smile on his face. "You must be my dear nephew, Joseph. You are every bit the strapping young man I hoped you might be. It's good to meet you son." Next, he turned to me, reached for my left hand, raised it to his lips, and he kissed the back of it with the charm of a prince.

Has my life suddenly turned into some fairytale? Has God Almighty granted us a reprieve from our ordinary mundane existence? Can it be that we are really going to prosper from the extreme good fortune of this generous man, a man Joseph and I have never set our eyes on before this very minute?

His gently caring demeanor instantly won my admiration. I sensed that Uncle Patrick is a refined gentleman, very well educated, a man of authority, and a man who knows what he wants from life, one who knows how to get things done.

He gestured for one of the hotel attendants to do something for him. I could not determine what the signals meant from a glance, but as we walked out the front door, a shiny black carriage appeared. Apparently the coach belonged to the congressman, because the driver, a well-dressed black man, referred to him as Mr. Adams; it gave me a degree of comfort that he did not address him as "Master Adams." Four jet-black horses, as shiny as the coach they were harnessed to, waited nervously for the coachman's command.

The attendant helped us into the coach, closed the door behind us, and received some sort of remittance for his eager and polite assistance. Uncle Patrick shouted, "Take us to the Harbor House Restaurant, Albert!" With a crack of the whip and the shout "Let's go, horse!" the coach began to move through the streets of the city of New Orleans.

I found the buildings along the city streets large, in comparison to those in the many other port cities we had visited. Most of these are built upon massive columns made of brick. The upper structures are made of wood and those with galleries have wrought iron railings. The bottom stories are constructed entirely of brick. Virtually all these large homes have brick chimneys becoming progressively smaller as they tower along the structures reaching for the sky above the rooflines.

The streets are bustling with activity; coaches and carriages, wagons and carts, people and animals everywhere, parading up and down the dusty roads. Uncle Patrick says the restaurant is seven blocks from the hotel at the corner of Conti and Burgundy Streets.

The coach ride was remarkably comfortable. Albert must be an experienced driver, moving such a large coach amidst all the clutter of these busy streets with four horses. To remain in steady control, this task cannot be undertaken by a novice, I thought. Then I heard Albert shout, "Whoa, horse!" with an authoritative tone, and the coach came to a standstill.

A restaurant attendant quickly opened the door of the coach and assisted me to the ground. Uncle Patrick gave me his arm, Joseph did likewise, and the two men escorted me up the huge stairway that led us to the entrance.

As we entered the dining hall, a black man playing an upright piano caught my attention. Like Albert, the man was well-dressed, and he had a pleasant disposition about him. He smiled as he saw me staring in his direction. I did not give him another thought, though his music was delightful, and it helped to create an elegant atmosphere in the dimly lit room.

We decided to allow Uncle Patrick to order for us all. He told the waiter we would have roasted duck, rice and gravy, a few steamed carrots and turnips, and for desert, we would like some bread pudding. We all asked for iced tea to go with the meal.

While I had examined the buildings and other sites on our way to the restaurant, Joseph and his Uncle Patrick were steeped in conversation. I only remember hearing that we would be taking the coach across the river by ferry in the morning and heading northwest along the course of the river to various stopping points which will ultimately take us to Brashear City. I heard this destination will mark the end of the second leg of our journey to the "promised land."

While we dined, Uncle Patrick shared that there will be a sailing vessel loaded with freshly milled lumber waiting for us at a dock along the Atchafalaya River. From there, the final day of our journey will take us to Deer Island. He told Joseph that all the tools, nails, and hardware needed to begin construction are also onboard. This information produced much excitement in all of us. We are getting closer to our new home every day. It won't be long now!

There was never a hint of politics raised in any of the conversation. It was obvious that Joseph's uncle was excited over sharing his plans for our future. He seemed to be embarking on an adventure far removed from his customary realm of activity; not unlike the radical changes we were experiencing in pursuit of Joseph's ambitious dreams.

"Deer Island is a place unlike any I have ever seen. It has been the focus of all I have dreamed of since I acquired the tract of land in 1834. You will never understand how I longed for the two of you to come here and help me turn my dreams into reality." With that emotional revelation, I could see that, though the perspectives may differ, Joseph and Uncle Patrick share the same hopeful dream for a good life. Now we will share that dream together as a family.

He told Joseph that the uncertainty of his political career was the driving force behind his insistence that we come to America to share in his good fortune. With Joseph's building skills and the resources to keep the project funded and supplied, the proposed settlement will soon be established. Uncle Patrick says that as time goes by, the fruit born from our decision to accept his invitation will demonstrate the wisdom of our choice.

Back at the hotel, Joseph and Uncle Patrick continued to explore plans and the ideas for their fulfillment. I decided to try to find my friend Mira. I needed a break from being third party to a two-way conversation. Begging their pardon, I removed myself from the room. I went to the lobby and asked an attendant to deliver a message to Ms. Mira Langley requesting that she meet me here.

Surprised by our unexpected reunion, Mira rushed over to greet me with a fond embrace. Trailing just behind her was a tall, lanky fellow she introduced to me as John Longstreet. "This is my fiancé," she proudly stated. John has dark curly hair and deep brown eyes. He has a distinguished look about him. A bit shy at first, but that soon changed when Mira and I began to cut up and have a little fun together.

We spent the remainder of the evening together. By the time we parted company, we had become more like a brother with his sisters than casual acquaintances. After saying good night, I returned to find the two men engrossed in serious conversation. I interrupted just long enough to say good night, and then I retired for much needed rest. The day had been filled with many pleasant experiences, but all my energy was consumed in the process.

Chapter Three

JOURNEY TO PARADISE
THE OVERLAND TRAIL
ALGIERS TO DONALDSONVILLE

June 4, 1840

Uncle Patrick had someone wake us at sunrise this morning. We were instructed to meet him in the lobby as soon as we are dressed. We will be having breakfast before leaving the city. We are anticipating another day filled with pleasant experiences as we hurry to get downstairs.

Over breakfast, Joseph assured Uncle Patrick that the "big house" will be as breathtaking as any home in the South. "I will use all my talents to provide you with a beautiful and comfortable retirement haven. I hope I can make it even more splendid than you have imagined it could be," he pledged.

To our astonishment, Uncle Patrick presented Joseph with a copy of his will and testament. Essentially, the document conveys the property known and described by an attached survey as Deer Island, an area of five square miles (or five sections). A second property included in the legal document is described in another survey. It is an area covering one square mile (or one section) located on the Bayou Du Large about twenty miles below the village of Houma. In the event of the congressman's death, these properties would immediately become the possession of Joseph and Josephine Addison.

Nothing could have prepared us for this. It all seemed surreal, unimaginable, and impossible; we have become heirs to vast land holding the day after arriving in America. Life in Louisiana was beginning to appeal to me in a way I never dreamed could be possible, and yet, it is true—there is tangible proof that it is true. It is strange that a few words and sketches could make such a profound difference in our outlook for the future. The degree of security a will brings to Josephand I can hardly be expressed in words.

I could not help noticing the patronage Joseph's uncle receives from the various clerks, waiters, bellboys, and other hired servants. The congressman has always been polite, mild-mannered, and generous to everyone we have encountered; I guess the gratuities he freely administers must be the precipitant that prompts such pampering.

I giggled to myself thinking that the only coddling I ever get, is from Joseph when he has amorous intentions, but that would not be a fair assessment of Joseph's coddling. He is a caring and sensitive husband with no pretense for his actions.

Albert was already prepared to leave once we finished breakfast. Our belongings are aboard the coach strapped down and covered in the luggage racks. The high spirited horses are standing at attention eagerly but patiently waiting for the coachman's commands. How elegant the glossy black coach with the four jet-black steeds presents itself to any curious onlooker in front of the Grand Hotel Orleans.

Having climbed aboard, I listened for Albert's command. "Let's go, horse!" and we were soon at some distance from our overnight lodge. I took one last look at the elegant hotel not knowing if I would see any other like it in my lifetime.

Just before leaving, Mira and John had come down from their room to wish us godspeed. I'm glad we had the chance to see each other again. Maybe we will meet again someday.

We are heading for the Esplanade Street ferry. Traveling downstream following the river's course, Albert brought us along Decatur Street. My position in the coach afforded me one last look at the front of the city. As we passed the open square that separated us from the Catholic Church, Uncle Patrick shared with us its history. This church was named after the patron saint of France, St. Louis. Peering through the wrought iron fence that surrounds the grounds, the majesty of the building was evident. Its twin towers rise above the front two sides with the center tower reaching toward the heavens.

Uncle Patrick told us that a disastrous fire in 1788 had completely destroyed the building along with over eight hundred other buildings. Prior to the completion of the reconstruction on the second church, another fire destroyed another two hundred building; but this time, the church was mercifully spared. Restoration was completed in 1794.

Subsequent to these two disasters by fire, the governing body of the city passed a new ordinance that required new buildings be fashioned with brick or stone walls and their roofs must be covered with slate tiles. The only structure which stands today representing true French architecture is a convent built for the Catholic nuns in 1734.

Uncle Patrick explained that most of the buildings which exist today are typically a combination of the Spanish influence, with the many courtyards, the ornate wrought ironwork, high ceilings, balconies, and arched windows and doors. The French influence appears in the mansard roofs (roofs having two slopes on all four sides, the lower slopes being almost vertical and the upper slopes being almost horizontal).

Uncle Patrick continued describing the local architecture. "Notice the buildings on either side of the cathedral, the one on the left is the Cabildo. Completed in 1795, it was the seat of government under Governor O'Reilly's administration. The building at the right side of the church is the Presbyter—intended for a rectory servicing the priests, when it was completed in 1813, it was never used for its stated purpose. It was leased for commercial shops. These two buildings demonstrate the two architectural types I described having both the Spanish and French influence incorporated in their design." Just as I was going to announce our soon coming reunion with Ole Sal, Uncle Patrick brought our attention toward the newly constructed United States Mint. "Constructed on the site of Fort San Carlos, this magnificent building was completed midway through the second four-year term of President Andrew Jackson in 1835. The structure is over eight hundred feet long and one hundred feet deep. The facility and its grounds are surrounded by wrought iron fencing," he proudly shared.

"We are coming to Esplanade Street. We will soon be at the produce market near the river," Uncle Patrick announced. "The ferry landing is just over the railroad tracks at the riverside of the levee," he added.

Albert drove our coach over the levee and across two sets of railroad tracks; he then followed along the river road heading toward the ferry landing. Soon we will arrive at the loading pier, where the steam powered ferry *Dixie Lee* lay waiting to receive passengers. "Whoa, horse!" was the order from above the coach; at once, the coach stopped. As we prepared to dismount from the carriage, an attendant approached my side of the coach and opened the door. "Can I help you, miss?" he asked.

Uncle Patrick and Joseph were going out the other door. I raised myself to the crouched position and extended my hand to the nice young man who helped me to the ground. "Thank you, young man," I said gingerly, thinking to myself that this pampering is going to require some getting used to.

CARROLLTON & PONTCHARTRAIN RAILROAD 1840

ALBERT SHOUTS:

Uncle Patrick began to tell us of the dangers associated with ferrying across the river. "It is unsafe to ride a coach onto a ferry. Just last year, a couple remained inside their coach. It was smaller than the one I own, pulled by a single horse. Once aboard, someone's horse bolted unexpectedly causing the young couple's horse to lose its balance. Carriage and horse went overboard, as the swift river currents made all disappear into the murky waters. Horse, driver, and the couple inside the coach all perished. That incident made a believer out of me. Dismounting before boarding is the wise decision," he warned.

Coincidentally, the ferry landing happened to be near the site where we docked the *Island Mistress* when we arrived in New Orleans yesterday. Strangely, the ship was gone; she must have relocated, I surmised. She couldn't have finished transferring cargo and passengers this quickly; that would be something I never thought possible, never having witnessed it before! She must have moved somewhere up or down river from here.

"Let's go get a basket of fruit for our journey," Uncle Patrick suggested.

I was first to respond. "Great! I was hoping to see Sal once more before leaving the city."

Making sure we were clear of the wheels, Albert proceeded to drive the coach to the landing pier, and there he boarded the ferry.

We began walking back over the levee and the two sets of railroad tracks. As we were nearing the market, a train passed us by, blocking Albert and the coach from view.

As we drew near to the produce stand, Sal saw us coming. Scurrying over to greet us, he heralded, "Top of the morning to you all! It is good to see the fine young couple so happy and gay in this our fair city. What can I do for you folks on this beautiful morning?"

"We would like a basket of fruit for our journey west," Uncle Patrick touted. As Sal began filling the basket, Joseph and I thanked him for making us feel so welcome in his beloved city. "You reduced the anxiety associated with being strangers in a strange land. For that, we will always be grateful," I shared. I gave him a kiss and left him blushing as he shook hands with Joseph.

As we headed back to the ferry, I turned back to give Sal a good-bye wave, and I shouted, "I hope we meet again someday!"

With a big smile and a bit of a chuckle, Sal retorted, "The pleasure would be all mine! Have a safe trip. I hope you enjoy the fruit! Farewell!"

When we arrived back at the ferry, Albert was tending to one of the lead horses; he was rubbing his head and speaking to him as you would a child. "We got a long way to go, ole boy, save your strength for the other side de river," he softly pleaded.

After letting Albert select the fruit of his choice, we headed for the roof deck of the *Dixie Lee*. The view of the mighty river was awe-inspiring. There were countless vessels—small sailing vessels, ocean-going sailing ships, steam-driven paddleboats—vessels of every size and description. There was a large boat sporting four masts under full sail heading downriver. I wondered if she might be bound for England as she rounded the big bend at the far side of the river.

The *Dixie Lee* has side paddles; most of the steam-powered riverboats I saw were stern paddle wheelers. Uncle Patrick says our ferryboat has been in service for thirteen years, ever since the ferry service began in 1827. We will be docking at the Algiers Point Landing, just above the great bend in the river where that large sailing vessel is traveling."

A loud blast from the steamboat whistle sounded our departure. I glanced over at Albert to see if the horses were shaken by the sudden loud noise. No problem! The four black beauties were standing at attention as the paddles of our steamboat engaged, challenging the river's currents to carry us across its broad expanse. I was amazed at the ease and the graceful posturing of our vessel as it seemed to have no trouble following its captain's wishes.

Initially, as we parted from the dock, we traveled upstream against the current. As we began to near the other shoreline, the captain slowed the engines, allowing the currents to carry us into position for the landing. Turning the bow into the current once again, we seemed to walk over to the dock. The loading ramp was placed into position after the boat had been tightly secured to the huge piles at each end of the wharf. From our vantage point atop the roof deck I watched how the various horses and horse teams responded to their handlers.

One by one, the coaches disembarked without a hint of trouble. Albert had the largest team of horses and the biggest coach to drive onto the ferry dock. I paid close attention as he barked commands, gently stroking the horses' backs with the leather of the long reins he clasped tightly in his hands. In a matter of moments, the coach was ashore, safely awaiting our company.

We waved good-bye to the skillful captain, who supervised the proceedings from his elevated pilothouse; then we left the roof deck and walked with the rest of the passengers to our various carriages.

"Good job, Albert!" Uncle Patrick lauded.

"Why, thank you, Mr. Adams!" Albert retorted with his predictable smile. After that brief exchange, we mounted the coach and following our coachman's command "Let's go, horse!" we headed north following the west side of the river along the suddenly crowded road.

"We are on our way to Donaldsonville," Uncle Patrick informed us. "We will spend the night there, before heading for the village of Houma, the second leg of our journey. We should arrive at Milly

Townsend's boarding house at dusk—that is, if Albert can keep all the wheels rolling," he said amusingly.

I certainly did not want to complain to anyone, so I kept my thoughts to myself, but the road we were traveling was not befitting the elegance of the carriage we occupied. The frequent potholes and the stubborn ruts caused sudden jolts that no one could prepare for; I hit my head against the coach walls too many times to mention. Now I know what Joseph's uncle meant by saying we "should" arrive by dark this evening, "if Albert can keep all the wheels rolling."

Aside from a few tiny villages I saw along the riverside roadway, Louisiana seems a vast wilderness. The countryside is densely forested. The only cleared land visible is the roadway, and once in a great while, a few acres of farm and pasture land surrounding the small settlements.

I have seen a handful of beautiful homes along the way. The affluence of their owners was evident. The large homes could easily house several families. There were black people everywhere it seemed; a few doing chores around the grounds surrounding the homes, others were working in the fields.

"Since 1796, when Etienne de Bore successfully crystallized sugar from the cane grown on his plantation, the sugar industry has flourished," Uncle Patrick explained. "It is common for a plantation of average size to have as many as fifty slaves. The large work force is needed for the strenuous task of working the cane fields. During the harvest season, for example, the adult slave may work sixteen hours a day. The grinding season usually begins in late September and ends around Thanksgiving. Using a special knife—like a machete, but having a hook on the back end of the blade—first they cut the leaves away from the cane stalk, next they lop off the top, then they sever the cane just above ground level. Skilled workers waste little motion in the rhythmical art of cane cutting." Uncle Patrick really knows plenty about the sugarcane business.

Uncle Patrick continued, "While some workers are busy cutting, others are loading the denuded stalks onto mule or ox-driven carts for transport to the mill. There, the stalks are unloaded and fed into steam presses for juice extraction. After the juice has been extracted, the stalks are ground. This by-product is called bagasse—this is some-times dried and used as fuel for the mill, it is often discarded as waste. The extracted juice is poured into huge caldrons where it is boiled. The brown crystallized sugar is stored in one thousand pound lots in large barrels known as hogsheads. It is then shipped to the planters' factory in New Orleans to be sold. The molasses residue, a by-prod-uct of the crystallization process, is also sold at the factors' market."

"It makes me tired just thinking about it!" Joseph remarked with a serious expression on his face. Sensing that I was a bit bewil-dered by the lesson on the sugar industry, Uncle Patrick shifted the focus of conversation to sharing stories. I told him of the unpleasant scene we witnessed at Mobile. Joseph and I took turns expressing our sentiments regarding the slave auction.

Uncle Patrick assured us that the plantation owners he knows treat their slaves with the dignity of any hired hand, furnishing them with adequate housing, food, clothing, medicine, even affording them parcels of land where they can grow their own food, supple-menting their provided needs. "To alleviate your suspicions regard-ing how slaves are treated, you will be afforded a firsthand look at how a sugar plantation functions. Tomorrow morning, we will leave Donaldsonville and head for Houma. Near the outskirts of that set-tlement is Sugarland Farms Plantation. The Henleys and I are good friends. In fact, we will be there for an overnight stay. How does that sound?" Uncle Patrick asked, hoping to lighten the atmosphere. That will provide us with a great opportunity for expelling any misgivings Joseph and I may have about the institution of slavery I reasoned.

By late afternoon, all the fruit in the basket had disappeared. Seeing we were making good time, Uncle Patrick asked Albert to make a rest stop. A few moments later, we drove off the main road and the coach stopped beneath the largest live oak trees I had ever seen.

We dismounted the coach. A stretch of my legs and an arm stretching yawn, and I was beginning to recover from the aches and cramps brought on by our bumpy excursion. Joseph came over and embraced me, looking into my eyes for any signs of how I was feeling within. Seeing nothing that gave him alarm, he kissed my forehead, saying, "I love you dearly, Josephine Moore Addison."

I reciprocated with a tender kiss and a gratifying sigh, meant to stimulate his masculinity, and to encourage his resolve to see his adventurous dream fulfilled.

Pointing to the gigantic trees draped with Spanish moss, Uncle Patrick told us that on Deer Island there are many trees this size and larger. "I know you will be amazed when you see the environment surrounding your future home," he boasted.

His remarks further excited us; though, I could not imagine how that was remotely possible—I thought we had already been stimulated beyond anyone's expectations by the many surprises we have already experienced. Uncle Patrick's alluring comments about our future homestead drove me to test the endless bounds of my imagination, spurring me on through a cavalcade of curiosity and wonderment.

Albert asked his boss if he was pleased with our progress. Uncle Patrick told him he had driven the stretch of roadway with the expertise of a master coachman. The bright whiteness of Albert's teeth bore testimony of the pleasant relief he felt over the congressman's compliment.

Strolling over to the power source that made this overland journey possible, I noticed the horses had worked up quite a sweat from the long trip. They were obviously well kept animals. Their stamina is proof of their humane treatment.

"They are a magnificent team!" Albert proclaimed. "The best there is anywhere in the South!" he boasted.

Uncle Patrick tried not to show his pride, but Albert's remarks brought a conspicuous smile that spoke louder than his efforts to be humble in our presence. After all, Albert was just stating the truth; they are a magnificent team of horses.

The large black coach was a bit dusty from the trip, but it is still a beautiful thing to behold. The luggage rack atop the coach is adorned with polished brass fittings, as are the matching headlamps at the front and on both sides of the carriage. Albert's seat has a brass railing on three sides. The mounting ladders are also polished brass.

The contrast between the sleek black wood of the coach and the polished brass accessories gives the vehicle an elegant look that only English royalty enjoys back home.

"It is time to get underway!" Uncle Patrick shouted. "I would like to see the animals attended before dark if it is at all possible, Albert!" he pleaded. As soon as my bottom hit the seat, I heard the command "Let's go, horse!" With the nudging of the leather straps against their backsides, the powerful team moved us along the road to Donaldsonville, leaving our rest site in a cloud of dust.

PLATTENVILLE TO HOUMA

June 5, 1840

After a leisurely breakfast, we mounted our coach for the second leg of our overland journey. I am told we should arrive at Sugarland Farms Plantation by midafternoon—that is, if Albert can keep all the wheels rolling. Lord knows I now understand what that means.

Milly Townsend's Boarding House was no Grand Hotel, but the accommodations were comfortable, and the food was good. I had expected Milly to be some old widow, but she is a woman in her thirties with a husband and two teenaged children. They work together, doing the majority of the duties associated with operating the family business. Her husband and son work in the kitchen, cleaning and preparing the food. Milly and her daughter attend to their guests, serving tables, etc. They employ two attendants; one is responsible for assisting visitors with their horses; the other cleans the floors, washes dishes, and makes the beds. They seem to manage their affairs very well.

"Let's go, horse!" Albert ordered, as the coach slowly traveled the deserted streets of the sleepy community. Approaching a bridge that crosses Bayou Lafourche, Uncle Patrick told us that most of the homes and business establishments are located across the bayou from the road we are traveling. We are following the left descending bank of the waterway.

We traveled about an hour before we arrived at a thriving community known as Plattenville. Uncle Patrick instructed Albert to make a stop at the general store. "Whoa, horse!" Albert ordered, and the coach was brought to a stop. As we dismounted, our coachman came down from his lofty seat to consort with his beloved horses.

Uncle Patrick wanted to purchase some roasted coffee beans and have them ground by the store's proprietor. Mr. Alcee Dupont spoke English, but with some degree of difficulty. Most of the inhabitants here are French. Since opening his store twenty-five years ago, there has been an increase of English immigrants; some stopping here, but most passing through to other destinations. Consequently, he had to learn our language.

Mr. Dupont shared that the first Englishman who came to his store had to point to the things he wished to buy. He says that as time passed, he learned more and more words. "Now I can hold a descent conversation. At times, without realizing it, I find myself using a French word when I really don't mean to, especially when I get excited over something," he told us.

The general store was well stocked. The coffee grinder held a prominent place on the store counter near the doorway; the aroma of fresh roasted coffee beans filled the air. The store walls were lined with leather goods, harnesses, yokes, horse saddles, etc. At the center of the store there was a large cast-iron stove. The potbellied stove was contained within a brick enclosed sandbox to protect the wooden floor from falling embers. Six straight back chairs surround the spot, and all but one chair was occupied by men smoking tobacco pipes steeped in conversation. There were various barrels of food staples—flour, rice, dried beans, etc. Behind the counter were tins of tea, sugar, molasses, tobacco, and many other items.

Upon one wall were hanging farm tools—cane knives, hoes, shovels, axes, various saws, hammers, and carpenters tools. In a large cabinet, whose doors were opened, several long barreled rifles were on display. Several powder horns hanging from their leather necklaces dangle from hooks mounted on the doors of the lockable chest.

Joseph's uncle led him to the rifle display case and told him to pick the one he wanted. After careful deliberation, he asked Uncle Patrick to recommend one to him. Grabbing the most beautiful gun in the case, he handed Joseph a muzzle loader with polished brass inlays from its butt plate to the end of the stock, which stops where the barrel ends.

"That's a fine choice, Congressman Adams. It's a Kentucky flintlock, affectionately called by some *Long Tom*. It's .45 caliber mini ball can be propelled to hit any target to a distance of three hundred yards, if your eyes are good and you have a steady hand," Mr. Dupont proudly stated.

"What are your names?" Mr. Dupont inquired.

"My name is Joseph, and this pretty woman by my side is my wife Josephine. I am the congressman's nephew. My wife and I are from Southampton, England."

"You can kill anything from a water snake to a bear with this baby. This past winter old Alphonse Dupuis, the man with the straw hat sitting near the stove, shot a 450-pound black bear as it was trying to rob his beehives; isn't that right, Alphonse?" Mr. Dupont queried in a teasingly boastful sort of way.

Removing the pipe from his mouth, he replied in the affirmative speaking in French and English, but we could understand his assertion.

Joseph had a sparkle in his eyes as he humbly but proudly accepted the handsome firearm. "Give him two powder horns, a thirty-pound keg of gunpowder, and enough .45 caliber miniballs, flint, and wadding material to use all the powder. Give him all he needs to keep it clean," Uncle Patrick ordered.

"Yes, sir! Mr. Congressman," the store owner happily announced.

While the men were getting ready for the hunt, I decided to exit the store to have a look around. Just down from the store was a large, well-kept field. There was a group of young Negroes jumping rope and having a good time enjoying the summer sunshine.

At the backside of the large, wide-open expanse, was a Catholic church. It was constructed entirely of brick except for the entranceway, which had a gabled roof to protect the front doors from the rain. To the left of the church is a splendid home, elevated by brick columns that extend about eight feet above the ground. That must be the rectory, I thought. At the other side of the church is the home of past parishioners—a cemetery.

Compared to St. Louis Cathedral, this church has a simple design; the open field trains one's eyes directly toward the structure from the roadway, just as the cathedral in New Orleans does. It is a rather clever way to advertise its presence in the community, I reasoned. The church building is clearly the center of attraction in this community.

I decided to have a chat with Albert while the men were conducting business inside the store. Albert smiled as he saw me approaching. "It's a good day for traveling, isn't it, Albert?" I hailed.

"Are you enjoying the trip, Mrs. Addison?" Albert politely asked.

"Yes, indeed! It could not be finer weather nor could I be any happier with our progress!" I answered approvingly.

Albert warned that if rain comes we would have to drive as quickly as possible to the nearest village to layover. If it rains hard enough, sometimes it takes several days before this heavy coach can travel again. "Dry weather is what I like and the horses like it better too!" he exclaimed.

I asked Albert where he came from, and he replied gingerly, "Well, Mrs. Addison, it is a long story, but I'll try to shorten it for you." He continued, "My full name is Albert Huie. I was born in Malanje, Angola. When I was very young, my parents and I were captured by slave brokers and taken by ship to Charlotte, North Carolina. We were sold at an auction together for $1600 to B. G. Caldwell and Company. When my father and mother got too old to put in a hard day's work, they set us free. One of the Caldwell's was a good friend of Congressman Adams. Mr. Adams paid for our transport to New Orleans and moved my parents into a house on a small farm that he owns on the outskirts of the city. My papa passed on. Mama and I live on the place alone now. I go everywhere Mr. Adams goes. I have been working for him for fifteen years now. He takes good care of me and Mama. I would do anything for him. He is a good man, that I can tell you. He calls me his shadow because I'm always behind him—that is, when I am not tending the coach and his horses. Did I answer your question, Mrs. Addison?" I told him that he answered very well as he showed the store attendant where to place the goods he was carrying from the store.

Joseph appeared on the front porch of the general store with his new gun in his hand and two powder horns hanging by leather straps from his neck. "I'm ready for bear!" he shouted.

Albert and I chuckled over my husband's enthusiasm. "Now I won't have to worry about eating, when we get to Deer Island!" I cautiously assured him. When we boarded the coach and heard the command "Let's go, horse!" from our trusty coachman, we resumed our downstream trek.

Chapter Four

JOURNEY TO PARADISE
THE OVERLAND TRAIL CONTINUES
SUGARLAND FARMS PLANTATION

June 5, 1840 (Midafternoon)

Albert steered the coach to the right, turning off the road beneath a canopy of greenery. Turning left after a short distance, he shouted, "Whoa, horse!" and that brought the coach to a halt. Through my window I could see a rising stairway leading to the veranda of a magnificent home.

"This is Sugarland Farms Plantation, established in 1827 by my good friend, William Harrison Henley," Uncle Patrick announced.

I was awestruck by the majesty of the beautiful structure that appeared before me as I exited the coach at the hand of a smartly dressed dark attendant.

A broad stairway leads to a veranda, which affords access to the main entrance to the house, located on the second floor. The balcony is highlighted by six large square columns equidistant, which support the roof and balustrade and which bound the parameter of the porch with one column at each side of the stairway.

Exiting the French-styled doors at the top of the steps and coming down to greet us was a man of dignified appearance, tall and lean, and fashionably dressed—not unlike Uncle Patrick's normal attire of suit, coat, and hat.

Greeting Uncle Patrick with a smile and a handshake, Mr. Henley then turned to Joseph to extend him the same courtesy. "Harry, this is my nephew, Joseph Addison, and his charming wife Josephine."

As Uncle Patrick was introducing us, the gentleman removed his hat in a gallant display; I offered my hand, which he promptly raised to his lips and kissed. He looked into my eyes and said, "Welcome to my home, Mrs. Addison. I hope your stay here will be most pleasurable."

Mr. Henley asked me if the journey from New Orleans had been an enjoyable one. "Yes, it has been pleasurable, Mr. Henley, and somewhat an educational experience as well. The congressman has given us a general history lesson about life in Louisiana, from the founding of the city of New Orleans to the growing prosperity of the sugarcane industry; a subject I am sure you have an interest in," I quipped.

"Indeed I do, madame! Indeed I do!" he answered with a chuckle. "I believe we are going to be good friends!" Mr. Henley pledged.

The young Negro attendant who helped me down from the coach mounted the carriage and took the seat next to Albert. He directed him to steer the coach the length of the semicircled drive. Turning left at the main roadway, they made nearly the entire circle from where I was standing before disappearing as they drove past the right side of the house and headed for the stable.

Sugarland Farms Plantation
Established 1827 by:
William Harrison Henley

Mr. Henley was engaged in conversation with Joseph and Uncle Patrick when Mrs. Henley appeared at the top of the elevated porch steps. She was elegantly dressed, wearing a flounced gown. The alternating navy and sky blue fabric was radiant, even in the filtered sunlight. Fitted around her neckline was an embroidered collar, trimmed with bobbin lace. The puffed sleeves were three quarter length, trimmed with bobbin lace and loosely fitted about the mid forearm.

A navy blue sash was trimmed with lace and fashionably tied at the waist presenting two contrasting lines down the front of the dress to the knees. Without a doubt, she was wearing the most beautiful dress I have ever seen.

Carefully descending the massive steps, Mrs. Henley greeted everyone with a hearty welcome. Her husband introduced Joseph and me after she had first given the congressman a fond embrace. The men resumed their conversation while Mrs. Henley and I got better acquainted. She asked me to refer to her as Greta, dismissing all formality. She then took me for a walking tour of the meticulously kept grounds.

A brick walkway established the path of the tour. Leaving the front of the stairs, we walked toward the left front of the house. Greta began to describe her residence. "Thirteen years ago, my husband and I left New Orleans to build a sugar plantation. We purchased two thousand acres of land that was already under cultivation. The original owner died. His wife sold us the land and moved to Virginia to live with her family there."

Greta continued, "William's father owns a cotton plantation in Natchez, Mississippi. William worked in New Orleans as a factor for several years, handling numerous clients in both the cotton and sugar industries. Wanting to change direction in his life, he saw a future in sugar, and now, here we are." She chuckled.

There are magnolia and crepe myrtles in full blossom, strategically placed throughout the grounds. Greta continued, "We keep up approximately seven acres surrounding our home and around the stable and row houses at the rear of the house. We have a fishing pond a few hundred feet to the left of our backyard. We will visit that area later."

"My husband," she said, "employed some of the best brick masons and carpenters to do the construction work on the house. The ground level floor is made entirely of brick. Built as a foundational substructure, the first story is only eight feet tall. The exterior and interior walls, as well as the floor at this level, are solid brick a foot thick. The below ground foundation for the four brick chimneys is eight feet deep, constructed with cement to support the massive weight of their columns. The chimneys are placed midway between the slope and the roof line on each side of the gable, front and back. All four columns rise about five feet above the roof's peak."

Greta began to describe the top story of the three-storied building: "Accenting the roof are six dormers, three protrude through the front slope and three through the back. The upper-story houses four bedrooms, a powder room, and a small parlor that we use for overnight guests. The center dormers light the hallway, which runs the depth of the structure. The other four light the bedrooms at each corner of the upper level of the house."

Then she described the floor plan of the second story: "The second level has a hallway down the center running through the entire width of the house, front to back. It has double French doors for entering or exiting the house onto the front and rear verandas. There is no access to the ground level from the rear porch. We use the spot for leisurely activity, and it facilitates a wonderful view of the estate. Midway down the hall to the left is a stairwell lending access to the ground floor. Our master bedroom is located at the front left of the center hall. To the right is a library and study room. Next down from the library is our powder room. The last room at the right side of the hallway is the parlor. To the left just to the rear of the stairwell is the dining area. Both the dining room and the parlor have double French doors lending access to the rear veranda. From the vantage point of the rear veranda, one can have a spectacular view of the courtyard, the fish pond, the cultivated acreage, the stable, the blacksmith shop, the row houses, and the back portion of the well-kept grounds that grace the homestead."

Just as I thought Greta might need to sit down and rest her voice awhile, she began to describe the ground floor. I remember thinking how vast the Henley property was and how intricately this woman was describing it all. I was getting tired just listening. "The ground level has two main entrances. The front and the rear verandas both cover brick galleries, which extend the entire width of the house and access the double French doors at the center at both the back and front of the house. Like the floor above, the center hallway travels through the entire house, front to back. Entering the front door to the left is the stockroom. To the right, there is a dining room and a lounging area for the house servants. Next down and to the left is the stairwell leading to the second floor level. Across from the stairwell, to the right side of the hall is our cook's living quarters. The last two rooms are the kitchen to the left and servants quarters to the right. That is where your coachman will be spending the night." Wow! I never heard such a complete and concise description of anything. She lost me somewhere on the second floor.

"Would you like to go sit in the breezeway below our cistern, Josephine?" Greta offered. I gladly accepted her invitation; I needed a respite.

We walked the brick pathway and approached a round-shaped enclosure, which supported a huge wooden storage tank about eight feet above ground. There was a natural breezeway created by the passageway that traveled completely through the circular structure. Greta ushered me to one of the two brick benches that followed the contours of the foundational walls—though they were functional as a seating area I do believe they added strength to the walls that were holding the cistern filled to the brim with water. Immediately upon being seated, I could feel the refreshing cool air caressing my sweaty face. The shape of the walls below the tank seems to draw the breezes over one's entire body.

"This is the coolest place on the farm. Can you feel what I'm talking about, Josephine?" Greta asked.

"Indeed I can feel it! The instant I sat down, I could feel it. Even the bricks we are seated upon have a cooling effect!" I declared, enjoying the sudden relief. Before my bottom got damp from the condensation that covered my brick seat, Greta beckoned me to follow her to continue the tour of the grounds around the left, back, and right sides of the mansion she called home.

Continuing to walk the brick pathway, I noticed the red and pink roses in full bloom along the left side of the house. There were fancy leafed caladiums forming colorful circles at the bases of all the live oak trees—the huge branches of the oaks reach upward, towering above the rooftops of the house, nearly touching its walls as they screen them from full sunlight.

Near the back left corner of the house, the brick walkway diverges. Directing me to the right, Greta said the other path would lead us to the fishing pond. "We will see that later, after we have had a good cup of tea," she told me.

The courtyard was surrounded by brick walls about six feet tall. Wrought iron gates allowed access to its interior space at three locations. There was a walkthrough gate located at the center of each sidewall. There was a large double gate that was at the center of the rear wall, lending access by wagon or coach to the back porch of the house.

The entire courtyard floor is made of brick. The various plants and flowers are contained in brick planters about two feet tall. At the center of the courtyard is a bronze statue of a woman, which focuses one's attention to the multi-tiered birdbath beneath her feet. The bottom tier of the water fountain empties into a shallow pond, which encircles the sculptured centerpiece. A series of wrought iron chairs, tables, and benches are strategically placed about the enclosed garden affording different views of the courtyard, depending upon where one chooses to sit.

On each side of the fountain approximately twelve feet distance is a magnolia. Perfectly matched in shape and size, these twins are a different variety from those outside the spacious courtyard. The leaves and the flower blooms are smaller; they must be dwarf magnolias, I reasoned, perfect for this setting. The fragrance of the magnolia flowers enhances the atmosphere in the courtyard at this time of the year.

Caladium-rich beds separate the rear gallery floor from the court square with six-foot openings at each end and a twelve-foot opening at the center of the house. If one would stand on the rear gallery at the center and look toward the three walls surrounding the courtyard this is the view one would see: the left wall is graced by the white flowers of the gardenias, which stand neatly trimmed about four feet tall; the back wall is lined with azaleas about the same height, neatly trimmed; among the azaleas equally spaced are alternating pink and red camellias whose beautiful flowers are showing off their charm; Carolina rhododendron line the right-side wall's base interrupted only by a ten-foot bed of crinum lilies with a creeping fig behind them clinging to the wall.

Encircling the base of the magnolias and the fountain are pink, red, and white begonias. Huge brass planters contain crepe myrtles in full bloom. I can hardly do justice to this splendid, magnificent display of natural beauty. You would have to see it for yourself. Unbelievable! That is what it is, it's unbelievable!

Exiting the gate at the right rear of the house, leaving the court-yard and heading toward the front, we passed beneath a roofed breeze-way that protects the Henley's elegant carriage from the weather. It's not as large as Uncle Patrick's, but every bit as beautiful. It sports brass headlights and all brass fittings for the trim work; its chestnut color, contrasted by the brass trim, is befitting any well-to-do owner. The roofed breezeway is connected to the house, occupying the space between the two massive chimneys; it extends out and away from the house about twelve feet, supported by three large cypress columns.

Greta said that they have four chestnut horses that pull their carriage housed in the stable out back. Reaching the front gallery, we finally made our way back to our starting point. We entered the house through the ground floor front doors. I was very tired from the lengthy tour; my feet were hurting, and I needed to sit down somewhere, anywhere!

Passing the stairway, we continued down the hallway to the kitchen area. I had not noticed Albert and the young attendant sitting in the servant's dining room.

Greta called out, "Flocie!"

A black woman appeared instantly and responded, "Yes, Mrs. Henley!"

"We will have tea in the parlor, and there will be four more mouths for supper and breakfast in the morning. Is Albert being treated to some of your sweet potato pie?"

"He's eating one right now," Flocie told her. "Albert and Beau are at the dining table right now eating pie and having some of my strong coffee," she added.

"I'll send Fannie Mae up to the parlor with your tea directly," Flocie pledged.

We returned to the stairwell, and we went upstairs to the par-lor to relax and wait for the servant to bring us tea. I sat down near the open doors, and I could see the vast stands of sugarcane, the leaves being shaken by a stiff southern wind. Two thousand acres of cultivated farmland! Such a massive plantation must need a large workforce.

Greta seemed to be curious about where the men were. "The men must be downstairs lounging in the courtyard, or they might be back at the stable arguing who has the best team of horses. You know how men are!" she quipped.

Before we were well seated, a young black woman appeared carrying a silver tray. On the tray was a decanter of hot tea, a sugar bowl, a creamer and a set of silver spoons. The young girl lightly set the tray down on a small glass table that was set before us.

"Fannie Mae, this is Mrs. Addison. She and her husband, Joseph, will be spending the night before continuing their journey tomorrow morning," Greta announced.

"Pleased to meet you, Mrs. Josephine," Fannie Mae said with a curtsy.

After a fine supper, we gathered in the parlor to have good conversation. I asked the two gentlemen who had the best horses, trying to stimulate the first contest of wit for the evening.

"The debate is still on-going," said Mr. Henley. "Perhaps you could be the judge of that. Tomorrow morning, we will meet the field hands and visit the stable so you can look the teams over. That would be fair, eh, Patrick?"

Uncle Patrick said that it would be a fair contest, especially since I would be an impartial judge in this matter.

Greta reminded me that we still needed to make a tour of the fish pond in the morning before the men steal me away from her.

"I would like to see the slave quarters in the morning, Mr. Henley," I suggested. "I meant the servant's quarters, of course," trying to correct my slip of the tongue. Seeing embarrassment on my red face, Mr. Henley tried to comfort me by explaining his position on the subject of slavery.

"Josephine, we own forty-three slaves. Twenty of these were born to married couples. Each family here has their own dwelling. Of the twenty children, Beau is the only one who does regular chores. He is the oldest of the twenty kids born here on my farm. We have twelve single men, ranging in age from eighteen to thirty-five who perform the hardest of the field chores. Flocie, our cook, has two children—Fannie Mae and Beau. Flocie and her husband had their own house out back, but since her husband died two years ago, she and her kids have taken up residence downstairs. The twelve single men live in the bunk house, the building nearest the stable.

"The kitchen and dining area for the field hands and other servants is located in a large building at the end of the row houses. They cook in a large fireplace just like the one in our kitchen. There is also a wash room for bathing, personal hygiene, and another for washing and storing clothes.

"Our slaves grow much of their own food in gardens tended in the back of the living quarters. This is supplemental food they wish to grow. The plantation provides adequate food for everyone. Everyone shares the responsibility for planting, maintaining, and harvesting the produce. I believe they cultivate about five acres for their own personal use.

"For meat, the men hunt for rabbit, squirrel, deer, coon, or whatever their taste buds fancy. A few of the men have their own hunting dogs. Every family has one shotgun for hunting—the men in the bunkhouse have three hunting guns.

"All the women share cooking chores, washing chores, and caring for the children. When needed, they help the men in the fields, usually accompanied by their children. Tomorrow, we will visit all the people and examine all the facilities. How is that, Josephine?" Mr. Henley concluded with an open invitation.

"That will be an educational adventure. I always welcome an opportunity to learn Mr. Henley," I replied with anxious anticipation.

Soon after the discourse on the personal slaves of William Harrison Henley, Joseph and I retired for the evening. It had been a long and interesting day. Now I lay me down to sleep, asking God my soul to keep. Amen.

June 6, 1840

The sun was up when I scurried out of my bed. I quickly dressed and gazed out of the dormer window. Our bedroom was on the third story located above the parlor. The view was fantastic. My eye level, I'm guessing, was at least thirty feet above the ground; this expanded my scope of vision. Two thousand acres of sugarcane is an impressive sea of greenery by anyone's standard. Joseph could be heard at the bottom of the stairwell summoning my presence.

He came into my room to inform me that we would be eating breakfast in the courtyard. "Everyone is ready to eat. Come downstairs to the courtyard as soon as you are ready!" he proclaimed excitedly.

I hated to leave the view from my bedroom window. I saw the stable, the blacksmith shop, the row houses; I saw the bunk house near the stable, the kitchen; I even saw the fishing pond. I reluctantly rushed downstairs to join the company of my hungry friends.

Breakfast consisted of biscuits, poached eggs, and grits (finely ground corn). After a cup of steaming hot coffee, Greta escorted me to the fishing pond. A privacy hedge of cane pole reeds (used for fishing and trapping) obscures any view from the kept grounds. If the brick walkway would not be leading me there, and I had not been previously informed about its existence, I would not have given this portion of the estate much attention.

Before reaching the hedgerow we crossed a drainage ditch, about six feet wide traversed by an arched wooden bridge. The brick path continued on the other side and soon took us through an *S*-shaped opening in the twenty-foot-tall bamboo stand. The layout for hiding the scene on the other side was impressive. I was beginning to wonder what the secret was, when suddenly I no longer needed to guess. There it was!

In plain and open view before my eyes was a very large pond. It was completely surrounded by huge cypress trees. The pathway continued past the hedge, through a narrow clearing in the trees, and led us to the foot of an arched bridge much larger than the one we had already crossed. Crossing the bridge, we arrived at a manmade island about fifty feet wide. The island was contained by a solid brick border; the brick ascended above the ground by about two feet. At the center was a gazebo, almost identical to Grandfather Moore's dairy farm. I could hardly believe my eyes!

Greta, seeing the look of astonishment on my face, asked, "What do you think of our fishing pond?"

"It's the most welcomed site I have seen since I left England. It reminds me of my family and friends back home. We enjoyed countless hours of fellowship beneath the roof of our gazebo," I answered in a somber tone, feeling a bit lonely.

One of the black men was fishing from a rowboat near the far end of the pond. Greta says that someone fishes the pond nearly every day. She boasted of the large catfish that have been pulled out of there. "One of the men caught a forty-five-pound catfish last summer. That one fish fed nearly our whole extended family. I thought Flocie was going to pass out when she saw the massive fish," Greta told me, obviously amused by the notion.

I suddenly found myself a bit envious of the Henleys' good fortune. I conquered my feelings by expressing my admiration and genuine gratitude for the kind hospitality and generous and caring attention that Greta and her husband had afforded us since our arrival. I also mentioned my appreciation for the kind and considerate attention which was afforded Albert, Uncle Patrick's coachman.

Greta informed me that Albert was like a member of the family. She thinks he is sweet on Flocie. Albert has been driving the congressman to Sugarland Farms Plantation for many years. "Since Edward, Flocie's husband, died, they have been keeping mighty close company whenever he is here. I would not be at all surprised if they get married someday," Greta speculated. That would really be something.

"Are you ready to meet our extended family, Josephine? The term *slave* is an accurate term used in reference to human beings who have been purchased, but we treat them with dignity and respect. I believe that counts for something; hence the term we use is servant," Greta informed me with no apparent reservations.

"Let's head back to the house. I know William and Patrick are anxiously awaiting a decision on who has the best team of horses. By now, I am sure they are wondering what is taking our tour so long," she offered with a chuckle.

I was enjoying Greta's company. In spite of her wealth, she has not been pretentious. She is a fine, dignified, smart, and caring person. I feel a kindred spirit. We have so much in common I know we will be lifelong friends.

"It's about time you ladies returned. We were beginning to wonder if you got lost, or maybe one of you fell into the pond," Mr. Henley teased, drawing a hearty laugh out of everyone. "Let's go see the horses!" he ordered.

Exiting the courtyard through the large wrought iron gates, a brick roadway extends about one hundred feet. Brick borders about thirty inches high and two feet thick follow the length of the road. Mr. Henley explained the purpose for this extended passageway.

"We use this brick roadway primarily during the grinding season. Our driveway gets so torn up and rutted during any rainy spell, it becomes a quagmire. The wagons carry mud on their wheels when traveling to the back of the house to deliver provisions. Making deliveries to the front of the house would totally wreck the place. With this brick path to the rear of the house, the wagons can have their wheels cleaned of mud before making the delivery. We only use the road that leads directly to the back during the grinding season. We avoid the semicircle drive at the front of the house. This has proven to be successful, preserving the appearance of the front of our home," Mr. Henley informed us.

As we approached the stable, Mr. Henley began to describe it to us. "The configuration of the roof is one that provides more room to accommodate storage of hay, sacks of grain, or anything else we need to stow away. The doors remain open during the summer months to provide cross ventilation. The building is seventy-five feet long and forty-eight feet wide. We have a row of stalls along each side of the open ten-foot passageway that traverses the building. There are eleven stalls, twelve feet wide, and eighteen feet deep. The twelfth stall is the tack room where bridles, saddles, harnesses, and other essential items are stored. The height of the doorway is twelve feet to accommodate carriages, or coaches the size of Patrick's," he informed us.

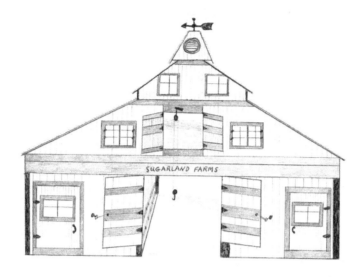

As soon as he mentioned the word coaches, Uncle Patrick's shiny black coach came into view at the far end of the stable breezeway. Mr. Henley had his blacksmith grease the wheels in preparation for our soon departure. Albert was tending Uncle Patrick's team of spirited black horses. Beau was doing the same with Mr. Henley's spirited chestnut horses.

Both four-horse teams were announcing their eagerness to serve. They were all engaging in enthusiastic snorting, whinnying, and stomping their hooves as they seemed to beg our attention. Uncle Patrick asked Albert how the horses were feeling this morning.

"They are fit and ready!" Albert responded.

"What about my horses, Beau? Are my chestnuts fit and ready?" Mr. Henley asked with confidence that they were every bit as ready as the congressman's black beauties.

"Your horses are mighty ready, Mr. Henley!" Beau quickly and playfully boasted.

Looking directly into my eyes, Mr. Henley asked, "What do you think of our horses, Josephine? Which of the two teams wins your favor?" You could feel the tense atmosphere as the two owners held their breath waiting for my response.

I walked from stall to stall examining the beautiful creatures very carefully—aside from their healthy appearance, I was ignorant of how one judges horseflesh; therefore I decided to deliver a coy announcement.

"It is good that these magnificent horses are not the same color. If they were, no one could be sure which team he was choosing. These eight horses are the most beautiful, capable, and high-spirited teams of healthy horseflesh I have ever set my eyes upon. The only real distinguishing factor is their color, which I find highly appropriate, seeing they are perfectly matched with the coaches they pull. How is that from a woman with no horse sense?" I quipped.

"I can see Patrick has been schooling you in the art of political savvy," Mr. Henley answered with a chuckle.

Everyone had a good laugh as we walked through the stable and out the back door. "This is our blacksmith shop," Mr. Henley stated as we entered the building behind the stable. "We are equipped to fix or repair almost everything on the farm. This shop is a very important element of our enterprise. During the planting and grinding seasons, things tend to break or need repair on a regular basis. When things are busy in here, we are losing precious time out there!" he sternly announced, pointing to the vast stands of sugarcane not far away from where we were standing.

Taking us back through the stable breezeway, Mr. Henley said we would visit the servant's quarters next. Exiting the front doors, we turned right and headed down the road. Already visible was the square shaped bunkhouse. There were several children playing around a string of houses built in a straight row along the right side of the roadway.

"We are coming to the bunkhouse. I can see Sam and Ed sitting on the front porch. Where is everyone else?" Mr. Henley asked.

One of the two black men walked over to us to explain, "The others are hoeing in their gardens, Mr. Henley."

The other man stood up an offered to go and fetch them. "That would be mighty fine!" Mr. Henley said approvingly.

"Sam Boles, this is Joseph and Josephine Addison. They are here visiting us with Congressman Adams. Mrs. Addison requested that I bring her back here to visit you all."

"I'm pleased to meet you all," Sam remarked with a pleasant smile and a polite nod of the head. "You all want to have a look inside de place?" he asked. "Follow me," he said, walking toward the bunkhouse door and beckoning us to follow with the motioning of his hand.

I suddenly realized that Greta had not accompanied us on our tour. How rude of me to have not noticed, I thought. My senseless curiosity has caused me to lose consciousness, I chastened within myself. I hope and pray that I did not offend her.

Just as I was beginning to sulk, Mr. Henley announced that his wife had stayed behind to prepare a surprise for our guests. "She wanted to do a little something for Joseph and Josephine to remember us by," he said with a broad and approving smile.

We entered the spacious one-room bunkhouse. The beds were neatly made; there was no odor, and the floor was swept clean with nothing dragging. I never expected that twelve men living together in one room could be so neat. There were three sets of double bunk beds on the east wall and three sets on the west wall. Walking through the front door, straight ahead in the middle of the room was a single long table with benches following along its sides. Looking directly over the top of the table, built into the north wall at the rear of the house, is the fireplace. To the right of the fireplace is the rear exit door. To the left of the fireplace were three shotguns and a blunderbuss, hanging conspicuously on the wall for easy access. Each of the four walls had a small wooden box secured to it; each box contained an oil lamp. The oil lamps were made of metal with a globe secured by wires mounted in an "X" fashion on the two sides not protected by the handle to help prevent the glass from breaking. The north wall had no windows, it had only the doorway; the other three walls had two windows each, with paned glass and protective shutters—now in the open position. This configuration supplies plenty of sunlight and cross ventilation. Closing the shutters in cold weather would certainly help the fireplace to keep the quarters warm. Interior walls were covered with horizontal planking; the boards on the outside walls were upright—board and batten construction. The ceilings were open, exposing the rafters and the ceiling joists. The roof was covered with shingles. The floors were made of tightly fitted planking with scarcely a gap to be seen.

As we exited the rear of the bunkhouse, eleven men with various garden tools in hand came to greet us. Mr. Henley introduced Joseph and me first, then the men began to identify themselves, all beginning with "pleased to meet you" or "mighty glad to see you." Then they gave us their names.

Sam Boles, the man who escorted us through the bunkhouse, stood by each man one at a time as they introduced themselves: Ed Caro, Joe Darby, Buck Holt, Ned Argus, Fred Nixon, Jack Dixon, Bow Jangles, Elijah Brown, Zen Gaston, Blue Diamond, and Tom Call.

Every face wore a smile that seemed genuine. They were all modestly dressed and wore shoes. All the men were cleanly shaven. Joseph and I thanked them for the visit. Mr. Henley bid the men good day, and we rounded the building and began to walk down the road again.

Our inspection tour lasted the rest of the morning. We met every soul—man, woman, and child. All the housing was of the same construction as the bunkhouse. Each building had a fireplace on its north wall, but the one in the kitchen was very large—like the one in the Henley kitchen.

Not far from the kitchen house was the change room. This building is where everyone did their cleaning up, where they washed their clothes, where they bathed. Every family has a designated spot for hanging or shelving their clothes. That is why the houses were so neat and odor free—no food to dispose of, no extra clothes or dirty shoes dragging around.

Row houses
Sugarland Farms Plantation

The row houses, or resident family houses, were all identical. A center wall separated the house into two rooms for adult privacy. The children usually play and sleep in the front room; at times, I'm sure some of the young ones sneak to the back to be with Mama.

When we got back to the Henley house, I was given a list of all the residents living at Sugarland Farms Plantation—a natural part of Mr. Henley's records. I have already recorded the names of the bunkhouse residents. What follows here is a copy of the record Mr. Henley gave to me.

Cabin no. 1: Assigned to Ed and Flocie East. Ed is now deceased. Flocie and Ed had two children while in the employ of the plantation—Fannie Mae, aged twenty-two, was born in the Henley home in New Orleans; Beau, aged thirteen, was born on Sugarland Farms soon after it was established.

Cabin no. 2: Assigned to Charles and Henrine Tomas. They have one child, Tyrone, who was born here on the plantation.

Cabin no. 3: Assigned to Row and Cecile Rich and their seven children, all born on the plantation—Rock, aged eleven; Jeb, aged nine; Boy, aged seven; Mattie, aged five; Sybil, aged three; April, aged two; Joy, aged one.

Cabin no. 4: Assigned to Wallace and Maggie Marks and their five children, all born on the plantation—Ike, aged twelve; Spike, aged eleven; Ira, aged ten; Missy, aged nine; Shelly, aged eight.

Cabin no. 5: Assigned to Slim and Margo Charles and their two children, both born on the plantation—Hattie, aged ten; Jack, aged seven.

Cabin no. 6: Assigned to Saxon and Dora Knox and their three children, all born on the plantation—Cary, aged twelve; Tara, aged ten; Fawn, aged four.

At fifty-five years of age, Saxon is the oldest slave on the farm; he is the blacksmith. His wife Dora is the chief cook among the servants; she oversees the servant's kitchen.

Rowe, from cabin 3, is Mr. Henley's coachman; he is also learning the art of blacksmithing from Saxon in his spare time.

My reflections on Sugarland Farms Plantation after careful consideration: Though the term *slavery* implies the harsh subrogation of one class of people for the benefit and pleasure of another, the condition of being subjected to specified influences could easily be applied to many circumstances among "free peoples"; therefore, one must be careful not to draw conclusions in ignorance. This would be most unfair! Mr. Henley's "slaves" are an extension of his family; they are treated better than many "free peoples" are treated in the bondage of their hire. Personally, I continue to oppose the institution of slavery on personal grounds and convictions; I will never own another human being.

I regret that we will be leaving so soon. I have enjoyed my stay at Sugarland Farms; it has been a learning experience. The Henley's have been very hospitable. I will leave feeling pampered by our gracious hosts.

Pausing as I started to mount the coach, I came down to give Greta a good-bye embrace. "I will forever remember your kindness Greta. God be with you," I prayed, as sentimental teardrops began to race down my cheeks. I mounted the coach and seated myself, as Joseph and Uncle Patrick said their final good-byes.

"Let's head west, Albert!" Uncle Patrick shouted.

"Yes, sir, Mr. Adams!" Albert responded. With the crack of the whip and "Let's go, horse!" we pulled away from the glory land experience of Sugarland Farms Plantation.

Ole Flocie could be seen and heard as she shouted to Albert from out in the front yard; waving a white kerchief, she hollered at the top of her voice, "You take care of yourself, Albert Huie. You get back here soon, you hear me! You get back here soon, Albert!"

"I hear you, Flocie! I hear you!" was the shout from atop the coach as Fannie Mae and Beau stood beside their mother waving with her. It was a moving scene. I bet Albert had tears in his eyes as our team of horses ambled west heading for Chacahoula.

CHACAHOULA

June 6, 1840 (Midafternoon)

The coach resumed its westward trek. Uncle Patrick says we will arrive at Chacahoula about an hour before sunset if Albert can "keep all the wheels rolling".

We will be spending the evening with a friend of the congressman. Her name is Pauline Longere, a woman he describes as a delightful French maiden, a woman he befriended while politicking along Bayou Lafourche several years ago.

The wagon trail leading us west was in good condition. The winding trail took us through dense forest, through a cypress swamp, through open fields with thriving grasses three feet tall—the grass was so tall that we could only see the backs of the cattle grazing there. We crossed shallow streams; we crossed arched bridges that spanned the deeper ones.

"*Chacahoula* is a Choctaw Indian word, which means *beloved home*, the place Mademoiselle Longere has chosen to call her home. Pauline calls her house *ma maison bien-amie* (my beloved home). There are only a dozen residences located at the tiny settlement. Pauline's dwelling is built on a natural peninsula, bounded by a stream on the west side, and almost completely encircled by a slough, a stagnant swamp for those unfamiliar with the term," Uncle Patrick told us.

"A picturesque site, the entire region is heavily forested by cypress trees. There are also gum trees, red maple trees, ash trees, live oak trees, and water oak trees. Oh yes, and there are countless palmetto plants—a tropical palm having long fan-shaped leaves. The Indians dry the leaves and weave baskets and make several other useful items with them. The finger of a ridge where Pauline's home is built stands about four feet above the surrounding swamp water. Her closest neighbor lives about a mile away," Uncle Patrick informed us with a simpering smile.

There seemed to be concern in the congressman's smile. Maybe he is worried about Pauline living in such isolation; I wonder if she is his girlfriend. His eyes seem to brighten when he speaks of her; time will tell.

Shadows were growing when I heard the coachman call out, "Here we are! I'm turning into the drive!" Albert brought the coach to rest at the rear of a quaint little house just a few feet from the back porch. It's been a pleasant journey from the Henley farm. Uncle Patrick kept Joseph and me in suspense as he described the natural beauty surrounding Pauline's home and now we could see it for ourselves.

Before we could dismount, a beautifully dressed woman appeared. The closer she came the more striking I found her appearance. As Uncle Patrick got out of the coach, Pauline rushed to him and gave him a tender embrace. She then proceeded to welcome us with a curtsy and a friendly smile, exclaiming, "*Bonsoir, madame et messieurs! Comment allez-vous?*"

Chacahoula – "Beloved Home"
Home of Pauline Longére
On a natural peninsula
Bounded by Cypress Swamp
And a stream to the West

"*Tres bien, merci!*" Uncle Patrick responded.

Uncle Patrick decided it was time to exchange greetings: "Pauline, I would like to introduce my nephew Joseph Addison, and his wife Josephine." Responding in her special way, Pauline said, "*Je suis enchantee de faire votre conaissance* (I am delighted to make your acquaintance)."

A gorgeous maiden indeed! Pauline is twenty-five years old. Her black hair is perfectly groomed and straight, flowing down over her shoulders and midway down her back. Her deep brown eyes are enhanced by her dark brows. Her complexion is impeccable, as is her smile with her bright white, well-shaped teeth. She seems elegantly dressed for such a rural community I thought, but what do I know? Lately, life has been full of surprises.

Pauline took Uncle Patrick's arm and Joseph reached for mine; we walked together, touring the grounds. There were a few large oak trees and a few pecan trees scattered around the "high ground" surrounding the house. The swampland was more pleasing to the eyes than I had imagined. A scenic stream flows through a ridge separating Pauline's property from the land to the west; that allows the water to flow to the slough on the opposite side of the road. There is an arched bridge that crosses the stream as the road continues toward Brashear City.

Joseph pointed to a family of raccoons resting in the upper branches of the pecan tree nearest the bridge. Across the stream is an impenetrable wall of greenery. Palmetto palms, dense brush, and small trees obscure any vision beyond a few feet. Spanish moss clings to the branches in the treetops, making darkness come prematurely. The cleared grounds surrounding the house span an area of nearly four acres.

Pointing to the bridge, Uncle Patrick informed us that early Spanish colonists used this same trail to drive their cattle to market from settlement to settlement. The final leg of our journey, beginning tomorrow, will follow the "Old Spanish Trail."

Turning my attention back to the scenery around me, I can only describe it as pure wilderness, but it does provide the viewer a splendid panorama.

The buzzing sound of dreadful mosquitoes and the weird sounds of the night creatures coming from the treetops, the swamp, and the forest, made me happy to hear Pauline say, "*Le soliel se couche* (The sun is setting; let's go inside!)"

Albert secured the horses in a small holding pen; they were settled and ready for a night's rest.

We entered the rear of the house and the first room we saw was the kitchen. Pauline said, "*Faites comme chez vous et mettez-vous a table* (Make yourself at home and sit down at the table)." Uncle Patrick seated himself at the table without hesitation, so we did the same.

Uncle Patrick wasted no time asking our hostess for a cup of coffee. "*Pauline, je desire prendre une tasse de café.*" As she walked to her wood burning stovetop, Pauline reached for a pot having a spout for pouring. "*Desirer -vous du the*? (Do you want some tea?)" she asked.

Before Joseph and I could respond, Uncle Patrick settled the matter. "*Non! Nous prefere prendre du café* (We all will have a cup of your wonderful coffee). *Merci.*"

This was a side of the congressman I had not anticipated; he can speak French. Sensing my bewilderment, Uncle Patrick offered clarification for his unexpected "*parley en Francais.*"

"Politicians who wish to win the respect and trust of their constituents must be able to communicate with them. In south Louisiana, many people speak French. Over the years, I have learned enough of the language to convince these wonderful people to vote for Patrick J Adams," he explained.

I was impressed! I hope Pauline knows as much English as Uncle Patrick knows French; otherwise Joseph and I will need an interpreter. Pauline soon dispelled my apprehension by speaking in English with a charming French accent. What a relief!

Poking a log in the fireplace to re–establish a flame, Pauline hanged a copper kettle over the heat source. Turning away from the hearth, she asked Albert to light a few lamps that were on the kitchen counter and place them throughout the house. "You know where to put them," she mentioned in a soft voice.

"*D'accord! Mademoiselle,*" Albert proudly answered, looking my way to see my reaction.

Joseph asked Pauline to describe life in the wilderness. He wanted to know how she managed, being alone in a community with only eleven other residents. He asked how she could be so happy, living in near isolation in such a remote location.

Pauline was very gracious. She answered all of Joseph's questions with delightful frankness; her explanations, given with an alluring French accent, served to captivate everyone's attention.

We dined on "*lapin cuire en civet*" (rabbit stew) a dish Pauline had prepared earlier in the day. "One of my neighbors—a young boy—shot the little creature, cleaned it, and delivered it to my back doorsteps," Pauline told us. This must be one of the benefits of being young, charming, and beautiful, I thought, trying desperately to disguise my jealousy.

Though Pauline had given a very detailed description of how she survives, relishing life in a swamp, I could not help wondering how life will be for Joseph and me on Deer Island. At least there is a road in the front of Pauline's home. We will be on a ridge called an island because that is what it is. Surrounded by marsh, rivers, and bayous, our only neighbors for miles and miles will be snakes, alligators, assorted reptiles and mammals, and a few birds—no people!

Conspicuously hanging on the wall, directly over the settee in Pauline's sitting room, is a portrait of our host taken in New Orleans in 1839. One could not help but gaze at the woman depicted. She was wearing a beautiful flounced gown; her gown resembled the one worn by Greta Henley back at Sugarland Farms.

Seeing my obvious fascination with the image, Uncle Patrick told me that it was one of the first daguerreotypes made in the State of Louisiana. I must admit that, whatever the process of reproduction, the image was the mirror of its subject; it was quite remarkable!

Uncle Patrick shared that he and Pauline were on a business trip together last year in the "big city"; he decided that having Pauline's portrait taken would make a fine birthday present.

Overhearing our conversation, Pauline said, "It was a wonderful gift, *n'est-ce pas?*"

Pauline's comment was simply matter-of-fact without any pretense of vainglory; she did not have to say anything—the daguerreotype said it all!

The delightful Pauline continued to fascinate us with stories of life in the "swamp lands." Her irresistible charm and selfless demeanor were bewitching. When she was not offering us coffee, tea, a glass of water, tending to our comfort, or telling fanciful tales, she was singing French folk songs, dancing about the room as she sung. "*Je danser, et Je chanter, de joie* (I dance and I sing for joy)," she says.

Pauline Longère
New Orleans, LA
1839

"*Pauline a toujours envie de danser* (She always feels like dancing)" Uncle Patrick informed us. This was a mute point, especially after hearing her own explanation for her jolly display; what a perfect hostess she makes!

Most amused by this dazzling beauty was Congressman Adams. I could see a sparkle in his eyes as he admired the young maiden's charisma. His infatuation with Pauline was quite understandable; I had to nudge Joseph in the ribs a few times during the course of the evening in an effort to distract him from her spell. The men seemed to be entranced by her innocent yet personable conversation.

I had lost all sense of time, when all at once Pauline said: "*Vous avez l'air fatigue, vous avez besoin de repose* (You look tired. You need some rest)." Sadly, I had to agree with her; reluctantly, I went to bed.

The lamps were burning low by the time we retired. As I lay in bed, I examined all of my preconceived notions about life in America, comparing what I imagined to what I heard from Pauline and Uncle Patrick during the evening.

My experiences at the Henley plantation had shed new light on my previously held convictions against slavery. I am certain experience will be my best teacher in regards to wilderness living. Deer Island will become my school, nature will be my schoolmaster; and the bell is about to ring.

June 7, 1840

This, the fourth day of our travel since leaving New Orleans, will complete the final leg of our overland journey. We will be taking the "Old Spanish Trail" as we head west to Brashear City.

When I was awakened by Joseph this morning, I wondered if I had gotten any sleep. The excitement of what lay before us had made it difficult to dismiss the wonderment; I wrestled with my pillow most of the night.

Ms. Longere had prepared a special breakfast. Joseph, having witnessed the preparation, explained what she had done with the ingredients. She made a corn bread batter—cornmeal, milk, and eggs. To the batter she added crispy bits of fried pork skins. She went to the fireplace and brushed aside the ashes and embers from last night's fire. Next, she poured the mixture directly on the hot brick surface. After a few moments, the mixture set—stopped oozing— and she shoveled ashes and embers over the top, sealing the "*farine de mais de porc en croute,*" as Pauline calls the dish.

I was offered the first bite. "*Goutez-y*! Taste it, Josephine. *Ca c'est bien bonne*! It's very good!" I could not believe such a dish would be edible—food cooked covered in ashes without a protective covering didn't whet my appetite. When Ms. Longere took the broad flat cake out of the fireplace, she placed it on a large tray to allow it to cool to the touch. Once cooled, she brushed away all the ashes from the encrusted treat. When she cut the one-inch thick flat cake into serving-size pieces, the aroma made my mouth water. Joseph insisted that I try a piece.

It was delicious. The combination of the pork flavor, the crispy crust, the bits of fried pork skins, and the firm texture of the corn bread produced a taste sensation I have never before experienced. I complimented Pauline on her unique concoction. Crusted corn batter stuffed with fried bits of pork skins; I'll have to remember that!

"*Merci, Madame Josephine.* I am very glad you enjoyed it," she responded with her usual feminine charm.

Albert was already harnessing the team, making the necessary preparations for our soon departure. Uncle Patrick was having conversation with Pauline in the distance; for the first time since our arrival, they were alone together. Joseph and I decided to take one last walk around the place to give them some space. I could not help wondering about their relationship. He is certainly in love with her; anyone could see that, but there was no display of the carnal aspects of romance in our presence. An occasional kiss, tender gestures, fond embraces, and love in their eyes for one another, but no announcement of a wedding. There is something queer about the relationship.

I admire moral character; Pauline slept in her room, Joseph and I were given the other bedroom, and Uncle Patrick and Albert donned couches in the sitting room for the night. I would certainly welcome Pauline into our family with open arms. Though Uncle Patrick is a bit older, his masculine charm and good sense would enhance the union. What does age have to do with love anyway?

There were several rabbits feeding on the dew-drenched grasses along the edge of the swamp. You would not think these furry, white-tailed little animals would like being around so much water. They must be plentiful here; we must have seen a dozen of them during our leisurely stroll. I had never eaten rabbit before Pauline introduced me to her rabbit stew. I think I will ask for her recipe before we leave this morning.

The call to board sounded. Uncle Patrick seems anxious to get to our next destination; Albert has already ascended to his position atop the coach. "Let's go!" Uncle Patrick beckoned. "Daylight is burning!" he shouted with a smile. "We have more places to go and people to meet!" he added.

I humbly asked permission to take the time to have Pauline write down her recipe for rabbit stew; we quickly disappeared into the kitchen to pen the cooking procedure necessary for succeeding with the dish. Lord knows I will need to learn to cook wild game on the island.

Pauline rushed to find pen and paper and jotted down everything I needed to do to make a proper stew. When she finished writing and explaining the details, we embraced. With my eyes beginning to shed tears, I told her how much I appreciated her hospitality, her encouragement, and her cooking skills. I said she would always be my special friend, and I hoped we would see each other again someday. I will always remember her beauty, her charm, and her graceful demeanor.

Pauline seemed to be touched by my comments. "*Vous etes bien aimable et je vous souhaite un bon voyage; soyez sage et Dieu vous benisse.* You are very kind and I wish you a good trip. Be careful, and God bless you, Josephine."

After a fond embrace, we said good-bye; I scurried to the coach, climbed the step, and seated myself, closing the door behind me. Waiting for the men to join me in the coach, I peered through my window; my attention was drawn to Mademoiselle Longere's attire. Not only was she impeccably dressed, but the woman displays such vibrancy and beauty that one would have to be blind not to take notice. I felt a bit envious, as I watched her charming the men, captivating all their attention, a spectacle like flies being entangled in a spider's web. Actually, I too found myself captured in the web she so craftily spun just by being herself. What a refreshingly delightful creature she is; I am glad I had this opportunity to make her acquaintance.

Albert shouted his familiar command. "Let's go, horse!" The coach began to move slowly out of the driveway. The fair maiden waved good-bye and bid us adieu as the crack of the whip announced our departure; we were on the road again.

As we began to pick up speed, the clattering of horseshoes atop the wooden bridge signaled that we were westward bound on the "Old Spanish Trail." The weather was perfect for the journey. It seems we will avoid the dreaded rain-induced quagmire that would prevent our wheels from rolling—something Albert was always mindful of, the weather.

BRASHEAR CITY

June 7, 1840 (The End of the Overland Journey)

Uncle Patrick announced that we would soon reach the end of our overland journey. He pointed to a fork in the road as we passed it by. "That road leads back to Donaldsonville. Albert and I will be taking that route when we head back for New Orleans in a day or two. The distance from Donaldsonville to Brashear City via this route is about the same as the distance from Donaldsonville to Houma. The time it takes to reach either destination using Donaldsonville as the starting point is virtually the same," he informed us.

After about two hours, the horses ambled through a quaint little settlement; I saw a large general store and two sizable boarding houses. The residential houses are small, but they seem to be well constructed: they were all built on brick or wooden piles about four-to-six feet above the ground. I suspect this area must be prone to flooding.

Just as we passed the blacksmith shop, Uncle Patrick instructed Albert to drive to Mr. Peltier's home. Mr. Irving Peltier is a political friend of Congressman Adams; he is a senator. We will be visiting the senator to review various documents and look over the sketches and drawings for our construction project on Deer Island. He has made a few copies for us to use at the building site.

We passed numerous carriages and a few wagons along the way, but none of them was large enough to need a four-horse team. In fact, none were drawn by more than a single horse. No wonder so many people were staring; we must be a curiosity to draw such attention.

We soon arrived at the front of a beautiful home. The coach slowed down, and after Albert's command, "Whoa horse!" we dismounted. After everyone was introduced, Mr. Peltier's wife Susan and I got acquainted over a cup of coffee. Though the Peltiers operate a farm, they live in the city. She told me they have eighteen slaves who live at the farm site in Pattersonville, just a few miles across the Atchafalaya River. There is an overseer living on the farm location to manage the workload; nevertheless, Mr. Peltier mounts his horse every day, when he is not away on business, and crosses the river on a ferry that takes him from Brashear City to Berwick. From there, he rides to Pattersonville to inspect the progress at the farm.

It was late afternoon when we pulled away from the senator's house and headed for the docks along the river. The Atchafalaya marked the western boundary of the city. As we journeyed along the waterfront, I noticed a sailing vessel heavily laden with freshly milled lumber on its decks. "Whoa, horse!" sounded from above the coach; this must be the boat we are looking for, I thought, as the coach came to a halt.

"There is your boat! The *Swamp Rat*, so named by its owner because she can take you anywhere!" Uncle Patrick remarked in an amusing manner.

What are we getting into? Just as I was about to get jittery, Joseph walked me over to the vessel describing it as we walked. "She appears to be about sixty feet long. She is a lugger I bet. Judging from her rigging with two mast heads sporting lugsails and jib sails off her bow, she would be highly maneuverable," he concluded.

Just then, a rough-looking character appeared on deck and proceeded to greet the congressman. "*Bon soir! Comment allez-vous? Monsieur Adams*" the man spoke in brash tones. Uncle Patrick introduced us to the captain and owner of the sailing vessel. "This is Francois Marceaux, but he prefers to be called Frenchy," Uncle Patrick suggested.

Joseph shook hands with the captain as I looked on from a distance. He nodded a hello toward me, and I did likewise.

"Don't be shy!" Frency said aggressively. "Come aboard and give my boat a good look over," he beckoned.

Joseph and I boarded the vessel. Examining the huge pile of freshly milled lumber, he informed me that it was cypress; cut from a tree common to South Louisiana whose soft wood is easy to cut and perfect for almost any construction—boats, houses, and furniture for a few examples.

I overheard Frenchy telling Uncle Patrick that everything was loaded and secured for the journey downstream. We would be leaving for Deer Island at first light tomorrow.

Uncle Patrick informed Frenchy that arrangements have been made for a labor crew to meet him at the mouth of Deer Bayou about noon tomorrow. He told him that with the lumber that he had already delivered to the construction site, this load of timber will be more than adequate to begin work. They agreed that there would be plenty enough material to make a good start. "I'll arrange for more deliveries to come out to you as progress continues. I want you and Carey to assist the Addisons in any way you can, Frenchy," he instructed.

"Who is Carey?" I wondered as we were entering the cabin. A pungent odor immediately caught my attention; this was no *Island Mistress!* I had to make several trips out the door to get some fresh air; I was becoming nauseous. Peaking back in, holding my breath, I saw the beds were so narrow that a small child could not lie beside me. If that was not startling enough, a young man suddenly appeared through a hatch in the cabin floor.

"My name is Carey Trudeau. I am Frenchy's deckhand. I am sorry if I scared you by coming out of the hold," he stated apologetically.

Joseph assured the young man that he had not scared anyone; that was only partly true. We returned to the dockside to hear Uncle Patrick's final words of encouragement; Lord knows I am in need of plenty reassurance as my knees are beginning to shake from the anxiety I was suddenly experiencing.

Uncle Patrick vowed to make a trip to the island in a few weeks to check on our progress. He told us that anything we needed would be ours for the asking. He said that Frenchy would be our courier and the primary means of transport for goods and services to and from the island. He asked Joseph to make a thorough inventory of tools and hardware so anything that is lacking can be acquired on the *Swamp Rat's* next trip to the city.

Joseph pledged to Uncle Patrick that he would be ready for more lumber in about three weeks. "Barring unforeseen difficulty, I should have the "little house" completed in a month."

Astonished by Joseph's bold statement, Uncle Patrick smiled and told him that if he fulfilled that time schedule, it would be quite an achievement. "I admire your aggressive determination. I am sure you will not disappointment me. After all, you are an experienced shipwright. Those woodworking skills will be a great asset for both of us. Good luck, son!" he affectionately concluded.

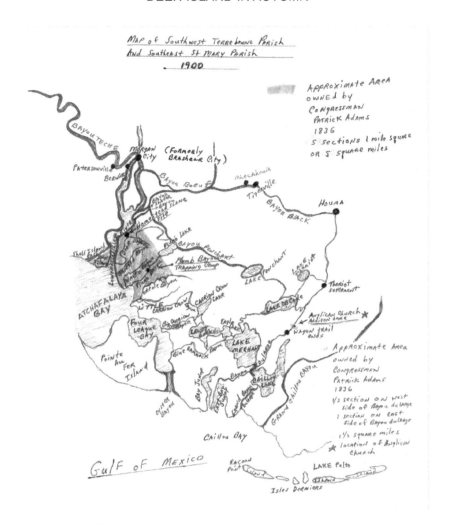

Carey was busy unloading our personal effects from the coach and placing them neatly in the storage area aboard the boat. In the process of his activity, I noticed that he was carrying two sealed wooden boxes I had not seen before. Seeing my curious glances, Uncle Patrick interjected, "Those are the special gifts from the Henleys that Greta secretly prepared while we were touring the plantation, remember? Greta instructed me to tell you not to open the boxes until you are secure in your new home, and oh, by the way, she said to be sure you keep them dry."

Upon closer examination, the boxes had brass hinges and they were securely nailed with copper nails to prevent accidental opening. There were keyholes at the front of each box with keys inserted. I removed them for safekeeping. The contents would have to remain a secret until construction is completed on the "little house" as per Greta's wishes.

I must admit that when Uncle Patrick pulled away in his stately coach, I cried uncontrollably. I can't explain why, I just cried and cried. I yelled at Albert to keep all the wheels rolling and not to forget what Flocie told him when we left the Henley plantation. I felt weak as the shiny black horses obeyed the coachman's command, "Let's go, horse!" and the coach sped away from view.

As usual, Joseph stood beside me in my moment of weakness. He embraced me to bolster my assurance that everything was going to be all right, lifting my courage by sharing with me his own. "With God's help, we will continue to have a prosperous journey. Our great adventure is just about to begin!" he roared with the confidence of a lion.

We settled inside the small cabin for the evening. Frenchy lit two oil lamps; I appreciated the light, but the lamps added heat that seemed to intensify the pungent odor that I thought I was beginning to manage. If that wasn't bad enough, it was already very hot and sticky before the lamps were lit. It is going to be a long night, and a long trip to the island tomorrow, I pondered sullenly.

As things turned out, the horrid pictures that were flashing inside my head aboard the *Swamp Rat* failed to materialize. The deck-hand was bent on making himself a spectacle. A lively sort, his playful antics diverted our attention from the heat and the smell. Before long, we were oblivious to everything, as Carey Trudeau began to blow a harmonica, which he pulled from one of his deep side pockets. He played the mouth harp very well and with wild enthusiasm.

Enthralled by the spider's web being spun by this sudden change in atmosphere, Joseph suddenly yanked me from my seat. Pretending to know the melody Carey was playing, he began to dance me all around the cabin deck. The unexpected rush to the dance floor upset my ability to adjust to the rhythm; I could not follow Joseph's lead, and my clumsiness made us all laugh the louder. With careless abandon, we had a grand time laughing and prancing inside the cabin of Frenchy's boat.

We had a glorious time on the old lugger, enjoying the merry melodious cantata of French songs and the striking and vigorous harping. All the excitement had stolen me away from sleep's grasp. It was two o'clock in the morning when the entertainment ceased; noise gave way to silent slumber. I lay awake gathering my thoughts and wondered to myself: what is Deer Island going to be like? Are there any Indians in this area? Is the Atchafalaya a dangerous river? Is Frenchy a good captain? Is the *Swamp Rat* fit for the occasion?

Sadly, no matter how long I pondered these questions, only tomorrow will provide me with the answers. Goodness! I suddenly realized that tomorrow for me begins in just a couple of hours. I asked the Lord for a safe trip downstream, and I told Him good night. Amen.

Chapter Five

JOURNEY TO PARADISE
(THE RIVER JOURNEY)
DOWN THE ATCHAFALAYA

June 8, 1840

Frenchy and Carey were awake before the sun. Though they tried to keep their voices down, I was awakened by their boisterous laughter. They apologized for disturbing me, but I don't think they really meant it. They weren't sorry at all; they just continued to engage in their playful antics. Their conversation was in the French language; I could not understand a word they were saying. One thing I know for certain, the subject of their conversation was moving them to uncontrolled laughter.

"*Serres comme des harengs*! Packed like sardines!" Carey lauded, seeing how closely Joseph and I were lying in bed beside one another. I couldn't find much humor in that!

What the heck! I thought, jumping from my crowded bed. I shook Joseph repeatedly, trying to get him up and out of the comfort zone he must have found. It didn't seem fair that he should get more rest than me; reluctantly, he arose from slumber and inquired what the fuss was all about.

"Today we are going home!" I clamored. "Today our adventure begins! Let's get this boat under sails! Time is wasting, let's go!" I sternly urged. That outburst of stored energy had all three men baffled. They looked at one another in a stupor. I guess I had made the statements with the force and authority of some general in the armed service; they weren't used to taking any orders from a woman.

Maybe I should pursue another course since it was obvious that they misunderstood my remarks. I was merely expressing my innermost feelings; I was trying to share my enthusiasm for covering this last leg of our long journey. I wasn't trying to take over the ship in some mutinous act. As I continued to muse over the reaction my outburst caused, the men continued their somber expressions.

Frenchy, pretending to be humble—a trait that would certainly have to be acted out—asked if we could wait for the sun to rise, begging my pardon.

A moment of silence and then the cabin was vibrating with rip roaring laughter; uproarious laughter, which continued until every face, including my own, was so filled with blood that barring efforts to regain our composure, one might perish.

Frenchy lit the oil stove and began to make coffee. I asked for a cup of hot tea, suggesting an alternative brew. He made a funny gesture, then with eyes wide open and a grotesque expression on his face, he quipped, "A cup of tea!"

"If you taste one cup of my English tea, you will never drink that black water again!" I challenged. Gruffly responding to my invitation to savor one cup of tea, he agreed to give it a try.

Searching through my belongings, I produced a tin of tea I had brought from home. Carefully watching my every move, the expressions on Frenchy and Carey's faces caused Joseph and me to burst out into laughter once again. "If this continues, we'll be too tired to set sail," I cautioned.

The "Swamp Rat"
Built in 1830
A Box-Keeled Sailing Lugger
Overall length - 69½ feet
Beam - 12 feet
Draft - fin down in sailing
position 8 feet
Draft - fin raised 30"

"There is no harm in having a little fun," Frenchy responded. I was happy that our boat crew was comprised of lively and witty characters. They have been the perfect remedy for the anxiety and apprehension that had gripped my heart when I first met them.

After two cups of tea, I asked Frenchy what he thought of the brew. While requesting his third cup, he said that it was all right, but it would take some getting used to; he was just being stubborn, I felt.

In the spirit of compromise, I told the men I would make coffee as soon as we get under way. "*Ca c'est une bonne idée, Madame Addison*," Frenchy responded as he walked out the cabin door, barking out orders to Carey as we prepared to make sail.

"*Allons mon motelot!*" Frenchy ordered authoritatively. I figured out the meaning of the French commands by watching their body language. Whenever Frenchy shouted to Carey, his hands and arms went into motion—one motion of his hands and the boat was untied from the wharf; another movement of his arms, and one at a time, the lugsails and jib sails were unfurled. Finally, we were underway, moving south a little faster than the swift river current.

While Joseph went on deck for some fresh air, I made the coffee I had promised. With two cups of fresh coffee in my hands, I joined him outside the cabin to take in the sights. The scenery was awe-in-spiring; I have never seen wilderness, at least not a wilderness consisting almost entirely of cypress swamp. It was magnificent, though a bit strange for a city girl.

Frenchy and Carey made quite a team. They worked well together and demonstrated a degree of affection for one another. Carey was an orphan child; his parents died of the fever. Frenchy took him in and taught him how to assist in the operation of his boat. "*Il est une homme bien, mais Carey manqué de bon sens* (he's a good man, but he lacks common sense)," Frenchy says. Now, with years of experience, he has assumed the responsibility of a deckhand. It was Frenchy who taught Carey to play the harmonica. Starting with the simplest tunes, he now plays like a professional. They have been together since Carey was three years old; he is now nineteen.

Massive trees can be seen floating downstream. Uprooted along the banks of the river's course, these huge obstructions make river travel hazardous. Frenchy is on a raised platform at the rear of the cabin manning the helm, carefully trying to avoid these dangerous obstacles.

Looking down the river from our vantage point near the bow-sprit, I could see three long slim boats exiting a stream to cross the river in front of us. The boats looked like logs with people on them. As we drew closer, I could see three men wearing no shirts paddling each craft just ahead of us. "Indians!" I shouted, not realizing I had shouted so loud.

Looking at Joseph to see his reaction, he seemed to greet this visual experience with the same casual attention one might give a seagull or a common sparrow. He did not even raise an eyebrow. I interpreted his "*laissez faire*" demeanor to mean that encountering Indians will be a normal occurrence.

Trying to dispel my fear, I waved as they passed us, hoping to get a friendly response of some kind. They did not look in our direction; it's as though they were carefully trying to mind their own business. They quickly disappeared into a narrow stream, now hidden from view by the dense cypress forest.

They are a handsome people, I thought; with a muscular build, long straight black hair worn to the shoulders, and a skin color somewhere between brown and red. Their total disregard for my friendly gesture—I know they saw us—produced some uncertainty within me. Are they friendly? Are they hostile? Were they merely indifferent, like my husband, over our chance encounter?

"The Atchafalaya is second only to the mighty Mississippi," Frenchy told Joseph and me as we sat down next to him near the helm. Further describing the challenges before us, he continued, "You have to remain alert while traveling this tricky channel. Between floating debris and sandbars that are always moving, it can be dangerous if you are not careful. Sometimes a captain's best efforts to be safe can be thwarted by a submerged log or being stranded on a sandbar that was not there on the last trip up or downstream. Many have fallen overboard and drowned, being pulled under by the whirlpools and the strong undertow in the deep waters of the main channel. It doesn't take much of a hit from a log or a sudden floundering on a bar to cause one to lose his balance. That is why I installed these railings around the helmsman's platform."

Frenchy continued: "I don't believe in taking chances, especially since my brother drowned in these waters three years ago. The current is too fierce to attempt swimming to safety without some form of floatation. If you fall in, look for something to grab onto, something that can float you into the shallows until someone can rescue you. *Prenez garde de ne pas tomber*; be careful not to fall!" he warned.

Frenchy had just scared the daylights out of me; I grabbed the railing and held on tightly, heeding the warning of our experienced and cautious captain. In a short time, I put my fears behind me and stood up to have a look over the top of the cabin. We were approaching a large expanse of water; I wondered if we were reaching Atchafalaya Bay. Just as I was going to ask, Frenchy began to explain where we were. "The land mass that has been on our left is called Bateman Island. At the southern tip of this island, the Bayou Shaver conjoins with the waters of the Atchafalaya, forming this bay, sometimes referred to as Sweet Bay. On the other side of this bay, the river narrows once again. That section of the waterway is known as the Lower Atchafalaya River." The currents there are much stronger, he says.

"There is nothing to worry about. The *Swamp Rat* can pass any test this old river wants to give her," Frenchy boasted. On that note, I decided to go for coffee; the captain's display of confidence lent me little comfort. I turned my head to ask how much sugar he wanted in his cup of coffee. "Two heaping spoonfuls, I like my coffee sweet!" he shouted.

The power of the river current could easily be felt as it worked against the movement of the hull. I was glad the boat wasn't any smaller. The sixty-foot hull seemed sizable while tied to the wharf, but the large expanse of water brought a different perspective, making the boat seem tiny and insignificant.

Returning with the coffee, Frenchy pointed to a sharp bend in the river: "Can you see the crescent formed by that large curve in the river?" he asked. Joseph and I trained our eyes on where he was pointing. "Once we round that large bend, we'll be heading due east to a point where the Atchafalaya heads south again, forming a cove against its eastern shoreline. That's the bend we are looking for," Frenchy informed us.

It wasn't long before we had navigated the huge river bend and the cove came into perfect view in the distance. Frenchy pointed. "If you find the center of that cove, you will be looking at a point just one quarter mile from the construction site that Congressman Adams has chosen to build his retirement home. From this bend, the entire shoreline along the left descending bank, all the way to where the river enters Atchafalaya Bay, forms the western boundary of the congressman's estate. He also owns the island on the west side of the mouth of the river; an island formed by clam shell deposits he calls *Shell Island*."

Joseph and I were overwhelmed by the site of our new homeland; we shouted with joy over the news. A large, densely forested ridge completely surrounded by water—the river to the west, the bay to the south, and bayous to the north and east—"it's Deer Island!"

Carey had remained aloof for the entire trip. Fearing he might have fallen overboard, I asked Frenchy what had become of him.

"Look over your head," Frenchy said with a hearty laugh.

Carey had been playing an innocent game of hide-and-seek; the only trouble was that no one was seeking. He complained that if he had fallen overboard, he would certainly have drowned by the time anyone had noticed he was missing.

"I am sure I would have heard the splash," I teased.

"*Ne vous genez pas; je sais nager!* (Put yourself at ease. I know how to swim!)" Carey boasted.

Soon after rounding the river's bend, we were heading south; cypress forest began to hide the ridge from view. Frenchy says the mouth of Deer Bayou will only become visible when we get there; finding the channel at night would be next to impossible, Frenchy told us.

Frenchy informed us that we were nearly there; we should soon see the mouth of Deer Island Bayou. We had been sailing for nearly two hours—thank God, without incident. Joseph engaged the crew, learning all he could about life in Brashear City; he wanted to gain insight from these two lifelong residents of the Atchafalaya Basin.

As the bowsprit drew near to a passageway running through the left riverbank, Frenchy proclaimed in an excited voice, "This is Deer Island Bayou! *Voyez vous-meme!* See for yourself!" he proclaimed.

Carey worked frantically to raise the sails, removing them from the wind's stubborn grasp and gathering them in; he secured each sail to its beam on the masthead. The two jib sails were furled to their support lines, which ran from the bowsprit to the foremast. He then jumped from the bow, which was nudged against the southern shoreline, having a rope in his hand. He immediately tied the line to a tree to prevent the swift river currents from pulling us away from our landing site.

With the sails no longer obscuring our view, Joseph and I looked over the future homestead in awe. Nothing could have prepared us for this moment. The narrow channel was shrouded by tall branches of the huge cypress trees, producing a natural, cavernous tunnel that beckons one to enter; clam shells and cypress knees line the bayou's shoreline, stifling erosion.

My wildest exaggerated notions of what I might find when I arrived here could not compare with the reality I was now experiencing. Joseph looked into my eyes, searching for signs within my being, trying to determine what I was feeling deep inside. He drew me to his chest and whispered softly: "See, honey, I told you this would be a great adventure."

I stood spellbound in his arms. Of course, he had promised that leaving Southampton for America to begin a new life in Louisiana would be an adventure—Indians and all! Four long years ago, a letter from Uncle Patrick resurrected a lifelong dream; now, I can relish in the splendor, as the realization of that dream transforms my life. The man I love, holding me in his arms, is all the reassurance I need. Everything is going to work out just fine, I thought.

This was our new home! Is this our back yard or front yard, I mused. Suddenly I was finding myself thrilled by endless possibilities; we may even have children—no better time to start a family than now!

We were not certain when our labor crew would arrive; meanwhile, Joseph's curiosity was stimulated when Frenchy ordered Carey to go below deck and raise the keel. Seeing the inquisitive look on Joseph's face, Frenchy began to explain. "The *Swamp Rat* has a specially designed hull. She is what we locals call a box-keeled sailor. She has a retractable keel. A specially constructed box receives the fin in the raised position. This unique design permits the craft to venture into shallow water under reduced sail or by using oars, which we are about to do."

Joseph was intrigued by the concept; he went below decks with Carey to witness the procedure. Joseph is always looking for new designs in form and construction. His love for boats is only surpassed by his love for me, but sometimes the tug-of-war is too close to call.

Joseph will most certainly build a boat for our own use, as soon as he has the time. I overheard him telling Uncle Patrick that he wanted to build a sailboat. His uncle told him to make a materials and hardware list, and he would freight it out to the island on the first available transport.

It is still hard to rationally understand the many fantastic events that Joseph and I have experienced since we left England. We have been introduced to many wonderful people, and in such a short space of time; I haven't had time to savor all these experiences. It's as though the clock has been racing faster than my mind; I can't keep up with what it is presenting to me. People who were strangers one week ago are now dear friends; this is indeed surreal. Everyone has been so kind and generous—and what about Uncle Patrick? He's the one who made this all possible.

Carey and Joseph came back from below decks carrying oars and swivel mounts that fit into the bulwarks on both sides of the boat. There are three oar stations located on each side; I was glad when I heard that I would not be expected to man one of them. Frenchy says that the manpower we need will soon be arriving. I could not imagine how Joseph and I, with no experience, could be the least bit helpful in the task before us, getting this heavy vessel up Deer Bayou to the last landing.

Carey disembarked, jumping onshore to climb a tall tree to look up river for signs of our labor crew. Suddenly he yelled, "Frenchy! *Les voila, et les voice!* (There they are, and here they come!)"

About a half hour later, three small vessels pulled alongside carrying six men in each craft; each boat was carrying a full load of timber, making them sit low in the water; far too close for comfort, especially in these swift waters. Frenchy asked for two men from each boat to come aboard to man the oars. The three dories had taken down their sails; the small craft will be easily propelled by four men at oars in the gentle currents of the bayou Frenchy told us. I wondered how six men would manage getting us upstream.

Carey strained to push us from the shoreline; we were stuck in the sand. Joseph jumped off the bow to lend a hand. After several attempts to make the boat move, it gave way suddenly. Joseph lost his balance and had a desperate hold on the bowsprit, struggling to keep himself from falling into the water.

"*Mefiez-vous!* (Watch out!)" Frenchy warned, but it was too late. Just as Carey was about to successfully climb over the bow, Joseph grabbed his leg in a panic, and both men fell into the water.

The episode was hilarious! You should have seen their faces when they lost control and fell from the bowsprit. We all had a good chuckle. Frenchy threw a rope ladder over the side to receive the "*pauvre bêtes*" (poor things) from the water.

"Strike oars!" Frenchy ordered. Once again, we were under way. Frenchy told us that the congressman had hired him a few years ago to carry a survey crew to this area. The surveyors spent a month mapping the topography, looking for the most suitable ground for the construction site—the highest ground. He told us that the spot that was chosen is not only the highest elevation, but it has a natural fresh water stream flowing through it. This information confirmed what Uncle Patrick had shared in his letter of invitation several years before.

Frenchy continued, "The spring runs its three-quarter mile course through clam shell deposits until it discharges into Deer Island Bayou. The clam shells look like giant pearls lining the bottom and sides along the course of the cold clear fresh water stream. The dense woodlands of the interior of the island are teeming with a wide variety of wildlife."

As we traveled upstream and finally began to penetrate the ridge, I saw many different types of fur-bearing animals that seemed to fearlessly appear for our inspection. There were many species of birds and water fowl that I could not identify since I had never seen them before. Already I have seen at least eight deer; only one had antlers.

Just as I was about to express relief that I had not seen any snakes, a huge serpent crossed before our bow. As it slithered ashore, I could not bear to watch the entire length of its body as it disappeared into the thicket. I ran over to Frenchy, asking if the dreadful creatures were plentiful on the island; to my utter disgust, he said they were abundant throughout all the fresh water regions of south Louisiana. Trying to calm my sensitive nerves, he said that they were just as afraid of me as I am afraid of them; I didn't find that notion very reassuring.

An alligator made its appearance, only to sink below the surface before I could get a close look at him. Well, I thought to myself, this is wilderness. What else would you expect to find in an area uninhabited by man. Joseph will always be nearby to protect me. I'll just remain close to the house, I reasoned.

Before I realized it, we were nearing a large gradual bend in the bayou. As we maneuvered around the bend to our left, Frenchy pointed to a large crescent formed by another large gradual bend that turns to the right, just about a half mile ahead. Frenchy began to explain where we were going. "At the deepest point of that large crescent, right in its center, is where we will land our boats. Soon, you will see the turbulence caused by the rushing water of the fresh water stream as it enters the bayou. This is the site of your new home."

Straining my eyes, I spotted an area of disturbed water protruding through the left shoreline: "My God, Joseph! We finally made it!" I shouted. I wanted everyone to know just how happy I was to be here.

Nosing the bow up to the bank just below the mouth of the bubbling stream, we landed. Carey jumped ashore to secure the boat. The pleasant sound of the clashing waters filled the air as Joseph and I took our first steps on "terra firma." Frenchy encouraged us to walk up the left bank of the stream to its head; he told us the fountainhead is three-quarter mile from where we were standing, and it is there that the construction of the two houses will take place. He told us that one-fourth mile further north is the center of the crescent in the Atchafalaya that he had showed us earlier.

"You two go on ahead of us. We want to give you some time alone to gather your thoughts and enjoy the moment. Take your time about it. We have plenty to keep us busy here. We will wait for your return," he politely added.

As we walked along the stream, Joseph noted that we were on a natural incline. He said the rise was gradual enough not to prevent it being used for transporting people and materials by small boat to and from the bayou to the homestead site. He said the transport vessels would have to be polled to go upstream; going downstream would only require some method for steering.

The water in the stream is so clear that it is difficult to judge its depth. Joseph found a stick and pressed through the water's surface to the bottom and estimated the depth to be two and a half to three feet; this is more than enough to accommodate a heavy-laden flatboat and not touch bottom, he said. The clamshells forming the bottom, added brilliance to the scene as they shone brightly, even in the filtered sunlight.

Reaching the summit of the ridge, the fountainhead presented us with its wondrous splendor. The gurgling sounds emitted by the fast escaping water created a tranquil atmosphere. Happening upon a fallen tree, we decided to sit down and take in the view. Joseph looked into my eyes and said, "*The Garden of Eden* had fruit trees, but I can take care of that. I would not ask God to improve anything He has done here. Deer Island has exceeded my wildest expectations."

I could not have expressed my feelings any better I shared with Joseph, as we joined hands and knelt for a prayer of thanksgiving. As my husband prayed, I thought about my family and friends back home. I asked God to give them peace that only He can give; to give them the faith to believe that we have arrived at our new home safe and sound.

While Joseph descended the ridge to return to the boat, I chose to stay behind. I saw a massive oak tree, larger than the ones we encountered on our journey from Algiers Point to Donaldsonville. Some of its gigantic limbs touch the ground; continued growth extends them upward again as they compete for sunlight with the surrounding trees. The trunk of this tree must be eight feet in diameter, I thought, as a squirrel's barking distracted me, momentarily diverting my attention. What a handsome specimen to grace our surroundings.

As I gazed around me, two other oaks of similar stature caught my attention. Like stalwart sentinels, they will help to shield us from the elements. Though the forest is densely covered with trees, shrubs, palmetto palms, bushes and vines, the large oaks have won the battle for the sun's rays; they have destroyed nearly all their competition. I don't believe a single tree will have to be cut down to make room for our two buildings. We'll nestle them in among these giants.

When Joseph returned, he told me the work crew was on its way with tents, cooking utensils, and other provisions that will afford us shelter and satisfy our appetites until the *little house* can be completed. After giving me the message, he returned to the crew to lend a hand.

The crew set up camp close to the construction site of the first house. Joseph told me the area near the fountainhead is reserved for the *big house*, Uncle Patrick's dream retirement home. Our house will be built three hundred feet downstream from the fountainhead.

While the workmen returned to Deer Bayou for more provisions, Joseph and I took the opportunity to get personal. We embraced; Joseph's dream was finally being fulfilled. Tears of joy ran down his face as he was overwhelmed by the moment. He did not have to say anything; it was all written on his face. I held him tightly, kissed him passionately on his lips, and told him how much I loved him. I whispered in his ear, "I believe it is time to start a family."

DEER ISLAND

June 9, 1840 (Our First Day)

When the sunlight awakened me this morning, I found myself all alone. The brilliant sunshine had already brought color to the trees. Apparently, the men had returned to the boats for supplies. I decided to make some tea.

After lighting the oil-burning stove that came from Frenchy's boat, I strolled over to the stream to fill my teakettle with water. How convenient to have a source of clean fresh water so near; it will be practically outside our front door. Cupping some water with my hand, I tasted it. I found it to be cold and refreshing—no aftertaste. It's just one more blessing to add to our growing list.

Countless squirrels played excitedly all around our campsite. They scampered up and down the nearby trees, chattering and barking at one another. I could not discount the fact that they might be expressing their disapproval over our intrusion, although they did not appear threatened by my presence. The chatter of the squirrels and the sound emitted by the swift waters in the stream compete for my ear as songbirds join in nature's orchestra chanting their blissful tunes. The wildlife seems to welcome us newcomers, willing to share with us their marvelous habitat.

They just haven't learned to fear us, I thought. I must say I wish things could remain exactly the way they are now. The many species of wild animals are a joy to see and hear. Though Joseph has never been an avid hunter (he did go pheasant hunting with my grandfather in England a few times) I'm sure he will eventually make use of his rifle. The gun Uncle Patrick bought for him at the Plattenville General Store is not only pretty to look at, but it will provide us with all the venison we can eat. When not on the menu, most of the edible local wildlife will be allowed to coexist with us.

After a cup of tea, I decided to walk downstream to see what the men were doing. Joseph was building a flat-bottomed boat. He says the design will accommodate a heavy load. The boat is squared at the ends and raked front and rear to allow the boat to slide across the water rather than having to plow through it; both ends can serve as the bow since the stream is not wide enough to turn it around.

When I showed up, the first flatboat was ready to be launched and loaded with lumber. Before long, a neatly stacked load of lumber was loaded aboard and ready to be transported to the fountainhead of the stream. Carey and another man volunteered to take the first load upstream. Donning long poles with wide points diverging from their lower ends, they climbed atop the lumber and moved the boat slowly up the stream. Not at all surprised by the success of the venture, Joseph announced, "Let's make another one!"

I followed Carey upstream to observe the technique he and his helper were using to move the heavy load. Working against the fast-moving water of the ten-foot wide channel with one man at each side, they began to walk the vessel upstream; they alternated their motions to insure that one pole remained lodged at the bottom at all times. In this manner, the swift current was prevented from sending them backward.

Joseph continued work on the second boat as the rest of the crew continued to unload the lumber that was aboard the *Swamp Rat*. Frenchy had already supervised construction on a wharf near the mouth of the stream. The structure jutted out from the downstream bank by about sixty feet. The support piles stood about eight feet above the water for easy mooring. The deck of the wharf was built to facilitate loading and offloading materials.

I told Frenchy that the dock looked good; someday we'll have our own sailboat to moor here, making good use of the project that he helped to build. Attempting to be modest, Frenchy said, "Thanks, Josephine, but I had a lot of help."

Joseph says the use of flatboats will save countless hours of backbreaking work. Frenchy watched previous work crews struggle as they carried hundreds of loads of lumber to the construction site; he said it was a nightmare. To Joseph, the notion of carrying this monstrous load of lumber by hand was unthinkable.

Not wanting to be in the way, I decided to return to the camp. The men would soon be tired and hungry; I'll go put a pot of beans on the stove to make myself useful. Carey was returning from his first load when I left the dockside. I announced to everyone: "The beans will be cooked in a couple of hours in case any of you get hungry!"

The men never stopped; they made one trip after the other. By midafternoon, they were using two boats. By the time the sun was low in the western sky, nearly hidden from view by the dense forest, they had made thirty loads of lumber and supplies.

Hungry and tired, there wasn't much time spent on small talk after supper. Frenchy said it best, "Tomorrow will be another day for hard work!"

Lying beside me, Joseph told me work would begin on the *little house* at first light in the morning. I knew he was exhausted, so I did not ask him to elaborate. I wonder what tomorrow will bring; God knows. Amen.

As I lay in my cot motionless, steeped in thought, I concluded that our lives had forever been changed. Though I have been married to Joseph for four and a half years, it seems our life together is just beginning. Each day of our long journey has presented us with experiences we could have never dreamed were possible. In view of this fact, it would be pointless for me to continue to burden myself with needless worry—a burden I have imposed upon myself since the moment we decided to accept Uncle Patrick's invitation. Since our departure from England, experience has taught me that worrying is a needless expenditure of energy. It is plain nonsense. In the future, I will try earnestly to remain focused on events as they present themselves—one day at a time.

Will I be able to adjust to wilderness living in such an unpredictable environment? I am a young woman; Joseph is both young and industrious. Together we will be well able to face the good and the bad times that lay ahead for us. With God's help, we can endure anything.

The hour is late; my eyes are heavy. As I snuff the lamplight, having laid down my pen, I pray God will go with us as we continue our new adventure. Good night and amen once again, Lord.

Chapter Six

LIFE ON DEER ISLAND
UNCLE PATRICK'S FIRST VISIT

August 3, 1840

The timely visitation by Uncle Patrick, three days after completion of the construction on the *little house*, brought excitement to what otherwise had become a mundane existence here. The sound of hammer, ax, and saw, the crackle of the flame in the open hearth of my outside kitchen, the drudgery of the same routine each and every day, was finally interrupted by a few days of leisure time, while plans for the *big house* are being finalized.

Joseph and his crew have marked the locations for the piles that will support the structure. Holes will have to be dug about six feet deep to ensure a good foundation. He and Uncle Patrick are discussing the material needs for completing this second project (third project if you count the wharf).

One of the men who escorted the congressman to the island, assumed the role of cook; he immediately began to prepare a dressed deer they had brought with them from the mainland. Though I am twenty-two years old, I have had no experience cooking wild game; I've only pan fried mutton and stewed a few chickens—not much of a menu, and useless, since neither of these meats are present around here. Poor Joseph!

Fortunate for me, there are many good cooks among our work crew. Since we feed fifteen to twenty mouths a day, I am glad these men have been considerate, graciously volunteering their services. Almost everyone takes his turn; like me, Joseph would not be of much use over a stove. I don't believe he has prepared a single dish in his life.

Harry Thompson, our newest cook, has pledged to teach me how to prepare venison stew. First he butchered the freshly killed deer. Into each of three very large cast-iron kettles he had suspended over the open fire of my outdoor hearth, he added a healthy measure of lard. He portioned the meat, putting an equal amount in each pot for browning. Once the meat was seared, he removed the meat from each pot for stuffing. To the remaining grease, he added several chopped onions. While the onions were being reduced, he stuffed the portions of deer meat with peppercorns and garlic. He added water to the onions and deer drippings and returned all the meat to the pots for stewing. After the meat had cooked a couple of hours, Harry added dissolved cornstarch to the broth to thicken the gravy. One hour later, the hearty meal was ready to be served over the rice he prepared on the oil stove.

Mark Mathews, the other man who escorted Uncle Patrick to the island, tended to the fire, stoking it with fresh wood and keeping the flames crackling. He's a nice young man; he and Harry have worked for Uncle Patrick before. Harry owns a sailboat that the congressman charters from time to time—*Lady's Dream* it is called. Mark is the deckhand.

With construction on the *little house* completed, and the materials being ordered for the *big house*, Joseph and I will get a much needed break, at least for a week or two. Joseph says it will take about a year to finish the retirement home, but when it is completed it will be an elegant thing to behold. Meanwhile, everyone is leaving for the mainland to rest and to pick up new materials. We will be all alone! That will be a novel experience that I am looking forward to; Joseph isn't saying much but I know my husband. The term "marital bliss" comes to mind.

The "Little House"
Built by Joseph Addison
Completed July 30, 1840
Location: Deer Island

Our entire crew seemed to be relieved that construction would be halted for about two weeks. They have been working very hard from sun to sun, having time for nothing else but to eat and sleep. Uncle Patrick congratulated everyone on a job well done. The atmosphere at the campsite was jovial; the men were steeped in conversation and joke-telling with the congressman.

Uncle Patrick told Joseph he knew that his shipbuilding skills would be an advantage, insuring the successful completion of his retirement home, thus fulfilling the dream he has had for many years. Now, his dream was becoming reality; you could see the pride he felt over the progress we have made in his never ending smiles. I haven't seen him this happy before now. I'm glad he is pleased.

Just before sunset, we dined on "peppercorn venison stew"; Harry could not have been prouder of his specialty. We had beans, rice, and gravy, to compliment the main dish; we all ate like we were starving. Amazing to me was how much food was eaten in that one meal. At the end of the evening, nearly all was gone, consumed by satisfied appetites, some a bit more than satisfied. What better testimony for the cook's success; there is none that I can conjure.

We talked by the light of the lard oil lamps that Uncle Patrick brought us; I had borrowed the one off Frenchy's boat until now. The moon traveled from the eastern horizon to a point directly overhead before we said good night. The workers all retired to their boats; Uncle Patrick slept with Joseph and me in the *little house.*

It had been a wonderful day. Uncle Patrick will board *Lady's Dream* at first light. He will join all the other men aboard the *Swamp Rat* and the three dories; the flotilla will head upriver for Brashear City, a place that seems so far away to me. There is so much distance between us and civilization, I'm feeling lonely already.

The men are all asleep. The only thing moving is the occasional flicker of the flame over my new lard oil lamp. Its light is most suitable for writing in the late hours of quiet darkness, when nothing is stirring except my pen and I. And now I lay me down to sleep; I pray the Lord my soul to keep, amen.

August 18, 1840 (Our Normal Routine)

Our fleet of boats carrying work crews and supplies arrived about mid-day today. They will be busy unloading for at least three days Joseph told me. He will be taking some of the men to the construction site to continue work on the foundation while waiting for more help; others will join him when the building material has been ferried from the bayou to the fountainhead.

August 20, 1840

The rustle of leaves in the windswept trees stirred me from my sleep this morning. Overcast skies portend rainfall, as I peer through the open shutters and the temperature of the surrounding air begins to plummet. As the thunderclouds begin their assault and the lightning flashes strike in the distance, the deluge was unleashed from the heavens.

As I struggled to close the shutters and seal the windows, I could see Joseph and his band of workers making a mad dash for the front porch. I brought clean dry rags from my wash basket so they could dry off before coming inside. The chill from the storm made some of the men shiver in their boots as they huddled around the dinner table. Frenchy recommended I make a pot of hot coffee to warm up their bones. I lit the oil stove and put the kettle on to boil.

Joseph told me that they were driving dowel pins into the sills to secure them to the foundation piles when the sky broke loose. They could see the storm coming, but they were trying to do all they could before having to quit for who knows how long. "Now there is nothing we can do but dry up, stay warm, and spend some leisure time in the *little house*, until the weather breaks. We'll make the best of it!" he exclaimed.

The foundation piles are buried six feet below ground and extend four feet above ground. The floor sills are placed atop the piles whose tenons fit tightly into the mortised hollows in the massive horizontal beams. Holes have been drilled through the beams where the tenons have been fitted, so dowels can be driven into them to hold the interlocking timbers firmly in place. The foundation of the *little house* was laid in this same way, but on a smaller scale.

August 22, 1840

Since we arrived on the island on June 8, construction has been halted only once to await materials from the mainland. That costly delay prompted Joseph to make sure that we don't run out of material again. When supplies dwindle, he will send the *Swamp Rat* to the mainland for more.

Joseph is making plans to expand the dock site to better accommodate the freight boats, since they are now traveling more frequently to and from the mainland. The heavy loads are cumbersome enough without having the added inconvenience of little or no mooring space. The way it is now, boats must constantly be shuffled to get to the wharf in order to safely unload. He says he'll have to take the time to get it done; in the long run, we will gain time by not wasting it at the bayou bank.

August 25, 1840

The new docking facility has been finished. Joseph says, when his crew gets focused on the task at hand, they are very good at seeing it through to the end. Now, our landing can handle at least two large boats and several small craft with no problem. In the future, when guests come for a visit with two or more vessels, they will be able to moor with a convenient walkway to bring them ashore. "That's the way I like things done!" Joseph asserted, with the admiration of his work crew.

Joseph is respected by the men who work for Uncle Patrick. Though he is much younger than most of them, they gladly follow his lead; they recognize the skill and craftsmanship that he acquired as a shipwright in England. There has not been a crossword exchanged between any of them.

Each time I sit down to write, I remember the smile on Greta Henley's face. I appreciated the hospitality and the kindness that she and her husband afforded us on our visit at their home. The presents that she had secretly loaded on Uncle Patrick's coach remained sealed until we had a roof over our heads as she had instructed. The day we occupied the *little house,* Joseph carefully removed the copper nails which secured the well-crafted boxes. Frenchy and Carey were present in the room looking over our shoulders to get a glimpse inside the small wooden crates. One box had a leather bound King James family Bible; the second contained a leather-bound diary. There was also a detailed sketch illustrating the cane harvest at Sugarland Farms last fall.

Grateful for the exquisite gifts, Joseph told Frenchy to be sure to communicate, by whatever means possible, to the Henleys that their gifts will be used each and every day, and that we hope to be able to thank them in person some day. Let them know how much we appreciate the kind and considerate blessings they have bestowed upon us. "Those are altogether my sentiments as well," I added.

Reflecting on our present condition, Joseph and I have much to be thankful for; moving into the comfortable spaces of the *little house* most of all. I must admit that living conditions during the days I spent under the canvas tent were less than desirable; it always leaked when it rained; once a strong gust of wind brought the wet canvas of the walled tent down upon our heads. I was happy that it kept us 90 percent dry most of the time, but I'm happier to be inside a solid wooden structure, which is better suited to protect us from the weather, mosquitoes, and creepy things.

August 26, 1840

Sometime in the month of July, Joseph and his crew built a roof over the open hearth. The roof is thatched using woven palmetto leaves; it has a whole in the center to allow the smoke to rise uninhibited. It is a temporary arrangement to be used until the permanent out kitchen can be built. It was built midway between the front porch and the freshwater stream, providing easy access to the water for cooking. A pole has been strategically placed above the open hearth to hang the cooking pots. Logs are placed around the outside parameter of the structure, providing a windbreak; these logs also serve as a welcome seat for the tired and hungry souls that tend to congregate there. The inner parameter of huge logs, are placed in a square surrounding the hearth itself; this directs the heat from the fireplace upward; it also provides a windbreak, making it easier to contain and control the fire within (the inside face of these logs is so close to the fire that they are charred).

Each morning, I stoke the fire in the open hearth to rekindle the flame; we try to keep it alive twenty-four hours a day. Of course the men do all the hard work; I am just the tender and the cook. I make the coffee on Frenchy's oil stove, but for cooking meals, I prefer to cook over the open hearth. Cooking over an open fire takes some getting used to, but it makes no sense to burn whale oil in the portable stove when firewood is so abundant, especially with all the small pieces of discard from the construction work.

Joseph has vowed to kill his first deer as soon as the weather gets cold enough to preserve the meat. When the temperature is near or below freezing, Frenchy says the carcass can be hung to dry; it will last for several days without spoiling. That would provide us with venison for nearly a week. Frenchy also shared that the meat can be smoked, but we will need to build a smokehouse—we won't have time for that now. Our trusty boat skipper has volunteered to teach us all we need to know about preserving meat and preparing it for consumption. "I'll cook Joseph's first deer for him if I am here when he shoots one!" he promised.

I am thoroughly enjoying the writing desk my husband built for me. Built entirely of cypress, the desk has pigeon holes for storage of small items, which might otherwise be easily misplaced; it also has a roll top. When I finish making entries in my diary, I can close the top, protecting the contents from dust; it will keep my inkwell from being accidently knocked over. The brass drawer pulls lend a bit of charm to the handsome piece of furniture.

September 18, 1840

Work on the *big house* has been steady for a month. The men who are helping us with the massive project will be going to Brashear City to visit with family and to get some well-deserved rest. When they return, they will be bringing more lumber and supplies. Joseph and I plan to make the best of our time alone.

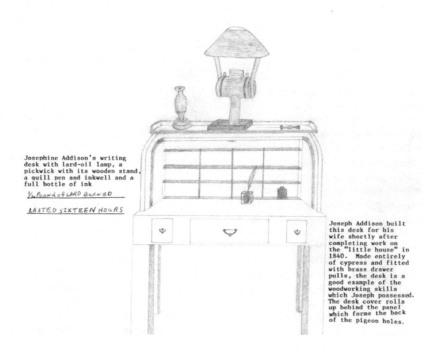

Josephine Addison's writing desk with lard-oil lamp, a pickwick with its wooden stand, a quill pen and inkwell and a full bottle of ink

½ Pound of LARD Burned

LASTED SIXTEEN HOURS

Joseph Addison built this desk for his wife shortly after completing work on the "little house" in 1840. Made entirely of cypress and fitted with brass drawer pulls, the desk is a good example of the woodworking skills which Joseph possessed. The desk cover rolls up behind the panel which forms the back of the pigeon holes.

Joseph has constructed a ladder on our front porch that will lend access to the attic through a hole in the ceiling. He says there is a walk space of at least twenty by thirty feet, which is tall enough for a grown man to walk upright without hitting his head. "It will make a nice bedroom for children and it can be divided into two rooms if we have girls," he teased.

Children! Each night I pray that God will bless us with our first child; His will be done. Amen.

146

AN UNEXPECTED VISITOR

September 20, 1840

Frenchy and Carey and the entire workforce left for the mainland early yesterday morning. Joseph is going to the bayou to strengthen one of the piles on the new section of wharf. He loaded a couple of cypress beams in one of the flatboats and headed downstream.

I put a pot of beans on the fire of the open hearth and sat on one of the outside parameter logs to enjoy a fresh cup of hot tea. The silence and solitude of being alone made me think of England; I was struggling with loneliness. When all the men are here, and activity is the deed of the day, I'm always interacting with someone or something—staying busy. It is at times such as this, that I am prone to tears.

I think of my mother and father, Grandfather and Grandmother Moore, the English countryside, the smoke stacks and the clouds of steam at the industrial works of Southampton, my girlfriends— Victoria Ramsey, Elizabeth Blackett, and Diana Eddington; these thoughts conjure up visions that are beginning to torment me.

I must not dwell on England! I must not allow myself to become so affected by melancholy! I must accept that my separation from my homeland is a permanent one! Just as I was about to succumb to my self-pity, Joseph walked toward me accompanied by several men I had never seen before.

Josephine! This is Captain Jean Laffite! He is a good friend of Uncle Patrick; he is the commander of five armed merchant ships in the American Navy. His ship, the *Osprey*, is on anchor in Atchafalaya Bay. He has been sent here to survey the congressman's estate and to find suitable timber for the servicing of his ships. He has made a deal with Uncle Patrick—timber in exchange for work crews to clear the proposed sites for the garden, the fruit orchard, the pecan orchard, and last of all, the cemetery.

I was about to say that I needed a larger pot of beans when Captain Laffite invited Joseph and I to dine with him aboard his ship; he reached for my left hand, raised it to his lips, and kissed it gently. With deep dark eyes he gazed into my own and said, "*Je suis enchantee de faire votre connaissance* (I am charmed to make your acquaintance), Josephine." I am certain his kind gesture made me blush.

Mr. Laffite was fashionably dressed, and his French accent was charming. It is easy to see that he has a way with women; there's nothing wrong with that. He is a handsome man, of medium build. His beard is neatly trimmed; he has a smile that could beguile any woman. He appeared to be a man with an adventurous spirit.

Joseph and I accepted his offer to accompany him to his ship, and after I removed the beans from the fire, we walked downstream with Laffite and his men, boarding a large row boat that was at the dock waiting for us.

There was something queer about the stoic silence and the lack of expression on the faces of Laffite's men. Their respect for the captain seemed to exceed old-fashioned discipline, but that was not a matter for my concern; Captain Laffite is a friend of Uncle Patrick, and that was all that really matters.

With six men manning the oars of the dory, in no time we were at the mouth of Deer Bayou. The *Osprey* was in clear site, only a few hundred yards into the bay. Joseph and the captain were steeped in conversation as we neared the ship. Curiously, I saw no flag flying from the aft mast—Joseph did not seem to care.

"The *Osprey* is one of five ships in my fleet. Each one of the 135-foot vessels is armed with at least ten heavy cannon, each has a displacement of four hundred fifty tons and carries an average crew of eighty-five able-bodied seamen. All the vessels carry square rigged sails on the foremast and the fore-and-aft mainsails with square main topsails, making them extremely versatile. The square sails drive the ships best in quartering winds and the fore-and-aft sails are effective when sailing to windward," Mr. Laffite proudly shared, giving a complete description of his ships to my attentive husband (he must have known Joseph would understand what he was talking about).

I could not help wondering why a merchant ship needed to be so heavily armed. I assume Captain Laffite had anticipated a few questions; I am sure he detected some modest alarm in my facial expression, sensing a bit of apprehension might be the source of my concern. Before I could ask any questions, the captain continued his oratory.

"My ships deal in merchandise from all parts of the world. The reason for my ships being armed is quite simple. Pirates have been raiding merchant ships along the gulf coast for a hundred years. Cannon fire is the only thing the scoundrels understand. It's the only way I can discourage them from attacking and preying on my ships. In all of my years at sea, I have not lost a single ship to pirates!" he explained without reservation.

His explanation seemed plausible—a bit boastful, but believable. He seems to possess a fearless resolve; it's uncanny the way he feels his good fortune is not by accident. I have never met a man like him. His dark brown eyes sparkled in the glare of the sunlight as we prepared to tie alongside his boat with the cannon over our heads peeping through the opened portholes—those cannon were a menacing sight!

Topside aboard ship, the scuffle of fast moving feet on the decks could be heard, as the gentle waves of the near calm bay slapped the side of the hull. "You brought us some company, eh, Captain!" one of the crewmen hollered as he leaned over the bulwarks just above us.

"That I did! Now you boys mind your manners in the presence of a lady," he staunchly recommended.

"Yes, sir, Captain!" The men respectfully replied, grinning from ear to ear.

We climbed a rope ladder and went aboard ship. The captain asked us if we wanted coffee or tea, as he ushered us into the captain's quarters at the stern of the ship. We sat around a table that was beautifully finished; Joseph and Captain Laffite continued to discuss the design of the ship—not my favorite subject. My husband, being a shipwright, is always keenly interested in the various crafts he has a chance to examine. Shipbuilding has been a deep passion of his ever since we met. As I have mentioned countless times, I believe Joseph's love for ships can only be surpassed by his love for me—I wonder!

The view of the bay through the cabin window was magnificent. I wondered how it would feel to sail in an armed merchant ship on the open gulf. I was glad for the break in the monotony of life on the island. We were losing some of our leisure time, but what is leisure time anyway. After all, Captain Jean Laffite will be helping us complete the congressman's plans for clearing parts of the island for our benefit as well as his—what a convenient relationship he and Uncle Patrick have, I thought.

A sailor entered the captain's quarters to announce that dinner was ready to be served. Captain Laffite instructed his crewman to have the cook accompany him when he returns with the food; he wants to introduce him to his guests. As ordered, before long a short man with platted hair hanging down his back showed up at the dinner table.

"Joseph and Josephine, this is my Chinese cook, Ta Lee. He is an excellent chef and a valuable member of my crew. In fact, I would have to say that next to me, the cook is the next most important man on my ship. To satisfy the hungry appetites of eighty-five sailors is not an easy task. Ta Lee is one of the best at doing just that," Mr. Laffite lauded.

The food was exquisite! We dined sumptuously on a bounty of seafood—boiled shrimp, boiled crabs, oysters on the half shell, fried fish balls, and a couple of items I did not recognize.

"*Comment trouvez-vous le boulette de poisson?* How do you like the fish balls, Josephine?" Laffite asked.

"Everything is delicious, Captain Laffite, especially good are these fish balls," I answered while still savoring the deep fried delicacy.

Mr. Laffite told Joseph that he had just returned from a cruise in the Caribbean Sea. The four other ships in his fleet are heading for Campeche Island, just west of the mouth of the Sabine River. The captain said that he and his brother Pierre run a distribution center on the island; they sell wholesale goods to the Texas merchants who frequent his establishment there.

Next we boarded a dory with a lateen rigged sail and headed for the eastern end of the Adams estate. Pulling out a chart of the boundary lines, Mr. Laffite informed us there were five bayous running through the congressman's land. He told us that we are going to scout everyone of those bayous together so Joseph can become familiar with the property. Uncle Patrick had marked and named the various bayous on a copy of the land survey he gave to Captain Laffite on his last trip to New Orleans.

Creole Bayou is the east end of the estate and the Atchafalaya River is the west end, the captain told us. Before the sun set, we were back at Addison's landing—the docks near the mouth of our stream. During the course of this one day, we visited Creole Bayou, Plumb Bayou, Palmetto Bayou, Crooked Bayou, and the last one of the five, Deer Bayou.

Captain Laffite declined our offer to spend the night on the island. He said he had some urgent business to attend to, but he did appreciate the kind offer. He told us that in one week, we could expect a visit from his brother, Pierre Lafitte; he will be bringing a special present with him when he comes. "*Croyez-m'en.* Take my word for it! He'll be here in seven days!" With this pledge, the captain ordered his men to strike oars and head back to the *Osprey.*

"*Au revoir Joseph, et Josephine, et a jeudi.* Good day to both of you, until we meet again! *Au revoir mes amis!*" Captain Laffite shouted, as his dory disappeared around the bend heading for the river.

Joseph and I strolled along the moonlit pathway which follows the left ascending bank of the stream. The owls were calling in the distance and the night creatures were making their special sounds as we arrived at our front porch. Joseph brought two chairs outside, and we sat and chatted before retiring for the evening. The day had been filled with new discoveries and newfound friendships. We are considerably amazed at the vastness of the estate and what it has to offer its inhabitants—it's massive and bountiful, densely populated with wildlife.

Regarding the charming Captain Jean Laffite, Joseph got a bit of background information on his relationship with Uncle Patrick. "They fought side by side at the Battle of New Orleans in 1815. The good captain is fifty-eight years old now, nine years older than the congressman. Ever since the war, they have been very close friends. Rumors that the Laffite brothers were killed in a naval battle in the Caribbean Sea back in 1826 are obviously unfounded!" Joseph interjected, with a hint of sarcasm in his tone of voice.

Recalling the fine dinner that Laffite's cook had prepared for us, I told Joseph that Ta Lee gave me the recipe for his fish balls. It is a blend of grated potatoes, fish flakes (sun-dried and salty), eggs, onions, a bit of ground peppercorns—mix the ingredients and roll a handful at a time into balls with your hands, coat with cornmeal, and deep fry until golden brown then serve hot.

"I really enjoyed those fish balls, Josephine. You're going to have to learn how to dry fish—if we ever get any!" Joseph teased.

Playfully responding to his culinary dream, I retorted, "We not only need fish, but we need a garden to grow corn to grind into meal, cultivated, so we can grow potatoes! Then I will make you some of Ta Lee's *boulette de poisson*," I chided.

Shocked that I remembered the French words for the fish balls, Joseph responded with "A bit more time around all these Frenchmen and you'll be speaking French." There's not much chance of that!

Looking into my eyes, Joseph drew closer; grabbing me by the hand, he whispered, "I'm going to need some help around here if we are going to eat so well. That won't happen if we just sit out here and dream about it." He rose to his feet, lifting me from my chair and he kissed me in a tender embrace. It was time to retire to the bedroom. Good night!

LAFFITE KEPT HIS PROMISE

September 28, 1840

Today is Joseph's twenty-second birthday! We have had a little over a week alone together; Joseph is not expecting the work crew back until the second week of October. I rose with the sun this morning. My poor husband is sleeping late today; that does not happen very often. The squirrels are scurrying through the treetops, barking and chattering in squirrel talk. They are a source of amusement each early morning and each sunset.

I poked around in the ashes of my open hearth and found there was still life in the leftover coals. I added a little kindle wood and encouraged a flame so I could brew some tea. I walked to the stream to fetch a kettle of water. As I stooped down at the water's edge, I glanced downstream for no apparent reason and saw a huge deer with antlers having a drink from the far side of the waterway, only a hundred paces from where I was kneeling. The wind was blowing from the southeast, keeping my scent away from him. When he spotted me, he did not show any sign of panic; he looked at me for several minutes, then he turned and disappeared into the thicket.

As soon as the tea was done, I went inside to see if Joseph was stirring in his bed. He was still asleep, so I grabbed my favorite chair and went out on the front porch to relax. The dense forest on the ridge obscures the sunlight until about nine o'clock in the morning. The same is true in the evening; by five o'clock in the afternoon, darkness seems to begin early because the trees act like a dark screen blocking the sun's view of us. We only get full sun for about three hours a day, when the sun is almost directly overhead. I think it will be different when the effects of seasonal changes begin to materialize.

Fall has just begun, and the leaves in the trees have not decided to fall on schedule.

As I was reminiscing about autumn in England, Joseph joined me on the porch. After kissing me on the forehead, he sat beside me for some peaceful time together. I walked to the out kitchen to get us each a cup of hot tea. We weren't finished with our tea when we heard someone calling our names from down the stream.

"*Bonjour, Joseph! Bonjour, Josephine!* Hello!" We wondered who it might be.

"I'm Pierre Laffite!" he shouted, as me and Joseph walked down the path to greet him. "I have brought to you the presents my brother Jean promised you," he told us.

He and Joseph shook hands, and as seems to be the local custom, he reached for my hand, which he promptly kissed. While he and Joseph got acquainted, I decided to give him the once-over. He seemed much older than Jean, but he appeared to be in good shape. He's handsome, well-built, a little shorter than his brother, and he has a neatly kept beard (a bit longer than his brother) and hair cut at his shoulders. You could tell he was French; that is for sure!

Pierre told Joseph his ship, *La Vengeance,* is on anchor in the bay. He said he and his men were instructed to deliver a stove and other cooking supplies to the island. He asked Joseph if his men could use the flatboats to facilitate transport of the goods upstream.

About eleven o'clock this morning, Pierre's cook, Kim Wong was introduced. He is the brother of Ta Lee, Captain Jean's cook. Pierre has instructed him to assume the cooking chores while he and his crew get the work done on the out kitchen.

Kim walked with me to the open hearth to prepare the fire for cooking a big meal. Several men showed up right behind us with two completely whole deer carcasses that were already dressed; they had a side of beef already dressed; and they had other foods like potatoes, dried beans, and several other goodies for the pots. I knew my open hearth could not possibly handle all those huge cast iron pots, but Kim had everything in control.

While he was tending the fire in the hearth, Kim's men were digging a pit. Into the pit, they threw sufficient firewood to accommodate our needs. They erected iron crossbars supported by a wooden framework over the open fire to hang the pots for cooking. They worked quickly and efficiently together. I could tell they had done this before.

Within an hour, all the food was cooking. I was impressed! Captain Pierre's men had everything up the stream, including the huge woodstove (a Queen Atlantic model) by midafternoon. Joseph and his newfound merry men were busy constructing the out-kitchen when the call to eat went forth.

"Come and get it! You snooze, you lose!" Kim Wong hollered.

You should have seen that sight; it was like pigs running for the feeding trough; they had worked up a big appetite. Pierre says they will be finished with the outbuilding by tomorrow morning. He'll be leaving for Campeche Island by noon. It is amazing how much work can be accomplished in such a short time. With a crew of hard workers totaling eighty-five men, things happened fast.

Kim Wong brought me two large crock jars filled with fish flakes. "Captain Jean told Pierre how much you liked the fish patties my brother fixed for you aboard the *Osprey*. He wanted you to have an ample supply. The flakes will last a very long time if you keep them dry," he informed me. "I also brought a crock jar filled with peppercorn and a grinder to reduce them—whole is for stuffing, ground is for stewing," he said.

Kim and I got to know each other very well during the long and busy day. He told me his extended family has a shrimp-drying operation about forty miles to the east, at a place called *Timbalier Island*. At the urging of his brother, he decided to become the cook on the brigantine, *Avenger*, six years ago. Pierre heard of his cooking skills and he stole him away one night, while his former captain was asleep; he's been on *La Vengeance* for about a year. He says he is very happy with his new job. "I only have one boss. I answer only to my captain," Kim shared, obviously content with his role as chief cook.

For the evening meal, Kim prepared a seafood gumbo to supplement the leftovers from the midafternoon meal. He used the following ingredients: to a huge pot of water, he added fresh oysters shucked into the pot, fresh shrimp, dried shrimp, crabmeat, trout fillet, pepper, onions, and garlic to taste. He served this dish over fresh steamed rice. The taste was so good that they had none left for anyone to make a second pass by the pot.

I asked Kim how he was able to secure such a large amount of fresh seafood. He told me there are men in the crew who know how to cull oysters from the shallow reefs that are abundant throughout the gulf coast. There are other men skilled with cast nets or seines to harvest shrimp and various fish. The scraps from the fish they catch (mostly their heads) are used on a string of hand lines set out between two buoys wherever they go on anchor; running these lines a few times, provides all the crabs they need. As a general rule, he says the supply of seafood is always somewhere around when they drop anchor. It's a moving seafood market conveniently available whenever needed—that's pretty good, I thought.

"Louisiana's coastline is teeming with all sorts of seafood," Kim heralded. "Anyone who goes hungry out here does not know where to look for food," he added.

After the evening meal, Mr. Laffite assembled his crew and ordered them back to the ship. "A few of us will return early in the morning to set up your new woodstove and then we'll be on our way out to sea; that is where we feel most at home, aboard our ship and on the sea," an expressed sentiment I knew he believed.

As the men left for the bay, Joseph asked Pierre to spend a little time with us on our front porch. He accepted the invitation and I prepared a pot of coffee using the freshly ground roasted beans that Kim Wong had given to me earlier. Pierre shared many stories with us; especially interesting was his description of an island he and Jean had frequented until around 1815, when Jean had a disagreement with Louisiana's governor—something to do with the governor's daughter he said. After that, we moved our distribution center to Campeche Island. "*Loin des yeux, loin du coeur.* Out of sight, out of mind," Pierre asserted, laughing heartily as he shared this bit of insight into his past (as well as his brother's).

BARATARIA

Pierre began to reminisce about Barataria Bay. "The bay was a convenient mooring spot for our ships. It afforded shelter from the stormy waters of the Gulf of Mexico being protected by two large islands—Grand Terre and Grand Island. For almost ten years, we considered the site our home. Many of our crewmen live on these islands today.

"With easy access from the mainland, especially New Orleans, the site has quickly become a watering spot for the affluent and the adventurous citizens who live in the various settlements surrounding the big city. Many fishermen make their homes there.

"There were people living on the islands before we arrived. Since we left, the population there has exploded. There are numerous cottages, many of which are owned by businessmen and plantation owners throughout the South. Some are used as summer resorts; some use them as permanent residences. Rental houses line the seaside beaches. The fishermen's huts are located on the back side (the bay side) of the high sandy ridge. The gray walls have never seen whitewash and are weatherworn, having been baked in the sun and aged by wind and rain.

"On Grand Island, there are two hotels and a general store. There is a seafood market where merchants come from the mainland to buy the day's catch.

"Acres of wildflowers grace the landscape. White chamomile, compete with yellow goldenrods for the attention of a wandering eye. Plantations of lemon and orange trees abound.

"The white beaches give the islands special character. Bathhouses and out-kitchens are common. Fishermen's wharfs extend out from the banks like sleek wooden fingers along the bayside shoreline. Reeds grow in the brackish water ponds in the low areas of the back side of the island.

"Swimming in the gulf is a passion for some, others ride horses along the beaches or on the worn pathways void of vegetation that traverse the islands from one end to the other—generally a wagon-path. When it is not raining, there are always groups of people (large or small) who enjoy a leisurely stroll on the beaches—talking, laughing, and singing joyful songs, enjoying the tranquility, enhanced by the constant sound of the waves tumbling onto the shore. *C'est la belle vie, n'est ce pas*. This is the good life, is it not?" Pierre lauded.

"Sailboats can circumvent Grand Island through two passes—Caminada Pass on the west end and Barataria Pass on the east end. Lateen rigged boats are often seen enjoying the protected waters of the two bays. Many fishermen use the lateen rigged sailboats to go after their catch. That particular design is very maneuverable and easy to manage, usually operated by one or two men—a favorite choice for the vacationer with little experience in sailing.

"West of Caminada Pass is Cheniere Caminada, a village occupied primarily by fishermen. East of Barataria Pass, the American Army is building Fort Livingston on Grand Terre Island to defend New Orleans from attack by vessels trying to reach the Mississippi River through Barataria Bayou, the backdoor to the city. Construction at the site began in 1834 and it is not yet completed.

"Since mosquitoes are a serious problem in the spring and summer, the local residents attract the purple martins by building houses affixed to long poles. Nearly every home or cottage has at least one nearby. Related to the swallows, the small glossy black birds have a voracious appetite for the pesky nuisance. The purple martin is the island's best friend. They are a welcome site when they appear each spring. Their chirping is music to the ears of every islander.

"I have nothing but praise for that spit of land that holds back the sea!" On that note, Pierre Laffite ended his oration with a smile, noticeably tempered by solemn consternation. It was almost as though he had just described the feelings he would have had if he had just lost a child or some close friend.

Knowing I am keeping a written legend—my diary—Captain Laffite offered to give me a sketch of the west end of Grand Island as a personal gift. "I know you will appreciate it," he told me. "I'll see you in the morning with the sketch in my hand," he promised.

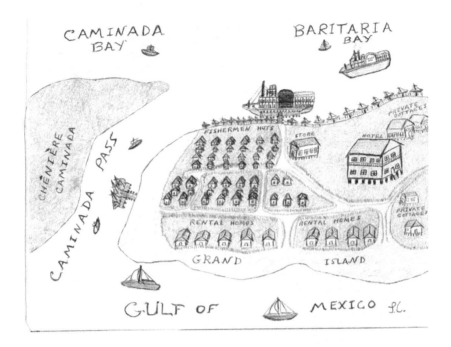

I adjusted the wick of my lamp to finalize this day's record. This fairy tale turned into reality continues to bewilder both Joseph and me; we know it will be impossible to sustain this level of extreme good fortune. We ponder what life will be like when the excitement prosperity affords is diminished. What will there be left after activity that would take a lifetime is started and completed in a few months—it is extraordinarily odd and totally inconceivable! Is it not? As most recipients of a benefactor's generosity would conclude, "I shall count my blessings, and thank almighty God for everything. May God bless Uncle Patrick. Good night and amen". It's been one heck of a birthday, eh, Joseph? Joseph was oblivious to my question now being sound asleep. So be it. It was a good birthday!

September 30, 1840

Pierre and his men left the island right on schedule yesterday around noon. I kissed him on his cheek and asked that he tell Jean how much we appreciated his many gifts. I told him I hopped we would meet again and Joseph and me bid him adieu. The diagram of the west end of Grand Island was very well done. I will insert it in my legend; in the bottom right corner, he signed with his initials "PL."

My Queen Atlantic stove has found a new home. The location of the out-kitchen is convenient; it will make cooking much less of a chore. Civilization has come to Deer Island!

Joseph and I will enjoy the next few days of solitude; we intend to relax and break in our new cook stove. We don't expect any more company until Frenchy and Carey, with the rest of our work crew, return with lumber and materials needed to continue work on the *big house.*

Chapter Seven

PROGRESS
THE HOLIDAY SEASON

November 27, 1840 (Thanksgiving Day)

This, the fourth Thursday of November, will be a day of celebration on Deer Island. The framework on the *big house* is nearing completion. Yesterday, the men finished cutting tenons on the upstairs ceiling joists to fit the mortised hollows cut in the top beams which traverse the second-story studwalls.

Frency and Carey are the only members of our work crew that stayed to share in the festivities; the rest of the men headed for the mainland to spend time with family and friends. Frenchy is an excellent cook, and he and Carey have volunteered their services; you cannot begin to imagine how glad I was to yield to their wishes.

Before sunrise this morning, Frenchy demonstrated the method for loading the Kentucky long rifle. They are going after our first kill; until this time, not a single deer has been shot on the island. By the light of the oil lamps they carefully went through the process—ninety grains of black powder down the muzzle, the .45 caliber miniball follows the powder down the barrel, the wadding or patch was coated with a little lamp oil and placed over the end of the barrel to be sent down the barrel by the ramrod to seat the charge, tapping it down lightly for a good seal. Once this was done, Frenchy explained to Joseph the mechanics of firing the gun. Pointing to the hammer, he told him there is a flint embedded inside this part. A small amount of fine gunpowder will be placed in the flash pan. When we spot a deer, you will slowly cock the hammer by pulling it back. You will aim the rifle right behind the big muscle of the front leg, about a foot above the belly. When you have taken aim, gently pull the trigger. This will release the hammer. The flint will spark over the flash pan and ignite the load of powder in the breach through the touch hole, exploding the charge and sending the projectile into the deer's heart."That's all there is to it, Joseph!" Frenchy said with his typical laugh. "Don't worry, I'll be with you to guide you through the shooting process. The gun is already loaded. We'll bring your powder horn to charge the flash pan. Now, finish your coffee. It's time to go!"

The wind was blowing from the north as the two men walked out the front door and down the steps, disappearing into the thicket beyond the fountainhead. Carey Trudeau was still asleep in the upstairs loft. I sipped my cup of coffee on the front porch. Right when daylight was breaking, a loud gunshot rang out; man, it sounded loud! Disturbed by the noise, Carey descended the access ladder that leads from the front porch to the attic bedroom.

"You think they got one?" Carey asked as he went inside to get a cup of coffee before joining me on the porch. I had my eyes trained in the direction of the fountainhead, anxiously awaiting the outcome. Frenchy appeared, dragging a deer by its hind leg; Joseph followed close behind with his rifle resting over his shoulder, his powder horn hanging from his neck.

"I killed my first deer, Josephine!" Joseph announced with a prideful smile.

"One shot! He killed him dead with one shot! That is pretty good for a greenhorn, or anyone else for that matter!" Frenchy acclaimed. "Of course, I had a good teacher," Joseph acknowledged, and rightly so—Frenchy had done a good coaching job.

The three men encouraged me to take it easy, relax, and enjoy this holiday. That is what I intend to do. I'll keep the coffee and tea hot for them; they can handle all the rest.

They hanged the deer by the hind legs and began to separate the hide from the meat; Frenchy told Carey to scrape the hide and salt it well to preserve it; he knows a tanner on the mainland who will cure the hide. He will bring it to the city on his next trip to have the procedure done and return it to Joseph as a reminder of his first deer. He's going to mount the horns on a plaque for Joseph to hang on our wall. I didn't know that killing a deer was such a big deal, but with men I guess it is, I reasoned.

Carey lit the fire in my new woodstove while the other two men prepared the meat for the pot. They cut away the hind quarter for our consumption; the rest of the meat was lightly salted and hanged to cure in the northern breezes. Tomorrow they will store the excess meat in a large crock jar and cover it with melted lard to keep it from spoiling. As long as it is properly sealed, it will last indefinitely. Thank God for Frenchy; he has taught us many things we will need to know to survive on this remote island. I honestly don't know what we would have done without him.

Joseph said that his rifle didn't kick back as hard as he thought it would. Frenchy got a good laugh out of that assertion. "As excited as you were when I pointed you to that deer, the gun could have knocked you to the ground and you probably would not have felt it," he teased.

"I am sure you are right, Frenchy. If you would not have steadied my aim, I may have not hit the deer at all," Joseph modestly responded.

I surprised everyone when I asked to be taken on a fishing trip tomorrow. Carey thought it was a good idea. "There are a few fishing poles aboard our boat. We can cast a net for bait and go and have a good time," he quipped. I anticipated an enthusiastic response from the other members of our party.

"Well, what do you two think of my idea?" I asked, a bit annoyed by their apparent indifference.

They pretended to be disinterested, but after a brief pause, they conceded that it was a great idea. We will be heading for Oyster Bayou in the morning, wherever that is. Our trusty captain says we will try for redfish; he says it is good for baking or frying. I can't wait! We will finally be doing something different, I mused.

I asked them to save some of the inedible parts to bait a few crab lines; I would like to learn how to catch crabs while we are fishing. Carey liked the idea; he says crabs are good bait for the types of fish we want to harvest. "We will need to learn all these things if we want to expand our menu list beyond boiled rice, boiled dried beans, hot coffee and tea," I teased.

"You said a mouthful!" Joseph proclaimed. "We definitely need to figure out ways to expand the menu. This deer meat is a very good start. As soon as we have the time and a few needed materials, Frenchy will help me build a smokehouse. When we learn how to smoke some of our meat, that will be one more step toward becoming self-sufficient," he added. "Whatever you want or need, it will be done for you, my dearest Josephine, you can count on that, my dear wife," Joseph teased, adding a little frivolity to the conversation.

It's my feminine charm, I silently reasoned. Those men will do anything I ask them to do, I mused. After all, I am the only woman on the island. I am the "*queen of Deer Island.*" Enough of this fanciful daydreaming!

Before dining on "*venaison a la Marceaux,*" Joseph led us all in a prayer of thanksgiving. We each took a turn thanking God for blessings too numerous to recall, not the least of which was the meat we were about to enjoy.

During the afternoon, the men exchanged tall tales—some true, most exaggerated, some the figment of a dreamer's imagination. Carey took out his harmonica, and we sang and danced until we were all tuckered out.

"The early bird gets the worm, and the one with the worm will catch the first fish," Joseph postulated.

"*Vous avez l'air fatigue,* et *vous avez besoin de repose.* You look tired, and need some rest," Frenchy shared, seeing that I was exhausted from the day's exuberance.

We all agreed it was time to get some rest. When Joseph went to sleep, I lighted my lard oil lamp, adjusted the wick for brightness, and recorded the day's activity in my diary. This was our first thanksgiving celebration; it was a wonderful experience. I hope we can celebrate this day with our friends every year, make it an annual custom. It is a good thing to have friends to share in the bounty; it enhances the satisfaction of the day's festivities. I thank God for good friends, and I hope someday to be thankful for at least one child; may God's will be done, amen and good night.

December 25, 1840 (Christmas Day)

Uncle Patrick arrived on the island yesterday. He brought a few provisions and some presents to celebrate our first Christmas. He will be spending the week with us. He says the Henleys promised to come out to share the New Year celebration with us; they are bringing Pauline with them when they come. He knew I would be excited with the news.

Harry Thompson and Mark Mathews, captain and deckhand of Uncle Patrick's chartered boat—the sloop *Lady's Dream*—have volunteered to assist in the food preparation. That was fine with me; there would be more time to enjoy our company.

Frenchy and Carey will be celebrating the holidays with us also; they have become a part of our extended family. Words cannot express the appreciation Joseph and me have for their tireless assistance in this huge endeavor; the establishment of a homestead on Deer Island has been quite a challenge.

Our labor crews have been hard at work on the *big house*; though still unfinished, progress has been steady, and the congressman's new home is shaping up to be a handsome structure indeed. Uncle Patrick is thrilled that it is nearing completion, and he is looking forward to the day he will be living on the island with us—I often wonder if his plans include Pauline Longere; does he plan to ask for her hand in marriage? I don't believe he is building such a large dwelling to live there alone; time will tell.

Three days ago, four men from Brashear City got surprised by a swift moving northwester. The storm was so violent that they sought refuge in Deer Bayou. When they spotted our landing with the *Swamp Rat* securely moored, they decided to try to find more comfortable shelter. They surprised us when they knocked on our front door. Drenching wet and cold, we invited them in to dry off and to warm up with hot coffee. The men spent the night aboard Frenchy's boat and headed for the mainland early the following morning. We have discovered that life is full of surprises.

I was awake early this morning; everyone was still asleep, so I made some coffee and tea. I decided to light my lamp so I could sit at my desk and make a few entries in my diary. I write nearly every day, but once in a while, when not much is happening, I skip my ritual and catch up later; hence, the notation about the men caught in the winter storm.

There can be no better reason for celebrating one day each year than this, I thought. Christmas! The day the entire Christian world commemorates the birth of the Savior, Jesus Christ, the King of kings and the Lord of lords!

It's cold and frosty outside; the trees are standing motionless in the absence of even a mild breeze. It's going to be a wonderful day!

About a half hour after sunrise, the house was bristling with activity. Gifts were exchanged, and there was joy on every face. Uncle Patrick presented Joseph with a W&C Scott double-barrel, eight-gauge, percussion-firing shotgun. It shoots reloadable brass shells with a cap that ignites the powder inside the breach when struck by the hammer. "It is the latest version of a fowling gun on the market," Uncle Patrick announced with pride. In addition to the gun, he brought more brass shell casings, percussion caps, gunpowder, and enough shot to last a lifetime—he also brought a press for reloading the brass shells and other paraphernalia needed to do the job correctly.

Frenchy and Carey were amazed to see such a fine firearm for duck hunting. They immediately asked where they might attain one for themselves. "There is a gun shop in New Orleans that had just received a shipment. I learned from a close friend of mine about the advantages this firearm has over the flintlock shotgun. The shop owner allowed me to test fire his new gun. After that experience, I just had to own one. A vast improvement over Joseph's Kentucky flintlock, I decided to pick up an extra gun and give it to him for Christmas," Uncle Patrick told the emulous boatmen.

The men are planning a hunting trip for tomorrow morning; they intend to scout around for a good spot this afternoon. They will compete to see which pair of shooters will best the other. It will be a battle between the flintlock and the percussion loaded shotgun. I'm guessing they know who will win already.

By midmorning, the Queen Atlantic stove was covered with pots filled to the brim with today's special menu. Carey was kneading dough for a pan of fresh bread. Now that we have an oven, biscuits and bread will be a staple around the dining table. Everyone was congregating around the out-kitchen, enjoying the aroma of the gourmet food. What a feast! I could not wait to get a sample, but to be polite, I restrained myself.

Uncle Patrick, accustomed to speaking his mind whenever he has an audience, began to extol the efforts and the accomplishments that have been made toward the realization of his dream for a retirement haven. Looking skyward, Joseph's uncle thanked God for his nephew's talents. He thanked God for all the blessings that had been bestowed upon him during the course of his lifetime. He thanked God for his many friends and business associates—he mentioned William and Greta Henley, Irving and Susan Peltier, Jean Laffite, and last but certainly not least, Pauline Longere. He closed his heartfelt prayer with this: "I thank God the Father for sending his Son to redeem mankind. I dedicate the remainder of this day for the celebrating of Christ's birth. Amen."

All present voiced a hearty "Amen!" and the festivities continued. Uncle Patrick walked over to me and gave me a hug; whispering in my ear, he said that he thanked God for me in a special way, because if I had not accepted his invitation to come to America, none of this would have been possible. He called me the key to his success. I must say I was most flattered by his remarks. It is nice to feel loved!

Christmas day was spent sharing the joy of the season. The effulgent sunlight, and the crisp cold air, produced an atmosphere that was perfect for the festivities. We dined on wild turkey, venison, roasted pork, and an assortment of vegetables.

About midafternoon, Melvin and Jennifer Lacache came for a visit. Joseph and I met them a few weeks ago; they live on a houseboat along Bayou Chene. We met by chance. One morning, Joseph and Carey had gone to the landing to check the mooring lines on the *Swamp Rat*; suddenly, a sailboat appeared, heading downstream for the river. When Joseph waved at them, the couple maneuvered their boat, swinging it around to say hello and to get acquainted. Joseph and Carey escorted them to the house so I could meet them. We had small talk and sipped on a few cups of coffee and tea. Melvin is a trapper and a fisherman; he has promised to help us learn how to trap the open prairie of the estate. Jennifer sews all her family's clothing, and she has promised to teach me everything she knows. These swamp people are so industrious and self-sufficient, it astounds me. I am glad everyone we have come to know is ready and willing to help us to assimilate.

Jennifer Lacache gave me a sewing box filled with the necessary implements for sewing—thimbles, needles, various spools of thread, etc. She told me she would bring me yards of material when we get together for our first sewing lesson, probably in the spring when the trapping season ends. I told her I appreciated her eagerness to teach me.

Melvin and Jennifer have three boys and one girl; all their children were visiting friends, so they decided to sail down Bayou Penchant to come for a short visit. We understand they have a nice bunch of kids. I hope we will have children; it's not that we haven't been trying. After a couple of hours, they headed back to their home; they were scheduled to pick up their young ones an hour or so before sunset. They promised to see us again this spring.

The sun was beginning to set when Uncle Patrick announced that he had a few more surprises for me and Joseph. We waited patiently as Harry and Mathew went to their boat to gather the presents. Meanwhile, he told us he had seeds for planting the garden—a garden that is not yet cleared for cultivation. "To demonstrate my full confidence that the garden will get planted, I have purchased these seeds," he explained with unshakable confidence. There are heads of garlic, seeds of corn, onion, okra, mustard, turnips, beets, squash, purple hull peas, green beans, and several varieties of vegetables and herbs. *Wow!* I thought. He has big plans even for the garden. I had to respect his resolve.

"*Vouloir c'est pouvoir*. Where there's a will there's a way!" Frenchy interjected after an extended silence.

Harry and Mathew returned from the *Lady's Dream* with the Christmas gifts. "These presents were sent to you from William and Greta Henley," Uncle Patrick shared. Harry handed Joseph a mahogany box, about twice the length of a cigar box. Inside the box was a large hunting knife. "It's a *Bowie knife*, named for Jim Bowie. He was made famous after he died heroically at the Battle of the Alamo during the Mexican-American War, about four years ago. Texas is now seeking to join the Union, a cause to which I am deeply committed," he voiced, with a determined look on his face.

Now it was my turn to open a present. Mathew laid a wooden chest at my feet as I sat on the end of my chair on the front porch. I opened the finely crafted, hinged chest. It was filled with feminine delights—clothing, shoes, perfume, and soap. I was ecstatic.

As the day was coming to an end, Uncle Patrick once again expressed his appreciation and his love for me and Joseph. He seemed to be somewhat in a state of melancholy as he shared his heartfelt sentiments with us. There was a hint of emptiness in his heart. He seemed lonely. Though he did not say it, to me it seems he is trying to forget someone or something. Maybe he will share it someday; I'm surely not going to ask.

While the men sat around the front porch having conversation, I went into the house to prepare for bed. Joseph continued to accommodate our guests while I laid down for a while. Later, when all is quiet, I'll get back up to record this day's activity in my diary.

As I laid down to rest, I wondered silently why such a fine, handsome gentleman remained unwed. Was there a romance that ended somehow, and left deep emotional scars that he finds difficult to dispel from his memory? What could be preventing him from engaging in the normal course of a male-female relationship? The cycle of a loving relationship—love, marriage, sex, children, these are the four steps necessary to solidify the bond between a man and a woman who are in love.

Joseph and I have the first three requirements for a secure relationship, now all we need is step four; we are trying. I guess that is how the old adage "Patience is a virtue" applies to me. I am trying to be patient; maybe when I stop worrying, the cycle of love for the Addisons will be complete. God knows.

December 28, 1840 (William and Greta Henley Arrive)

About midmorning, we were graced by the presence of William Harrison Henley and his wife Greta, owners of Sugarland Farms Plantation from the village of Houma. Accompanying them was Mademoiselle Pauline Longere, Uncle Patrick's beautiful and charming lady friend from Chacahoula.

Joseph and I thanked William and Greta for the Christmas presents they had sent with the congressman. We also thanked them for the leather-bound books (the Holy Bible and the diary). We shared with them our sincere appreciation for all the gifts they have given to us since we first met back on the plantation. I told Greta that both of our books have been used on a regular basis. Joseph reads at least one Bible verse each morning over a cup of tea or coffee. I showed her the many pages already recorded in my written legend. I could tell it made her happy to see how we were enjoying the special gifts.

Greta informed me that her husband had purchased the two books while on a trip to South Carolina. He bought them from a friend of his that owns a sugar plantation near Charleston. I was so excited over the arrival of our guests, that I forgot I was supposed to be the hostess.

Harry Thompson was busy offering coffee or tea, to everyone who wanted a cup, when I regained my senses. I'm glad he decided to assume that responsibility; I could spend more time with Pauline and Greta. All the men had gathered around the out-kitchen; they were discussing politics—a subject that does not interest me.

Frenchy and Carey are on a duck hunt; they left before daylight. I hope the shots I heard hit their marks; we are planning to have pot roasted duck for our main course. There hasn't been any shooting for a while; they must be heading back with dinner—I hope!

Pauline and I listened as Greta informed us that her son was not able to attend the holiday celebrations due to a bout with the flu. She received a letter from him on Christmas Eve (I didn't know she had a son!). She went on to tell us that her dear son, William Harrison Henley III, is attending college at Virginia Military Institute (VMI); the university opened its doors for students in 1839. William is half-way finished with his sophomore year; he is studying agriculture, political, and military science. She told us young William has aspirations of running for some political office; he would like to follow in the footsteps of our dear friend, Congressman Adams. She says Patrick advised her son that a military background and a keen understanding of agriculture would build a suitable platform from which he could launch a political career. Greta says she and her husband have great hopes for their son's future. (I never knew the boy existed until now, but I am already impressed by his potential. They must be proud of him; he is only twenty-two years old. We are the same age—how different are the courses that are afforded to each individual, I pondered.)

Pauline politely listened as Greta continued to fill our ears with interesting facts about her son and how his going away to school has affected their lives. She says Billy (William's nickname) has been running the plantation in the summer months, when the cane crops are laid by. My husband and I were accustomed to taking extended vacations—visiting friends, mostly other planters, from Louisiana to the Carolinas. "Now that our son is in school, we will have to make shorter trips," she told us with a degree of disappointment, barely discernible. I don't think she was trying to invoke sympathy; that would be impossible!

Greta continued to entertain us with her oratory. "Year before last, we visited cane, cotton, peanut, and tobacco growers in Mississippi, Alabama, Georgia, North and South Carolina, and Virginia. My husband says its good business to stay in touch with all the growers he befriended during his days as a factor back in New Orleans. I most enjoy sharing recipes with the wives of all those Southern gentlemen," she commented in a flirtatious manner befitting her Southern charm. (She wasn't being pretentious or condescending; she was just being Greta. She does have a different circle of friends—a condition of circumstance I reasoned. Joseph and I also have friends; it's just that our circle is much smaller.)

"It must be the vitality of youth, Greta! I don't believe I could keep up with your fast-paced lifestyle! I must say, I am envious of your carefree existence and the wide range of your experiences. It is plain to see why Congressman Adams cherishes your friendship and why you enjoy having him in your circle of friends. You have so much in common—you seem to have a kindred spirit!" I surmised.

Greta was obviously flattered by my assertions. I decided to get Pauline to participate in our conversation. Pauline is the epitome of what every woman I know would like to be: charm, beauty, a radiant smile, a perfect figure, there is nothing about the feminine anatomy that she could improve. This I know; she can charm any man without saying a single word. Always fashionably dressed, no duchess in England could boast in her presence; now that is saying something!

Frenchy and Carey were returning from the hunt. When they took one look at Pauline, they were both speechless. "What is the matter? A cat got your tongues?" I teased. "This is Mademoiselle Pauline Longere. She is here visiting us from the tiny settlement of Chacahoula," I told them, hoping they would catch their breath and say something. While they were trying to gather their thoughts, I introduced Greta.

"*Bonjour, Mademoiselle,*" Frenchy barked in his customary gruff voice. "*Bonjour, Mademoiselle,*" Carey announced with stammering lips, exposing his shyness in the presence of a beautiful woman.

"Pauline, this is our captain and fellow laborer Francois Marceaux. The young man with him is his deckhand, Carey Trudeau,"

I announced. Two Frenchmen and one French maiden meet for the very first time; it was as though a dam broke with the water behind the structure suddenly pouring through a narrow channel.

I didn't know that French could be spoken so fast. Pauline had the two men enthralled in conversation in their natural tongue. It was something to see. While they were enjoying each other's company, Greta and I went for a cup of tea.

When I saw there was no end to the getting acquainted scene in the front yard, I reminded the trusty hunters that there were ducks to be cleaned and cooking to be done. "There will be plenty time for frolic during the course of this holiday period," I advised.

Greta and I whisked Pauline away from the gawking Frenchmen, deciding to go inside for some woman talk. "How are things at Chacahoula, Pauline? Have you been well?" I asked.

Forgetting she was now speaking to people who did not understand her language, she retorted, "*Tres bien, Madame Josephine. Merci.*" Sensing the *faux pas*, she continued, "*Pardonez-moi s'il vous plait.* I am sorry; I was enjoying speaking in French with those two gentlemen. I forgot myself for the moment."

"All has been well with me, Josephine, and how is life on the island treating you?" Pauline inquired in her soft, gentle voice.

"It will take some time to adjust to wilderness living, but with all the assistance and emotional support from the many friends we have made, I think we will be just fine. Loneliness! That is what I fear most. Once the construction is finished, and all the work crews have returned home, who will visit us then?" I shared.

"Not to worry," Pauline consoled. "Congressman Adams will be here. He will introduce you to many of his good friends. There will always be someone coming to the island to visit, you will see! I'm telling you the truth! Patrick is well-liked among his constituents. You will have more visitors than you can wish for. Remember what I am telling you, you will see!"

"Thank you for the pep talk, Pauline, I needed a little solace. I appreciate your candor. You and I are going to be bosom friends," I responded with all the sincerity that I had within me. "We'll be like sisters!"

I told Greta we could all be like sisters; she is the oldest at forty-eight; Pauline is twenty-five; I am twenty-two. A fine trio of sisters we will be. It is amazing how good having friends can make someone feel; there is some degree of security in knowing you are not alone.

I recommended we go for a walk. Frenchy and Carey had cleared a pathway from the rear of the *big house* to the bend in the river. I told my sisters the scene from the river bank there is fantastic and off we went down the quarter-mile trail. It finally dawned on me that this was Greta and Pauline's first visit to Deer Island. That explains why they were filled with amazement and wonder over the serenity of the location. They must have been shocked to see the progress—the new wharf, the *little house*, the out-kitchen were all completed; construction on the *big house* was nearing completion. All of this was accomplished on a remote island deep in the wilderness. I could see it in their eyes; they were impressed! Why not? It is inspiring to see a homestead built on an island! I am sure this is a unique endeavor.

Just before we reached the river, we startled a deer; you might say the deer startled us. We soon emerged through the dense thicket that lined the *beaten path* and witnessed the vast expanse of the swift moving water of the Atchafalaya River. The fresh air, the abundant waterfowl feeding in the calm water behind the sandbars, which rise above and sink below the water level with each change in the river's course—a hazard to passing vessels, the channel never stays the same; it is constantly changing. From the clam-shelled bank we could walk up to the water's edge. I pointed to all the driftwood that was lodged against the shore. Our source of fresh firewood never diminishes; nature is taking good care of us, making regular deposits for our consumption.

On our way back to the out-kitchen (it was time to eat), Pauline lauded the beauty of the island and the environment surrounding the estate. Greta proclaimed that she found it peaceful, exhilarating, a wonderful experience.

"The first time I walked to the river, I was spellbound! To breathe the clean freshness of the open air to witness life exuded by the motion of the swift moving river current; in stark contrast is the environment contained by the dense forest where our new home is located. The difference is evident, but notice how one environment compliments and enhances one's appreciation for the other," I declared.

Without any forethought I asked Pauline a deeply personal question: "What about the congressman? Are you going to marry him?" I was ashamed that I let that slip out. Greta seemed shocked by my lack of sensitivity; nonetheless, she anxiously awaited her response.

"I am very fond of Patrick," Pauline admitted. "But you are seeing only the obvious aspects of our special relationship." She continued to address the subject. "Patrick Adams is a close friend of my father. My father is involved in a serious business that many find difficult to understand. My father has borne the brunt of vicious attacks on his character. There are many officials in the American government who would much prefer to see him dead. Patrick, at the urging of my father, agreed to care for me. I am the ward of Patrick Adams. I am like a member of his family, like you, Josephine. He is my surrogate father," Pauline lamented.

"Yes, I love him and he loves me, but I believe the love he has for me is the love of a father for his daughter," she bemoaned. She continued, "My name has been changed to protect me from anyone who may be bitter toward my father. My name is not really Pauline Longere. It is Pauline Laffite. I am Jean Laffite's daughter," she asserted. "My father is a privateer!" Pauline exclaimed. "Do you know what people that hate him call him?" she asked. "They call him a pirate. They want to be rid of him!" she announced with tears flowing down her face.

Greta and I tried our best to console Pauline in her moment of painful reflection. We told her that we all loved her and that as long as we lived we would support her in any way we could. "We do now, and we always will, consider you as a member of our family. I would be proud to call you Aunt Pauline or sis, whichever title suits you," I shared. I wiped away her tears, and I embraced her. "I love you, sis!"

Greta had never met Pauline's father, but she overheard Patrick and her husband speaking of Captain Laffite on several occasions. She was surprised to learn that Jean Laffite had visited Joseph and me back in the month of September, a week before Joseph's birthday. Greta marveled that Jean's brother, Pierre Laffite, brought us our Queen Atlantic stove. "That's not all he brought us!" I boasted. "He gave us items of cast iron cookware, and he and his crew were responsible for building our out-kitchen. What do you think about that?" I posed.

Greta responded, "I don't know what to say, Josephine! Such generosity is always commendable! I suppose the adage 'actions speak louder than words' would be an appropriate observation. Clearly, there is evidence of a deeply personal relationship between Jean, Pierre, and Patrick Adams," she deduced.

Pauline told us she could not have said it better: "These men were all *compagnons d'armes*, comrades in arms, they fought side by side during the Battle of New Orleans. Their friendship has been tried in the fire!" she proudly shared.

I told Pauline about her father and her uncle's trip to the island; I made it clear to her that they were not only handsome, but they were polite and eager to lend us their assistance. I told her that Jean had promised to send his brother bearing useful gifts in one week, and so it was that Pierre arrived one week later—on Joseph's birthday. I told her that her father was dignified in appearance and a perfect gentleman; he spared no means to make us feel welcome aboard his armed merchant ship. At the request of the congressman, your father brought us through all the bayous that run through the estate, demonstrating the vastness of the land Patrick owns, giving us a first-hand look. He was a charming host, and he made it quite clear that he has a great deal of respect for Patrick Adams.

Because what was discussed was said in confidence, and we did not want to violate the agreement between Captain Laffite and Patrick Adams, Greta and I agreed with Pauline that the matter should be kept secret. It is for everyone's good. Your name will remain Pauline Longere. We all agreed we would not bring up the subject again.

I had to interject one more thought into the conversation. "It is my opinion that Patrick Adams is truly in love with you, Pauline. The two of you have no blood relationship, and the legal aspects regarding his guardianship of you would not stand in the way of a nuptial union. I do not believe the difference in age is relevant. Love is the only thing that matters, and happiness follows close behind. That is my heartfelt opinion!"

Greta concurs with my perception of their relationship. "It is clear to me that the love you and Patrick share is more than platonic. Marriage is the natural next step in my opinion."

"*Les les faire*," Pauline proclaimed. "Let things be! If Patrick asks for my hand in marriage, he may have it. He is an honorable man and a true gentleman. I would be proud to become his wife," she aspired.

"Well, that is that!" I shouted, striking my hands together to signify the end of the matter.

"Let's go see what the boys are doing," Pauline suggested with a coy expression that was a customary feature of her charming demeanor, just one of the reasons she drives men crazy. She is such a delightful creature, I thought, as we sauntered back to the cabin.

January 1, 1841 (New Year's Day)

It has been four days of fun, food, and frolic, and three nights of music, song, and dancing. Greta, Pauline, and I are worn and weary; we never declined an invitation to step in time with the rhythmical motions inspired by the fiddle-playing of Jerry and Tom Richardson, the banjo-playing of Mark Mathews, and the harmonica playing of Carey Trudeau. It has been a holiday season to remember.

Special mention must be given to the crews of the three vessels that have ferried our guests from the mainland to the island. They did all the cooking and the hard work necessary to make this a special occasion. Joseph and I expressed our deepest appreciation to Francois Marceaux and Carey Trudeau (captain and deckhand of the *Swamp Rat*), Harry Thompson and Mark Mathews (captain and deckhand of *Lady's Dream*), and Jerry Richardson and Tom Richardson (captain and deckhand of *Sugar Baby*); without their assistance, the festivities would have been more toil and less tranquility.

By midafternoon, Joseph and I were alone once again. Last to leave were Pauline, and Greta and William Henley aboard their sail-boat, *Sugar Baby*. We waved good-bye until they rounded the northern bend in the bayou. Their crewmen, the Richardson brothers, told us they would be back at the wharf in the front of Sugarland Farms by sunset.

Watching that last group of guests vanish into thin air, I broke down and cried. It wasn't because I was sad; it's just that the quietness that solitude brings makes me lonely. My thoughts immediately focused on the day I waved at my family and friends for the final time as the *Island Mistress* stole me away from my childhood home in Southampton.

"What is wrong, dear?" Joseph asked in a soft, sympathetic voice.

"I'm sorry, Joseph, it's not your fault. It's just that seeing all these good people leave reminds me of England. I will be all right in a few minutes," I promised.

"I love you, dear. As soon as we start having children, these bouts with loneliness will dissipate," Joseph consoled.

"Do you ever get lonely, Joseph?" I asked, wiping the tears from my eyes.

"Yes, there are times I get lonely, but I choose not to dwell upon the circumstances that spawn this emotion within myself. To do otherwise would only serve to make the annoying sensation harder to overcome. Come now, let's go back to our cabin for a cup of fresh hot tea," Joseph beckoned, reaching for my hand to lift me from my seat on the wharf.

And so the New Year has begun; the first day has passed, as the night creatures announce the coming darkness. The weather has been perfect for our week of celebration; the temperature has remained above freezing, and we had clear skies and sunshine. It may be hard to understand, but I am already thinking of our next Thanksgiving, Christmas, and New Year's Day celebrations. The thought showers me with good memories as I look forward to adding even more pleasant experiences to my memory bank.

As Joseph and I sipped our tea sitting in our favorite chairs on the front porch of the *little house,* we began reflecting on current events. Joseph told me that Uncle Patrick has instructed him to make a materials list for the building of our own sailboat. He told Joseph that Frenchy would take over from there—he will deliver the list to the mill at Patersonville, demanding only the highest grade wood for the hull and the mast poles. He will order the hardware from the Bayou Boeuf General Store; Mr. E. B. Blanchard will secure all those necessary items for us.

Joseph's eyes began to sparkle; his head was in the clouds as he mused over the notion that his dream of building his own boat would soon be realized. I told him that once the boat is finished, our isolation will be eliminated. We will be able to come and go at will; we can visit the Lacache family at Bayou Shaver. We can go to the store at Brashear City; we will be free to do whatever we please. I told him that my spirits were lifted by the promise of someday having our own transportation. That expression of solace made my husband very happy.

"Let's go to bed early, Josephine!" Joseph suggested. He lifted me from my chair on the front porch, and he cradled me in his arms, carrying me through the threshold as though it was the first time.

"All is well!" I lauded. "All is well!" And with that, I will say good night, and amen.

October 28, 1841 (An Accident)

Ridgefield Ramsey fell from the rooftop of the *big house* this morning. Ridgefield, one of our carpenters, was nailing shingles when he lost his footing and tumbled to the ground. The fall knocked him unconscious; we were all extremely concerned over his condition.

He soon recovered, and aside from feeling sore, he was all right. After dinner, he climbed back atop the roof and started nailing shingles once again, much to everyone's relief.

Joseph says the roof will be finished by tomorrow evening if the weather holds.

November 27, 1841 (Thanksgiving Day 1841)

Uncle Patrick arrived yesterday on his chartered vessel, *Lady's Dream*. He was escorted to our cabin by his boat crew, Harry and Mathew about midmorning. Right away, Joseph proudly announced that the exterior of the *big house* is complete; all that remains is the installation of the glass windows.

Most of our work crew went in for the holiday season; they will return the first week of January to resume construction on the interior of the house. A skeleton crew of about six men will be returning in a couple of days to help install the windows.

Uncle Patrick informed Joseph that the order of wood he placed for his sailboat has been filled; it is in storage at a warehouse at Brashear City. Senator Peltier owns an interest in the establishment; we can leave the lumber there until it is needed. He paid Mr. Lafont for the lumber and ordered another one thousand board feet of two-and-a-half-inch thick plank. "I know you will make good use of it," Uncle Patrick offered with a grin.

"The mast poles you ordered, made from Siberian spruce, were a special order. They had to be shipped from New England, but they have also been stored in the warehouse. I had to get them shipped from the East Coast by rail. They arrived in New Orleans in October. The foremast is sixty-five feet long, and the aft-mast is seventy feet long. They are beautiful pieces of spruce. There is none better," Uncle Patrick was happy to report.

"The brass collars, mast foot plates, the pulleys and rope, the anchor, and all the other special materials you ordered are at the Bayou Boeuf General Store. Mr. Blanchard is storing them safely for when you need them. What about the sails?" Uncle Patrick asked.

"Any skilled sailmaker who has been given the dimensions of the masts, if he knows that my boat will be a sixty-five-foot schooner with jib sails of ordinary size, that man can fashion the proper sails," Joseph responded with a matter-of-fact manner.

"Write all that information down so I can carry it back with me to New Orleans. I'm sure I can find a good sailmaker somewhere in the city. I'll place an order right away so I can bring it to Mr. Blanchard on my next return trip to the island," Uncle Patrick instructed.

Uncle Patrick informed us that William and Greta will not be able to come for Thanksgiving; they are in the middle of the cane harvest. He reported that William Henley III is doing very well at

VMI; if all goes well, he plans to accompany his parents to spend the winter holidays with us on the island. They send their love.

He told us further that Pauline is not feeling well; it's nothing serious, a little cold and fever. She sends her love and pledges to be with us for Christmas and New Years, God willing!

I was happy with the news that we would all be reunited for the winter holidays. I look forward to seeing everyone. Uncle Patrick marveled over the progress being made on his future home. He praised Joseph and his work crews for their skilled craftsmanship.

The congressman informed Frenchy and Carey that there is a big bonus awaiting them when all the work has been completed. "I intend to demonstrate my appreciation for your faithful service to the Addisons. They have informed me of all the help and emotional assurance you and your deckhand have given them. My deepest thanks to both of you," Uncle Patrick gratefully announced, shaking our boat crew's hands.

Harry and Mark are busy in the out-kitchen, cooking dinner on my Queen Atlantic stove. That stove has been a tremendous blessing. Now we can cook several dishes all at once on the stovetop; at the same time, we can cook a large roast and bake bread, biscuits, or pastry in the oven. It certainly makes cooking, large or small meals, much less a chore.

Roasted wild turkey and venison stew, what a meal! Side dishes of rice, cornbread, and apple pie will enhance the main course. I can smell the aroma of the cook's progress from the front porch, with the assistance of a mild north wind. I'm getting hungry already.

While the other men continued with the food preparation, Joseph, Uncle Patrick, and I sat down on the front porch of the *big house* to relish in the splendor of the day. Joseph began sharing with his uncle the status of our homestead development.

Joseph started his elucidation. "Things are really shaping up around here. We now have a manageable vegetable garden that produces enough to compliment any of the wild game we choose to eat. We have constructed a corn crib for storing non perishable food items—corn, potatoes, pumpkins, etc.

"We have a chicken coop occupied by a dozen barred-rock-hens and one jet-black rooster we lovingly call *Daylight*. Each morning about 5:00 a.m., the customary quiet around the homestead is interrupted by his endless crowing. He does seem overzealous when it comes to awakening everyone within the sound of his voice. We hope to raise baby chicks this spring to increase the size of our flock so chicken can be on the menu more often. Josephine wants to raise another rooster, so Ole *Daylight* can have competition. We intend to name him *Sunset*—no kidding!"

That brought a chuckle out of the congressman!

Joseph continued: "Our pig pen is graced by the pregnant sow you had Frenchy bring us last month. We keep the boar in a separate pen to protect the newborn piglets when they arrive. Carey says the males have been known to eat their young. We are expecting a litter before Christmas. Carey says it is common for a healthy sow to have six to eight young ones. If that is even close to right, we will soon have pork-a-plenty—one more dish for the dinner table.

"Two of our six beehives are occupied. When the bees swarm, we hope to attract more colonies for the remaining houses. In addition to furnishing fresh honey, the buzzing little creatures will pollinate our crops and our fruit orchard when it is finished—now that may take awhile!" Joseph concluded.

"Dinner is served!" Thus the cry came from the out-kitchen. We ambled around the side of the house to join the hungry souls beneath the roofed breezeway of the kitchen where a large table awaited us and food fit for a king. "Solomon did not eat better than this!" Joseph proclaimed.

As we congregated around the table, Uncle Patrick offered a prayer of thanksgiving: "We thank you, Lord, for the many blessings you have seen fit to bestow upon all of us here. Thank you for sparing Ridgefield from serious injury when he fell from the rooftop of my new house. Thank you for the food we are about to eat, and thank you for the fellowship we are having this wonderful and beautiful day, amen."

With everyone sounding a hearty "Amen!" we indulged our-selves with the fine cuisine, which had been prepared for our joy and fulfillment.

Thanksgiving Day's afternoon was spent playing horseshoes and badminton. I must say that I did not fare very well in either competition, but I thoroughly enjoyed the company and the good conversation. Carey Trudeau bested everyone in horseshoes and bad-minton; no one could compete with his accuracy or his agility.

Later, we all took a leisurely stroll down the *beaten path* to the river bank to watch the sunset. The burnished orange, red, and mauve-colored clouds painted a spectacular scene across the west-ern horizon, as the sun slowly disappeared and took the surreal pan-orama with it.

"What a fantastic sunset!" Uncle Patrick raved. "Was it not as beautiful a sight as anything any of you have seen anywhere?" he challenged. None of us could disagree with that.

Carey entertained us with his harmonica for awhile and then we retired for the evening, having thoroughly enjoyed the events of the day. Owls called in the distance as I blew out the lamp over my writing desk. The hooting of the owls summoned my subconscious, as I suddenly lost their voices in an autumn slumber.

December 7, 1841

Late this afternoon, Joseph met with the entire work crew. The main structure on the island has been completed, with the exception of the cabinet work and the furnishings. Work on the four twelve-by-twelve bedrooms in the attic of the *little house* has been completed. The outbuildings, including the two out-houses, the corn crib, the bee houses, the chicken coop, the hog pens, the firewood storage area are all done. Joseph thanked them for their magnificent work and told them they would be welcome to come and visit the island anytime.

He informed them that their pay was forthcoming and could be picked up at the Bayou Boeuf General Store. Mr. E. B. Blanchard has been charged with the responsibility of distributing the funds.

Everyone will receive a handsome bonus from the congressman for their faithful service.

It was a bit sad to see all those workers, men who had become our friends, leave us for good. We may never see them again, but we parted on good terms. I will miss them.

December 15, 1841

Late last evening, Uncle Patrick arrived from the mainland. Progress on the *big house* has been steady, but a bit slower than expected. The work crew was released from their duties last week because most of them were not cabinet or furniture makers. Joseph will finish the remainder of the work with the help of Frenchy and Carey. Joseph says that the finish work is slow and tedious, but he pledges to be finished with the inside of the closets and cabinets soon; the furniture will come later.

Joseph took Uncle Patrick for a tour of the upstairs of his new home. He informed him that the closets were finished, and the beds are ready to receive the moss filled mattresses that were ordered six weeks ago. There is still work to be done on the inside of the closets—building storage shelves and hanging racks. There are other furnishings for the upstairs bedrooms that have not yet been addressed.

Uncle Patrick gave Joseph a list of furnishings he would like him to build for the first floor level—a cupboard, a library filled with bookshelves, various sorts of tables and chairs, a large pantry for food storage, a freestanding hat rack, lamp holders on every wall, interior doors separating every room, shutters on every window, and the list called for many other more refined details.

Joseph enjoys a challenge. He loves building things that are new and different; he thrives on such tests of his woodworking abilities. I pity the day when he starts work on his sailboat; once he gets caught up in his work, even his spare time will be consumed in contemplating his next step in the construction process. "Woe is me!"

Carey showed Joseph how to construct a rabbit trap. It is and elongated box about thirty inches long; the interior space is a square about eight inches by eight inches, closed at the back end, and having a trap door at the front. When a curious rabbit enters the darkness of the restricted hole, he hits the trigger mechanism with his head and there is no escape—no room to turn around. When the trap is sprung, the hunter reaches for the rabbit inside the trap by its hind legs; once the animal is clear, a swift chop of the hand behind the animal's neck and it is ready to be skinned, then cleaned and thrown into the hot grease on the stove. Simple!

Believe it or not, the trap proved successful; now we have six of them to be set out as needed. Soon we will be almost totally self-sufficient with little need for store-bought goods. With a wide variety of wild game to choose from, and the introduction of hogs and chickens and the vegetable garden, our need for provision from the mainland has diminished considerably.

The last time the *Swamp Rat* went to town, Mr. Lafont told Carey that the Peltiers were planning to visit us for the winter holidays. Uncle Patrick invited him, but he had to decline the offer since he had previous plans.

Frenchy is preparing to leave for Brashear City to pick up sixteen moss mattresses before our guests arrive so they won't have to sleep on their boats. "They should be finished!" Uncle Patrick declared. He is to go to the establishment of Ms. Emily Trahan, the local seamstress. "If they are not all finished, get what you can!" Uncle Patrick ordered. "Make haste, Frenchy! We are counting on those mattresses," he urged.

With that last word of encouragement, the *Swamp Rat* set sail for the mainland. They promised to be back with our new bedding by tomorrow evening. Barring unforeseen difficulty, that is entirely probable. We'll have just enough time to prepare the bedrooms in the upstairs of the *big house* before our guests arrive.

Ms. Trahan, a widow of ten years, opened her seamstress shop about eight years ago. What started as a work of necessity, making clothing for her immediate and extended family, has turned into a prosperous business. Widely acclaimed for her overstuffed moss mattresses, Emily makes a product that is in big demand in this region. She made six of them for the *little house*—four for the upstairs bedrooms and two for the two bedrooms on the first floor level. They are quite comfortable and are easy on the back; they provide a soft but firm sleeping surface.

LET'S DO IT AGAIN

December 18, 1841 (Our Second Winter Celebration)

About 9:00 A.M. a crowd of colorfully dressed men, women, and children made their appearance in our front yard. Uncle Patrick was leading the group as they made their way to our front porch. I hollered for Joseph, who was busy working inside the *big house*. "We've got company!" I shouted.

Poking his head through one of the dormer windows, he said he would be down in just a minute. "Serve the coffee and tea!" he ordered before ducking back inside.

Harry Thompson, Mark Mathews, Francois Marceaux, Carey Trudeau, Jerry and Tom Richardson, and Ron and Paul Dumond will team up to care for everyone's beverage, food, and incidental needs. The latest boat crew to grace our fellowship is Ronald Dumond, captain of Senator Peltier's fifty-foot sloop *Sara's Dream*; Paul Dumond is his deckhand.

You cannot possibly imagine what it means to me, when playing hostess to all these guests, to have all the chores designated to the willing servants of these three affluent gentlemen. These festivities would not be possible without the assistance of these fine men who are all faithful employees. Now it is time to greet my guests.

Susan Peltier, Greta Henley, Pauline Longere, and Emmaline Henley walked into the house with me for a cup of tea. The men disappeared—the cooks to the kitchen and the rest to tour the congressman's new home.

Susan walked out onto the front porch to summon her three grandchildren to instruct them on how they should conduct themselves. Once she gave them their orders, she brought them into the cabin to introduce them to us. "These are three of my seven grandchildren," she said. "The two girls are Tanya and Patricia, aged nine and seven. This young man is Donald, aged five. I have two more grandsons and two more granddaughters visiting with their father and mother elsewhere. Irving Jr. and his wife Gladys are in New Orleans for the holiday season," she volunteered.

"You have some fine grandchildren, Susan," we all agreed. Next, Greta Henley introduced her daughter-in-law.

"This is William Harrison Henley III's wife Emmaline. William brought a wife home for Christmas. They met in Virginia while William was at VMI during his freshman year. They got married this summer. Isn't she beautiful?" Greta asked.

Naturally she had to be pretty; Emmaline was the youngest among us. She was well-dressed and well-groomed. She has sandy blond hair, cut just below her shoulders and eyes that are bluer than the sky on a clear winter day. She is very attractive. Pauline still out-shines us all, in every category. Discretion demands that I keep these observations to myself.

Pauline, three years my senior, is by far the most beautiful woman I have ever seen. Her flawless complexion and brilliant smile, her French accent, her deep brown eyes and long straight black hair, her dark brows, her sparkling white teeth, her full lips and chest and her hourglass figure place her in a class all by herself. "That's Pauline!"

Greta Henley's appealing smile and pleasant demeanor compliment her elegant attire and give her a distinctive edge over any average woman who cannot afford to dress as well. Pauline could wear rags and it would not take away her beauty and charm; she is the loveliest girl in the region.

I am sure I am not alone in this seemingly obsessive compulsion I have for sizing up other women. I assume all women do it for one reason or another. As for myself, I don't know how women, or men for that matter, perceive my appearance. I believe I fall somewhere between Greta's sophisticated charm and Emmaline's youthful innocence, though I see myself as a bit better looking than either of those two. "How vain I must be to think such thoughts!"

I shouldn't be bothered with such nonsense anyway. Who cares? Joseph thinks I am beautiful, and that is all that really matters. I really don't know why I compare myself with other women in the first place. Pauline is a special flower; God has permitted her to bloom in our midst. I believe that makes all of us the richer, because she is the charming creature that God intended her to be. Maybe that is the thing she possesses that I envy; she makes people happy. "What an amazing attribute for one to possess!" I thought to myself.

Pauline awakened me from my extended daydream by asking me if I wanted another cup of tea. We carried on with lady talk until the gentlemen rejoined us on the front porch of the *little house*.

"Tomorrow we will set sail for Raccoon Point, about twenty miles east of the lightship anchored off Ship Shoal Island. We'll have a good time on the beach; when we return, we will stop at some shallow oyster bed and cull enough of those to satisfy our appetites. How does that sound?" Uncle Patrick asked, knowing the excitement he had just created. "We will all be going; not a soul will be left on this island. It will be a day of fun and leisure. The weather will be mildly cold but our boats can anchor close enough to the beaches that no one should get wet above the knees," he promised.

Everyone expressed delight over the planned trip to the coast. This will be my first opportunity to see the Gulf of Mexico since our arrival here, although Joseph told me the Atchafalaya Bay is essentially the northern gulf.

Once everyone had eaten dinner, we spent the remainder of the day enthusiastically exchanging information to bring each other up to date with all the current events.

William Harrison Henley III is a handsome young man with the wit and charm of a dashing young prince whose whole purpose in life is to one day occupy his father's throne. He is intelligent (top of his class), full of energy, motivated to make something of himself; he might make a good political candidate some time in his future. There isn't a shy bone in that boy's body. He and Emmaline make a nice couple.

Young William called for everyone's attention. "My wife Emmaline and I are expecting our first child," he heralded.

This was the first time the news was announced; even his parents did not know that Emmaline was with child. Greta tried to hold back her tears, to no avail, as everyone shook hands and shared in the joy of the moment.

One day, I will be making that announcement, I thought to myself. I could not help feeling a bit envious of William and Emmaline. The couple has only been married for seven months, and she is already bearing him a child; some people are just lucky that way, I reasoned.

"How many children do you have, Susan?" I asked. Mrs. Peltier said she has only one child, a son, Irving Peltier Jr. He is making up for their lack of childbearing having produced three boys and four girls—seven grandchildren.

Greta Henley had two sons—William Harrison Henley Jr. died of typhoid fever when he was nine years old, and of course everyone knows William Harrison Henley III; he has Greta's first grandchild in the oven (so to speak).

Greta told me that she and Susan are not examples of the normal family in south Louisiana. They told me the average size family has five to seven children and many have as many as twelve to fourteen. It is a matter of practicality; the more children, the more help earning a living, whether it be farming or trapping and fishing. Children are a blessing from above they shared. I could not disagree with that assertion. I do want children, and I will be happy with as many as God's grace will allow me to have, but the number twelve never entered my mind. How can anyone manage a tribe that size? I wondered. That is a frightening thought!

"Do you wish to have children?" Pauline shyly asked me in her characteristic soft voice.

"Oh yes, Pauline! Each night I pray that God would let me conceive a child," I solemnly attested.

"Don't fret," Greta pleaded. "William Harrison Henley III is our only child. I lost one to the fever. When I delivered young William, I had complications that left me unable to bear again. My husband and I wanted to have four or five children," she lamented. "But I thank the Lord for my healthy son. He is very dear and precious to us, especially since we know he will be our only child."

Harry announced, "Supper is served!" We relocated to the dining table under the covered breezeway of our out-kitchen. After the good meal, the men went to smoke their pipes on the front porch of the *big house*; the women congregated on the back porch of the congressman's home to watch the sunset.

January 1, 1842 (A New Year Comes and Our Guests Leave)

This past two weeks went by so fast it is frightening. Right when I was getting accustomed to the joy of sharing my life with the many friends that have graced this island for our winter holiday season, it was all but over. This afternoon everyone, including Fenchy and Carey, will be sailing for the mainland.

Senator Peltier's grandchildren were three of the most well-behaved kids I have ever had the pleasure to meet. They were never the least bit of trouble; in fact, they added to the joy of the Christmas experience. After all, what is Christmas without children?

About midafternoon, our guests ambled down the pathway to our boat landing at the mouth of the stream. After we exchanged sentiments and wished each other a prosperous new year, one by one, the three sailing sloops received their passengers and headed for home. Following close behind was our faithful captain and deckhand aboard the *Swamp Rat* heading for Brashear City.

Joseph and I walked up the ridge beside the fresh water stream, taking time to enjoy the abundant wildlife that frequently visits its banks. We sat down on our front porch to enjoy the remaining daylight. After sharing thoughts, I posed a question: "Joseph, What is a privateer?"

"A privateer is someone consigned by one government to sink and pillage the ships of another," he asserted. "Why do you ask, dear?"

"I was merely curious, that is all," I told him. I quickly changed the subject to avoid further probing by my husband as to the reason I would have asked him such a question. "When will Frenchy and Carey return?" I queried.

"Uncle Patrick has instructed Frenchy to secure the services of the local coopers (men with special skills who make barrels, casks, and cisterns) to construct three one-thousand gallon water storage tanks—two for the *big house* and the other for the *little house*. Cisterns are in high demand, and they will probably have a waiting list; it may take several months to fill our order. Meanwhile, Ridgefield Ramsey and his brother, with a small work crew, have been asked to help with construction of the foundation for the three large containers at their convenience," Joseph informed me.

I told Joseph we would have at least a week of privacy; there will be time for rest and relaxation. Meanwhile, we'll continue trying to expand our family. Joseph laughed with an expression of delight on his face when I shared that sentiment with him.

We walked the *beaten path* to the river to enjoy the sunset. We sat on a log that had been deposited onshore by high tide; it was still water-soaked, but that didn't bother us. We were steeped in conversation, sharing with each other our impressions of the events that have transformed our lives forever. Our experiences have been strange, foreign to two young immigrants from such a faraway land. Much like the sun has turned its back on the east, we have turned our backs on England; soon, all thoughts of returning home will disappear over the horizon and be gone—for now.

Once I put Joseph to sleep, it was time once again to light my oil lamp and record these events of the day in my legend. As I reflected on the winter celebration just past, the highlight for me was our excursion to Last Island. Sailing Louisiana's coastline for the first time was nothing short of an adventure. As we rounded Point au Fer Island, the vastness of the Gulf of Mexico captured my attention. The light boat at Ship Shoal Island, which warns ships to avoid the sandbars and shallow water surrounding its anchorage, could barely be seen to our southwest. Now we were heading due east for the western tip of *Isles Dernier* (Last Island). Fishermen call the spot Raccoon Point (Lord only knows why); we will be going ashore to comb the beaches for keepsakes—seashells, sand dollars, floatage, etc.

The weather was friendly; the sky was blue. A mild northwest wind filled our sails, sending us to our destination with ease. The gulf was near calm and easily managed by our experienced captains. I was amazed that our lugger was keeping pace with the three schooners. Our boat is for working; the others are swift, sleek, and elegant, desirable characteristics for any affluent owners.

We towed our two flatboats to the island to facilitate a dry landing. Once we reached our desired location, the small boats were used to ferry everyone who wanted to avoid the cold water. First to board one of the transfer craft were Emmaline, Pauline, and Greta. The second boat ferried Susan, her three grandchildren, and yours truly. The men all jumped overboard and waded to the beach; I guess it's a man thing!

We had to cast anchor about one hundred yards from the island to prevent the vessels from going aground on the shallow sandy bottom. Once all of us were ashore, Joseph boasted about how well suited the flatboats were for beaching. The rake at the front and rear were perfect; we were able to kiss the shoreline and step out on dry sand.

I could not help noticing the way Pauline gracefully went ashore with no assistance. The rest of us were a bit clumsy and needed a little assistance getting out the boats. Not Pauline! She jumped into her flatboat with the agility of a cat and she exited the same way; it seemed like she had a great deal of experience—she does live in a house surrounded by swamp; maybe she is accustomed to traveling is small boats, flat-bottomed canoes the French locals call "*pirogues.*"

Uncle Patrick said there is a fishing village about five miles to the east of Raccoon Point. I could not help but wonder about the men and women who made their home at the edge of the sea. They must be a special breed! I thought we were isolated; these people live in harm's way and much farther from the mainland than we do; that's fascinating!

We collected a huge variety of seashells, many still occupied by the hermit crabs that call them home. We found sand dollars, sea beans, and several very large bamboos of different lengths—the tube holes were four or five inches in diameter. Uncle Patrick says the bamboo that was washed ashore probably came from West Africa or somewhere in South America.

On our return trip, we stopped to cull oysters from a shallow reef head that was protruding above water at low tide. When we left for Deer Island, we had more than enough of the mollusks to satisfy everyone's appetite. Need I say more?

They were delicious fried, stewed, or eaten alive on the half shell. Our leisurely excursion was most gratifying in every respect.

I don't know of anything that could have been more exhilarating, a full day of fun with friends on a remote island. Doesn't that describe where I live? I am sure there are many people who would love to take my place.

I conclude this entry in my diary with a simple prayer: "Thank you, Lord, for leading Joseph and I here. I am sure it was your plan all along, amen." It is time for some much-needed sleep, as I count my blessings.

Chapter Eight

GOD ANSWERS PRAYER
GOOD NEWS

February 14, 1842 (Good News Comes to Deer Island)
Changes in my body have confirmed what I have expected for nearly two months now; I am with child. I informed Joseph, and word quickly spread. Frenchy and Carey were the first to help us celebrate the good news. Words cannot express what this means to me and my husband.

Frenchy knows a midwife who lives in Brashear city; Madame Theresa Blanchard has delivered hundreds of babies. He will notify the woman of the pregnancy when he goes back to the mainland. The child should be ready for delivery in September or October. The midwife is accustomed to spending several weeks with her patients--to be there when it happens, and to help with the recovery. She sounds very professional, I thought.

Heavenly bliss! Overwhelming joy! Wild anticipation! Those emotions express my feelings. Joseph is just as excited, but he tries to appear subdued, as though he never doubted this day would come. That's my man! He tries to keep his emotions on an even keel—calm, cool, and collective.

The men have been trying to choose a name for the child, but all the names are for a boy; not a single girl's name was ever mentioned. They are all confident it will be a man child. I asked them why they insisted I would have a boy. "Only the Lord above knows if I will have a girl," I postulated.

"None of us doubt the truth of your assertion, but we are sure it will be a boy," Joseph insisted. "God's will be done!" he concluded.

March 25, 1842

Our work crew, led by Ridgefield Ramsey, has finished the foundations for our three water-storage tanks. The structures are quite impressive (extra sturdy), but they have to be strong to support the weight of a thousand gallons of water each. Over four tons will be resting on each of the support platforms when the cisterns are full.

Joseph remains focused on the interior of the *big house*. All the cabinet work is done; there is a bit more window dressing (decorative finish work)and a few more pieces of the furniture need to be made. He expects that all his work will be done in two or three months. I hope so, he has worked tirelessly to see the project completed; it is time for a break. He never complains, but I know he is suffering from fatigue.

Ridgefield informed us that the three cisterns will be ready for shipment in a few days. The crew is going to the mainland today, but they will be ready to lend a hand when Frenchy halls the large storage tanks to the island. "It will be no small task to get those huge barrels up this ridge," he warned. The plan is to lay them on their sides and roll them gently up the hill. That sounds easy enough, but what do I know? I reasoned.

The construction work on the homestead is nearing the end. Once Joseph finishes all the furniture and the three cisterns are in place, all that will remain will be the clearing of the areas for a large garden, a fruit orchard, the pecan orchard, and the cemetery—no small task! I jest! Yes, there is still a tremendous amount of work to be done! Trees must be cut, and their roots cleared for cultivation; you might say, the next phase of our project will be a monumental task! Only the Lord knows how this will ever get done. Amen!

June 7, 1842

Ridgefield and company assisted Frenchy, Carey, and Joseph in putting the large water storage containers in their place. It took only two days to accomplish the task. The work was completed without incident; no one was injured. They are installing the downspouts that will direct water from the rooftops into the cisterns. Each tank has a spigot near the bottom to access the water inside.

This will be the crowning achievement for all the hard work that Joseph and his merry men have endured. Uncle Patrick will be well pleased. The next phase in the development of the homestead will take several years; even so, one day it will all be done. The congressman's vision of a retirement haven is within his grasp, a dream turning into reality.

July 23, 1842

Our boat crew has decided to go home to visit with family members. Frenchy and Carey have spent most of the last two years with Joseph and me. Joseph advised them to go in for a few weeks of leisure time, a well-deserved vacation. They headed for the mainland at first light this morning.

Once again, Joseph and I are all alone. The expectation of the blessed event has been a genuine source of comfort to me; the baby has been very active inside my womb. The steady movement and the relentless kicking I have been forced to endure leads me inclined to believe that the men might be right; the child could well be a boy.

In addition to the good news of the impending childbirth, work on the *big house* is now complete; after two years of steady progress, the last thing has been done. We now have twin swings on the back porch; one a little left, and the other a little right of the kitchen door.

The swings face each other and will accommodate six persons, eager for conversation, or for a reprieve from their day's activities.

Joseph is excited that he will finally have time to work on his sailboat; he is hoping Frenchy and Carey will remain in the employ of Congressman Adams to help him with the construction. He promises to work at a leisurely pace, but I think that hard and steady work is the nature of the worthwhile endeavor, whether he wants it to be so, or not. He estimates it will take him a year, from laying the keel, to setting the two masts.

I told Joseph that I felt sure Uncle Patrick would continue to pay for the help needed to complete our sailboat. The materials have already been purchased; they await our orders to have them shipped to the island. "He is well aware of the work involved in building a big schooner," I declared.

My time with child is steadily progressing. This being my first baby, I must admit that anxiety is part of life for me now. I can't say I'm fearful; I have experienced only modest discomfort thus far. The fact that a seasoned midwife will be with me when my time draws near is reassuring. No doubt she will be able to prepare me for what is ahead. Having children is a natural occurrence for most women; why should my case be any different, I reasoned.

As usual, my loving husband has been kind and considerate; he makes me feel stronger than I sense I really am.

TERRIBLE NEWS

July 26, 1842 (Terrible News Comes to Deer Island)

Frenchy and Carey arrived unexpectedly bearing sorrowful news. Uncle Patrick has died!

"While en route to New Orleans from Bayou Lafourche, he died suddenly in his coach. When his coachman dismounted to board the ferryboat at Algiers Point, he noticed the congressman made no attempt to get out of his carriage, as was his usual practice. When Albert opened the coach door, he discovered that his friend had expired. This took place in the late afternoon of July 22, four days ago," Frenchy reported.

I was speechless! Joseph's voice trembled when he asked about funeral arrangements.

Frenchy continued, "Senator Peltier told me to discuss the burial arrangements with you and Josephine. He says that since the congressman was such a prominent political figure, there will be many dignitaries who will wish to attend his funeral. The senator is certain that his friend would like to be buried on the island he had so loved and admired. I was asked to consult with you so we can prepare a suitable burial site here on Deer Island."

July 27, 1842 (Choosing a Burial Site)

Frenchy, more than anyone else, knows the topography of the Adams estate. He was assisting the survey crews when they mapped the site. He was the one who ferried them to and from the mainland; he traveled with them wherever they went. He knows the location of the highest ground; he knows the sloughs, the swampland, the prairieland, and the ridges that generally follow the course of the bayous. Consequently, Joseph delegated the responsibility to him; he will choose the burial site.

Understandingly, the mood around the homestead has been grim. Nothing could have prepared any of us for such a shocking event. Uncle Patrick has been our source of encouragement; he was our financier. He provided us with all of our needs; the man had a vision, which included our future. He will be sorely missed. Lord, help us now! I lamented.

July 29, 1842 (Guests Begin to Arrive)

William and Greta Henley arrived this afternoon. Pauline will be coming to the island with young William and his wife Emmaline tomorrow morning. Many state dignitaries plan to be here in the morning. Senator Peltier has assumed the responsibility of transporting the congressman's body to the island.

Greta and William offered their condolences and assured us that if ever we need anything, they would consider it a privilege to render their assistance. It was indeed reassuring to know that we have such caring and honorable friends.

Our guests will be staying in the *big house*. Now that it is completely finished, it will serve as a comfortable accommodation for as many guests as necessary. Plans call for the congressman to be laid out in the sitting room. The Anglican priest, Parson Michael Stanley from Brashear City, will preside over the ceremony.

The night was spent exchanging sentiments about the distinguished statesman from Louisiana, Congressman Patrick J. Adams. We have been told that Uncle Patrick had many friends and acquaintances in high positions of state government. Due to his competency in office, his significant influence was a benefit to many successful businessmen. Admiration of his impeccable character was universal; he had no enemies, political or otherwise.

The litany of Uncle Patrick's achievements is quite long. After solemn prayer, we retired for the evening.

July 30, 1842 (The Funeral)

We awakened this morning before sunrise. *Daylight*, our black rooster, was confused by all the activity, and he sounded his call much earlier than normal. Our overnight guests met Joseph and me in the kitchen of the *big house* for coffee, tea, and biscuits.

Since the news of Uncle Patrick's untimely death, we have had ample time to console one another over his passing. As each of us struggles with grief, the mood is still a somber one. We have accepted the tragedy as one of the many aspects of life that cause grief and sorrow—though difficult to endure for a season, with God's help we will find peace in the midst of heartache. Sometimes tears shed in earnest, provide a remedy that no medicine can offer.

William described his relationship with the congressman over the past thirty or so years. They met when he was a factor in New Orleans; Patrick had just been elected to congress. "Patrick had the right personality to hold any political position. I believe he could have run for governor of Louisiana. I sincerely believe he would have won!" William interjected. He told us that the congressman was a good communicator, he always had his ear open for advice, and he welcomed criticism from his constituents. In order to win the hearts of the Louisiana Southerners, he learned how to speak French; he never perfected the language, but he spoke it well enough to win their confidence. He told us that Patrick's willingness to travel among the people, visiting village and city, rich and poor, prince and pauper, without prejudice, made him a very popular man in this state. He and the congressman spent many hours together over the years; they shared stories and told the latest jokes. He was always the gentlemen; he served Louisiana with dignity and he has fulfilled his axiom (personal code of conduct). "When duty calls, I will answer with zeal!" That was his maxim; he honestly felt that serving the public was his destiny. "He was a man of sound character and high morals. He was my best friend," William lamented.

The responsibility for food preparation will rest upon the shoulders of Frenchy, Carey, and the Ramsey brothers. The crew of the *Swamp Rat* arrived late yesterday afternoon; the Ramsey brothers, Ridgefield and Scott, slept aboard their small boat and found their way to our kitchen before dawn this morning. Their unexpected arrival was a welcome surprise.

While the men discussed the menu, the sunlight became apparent, and Joseph escorted us to the front porch to witness the beauty of "sunrise on Deer Island." Joseph and William asked our crew of servants to gather all the chairs they could find and place them around the sitting room; if there aren't enough with those, they are instructed to run to the *little house* and gather all they can muster.

The "Big House"
Built by Joseph Addison
Completed July 27, 1842
Location: Deer Island

Melvin and Jennifer Lacache, our good friends from Bayou Shaver, appeared. We exchanged expressions of delicate and sensitive feelings, then they joined us in consuming hot liquid refreshment, prepared for our guests by our faithful servants.

MIDMORNING

About 9:00 a.m., a throng of humanity suddenly appeared in our midst. William H. Henley III and his wife led the procession. The casket was being carried by eight gentlemen wearing long black coats and top hats, sporting black trousers, white shirts and black ties. My first impression was that these pall bearers must be men of superior social status based on the dignity of their attire. I later learned that they were senators and congressman from the Louisiana state government, Senator Peltier among them.

Following close behind the coffin in the long procession were various businessmen from New Orleans, Baton Rouge, Shreveport,

Brashear City; they hailed from all over the entire state. I recognized Salvadore Cortez and his wife Amanda; Albert Huie and his mother were there. Mr. Lafont, Mr. E. B. Blanchard, Mr. Claude Peterson, and Mr. Augustine Champagne (all businessmen from our hometown, Brashear City) had taken time to come to the island to pay their respects.

Thank God that Joseph had the foresight to make several benches to accommodate our guests. I believe that over two hundred men and women assembled around the front porch of the congressman's home, a home he would never get the chance to enjoy.

The casket was set atop a table in the sitting room. Once it was in place, people began to file past the coffin; it is a traditional gesture of respect in honor of the deceased. Some prayed, some made the sign of the cross, some bowed their heads for a moment of silence, and some touched the bier and walked on. Many of the women wept, some shed mournful tears; the children walked hand in hand with their guardians with looks of bewilderment on their sorrowful faces, recognizing the solemnity, but not understanding why they were there.

All rooms on the first floor of the *big house* were filled with mourners. All the windows and shutters were opened so everyone could hear the proclamations being made by the speakers in the sitting room, those closest to the coffin. They spoke of Congressman Adams, expressing his dedication to his country, his service to his state, his loyalty to his friends. They boasted of his tireless efforts to make Louisiana a welcome place for its current and future citizens; he fought hard to defeat the notion of cultural and spiritual separatism. "A strong Louisiana is a united Louisiana!" he would proclaim with full conviction. They said he sought ways to try to improve the methods for the acquisition and distribution of slaves; he called for reform to improve public opinion concerning that institution. "If the South wants to continue on the road to prosperity, she must move from slavery to indentured servanthood; we must offer freedom to the Negro in exchange for years of service. There is dire need for improvement in our approach to industry and the way we treat those who make prosperity possible, our workers!" He urged his colleagues to press this issue, and he warned that to do otherwise would mean certain destruction.

William Harrison Henley took the floor attesting to the congressman's noble character: "Patrick was a faithful servant of our beloved state. I've never met a man who was more dedicated to the cause of the humane treatment of slaves. He promoted the notion that all men deserve dignity with no regard for color. He said the Bible warns us not to esteem one man above another for we are all his handywork, made in God's image. 'The whole world is one blood' is what he would quote to justify his convictions. Yes, he was a man with high morals. Patrick Adams was a loving man, a trusted friend, a man whose congeniality was universally appreciated—all the way to the White House. The world was a better place with the Honorable Patrick J. Adams around. I, for one, will miss him dearly."

Parson Stanley led everyone in a prayer and suggested we walk the funeral path to the graveyard.

Slowly, the procession moved along the pathway leading to the congressman's final resting place. Songbirds sang as beautifully as I have ever heard, as were traveled through the dense forest that was home for a host of wildlife, which includes an enormous population of deer.

The children held their peace, with a solemn dignity that is seldom otherwise experienced. Uncle Patrick had earned the respect of all who knew him in his lifetime; that high regard for this noble statesman is following him all the way to his grave. I am happy I shared part of his life with Joseph; Uncle Patrick was our dearest friend.

Intermittent breezes carried the sounds of nature to every ear, competing with the Parson for our attention. The man of God delivered his eulogy and commended Uncle Patrick's soul unto the Lord, as the casket was lowered into the hollow darkness of his grave.

After the graveside ceremony, Pauline Longere, Uncle Patrick's ward and confidant, carried a rose stem she had cut from a pink floribunda. She placed a vase, filled with water to preserve the magnificent rose blooms, at the foot of the congressman's burial site. The congressman's princess stood over the grave void of any noticeable emotion, stoic in appearance. I knew her well enough to know that her true feelings did not have to become a spectacle for others to see. I know that the sound of her silence speaks louder than any verbal expression or outburst of passion and grief. I am sorry for her loss.

Joseph told Pauline that he would try to grow a rose bush from the stem she left at the gravesite. Once the flowers have shed their pedals, he will bury the stem at the foot of the grave; with a little care, he believes he can make it grow.

"It will be a fitting memorial," Joseph shared.

Pauline, Joseph, and I were the last to leave the cemetery. As we strolled back toward the *big house*, Albert Huie approached us so he could introduce his mother.

"This is my mother, Jessica Huie," he proudly announced. "Mama, this is Joseph Addison and his wife Josephine, and standing beside them is Mademoiselle Pauline Longere, the congressman's ward I always was talking to you about."

"We are all very pleased to meet you, Mrs. Huie. You have a fine son. Albert made our journey from New Orleans to Brashear City a delightful experience," Joseph told her. "Albert, we want you to have the congressman's coach," Joseph stated. "We have no use for such an elegant vehicle. Those black horses are like a part of your family, take the team of horses and the coach with all of our blessings. I know Congressman Adams would have wanted you to have them," Joseph concluded.

I don't know who cried more, Albert or his dear mother. We told them that they would always be welcome on Deer Island. Albert shook Joseph's hand and hugged Pauline and me. I asked him if he was going to marry Flocie; he just laughed and said that I should know that things like that take time. He told us he had to go, then he scurried to find his ride back to the mainland.

"Don't forget Flocie, Albert Huie! She's back at the Henley plantation waiting for you!" I hollered.

"Yes, Madame Josephine! Don't I know she's a waiting?" Albert yelled back with a friendly wave.

"Don't you let her get away from you, Albert Huie!" I warned. I sincerely hope he heeds my advice.

Mr. Salvadore Cortez and his wife Amanda walked over to exchange sentiments before they headed back to New Orleans. We shared with Amanda the joy her husband's playful antics gave us when we first set foot on Louisiana soil. "We didn't know a soul when we arrived. Ole Sal made us feel right at home." Mr. Cortez told us to be sure to stop at his produce shop if we ever return to New Orleans.

"You are quite a character, Mr. Salvadore!" I teased.

"You call me Sal, Josephine. We are not strangers anymore," he responded, with his customary jovial manner. On that note, the produce vendor left our company, seeking a ride to the mainland.

MIDAFTERNOON

When we arrived back at the *big house*, the remaining guests were famished. They had patiently awaited our return before eating. I immediately instructed our cooks to start serving. "Children form the first line for the serving table!" Carey shouted to be heard over the noisy conversation of the large gathering. Frenchy, Carey, and the Ramsey brothers were splendid hosts; they quickly organized the serving lines and distributed the food to our hungry guests.

Once everyone had satisfied their appetites, individuals and family groups from the various boat parties began to seek out Joseph, Pauline, and me for final well wishes and comments about their deceased friend. Slowly, but deliberately, the huge crowd dwindled, as they walked down to the dock site and boarded their vessels to begin the journey home.

The last family to leave was Senator Peltier, his wife Susan, and their three grandchildren. The Senator reminded Joseph that all the materials for the building of his sailboat, including the two masts and the sails, are safely stored in his warehouse at Brashear City; Frenchy knows where the building is located and he will have access to its contents. He informed Joseph that there is another one thousand board feet of high grade planking stored at the same location. "Mr. E. B. Blanchard at the Bayou Boeuf General Store is housing all your hardware, including those brass mast plates you ordered," he added.

The senator informed Joseph that he was the executor of Uncle Patrick's estate. "I will not go into the details of what that means now. When I have convenient time, we will meet to discuss the matter to the smallest detail. You can take comfort in knowing that the congressman was not only wealthy in land holdings and real estate, he also had money in several banking institutions. In short, he was a very wealthy man," he shared. "You and Josephine will not have financial worries," he assured us.

We thanked Senator Peltier for his kindness and consideration. He pledged his continuing assistance and told us that if we required his services for anything, all we had to do was ask. Once all was said, the Peltier family boarded the *Sara's Dream*, where their captain and his deckhand were anxiously waiting to get under way.

"We'll see you for Thanksgiving!" the Senator hollered as his sloop rounded the north bend in Deer Bayou and disappeared.

OVERNIGHT GUESTS

Only a remnant of the day's visitors remained when darkness came. Pauline, the Henleys, Frenchy and Carey, and the Ramsey brothers, were all that remained of the congressman's entourage. After supper, we congregated on the veranda of the *big house* to speculate about what the future might bring to Deer Island.

Frenchy and Carey will continue in the employ of the Addisons, helping Joseph with construction of our sailboat. They will continue to ferry materials and goods to the island from Brashear City. Ridgefield and Scott Ramsey will assist us if the task is greater than our regular crew can handle.

William pledged to stay in touch; he and Greta will return to the island to visit as often as they can, especially during the winter holiday season when the cane harvest is complete. Greta asked me, "How about that baby?"

"There is a midwife who resides at Brashear City by the name of Madame Theresa Blanchard. Frenchy told me all about her. She has a good reputation for birthing children. When my time draws near, she will come to the island to assist me in delivery, and she will stay as long as necessary for my recovery," I answered with confidence. "Me and the baby will be fine," I added.

Our focus turned to Pauline. We asked what her future plans were, since her guardian and confident had died. "I have no certain plans," she told us. "Now that Patrick Adams is gone, I will need time to sort things out, but I cannot honestly say I have given much thought to my future," she lamented.

I could not help myself; I had to say it. "As beautiful as you are, there will always be suitors," I mused.

"There has never been a shortage of interested men, but the right man has eluded me thus far," Pauline shared, with no apparent sign of urgency—after all, she's only twenty-seven years old; no need to rush.

"Why don't you move to Deer Island? We have two houses! We are family, you and I are surrogate sisters, are we not? Please come and live with us," I pleaded.

"I am flattered by the kind invitation, but for now, I will remain at my home in Chacahoula. I will come to visit whenever the Henleys stop long enough to pick me up on the way to the island. The route they take, through Bayou Black, runs near the back of my home. I will be glad to come, especially during the winter celebrations. I might even spend a few days with you on occasion," she promised.

William brought up the subject of our two houses. "You and Joseph should live in the *big house*. I know that is what Patrick would have wanted," he declared. "Joseph is the sole heir to his estate. It is a privilege he bestowed upon you, it was his will," he proclaimed.

Joseph responded with wide eyes, and with a playful gesture, he said, "Well, no matter what we decide, we will always have plenty of room to accommodate our guests."

We all grew weary; everyone was yawning, except Pauline. I am sure it was after midnight when peaceful repose prevailed at the homestead. Everyone is leaving us in the morning. Frenchy and Carey are going to the mainland to get our first load of lumber to be used in the fabrication of our dream sailboat.

July 31, 1842 (The Wee Hours of the Morning)

Just as I was about to put down my pen and blow out my lamp-light, I was startled by the violent clashes of thunder and flashes of lightning that lit up the sky. The summer storm brought heavy rainfall down upon our rooftop, playing a soothing chord amidst the disharmony of the horrific thunder. Without warning, a subtle seduction was befalling me, and I lost myself during the unexpected interlude shortly after my head rested upon its pillow.

Chapter Nine

LIFE GOES ON
ENLARGING THE FAMILY

August 12, 1842 (Go, Frenchy! Go!)

Joseph dispatched Frenchy and Carey to Brashear City to rendezvous with Madame Theresa Blanchard at her home; they are to bring her post haste to my bedside on the island. I went through a sleepless night due to the extreme discomfort of labor pains.

Joseph is trying to remain calm, but it is obvious he is in a situation he finds most uncomfortable. He has been nervously pacing the floors, refusing to go outside, choosing rather to remain within earshot of my voice. I must admit that his pampering is a source of joy to me, lending some relief from my physical anguish.

I can only hope the midwife arrives before the baby. I would hate to see anxiety and worry turn into chaos and panic, severely testing Joseph's ability to maintain his composure. My dear husband is a thoughtful and deliberate man; he is well liked by everyone, fruit from the same tree as his Uncle Patrick. Politics aside, I believe his legacy will rival that of his uncle.

August 13, 1842 (Early Next Morning)
The midwife was delivered to the island at first light this morning. My birth pains have diminished; Madame Blanchard and I went through a series of questions and answers.

Joseph expressed his relief that Frenchy arrived with our nurse before it was too late. He said he was insecure; he felt helpless since he had no knowledge or experience in matters relating to childbirth.

Frenchy had his moments of nervous tension also. Carey told us, "The captain had little sleep last night. He was worried that he would not get back to the island in time."

"Yes, I will admit that I was very concerned. There is nothing wrong with that! *Nous sommes arrives juste a temps.* We arrived just in time!" Frenchy shared, breathing a sigh of relief, as time marched toward the big event that would soon come.

IT'S A BOY!

August 15, 1842
I gave birth to our first son at 4:00 a.m. this morning; all went well. Madame Blanchard was a true blessing; her assistance was invaluable. What a relief for all of us. I broke water about 10:00 p.m. last evening, and *voila*, in no time it was all over. The midwife says I had an easy delivery. "The little tyke just slipped out!" she told me.

John Quincy Addison is a fine, healthy baby with strong lungs for expressing his dissatisfaction over his new environment. Once he suckled upon my breast, he became gentle, and he seemed to welcome mother's milk and cuddling. The pervasive disquietude that was here before has vanished; it is time to relax once again.

Joseph and his two companions are so relieved that they are going on a fishing trip. "It's time to celebrate John Quincy's arrival with some fun in the sun," my husband declared. Meanwhile, Madame Blanchard will tend to my needs and do the household chores to enable me to have a quick recovery. "I will stay with you as long as you need me," she assured me. "You don't worry about anything but yourself and that newborn baby," she urged. That is exactly what I intend to do.

August 20, 1842 (The Keel Is Laid)

Steady progress is being made on our sailboat. Joseph says his special design of the fin keel will allow it to be retracted into a hollow receptacle for traveling in shallow water. Joseph is copying the design from some of the local sailboats whose owners use this method to increase their accessibility to areas they could not otherwise navigate. Our boat will be a schooner; it will have two large masts (the mainmast being abaft of and taller than the foremast) both of which will be rigged fore-and-aft. She will be built to slide across the lakes and streams like a flat stone skipping along the surface of the water. Joseph provided me with all the nautical details for my record.

The baby is adjusting to life outside the womb. My midwife was ferried back to the mainland yesterday. She definitely knows what she is doing when it involves delivering babies, and she was a tremendous help maintaining the housework. If God sees fit to bless us with another child, she will be the person we call.

John Quincy Addison is named after an American president who is somehow related to Joseph. Uncle Patrick spoke of him oftentimes. I am glad we chose to name him after one of our distinguished relatives.

A NEW TRADITION

November 1, 1842 (All Saints' Day)

This November 1st will mark the first celebration of this holyday on Deer Island. Uncle Patrick's untimely death and subsequent burial in our new family cemetery has prompted the beginning of this new tradition. We will visit the gravesite, praying that all of us will someday be worthy to stand in the presence of Almighty God.

Joseph quoted from a verse of scripture that Paul the Apostle wrote to the Corinthians. "Therefore we are always confident, knowing that, whilst we are at home in the body, we are absent from the Lord (for we walk by faith, not by sight). We are confident, I say, and willing rather to be absent from the body, and to be present with the Lord. Wherefore we labor, that, whether present or absent, we may be accepted of him. For we must all appear before the judgment seat of Christ; that everyone may receive the things done in his body, according to that he hath done, whether it be good or bad" (2 Corinthians 5:6–10). Amen.

Frenchy and Carey were our only guests for this first annual celebration. We spent the day in conversation, reflecting on the lives of our dear family members and friends that have gone before us.

Melvin and Jennifer Lacache and their three children came for a visit last week. Besides our boat crew and our midwife, members of the Lacache family are the only people who have seen our new child. I am sure that, by now, the word has spread to most of our friends.

November 25, 1842 (Thanksgiving)

The ducks were flying at daybreak this morning. Senator Peltier and his wife came out yesterday afternoon so he could participate in the duck hunt. Joseph, Frenchy and Carey, and Irvin have been making use of their ammunition; I don't know what cannon fire sounds like, but in the still quietness of the early morning, the blasts from their gun muzzles is startlingly loud. As yet, we don't know if they have killed anything, but the number of shots fired is proof that they are trying very hard.

Susan and I are enjoying a cup of hot beverage on the veranda of the *big house*, anxiously awaiting the results of the hunt. Susan has John Quincy cuddled in her arms, singing lullabies and rocking him to sleep. There is a chill in the air; there was a light fog earlier, which has already dissipated; the weather is perfect for the day's festivities.

As you might have guessed, some of the shooters hit their marks and they returned from the hunt with enough waterfowl to provide the main course for our Thanksgiving Day meal. The men had a fun outing, and it is certain we will enjoy the bounty they have taken.

"I hope you marksmen left a few birds to reproduce for next year's hunting season," I postulated.

The hunters all got a hearty laugh out of that inquiry. The senator responded by saying, "Josephine, we scared the feathers off of many more birds than we killed; we left more than enough to protect the species from extinction." Those jovial exchanges set the mood for the day's activity.

We feasted on pot roasted duck, stuffed with garlic cloves and peppercorns. Frenchy seared the duck entrails (livers, gizzards, and hearts); once they were suitably browned, he then smothered down a generous amount of chopped onions, mixing them with the duck parts and gravy; last he added chunks of fresh potatoes and turnips to the pot. The resulting stew was delicious.

I never dreamed that the entrails of a duck could taste so good; these native swamp people don't waste anything that can be used for food. They know how to prepare the strangest things and make them into something that is pleasing to the palate.

The afternoon was spent playing horseshoes. Carey Trudeau was again the champion. It was good fun.

The tranquil sound of the fountainhead feeding bubbles to the stream, about fifty feet from the front porch of the *big house* is soothing to the soul; that is why everyone raves over the majesty of the location Uncle Patrick chose to build his house. I have a feeling the front porch will be the center of attraction at our homestead for many years to come, maybe even for generations. God knows!

Joseph has the ribs fitted to the keel of our future sailboat. He is hoping to have her outside planked by the middle of January. Once the decks are finished, he will set the two masts, build the cabin, and install all her rigging. Work is slow but steady; sometime early next year, we should be unfurling her sails. Freedom at last! I look forward to that day.

John Quincy is a good child; he has been little trouble. Once he gets his belly full of mother's milk, he often falls into peaceful sleep. He has been a source of novel entertainment for all of us. Right now, he is nestled up close to his father under the bed covers.

I love the quiet darkness when everyone is soundly asleep. The glow from my lamp is soothing to my spirit as I record the events of the day in my record. I can hear the sound of thunder to our northwest; there must be a front moving through. The wind is suddenly picking up; the rustling of the leaves is evidence of a strong blow. Heavy rainfall will soon follow. It is time to blow out my lamplight and join my husband and my newborn son in our bed.

I adjusted the covers and lay my head down when the heavy rain began singing its familiar lullaby, inviting me to enjoy its constant serenade—serenity personified! Amen.

November 26, 1842 (Legal Affairs)

Senator Irving Peltier arrived this morning to handle business affairs regarding the Patrick Adams estate. Pauline was in his company.

"As I informed you earlier, Joseph, you are the sole heir to your uncle's estate. As executor, it is my obligation to have all the necessary documents signed; duplicates will be on file at my law office for safekeeping, provided you have no objections. Documents transferring title deeds to the various land holdings he owned, some of which are in Orleans Parish, will be filed in the Terrebonne Parish Courthouse," he informed us.

"I have prepared a list of all his known possessions for your records. Together with copies of all the legal transactions we handle this day, these papers should be kept in a safe. One of my boat's crewmen should have your safe on the front porch waiting for instructions on where you want it placed. It is quite heavy. The combination will be demonstrated to you before we leave. The numbers and sequence of right-left maneuvers should be recorded and secured in some secret place. These documents are very important," he warned.

"Patrick Adams had his money in several banking institutions, two in New Orleans and one in Baton Rouge. I suggest we leave those accounts in place until a more convenient location for the funds can be established. The documents for the transfer of the accounts to your name are in my briefcase. Sign these and that will be done. The money can be accessed at any time, once these papers are in the bank's files. These bank records should be locked in the safe with all the other documents," he suggested.

"There are still things that will need to be accounted for—movable items, personal belongings, items he may have left at his congressional office in Baton Rouge. I have a few of my assistants trying to locate everything. When we have secured all we can find, I will meet with you again to see what you wish to do with them," he informed us.

"Regarding Patrick's coach and team of horses, it is my understanding that you wish Albert Huie to have them; is that correct?" he asked.

Joseph told our lawyer, Senator Peltier, that we wished to give the coach and four-horse team to Albert. "What about the home his mother lives in on the outskirts of New Orleans? Can we donate that residence to them?"

"If that is what you want to do, I can arrange for the transfer; I will have to present you with further documents to sign, but it is a matter we can handle over the winter holidays. You are planning to invite us, aren't you?" he teased.

"You may be wondering why I brought Pauline with me. For one thing, she is here to sign the documents that require witnesses. Ron Dumond will serve as the second witness. His brother will not be needed for signing anything. More to the point, Pauline is here on legal matters also. Joseph, it is commonly known that Pauline was the ward of Patrick Adams. Though not an heir, she was his confidant. I know, and my wife can bear witness that what I am saying is the truth, he was going to ask her to marry him after the *big house* was finished. Sadly, he died before the fulfillment of his plans," he asserted.

"Pauline has not asked for anything. She does not need money or a home; that was provided by her father. Pauline has agreed to use me as her attorney. She will not become my ward. She is able to fend for herself. I will be her councilor and adviser in any business matters that may arise. I brought her here so everyone would understand where she fits into the Addison family. There are no blood ties, but there is the knowledge that she and Patrick were in love. With all sincerity, it is my opinion that whether through marriage, or adoption,

Patrick intended to make his princess a part of his family," he related in solemn tones, obviously sincere in his presentation of the facts.

"Pauline, you know we love you; you know I told you that we were surrogate sisters. I know the sentiments that have been expressed here are true. Joseph and I would love for you to come live with us on the island. We talked about it before Uncle Patrick died. I anxiously anticipated, in fact I prayed, that you and the congressman would be married soon. The *little house* is yours for as long as you live. If you marry and have children, they will be welcome here also. We will put that in writing for you," I pledged.

"Joseph, do you agree with what Josephine just said?" Senator Peltier asked.

Joseph declared without hesitation: "I agree wholeheartedly with what my wife just said. Pauline has been, and she will continue to be, a member of the Addison family. I want Pauline to have the *little house*. The only stipulation I make is that whether she marries or not, the land will never be separated from the Adams estate in perpetuity, agreed?" Joseph declared.

"What say you, Pauline?" the senator posed.

"I am flattered by the offer of kindness from my dear surrogate brother and sister. The proposal is both generous and fair. I don't feel I deserve to be considered one of the family, but I do wish to assume that role if they will have me," Pauline replied with her usual charming smile.

"I will draw up the paperwork and we will have the agreement in writing during the Christmas holiday season when I return to the island, if that is agreeable to everyone," the senator candidly offered. "I hereby declare that Pauline Longere is officially a member of the Addison family, with the love and respect for each other that, only brothers and sisters can know!" he proclaimed.

With a hearty "amen!" We concluded our handling of all pending legal affairs—annoying but necessary.

December 15, 1842 (Our Winter Guests Begin to Arrive)
William, Greta, and Pauline arrived from the mainland aboard the schooner *Sugar Baby* with their captain and deckhand, Ron and

Paul Dumond. William III and wife will be coming in a few days; they also have a newborn baby, a boy they named Patrick. In honor of his mentor, young William chose the name for his first son.

My two lady friends and I entertained ourselves around the kitchen table with John Quincy while the men all congregated on the veranda to discuss current events and get reacquainted.

William was very impressed with the progress being made on our sailboat. Curious about the size, he asked Joseph to give him the dimensions.

"Our boat will be approximately sixty-five feet in length, seventy-three with the bowsprit. She will be twelve feet wide at the beam with a draft of ten feet with the keel fin in the lowered position, twenty-eight inches with the fin raised, the mainmast will be abaft of, and taller than the sixty-five-foot foremast. She will have a cabin between the two masts and a second cabin about three feet behind the mainmast," Joseph informed him.

The evening was spent in merriment, with Carey playing the mouth harp and Ron and Paul Dumond on fiddle. Pauline sang French folk songs to the music and danced gracefully all across the veranda, enthralling everyone present.

December 18, 1842 (William Harrison Henley Arrives)

William Henley and his wife Emmaline arrived with their new son, little Patrick, around dinnertime today. Patrick is about to begin walking; he crawls all over the place but "his balance is still a bit off," Emmaline told us. I hope he and John Quincy will grow up best of friends.

The men are loading provision for a two day hunting trip at Plumb Bayou. The *Swamp Rat* will provide shelter, but I don't envy them the odious atmosphere and the cramped quarters. The excitement over the possibility of bagging a few geese will dispel any inconvenience or smelly sleeping accommodations, of that I am sure.

Pauline asked Carey to show her where he had the rabbit traps set; if we get lucky, she will be able to cook her famous stew while the men are away.

Frenchy boasted that they would bring back enough birds to stuff several pillows with their down. We escorted the motley crew to the landing and saw them off, wishing them good luck on their hunt. Soon the *Swamp Rat* rounded the south bend in Deer Bayou and headed for their happy hunting grounds.

We dined on boiled potatoes seasoned with salted pork and enjoyed conversation covering topics ranging from child rearing to thwarted romance. Joseph and I have never slept apart since we were married. It will be a strange, almost empty feeling to know I will be alone these next two nights.

The weather is cold, near freezing; I hope Frenchy's furnace will be adequate. There is nothing more welcome than the warmth of a fire when the temperature is falling outside the cabin door.

December 21, 1842 (The Hunters Return)

Braggadocios! That is what they all are, with tall tales of expert shooting. Their claims were not without merit, having nearly a hundred geese on the deck of the boat. We offloaded enough birds to fulfill our needs; each man took one goose in each hand.

Frenchy and Carey untied the mooring lines from the landing; soon they rounded the north bend in Deer Bayou, heading for Bayou Penchant, navigating the Big Horn and Little Horn Bayous along the way. They are making the trip to the mainland to distribute the excess feathered bounty among our friends and distant neighbors.

When the *Swamp Rat* is lightened from her loads, her keel fin is raised; in the raised position, she can easily travel the shallow waters of the inland bayous, and avoid the swift currents of the river. Spring floods, and strong north winds in the winter, make a trip to the mainland both slow and hazardous in the Atchafalaya.

Most visitors to Deer Island take the inland route (going north from the island: Deer Bayou to Big Horn Bayou, Big Horn Bayou to Little Horn Bayou, Little Horn Bayou to Bayou Penchant). This route lends access to Bayou Chene, Bayou Black, Bayou Boeuf, and Bayou Shaver, leading to the front yards of our friends who live in Chacahoula, Houma, and Brashear City, as well as those who dwell in houseboats, like the Lacache family.

Joseph, always quick to give me detailed descriptions of every vessel he sees, provided me with the following observations: "The Henleys have a magnificent schooner, with two masts fore-and-aft-rigged (the mainmast being abaft of and taller than the foremast). The Peltiers have an elegant fifty-foot sloop, with a single mast fore-and-aft-rigged, having a short standing bowsprit and a single headsail set from the forestay."

Joseph continued to describe the boats more commonly used by the local trappers and fishermen: "Some have chosen a modified version of a sailing lugger. These have round bottoms for maneuverability in the shallow bayous, and are shaped much like the sharpies used along the east coast, with a single mast sporting a lugsail (a quadrilateral sail lacking a boom and having the foot larger than the head, bent to a yard hanging obliquely on the mast) and one or more jib sails. Others prefer to use a smaller boat, with a removable mast for versatility and convenience, looking much like a dory (narrow, flat-bottomed boats, with high sides and a sharp prow, sporting a lugsail)."

Joseph has chosen to build a schooner; she will be sleek and elegant and seaworthy. She will be designed more for comfort and leisure, than for bearing the burdens of a freight boat like the *Swamp Rat* (a lugger). Joseph says that building a sloop, if we find it better suits our needs, may come later.

For now, utility is more important than elegance and beauty; Joseph says having Frenchy perform the heavy tasks cannot be taken for granted. One step at a time! Only the Lord knows how many steps it will take to complete all the plans, as yet undone, for the entire homestead. If anyone would give the task much thought, he would soon become disheartened.

Reflecting on the day's activities, what can I say? I have quickly learned that much of what people find enjoyable in south Louisiana is focused on, or around, the dinner table. Most of the men are excellent cooks; in many cases (especially when game is on the menu) they are better at preparing the dishes than their help mates. We dined sumptuously; we enjoyed exchanging commentary on current events in each other's lives; relating amusing incidents, designed to interject humor into the conversation; there was musical entertainment, dancing—a day of frolic and fun (wholesome fun). Another blessing on this day worth mentioning was the collection of two flour sacks filled with goose down—not quite enough for one well-stuffed pillow, but a benefit nonetheless.

The untimely death of Joseph's uncle has brought with it time for quiet introspection and solemn prayer. "Time heals all" is proving to be a true axiom. Though sorely missed, life goes on for those who inhabit the island he so loved. Joseph and I, with the help of our dear friends, will try to continue to lay the foundation for a family legacy, built in his honor. It's time to rest; the baby is asleep, nestled close to his father. All is quiet, save the gurgling sound of the aquifer singing its ever-present lullaby. Peaceful repose! God's will be done, amen.

GOOD ADVICE

December 23, 1842 (A Camp at Plumb Bayou)

Our good friend, William Henley, recommended to Joseph that he establish a campsite at Plumb Bayou. "An Indian shell-midden was spotted along the left canal bank. It's just about a half-mile from the beginning of the ridge, just around the first deep bend in the watercourse. That would be a choice spot for a hunting camp. The high ridge and spent clam shells will make a perfect foundation for several small buildings. The large oak trees and dense shrubbery will shield the structures from storm winds. It is a perfect location," William suggested.

Joseph was excited over the discovery of an abundance of muskrat mounds throughout the vast prairieland of that part of the estate. William says that the furs of the rats are in demand; trappers can make a good winter's wages by harvesting the little creatures. Of course Joseph will have to learn how and where to set the traps. He will need to learn how to skin, stretch, and dry the hides for sale at the fur market.

William began to explain the importance of making use of all the land included in the Adams estate. ""In Louisiana, you must improve the land and work the land to protect ownership," William cautioned. "Your vast tracts of land will need to show signs of use and management to insure your rights," he added. "To accomplish this, you could plant fruit trees along the banks of the bayous that traverse the estate. Build a hunting camp for the purpose of hunting and trapping the land. These are two examples of how you can demonstrate ownership," he urged. "In Louisiana, possession is nine-tenths of the law, especially when it comes to land," he cautioned.

Joseph explained his situation to William. "I still have much to accomplish on Deer Island itself. As of now, I haven't set foot on Shell Island, the westernmost part of the estate. I've only seen it from a distance. Plans for the homestead include a clearing for a fruit orchard, a separate clearing for a pecan orchard, a third clearing for a substantial garden, and last of all but equally important is a clearing for a family cemetery. That is enough work for two lifetimes!" Joseph expressed, demonstrating the difficulty of completing the massive project.

Joseph continued, "You've seen the schematic drawing of Uncle Patrick's adventurous plans. He believed that completing the project was not just a possibility, but a certainty. He must have had some reliable scheme to see his dream become reality in his lifetime.

"Don't misunderstand me, Mr. Henley, I am taking your sound advice very seriously. I just can't see how it will be possible to do all that is required without a tremendous amount of help—from the good Lord up above and from an army of living souls willing to work this earth along side of me," Joseph lamented, overwhelmed by the challenge.

William expressed that he was aware of the size and scope of the plans for the homestead. "It is a bold and daring undertaking, that is certain. God sometimes works things out in mysterious ways; let's just sit back and let His will be done," he encouraged.

Frenchy suggested that Joseph acquire the assistance of the Lacache family. "Melvin and Jennifer are trappers, maybe they would be willing to trap the Plumb Bayou area and pay you a percentage of their earnings," he hinted.

Mr. Henley thought Frenchy's suggestion was worth considering. Joseph will offer the proposal to Melvin Lacache on his next visit to the island. William says he believes that hiring the Lacache family to trap during the winter will be a very good start; it will demonstrate that the land is being used. That is what is most important.

"What about the land on Bayou Du large?" Joseph asked.

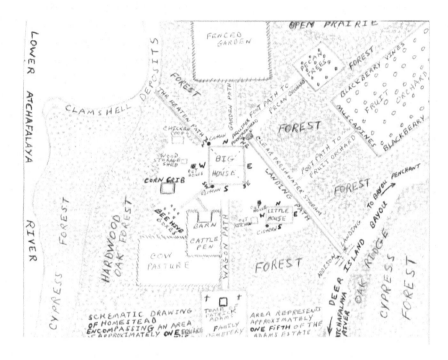

William said that there is talk of the railroad companies needing logs for crossties. "I have been to the property on Bayou Du large. It is rich in virgin timber, suitable for their needs. If you wish to clear the land for future use, that might be the way to do it. You can sell the trees, have your land cleared and demonstrate ownership all at the same time. You might check with Senator Peltier next time you see him. He is your lawyer now, is he not?" William asked.

Joseph responded, "I believe we have the best lawyer and the best counselor we could find anywhere! We will follow your wise counsel, and we welcome any other advice you care to give. Josephine and I will always be in your debt Mr. Henley."

"Think nothing of it, Joseph. I consider it a privilege to render whatever assistance I can for my best friend's family," Mr. Henley graciously stipulated.

Things have been happening so fast it almost seems surreal, and yet I know it isn't fantasy or some figment of my imagination. I am at a loss for choosing the right words to describe the feeling I have. In my wildest dreams, I couldn't have conjured up such ideas of blissful prosperity. It is sad that Uncle Patrick won't be here to relish in the splendor of his achievements (though not yet fully realized).

Uncle Patrick must have been a very busy man, I thought. To manage so many properties in so many diverse locations, I wonder how he did it. He was larger than life; so it was with him, and so is it with his dreams. Wow!

December 25, 1842 (Christmas Day)

The sun was obscured by a gray overcast sky this cold, damp, Christmas morning. With the temperature only one or two degrees above freezing, the moist air seemed to exaggerate the chilling effects of the moderate northern breezes. It was a gloomy day.

Joseph and I got out of bed when John Quincy began crying for a meal; it was 4:00 a.m., his normal feeding time. He is a healthy child with a good set of lungs; he is capable of wild displays of his vitality from time to time. Once nursed, he customarily returns to a state of deep sleep, which usually lasts until he is disturbed by movement around the house.

As soon as the teakettle began whistling, Frenchy entered the kitchen of the *big house* through the rear porch door. "I am ready to enjoy my first cup of coffee," he announced.

"Merry Christmas, Frenchy," I lauded. Frenchy responded in kind, expressing joy and confidence that the holiday would be a good one in spite of the weather.

Sunrise, our young Rhode Island Red rooster, refused to get out of his coop into the damp cold air. We could barely hear him crowing; his cock-a-doodle-do was muffled by the surrounding walls of his hen-filled harem. He was sounding off before the sun, fooled by the sounds being made inside our kitchen. It isn't the first time his clock was off!

Frenchy told us that the main course for the day's special meal was ready for roasting. The two sides of the big deer are dressed and stuffed with garlic and peppercorns. He and Carey are planning to slow roast the meat over the open fire of our first outdoor cooking spot. Even if it rains, the roof over the open-pit fire will protect the cook from getting wet outdoors. Dry firewood has been stored nearby to fuel the flames; it too, has been covered to protect it should it decide to rain.

Everyone is here for a vacation, except the Peltier family. They sent word that they would be celebrating at home, to spend time with their son, his wife, and their seven grandchildren. Irving and Susan plan to join us for our New Year's Day celebration.

When all our guests congregated in the sitting room of the *big house,* we exchanged well-wishes and gifts, sharing in the joy of the holiday. The day was spent exchanging stories, eating good food, and making plans for a fishing excursion to Point au Fer Island in the morning. Bad weather would be the only factor that could change our plans.

If we do make the trip, the men will be fishing along the banks of the island for redfish. Pauline and Greta will fish for crabs with hand lines around the sides of our boat. Emmaline and I will stay inside the cabin to nurse our children and keep them warm. I hope the weather breaks, but full sunshine won't be the criteria for moving forward with our plans. It is rain, or rather the lack thereof that will make the difference. This was the third Christmas celebration on Deer Island. Each year it seems to get better; after all, it is the birthday of the Savior, the Lord Jesus Christ.

March 17, 1843 (Freedom for the Pigs)

All of our pigs broke out of their holding pen this morning. Lord only knows where they have gone. Joseph, Frenchy, and Carey tried valiantly to round the stubborn creatures up without success. Our only hope is they will settle down; when they get hungry, they might return to their pen for food.

Twelve sows and two boars have gone into the deep woods. Frenchy says they may turn wild; if that happens, we will have to hunt them like deer. I hope they return, but I am not very optimistic.

The exterior planking is finished on our schooner; the slow progress has been a source of irritation for Joseph. Everything Joseph does, he does it to the best of his ability; if it takes two years to finish the boat that will be fine.

November 15, 1843 (Our Boat Is Coming Along)

Joseph finished the interior planking on our schooner on August 15; the decks were completed yesterday. After a bit more refinement, he will secure extra help. It will be time to roll her off her land locked perch and into the water; the moisture will swell up her planking; after a few months of soaking, the heavy masts will be set in place.

January 5, 1844 (Another Year Gone By)

Frenchy and Carey are on a month's vacation. They will be returning in mid-February to help finish our boat. Melvin and Jennifer Lacache, along with their four children, are at their trapping camp for the winter. Last year, they had a good season—the muskrats were plentiful, and the price was very good. They are hoping for another profitable trapping season this winter.

John Quincy is running all over the place; his vocabulary is expanding as well. The boy is a chip off the old block; he is going to be his father's double.

William H. Henley III graduated with honors from Virginia Military Institute. He has a commission in the army with the rank of second lieutenant. He wore his dress uniform, enticing us to gawk at him; he is very handsome in his military attire.

Joseph and I will enjoy a reprieve from all activity for the next few weeks. We are looking forward to the temporary hiatus, and we plan to make the best of our time together. Three and a half years of steady production has made us grow weary. We are hoping to revive our enthusiasm so we can resume our work.

This winter has been exceptionally cold. The swift moving water from the fountainhead of our stream prevented it from freezing all the way across, but ice was able to form along its banks. Deer Bayou has ice extending about ten feet from its banks; now that is cold! The temperature has remained below freezing for the last three days. It is good weather for remaining inside, cuddling and coddling; that is what we intend to do until February.

January 14, 1844 (Our Boat Is Launched)

As is the custom, we had to decide on a proper name for our boat. Joseph asked me to pick the name. All the workers stared at me waiting to see what I would call the new vessel.

"How about *Dreadnought*," I suggested. "Joseph, do you remember how fearful and full of unnecessary anxiety I was aboard the *Island Mistress* when we crossed the Atlantic? I believe I have overcome my fear of sailing. In fact, I can't wait to sail with you aboard our new schooner. We could travel Louisiana's coastline," I raved.

Surprised by my sudden newfound zeal, Joseph conceded that the name for our vessel would be *Dreadnought*. "She will be fearful of nothing!" Joseph proclaimed.

Joseph, with the help of several men, launched our schooner. She rolled into the water with ease and without incidental damage. She sure looks good floating on the water. The boat will be allowed about three months to soak and make her hull planking swell; a necessary procedure before we can set the heavy masts in place. I am getting excited!

March 25, 1844 (The Two Masts Are Set)

With the aid of Frenchy's rigging onboard the *Swamp Rat*, the two massive timbers (Siberian spruce brought from New England) that constitute our masts were gently lowered into place, through the deck holes, and down into the brass sleeve that will seat each mast on a brass plate bolted to the keel.

The delicate procedure took nearly all day, but they accomplished the massive undertaking without injury to the boat or any of the workers. With that major task done, the vessel had taken on her final dimensions; the bowsprit had been mounted about a week ago. With the added weight of the two masts, she sits a few inches lower in the water. Our new schooner is quite impressive to look at; she looks both graceful and eager as she awaits the remainder of her rigging—the jib booms, blocks and ropes, and ultimately her sails.

Before the final rigging can be completed, Joseph and a few men will build the two cabins—one between the two masts and the second abaft of the mainmast. The slow work continues. *Dreadnought* is nearly ready for sailing.

PLUMB BAYOU HUNTING CAMP

June 17, 1844

We have been living aboard the *Swamp Rat* for several days. Joseph, Frenchy, and Carey are hard at work on a hunting camp at Plumb Bayou. Sixteen piles have been buried three feet down in the clam shell heap that overlays the high ridge chosen for the site. The floor's foundation will be eight feet above the ground level, following the advice of William Henley. This will give the camp a better chance of surviving any tidal surge from a violent storm at sea; something we heard is not that uncommon. We intend to use the space below the camp to store trapping poles; we may decide to have a few chicken boxes installed, so we can have fresh eggs while we are out here.

The location of our future camp is about one-half mile from where the ridge of the island begins. The sharp bend in the watercourse, as it passes through the high ground, is shaped like an "S" (similar to the one in Deer Bayou); the second cove formed by the "S" curve is and Indian shell midden (the construction site).

Entering the bayou from Atchafalaya Bay, the watercourse travels through open prairieland. After penetrating Plumb Island, the watercourse is straight for about a half-mile heading nearly due east. After negotiating the "S" curve, there continues a narrow ridge that follows the right bank of the bayou all the way to Plumb Lake; everything north and east of the left bank is open prairie as far as you can see.

Plumb Island is a high ridge superposed with live oak trees; it's about three hundred feet wide. The high ground continues until it reaches the top of the "S" curve; there, the Island part of the oak ridge ends. Prairie forms the left bank all the way to Plumb Lake. Surrounding the island is a vast tract of golden prairie, looking like wheat ready to be harvested. The prairieland continues for miles to the west and north of the campsite. "*Le paradise de rat musque*, muskrat heaven!" that is what Frenchy calls the prairie.

For someone who has never seen the cypress forests, the islands and ridges, the swampland and the prairie of south Louisiana, it would be difficult to imagine with the mind's eye, the beauty and serenity this wilderness area exudes.

An Indian shell-midden is usually found near an abandoned camp site. In the truest sense, the word *nomad* accurately describes the life of the indigenous peoples that preceded the invasion of the "white man." Moving from area to area in search of food, evidence that they once camped at any given site is the shell midden; essentially, it is a garbage dump—discarded clam shells, bits of broken pottery, the skeletal remains of various fish and animals that they hunted. The larger the mound of discards, the longer the spot was used for a campsite; the location we chose must have been used for a very long time.

Joseph and I have another child on the way. I should be ready to deliver sometime in late September or early October. My midwife, Madame Theresa Blanchard, has been alerted; she has agreed to assist in the delivery.

Mosquitoes have been a problem, especially at night. The men aren't complaining, but it is difficult for me and John Quincy to hide our misery. I will be glad to get back to our comfortable home on the Deer Island.

The wildlife is abundant! It is common to see deer swimming across the bayou from the cabin windows of the *Swamp Rat*. Some of the alligators are so large, it frightens me. It is easy to understand why the Indians who lived here before us chose this place to set up camp.

Our schooner will be complete by the end of the month. Joseph is perfecting the rigging, and it should be ready for a trial run in two weeks. We are all excited about the benefits of having our own boat;

Joseph has not given any thought to a deckhand. He will certainly need one.

July 7, 1844 (Camp Addison Is Completed)

Work on the hunting camp at Plumb Bayou has been completed. The one-room structure will sleep ten men comfortably—more, if they don't mind sleeping on the floor. Joseph has constructed five sets of double bunk beds.

Frenchy donated a woodstove he had obtained from the family of a deceased relative. The camp is not fancy by any means, but the twenty-foot by twenty-foot structure will provide warmth and comfort for hunters during the cold of winter. The Henleys and the Peltiers will be the first to recognize its superior relief in comparison to the tight quarters of a sailboat's cabin.

"We are now showing signs of use and improvement on our land holdings," Joseph asserted. "With the establishment of this camp, and with the Lacache family running traps all over the prairieland, we are definitely showing possession and ownership of this property," he further stated, with confident relief that he had followed William Henley's advice diligently.

Having an appreciation for my husband's assertion, I told Joseph that I was extremely proud of him; I decided to walk over to him and gave him a tender loving kiss.

Emotionally moved by the moment, Joseph pledged, "You make all the work I am doing worthwhile. There is nothing I would not do for you and John Quincy, and that baby that will be with us soon."

"I envy you both," Frenchy told us. "I feel the same way," Carey shared.

"Frenchy, you and Carey are like members of our family now. Don't you start working my emotions. You will have me crying crocodile tears, if you don't watch what you say," I teased.

We will be leaving for Deer Island in the morning.

July 30, 1844 "Dreadnought"

Four months after the masts were set into position; *Dreadnaught* is now ready for her maiden voyage. The jib booms are in place; the two cabins are finished. All blocks, tackle, and ropes are rigged for use, and the sails are ready to be unfurled. The Ramsey brothers are on the island lending a helping hand. They are going to sail behind us to watch how our schooner handles on her first trip.

Frenchy and Carey will be tutors on the first few trips until Joseph is confident he can captain the boat. Joseph is a master boat builder, but he has absolutely no experience as a captain on any size boat. He unashamedly welcomed all the help he could get. To begin the first lesson, Frenchy feels it is best to take the schooner into Atchafalaya Bay where it will be safe to see how she maneuvers in the wind.

About 9:00 a.m., we boarded the two sailboats and struck oars, heading fair tide for the mouth of Deer Bayou. Everyone was excited, and I mean everyone! Once we reached the swift current of the river, Carey went to work on unfurling the sails, with Frenchy firmly in command.

With a display of little effort, the sails of *Dreadnought* were hoisted. With a sudden jolt, the wind filled her expanded canvas. "Yippee!" I hollered from the top of my lungs as our sleek craft ploughed through the water with ease. "Free at last! Free at last!" I shouted. "We can leave when we want to leave! We can go where we want to go! We can visit people when we choose! We can go shopping at the Bayou Boeuf General Store! Hurrah! Hurrah!" I shouted with excitement. I never knew sailing our own boat would be so exhilarating!

I was almost out of control with exaggerated euphoria; I can offer no explanation but the honest truth! My husband has given birth to a fourth key member of our expanding family. He has presented me with our first form of transportation. The isolation of island living is forever behind us; we are free to do as we please for the first time since our arrival in America. This marks a profound change in our lives! I thank God for Joseph and his talents; I guess that is all I can say on the matter.

Frenchy has a look on his face that tells the whole story of how he feels: "She is a fine sailboat! She handles like nothing I have ever had the pleasure of steering. She is gliding through the waves with ease; she is a magnificent vessel Joseph! Congratulations are in order," he lauded.

Joseph was speechless, but he had that unmistakable glow upon his face; he had that sparkle in his eye. I have only seen him act this way three times; once when we were married, again when Madame Theresa Blanchard said, "It's a boy!" and today when he realized the significance of this latest accomplishment. I will be seeing that look again very soon.

September 28, 1844 "It's Another Boy!"

Madame Theresa Blanchard came to our home in the nick of time. She arrived on the island late yesterday afternoon, just before sunset. I had my second son at 1:00 a.m. this morning.

Alexander Patrick Addison is a fine healthy boy with the same powerful lungs as his older brother. It took awhile for him to settle down, but like his brother, suckling my breast quieted him.

Thank God for Madame Blanchard! Joseph was far worse than last time. His nervousness nearly drove me crazy. He means well, but he and I were both relieved when the midwife arrived.

"I can hardly handle this anymore," he told Frenchy over a cup of steaming hot coffee.

Frenchy, a bachelor with no nuptial intentions, tried desperately to convince my husband that he personally understood his anxiety. Joseph saw a bit of humor in the gesture and that brought him a degree of relief.

Now that the excitement is over, everyone seems to have relaxed. Joseph is strutting like a peacock. Frenchy, Carey, and Joseph are sitting in each his rocking chair; three men smoking corncob pipes in celebration of our new family member.

John Quincy is still in a deep sleep. I bet when our black rooster sounds his customary alarm, he will wake up and wonder what I am holding in my arms.

It's an hour or so before sunrise and Madame Blanchard is already hard at work preparing one of her special dishes for us—pork and venison stew, with fresh potatoes, turnips, and carrots. "That sounds good to me!" I told her.

I just thank the Lord it's all over! Amen.

Chapter Ten

CURIOUS COMPANY
CURRENT EVENTS

July 1, 1845

Work was completed on our new smokehouse yesterday. Joseph insisted Frenchy and Carey take time off to enjoy the Independence Day celebration with family and friends on the mainland.

The next phase of the development of the homestead will require years of back-breaking labor. Joseph plans to begin clearing the area north of the *big house* for a garden. Trees must be cut and uprooted and the dense brush and briar patches must be removed so the land can be cultivated.

John Quincy will be three years old next month. He enjoys following his father wherever he goes; if you see Joseph, our oldest son will be nearby. His favorite activity is riding in the flatboat when his father goes downstream to check the boat; the experience is so thrilling to him, he never refuses a chance to make the trip.

John Quincy loves Frenchy and Carey; he dances to Carey's harmonica playing while trying to imitate Frenchy's hilarious monkeyshine. Our son is destined to be a comedian if the *Swamp Rat* crew continues to influence him; they spend much of their free time entertaining their tiny friend.

Little Alexander Patrick is trying very hard to manage a few steps without assistance. At ten months old, he is very active and he demands most of my attention. I am relieved that his older brother clings to his father's legs instead of my apron strings; it makes the job of caring for Alex much easier.

July 4, 1845 (Making Future Plans)

Melvin and Jennifer Lacache came from their home on Bayou Shaver for a visit; they brought their children along with them—Terry, Troy, and Terrence are their three boys and Denise is their only daughter.

Jennifer has volunteered to cook the meal today. Melvin has been catching alligator turtles for the market; he separated one of them from its shell and prepared the meat for the pot. We will be having turtle soup for dinner.

While the soup was in process, Jennifer began to encourage me to learn how to sew. She says it is a practical skill, and it can be enjoyable, especially when several women gather together to make quilts, blankets, or clothing for their families. She has pledged to invite me to one of her sewing sessions with some of the local housewives. "We drink coffee, bake cookies, share stories, and sew—it's fun," Jennifer posed, trying to captivate my interest.

Denise Lacache, Jennifer's eight-year-old daughter, is a charming young girl. She is her mother's trusty helper; she helps with the housework, she washes clothes, she helps with the cooking, and she is learning to sew under her mother's tutorship. "That girl can skin a muskrat a minute!" Jennifer lauded. I bet she will make some man a very good wife someday.

Melvin is trying to encourage Joseph to try trapping with them one winter. Now that we have good living accommodations at Plumb Bayou, he says that the Addison and Lacache families could trap the furry creatures together for the three month winter season. He pledged to teach Joseph everything he needs to know to become a skillful trapper.

Melvin told Joseph that his three boys are very good at catching, skinning, and stretching the hides of the muskrats on the rat molds. "My sons love the trapping season. They like the challenge. They enjoy the work. Most of all, they like the monetary reward the season brings. Those attributes make them very good at anything they do. I am very proud of them. You need to see my daughter skin muskrats. She's so fast she makes the boys blush," he boasted.

"Let's plan to make a winter of it this year; you won't regret it. I promise!" Melvin posed.

Joseph responded, eager to take the Lacache family up on their offer to teach us the trade: "Well, the kids are both healthy; Josephine has already recovered her strength since the delivery. The Plumb Bayou camp is ready for occupation. I can't see any reason we should not make this winter season our first trapping experience. After all, we need to demonstrate ownership of that portion of the estate, right, my dear?"

Of course Joseph knew I would welcome this new adventure, but for the family record, I told him, "If Jennifer and Denise can do it, so can I. I'll keep the stove warm and productive while all the rest of you do the real work!"

Everyone was amused by my comments, and we all had a hearty laugh.

The turtle soup was very tasty; the turtle eggs were especially good. The day was spent in leisure. Relaxation was the ultimate goal; this Fourth of July celebration was filled with the joy of living on Deer Island.

As I lay me down to sleep, I pray the Lord my soul to keep, amen.

July 10, 1845

There was heavy dew on the ground this morning. When I sat down in my favorite rocking chair on the front porch, the dew drenched tree leaves were shedding the excess moisture like raindrops. The children were asleep as I enjoyed a cup of hot tea wondering where my husband had gone.

Squirrels are dancing in the treetops as the sounds of songbirds lend cheer to the spectacle of nature coming alive with the dawn of a new day. The rushing waters of the fountainhead are emitting tranquil sounds that seem exaggerated due to the stillness of the forest absent a breeze.

A large female raccoon, with four of her offspring tagging along, has decided to taste the cold water of the stream not more than twenty paces from where I am sitting. The mother has seen me, but my presence does not seem to bother her. Once the baby raccoons satisfied their thirst, she casually led them away, disappearing in the dense underbrush on that side of the stream. I wondered if this was how things were in the Garden of Eden.

Joseph suddenly appeared from the backside of the house, carrying two rabbits by their hind legs. "I picked a dozen eggs this morning," he informed me. "The eggs are in the basket on the back porch."

This is one example of the leisurely business of life on "Deer Island." With construction completed and our sailboat now functional, it is just a matter of finding food, preparing it for the pot, consuming it, and enjoying the splendor of nature with my spouse and children. This must be what God intended. Joseph and I have everything we need to live a happy and productive life. The few things we lack can be obtained by exchanging what we do have for what we don't have at the city markets.

Life in America has been a wonderful experience. I regret that Uncle Patrick is not here to enjoy the fulfillment of his dream, the establishment of this homestead. There is a life lesson to be learned by his absence. We try to live each day as though it may be our last, for no one knows what tomorrow may bring. This was a hard lesson, but one that Joseph and I will keep close to our heart.

Joseph has expressed his concern regarding the enormous task of completing the work on the four clearings the congressman had outlined in his schematic of the island. He says the magnitude of the project is overwhelming; it doesn't seem possible. Feeling a bit melancholy, Joseph turned to prayer, asking God for strength and a firm resolve to see the job through to the end. God's will be done. Amen.

July 12, 1845 (Did God Answer Joseph's Prayer?)

(Two days ago Joseph was on the verge of despair; he pondered whether his uncle's plan for the estate was just a dream, or did he have some arrangement that he failed to disclose for insuring the job would get done. He could not have expected that I could do it alone, he lamented.)

About midmorning, we had a visitor. "*Bonjour, Madame et Monsieur Addison! Comment allez-vous?*" It was Captain Jean Laffite.

Joseph and I exchanged greetings with the captain and invited him to sit with us on the front porch. While he and Joseph got reacquainted, I went inside to make fresh coffee. They discussed the untimely death of Congressman Adams. Jean said when he heard of the congressman's passing, it was too late to attend the funeral. He offered his condolences and said he regretted the loss of his dear friend.

Jean began to express his intentions. "I will now explain to you and your wife why I have come today. Patrick had informed me in great detail his plans for a retirement home here. You might recall when we met last, that I had a survey of the Adams estate in my possession given to me by Patrick on one of my visits to New Orleans. Well, he had also given me his plans for the homestead—a schematic drawing outlining all his plans for improvement."

Captain Laffite continued, "I know from the information I have that there are four locations where trees must be removed to clear the land for various uses—the garden clearing, the pecan orchard clearing, the fruit orchard clearing, and the cemetery clearing. By any standard, that will require a great deal of work!"

Joseph was speechless; he could not believe what he was hearing. He kept quiet so he could hear the end of the matter before he made a fool of himself by saying something he shouldn't say; he did not know what to say.

"I have come to offer my assistance. I will help you finish the job that Patrick wanted me to finish for him. Remember what I told you about the arrangements that Patrick made with me years ago:

'I will give you the trees for the timber you need to service your fleet of ships; you will clear all the trees from the island at the specified locations; that was our deal, a deal is a deal!' Jean emphatically proclaimed.

"Well! But how! Gee! I can't! Joseph seemed to be unable to express himself. Due to all the excitement, I nearly forgot that I had to remain at the house to care for the children when the good captain stood up and walked down the front porch steps. I knew something was in the air, and I would have liked to see firsthand what that something was.

"Follow me!" Laffite ordered, grabbing Joseph by the arm. I continued to watch the two men as they quickly disappeared down the pathway to Deer Bayou—Addison Landing.

In about an hour, Joseph and Captain Laffite reappeared with a host of men following behind. Two very large oxen wearing yoke and harness were being escorted to the north side of the *big house*, the site for the garden clearing. The men were armed with crosscut saws, axes, pickaxes, and shovels. The entire group proceeded to the designated location and they began working straightway.

AN ISLAND INVASION

July 13, 1845

Ta lee and Kim Wong accompanied by a small army of men bearing food and spices and a large variety of pots and cooking utensils, arrived at the homestead at first light this morning. They have been charged with the responsibility of cooking for the workers. They have been instructed to construct an open-hearth kitchen near the worksite.

Joseph and Jean were at the boat landing before daybreak to greet the newcomers. Ta Lee told me they would soon return from the bayou for coffee and tea. "Expect four more men for coffee," he informed me.

Each morning, Joseph walks the *landing path* to check our boat to make sure all mooring lines are secure and to check the bilge for excess water. On his return trip he checks the rabbit traps (if they are set) to see if he has caught one or two for the table. The last thing he does before joining me for tea on our front porch is to gather the eggs from the hen house. This concludes his everyday early-morning routine.

Jean and his brother, Pierre Laffite, were with Joseph when he returned from the landing. Three other men were following close behind them. I went toward the fountainhead to greet them and to let them know the coffee and tea was ready to be served.

Captain Jean Laffite introduces his captains: "Josephine, you have already met the captain of *La Vengeance*, my older brother Pierre. I would like to introduce you to my other three captains—captain of *La Diligent* Rene Pinchot, captain of *Sophie* Vincent Gambi, and the captain of *Dorada* Pierre Cadet."

"My captains have volunteered eighty men each to help the Addison family complete all the plans for their homestead—that's four hundred men. They have also volunteered one cook with four helpers from each boat—that means there will be an open hearth cooking station at each worksite and one here next to the fountainhead. In addition to all the manpower, we have another pair of oxen headed this way. We will need all the pulling power we can get to uproot these large trees. A pair of mules is also forthcoming for transporting the freshly cut logs to Deer Bayou so they can be rafted together and floated to our vessels on anchor in Atchafalaya Bay," Captain Laffite informed us.

"One thing was not on any list—cattle. Since I know the congressman enjoyed a good steak dinner, I decided it might be a good idea for you to maintain a small group of cows. To service those cows you will need a bull. As I speak, one young bull, three cows, and one calf are on their way here. Some of my men have been instructed to quickly erect a small barn, complete with stalls and hay loft. Since hay will not be available on the island, Joseph can secure the necessary corn and hay from the mainland. Now, you are in the cattle business—a special gift from me to you!" Captain Jean Laffite authoritatively proclaimed.

"Work should progress at a fast pace if the weather holds," Jean pledged with unbridled enthusiasm.

July 20, 1845 (The Garden Clearing)

The last stump was removed from the garden clearing today. The mule team has been steadily hauling logs to the northeast side of the landing for shipment to the bay. The log run has been made east of our freshwater stream to prevent damage to the *landing path* we use to travel by foot from our boat landing to the houses. Laffite's men cleared a twelve-foot-wide pathway for this purpose. The salvaged logs Laffite can use for his boats from the garden clearing, the pecan orchard clearing, and the fruit orchard clearing will be transported through this avenue. Another twelve-foot-wide swath of trees is being cut south of the stream for removal of the logs from the cemetery clearing. Undesirable trees are being corded for firewood; underbrush and debris is being stacked around the outer parameters of each clearing to serve as a windbreak. It is a massive undertaking, but the seamen are hard workers and they don't waste time for anything—the noon meal is almost consumed on the run.

Captain Jean presented Joseph with a new plow with all necessary hardware and implements needed for plowing—harnesses, yokes, and miscellaneous items. He told Joseph that the two teams of oxen and the team of mules will be given to him when all the work is finished. "You can slaughter the oxen if you have no further need of them; preserve the meat by hanging it in your smokehouse. The mules can be used to pull the plow, or if you prefer to use the oxen, the mules can be sold to some farmer at Brashear City. Good mules are always in demand," he assured us.

I can only believe that Laffite and his men are a godsend; what else can I say? When Frenchy and Carey return, they will think the island has been invaded. What else could they think when they see the flotilla moored around our docking facility. What will they do? Turn and run back to the mainland, or will they come to the *big house* to see what all the commotion is about? I can hardly wait to see their facial expressions when they become eye witnesses to what has been accomplished in such short order.

Each evening as the shadows grow tall and the sun loses its intensity, five groups of men gather around each of their five open-hearth kitchens to fill their empty bellies. Such comradeship as I have never seen before ensues; first a fiddle or two begin to play, next a few guitars are being strummed, add the accordions and harmonicas, and you have five different locations filled with the excitement of men singing and dancing into the late hours of the night to the merry melodies of French folk tunes. Numerous flambeaus are lighted to enhance the light of the quarter moon. It is quite a spectacle! The delightful atmosphere thus created is in sharp contrast to the quaint sound of the night creatures ushering in the darkness, and the solemn quietude that follows.

Jean, Pierre, and the three other captains are using the *little house* as their sleeping quarters. The rest of the men sleep in tent camps at each of the four worksites. A skeleton crew remains aboard their ships to make sure the vessels don't run aground if some unexpected storm should strike. The weather has been perfect thus far, one more sign that God is with us in this endeavor.

John Quincy and Alexander Patrick have been fascinated by all the activity, especially when the night-time merriment begins. Joseph and I have been pleasantly surprised by the jovial spirit of all our hardworking seamen. They work hard in the daytime, and they play hard at night; I wonder where they get all that energy. They do partake in a bit of rationed wine. There are several empty casks being used as makeshift seats around the out-kitchens.

As is my usual custom, around midnight in the quiet darkness, the last sound to be heard is the scratching of my quill pen upon the paper in my legend. My writing strokes defy the tranquil peace that nature inflicts on weary human souls, challenging the ominous solitude that life on a remote island brings to all its residents.

There must be a balance between man and his environment in which neither is threatened with destruction. Is this not what we have come to understand as civilization? I hope our intrusion will not destroy the splendor that has been evolving here for centuries; time will be the judge of our actions today. I hope we are making the right choices. God help us. Amen.

August 2, 1845 (Frenchy and Carey Return)

About midmorning, Frenchy and Carey returned to find a much expanded landing site; for convenience, Captain Laffite had instructed his men to use some of the timber cut from the clearings to enlarge our docking facilities. Our band of merry men have completed work on the garden clearing and the pecan orchard clearing. Work is now in progress on the fruit orchard clearing.

They were amazed at the progress that has been made since they left the island for a much-needed hiatus. Frenchy, excited about what little he had seen, spoke first, "*Qu'est-ce qui s'est passé*; what has happened? *C'est miracle!* It's a miracle!"

Next it was Carey. "*Comment avance le travail.* How is the work coming along?"

Whenever Frenchy and Carey speak in the French language to us, it's a sure sign that they are excited beyond belief. This is a rare occurrence indeed!

"It is hard to imagine so much good fortune in such a short period of time could befall anyone Madame Addison," Frenchy raved. "It is nothing short of a miracle!" he insisted.

"Who are all these men? Where did they all come from?" Carey Trudeau asked, obviously overcome by wonderment.

"These are all crewmen from Captain Laffite's five ships that are on anchor in Atchafalaya Bay," I told him.

"Is Captain Laffite's name by any chance Jean?" Frenchy delicately asked, unable to disguise the menacing look on his face.

"Yes, that's right, his name is Jean Laffite. He is a merchant seamen working for the American Navy. He has five armed merchant ships on anchor in the bay. He is a privateer; his ships are armed to defend them from pirates," I asserted without apprehension.

Frenchy seemed uncomfortable with my response, but he did not offer any reason for his apparent uneasiness. He changed the subject and asked how the children were doing amidst all the noise and activity.

"John Quincy is with his father at one of the work sites. Alexander Patrick just had his morning feeding, and he is sound asleep in the sitting room," I informed him.

Frenchy was curious about the cooking arrangements for the vast number of workmen. I explained about the establishing of five open hearths—one at each of the four work areas and one right there, just north of the fountainhead.

"So much has happened since you and Carey left the island. I don't know where to begin. We now have a barn with a hay loft, three cows and one young calf, one bull for servicing the cows, two yokes of oxen, and one pair of mules. Now just that alone would have been unimaginable without the efforts of Captain Jean and his hard working sailors," I shared.

I ushered my two good friends into the kitchen for a cup of hot coffee. "Joseph intends to ask both of you to supervise the fencing of the cattle pen and the garden clearing. Jean will provide the work crew and the materials needed to accomplish the task. That is no small job!" I warned.

I informed Frenchy and Carey about the regular evening festivities. "After the evening meal each day, the men gather in groups and sing and dance and play music until midnight. Lighting flambeaus to dispel the darkness, the merriment is stimulating and exciting to watch. After a while, when the wine has worked its charms on the jovial participants, the hoopla intensifies. The merrymaking reaches its limits and it is suddenly brought to a swift conclusion when the various captains order everyone to their tents. Within half an hour all is quiet. The transition happens so fast it's like blowing out my oil lamp after making a final entry in my diary."

Frenchy expressed concern that he and his deckhand would soon be out of a job; I allayed those fears very quickly. "Joseph has been advised to fish the streams, trap the land, and plant fruit trees along the banks and ridges that follow the courses of the five bayous that traverse the estate. Those activities and improvements will demonstrate possession and ownership, but Joseph and I will require much more help as time marches on. Who will help us milk the cows, work the garden, and maintain the numerous activities that will need daily attention?" I courteously asked.

I informed him that Jean has estimated about three more weeks and all the work on the homestead will be totally finished. He is well pleased with the thousands of board feet of lumber the logs he was able to harvest will yield for use in servicing his ships. Raft after raft of bundled logs have been floated to the bay ultimately bound for Campeche Island.

I told Frenchy that he and Carey would be with us for as long as they wish to be in our service. "If we ever separate, it will be a voluntary choice," I pledged.

August 15, 1845 (A Birthday Celebration)

Today was special in many ways. Captain Jean had secretly instructed his cooks to prepare various pies for dessert after the evening meal.

In celebration of John Quincy's third birthday, the captain suspended all work on the cemetery clearing to plant sixteen pecan trees in the pecan orchard clearing. He also planted our fruit orchard with ten each of the following—pomegranate, peach, pear, plum, orange, grapefruit, persimmon, fig, and date palm.

After supper, everyone joined together to sing happy birthday to John Quincy. With the numerous voices joining in song, I am sure the sound was carried by southerly breezes all the way to the mainland. It was a touching few moments that brought forth tears from my eyes.

Work on the cemetery clearing is nearly complete; the cattle pen clearing has been finished. Fencing is up around the garden parameter and the cattle clearing (pasture). Captain Jean Laffite and his captains and crewmen will soon desert the island as quickly as they came. How will Joseph and I ever be able to pay for his kindness and generosity? What words will I utter to him when he prepares to leave here? I pray God will put the right words in my mouth when I tell everyone good-bye.

A DAY TO CELEBRATE

August 20, 1845 Midday (Laffite Prepares to Leave Deer Island)
The last stump has been removed from the cemetery clearing. The pink floribunda that Pauline planted at the gravesite of Uncle

Patrick looks beautiful in the full sunlight; it will flourish now that the brilliant rays of our daytime host have been magnanimously freed.

The discard from the massive undertaking has produced multiple cords of wood that will be fuel for many a stove fire—enough for several years if properly shielded from the rain. The remaining brush and the giant roots from the uprooted trees have encircled each clearing. They will serve as wind breaks, and they will be the perfect natural trellis for the blackberry vines that will certainly cover them over. Blackberries! I wish I had a few. The season for the berries is over until next spring; it will be one more thing to look forward to for our eating pleasure.

Deer Island has forever been changed. Everyone boasts of the clever way that Uncle Patrick had set up the homestead. Each clearing is surrounded by dense forest. The long pathways that lend access to each site are perfect for conveniently finding what you are searching for. Without the designated pathways, one would have a difficult time locating each clearing because they are so well hidden among the trees. I thing the idea was to maintain the integrity of the island's natural appeal—wilderness. The various clearings are hidden from view intentionally to enhance the experience of exploring the natural beauty that is all around you. What a brilliant well-thought-out plan he proposed.

Captain Laffite has announced plans for a big celebration tonight. Everyone is looking forward to the event with great anticipation. Frenchy and Carey have joined the fun each night, adding their mouth harps to the musical mix of instruments. What a sight! I wish everyone could see those two trying to compete for attention among so many gifted musical talents. I don't know how we would have gotten along without them.

Excitement began to build as Gambi, Pinchot, and Cadet, three of Laffite's captains, supervised preparations for our *Soiree Musicale*. Flambeaus are being hung from the low tree branches between the two houses to provide light for the evening's festivities. Kegs of wine stand ready to be tapped and consumed by the host of men who have labored so hard for the past forty days.

Joseph has been discussing ship design with the Laffite brothers. Pierre complimented Joseph on the fine boatbuilding skills he demonstrated on our new sailboat, *Dreadnought*. Joseph told me he had many compliments from Laffite's men on the quality of the newly finished vessel.

The events that have led Joseph and me to this point are too bizarre to be anything short of miraculous. It is as though we are living a fairytale where even tragedy is ultimately turned into good fortune. It might seem callous to view someone's death as good fortune, but Uncle Patrick's untimely demise has spawned a series of events that can only be construed as divine providence. Beyond providence, there is no rational explanation for what has happened to us.

Earlier this afternoon, I hailed Jean on his way down the *landing path*: "Captain Laffite! Can I speak with you a moment?" I shouted.

"Yes, Madame Addison, what can I do for you?" he asked as he drew closer and greeted me with a charming smile and those penetrating brown eyes of his.

"I know that Pauline Longere is your daughter. I want you to know that we have accepted her as a member of our family. In fact, we have given her the *little house* and an open invitation to come to the island to live with us. She and I have agreed to be surrogate sisters," I informed him, nervously awaiting his response.

Jean responded soberly with a question: "Does Joseph know about my daughter?"

"No! I promised Pauline I would honor the agreement between you and Uncle Patrick to keep your daughter's identity a secret, knowing that she might otherwise be in danger," I shared.

"I appreciate your frankness and your honesty. I sense you had great respect for my dear friend, Congressman Adams. When we leave the island, you may inform your husband about Pauline. I sincerely appreciate your kindness and continued friendship with my daughter. I will ever be in your debt for that," Jean told me.

"Captain Laffite, how will we ever be able to repay you for all your kindness and generosity?" I asked.

"*Tu etes un ange*. You are an angel, Josephine! *Notre Dieu, Il avait donne sa benedicite a ce projet*; our God, the congressman's plan had His blessing. *N'est-ce pas?*"

I could not disagree with his second comment; as for me being an angel, that is something I should aspire to become.

Laffite continued, "As far as payment for any perceived debt owed to me, or to any of my men, you and Joseph have already paid in full—you owe us nothing! Yes, you have already paid in full!" He reiterated, bowing his head in pensive reflection. "We will speak again this evening," he added, as he continued his walk downstream on the *landing path*.

In my absence, Carey Trudeau was minding Alexander Patrick from a chair on the front porch of the *big house*. My son was resting his head on a pillow on the floor; southerly breezes were blowing his hair away from his brow. For a brief period, quiet solitude was the order of the hour, so I instructed Carey to wake me if I nap too long.

A FINAL TRIBUTE

The night of music and merriment seemed short-lived. Before I realized it, it was nearly midnight. The wine had disappeared, and everyone was nearing exhaustion from all the dancing and horseplay. With Joseph's hearty approval, I am sure I danced with every man on Deer Island (it is difficult being the only women). I danced several waltzes with Pierre and Jean; they proved to be very good dancers. All the musicians had stopped playing except one man on accordion and one on fiddle when Captain Jean Laffite climbed atop a wine casket and asked for everyone's attention.

"I would like everyone to pause for a few moments of silence in honor of my fellow comrade in arms and my dear friend, the Honorable Patrick J. Adams," Jean requested.

After an extended silence, Captain Laffite began his tribute: "In memory of my dear friend and comrade in arms, I wish to present this token of our friendship to his family. Joseph and Josephine, would you come closer to receive this gift from me to you," he asked, beckoning with his free hand.

"As a token of the friendship I had with Patrick Adams, I present you with this cutlass. Let everyone within the sound of my voice bear witness. My friendship with Patrick Adams was not in vain. I pledge the same loyalty and friendship to Joseph and Josephine Addison until there is no more life in my body. What say you all?" he queried.

"Aye, we all bear witness!" the men announced with fervor.

Captain Laffite presented us with a beautifully engraved cutlass. The blade was made of silver and the hilt was cast in pure gold with an inscription on each side of the handle—one side commemorating the Battle of New Orleans and the other side was his congressional tenure. The butt of the cutlass had the initials—"*PL*."

After the presentation, I thanked Captain Laffite for everything he had said and done. Curious over the initials on the butt of the short heavy sword, I drew him closer so I could whisper in his ear: "Does the PL signify your brother Pierre or do they represent your daughter?"

"What do you think?" Laffite responded with a leading question.

"Pauline Laffite," I softly suggested in a voice a bit louder than a whisper.

"No!" Lafitte smugly retorted. "Pauline Longere!" he uttered with a smile. "Remember, they are one and the same," he teased.

Frenchy and Carey each had one of our children cradled in their arms. Joseph showed the elegantly crafted cutlass to them in the dim light of the flambeaus nearby; a tailored leather scabbard was given for the protection of the sword when it is stored. Frenchy put John Quincy down so he could sheathe the sword so Joseph could return to the wine cask pulpit now vacated.

Joseph mounted the wine cask where Captain Laffite had made his brief speech and asked for everyone's attention. A bit nervous, his voice trembled due to the emotion he was feeling from deep within. With a quiet audience, he began to speak to the enormous crowd of seamen.

"Words cannot begin to express the heartfelt gratitude my wife and I wish to convey to all of you before leaving our homestead. Know this!

"You will always be remembered by the Addison family. You will always have a place in our hearts. Should you choose to come and visit us again, you will ever be our welcomed guests. Thank you all, and godspeed!" he asserted with teary eyes.

Everyone let out a cheer, as Jean and his four captains took turns bidding us farewell.

Captain Pierre Laffite was first: "Joseph, I wish to inform you that your corncrib has been stocked with sacks of seed, all suitable for planting this fall, with enough for next spring as well. *Se rappeler; il est vrai que Laffite se soucie des amis. Bonne chance!* Remember; it's true that Laffite cares about his friends!"

Captain Rene Pinchot was next: "Joseph, I hope your team of mules will be as productive pulling your plow as they were a tremendous benefit helping pull all those trees to the bayou side for rafting. *Bonne chance!*"

Third to speak was Captain Vincent Gambi. "Joseph and Josephine, I pray the citrus and fruit orchard, as well as the pecan orchard we planted, will grow quickly, that all the plants may remain healthy, and I hope they will all bear in abundance. *Bonne chance!*"

Captain Pierre Cadet could not speak English. He began rattling off several things in French; he was speaking so fast that Jean had to stop him so he could interpret for us:"Pierre would like to tell Josephine that he hopes the plow he gave to her husband will help him produce an abundance of crops. He also wishes you, and your whole family, long life, and prosperity on Deer Island."

Pierre had a look of consternation which was promptly dispelled when Jean explained to him. "*Je l'explique pourqu'elle comprenne.* I'm explaining it so she may understand."

Cadet responded with a broad grin: "*Tres bien merci. Bonne chance!*"

After this final exchange, Jean and his four captains ordered the men to the dock site. In a matter of minutes, there was no evidence that anyone had been here. All that remained were the five captains and twenty empty wine casks. One by one, we shook the hands of the gallant seamen who orchestrated the modern miracle that now would forever grace Deer Island—completion of all Uncle Patrick's dreams for his retirement haven.

"*Bon soir mes Amis, bonne chance!*" was the parting chant. "*Bon soir mes Amis, bonne chance!*" they shouted as they soon disappeared in the darkness that obscured the *landing path* from any distant view. "*Au revoir mes Amis, Au revoir!*" someone hollered, his voice muffled by the faraway distance of the caller.

Joseph and I joined Frenchy and Carey on the front porch of the *little house*. I made coffee while the men had a smoke with their corncob pipes. After a cup of coffee, I escorted my two little boys to the *big house* for some long-overdue rest. After I was sure the boys were asleep, I returned to join the men next door.

"What's next?" I asked.

"Who knows?" Joseph answered, before drawing enough air through the stem of his pipe that it produced a brilliant orange-red glow near the top of his tobacco bowl.

"*Le projet pour la propriete a bien reuse, n'est-ce pas?* The plan for the homestead turned out well, did it not?" Frenchy lauded.

"Josephine and I will have much to mention in our prayers this evening; the blessings we have received are too numerous to mention in casual conversation" Joseph thoughtfully responded. "Frenchy, you and Carey are a blessing to us as well; we thank God for both of you," Joseph added.

We had a lengthy conversation beneath the starlit sky enhanced by the light of the full moon. Owls were calling back and forth across the ridge. The sound of the rushing water in the stream and the gurgling sounds of the bubbles being exuded by the fountain-head redouble the tranquility that is necessary to soothe one's soul. Intermittent breezes stir the leaves above and below us as we sit with newfound wonder and amazement as nature once again becomes our only companion.

As I prepared to snuff out my lard oil lamp and pen the last entry in today's record, I heard a queer noise. At first I thought it was thunder, but that notion was soon dispelled by consecutive booms whose sounds were coming from the direction of the bay. Captain Jean Laffite and his men were saying their final good-bye with cannon fire as they set sail for Campeche Island.

> Farewell Captain Jean Laffite
> I hope again one day we meet
> To share in life before we sleep
> And go below in earth or deep
> Farewell.

Chapter Eleven

TRAPPERS
TRAPPERS WE WILL BE

September 1, 1845

On July 7, 1844, work on the Plumb Bayou trapping camp was completed. This winter, Joseph and I intend to spend three months hunting for fur. We will accompany our good friends from Bayou Shaver, Melvin Lacache and his family. A native of the Atchafalaya Basin, he has been a trapper since he was old enough to walk. Since the winter of 1842 (at our request) they have trapped the estate so we could demonstrate ownership of the land. Upon the advice of William Henley, we collected a small percentage of the proceeds from their trapping season each year to insure our land claims remain legal.

Melvin Lacache and his wife Jennifer are both of Portuguese descent. Melvin's father was a crewmember on Vincent Gambi's brigantine *Sophie* until old age ended his career as a seaman.

Plans are being made for an early trip to Plumb Bayou. Joseph and Melvin will be rendezvousing with the *Swamp Rat,* which is freighting a new cistern from the mainland to our trapping camp. In addition to making a foundation to secure the water storage tank and raising it into place, they will be fabricating an outhouse and all that entails (digging a deep hole beneath the structure). They will be checking the camp for necessary repairs (shingles may need repair or replacement, for example). They will be clearing any brush or debris from the area surrounding our winter home. They believe the work will keep them busy for the next two or three weeks.

Melvin and Jennifer fish, hunt, and trap for their livelihood. Their entire family is involved in everything they do; they work together. With three healthy boys and one daughter they have plenty of help. It soon became apparent to Joseph and I just how valuable an extended family can be.

Melvin owns a fifty-foot sloop he calls *Cracker Jack*. It is a versatile craft, well suited for travel up and down river as well as navigating the small bayous that seem to be everywhere in this general area.

In the winter, the Lacache family traps; in spring and fall they seine for fish and shrimp. They set hoop nets for buffalo fish and freshwater catfish; they set bush traps to catch soft-shell crabs. In summer, they pick moss and hunt for turtles. They are very industrious.

With Melvin's help, we hope to have a productive trapping season; Joseph has much to learn, and he knows Melvin will be a good mentor. *Dreadnought* will leave in the morning, loaded with necessary building materials and provision. Joseph says when they return, the camp will be ready for occupation, with every possible convenience to make our three month stay pleasurable.

September 2, 1845 (Plumb Bayou, Here We Come)

At first light this morning, the Lacache family moored their boat at Addison Landing. Melvin and his three sons—Terry, Troy, and Terrence—joined Joseph aboard our sailboat; they headed around the south bend in Deer Bayou to meet the *Swamp Rat* at the rendezvous point, the mouth of the Atchafalaya River.

After seeing Melvin and the boys off, Jennifer and her daughter Denise appeared on the front porch of the *big house* just as I was about to make tea in the kitchen. "Hello!" Jennifer shouted.

"Come on in and have a fresh cup of tea with me; I'll make some coffee for you later," I answered, welcoming their company. Jennifer brought a few yards of fabric and her sewing paraphernalia with her. I know what that means; she intends to give me lessons.

I know our time together will be enjoyable; she and her daughter are both vivacious characters. They are always happy-go-lucky and fun to be around. This will be our first extended visit together; I know they will dispel any loneliness I may have otherwise endured in Joseph's absence.

September 20, 1845

Joseph and company arrived back on the island about mid-morning. The cistern and outhouse are functional, and the grounds are cleared of brush and debris. Our trapping poles are neatly stored beneath the camp; the traps have been checked and they remain stored in the wooden casks inside the camp.

Melvin reported that there are numerous muskrat mounds all over the prairie. He began sharing with us his optimistic observations: "There were several otters swimming playfully in many of the shallow water ponds. Raccoons, squirrels, and rabbits are so plentiful I could kill them with a stick. Things are really looking good. The signs are promising. Now, all we need is a good price for the furs. One thing is for sure, we won't go hungry!" Melvin confidently boasted.

We spent the remainder of the day speculating about the money we would make this winter; most of all, we agreed the experience will be gratifying for all of us, even John Quincy and Alexander Patrick.

November 22, 1845 (Thanksgiving Day)

Our guests began arriving yesterday. The Lacache family is spending a couple of days with us as we make final preparations for our trip to the trapping camp; we will be leaving sometime tomorrow. Everyone is excited, especially Joseph and me; this will be one more new experience to add to a growing list.

Frenchy and Carey brought several dressed turkeys from the mainland. They began cooking as soon as they arrived this morning. After the day's festivities they will be going home for the winter. We will see them again next spring.

The food was good, the company delightful, but more important than anything else was the growing relationship that was bonding us together. The Lacache family has become our dear friends. It feels good to have friends.

December 1845 (Our First Season Begins)

The day after Thanksgiving we left our home on Deer Island for the Plumb Bayou trapping camp. We arrived safely before sunset. The first order of business for Melvin and Joseph was to build a fire to ward off the mosquitoes; this would allow them more time to get things ready for an early start in the morning.

Within two days, all our traps had been set at well chosen locations. Joseph, Melvin, Terry, Troy, and Terrence are spending much of their time clearing small ditches; cutting through the floating vegetation will provide better access to nearly all the ponds. Using special rakes, they pull the green matting to each side of the desired channel course; the result is a narrow passageway wide enough for a pirogue to pass. This gives easier access to more areas of the prairie; more area means more traps can be set, giving a better chance for a good harvest. This has proved a difficult task, but Melvin says that each year this job of channel cutting will become easier, since we will be reopening existing channels. "The first pass is always the most difficult," Melvin says.

As time passed, Joseph began to use his push pole more effectively as he maneuvered his pirogue through the narrow ditches the local fishermen call a *trainasse*. "This is much easier than trying to walk the floating marsh (*marecage tremblant*) to get to the trapping runs," Joseph proclaimed with a determined smile.

Joseph asked Melvin if he thought dugout canoes would be better than pirogues; he feels that the round bottom of the canoe would slide through the narrow ditches easier than the flat-bottomed boats, especially when the water is low and the ditches have become nothing less than soft mud.

Melvin said the round bottom of the canoe would be an advantage, but the dugouts are difficult to make. Joseph pledged to have two dugout canoes ready for next season. "Good luck with that ambitious project!" Melvin challenged.

In an effort to allow Joseph to build self-confidence, Melvin gave him several traps and poles and told him to give it a try. "Experience is the best teacher," he asserted.

The next day, Joseph set out a few dozen traps. When he got back from the run, he was very tired; unaccustomed to walking the floating prairie, he sought the comfort of a chair right away. When he returned to his set of traps, he found they had all been set in the wrong places. He did not catch a single muskrat. He was discouraged, and that is expressing it mildly. "What a disaster!" Joseph lamented.

"At least you tried," Jennifer replied, trying to reassure him in the midst of his apparent embarrassment. "It's a learning process," she added.

"That's right, Jennifer," I said. "Joseph, I am proud of you. You did try very hard. In due time, with Melvin's help, you will learn how to trap. You have no reason to be ashamed," I consoled, trying to lift his spirits.

Joseph killed a raccoon. The fur was badly damaged, and it was not marketable, but it was not a total loss; he ended up in Jennifer's pot, and the furry creature was very tasty.

January 1846 (Our Second Month)

It has been a cold winter. Melvin says that is a good thing; cold weather produces a higher quality fur and that means we will get a better price at the fur market. "Fur buyers love cold weather; everyone makes money!" Melvin proclaimed. It has been so cold that the men have to break through ice to run through their trapping ditches.

Melvin's daughter, Denise, came down with some type of persistent fever. She was sick for three days. The boys had colds, but none of them contracted any fever. During this temporary bout with sickness, my two young ones got restless, having to be kept inside to avoid the cold damp atmosphere, hoping to prevent any further spreading of the ailment. Melvin and Joseph remained healthy, but they were a bit more cautious about staying dry and keeping warm. Jennifer and I had become nursemaids to them all; with so many of us remaining in such close quarters, our confinement did spawn a degree of discontentment, but that was short-lived.

Melvin shared that Joseph was coming along very well; he asked him to give us the proper procedure for skinning a rat. Joseph was eager to share what he had learned. "First, you must have an animal to skin," he teased. "I had to learn where to make the proper cuts so the hide could be separated from the flesh without any unnecessary damage. The hide is turned inside out so any meat residue or fat can be scraped from the pelt, another careful procedure. First, a slit is made from one back leg to the other across the body; the carcass is then separated from the hide by pulling away the pelt toward the head, turning it inside out. Finally, the skin is cut away from the eyes, preserving as much of the fur as possible. Turned inside out, the pelt is scraped to remove any excess meat or fat residue before it can be stretched over a mould to dry. Care must be taken to avoid excessive exposure to moisture; for example, they must be taken into a shelter if it rains or even if the humidity gets very high. The midday sun is best for proper drying, which normally takes three or four days. Once dried completely, the pelts are stacked atop each other in some dry place—commonly stored inside the hunting camp, which is usually kept warm," Joseph proudly announced. We were all impressed with my husband's newfound knowledge; I am very proud of him.

Our camp is filling up with muskrat pelts at varying stages of the curing process. The intrusive odor is difficult to describe; somehow it makes one feel dirty. Before long, even our clothing had absorbed the nauseating smell. Next year, the men promise to build a drying shed for both the convenience of storage and relief from the pungent smell.

Joseph got a tutorial for the skinning of the other furbearing animals also; he is learning to process the hides of beaver, raccoons, otters, mink and opossum. Yes, one might say that Joseph will soon be a bona fide trapper.

Jennifer is a very good cook, especially when it includes wild game of any sort. Whether she is preparing ducks, geese, rails, marsh hens, rabbits, squirrels, raccoons, or deer meat, when she says dinner is served: everyone scrambles to the table. There is no such thing as leftover dinner. I yielded to her skills and allowed her to cook the main courses.

I have been the breakfast cook: biscuits, cornbread, and the customary coffee and tea to wash it down with. Jennifer brought several jars of fig and pear preserves and muscadine jelly that she had processed last year. She has promised to teach me her method for preserving fruit. We have made a good team; there has not been a single complaint. Believe me when I say that cooking is the most important aspect of any happy camp life. Work, eat, and sleep; that's about all there is to do at the Plumb Bayou trapping camp.

Adding to the list of improvements we wish to make to demonstrate possession of the land, Joseph intends to plant fig trees on all the high ground, following the courses of the various bayous that traverse the estate. This plan will provide another food source for the Addison diet if it is successful. Melvin says the alluvial soil along the bayou banks is rich in nutrients and should support the healthy growth of anything we choose to plant. That is encouraging.

We had brought a dozen hens with us to the campsite, thinking we might enjoy fresh eggs. In short order, they began to disappear. The last chicken was spared the fate of her sisters; we killed her and made soup. One day, Melvin's son, Troy, was walking the ridge to pass the time. Not far from the camp, he found a pile of chicken feet. Melvin says the culprit was either a mink or a raccoon, both of which are notorious chicken eaters.

Learning from this mistake, next year we will enclose the bottom of the camp with chicken wire to ensure the safety of our prize hens. "If at first you don't succeed, try, try, try again"—isn't that how the saying goes? I am sure our efforts will pay off with fresh eggs next winter. One can only hope.

February 1846 (Seeing the Finish Line)

The men have been moving the trapping poles in search of more muskrats. As one run plays out, they start another at a different location. You can sense that the season is nearly over.

We haven't seen any alligators since the first day we arrived. Melvin says they hibernate in cold weather, but it is not uncommon to see a few during a mild winter; that can spell trouble. He told us that in a mild winter, if the gators become active, they can be a severe nuisance; they will eat anything caught in a trap.

In addition to our many plans—a drying shed, more secure protection for our chickens, making two dugout canoes—Joseph and Melvin have discussed construction of a pig pen to hold a few young piglets. That's one more idea for the dinner table. Wild game tastes good, and fresh pork would be a welcome dish, but I don't think expanding the menu with fresh pork meat was what Melvin had in mind.

Melvin explained the reason for wanting pigs during the trapping season: "Pigs will eat anything! Most trappers I know bring pigs to their winter trapping sites so they can eat the carcasses of the animals they skin. It's a good way to dispose of the meat (saving the trouble of having to find a place to dump the carcasses) and the pigs will get fat on a steady diet. Once the season ends, the trappers bring the pigs back home and purge them with corn for several weeks. By the time Easter comes, they will be ready to slaughter. Corn-fed pork! That's the best tasting pork there is!"

I must admit that Melvin's explanation raised a few eyebrows. Joseph and I must have appeared to be in a state of temporary shock; we were speechless for a few minutes. Jennifer, sensing we were bewildered by the notion of feeding raw meat to the pigs instead of eating pork during the winter, made us laugh by saying, "You wanted to become trappers, and this is part of what trappers do! You will get over your perplexity when you taste some rat-fed corn-purged pork meat in the spring!" The laughter was brief, but soothing to the soul; I hope Jennifer is right!

I could not help but recall the sight of the big alligator that was sunning himself on our campsite wharf when we arrived the day after Thanksgiving. He was huge! A young piglet would make him a good meal. I hope next winter is cold enough to avoid any close encounter with the menacing beast. After all, we are occupying the same hunting ground.

It is the end of February. We have had good success. Ice is coating the water surface less frequently, a sign that spring is not very far away. Warmer weather will be a welcome relief.

Jennifer's sassafras tea has been an amazing remedy for nearly everything that ails you. It is one more beverage for our steady consumption, and it has medicinal qualities that coffee and regular tea don't have. Chips of wood from the roots of the common sassafras tree are boiled in water resulting in a light green tea; add a bit of sugar and serve hot, it's tasty. The sassafras tree is useful for an additive the locals call *file*; added to gumbo, it produces a special flavor, and it thickens the watery dish. So we can use dried leaves ground to powder for *file,* and roots chipped and boiled for tea. Jennifer says this tree variety is plentiful; she has promised to teach me what they look like, so I can learn to identify them myself.

Melvin shared a story with us about an incident his father had this summer. "My father, Raymond Lacache, Ray for short, lives on a houseboat, much like the one Jennifer and I own, moored along Bayou Chene. Living nearby, on another houseboat moored about a hundred paces from papa's dock site, lives a family friend, Mr. Eugene Lejeune.

"Mr. Lejeune had been suffering from acute dysentery for several weeks. He is seventy-five years old. Each morning and each evening, Ray visits Mr. Eugene to make sure he has adequate food to eat, and he stays with him for a time to try to help him cope with loneliness, something any friend would do for another in need.

"One evening this past July, papa went for his customary visit at Mr. Lejeune's home. After about a three-hour visit, Ray told Gene goodnight and headed back home. It was about 9:00 p.m.

"About halfway back to the Lacache houseboat, Papa heard something very heavy hit the ground just ahead of him with a loud thump. Was it a large branch that had fallen from a nearby tree he wondered?

"Straining his eyes to see ahead of him, with only the light of the moon to show the way, Papa spotted a large black bear ambling along the pathway leading to his house. Having no gun for protection, papa was worried; he said the bear was between him and his house. Ray later shared with everyone that he was glad the bear decided to go about his business. There was no roar and not even a hint of aggressive behavior.

"Since Papa was unarmed, having no defense against a possible assault by the bear, he felt the good Lord up above had protected him from what could have been a dangerous encounter. He said he was more startled than shaken at first, but when he finally made it home, the relief he felt that nothing bad had happened to him made him tremble; this demonstrated the level of fear he had really experienced," Melvin shared.

"Wow! I hope nothing like that ever happens to me!" Joseph exclaimed, obviously nervous over the possibility that there might be more bears around Deer Island than he was aware of. "No one told us there were bears near here! We've had no signs of them up to now!" Joseph stated in a serious voice.

Seeing his story had rattled Joseph's nerves, Melvin told us that the event he described was a rare incident; he said his father has only seen four or five bears in his entire life. He is now sixty-eight years old. "I personally have not heard anyone say that they ever saw a bear on Deer Island," he shared, trying to relieve our anxiety.

Joseph seemed to be comforted by that information, but a single bear in my presence would be one too many for me I quietly reasoned.

The men have been speculating about how much money we have made this season. It's a good feeling to know we will soon be rewarded for all our hard work. Everyone has something special they would like to purchase.

My youngest son, Alexander Patrick, is only two years old, but John Quincy is four, and he is well aware of the coming events at the general store. He wants candy, and I'm sure he will have some.

Jennifer's three sons all want new pocket knives; Denise wants a new dress. We adults didn't reveal our wants, but we have some, of that I am sure. It is fun to spend money, especially when it is hard-earned money.

February 28, 1846

Tomorrow we head for home. *Dreadnought* will carry home our payload of furs. Preparations for our departure are nearing completion. The trapping poles have been retrieved from the marshland and stowed away beneath the camp. The traps have been greased with lard and stored in our oak barrels. "They won't smell good, but they won't be frozen by rust," Melvin confidently boasted. This confidence can only come from experience.

March 1, 1846

We arrived back at home on Deer Island late this afternoon. Everyone was tired and weary. Melvin and his family quickly boarded their boat, the *Cracker Jack,* and headed for their houseboat at Bayou Shaver. We agreed to rendezvous at the fur buyer's dock on the fifteenth of March to settle up for this winter's trapping season.

Joseph and I were exhausted; we would soon find our beds for some much-needed rest. The kids were asleep in our arms when we disembarked; they remained quiet and motionless when we put them to bed. Reflecting on the experience of our first trapping season, I found it both gratifying and adventuresome. With nonstop activity since our arrival, time seems to have been insignificant; we are closing in on six years of life on Deer Island. How time flies! Amen.

March 15, 1846 (Early Morning until Midday)

We rendezvous with the Lacache family at the fur buyer's shed at Brashear City today. We are supposed to meet them around noon so we will be getting an early start.

The Bayou Boeuf Trading Post is cooperatively owned by two gentlemen. The fur buyer shed is managed by Mr. Augustine Champagne, and the seafood dock is managed by Mr. Claude

Peterson. The two establishments are side by side and together they combine to form the trading post.

Joseph was excited about what lay in store for us today; "Time to cash in!" he told me as we were heading up the Atchafalaya River to receive the reward for our labor. This would be my very first trip to the mainland, and I am enjoying every minute of the journey. The change of scenery was refreshing.

Melvin and Jennifer were at the dockside when we arrived at the Bayou Boeuf Trading Post. Mr. Champagne, the fur buyer, was aware of our good fortune when we docked our boat. Melvin said he couldn't keep the good news to himself. "I had to spill the beans!" he announced.

It was totally understandable; even though Melvin is an experienced trapper, he made no secret that he thought that he and Joseph had done very well; in fact, his exuberance did not exceed the joy I witnessed on Joseph's face over the results of our first season together. I can only hope that next season will be as good.

I must say that for my first visit to the mainland, this experience will be one to remember; just being near a city is stimulating enough for me. Buying store-bought clothing for myself will only serve to add to the joy of our visit here; meeting new people and starting a longtime relationship with the proprietors of the local businesses (some of whom we have done business with for the past several years) will also be gratifying.

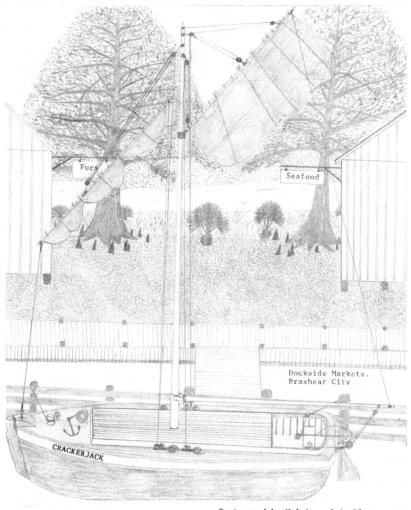

Furs

Seafood

Dockside Markets.
Brashear City

CRACKERJACK

Boat owned by Melvin and Jenifer
Lacache

Two young men immediately went to work unloading our furs from *Dreadnought*. Mr. Champagne was smiling from ear to ear. "Joseph, be prepared for a shock when I pay you for those pelts. Fur prices are sky high and in big demand. That is good news for all of us," he unrestrainedly bragged.

With the certainty that we had a good trapping season, we decided to walk over to the seafood dock to see what was happening there. Mr. Peterson was supervising the transfer of two large turtles from a boat onto his storefront dock. "Be careful! Don't let those alligator turtles get back into the water!" he cautioned in a stern voice. Turning his attention toward us, he asked, "How are you folks today?"

"Everything could not be finer. No, sir, things could not be better!" Joseph remarked with a joyful demeanor.

"I could tell by all those smiling faces that you had a good winter," he teased.

"Yes, sir! We had a good season!" Melvin exclaimed, noticeably proud to share the good news. "What price will those two turtles bring?" Melvin asked.

"They will bring about thirty dollars apiece," Mr. Peterson said. "Depending on the demand, I have paid higher prices than that. Right now, this is the fair market price," he told us. "I pack the turtles in wooden crates and ship them by steamboat to Shreveport. The people there love turtles. They make sauce piquant and soup with the savory meat," he explained. "Will I be seeing turtles from you this year?" he asked Melvin.

"Yes, indeed! At that price, I will be doing all I can to help you fill your orders," Melvin gleefully responded.

"I'll take all you can bring me, Melvin, and that would include your turtles also, Joseph," Mr. Peterson offered, trying to encourage Joseph to do likewise.

"I will give it a try!" Joseph exclaimed. "If Melvin will teach me how to catch the creatures," he added.

"Good luck!" Mr. Peterson emphatically asserted, just as we were being hailed to return to the fur buyer's establishment.

We were escorted by one of the dockworkers to Mr. Champagne's office where he was anxiously awaiting our arrival. "After all expenses, Joseph, you and Melvin made nine hundred dollars," Mr. Augustine proclaimed, as he extended his hand filled with cash.

We were speechless. Even Melvin, an experienced trapper, found the settlement hard to believe. "This will be a good incentive for trying again next year," Joseph spouted with wild enthusiasm.

"Congratulations on a fine season, and I wish all of you god-speed!" Mr. Champagne lauded. After shaking everyone's hand we headed for the boats with the bounty.

We loosed our mooring lines and headed downstream for the general store at Bayou Boeuf Landing. We are all anxious to spend some of our newfound means of exchange.

As we approached the landing, the prominent scene was the steamboat *Southern Star*; she was taking on wood and provisions. I had seen this side-paddleboat before; she makes biweekly excursions carrying vacationing passengers to Last Island. I have heard her whistle sound, morning and evening, as she makes her regular runs on Mondays and Fridays.

I have often scurried up the *beaten path*, summoned by the sound of her whistle, to watch her as she gracefully negotiates the sharp southern bend in the river. I enjoy waving to the many happy people onboard as she supplely passes me by. Though I have seen her countless times, this is the first time I have seen her up close.

I have been told that the village on Last Island has numerous cottages and even a hotel or two for rent. Located about twenty-five miles east of Atchafalaya Bay, Last Island is reputed to be a favorite watering spot for the affluent in this region. Now that I think about it, the remote island could be compared with what Pierre Laffite described regarding Grand Island. I have visited the westernmost end of Last Island, but I have not yet visited the village.

I would like to make the journey aboard the steamboat some-day. A leisurely vacation, a little fun in the sun, walking the sandy beaches and swimming in the surf would be a new adventure, espe-cially enjoyable would be the opportunity to mingle with strang-ers—"fresh faces" so to speak. The smiles on all the faces of the pas-sengers now boarding the vessel, testify that the trip to Last Island must be a worthwhile experience.

Suddenly, Joseph grabbed my arm, inviting me to accompany him inside the store; he wants me to try on a few dresses. As soon as I entered the building, I was introduced to the store's owner, Mr. E. B. Blanchard. "How are you today, Mrs. Addison?" he asked. I told him I was fine, and I was glad to make his acquaintance (I had met him at Uncle Patrick's funeral, but I didn't really know him).

To please my husband, I tried on several articles of clothing, and he purchased them all. I picked out a pair shoes and a pair of rubber boots, then I heard the familiar sound of the steamboat whistle.

I hurried out the storefront door to see her off. The boat captain was looking in my direction from the pilot house. With a smile, I waved good-bye to him. He returned my gesture with a wave of his own as he moved the large vessel away from the dock and headed for the Atchafalaya River.

When we finish with our shopping and board our boats filled with store-bought goods, we will be going to Bayou Shaver as the guests of the Lacache family; we plan to spend a week or two on their houseboat before heading back to Deer Island.

When we reached the river, I caught a final glimpse of the smoke stacks of the *Southern Star* as she entered Bayou Teche from Berwick Bay. She sounded one more blow of her whistle before disappearing.

I found myself reflecting on past events—our ride across the Mississippi River aboard the *Dixie Lee* from New Orleans to Algiers Point: the fresh produce market and Mr. Salvadore Cortez; the coach ride with Uncle Patrick and his driver, Albert Huie; visiting with the Henleys at Sugarland Farms; Pauline Longere and her beloved home, Chacahoula; a myriad of thoughts about so many wonderful experiences captured my mind completely. I became lost in the fantasy.

"Josephine! Josephine!" Joseph shouted, seeing I was in a trance. His sudden outburst startled me. "What were you thinking?" he asked.

"Oh, I was just thinking!" I exclaimed in solemn tones.

"Are you all right?" Joseph asked me.

I assured him that I was fine. "I was merely having a daydream," I explained, using sullen tones I could not restrain.

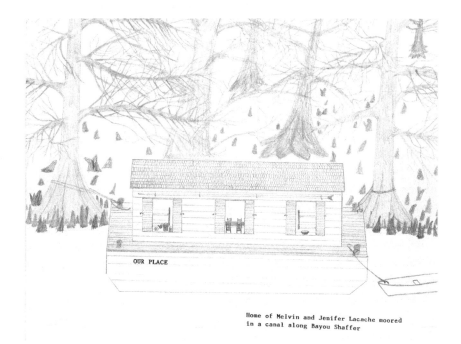

Home of Melvin and Jenifer Lacache moored
in a canal along Bayou Shaffer

There is something about a wave. In my mind's eye, I can still see the smile on the steamboat captain's face as he waved good-bye. The kind gesture reminded me of the Southampton docks; the good-bye waves we exchanged with family and friends, seeing their faces and knowing they were seeing each other for the very last time. Yes, there is something about a wave that incites deep personal feelings within me.

March 15, 1846 (Late Evening)

We arrived at the home of Melvin and Jennifer Lacache just as the sun was setting. Their house boat is moored to large cypress trees along Bayou Shaver. Melvin's children raced out to greet us, wanting desperately to know what took us so long. Once Jennifer pulled out the bag of treats, they scurried away to share their just desserts. "Now you boys share with your sister," she advised.

"Okay, Mom!" was the reply.

The Lacache children are a well-behaved bunch. They are obedient, considerate, respectful, mild mannered, and they are always ready to lend a hand even if they aren't asked. Their oldest son Terry is fifteen; next is Troy, he is twelve; their youngest son is Terrence, he is nine; and the end of the family train is their daughter Denise, and she is eight years old and pretty as a peach. She takes after her mother.

During the past three months, living in cramped quarters, I never heard the Lacache children have a single argument. Differences were settled peacefully. They obeyed every command without murmuring or complaining, and with no procrastination. I can only hope that my children will follow their wholesome example as they grow up together.

I intend to bare as many children as my reproductive health permits; the boys to help Joseph around the estate, and girls to give me a helping hand. That would be nice.

June 7, 1846 "Muskrat"

Our sailboat *Dreadnought* has proven to be a wonderful asset, especially for carrying heavy loads of building materials downriver to the homestead. She is perfect for sailing in Atchafalaya Bay and along the Gulf Coast. Now that the heavy lifting has been finished, it is time for us to build a smaller vessel that would be easier to maneuver through the inland bayous and shallow water streams.

Soon after our first boat was built, Joseph realized she was too big to be practical. The sloop the Peltiers own, *Sara's Dream*, will serve as the prototype for the hull that Joseph and Melvin intend to build (just a little smaller). The Henleys' boat, the schooner *Sugar Baby*, is a luxury vessel more than a work boat; our vessel will be designed for utility and not so much for elegance.

When William Henley and his family come to Deer Island for a visit, they board their boat from a dock in front of their house. They travel up Bayou Black to Tigerville; turning west, they enter Bayou Chene. They continue on a westerly course until they reach Bayou Penchant; once they enter Bayou Penchant, they head south until reaching Little Horn Bayou. They travel that course, heading further south before entering Big Horn Bayou; finally, they enter Deer Bayou traveling southwest, until they reach Addison Landing. This course is charted through inland waterways, something *Dreadnought* would find nearly impossible to manage.

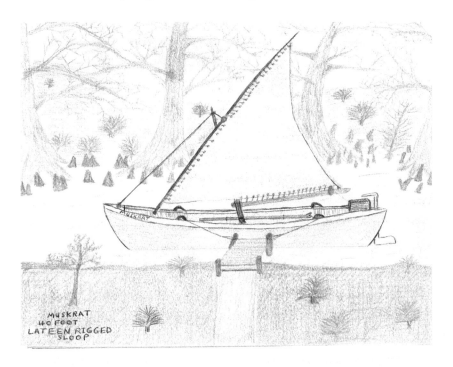

Because *Sara's Dream* is light, she has a shallow draft, and with lateen rigging she is highly maneuverable; she is perfect for traveling the inland bayous and streams. This will be a more practical design for our purposes than our first boat. Anxious to get our forty-foot sloop with lateen rigging in the water, Joseph and Melvin began laying the keel this morning.

July 4, 1846
Today we launch the newest member of our growing fleet of watercraft. *Muskrat* is in the water! Joseph and Melvin will be taking her to the bay to see how well she maneuvers.

Joseph always seems to be happiest when he is building or repairing some boat. The two men are very proud of the results of their handy work.

July 8, 1846

Today we will make our first trip to the mainland through Bayou Penchant in our new boat. If all goes well, we will be able to visit our friends on Bayou Chene, Bayou Shaver, Bayou Black, and any other destination reachable by water. Today is a happy day! Freedom at last! Freedom at last!

Joseph shouted a hearty "Amen, sister!" as he laughingly observed the joyous exhibition I was unashamedly displaying as *Muskrat* skimmed through the water at a good clip, aided by a stiff southeastern wind.

I told Joseph how much I loved him, and I shouted gleefully. "This will be a day to remember! Now we can travel to Chacahoula to see Pauline when we get the notion," I proudly asserted.

The melancholy associated with loneliness is forever dispelled—thank God! *Muskrat* is proving she is just what we needed. With a shipwright for a husband, I should expect the best, and he always delivers.

THREE YEARS LATER

MEMORIAL

November 1, 1849 (All Saints' Day)

Today we were visited by Senator Irving Peltier. With him he brought another degree of pride to the Addison family. He presented Joseph with a bronze plaque authorized and commissioned by the first president of the United States from Louisiana. Inscribed on the plaque are the following words:

Here lies Patrick J. Adams
Born July 4, 1791

Died July 2, 1842
A good soldier
A distinguished statesman
A close friend
I knew him well
Gone but not forgotten
Zach Taylor

Words cannot describe what we were feeling when we read the tribute to Congressman Patrick J. Adams. We always knew he was well respected by his peers. We were told he was a man of great influence, influence that reached all the way to the White House and the twelfth president of the United States, Zachary Taylor.

Senator Peltier also delivered wrought iron fencing and a gate to enclose a parameter around the gravesite. "He was the center of everyone's attention when he was alive; even after his death, the attention will not waver," Senator Peltier lauded.

November 10, 1849

Uncle Patrick's gravesite has been enhanced by the bronze plaque and the wrought-iron fencing. A gate lending access to the front of the tomb focuses one's attention directly toward the commemorative accolades inscribed on the plaque, which can be clearly read from a distance. The ever-expanding pink floribunda shows off its blooms adding a dignified floral tribute to the scene.

Pauline is certain to be affectionately touched, as we were, when she comes for her next visit. I regret she was not here to share in the solemnity of this moment with us. The congressman's gravesite without any doubt will serve as the anchor that will summon generations to come to this island. The Addison family will always be attached to Deer Island and its cemetery.

FIVE YEARS HAVE PASSED

October 1, 1854 (Another Boy)

Theresa Blanchard, my trusted and faithful midwife, has performed her duty for me once again. Boy number 3, Sanders Addison, was born this day. We have another man child, another pair of hands to help us around the estate. Like his two older brothers, Sanders will be a blessing, especially as he grows in strength and vitality. Joseph and I are thirty-six years old; Sanders was a bit of a surprise. John Quincy and Alexander Patrick were born two years apart. It has been ten years; we thought my childbearing days were over.

There is not a single day on this island that anyone could responsibly say that there is nothing that needs to be done today. Whether it is raining, sleeting, snowing (a rare occasion) or hailing, there is always something that needs attention.

A few examples of our routine activities will demonstrate the necessity for diligence. Our garden now produces enough vegetables to offer for sale at the city markets. Every year we raise enough piglets to sell some of them. The abundant harvest we gather from our fruit and pecan orchards allow us to bring untold bushels to market. Joseph has become very productive as a trapper. John Quincy and Alexander Patrick have become skilled woodworkers; their chairs, tables, swings, and even bird houses have been in high demand because of the quality of their workmanship—they bring a good price at the general store.

I guess you could say that we have become very prosperous, but believe me when I say there is a lot of sweat and hard work involved in our success. With the help and support of our close friends and associates, Joseph and I have become productive Louisiana homesteaders; we have become self-sufficient in many ways.

Madame Blanchard, my midwife, says I have been among her easiest patients. Having delivered hundreds of babies, she should know. "Your babies pop right out," she often muses. Theresa will remain on the island for at least a week, allowing me time for full recovery. She has been a sweetheart, a true blessing. It is a common sentiment that Madame Theresa Blanchard is the best midwife in the region; I obviously concur with that notion.

All is well with the Addison family! I look forward to tomorrow! God bless us everyone, Amen! Good night!

THANKSGIVING 1855

November 25, 1855 (Thanksgiving Day)

Our guests have been arriving for several days. Last evening, Frenchy and Carey joined us for the festivities. William Harrison Henley, his wife Greta, William H. Henley III with his wife, Emmaline and their son Patrick have been here a week. Pauline Longere, beautiful as ever, came with the Henleys aboard their sloop *Sugar Baby*. Senator Irving Peltier and his wife, Susan arrived day before yesterday. Melvin Lacache and his wife, Jennifer arrived yesterday morning with their four children: Terry, Troy, Terrence, and Denise. It is a long guest list of families and close friends.

I was stirring around in the kitchen of the *big house* before anyone else this morning. My two roosters *Daylight* and *Starlight* got confused by the lamplight and movement inside the house. They were both sounding off their customary morning wakeup calls: "*Cock-a-doodle-doo! Cock-a-doodle-doo! Cock-a-doodle-doo!*" they announced in unintended disharmony. It was two hours before daylight.

I am getting the stove hot for a huge breakfast—biscuits, cornbread, milk, coffee, and sassafras tea. My female guests have pledged to lend a hand with the remainder of today's food preparation.

I could see activity at the out-kitchen behind the *little house*. Frenchy and Carey are firing up the Queen Atlantic stove in preparation for a long day of cooking.

This will be the biggest menu ever for our Thanksgiving Day celebration. We are having pot roasted duck, venison stew, pan fried rabbit, pan-fried squirrel, and pan-fried raccoon. A large pig will be roasted over a fire in the open hearth near the freshwater stream. We are having a variety of garden vegetables. Numerous pies (apple, peach, pumpkin, and pecan) are ready for tasting—baked last night by our best pastry cooks.

The Peltiers brought several jars of assorted jellies and jams; they also brought a two-gallon cask of fresh honey. The Henleys brought a three-gallon cask of fresh cane syrup with a storage rack to support it in the horizontal position; it was tapped with a spigot for easy access.

Did King Solomon ever have such a meal? I wonder! This is shaping up to be our best celebration ever; of course, next year I will probably be boasting about the same thing. Everyone is healthy and filled with exuberance.

Fur prices are expected to be low this winter according to our buyer, Mr. Champagne. The past few years have been so productive that the factors in New Orleans complain that the furriers have excessive inventory from last year's season; consequently, since demand is low, prices will be low also. That spells trouble for both the buyers and trappers. Joseph and Melvin will not trap this winter, hoping that next year the market will be fluid once again. In the meantime, we will make the best of the reprieve and enjoy a full winter holiday from Thanksgiving through New Year's Day.

Many of our welcome guests have pledged to stay with us throughout the holiday season; some will be with us for forty days or more. Joseph and I could not be happier; every day will be like Christmas. With both houses furnished upstairs and downstairs, we can comfortably accommodate everyone. I wish Uncle Patrick could be here to see what has been accomplished here on Deer Island and to share in our joyous annual traditions. We miss him.

The men plan to do a great deal of hunting; they will be making several overnight trips to Camp Addison (Plumb Bayou trapping camp). Knowing the women are eager to have wild game in the pots, this has proved to be a good incentive for them to try hard to bring home the kill. How I love Southern hospitality!

While the men are away on the hunt, we women will be cackling like contented hens, enjoying conversation while maintaining the household chores. We never run out of things to talk about.

As the sun peaked over the horizon, *Daylight*, one of our Black Rock Rooster is competing with Starlight, our Rhode Island Red rooster for our attention (their two predecessors were both made into chicken stew last winter). These two young birds are focused on one thing throughout each day; they keep the hens on the nest! I must say they do a very good job of keeping the eggs fertile; there's a dot in every yoke.

I am beginning to hear movement throughout the house; this second sounding by our roosters has done its job. It is time to put down my pen and get to work. Tonight we will congregate around the front porch for storytelling; another activity I always anxiously anticipate; it is exciting to hear all the tales (some true and some fabricated) just for the fun of it. I thank God for His countless blessings! Now, it's time I get to work in the kitchen. Amen!

With the breakfast cooked, and the coffee and teas dripped, the kitchen quickly filled with hungry, sleepy-eyed souls, all happy to be guests on Deer Island, hosted by the Addison family.

Chapter Twelve

THE GREAT STORM

January 1, 1856 (New Year's Day 1856)

Today will be filled with the usual activities - food, fun, and fellowship. The men have cast nets for shrimp, and they have culled a huge pile of fresh oysters from a reef in Atchafalaya Bay.

Guess what's for dinner? We are having boiled shrimp, oysters on the half shell, and seafood gumbo. Jennifer Lacache is planning to cook shrimp and oyster stew. There are pies of every sort, all prepared yesterday with joyful anticipation of the coming new year.

Things have been very busy these past few weeks; neither of our two stoves had time to cool off. Today begins our sixteenth year on Deer Island. I could have never imagined that life could be fulfilling so far from my homeland. John Quincy is thirteen, Alexander Patrick is eleven, and our youngest son, Sanders, made one year old this past October first. We almost caught up with Melvin and Josephine; they are still one child ahead of us, and she is a girl.

March 15, 1856 (The Railroad Is Here)

The New Orleans, Opelousas, and Great Western Railroad completed a section of tracks that reaches the Bayou Boeuf terminal at Brashear City. Anticipating the railroad's soon arrival, the terminal was already under construction and nearing completion when the last section of track was laid. The railroad has also established a terminal at Chacahoula we have been told.

Frenchy and Carey brought us the news this morning over a hot cup of coffee. "For your record, Josephine, work on the railroad terminal was completed on February 24, 1856." Frenchy informed me, with his usual antics and his contorted facial expressions. There is no doubt that Frency can be a very funny man; he's a character you might say. We love him.

We all agreed that changes were coming fast and we are hoping that the changes will be for our good. "Sometimes progress can be a two-edged sword!" Joseph mused.

May 15, 1856

Our garden is planted. Though Joseph and I were not acquainted with agriculture before moving to America, trial and error, and good advice from some of our friends, has made my husband a fair gardener. All we can do now is hope and wait for a good harvest. Joseph made the effort; the rest is up to God and the weather.

We recently enlarged the chicken coop. We now have the shelter divided (one side is for roosting and the other is for nesting); we hope to produce more chicks, which will provide more eggs for our consumption. We have been very successful in propagating our chickens; this latest improvement will better accommodate our growing flock.

We have acquired a few domestic turkeys, ducks, and geese, almost doubling our stock of poultry. These additional birds make their nests on the ground and are not particularly fond of an enclosed shelter, preferring to stay outdoors. These birds have become a welcome addition for our dietary needs, providing us with other sources of eggs and meat.

Our corncrib is filled with dried ears of corn. This provides us with feed for all our animals—pigs, poultry, cattle, and mules. Each year we devote a sizable area of our garden to grow feed corn.

We have deer meat hanging in the smokehouse. Joseph learned how to cure the meat using smoke and a little salt. This process has been a successful way to extend the shelf life of the deer he kills. It is safe to eat even after being hung for several months. This has helped tremendously, not only in the preservation of the meat, but most importantly, there is little that goes to waste.

Our pigs have given us trouble from time to time. They burrow beneath the fencing and escape to Lord only knows where. Some return for food, others do not. We try to keep a dozen or so confined to a pen for the obvious reasons (more pigs). Once a sow is bred, we isolate her from the rest of the pigs so she can bare her young safely. It is not uncommon for a sow to deliver up to eight piglets; now that's a pork factory, one might say.

When Joseph dresses a pig for consumption, he builds a large fire beneath a huge cauldron filled with water. Once the water is boiling, the disemboweled pig carcass is doused with scalding hot water and the hair is scraped from the hide. Once butchered, the fat is trimmed and cooked in a large vat where it is rendered into oil that is poured hot into crock jars where it will solidify into lard. The skin with residual fat is cut into small chunks and fried; once crispy, the pork rinds are removed from the pot, sprinkled with salt, and popped into the hungry mouths of those lucky enough to be present at the time. It makes a tasty snack.

We only kill a pig during the winter; it is more practical. When the temperature is near freezing, the carcass can be halved and hung to dry in the open air for easier butchering. The same can be done for a calf or a deer. The firmer dried meat is easier to cut into pieces than the soft meat of any fresh kill. One small pig can feed our entire family.

June 15, 1856

Joseph and the boys caught a few turtles. Melvin Lacache and his three sons are coming to lend a hand. The large creatures are very heavy, and they can be dangerous if not properly handled. The men will remove them from the holding pen and load them into crates for shipment to the seafood dock at Brashear City.

While the men are occupied with the alligator turtles, Jennifer, Denise, and I will continue sewing on a quilt we started about a month ago. Jennifer is the expert; each time we sew together she gives me a tutorial. It is a good way for us to pass the time, and we enjoy making the useful blankets for our families. These quilts are especially welcome in our houses in the cold of winter; in the *big house* our bedrooms are all upstairs, away from the warmth of the woodstove.

August 1, 1856

Announcing her passage around the deep bend in the Atchafalaya River to warn unsuspecting vessels that she is coming, the steamboat *Southern Star* is headed south for Last Island. Each Monday and Friday, the sound of her whistle fills the air, both morning and evening, as she delivers passengers to and from the island resort. She sounds her passage about an hour after our rooster crows in the morning; about the time the chickens go into their coop to roost, she makes her evening blast, returning from her twelve-hour round trip.

I often wonder what it would be like to spend a week on Last Island. What would it be like to stay in the hotel and eat in the restaurant among strangers? I wonder what it would be like to experience the lapping of the waves against the shoreline in the quiet of night—lying on a blanket on the sandy beach and starring at the moon and stars. How nice would it be to make new friends and acquaintances from all regions of the south? All these thoughts stimulate my imagination. I wonder!

It must be a worthwhile experience, since the biweekly journey to the resort by steamboat has become popular to so many people. Whenever I walk the *beaten path* to see the *Southern Star* as she passes, she never seems to be short of passengers. It has to be a pleasurable excursion! Someday, I will see for myself; I'll then know firsthand what it is all about.

August 4, 1856 (Early Morning)

Once again, Melvin and Joseph are freighting turtles to the mainland. The boys are bringing some of their swings and tables to the general store for sale. Jennifer and Denise will visit with me during their absence.

Joseph will be using some of the proceeds from the sale of the turtles to buy sugar, rice, cornmeal, and a few wicks for my lard oil lamp. I also ordered a couple bottles of ink for my quill pen.

Jennifer has been teaching me how to prepare a few local dishes. To a pot of hot water, add cornmeal, a pinch of salt, and a little bacon grease and you have grits. A pat of fresh churned butter will enhance the flavor of the dish; serve with biscuits and fried eggs, and you have a good wholesome breakfast. It's pretty good.

Our new boat, *Muskrat*, has been the best thing for improving our lives on Deer Island. The freedom the boat has provided cannot be stressed enough. We visit often now; this is something that was not at all practical in our big boat.

Joseph called our vessel *Muskrat*; he says the name will serve to remind us that the proceeds from the sale of the hides of the furry creatures paid for all the materials needed for her construction. I could not see the need for such a silly reminder. I would have chosen some other name. If it were up to me, I would have chosen *Island Belle*; that sounds better than the name of the rats we trap I thought.

Going to the mainland through Bayou Penchant takes considerately less time than it does when fighting the swift current of the Atchafalaya. Consequently, we make trips to the city more often—not out of necessity, we just enjoy the outing.

At times, when Joseph has to go to Bayou Boeuf Landing to conduct business, I get him to drop off the boys at Bayou Shaver so they can spend time with the Lacache boys. We pick up Melvin, Jennifer, and Denise and head for Bayou Chene to join friends for a sewing party. Melvin usually accompanies Joseph to the mainland.

When Melvin and Joseph return, they generally stay awhile. They join up with a few of the nearby men and smoke tobacco in their corncob pipes; they tell jokes, discuss current events, and there is no doubt that politics is always a topic of interest.

I always enjoy our trips to the mainland; many times I make new friends. Most of us have a common existence; we make our living from the bountiful Atchafalaya Basin. Though none of us consider ourselves as wealthy, Joseph and I are considered by some to be very wealthy because of our vast land holdings. Land does not put money in your pockets unless you work it; rich or poor, we all must work the land and farm its resources.

The swamp people are generous, always willing to lend a helping hand. Hospitality is a way of life; it seems to come naturally to these bayou people. Maybe it is because we all have so much in common; whatever the reason, their kind disposition has made my life much more pleasurable.

August 4, 1856 (Late Afternoon)

Joseph arrived back from the mainland near sunset. He brought Melvin and all the kids with him; since it is too late to bring Jennifer and Denise home, they will be spending the night on the island. The turtles brought a good price, so Joseph bought a few extra things that were not included on my list. He has never been reluctant to spend money; after all, that is what the means of exchange is for, isn't it?

Our oldest son, John Quincy, will be fourteen on the fifteenth of this month. Joseph and I have a surprise for him; the special item was ordered several months ago and it has finally arrived at the general store. My husband picked it up while my son's back was turned; it was sneaky but necessary I reasoned. I can't wait to see the look on his face when he sees what we bought him. He will have a happy birthday, of that I am sure.

We had a good meal, and after several hours of storytelling, we retired for the evening. Good night, Lord. Amen.

August 5, 1856

The Lacache family headed for Bayou Shaver about midmorning. Joseph promised we would go for a visit and spend a day and a night with them in a few weeks.

The day was spent relaxing and enjoying the pleasant weather. Joseph and the boys went fishing at the landing without success. The boys reported that they had fun trying. I am inclined to believe they were more interested in swimming than catching fish, since everyone of them, including Joseph, returned soaking wet and full of laughter.

Since completion of the railroad to Brashear city, the Bayou Boeuf terminal has been invaded by adventurous sorts—vacationers wanting to experience all that an excursion to Last Island has to offer.

Evidently, the accommodations and easy access provided by paddleboat have been much publicized. There has been talk of using the *North Star*, sister ship to the *Southern Star*, to make additional trips to Last Island to accommodate the increased demand—at least for the summer months. Some say, within a year, island excursions may become a daily routine. The railroad, with the benefit of good advertising, has certainly drummed up more business; that's for sure!

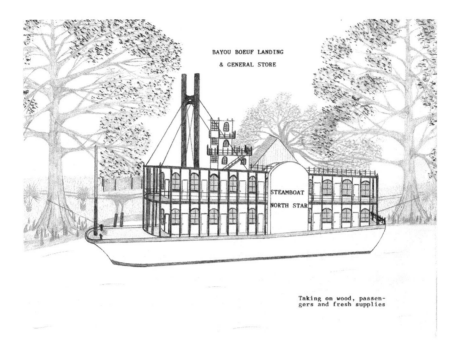

BAYOU BOEUF LANDING
& GENERAL STORE

STEAMBOAT
NORTH STAR

Taking on wood, passen-
gers and fresh supplies

Before the railroad arrived, vacationers to our east, looking for a good watering spot, took steamboats from New Orleans through Barataria Bayou, traveling through the bay to the backside of Grand Terre Island, Grand Island, or Cheniere Caminada. Those locations became immensely popular, especially after the War of 1812. The area had seen much improvement since it was occupied by our privateer friends and their acquaintances. The allure of something new has become the catalyst for the interest created in those with adventurous spirits.

August 7, 1856 (Another Loss)

Sadly, news of Captain Laffite's death reached us today. Jean Laffite died on May 5, 1854, at the age of seventy-two. Joseph and I will miss his unusual character and charm. His daughter, Pauline Longere, will remain an important member of our family. Once we know she has learned of his death, we will send her word that we hope she will reconsider coming to live with us here on Deer Island.

Senator Peltier passed the news of Jean Laffite's death to Mr. E. B. Blanchard at the general store. Melvin was buying a few provisions and he was charged with delivering the message. After delivering his store-bought goods to his home, he picked up Jennifer and Denise and came downstream to inform us of the bad news.

August 8, 1856 (Friday Late Evening)

It rained the entire day today. Intermittent thunderstorms have obscured the customary sound of the steamboat whistle, which usually announces the passage of the *Southern Star* each evening. The sun never appeared. It has been a gloomy day; none of us ventured outside the house due to the terrible weather.

The animals have been acting a bit strange of late; the cattle are lowing, as though they are frightened. The seagulls are flying inland, making their shrill cries as they fly over the homestead, the pigs seem restless, our roosters never made a single sound today, and none of the chickens left the coop for a stroll in the yard. The boys sat on the back porch swings, patiently waiting for the weather to change, whittling sticks with their pocket knives and exchanging jokes.

THE WEATHER IS QUEER

August 9, 1856 (Saturday)

The rain has not subsided; in fact, it has intensified. Strangely, the winds are blowing from the north; this is summer! Even the seagulls are seeking safehaven; their shrill cries once heard overhead have disappeared. The sky is much darker than yesterday; there is definitely something wrong.

Joseph and the boys are heading to the landing to secure the mooring lines on all of our boats due to the high winds. "It is better to be cautious. It's far better to be safe than sorry!" my husband proclaimed with some degree of consternation.

I totally understood Joseph's serious concern. We have never experienced weather this persistently ferocious. We have taken the precaution of closing all our shutters, and we have secured the *little house* as best we could. Now all we can do is ride out the storm and try to stay dry.

August 10, 1856 (Sunday, Midday)

Wind–driven rain is assaulting our windows. Joseph and the boys are doing all they can to prevent water from seeping into the house. A few shingles must have been blown loose by the intensity of the relentless storm; water is beginning to cover the floors upstairs. Joseph is trying his best to remain calm, but we are all shaken by the persistent onslaught.

August 10, 1856 (Late Sunday Night)

The full forces of the storm are upon us; the wind is howling at a level I could never have imagined. It is an eerie feeling! Outside, we can hear tree limbs cracking and then falling to the ground with a heavy thump; the wind, now penetrating the narrow cracks in our roof and walls, is whistling. The combination of spine-chilling sounds, with the uncertainty of what would happen next, has begun to shaken our resolve. The flames above our lamp wicks are ready to be extinguished by the uninvited winds that have found a way to come indoors. Though our dwelling has been soundly constructed of only the best materials, and even though I am confident that my husband was careful to incorporate every bit of his skill in the process, we found ourselves kneeling on the kitchen floor near the woodstove praying for a reprieve. Lord, help us all!

August 11, 1856 (Monday Morning)

The wind has diminished. Joseph and the boys are going to the landing to check our boats after they assess the damages to our two dwellings and outbuildings. We heard a large crash that sounded like an entire tree falling; we fear it may have fallen on one of our buildings during the night. I am anxiously awaiting a report. A drizzling rain and an overcast sky persist, but thank God, the terrifying tempest is dissipating.

When Joseph returned, he gave his report: "The gulf waters must have risen above the bayou banks. The small boats were all lodged between trees, about four feet higher on the ridge than where we left them. They suffered no damage. Thanks to the tall piles that secured our mooring lines, the *Dreadnought* and the *Muskrat* were able to rise and fall with the tidal surge. Both vessels escaped any damage. A large branch has penetrated the roof on the south side of the *little house*, and the corn crib was blown over by the wind with little damage. The barn, the smokehouse, the beehives, and the two cisterns, the out-kitchen behind the *little house*, and the out houses and the chicken coop, have all been spared any damage. There are several shingles blown from the rooftops of both houses. Considering the magnitude of the storm, we can consider ourselves very lucky," Joseph solemnly concluded.

I could not help wondering how things went for all our friends. This storm uprooted trees, snapped large branches from their trunks like they were twigs, and denuded much of the foliage of those that survived the powerful wind. It is hard to believe there could be so much destruction inflicted in such a short period of time.

August 11, 1856 (Monday Midday)

Melvin Lacache and his family came down Bayou Penchant to check on our situation. Melvin reported that the settlements on Bayou Chene and Bayou Shaver sustained little damage. There were a few fallen trees and minor roof damage on some of the dwellings. No one was injured. "We were very fortunate!" Melvin declared.

Melvin informed Joseph that several men in our community have offered their assistance to help us repair all the damages. They will come to Deer Island in a few days, when the weather has dried up the ground a little.

August 11, 1856 (Monday Night)

We shared our experiences over the supper table. We were all grateful that the ordeal was now over. Repairs will be minimal. Joseph feels there will be no need for outside assistance; he believes that with the help of Melvin and his sons, the Addisons will be able to manage.

After a few hours of reflection and sharing our emotions, we all grew weary and decided it was time to retire. As I lay in bed, I prayed for God to be merciful to those who were less fortunate, as sleep overwhelmed my thoughts.

August 12, 1856 (Tuesday Early Morning)

A steamboat whistle sounded early this morning; a second whistle sounded about an hour later. Joseph and I exchanged looks of consternation. "Something is wrong! Something is terribly wrong; something very bad must have happened!" Joseph asserted.

After considering the matter, Joseph offered his thoughts: "Those poor souls who were on Last Island when the storm's fury was unleashed, what became of them? The onslaught stirred the seas and raised the water level high above the sandy ridge. How could anyone survive under those conditions? They had nowhere to run; they had to face the wind and sea naked, as if they wore no clothes. The very thought of what they must have been forced to endure frightens me," Joseph lamented.

Joseph has decided to go to bayou Shaver and pick up Melvin. They will head for the mainland to try to get more information. The boys and I will accompany him to the Lacache houseboat; there we will visit with Jennifer and her children while the men try to discover what has happened.

August 12, 1856 (Tuesday Midday)

Mr. E. B. Blanchard, owner of the Bayou Boeuf Landing, informed Joseph and Melvin that the fishing village and resort facilities on Last Island have been completely wiped out, with tremendous loss of life. Mr. Blanchard continued, "The *Southern Star* has not been seen since Friday morning. Two rescue vessels, the steamboats *North Star* and *Major Aubrey*, were dispatched at first light this morning to search for survivors. The true extent of the death toll and damages will not be known until firsthand knowledge can be received from someone who has returned from the site; someone who can substantiate all the rumors. God help us all!" Mr. Blanchard woefully proclaimed.

August 12, 1856 (Tuesday, Late Afternoon)

Melvin and Joseph arrived at the Lacache houseboat just before sunset. Joseph delivered the somber news: "The scene Melvin and I witnessed at Bayou Boeuf Landing is difficult to put into words," Joseph shared, as everyone listened intently to his report. "The first survivors were arriving aboard the *North Star*; the *Major Aubrey* was following close behind, so we moved our boat away from the dock site to make room for the two returning rescue vessels. The wailing and weeping of so many people who were waiting at the landing to discover the fate of friends and relatives who were vacationing on the island was difficult to bare. Unable to endure the morbid scene, I asked Melvin if we could leave for home. I had seen enough," Joseph volunteered, with his head bowed and tears flowing down his cheeks.

Melvin, a native Louisianan, said that this was the worst storm anyone could remember. "The loss of life can only be imagined; this was a horrible tragedy!" Melvin shared, visibly shaken by what has happened.

Joseph had made plans with Melvin to spend a few days on his houseboat. After a light supper, we continued to share our emotions; the mood was melancholic to say the least. After a prayer of thanksgiving, we asked God to lend comfort to those who have lost loved ones. We then retired for the evening.

August 15, 1856 (Friday)

We arrived back at Deer Island late yesterday evening, after spending a few days at Melvin's place. This morning, the absence of the sound of the customary steam whistle, reminded Joseph and I that changes are coming. No one can predict how long it will take for the people of our region to recover from this emotionally traumatic event.

John Quincy is fourteen years old today. We celebrated the event alone, thankful for the solace we found by embracing one another; there is strength in family. I know this is true. Joseph gave John a twelve-gauge Lefaucheux double barrel shotgun for his birthday. Imported from France, the gun sports outside hammers and side locks and uses pinfire cartridges. John Quincy was thrilled with the unexpected gift, and he immediately bragged how many ducks he would kill this winter.

Life can be so good, I thought, but it also presents challenges that can be bitter and hard to overcome. For whatever comes my way, this I know—I have a caring family that loves me and a relationship with the God of all the earth who loves me; with His help, I will be able to withstand the hard things as well as the good. May the Lord grant us mercy, for I know, by the Holy Scripture, that His mercy endures forever, amen.

ENDING A TRAGIC YEAR

November 24, 1856 (Thanksgiving Day: A Day of Reflection)

Our regular guests have arrived. Frenchy and Carey were unable to attend the festivities because he and his boat have been hired to help with the storm recovery efforts that are ongoing.

When Pauline arrived, we immediately expressed our condolences over the death of her father, Jean Laffite. Joseph and I pleaded with the fair maiden to come and live with us on Deer Island. She respectfully declined our offer, but I believe I detected a bit of indecisiveness in her response. Her home at Chacahoula sustained no damage from the storm. Joseph reminded her that the *little house* was her home and still unoccupied. She smiled at that notion and said, "Maybe someday, I don't know when, but maybe someday we will be neighbors," she teased.

The aftermath of the storm was the topic of discussion. Senator Peltier gave us the sordid details: "Just over two hundred people survived under horrific circumstances that can only be described as divine providence. Estimates of lives that were lost range from two to four hundred souls, we will never know for certain. Not a single structure remains on the island. The entire village was wiped out. Life on this part of the Gulf Coast will never be the same. The ship shoal light-boat has vanished; it is presumed to have sunk somewhere offshore in deep water," he informed us with a noticeably sad countenance.

After a day of feasting and sharing our heartfelt prayers of thanksgiving, we retired for the evening. Good night, Lord. Amen.

November 25, 1856 (Midmorning)

Melvin and Joseph are making plans to go to Plumb Bayou to inspect our trapping camp. If the structure has survived the storm, they will assess any damages and return with a materials list for making any necessary repairs. While they are at the site, they will scout for any signs of muskrat to determine if we will trap this winter.

November 25, 1856 (Evening)

Joseph and I joined our guests on the front porch of the *big house* for a night of storytelling. The entire evening was filled with wonderful accounts of true-life experiences and folk tales. It was an enjoyable evening.

The Henleys and the Peltiers will be heading for home in the morning. Pauline has decided to stay with us for a while longer. I cannot help but wish she would decide to move to the island to live with us. Pauline told us she would return to her home by way of the railroad. Joseph can deliver her to the Bayou Boeuf railway terminal when he goes to the mainland to buy provisions. From there, she will board the next train headed for the Chacahoula terminal, not more than a mile from her house. "I can walk home from there," she told us.

With attentive ears, we all listened as the mild-spoken Pauline paid tribute to her father. "My father died peacefully at his home in Alton, Illinois. His wife and son were beside him when he passed. I don't believe he ever told his family that he had a daughter living in the swamplands of Louisiana. Knowing Senator Peltier was a close friend of Congressman Adams (my father's dear friend and confidant) my father's family passed on the news to him, knowing the word would eventually reach his friends, the Addisons. The only reason I know anything is because the senator traveled to my home to give me the sad report," she told us.

After a brief pause, Pauline continued, "I've lived without my father for most of my life. I don't remember my mother at all. She abandoned me when I was young, leaving me in the hands of one of my father's friends in New Orleans. When I reached the age of fifteen, my father bought me a home in Chacahoula and asked Congressman Patrick J. Adams to care for me. My home and my friends have been my only source of security for as long as I can remember," she shared.

Pauline is a "chip off the old block" I sensed; her resilient defiance seems to spawn her desire to remain independent.

Pauline continued, "My father paid me a visit about ten years ago, it would be our last. He had just finished his commitment to the Addison family and he was proud to share with me all that he had accomplished on Deer Island. 'Patrick Adams would be proud of what I did for his family, my father told me.'

"Two years after my father visited me, I learned through a mutual friend that he moved north. In 1848, he moved from Campeche Island to Alton Illinois. He was born in 1782 at the small village of Pauillac, situated on the west bank of the Gironde estuary between Bordeaux and the Bay of Biscay in France. He was baptized in France in 1786. He lived a full and adventurous life and died at the age of seventy-two." With little sign of emotion, she ended her story.

Pauline is a woman of strong character; who else would be content living alone in the middle of a swamp? I will always admire her intestinal fortitude. After her tribute to her father, we disbursed to each our bedrooms for a good night's sleep. As I lay in bed my thoughts were of the gallant seaman who graced the island at a time of great need. I am glad I got to meet him; he was a man of integrity and loyal to his friends. I will miss him.

November 30, 1856

Melvin and Joseph returned from Camp Addison at Plumb Bayou. One of the giant oak trees was spared from being entirely uprooted by one of its huge branches, which thankfully touched the ground, stopping it from being toppled by the treacherous wind. A few planks from the walkways floated off with the high water; they were deposited some distance away in the marsh. "We were able to recover most of the boards while we were scouting the trapping grounds." Joseph informed us.

"The trees and brush must have shielded the camp from the strong winds. With little need for repairs, we will be able to trap this winter," Joseph proudly announced. "The muskrats are plentiful and begging us to undress them," Melvin teased.

Jennifer asked Pauline if she would like to come and spend the winter with us, but she declined the offer: "No, I will accompany Joseph to Bayou Boeuf railroad terminal when he goes to the city for provisions. I'll take the next train to Chacahoula terminal and walk the short distance home from there. It is time for me to get back home," she told us with a determined look on her face.

About midday, Joseph and the boys boarded the *Muskrat* and escorted Pauline to the mainland. As they were pulling away from our wharf, Pauline shouted, "I'll see you and Jennifer next Thanksgiving!" With a final wave, the boat disappeared, rounding the north bend in Deer Bayou and heading for Bayou Penchant.

FOUR YEARS LATER

December 25, 1860 (Christmas Day)

Joseph bought several kerosene lamps for the homestead. Mr. Blanchard, owner of the general store, told Joseph that these mineral petroleum lamps have only been on the market for a year; he had just received a large shipment by railcar from New Orleans. He told Joseph they are selling like hotcakes.

Joseph says the fuel burns clean and without the strong odor my lard oil lamp exudes when my wick is burning. The glass globe that protects the flame of each lamp from drafts also makes a properly adjusted wick shine much brighter than my old open-air lamp.

With my new lamp, I won't have to strain my eyes when I sit at my desk to write. I will stow away my lard oil lamp in the morning. It has served its purpose; I have no complaints, but brighter light is better.

Melvin and Joseph have decided to forego the trapping season this winter; fur prices are down, and there is little demand for musk-rat hides. Whenever this happens, Joseph is sure to pass the word to everyone that the winter celebrations on Deer Island will be forthcoming. "Everyone is welcome!" Joseph proclaims.

Our holiday guests have pledged to remain on the island until after our New Year's Day celebration. The winter holiday season has always been a source of great joy for all my family. Every year, our sons have more boys and girls with which to enjoy frolic. It is my favorite time of the year, and we will continue this tradition as often as we can.

When we go trapping, we are limited to only two days of festivities in the fall—All Saints' Day and Thanksgiving—then we head to Camp Addison for the winter. I must admit I would rather spend the winter months with our beloved friends than three months of processing furs for the market. I would not dare try to discourage Joseph; whatever he decides to do is fine with me.

Susan, Greta, and Pauline (my surrogate sisters) have added Jennifer Lacache to our close circle of female friends. Jennifer's daughter, Denise, is now twenty-two years old and radiantly beautiful, much like Pauline; she has become my fifth sister. I am proud to know them all. We are so compatible it is uncanny; we share a kindred spirit—there is no doubt about it.

Another year will soon pass us by; we have lived on Deer Island for twenty years. It doesn't seem that long. How time does fly! Living here has been most enjoyable, filled with unexpected events and overflowing with excitement.

Chapter Thirteen

WAR
IN THE BEGINNING

January 15, 1861

There has been much talk around the general store that there will soon be war. There seems to be some confusion about why Louisiana would join with other southern states to fight against those in the north. Joseph has tried in vain to explain to me the reasons behind all the turmoil. "Louisiana has not yet seceded from the union. Before any action is taken, it must be approved by the state legislature," Joseph informed me, looking somewhat dispirited by the news.

Only a wife and mother could feel the gambit of emotions created by such troubling news. My immediate reaction was fear; a fear that the men in my life might be forced to participate in this war, if war is declared. Lord, help us all!

February 1, 1861 (Early Morning)

An important meeting has been called to discuss the possibility of forming a militia of volunteers to protect our community if it becomes necessary. The rendezvous will be held at Bayou Boeuf Landing and General Store; the men have been asked to be there for noon.

Joseph and the boys are leaving for the mainland at first light to be sure they will arrive on time. I will stop off at the Lacache houseboat and spend time with Jennifer and Denise while the men conduct their business. These are troubling times; everyone I know is in a heightened state of disquietude. I do not like the way I am feeling. I won't know more until they have returned.

February 1, 1861 (Late Evening)

More bad news! Joseph says the Louisiana legislature has voted to break away from the Union. All the men have signed up for military service with the exception of Sanders, because he is too young. Joseph said that Frenchy will bring us more information when he comes to the island for his next visit.

March 30, 1861

Louisiana has officially declared itself to be a member of the Confederate States of America as of March 21, 1861. Volunteers have been asked to report to the Bayou Boeuf railroad terminal posthaste for immediate transport to a training facility at either Camp Moore on the Amite River, or to Camp Roman near New Orleans.

One can scantly imagine the anxiety I was feeling. Tears could not dispel my discomfort; I was getting stomach cramps. Fear gripped my heart. The uncertainty of what lay ahead was robbing me of my senses. What am I going to do? How will Sanders and I manage without the men? How soon must they leave? I posed many questions within myself trying desperately to maintain some degree of self-control. I must be strong for the boys, I reasoned.

Joseph, John Quincy, and Alexander Patrick were exhibiting a stoic resolve; they seem very strong and determined to do their duty (a family trait that has been passed down for several generations).

"The boys and I will face the challenges before us and, God willing, we will return at our earliest convenience," Joseph shared, trying to ease my concerns.

Melvin and all three of his sons are going to fight for the South. He and Joseph will relocate the houseboat to Addison Landing as soon as possible. Jennifer and Denise will move into the *big house* with Sanders and me for the duration of the conflict. Sharing the ordeal with the Lacache women will be a source of comfort and emotional support. I am glad for that arrangement; it will be mutually beneficial.

April 3, 1861

Frenchy and Carey will ferry all the men to the railroad terminal aboard the *Swamp Rat* this morning. They promised me and Jennifer that they would keep company with our men until they all board the train. Frenchy has pledged to keep us aware of any new information he can gather.

Hugs, kisses, and tears describe the scene at Addison Landing as the men boarded Frenchy's boat and went off to war. There was an empty feeling that overwhelmed me when the vessel rounded the north bend in Deer Bayou, heading upstream for Bayou Penchant.

Jennifer, Denise, Sanders, and I bowed down upon our knees and prayed for our loved ones safe return. After a few moments of silence, we arose and went up the *landing path* to drink a cup of coffee. "They are in God's hands now!" Denise lamented, expressing heartfelt concern for her father and three brothers. Jennifer and I know just how she feels.

Sanders was ambivalent, torn between the desire to be a little man, and the temptation to cry like the rest of us; his father would be proud to know that his son chose the former over the latter. We were all strengthened by his display of courage. He is a "chip off the old block," as the old saying goes.

July 15, 1861

Frency and Carey arrived about midmorning with Pauline Longere, my older sister. "Things are happening so fast I decided it would be unsafe for me to stay at home alone. All the able-bodied men have gone off to war, I felt abandoned," she commiserated, obviously distressed by what was happening around her.

Once all her belongings were stored in the *little house*, we all insisted she move into the *big house* with the rest of us. "There is no reason for us to separate now," I shared.

"Denise and Sanders will be like brother and sister by the time this trial is over," I spouted. "They have always enjoyed each other's company," I shared. Privately, I knew Sanders was a bit infatuated with Denise; I can't say I blame him. She's such a pretty girl.

"We will all try our best to weather this storm in as much peace and harmony as is humanly possible," Pauline interjected.

"We are glad you decided to come to live with us," I responded. "If it's all right with you, Pauline, I would like to start calling you sis."

"Okay, sis!" Pauline retorted with a broad smile.

July 17, 1861

Sanders reported that he saw two dugout canoes traveling downstream, heading for the Atchafalaya River. Each boat was being paddled by four men. It is not altogether unusual to see fishing or hunting parties traveling the backwater bayous and streams; we have seen them countless times. We have never had trouble with any of them. They pretty much stick to themselves, rarely paying anything but passive attention to us.

Personally, I have never seen an Indian face-to-face, but Pauline and Jennifer have both spoken to a few individuals at the trading posts. "Some speak French, some speak English, some speak French and English," Pauline stated.

Denise and Sanders volunteered that they had spoken to several Indians; they even know some of them by name. I was amazed by this new revelation.

"You don't get out enough, Josephine," Jennifer teased. "The Chitimacha Indians have a village at Charenton. Since most of the settlers who came to inhabit this region (their region) were English, in the process of time it was natural for the natives to learn to communicate in English," Jennifer informed me.

"In my tiny settlement, nearly everyone speaks French. The natives in our area, the Houmas Indians, have learned to speak French," Pauline added.

"It makes sense that the natives would begin to assimilate with the peoples who, not only have them outnumbered, but now occupy most of the land that may have once been their hunting and fishing grounds. It does seem like the white man's intrusion would instill a great deal of resentment, especially in the men who are old enough to remember the times before we arrived," I speculated, a little nervous over the degree of resentment that the natives may feel toward us. What better time to carry out revenge on us than now, when we reside here unprotected.

I told everyone that I was feeling insecure, knowing there are hunting and fishing parties traveling Deer Bayou, with no men here to protect us. "Under the right circumstances, and with little or no provocation, resentment could be turned into hatred," I suggested.

Pauline sensed that my imagination was getting the best of me and that the unfounded notions I had just postulated were clouding my thinking. In order to calm me down through reason, she began to voice her feelings on the matter. "Josephine, these local Indians have been living among us in peace. Missionaries who came here after the American Revolution were successful in converting many of them to Christianity. There have been no incidents of violence of which I am aware," she shared.

Jennifer was of the same opinion; Pauline and Sanders and Denise concurred, so I decided to put my unsubstantiated fears behind me. I was thankful for the consolation; secretly, I was hoping they were right.

August 1, 1861

Frenchy brought us unsettling news this morning: "Confederate forces under General Pierre Gustave Toutant de Beauregard fired on federally-held Fort Sumter in Charleston Harbor in South Carolina. Jefferson Davis has been elected president of the Confederate States of America. The war has officially started," he lamented.

This was somber news indeed! Frenchy continued, "Joseph and Melvin were dispatched to Camp Moore, just north of Amite for training. All the boys were sent to Camp Roman near New Orleans. That is all the information I have to share with you at this time," he told us with an unusually sad countenance.

"Cheer up, Frenchy! Though you are the barer of distressing news, we believe that all our men are in the Lord's hands; because we believe that God hears prayer, we know he will give us the strength to endure whatever happens next," I shared, trying to dispel the anxiety I was feeling.

"I admire your faith, Josephine! We need all the help that God can give us, so keep praying," he advised sincerely. "I will return to you as soon as I have more to report," he pledged.

ATCHAFALAYA NATIVES

September 1, 1861

My only encounter with the local Indians happened on my first trip downriver aboard Frenchy's boat, the *Swamp Rat*. A group of dark-skinned men were paddling a large dugout canoe across the waterway, passing near the front of our vessel, only a hundred yards ahead of us. My first impression was that they were unfriendly; I know they saw me wave, but they pretended not to see my friendly gesture. They just continued on their way and disappeared into the cypress swamp. That was twenty years ago.

Pauline says the Indians sell or trade their handcrafted merchandise at the trading posts, the general stores. They weave the dried leaves of the local palmetto palm into hats and baskets; they use the local clay to make jars and various types of pottery. They sell dried fish and smoke cured deer jerky; they dry the leaves of the sassafras trees, grind them into powder, and sell the *file* as a thickening ingredient for a local dish called ""file gumbo." They also trap muskrat and offer the hides for sale or trade, just as we do.

About midday today, we got an unexpected surprise. A man whose voice none of us recognized appeared at the foot of the steps of our front porch: "Hello!" he shouted. "Hello!"

We were seated at the dining table, eating the noon meal when the visitor hailed us to come out to greet him. Sanders was in the backyard gathering eggs from the chicken coop. Not recognizing the voice, we curiously walked to the front door to see who it was.

"My name is Macha Joe, and I brought you some fresh deer meat," the man announced with a pleasant smile.

I was dumbfounded, unable to speak. Pauline broke my silence. "Thank you for the meat, Joe, we all like roasted deer meat, and it will be consumed forthwith," she told him. Pauline reached for the meat, and Joe turned away and headed down the *landing path* for the bayou.

"Wait!" I shouted. "Would you like a cup of sassafras tea?" I asked in a loud voice.

Joe hesitated for a moment, then he returned to the porch. "I'll take a cup of hot coffee," he said. "I have three young men waiting for me at the mouth of your stream," he informed us.

Just then, Sanders returned from gathering the fresh eggs and immediately greeted Joe by name. "Hello, Macha Joe," he shouted, clearly excited over his friend's presence on the island.

"How are you, Little Chief?" Joe countered. "Would you mind going down to the bayou and inviting my men to come and drink coffee with us?" Joe asked my son. Looking first for my approval, Sanders then hurried down the *landing path* to fetch the remaining men in Joe's party.

"I know all of your men have gone to fight the war. I figured you could use some fresh meat," Joe offered as a good will gesture.

I told him we had a sufficient supply of poultry and pork, but we haven't had any deer meat in a while. "We appreciate the meat," I told him.

Macha Joe knew everyone but me. While they were exchanging greetings, three young men appeared suddenly behind us. Like Joe, they were wearing ordinary clothing; they seemed to be a bit coy; they remained silent.

Joe identified the men as three of his relatives: "From left to right, this is Mark, Luke, and John," he told us.

Sensing we were perplexed by the introduction, Joe began to explain, "Yes, Mark, Luke, and John are their Christian names. The English names are much easier for non-Indians to pronounce and remember. Their true Indian names would be foreign to your native tongue. These names work better for everyone," he shared.

All four men had black hair and olive skin; they were all young and handsome. Their only distinguishing feature was their jet-black hair.

Denise, twenty-three and beautiful, did not escape the wandering eyes of our new guests. I believe their attention made her blush. Jennifer did not seem to be bothered by all the admiring stares. After all, boy meets girl; what could be more natural than admiration at first sight, I mused.

"You didn't think Joe was my real name, did you, Mrs. Addison?" Macha Joe teased.

"Well, I honestly did not know," I told him. "Sometimes my husband affectionately calls me Josey; real name or nickname, either one identifies me," I shared.

"That is a good point," Joe asserted. "You can call us by our nicknames. Now we know each other," Joe declared with no hint of sarcasm.

"Did you know that *Atchafalaya* is a Choctaw Indian word? *Hacha* means *river* and *felaia* means *long*. So the literal meaning of the name *Atchafalaya* is Long River. Another Choctaw word is *Chacahoula*. *Chuka* means *home* and *hullo* means *beloved*, so the literal meaning of the name *Chacahoula* is *beloved home*," Joe proudly informed us.

Macha Joe continued, "We are Chitimacha *Indians; Chitimacha* literally means "people of many waters." Our village is located at Charenton. It's about twenty miles up the river from here."

"The Houmas Indians originally settled near Baton Rouge, but they migrated south and now live along the bayous southeast of here. The Choctaw word *humma* means *red*. *Iti* means *stick*. *Iti Humma*

303

means *red stick*. The French translation is *Baton Rouge*," Joe informed us, as he concluded our vocabulary lesson.

"Someday, I would like to bring my wife (squaw) to meet you, Mrs. Addison. Would that be okay?" Macha Joe queried. "My woman is a big talker. Her name is Cachita. She will not come here with me without an invitation," he submitted.

"All of you are welcome," I spouted without much forethought. I love company, but I did not intend to give the impression that they could relocate their village to Deer Island. I hope they did not misconstrue my offer of Southern hospitality.

Macha Joe did all the talking. Mark, Luke, and John were attentive, nodding their heads and smiling once in awhile. After a two-hour visit, Joe announced it was time to head back to the village. Denise and Sanders tagged along with them as they walked down the *landing path* to the bayou. About a half hour later, they returned; each was proudly carrying a blowgun.

Sanders, filled with excitement, enthusiastically reported what happened at the dock site. "Mark jumped in the canoe and picked up a blowgun and gave it to Denise. Luke did likewise, and he gave me one also. They made us promise to practice shooting using acorns. They said when we get good enough to accurately strike a small target we will be ready to learn how to hunt with them. Next time they come, they promised to teach us how to shoot darts at small game. The key to becoming a good hunter is practice, they told me."

"Denise, what do you think of Mark?" Pauline teased. "It might be a case of love at first sight," she posed, just to see her reaction.

Denise never blinked an eye; she is not shy. She answered respectfully, "He seems like a nice young man, but there are a lot of nice young men," she stated in a way that showed her maturity and clearly demonstrated that she was a virtuous woman.

The notion of anyone else loving Denise made the much younger Sanders squirm in an obvious exhibition of childhood jealousy. His face was red with embarrassment. He tried desperately to recover his composure, but the cat was out of the bag; Sanders is in love with Denise.

The Indian visit was the highlight of the day's activity. Everyone retired early this evening. I wish Denise was closer to Sanders in age; she is sure to unintentionally break his dear heart someday. She's going to make some lucky man a good wife. She is not lazy, and she would be a perfect daughter-in-law; some things are just not meant to be, I thought to myself. The owls are hooting in the distance wooing me to find peaceful repose in the comfort of my moss stuffed bed. Good night, dear Lord; keep a merciful eye on our men please. Amen.

THANKSGIVING 1861

November 23, 1861 (Thanksgiving Day)

Our annual celebration will seem strange this year. Frenchy and Carey arrived early this morning, surprising us with a freshly dressed turkey to roast in the oven and half a pig for roasting over the open hearth near the stream. The weather was perfect for the occasion. Though our loved ones are always in our thoughts and prayers, we will do our best to enjoy the day in their absence; I know they would want us to do just that.

To our surprise, Macha Joe and his wife Cachita hitched a ride aboard Frenchy's dory (his nameless craft is a small, flat-bottomed vessel with high sides and a sharp prow; having a single mast and lateen rigged sail, it is highly maneuverable and can be handled by one man). They came to spend Thanksgiving Day with us and they came bearing gifts; Cachita brought a clay jar filled with fish flakes (fish cured in salt and dried in the sun) and several woven baskets and hats made from dried palmetto leaves.

While Joe and his wife were enjoying coffee on the front porch of the *big house*, Frenchy and Carey were tending the fire in the open hearth and seasoning the pig for roasting. Pauline and Jennifer were getting the turkey ready for the oven in the kitchen.

Cachita began to share one of her recipes using fish flakes. "To make fish balls, the first step is to place a measure of the salty fish flakes into a bowl of fresh water to rehydrate them and to get some of the salt out. Let the flakes soak in the water for about an hour then strain out the water and spread the flakes out so they can dry. During this time, you can chop your onions and parsley. Beat a dozen eggs and add the chopped seasoning, mixing them in a bowl. Boil several pounds of fresh potatoes, cook until soft, drain, and allow them to cool. Take the fish flakes and add them to the egg and seasoning mixture and combine them with the potatoes in a large bowl. Using your hands, roll portions of the mixture into round balls, drop the balls into a kettle of hot grease, and cook until golden brown," Cachita instructed.

This recipe sounded familiar. Ta Lee, Jean Laffite's cook, prepared fish balls for us aboard the *Osprey* when we were invited to eat with him, I recalled. I asked Cachita to help me write down her recipe in my legend for safekeeping while Joe was boasting how good his wife's fish balls taste. If they spend the night with us, I will ask her to demonstrate the correct process for making the dish; we have all the ingredients. In fact, I believe we still have fish flakes that Captain Laffite gave us, stored in a large crock jar. I was told as long as they are kept dry, they last forever. We shall see.

Macha Joe and Cachita are in their mid-thirties; they still have no children. They are an affectionate couple. Since I did not know them well enough to ask, I refrained from mouthing my curiosity over the absence of kids.

"A turkey in the oven and pig roasting over the pit. We will be eating a good meal today!" I announced, trying not to show the mixed feelings that were troubling me inside. Our thoughts are with our loved ones; that can't be helped. Frenchy and Carey could sense our sullen dispositions, but they did their best to keep us from being depressed. They laughed and cut up to try to lighten up the atmosphere.

Frenchy told us that the Peltiers and the Henleys are staying close to home; they feel safer there amidst all the uncertainty. "News is slow to get around. We are all pretty much in the dark," he told us. "Each of us are fending for ourselves. The isolation this has caused is making life most unpleasant," he added.

"Confederate soldiers are building fortifications on both sides of the river (one at Brashear City and another at Berwick). They told me they were trying to prevent Union gunboats from going up river. It is frightening to see these defensive emplacements being constructed in our front yard," Frenchy informed us. "War is coming to the Atchafalaya River Basin!" he lamented.

"I hope those gunboats don't come!" I emphatically stated with tempered skepticism. Everyone within the sound of my voice followed my assertion with a heartfelt "Amen!"

The lack of information about our family members is vexing our spirits. Countless unanswered questions are racing through our minds: Where are they? How are they? Are they serving together? How long will the war last? Will we ever see them again? How can anyone rest in peace with such serious contemplation wearing down and weakening our resolve? I am afraid for our men.

There were times during the course of the day that everyone was silent; we each bowed our heads in silent prayer. There is nothing else we could do. The only thing that offered me some degree of comfort was that our guests have decided to stay with us on the island through New Year's Day. At least we will be able to try to lift one another's spirits through mutual sharing I reasoned.

January 1, 1862 (New Year's Day)

Our guests have been here for nearly six weeks. The time we spent together was filled with storytelling and we had the finest cuisine. Cachita, Pauline, and Jennifer (all fine cooks) taught me all they could about food preparation. It was fun. About midday, everyone prepared to leave for the mainland.

Macha Joe and Cachita will soon board Frenchy's dory and hitch a ride to the mainland where they have their canoe stored. From there, they will head back to their village at Charenton. During the course of their extended visit, they were able to change my nervous apprehension to a comfortable acceptance of the Indian presence in our region of South Louisiana. If all the Indians are like them, I will be proud to call them my friends.

As Frenchy pulled away from our landing, he pledged to keep us informed, "If I get any news, I will get out here and share it with you," he promised.

I told Joe that he and Cachita could come to visit whenever they are fishing or hunting in our area. "Sanders is excited about learning to hunt small game with the blowgun that Luke gave him. Maybe Mark might want to teach Denise how to shoot the one he gave her," I quipped.

Denise could not hide her embarrassment, as we all waved our final good-byes, and Frenchy's boat disappeared around the north bend in Deer Bayou, heading for the mainland by way of Bayou Penchant.

I could not dispel the feeling of melancholy as the day came to an end. As I record these last few lines, I pray for God to extend His mercy toward all of us. It's time for me to get to sleep; I can only hope for a peaceful repose.

January 15, 1862

This has been a very cold winter. The temperature has been below freezing for days. Early this morning before sunrise, Pauline assisted Sanders in loading Joseph's rifle, and they went on a hunt together. They left before the break of day to try to shoot a deer. Pauline will assist him by directing his aim to hit the target; the gun is heavy for a seven-year-old boy to hold steadily in the shooting position. This will be his first hunt with his father's rifle.

The sound of Joseph's Brown Bess Kentucky Long Rifle rang out like the boom from some cannon in the distance about nine this morning. Jennifer, Denise, and I are anxiously awaiting the results. If they were successful, we will dress the deer and hang the meat from the jib pole of our smokehouse to drain some of the blood from the carcass. This cold weather is perfectly suited for hanging meat, I thought.

Sure enough, Sanders and Pauline returned with a young buck with four points on his rack of horns. "He shot him dead!" Pauline proudly boasted, building up confidence in my youngest son's heart.

"You are going to be a good hunter, Sanders. Your father will be proud of you when he learns your first hunt produced a young male deer," I lauded. "We are all proud of you!" Jennifer and Denise declared with one voice.

"Now we have to go to work and clean the beautiful creature," Jennifer confidently suggested. "I have had plenty experience cleaning Melvin's deer," she told us. In a little over an hour, with a little help from the rest of us, the animal was dressed, split down the middle of the carcass, and hung by its legs from the pole that protrudes through the rear gable of the smokehouse.

We dined on Pauline's rabbit stew; that girl makes the best stew. After the tasty meal, Sanders went down the *landing path* to check the boats. Denise, Pauline, Jennifer, and I resumed our sewing. We have several yards of fabric and many balls of yarn. We have been spending our afternoons sewing and knitting clothing and quilts for our personal use. This activity has helped us pass the time and it is far more fun than tedious. There is genuine satisfaction knowing that we are being productive. The quilts and blankets will be put to good use by our families. The sewing sessions have been a good nerve pill.

GLOOMY NEWS

July 30, 1862 (Midmorning)

Frenchy arrived about 9:00 a.m. to bring us news from the mainland. He came alone, having sailed his dory to the island without difficulty. This was the first time he attempted to sail alone. He told us that Carey Trudeau, his trusted and faithful deckhand (more like his adopted son), left for Camp Pratt on the twelfth of June. After a month or so of training, they will be sending him north to the battlefront.

"Where is Camp Pratt?" I asked.

"Camp Pratt is located about six miles northwest of New Iberia. Because there is a shortage of fighting men, the Louisiana Legislature has passed the Conscription Act on April 16, 1862. All able-bodied men from eighteen to thirty-five are ordered by law to come to the aid of their Southern brothers," Frenchy informed us.

"Carey is forty-five. He volunteered to join his friends in the war effort. I am sixty-five years old. If I am needed, I will go and do what I can for the Confederate cause," Frenchy pledged.

"Godspeed, Carey!" I proclaimed. "We have all become closer than friends. The mutual sharing of all our life's experiences, and the countless hours we have enjoyed keeping each other company has made us a close-knit extended family," I added.

"I hope Carey is sent to join forces with our men, wherever they are," I stated. "Is there any more news?" I asked.

With a look of consternation, Frenchy bowed his head and somberly announced that New Orleans surrendered to Federal troops on April 25, 1862. "Farragut then turned his attention toward Baton Rouge, moving his warships upriver. Confederate troops surrendered to the Union forces at Baton Rouge on May 12, 1862," he told us, showing signs of surprise and grief.

"Surrender so soon!" I shouted. "What could have gone wrong?" I asked.

"Only God knows! There is more bad news to report" he told us. "I have been informed that there are federal gunboats on anchor in Atchafalaya Bay. No doubt they intend to move upriver to give our boys hell," Frenchy asserted with a disappointed look on his face.

"Some of our men removed the channel markers in the river. Those Yankee gunboats will have a hard time maneuvering around the sandbars with no way to find the proper channel," Frenchy shared with a hearty laugh over this small confederate victory. "At least our boys are trying to make it hard on those men in blue," he added. "I am sorry, but that is all the news I have to share with you," he concluded.

"It's a sad time for the south. It's a sad time indeed!" I mumbled in muffled tones. "How gloomy can things get?" I asked, not expecting any response and not receiving any. It is indeed gloomy news, I reasoned. My heart is nearly overwhelmed with sorrow. God help us all!

September 8, 1862

Macha Joe and his three young relatives showed up with several baskets full of fresh corn and a fully dressed deer cut in quarter sections this morning. He handed me a clay jar filled with powdered sassafras (gumbo file) that his wife Cachita made for us.

Sanders went straight to the smokehouse with Mark, Luke, and John, to hang the fresh deer meat. Mark brought an eagle's feather with him and he slid it through Sander's hair, calling him "Little Chief." I wish everyone could have seen the grin on that boy's face; he immediately began to boast about the young buck he had killed with his father's gun. Denise and the boys congregated on the back porch of the *big house*, occupying the two swings.

I could not help wondering if sparks were beginning to fly between Denise and Mark. Sanders sat between them on the swing they shared, trying to shield his true love from any possible advances that the handsome Mark might attempt. Mark does seem to be a nice young man, and I detected a sparkle in Jennifer's daughter's eyes. "Poor Sanders," I mused silently as I watched him through the kitchen door.

After brewing fresh coffee, I joined the rest of my guests on the front porch to catch up on any news that Joe may be able to provide, serving everyone a cup of the steaming hot beverage.

Joe brought no news with him except for new regulations that he and his people are being subjected to. "The Indians of my village don't venture very far from home anymore for fear of the ongoing struggle that they are witnessing around them. My people have been warned to stay away from the soldiers from either side. If we obey this rule we have been promised that no harm will befall us. Cachita and I waited for a safe time, and we slipped through their lines before sunrise this morning," he shared. "We were in no real danger," he confidently asserted.

Macha Joe, his wife, and the three young men they brought to the island with them, will spend a few days in the *little house*. They vowed to keep their promise to take Denise and Sanders on a rabbit hunt with their blowguns; that should be interesting. I know they will have fun trying.

The good Lord knows how to lend comfort to those who are in distress, I thought to myself. God has blessed me with sons and with good friends—what more can I ask of Him? Thank you Lord for all of them, bless them and keep them from harm, have mercy on us all. Amen.

THANKSGIVING 1862

November 27, 1862 (Thanksgiving Day)

Sanders, Denise, Pauline, Jennifer, and I will celebrate Thanksgiving alone this year. We haven't seen Frenchy since the thirtieth of July. We can only hope that he is all right.

Last week, Macha Joe and his wife came for an afternoon visit. He informed us that Union gunboats occupy Berwick Bay; Confederate forces have been driven from the area. He told us that for now, it will be too dangerous for him to travel this far from the safety of his village. He promised to come again as soon as it is safe enough to do so.

I asked Joe if he knew anything about Frenchy. He told me that Union troops hijacked his boat; he has not seen the *Swamp Rat* for at least a couple of weeks. Joe said they also confiscated Frenchy's dory; he has no way to come to the island anymore.

In spite of all our woes, we determined with one accord not to allow our troubles to keep us from giving thanks: "Thank you, God Almighty, for your countless blessings. May you bless and keep us. May you give us the strength and the faith to endure whatever is yet to come. Amen." Then everyone said, "Amen."

January 1, 1863 (New Years Day)

Another holiday alone! Chicken gumbo, thickened in each bowl with a spoonful of Cachita's powdered sassafras, is today's entire menu—simple to make, but pleasing to the palate.

We pray for peace, so our men can return home. Lord, have mercy on us all. Amen.

FAMILY REUNION

January 23, 1863 (A Big Surprise)

Frenchy appeared unexpectedly at the front door of the *big house* this morning, shouting, "I have a big surprise for you! Melvin and Joseph have come home safe," he announced.

We rushed to the front porch to greet our husbands; they were standing on the porch in their gray Confederate uniforms. They looked worn out and they were both thin, but they were in good spirits.

Pauline just stood there with Denise and Sanders, watching the homecoming celebration. Jennifer and I were not emotionally prepared for this wonderful reunion; we shared tears of joy as we embraced our war heroes.

Everyone was excited; love was triumphant over grief. It was joy personified! After several hours filled with small talk, lighthearted stories, and laughter, the euphoria waned. Joseph began to expound on the reality of both current and past events.

"Confederate forces have retaken the lower Teche, Berwick Bay, and the lower Atchafalaya River, including Atchafalaya Bay. Those areas are now free from Union gunboats. The Lafourche railroad crossing has been cleared of northern troops. In the larger scheme of things, these are token victories, but they are victories none the less. Once this region was secured, our commanding general, General Green, handed us our discharge papers. He told us to go home. After a final salute, we hurried over to Bayou Boeuf Landing where we eventually located Frenchy. We boarded his dory and headed for home and here we are!" he was glad to announce.

"Thank God you two are safely home!" I proclaimed with solemn gratitude. Joseph and Melvin served together throughout their time in the army. They had nothing to report regarding any of our sons; that was disheartening to say the least. Now all we can do is hope and pray for their safe return.

If I recorded all the sentimental expressions that were exchanged this day, I would run out of paper and ink. Weary from all the excitement, we all retired early. My final entry for the day is a heartfelt prayer: "Lord, thank you for bringing our husbands home safely. I respectfully ask that you do the same for our sons. Amen."

July 1, 1863 (Alexander Returns Home)

Frenchy brought our son, Alexander Patrick, home about midafternoon. The joy we all felt for his safe return was short-lived and was soon turned to sorrow and grief; not because he was walking with a limp, but because of the news he brought home with him. We gathered on the porch to listen to his somber report.

"John Quincy and I had three months of training at Camp Roman near New Orleans. Melvin's three sons were trained there with us. John Quincy and I were dispatched by rail to Corinth, Mississippi, around the first week in August of 1861. There, we served under the command of Colonel Alfred Mouton charged with defending the railroad crossing at that location. This key junction is where the Memphis and Charleston Railroad crosses the Mobile and Ohio Railroad. Our commander informed us that this crossing was the most important railroad junction in the Confederacy. It is the main supply line from the Trans-Mississippi to our armies in the east."

Alexander continued, "On April 6 and 7, 1862, we engaged Union forces at Shiloh, a battle that resulted in the wounding of our commanding officer. After Shiloh, John Quincy and I were redeployed to strengthen Confederate forces at Corinth, twelve miles to our south.

"Under General Earl Van Dorn's command, we were engaged in heated battle with Union forces over the Corinth Mississippi railroad junction. After a two-day struggle, October 3 and 4, 1862, we withdrew from our position, falling back to reconnoiter and regroup late the second night," Alex stated.

"After the Battle of Corinth, John Quincy and I were sent to join General A. P. Hill's division, under the command of Robert E. Lee. At the Battle of Chancellorsville, April 27–May 3, our commanding officer, General Hill, was severely wounded. J. E. B. Stuart took command, and we followed his lead. On the last day of the battle, May 3, 1863, John Quincy was killed. Seven days later, I was wounded during a small skirmish with Union troops about fifteen miles from the battlefield at Chancellorsville. I was wounded on May 10, 1863, transferred to a hospital unit where I was treated, and eventually I was discharged from military service. Here I am! I am a bit shaken, but I am glad to be home," he sadly declared.

Melvin asked Alexander if he had any news regarding his three sons. Alexander told him that after they left Camp Roman, they were separated. All he could say was that Troy, Terry, and Terrence were sent north by rail.

The mood around the homestead can only be described by using one word: "Melancholy!" The day was spent in near silence, as we all tried to cope with the bad news. May God help us all!

July 5, 1863 (a Day of Reflection)

Today, Joseph, and Melvin decided to share some of their wartime experiences. I guess this will be a part of the healing process; they feel they have to express the details of what they went through with someone.

Joseph began, "Melvin and I were trained for six months at Camp Moore. In October of 1862, we were dispatched to Vicksburg. We remained there until we were sent to join the Eighteenth Louisiana Regiment under the command of General Alfred Mouton in January of 1863. General Alfred Mouton was promoted after recovering from the injuries he sustained at Shiloh on April 7, 1862. He was promoted from colonel to brigadier general."

Joseph continued, "General Mouton was in command of several small infantry companies in addition to the Eighteenth Louisiana Regiment. Our troop strength was about fourteen hundred men. We fought together in battles from Lafourche Crossing to Irish Bend along the Teche.

"With the coordinated assistance of General Green and Colonel J. P. Major, General Mouton succeeded in clearing the entire region of all Federal troops. As of June 24, 1863, Confederate forces once again controlled the area from Lafourche Crossing to Irish Bend, securing the entire Atchafalaya River basin," Joseph informed us.

"The plan for the Confederate attack was orchestrated by Major General Richard Taylor, who is in command of all Confederate forces in the District of Western Louisiana. He is the son of President Zachary Taylor and the son-in-law of Confederate President, Jefferson Davis," Joseph added.

"On June 25, 1863, Melvin and I were discharged from military service by General Green and sent home," Joseph announced, concluding his report. Once Melvin told us that he had nothing to add to Joseph's account of their military action, he and Jennifer walked the *landing path* to their houseboat for some time alone.

Denise decided to keep Pauline and I company, allowing her mother and father some time for privacy. Pauline shared an hour or so with me and Joseph before going to rest in her new home, the *little house*. She invited Denise to accompany her to give Joseph and me a little space to gather our thoughts, as we try to adjust to all that has happened.

Alexander and Sanders spent the day practicing with his blow-gun; Little Chief, proudly wearing his eagle feather, pretended to be a young Indian brave hunting for his diner while Alexander sat around watching him try.

Joseph and Sanders fell asleep early, retiring shortly after supper. I was the last one awake when my pen ran out of ink and my body told me it was time to shut it down. Good night, Lord. Amen.

August 30, 1863 (More News)

Frenchy arrived with more bad news from the warfront. Vicksburg surrendered to Union troops on July 3, 1863. Port Hudson fell into union hands six days later on July 9, 1863. He had no further information to share; no news on Carey Trudeau or any of the Lacache boys. "Sometimes no news is good news," Frenchy posed.

That notion was well-intended, but it provided no consolation for Melvin, Jennifer, or Denise. I could see the torment in their faces. It is a hard thing to endure; all three of their sons remain unaccounted for. Two of my sons went to war; one will never come home. In time, our loss will be just a sad memory; the war is over for Joseph and me.

Once again, I began to question what went wrong. No one dreamed the war would last this long; certainly, no one considered that we might lose the war. I never thought I would lose one of my sons. What a sad commentary for the nobility of the south. I have nothing more to record. It is difficult to think of anything else. This is one of the many consequences for waging war I reasoned.

January 1, 1864 (Terry Lacache Comes Home)

Another hero came home today. Running to embrace his parents and his sister, Terry Lacache arrived safely home. The joy of the homecoming was short-lived. We could tell by the look on his face that what he was going to share would bring with it much grief. With tears flowing down his cheeks, Terry began to share with us the source of his inner pain.

"My brothers and I were sent to the same training facility as the Addison boys. We stayed together at Camp Roman near New Orleans for three months. After our training was complete, we were separated. John Quincy and Alexander Patrick were sent north on one train. Troy, Terrence and me were sent north on a different train, and to a different destination. We never saw each other after training camp.

"All three of us Lacache boys were sent to Virginia. We were under the command of General Robert E. Lee and assigned to General Longstreet's division. At the Battle of Gettysburg, we were separated—I remained with Longstreet. Troy was assigned to General Pickett. Terrence was assigned to General Ewell's command.

"There is no easy way to share what happened next, Mom and Dad," Terry mournfully related. "Terrence was the first to be killed. He died during the Battle for Cemetery Hill on July 1, 1863. Two days later, Troy was killed during Pickett's charge up Culp's Hill and Big Round Top on July 3, 1863.

"I survived Gettysburg and went on to fight under Longstreet at Chickamauga (September 19–20, 1863). I fought at the Battle of Chattanooga (November 4–24, 1863). I fought at the Battle of Knoxville (November 29–December 4, 1863). It was on December

4, the last day of the battle, that I was wounded sufficiently to be discharged and sent home," Terry concluded his woeful story.

There was complete silence for at least a half-hour when Terry proclaimed, "I am glad to be alive! I am deeply sorry that John Quincy, Troy, and Terrence aren't here to celebrate my homecoming. Now we must learn to accept what has happened. We are all suffering from the casualties of war," he told us.

The grieving process began anew—everyone broke down and cried. "Melancholy!" That is what it is. "Melancholy!" That describes how we all were feeling. How hard can life be?

As I prepared to retire for the evening, I thought about the horrors of this War Between the States. How much pain are mothers and fathers in the North and the South being subjected to; I can't begin to imagine. I know when I put my pen to rest, that finding peace within will be hampered by many challenges; I know it will be difficult to fall asleep. Melvin and Jennifer were devastated by today's news, and understandably so; I can see their mournful faces even now. Dear Lord, give us all the strength we need to endure the aftermath of this senseless war; amen. Lord, help us all!

April 17, 1865 (The Conflict Ends)
Frenchy brought us the news we had hoped and prayed one day would come. The war has ended.

On April 10, 1865, General Lee surrendered to General Grant at Appomattox Courthouse. "Hurrah! The war is over at last!" Frenchy loudly proclaimed. It was difficult to get excited over the news. Yes, we were all happy it was over, but now we will have to live with the terrible memories this senseless exercise in futility has forced upon us.

Who can help pondering, each in his own way, what justification can be found for the carnage? It seems everyone has lost at least one relative, or some friend or acquaintance during the course of this unfortunate historical event.

My personal feelings I will share: War for what? Did anyone really win? How many men had to die? They died for what? What now? Whom did this struggle benefit? I am angry! This is how I am feeling right now! I can't dispel the anger; disappointment has taken control of my mind! The process of healing will take a lifetime. I don't know if anyone can recover the quality of life that existed before this disaster struck! I am mad! I just don't feel like writing anymore.

June 5, 1865 (Our Last Hero Returns Home)

Frenchy's deckhand and a close member of our extended family, Carey Trudeau, arrived at Bayou Boeuf railroad terminal last night. He and Frenchy arrived at the island about midmorning. Carey came through the war without a scratch, though he told us there were many close calls. He told us he served under the command of General Hood for most of his time in service.

Frenchy asked him to share his experiences with us, and so he did. "Under the command of General Hood, I fought in countless battles; the last battle under him was the Battle for Atlanta."

Carey continued, "After Atlanta, I was reassigned to General Pickett's brigade. We suffered a defeat at the hands of the Union commander, General Sheridan at a place known as Five Forks on April 1, 1865. I was taken prisoner and held until April 10 when Lee surrendered to Grant, ending the war. I am glad it is over, but it will be hard for me to forget the things I have witnessed. It is good to see all of you. I am glad I made it home. I love each and every one of you," he sincerely shared as he concluded his report.

What could I add that would be meaningful, after hearing Carey Trudeau's story of this never-ending war? The shooting has ended, but the war continues in our minds. When will it ever be behind us? Only Almighty God knows!

AFTERMATH OF THE CIVIL WAR

September 5, 1865 (Legal Matters)

Our good friend and legal advisor, Senator Irving Peltier, and his wife, Susan, came for a visit today. The topic for discussion was the disposition of the Adams estate following the Civil War. The Senator began his briefing by giving us the entire picture of what has transpired since our last meeting so we could fully understand our present financial situation.

The senator began: "By October of 1861, most if not all, Louisiana banks had transferred their hard currency (gold and silver on deposit at each establishment) to either Richmond, Virginia, or Atlanta, Georgia. The primary reason this was done was to finance the Confederate cause. Secondarily it was done to prevent the assets from being seized should Federal forces prevail in the conflict, especially along the Mississippi River.

"In exchange for the hard currency, the banks in New Orleans and Baton Rouge were issued Confederate War Bonds. Confederate money (paper currency) was already in circulation before New Orleans and Baton Rouge were occupied by Union troops.

"In late 1861, the Union blockade at the mouth of the river began to have its desired effects. Food and commodity prices were soaring, cotton bales were being destroyed by the ton to keep them out of Union hands. The Louisiana economy had virtually come to a standstill.

"By the time Union forces took total control of the Mississippi (New Orleans fell on April 25, 1862, Baton Rouge fell on May 12, 1862, Vicksburg fell on July 3, 1863, Port Hudson fell on July 9, 1863) the Louisiana economy had entirely collapsed.

"As someone more astute than I am put it: 'for the South to separate itself from the Union was tantamount to suicide.' I am persuaded now that his assertion has proved to be correct. The war was a tragic error in judgment by our leaders.

"Confederate paper money was losing its value, almost from the time it was issued. During the war, one person who endured the Federal occupation of New Orleans said that the use of Confederate money reminded her of the Continental currency issued during the American Revolution when seventy-five dollars of that currency was exchanged for one silver dollar.

"After the war, the Confederate War Bonds issued to Louisiana banks on behalf of their depositors, wasn't worth the ink used to print the paper it was written on.

"When Union forces began to make demands on Louisiana's elected government (which to true Southerners meant acting against their own people), I resigned my Senate seat and returned to Morgan City (Brashear City) to attempt to resume my law practice. My home and plantation escaped destruction, but all my slaves fled to regions unknown. My cane fields are growing up in weeds.

"William Henley's plantation will resume sugarcane production next year. Union activity in the Houma area was limited. Consequently, his operations were spared destruction. The best thing that happened to William is that his labor force (formerly referred to as slaves) remained on his plantation for the duration of the war. Not a single one of his workers left; probably because he had a good relationship with them before the war broke out. Some speculate that since the union army never occupied the area, there was no one to coax them into leaving. William's workers are now referred to as indentured servants. They will be paid for their services and they are free to leave if ever they should desire to do so.

"Both William and I had the foresight to withdraw modest amounts of money from our bank holdings before hell broke loose. We both have enough cash to pay the newly imposed land taxes. Unlike many who were not so diligent, we will be able to keep what we own. Since we have no money to withdraw from our former bank holdings, we will be starting all over again—that's not such a bad thing. At least we have something to start with.

"A full recovery is not in the immediate future for any of us, but we are confident and cautiously optimistic, that someday we will make a full recovery. One of our good friend William's favorite old sayings is the adage 'Slow and steady wins the race!' That will be our credo from here on down the road.

"As the attorney representing the Adams estate, and also with the charge of looking after Pauline, I will now present you with the status of your holdings. Pauline, I will deal with your affairs first— your house was burned to the ground by Union troops when they fought with our boys for control of the railway system. The land absent the home is of little value. I have enough cash resources from your father that I keep in a safe at my office to pay the taxes on your property until it can be sold. There is a modest amount of money for your necessities, if you should have any in the future.

"The Adams estate had resources in New Orleans banks and banks in Baton Rouge, as did Pauline Laffite. As I did for her, I also did for you. I have enough money in a safe at my office to continue paying your property taxes for the next few years. The bulk of Patrick Adams' cash assets—a sum in excess of 250,000 dollars—were exchanged by those banks for Confederate War Bonds. Those bonds that had been relegated to a stack of worthless paper were promptly burned by the Union occupiers. In a sense, this action was a blessing. It saved the bond-holders the pain associated with watching their entire savings go up in smoke.

"I was already aware that Pauline had decided to move to Deer Island. In an earlier discussion of previous legal matters, I remember that the Addison family donated the *little house* to her. In so doing, that made her a de facto member of the Addison family. It is now a foregone conclusion that she will be living on Deer Island.

"The good news, as I see things, is that you have nearly achieved self-sufficiency through the ways that you have developed and managed the homestead. I see no reason why you should not be able to continue to maintain the lifestyle to which you have grown accustomed. Continue to use your land. As I have told you before, 'Possession is nine-tenths of the law for land ownership in Louisiana.' Never forget that important condition, and you will be just fine.

"Reports I have received from people who know, maintain that though Louisiana will struggle to regain some degree of economic recovery, we are far better off than many of our Confederate brothers to the east. Virginia, Georgia, and Alabama are reported to be in ruins. Reconstruction will be a *hard scrabble* for sure. With God's help, we will persevere and eventually, we will overcome our financial losses.

"Many former affluent Southerners are now paupers, destitute for money, and devoid of property they once possessed. For them, it is a sad state of affairs. Considering the cost everyone paid in blood, and the prospect of having to cope with horrific nightmares that can scarcely be imagined, Louisiana should have never seceded from the

Union. It has been often stated that hindsight is better than foresight. The tragic consequences of that truism will remain with us for our lifetimes.

"The North paid a high price in blood as well. The victory was certainly tempered by the grief that those families are now forced to endure. They lost many family members and friends just as we did. Someday historians will record that this struggle was a sorrowful and costly exercise in futility. Men should have been able to come to agreeable terms without the slaughter of those they were elected to serve. It is difficult to imagine the carnage inflicted by both sides. I don't believe anyone with a conscience can say, 'It was all worth it!' I for one can't see how!

"The freed slaves will suffer through the changes like everyone else—the transition may be more difficult for them. No doubt some who were fairly treated on the plantations will someday long for the security that was provided by their former masters—food, clothing, medicine, and shelter. In stark contrast, they will now find themselves under a new taskmaster, the United States government. Lord, help us all!

"Melvin Lacache and his family will weather the storm. I know they are some of your closest friends. Their lifestyle, like your own, will be little affected by the turmoil that is sure to ensue.

"John Quincy Addison, the Lacache boys, and many others have been forever lost. Sleep is pleasurable and a bed is the pauper's paradise, but there will be many who will lay on their pillows with faint hearts most sorrowful. Grief will be difficult to erase.

"This winter, William and his family, and me and my family, are making plans to return to Deer Island to be with you for the joyous celebrations of the Christmas and New Year's holidays. We are hoping we can rekindle the happiness we once may have taken for granted.

"William Henley III was incarcerated in Andersonville prison for a year after he was wounded at Gettysburg. He is recovering from a severe leg wound. He was spared amputation, but he will always walk with a severe limp. Young William was a witness to much carnage during the war. He believes there's no justification for complaining. He is just glad that he survived.

"I believe I have given you a full account of everything I know, and I would now be happy to answer any questions you might have."

Since the only subject that was not mentioned was the status of the property along the lower end of Bayou Du large, Joseph asked Mr. Peltier to address that matter. He informed us that there was enough money to continue paying the taxes, but it would be wise to try to find some way to demonstrate use and ownership of the property there. Harvesting trees was one of his suggestions. He and Joseph agreed to collaborate on making sure the land holding there would remain secure for future use.

After a good meal and a time of leisurely conversation, our friend and legal advisor departed for the mainland.

THANKSGIVING 1865

November 21, 1865 (Thanksgiving Day)
Today is more a reunion than a festive occasion. Appropriately, we celebrated with a feast; we all have much to be thankful for. Our guests for the day's activities were as follows—the Henleys, the Peltiers, Macha Joe and his wife Cachita, Mark (Denise's boyfriend), Frenchy and Carey, and the Lacache family. Pauline is my surrogate sister and no longer considered my guest, since she is now a member of our family in the truest sense.

Greta gave me news regarding the state of affairs on her plantation and the situation with their son: "William H. Henley III rose from the rank of first lieutenant to colonel before resigning his commission after the war. He was wounded at Gettysburg and imprisoned at Andersonville for a little over a year. He is recovering from his wound. His family is doing well. Many of the slaves who were freed by President Lincoln decided to remain on the Sugarland Farms Plantation with us. They are now considered tenant farmers. They sharecrop, using some of the proceeds from the sales to pay their rent."

Senator Peltier reported that his son, and all his grandchildren, escaped harm during the conflict. His son and three grandsons all served in the Confederate army, but did not see a lot of action. "My family was spared, thank God!" he lauded.

Before our main course was served at the dinner table, Joseph prayed this heartfelt prayer: "This is a time for healing, a time to remember how precious life is, a time to be thankful for all that God has given to us, a time to petition God for the faith and courage to endure whatever is ahead for us. Amen."

The remainder of the day was spent enjoying each other's company and sharing our love for one another. Is this not all one can expect for oneself? I believe it is.

William Henley brought me a special gift on this holiday celebration. He was visiting friends at a little settlement known as Tigerville; there is a tribal village of Houmas Indians living there. He had an artist sketch for me a portrait of an Indian princess.

The oldest of three daughters, Callie's father is the Houmas chieftain. The images associated with her portrait give a perspective of native tribal life in Terrebonne Parish. Princess Callie looks dignified in her customary attire and she is a credit to her people; she is quite beautiful! I hope to meet her someday.

November 22, 1865 (A Little Ray of Sunshine)

Pauline Longere has decided to become a permanent resident of Deer Island. She intends to sell her property at Chacahoula as soon as Senator Peltier can secure a buyer. She has been living in the *little house* since Melvin and Joseph returned from their military service. Since her home was destroyed during the war, she will remain a resident here; we're glad to have her, she's been such a blessing.

Princess
Callie

Tigerville
1865

Melvin and Jennifer left for home shortly after the noon meal; they relocated their houseboat to its mooring site on Bayou Shaver last month. Denise and Terry promised they would visit us more often. We have made no decision on the trapping season as yet. Our fur buyer, Mr. Augustine Champagne, is exploring the market to see if furs will be in demand; it may be too early to resume ordinary commerce so soon after the war. Melvin will keep Joseph informed.

Trapping season or not, Melvin and Joseph are planning to spend a few weeks at Camp Addison this winter; our families can share some leisure time together away from our homes. We will take a much needed vacation.

Macha Joe, Cachita, and Mark left for their village at Charenton this morning. They will visit us from time to time when they are hunting in the lower Deer Bayou area.

Frenchy and Carey said they would see us next spring.

Everyone has left for home. Joseph, Alexander Patrick, and Sanders are asleep; Pauline just left for her house next door after enjoying a final cup of hot coffee on the front porch of the *big house* with me. Now, it's just me and my pen once again. I am tired and weary from grief; it is hard for me to continue writing in my legend when there are few good things to share. On that note, I end this day writing: "Good night, Lord. Amen."

(A final note from twelve-year-old Nora Addison. This was the final entry in my great-grandmother's diary. No one knows why; maybe the grief of losing a son in the Civil War was too hard for her to bear; only God knows.)

Epilogue

Since 1916, when I first received my Great-grandmother Josephine Addison's diary, I was inspired to begin a diary of my own. Over the past five years, I have learned much more of my family's history by carefully listening to the stories old people tell. I write down all that I can from memory; I then read the text to the person who told me the story. Once I am sure I have the right information, I transcribe my notes into my written legend. I have found this endeavor extremely gratifying, especially when I am praised for its contents.

Nora Addison, autumn 1921

INTRODUCTION TO VOLUME TWO

THE YEAR IS 1921

September 17, 1921

One hundred and three years ago on September 17, 1818, my Great-grandmother Josephine Addison was born. I thought it would be a good day to invite the reader to continue to follow the

Addison family legacy by reading volume two entitled: "Deer Island in Autumn: Carrying on the Legacy."

November 22, 1865, was the final entry in Josephine Addison's diary. One can only speculate over why she stopped writing. Even though her recorded legend ended shortly after the Civil War, the life and times of the Addisons has been preserved in the oral tradition.

I made fifteen years old on August 6, 1921. My family and I are looking forward to the trapping season again this year. It has been a family custom for three generations to share the winter holiday season with family members who live on Deer Island, founded in 1840 as a retirement haven for my great-uncle, Patrick J. Adams.

I especially enjoy time spent sitting on the veranda of the "big house" listening attentively to the storyteller whose turn it is to share some story with the captive audience—verifiably true or pure imagination. It is great fun; the older members of my family are excellent storytellers. I wonder what stories will be shared this year.

"Deer Island in Autumn, Carrying on the Legacy" is my story, the story of Nora Addison and my experiences during the holiday season with family members on Deer Island during the autumn months of 1921. My obsession with keeping the family history by recording it in a diary ensures an accurate portrayal of the life and times of our family for generations to follow. Born in Southampton, England, my ancestors arrived in South Louisiana in 1840; they established a settlement on a remote island in the Lower Atchafalaya River Basin. The Addison family legacy covers a period of time from 1836–1921.

September 17, 1940

This year is the centennial of the establishment of the homestead on Deer Island. Over one hundred direct descendants of Joseph and Josephine Addison will be gathering together to celebrate this event in the front yard of the "big house." The tradition of storytelling continues to be the mainstay of the day's activities. For one hundred years, Thanksgiving Day has been the most anticipated day of the year for my family. At thirty-four years of age, I have never lost the enthusiasm I had as a child growing up in the Addison family; I love to visit the island.

Many of my ancestors have been buried at the gravesite with Uncle Patrick, but they are alive today in the minds and hearts of their offspring. The graveyard has been the anchor that has kept the family coming back to the remote location. Many people with little or no means have been buried in our family cemetery, a sort of pauper's burial site. I am proud that we have had compassion on the less fortunate; I am certain Uncle Patrick would have approved.

There are only two of my family members who still call Deer Island home. They are the caretakers of the estate; everyone else has settled in the various towns and cities in the region, choosing the comforts that those locations offer over the isolation of wilderness living. I remain at home with father and mother on Bayou Du Large.

I have not yet married; writing has been my life since I can remember. It is a gratifying pursuit that I enjoy very much. I hope those who read my family's stories, will understand those heartfelt emotions that I have sincerely tried to share with them. I hope we will meet again in volume two;
God-willing, it will be so.
Nora Addison, 1940

The end of volume one

Deer Island in Autumn

VOLUME TWO

by

ROBERT J. BLACKWELL JR.

Abstract

Deer Island is a real place! Though fictionalized, the characters accurately portray life in the lower Atchafalaya Basin (specific to Terrebonne Parish, Louisiana) and its tributaries from 1840–1921.

The Addison family legacy is expressed in the form of the meticulously kept diaries of three generations of the family's matriarchs.

Each of the two volumes can stand on its own merits, but the story invites the reader to experience both.

The Author

Comments from a couple of readers:

"When I began reading *Deer Island in Autumn,* I just could not put the book down; it brought back many of my childhood memories. I could have been either of the two young girl characters. I believe this book is a cross between *Treasure Island* and *The Swiss Family Robinson*; it has elements of both."

—*Alma C. Richard*

"For readers in like mood for a rare story of life in *Bayou Country, Deer Island in Autumn* is just the thing. Whether it's explicating, justifying, or celebrating life in Terrebonne Parish in the mid-nineteenth century, this story goes down quickly and easily, just like a glass of ice tea in the summer."

—*Alice R. Fields*

Deer Island in Autumn
Volume Two
Carrying on the Legacy
A novel by
Robert J. Blackwell Jr.

There is no intended resemblance between the characters of this novel and any people, living or dead.

Though the geographic areas are readily identified on any map of
southeastern Louisiana, the characters of this story who settle these
locations and who contribute to the establishment of the various
communities never existed; the colors used to paint their portraits,
however, are definitive and recognizable and true.

Robert J. Blackwell Jr.

ACKNOWLEDGMENTS

This novel is dedicated to the memory of Alma C. Richard who was the first person to completely read and critique its contents. Her evaluation was inspirational, and it was she who farmed out the manuscript for other educators to review. She orchestrated an invitation for me to appear before the Terrebonne Parish Literary Society and to give a presentation of *Deer Island in Autumn*. Several of the society members had read my manuscript by this time with rave reviews. They received me well and encouraged me to pursue publication. Their confidence in the book's merits continued to influence the course of my efforts to publish, and I am sincerely grateful for their assistance.

I would also like to thank Tammy B. Daigle for her assistance in preparing the manuscript for final editing; I recognize the hard work she offered was a true blessing.

I would like to thank Hugh Paul St. Martin III for his encouragement and advice for getting this work into print for the general public to enjoy.

I would like to thank my son, Robert J. Blackwell III, for his contribution to this work. All signed pictures are examples of his hard work.

I would like to thank Callie Rose Courteaux, a direct descendant of a Houmas Indian chieftain, for the use of her image as inspiration for the two sketches of Princess Kallie.

Preface

In the beginning, American politicians quickly began to translate their power and influence into money and vast land holdings (after all, it was there for the taking). A young Louisiana congressman, Patrick J. Adams, knew the privileges that were afforded to ambitious political devotees. A consistent rise in his means for living, since his election to office twenty years earlier, prompted him to write a letter to his nephew in Southampton, England.

Joseph Addison, the congressman's nephew, was preparing to marry his beloved Josephine Moore at the time the letter of invitation was sent. This is where the story in volume one begins. Josephine Moore shares plans for her wedding in a diary she had just begun to write. Her first entry describes their nuptial arrangements and continues with events surrounding their marriage ceremony. The "big event" took place on January 5, 1836.

Josephine records events that led to their decision to leave England for an American Louisiana. She shares her experiences while taking the journey, which culminates in the young couple's arrival at the site that would become their new home.

Establishing a family tradition, the Addisons celebrate Thanksgiving Day shortly after completing construction on the "little house." God's hand in their destiny became increasingly evident as they recalled their open sea passage from England to New Orleans. Uncle Patrick's willingness to share his good fortune, and his plans for the establishment of a settlement on a remote island in the Lower Atchafalaya River Basin held great promise and a bright future for Joseph and Josephine Addison. Now, with a roof over their heads, it was time to give thanks.

The arrival of fall is being announced by brilliant colors and changes seen in the virgin forest, which is poised atop ridges and standing in the swamps along the lower river basin. A vast network of bayous and streams lend access to the high ground as they wind through endless miles of cypress and hardwood forest and vast tracts of open golden prairie, undulating with each rise and fall of the tide. Northern breezes portend imminent cold, as the approaching winter helps set the stage for the festive occasion that nature will host in the wilderness paradise.

Volume I follows the Addison family from their marriage in 1836 through the tragic times of the Civil War in 1865. The story portrays the life and times of one English family who decided to risk everything that was dear to them for an adventurous life in a young, untamed Louisiana.

Volume II focuses on a special time in the life of one of Joseph and Josephine's descendants, Nora Addison; it was she who the family members entrusted with the responsibility for carrying on the legacy, an amenability she embraced without hesitation.

Prologue

There is a wilderness paradise where time is only significant when it welcomes, or bids farewell, to one of its consumers. Those who are bid adieu are preserved, for posterity's sake, by sharing their lives and experiences through the art of storytelling.

Deer Island is a place where the fabric of life is tightly woven; mutual interests are cultivated. Each shared expression of some heartfelt emotion, each account of some uncommon event, each expounded detail of some ideal or conviction, each celebration of life and living communicated unashamedly and in a forthright manner, produces a colored fiber. The hues of these threads may be brilliant and appealing, or they me dim and dismal, but each is applied to the pattern of the weave for all to witness.

This "Garden of Eden" is the place where love drives the potter's wheel and guides the potter's hands. Each artist does his part in fashioning the ever-changing masterpiece; as new pieces of clay are added and others removed, the essence of its character is enhanced—whose substance is the family legacy.

Autumn is a special time of the year on the densely forested ridge, a season when nature hosts and affords the means for the fulfillment of the wildest aspirations of its guests who follow in the footsteps of the young couple who left Southampton, England, seeking adventure and braving every uncertainty for the opportunity to begin anew in a distant land, in America when she was not yet assured of her sovereignty.

In 1918, twelve-year-old Nora Addison is determined to keep the family history alive. She begins to record her own diary, lending us her personal perception of all the characters in her family's play, using the written and the oral traditions of her ancestors.

Nora, an avid reader, has practically memorized the diary of her great-grandmother, Josephine Addison. Uncle Justin gave her the leather-bound record as a present on her tenth birthday. The massive diary is her most prized and cherished possession, a source of strong inspiration and contentment.

Robert J. Blackwell Jr.

Illustrations

21. Princess Callie 1865
22. Push Skiff
23. Princess Kallie (1875)
24. 1919 Packard

Deer Island in Autumn
Volume Two
Carrying on the Legacy

Chapter One

CONTINUING THE HISTORY

(Uncle Justin decided I would become the new Addison family historian. As a source of inspiration, he gave me the diary of my great-grandmother, Josephine Moore Addison, for my tenth birthday. The following are excerpts from my diary.)

August 6, 1918

Today is my twelfth birthday. Two years ago, I was given my great-grandmother's diary as a present while we were spending the fall holiday season on Deer Island with family members. For the past two years, I have nearly memorized its entire contents.

Knowing I am an avid reader, Uncle Justin felt the time was right to entrust me with this valuable family treasure (Josephine's diary, 1836–1865). His expressed desire was that I should continue to record my family's history, beginning where Great-grandmother Josephine Moore Addison stopped writing, using the oral tradition as a resource for my material. Storytelling is the key.

The following information was taken from Josephine's diary; much more was gathered by listening to the old stories shared with me by Uncle Justin, stories about my ancestors from 1840 to 1921. This information was recorded in my own personal legend for posterity's sake; it is the history of the Addison family.

Patrick J. Adams was my great-great-uncle on my father's side. He was born on July 4, 1791 in New Orleans, Louisiana; he died on July 22, 1842. He was only fifty-one years old; he was the first person buried on Deer Island.

A brief history: Patrick Adams was a native of New Orleans. He fought in the Battle of New Orleans on January 8, 1815. He ran for political office and became a Louisiana congressman, a position he held until the time of his death (1816–1842). He served under the following presidents: James Monroe, 1816–1824; John Quincy Adams, 1824–1828; Andrew Jackson, 1828–1836; Martin Van Buren, 1836–1840; William H. Harrison, 1840–1842.

On September 4, 1834, Patrick Adams acquired five square miles (five sections) of uninhabited wilderness located in the lower Atchafalaya River Basin. His dream of establishing a settlement on this large tract was realized in 1840, when construction at the site was begun.

Another one-square mile (one section) of land was acquired in the same transaction. This second location was not developed until part of it was used to establish an Anglican Church in 1875. Two years later, a family residence was constructed on the remaining portion of the property on Bayou Du Large.

My great-grandfather (father's side) *Joseph Addison* was born at Southampton, England, on September 28, 1818; he died on February 17, 1890. He was buried on Deer Island. He was the nephew of Patrick Adams.

My great-grandmother (father's side) *Josephine Moore Addison* was born at Southampton, England, on September 17, 1818. She died on July 27, 1905, on Deer Island; she was eighty-seven years old. She was buried on Deer Island. She was Joseph's wife.

A brief history: Joseph and Josephine were married on January 5, 1836. They resided in Southampton, England, for the first four years of their marriage. After lengthy and careful deliberation, the young couple decided to accept the invitation of Joseph's uncle, Congressman Patrick J. Adams, and moved to America.

On June 8, 1840, they landed at Deer Island and established a settlement there. Through the course of their lifetime, they built and occupied the homestead in accordance with the plans that were introduced to Joseph by his uncle. They had three children—all boys!

DEER ISLAND

THE FIRST GENERATION

John Quincy Addison was the first of three sons born to Joseph and Josephine Addison; he was my great-uncle (father's side). John was born on Deer Island August 15, 1842. He was killed during the Battle of Chancellorsville on May 3, 1863; he was twenty-one years old. He had no children.

Alexander Patrick Addison was their second son; he was my great-uncle (father's side). He was born on Deer Island on September 28, 1844; Alexander was wounded (just seven days after his brother was killed) during a skirmish with Union forces about fifteen miles from the Chancellorsville battlefield on May 10, 1863. He died from complications due to his Civil War wound August 12, 1873; he was twenty-nine years old. He was buried on Deer Island. He had one son.

Sanders Addison was the youngest of three sons; he was my grandfather (father's side). He was born on Deer Island on October 1, 1854; since he was only seven when the Civil War began, he was spared the misery of war. He died on Deer Island of natural causes on March 7, 1916; he was sixty-two years old. He was buried on Deer Island. He had three sons.

THE FAMILY GROWS

DEER ISLAND

THE SECOND GENERATION

Alexander Patrick Addison married *Elizabeth Cotton Addison* on June 30, 1869. They lived together in the *little house* on Deer Island. They had one son, *Justin Addison*; Alexander died before his son's second birthday. Living in the house together, Elizabeth and Pauline Longere were like two sisters; they formed a very close relationship, and they shared the joy of raising Justin together. Elizabeth remained on Deer Island until she died. Elizabeth was born in New Iberia, Louisiana, on October 12, 1845. She died on Deer Island of natural causes on February 12, 1909; she was sixty-four years old.

Pauline Longere was an adopted family member who was both ward and confidant of Uncle Patrick. Formerly a resident of Chacahoula, she moved to Deer Island when the Civil War began in 1861. She occupied the *little house*, the house that the family had given to her when Uncle Patrick died. Pauline never married despite being pursued by countless suitors; she was born in New Orleans on September 7, 1814. She died on the island on July 1, 1900. Great-grandmother Josephine often boasted to my Great-aunt Elizabeth about the degree of comfort she brought to the homestead during those trying times (the war years).

I sincerely wish I could have met Pauline. Grandfather Sanders knew her for most of his life; he fell in love with her the first time he saw her. Unfortunately he was only seven; she was forty-six when she moved to Deer Island.

Sanders Addison was my grandfather; he married *Martha Lamb*, an immigrant who arrived in America in June of 1870. Martha was born in Birmingham, England, on March 15, 1856; she was living in Houma, Louisiana, when they met. They were married on June 14, 1877. Both houses on Deer Island were occupied at the time of their marriage; in 1875, however, my great-grandfather, Joseph Addison, donated a parcel of land for the establishment of an Episcopal Church. On July 4, 1875, the church building was completed. After Sanders and Martha wed, they decided to develop the remaining portion of the family land; they built a family residence there.

Grandfather Sanders Addison and his wife *Grandmother Martha* had three sons while they were living at their first residence on Bayou Du large. Their oldest son was my *Uncle Arthur Addison*; he was born on Bayou Du large on February 16, 1879. Their second son was my *Uncle Sanders Addison Jr.*; he was born on Bayou Du large on October 14, 1882. My father, the third of the three children, *Adam John Quincy Addison* was born on Bayou Du large on September 7, 1885.

After raising their three children, *Sanders* and *Martha* moved to Deer Island in 1904 to care for his mother, Josephine, who was not well. They occupied the *little house* for the rest of their lives.

THE FAMILY CONTINUES TO GROW

DEER ISLAND

THE THIRD GENERATION

Uncle Justin Addison was the only child of Alexander Patrick and Elizabeth Addison; he was born on September 15, 1871. He married *Clara Southern* on July 14, 1892; Clara was born in Morgan City on January 3, 1869. Justin and Clara had no children.

A brief history: My uncle *Justin Addison* met *Clara Southern* in Morgan City just after its name was changed from Brashear City. After the wedding, they moved into the *little house*. In 1904, they moved into the *big house* to care for his aging grandmother, Josephine. Josephine died on Deer Island in 1905. Justin's mother, Elizabeth, died on Deer Island in 1909; Aunt Clara died on Deer Island later that same year during the Storm of 1909.

After several years of living alone, *Justin* met *Sarah Blanchard* and married for a second time; on October 5, 1917, they wed and Justin adopted Sarah's two children. Sarah was a native of Thibodaux, Louisiana, born on July 17, 1890. At the time she and Justin met, she was a widow; her first husband, Oxford Blanchard, died of the fever in 1915. The two adopted sons are *Felix Addison*, age twelve and *Gustave Addison*, age three. Together they moved into the *big house* on Deer Island and they occupy that residence to this day.

Uncle Arthur Addison married *Claire Brown* on April 7, 1900. Aunt Claire and Uncle Arthur reside in Morgan City, Louisiana. They have two girls—Shannon Addison, age seventeen, and Stacey Addison, age fourteen.

Uncle Sanders Addison Jr. married *Kathleen Wright* on October 14, 1882; Aunt Kathleen and Uncle Sanders reside in New Iberia, Louisiana. They have three married children: *Cassy Addison*, age thirty-two, married Bernard Dupont and they have three girls (Patty Dupont, age twelve, Kathleen Dupont, age ten, and Linda Dupont, age seven); *Greta Addison*, age twenty-seven, married Mark Richard, and they have two children (Todd Richard, age seven, and Melissa Richard, age four): *Joseph Addison*, age twenty-four, married Edwina Marcel and they have a son, Melvin Addison, age two.

My father, *Adam John Quincy Addison*, married *Ida White* on October 17, 1902; my father and mother were childhood friends. Both were residents of Bayou Du Large and attended the Episcopal Church together for as long as they can remember. Adam and Ida were married on October 17, 1902, and lived with Adam's mother and father, Sanders and Martha, for two years in the family home. In 1904, Sanders and Martha moved to Deer Island and gave their house to Adam and Ida.

THE ADDISON FAMILY

THE FOURTH GENERATION

Adam John Quincy Addison and Ida White Addison had four children on Bayou Du Large—*Lee Robert Addison*, born December 5, 1903; *Brad Braxton Addison*, born May 5, 1905; *Nora Emily Addison*, born August 6, 1906 (that's me!); *Alma Mary Addison* was born on August 12, 1914.

My father, Adam John Quincy Addison, was named in honor of his great-great-great uncle, Patrick J. Adams, and also his great uncle, John Quincy Addison who was killed during the Civil War.

October 1, 1918

My family and I are anxiously anticipating our customary journey from Bayou Du Large to the Plumb Bayou trapping camp. Every year, about the middle of October, we begin to make preparations for the trip to our winter home.

Once everything is delivered to the campsite and secured, we will head for Deer Island to visit with Uncle Justin and Aunt Sarah and their two boys, Felix and Gus. I can't wait!

In the meantime, I thought I would try to consolidate the lengthy family history into a few pages for my diary. I have written many notes to ensure that I record the information accurately. When we visit Uncle Justin this fall at Deer Island, I will ask him to review my text to see if I've got it right. It is important to me that when I record the notes from all the stories I have been told that what I am writing is true.

October 2, 1918

The Addison family first arrives at Deer Island--the vast area surrounding the island settlement was unscathed wilderness in 1840, and it remains virtually unchanged to this day. Arriving at Deer Island on June 8, 1840, Joseph and Josephine immediately pitched camp, setting up a large canvas tent to protect them from the rain and the mosquitoes.

Construction on the *little house* began the following morning. Their small home was completed on July 30, 1840; the young couple finally had a roof over their heads.

Construction on the *big house*, the future home of Joseph's uncle, Congressman Patrick J. Adams, began almost immediately after construction of the *little house* was completed. The arduous task of building such a large home at the remote site can hardly be imagined.

Frenchy and Carey, the crew of the *Swamp Rat*, made many return trips with lumber and construction materials from the lumber mill and the general store at Brashear City. Anything that Joseph requisitioned was supplied by the congressman until the work was completed.

Meant to be his retirement home, the *big house* was completed on July 27, 1842, shortly after Uncle Patrick's untimely death.

My great-great uncle, Patrick J. Adams, was the first member of the family to be buried in the Deer Island cemetery. Joseph and Josephine established the burial site in his memory. They fashioned a brick tomb to enhance the grounds for our sake. Thus, the family cemetery became part of life on the island from that day forward.

Great-grandfather Joseph had brick masons construct a beautiful monument over the grave. Later, at the request of the Louisiana delegation, President Zachary Taylor authorized that a large cypress cross be erected at the head of Uncle Patrick's tomb. The president also authorized that a bronze plaque be affixed to the tomb, citing the meritorious service he granted to the Congress of the United States from 1816 to 1842, and last of all, he authorized that a wrought iron fence be placed around the congressman's burial site. That work was completed on July 4, 1850, the day that would have marked his fifty-ninth birthday.

Many dignitaries made the pilgrimage to Deer Island to see the congressman laid to rest. Boats of every conceivable description docked at the wharf at the mouth of the freshwater stream that flows from the fountainhead near the front of the *big house*. Gallant men, dressed in long black coats and wearing top hats, escorted fashionably dressed ladies with tear soaked kerchiefs along the left bank of the stream which led to the Adams home. After the coffin was brought into the sitting room of the *big house* for viewing, several eulogies were delivered. After a brief prayer from the Anglican priest, Parson Stanley, the casket was carried in procession to the burial site.

My great-aunt, Elizabeth Addison, recorded thoughts about the events on the day of the congressman's burial as told to her by Josephine: "In spite of the pomp and ceremony, it was an austere occasion. The congressman had enjoyed an elegant lifestyle. It was a befitting tribute to observe the way his patrons and comrades in office pampered him, even after he died. An epitaph for a Southern gentlemen better left unscribed."

Elizabeth continued, "Pauline Longere came to pay her respects. As usual, she was brilliantly attired and as beautiful as a picture. She donned a red velvet parasol that caused no small stir among the other ladies present. By far, she was the most beautiful and elegantly dressed woman to grace the island that day. She left a stem of roses beside the congressman's grave—a cutting from a pink floribunda. My husband Joseph planted the cutting, and it took root. From that day forward, each time someone is buried in the family cemetery, a cutting is taken from the rosebush started from that stem of the pink floribunda that Mademoiselle Pauline Longere left beside her confidant that day."

Each year, on All Saints' Day, my family and I pay homage to the man who forever changed the lives of my ancestors by visiting his tomb in the family cemetery on Deer Island, the island he so loved and admired but never had the chance to enjoy.

During the twenty-one years of life on Deer Island preceding the beginning of the Civil War in 1861, the Addison family succeeded in completing all the plans for the settlement as they were presented to Joseph by his uncle in 1840. The schematic of the plans for the retirement haven have been copied; I am preserving the document, including it in my recorded legend.

Adam, my father, married Ida White on October 17, 1902; they made their home on Bayou Du Large, briefly living with his mother and father. As a wedding present, Sanders and Martha gave their home to Adam and Ida; they lived together with the newlyweds for about two years before moving to Deer Island to live in the newly vacated *little house*. They lived on the island for the remainder of their lives.

Grandfather Sanders died of natural causes on March 7, 1916. Grandmother Martha died from grief over the death of her husband on March 3, 1917. They were both buried on Deer Island.

August 12, 1920 (Alma's Sixth Birthday)

Today we are celebrating my little sister Alma's birthday. Mama has made several pies, and we are going to spend the day with

Grandmother White (my mother's mother). We are going to have a big feast; it will be great fun. I can't wait!

Papa is hollering for me outside the house. Everyone had been seated on our buckboard wagon, and they are anxious to get under-way; the horse is hitched and they are ready to go up the bayou. "Come on, Nora! We'll leave you behind if you don't hurry out that door!" Papa yelled.

"I am coming!" I replied as I scurried out the front door and jumped aboard the rear of the wagon between my two fun-making brothers, Lee and Brad.

"I bet you two can't wait to see Cousin Susan," I teased. They just gave me a pair of eyes, suggesting that I struck some kind of nerve. "Don't worry! I'll be taking up all Susan's time, as we catch up on all that has been happening on the bayou," I prodded my two silly brothers further.

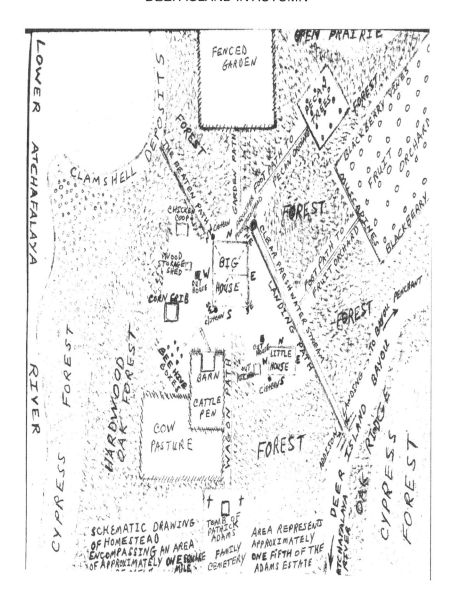

Lee gave me a pinch on my side that was so hard that I yelled, prompting Mama to issue a warning for us to behave ourselves. This describes the activity that lasted the entire day. We had a wonderful time. Cousin Susan made my brothers blush several times; she's beautiful and outgoing and they are shy and reserved—what a spectacle they made of themselves.

Alma, the birthday girl, got a new ragdoll from Grandfather White. Once she received that doll, she lost touch with the rest of us as she played enthusiastically throughout the day with her make-believe friend. That girl has one heck of an imagination. She carried her doll everywhere; she had more conversation with that ragdoll than I've heard from her in a week.

August 15, 1920 (More History)

After the untimely death of Congressman Patrick J. Adams, Joseph and Josephine moved from the *little house* to the *big house*; it was there that they raised their three sons—John Quincy Addison, Alexander Addison, and Sanders Addison.

During the Civil War, Joseph and his two older boys joined the Confederate Army. John Quincy died heroically at the Battle of Chancellorsville in 1863. Alexander was wounded just a few days after his older brother was killed not far from the Chancellorsville battlefield; he recovered sufficiently to return home. Joseph returned from the war without a scratch after helping his Confederate comrades secure the Lower Atchafalaya Basin by driving Union troops from the area. Sanders, was only seven years old when the war began.

August 21, 1920 (Anxious Anticipation)

Soon it will be autumn! Lee, Brad, Alma, and me will accompany our parents to Deer Island for the annual All Saints' Day and Thanksgiving Day celebrations with Uncle Justin, Aunt Sarah, Felix, and Gus. Everyone is excited; I can't wait! I wonder what stories will be shared from the front porch of the *big house* at storytelling time.

I often contemplate why Josephine stopped writing her diary; her last entry was dated November 22, 1865. Did the tragedy of war steal her joy for writing? God knows! The record of her experiences that she did write lends to my mind's eye impressionable images, making my ancestors seem vividly present in my heart and in my memory. My great grandmother's references to others she came to know and to love introduce me (in a way not otherwise possible) to those who played important roles in her life throughout her descriptive legend.

Those members of my family, who knew and loved Josephine, added both color and style to her written accounts. My Great-aunt Elizabeth continued to preserve the family legacy. Having shared the *big house* with Josephine and Pauline after Joseph's death in 1890, Elizabeth became familiar with the history of Deer Island from the stories they shared on the veranda, as they rocked in their favorite chairs within earshot of the bubbling fountainhead.

From the time he was old enough to understand, Uncle Justin enjoyed listening to conversationthe three women shared on the front porch. He says the only thing more consistently heard, other than the three women's sentimental storytelling, was the perpetual sound created by the fountainhead of the natural stream, as it excitedly escaped the grasp of its underground captor just a few feet from where they were seated.

Like the fountainhead of the natural stream, Pauline, Elizabeth, and Josephine were wellsprings of experiences, experiences bursting forth through the grasp of their vivid memories that their minds have held captive, bustling forth in an expression of words escaping their source, a source that was never found depleted.

There are times when I lay awake at night; it's almost as though I can hear my Great-grandmother Josephine, my Great-aunt Elizabeth, and that true southern belle, Mademoiselle Pauline Longere, speaking of bygone days (rocking chairs creaking) as the fountainhead gurgles out its special rhapsody, competing for an audience.

Well, I believe I have compiled enough of the history of Deer Island, for now, but I am sure there will be more interesting things to record in the future. Now it is my turn to carry on the legacy. I look forward to the shared experiences that will inspire me to continue this worthwhile endeavor. May God be with me as I write. Amen.

September 1, 1921 (Memories of Last Autumn)
Last summer, Uncle Justin purchased two young Indian ponies. They are beautiful creatures and they were both saddle-broken. Felix and I rode double so I could get a feel for riding, and he instructed me on how to handle the reins.

Exhibiting the patience of Job, Felix taught me to mount and dismount; once I mastered climbing aboard, he led me and my horse through the pasture surrounding the barn. Stopping long enough for Felix to saddle the other horse, I sat on my mount waiting anxiously for my first solo ride to begin.

We spent at least an hour riding around the estate, traversing the entire property that was accessible; we even rode to the river bank, passing through the *beaten path* to get there. The view of the mighty Atchafalaya from atop my horse was something special. We waved at the crew of a sailing vessel as it passed us by, heading south for the bay.

Once I was comfortable with what I had learned about riding, Felix taught me how to secure the saddle belts around the girth of the horse's belly; I learned to knee the horse in the belly to have it exhale, so the belt can be tight enough for safe mounting.

During our last autumn visit, Felix and I made at least a dozen rides on the two newly acquired animals. Both horses are mares; they are very gentle and well behaved. It was all great fun, and we had no bad incidents. The mare Felix assigned me was named *Patches* because she has large gray patches all over her white body. The horse Felix rode was named *Beauty* because her black patches contrasted well with her white body; I must admit I found her the more handsome of the two.

Uncle Justin had just refurbished the barn before he acquired the two horses. I had Gus make a sketch of the structure for my record. He is quite the artist; he sells some of his work at the general store in Morgan City. The blacksmith shop has long ago lost its purpose for existing, though all the hardware is still sheltered by the outbuilding. There is no longer any need for hinges or nails; there is no longer any need for spikes used in the construction of the wharfs. The old workshop has been relegated to nothing more than a historic curiosity.

Felix and Gus taught me how to blow a duck call; they even taught me the feeding call, which requires a bit more skill. They promised to take me on a hunt this year if I can convince Papa to let me borrow his L.C. Smith 410 gauge double-barreled shotgun.

Papa bought the new gun from Doc Fursom's General Store after the last trapping season. I believe he will agree to let me go duck hunting with the boys; he has taught me the proper way to handle the gun, and I've actually shot at a few tin cans. Believe it or not, I'm a pretty good shot.

Brad and Lee each have Parker 12 gauge double barrels; they are very good shots. They generally hit anything they shoot at, including high flying geese and the swift canvasback. The boys have hunted together at Uncle Justin's for the past two years. This autumn, I'll have a chance to see what the excitement of the hunt is all about.

Horseback riding and duck hunting will be two activities that will make our stay on the island an ever more pleasurable experience. When I begin to anticipate all the fun we are sure to have, I find it difficult to fall asleep; it's a struggle I am happy to endure. It makes life exciting, and it satisfies my insatiable quest for new adventures; it stimulates my imagination.

Oftentimes when I lay in bed at night, and I hear the night creatures singing their curious songs, I imagine life on Deer Island; I can hear the gurgling sounds emitted by the fountainhead just a few yards from the front porch of the *big house*. I can hear the owls calling from the distant treetops and the grunts of the pigs, which have been disturbed by some unexpected activity in Uncle Justin's back yard; I hear the milk cows emitting their deep bellowing sounds during the night as though a bull from the mainland might hear their mellow voices. I can hear Aunt Sarah's high pitched voice as she scolds a goat for visiting the screen door from the porch side of the kitchen. I can anticipate the wakeup call from one of my aunt's two roosters; though they have had many names, and though the breeds have varied, they always get us out of bed a little earlier than we may have intended.

There is so much to look forward to that I get restless when September comes each year. Each visit to the island provides me with never ending cavalcades of emotions, inspiring me to record what I remember for posterity's sake. Oh, I do love to write. Good night, Lord. Amen.

September 17, 1921 (Curious Thoughts)

As I read my Great-grandmother Josephine's diary over and over these past few years, I learned much about my imaginary princess, Pauline Longere. There remain many unanswered questions I have about her life on Deer Island after the Civil War ended. I read that there were some mysterious connections between Pauline and Jean Laffite, the infamous privateer.

Storytelling time thus far has yielded no solid evidence to prove whether or not she was really his daughter. The usual custom for sharing stories is that if the story is really true, it must be supported with tangible proof; otherwise, we have the right to assume the account presented was fabrication.

It was said of Pauline (and it was written) that she was the most beautiful woman in all the Louisiana Territory. That is a fantastic claim; there are many beautiful women that I have seen with my own eyes. I often try to imagine what special qualities the people who knew her (both men and women) must have seen in her to make such an unusual boast: "The most beautiful woman in all the Louisiana Territory!" She must have been something!

Near the end of Josephine's extensive record, a record which began in 1836 and ended in 1865 (right after the War Between the States had ended) there was a reference to a real princess; not an imaginary one.

Josephine wrote of a Princess Callie, the daughter of a Houmas Indian chieftain. There was no information at all written about her; there was only the mention of a portrait of the woman. It was presented as a gift to my grandmother. I do recall reading about her reaction when she first gazed at the image; she wrote that the young woman was beautiful, and she would like to meet her someday. Did they meet sometime after the diary was discontinued? I wonder.

Curiously, Princess Callie has not been spoken of during any of the storytelling I have participated in, and I've been listening to stories on the front porch of the *big house* since before I was old enough to understand what was being shared.

I intend to pursue this matter of the Indian princess when we get to Deer Island this autumn. Uncle Justin is an expert on all things

Addison, since he has lived on the island for almost his entire life. I am sure he must know something that will stimulate my imagination about the woman Josephine described as beautiful and fascinating; thus prompting her to express a desire to meet her.

I can imagine, with my mind's eye, a young woman dressed in her native clothing and appearing dignified, a person worthy of respect. Princess Callie! What will I learn about you? Only the Lord knows! Good night, Lord. Amen.

Chapter Two

GETTING READY FOR THE WINTER

October 15, 1921 (Nora Is Fifteen Years Old)

This is the third season of the year; nature is preparing itself for the cold onslaught of winter. Northerly breezes come and go, but with increasing frequency, dropping the temperature to a very comfortable level. Deciduous trees are undressing themselves with each hint of a wind. Migratory birds are filling the sky as they search for feeding grounds and roosting sites. All these changes around me stir my senses and make me happy to be a resident of *bayou country*.

Mid-October, for the Addison family, is the most exciting time of the year. Our seines are safely stowed away in our attic, where they will remain until next spring. Papa and the boys are inspecting the traps, making sure they operate freely and seeing if any need to be replaced.

My two brothers have already gathered the bamboo poles that Papa uses to secure the traps along his trapping runs. They stripped the cane poles of their leaves, cut them in six-foot lengths, and tied them in bundles so they can be loaded atop the cabin of our boat when we prepare to leave for our trapping camp.

Mama is going through all of our clothes, mending tears, and sewing buttons. Our food staples have been allowed to dwindle in preparation for our departure. Each fall, Mama tries to use up our old provisions, so we can leave with the fresh supplies Papa will purchase from the general store up the bayou.

I have been assisting my mother in packing the things she wants to take with us to our winter home. My little sister, Alma, is supposed to be helping us, but she is more interested in playing with her ragdoll than helping us with our chores.

Residents of Bayou Du Large know the fur harvesting season is approaching when they see the Addison family preparing to leave for the winter. Everyone knows that we leave for our trapping grounds early so we can finish our chores there in time to proceed to Deer Island for the celebration of All Saints' Day with our family members who reside there. We are always gone two weeks before the other trappers prepare to leave for their cold weather homes.

Fur season begins on the first day of December each year. We usually leave for our camp on the twentieth of October. We never miss that scheduled departure by more than a day on either side. If the twentieth falls on a Saturday or a Monday, we usually leave after the church service on Sunday. If it falls on any other day of the week we leave right on schedule.

Mama is preparing a list of items that she will need to sustain the family through the cold months ahead. Trying desperately not to overburden Papa, she tries to keep the shopping list as short as possible, listing only necessities.

The top of the list always begins with sacks of flour, sugar, rice, dry beans, and salt. It continues with things like coffee, tea, cornmeal, lamp wicks, and kerosene for the lamps; after these items, the list continues with things that are important but not essential. The lower an item appears on the list is an indication of how necessary the item is. Papa always makes the final determination about what will go on our bill and what will not.

My brothers and I are very careful about asking Mama for anything (Alma is always too busy with her doll to ask for something). If Mama deems a request selfish or foolish, the one making the request is in for a mild scolding. "Papa has enough on his back without you youngsters putting more in the sack to weigh it down," she would warn. None of us wanted to be guilty of that charge; it would be unbecoming of any child who loves Papa to be selfish.

Tied to the dock at the edge of our front yard is Papa's most prized possession, the *Early Rose*. My great-grandfather, Joseph Addison, built the boat shortly before his death in 1890. Though the boat is older than Papa, he says she is as fit as the day she was launched.

Originally built for my great-grandfather, the *Early Rose* was passed down to my grandfather, Sanders Addison, before he died. My grandfather, Sanders, passed the vessel down to my father, Adam Addison, before he died. When grandfather had the boat, it was different; he kept her as she was originally built. The *Early Rose* was designed with a special retractable keel (a boat of this type was known as a box-keeled sailor). She sported a single mast and had a big fin underneath the hull, which could be raised into the hull's interior into a receiving box which is built above water level; this allowed the vessel to travel in very shallow water. She had four oar stations to facilitate her movement through the shallows when not under sail. The sail was generally used on the open lakes and in the Gulf of Mexico but could also be used to travel the bayous and streams that traversed open areas of prairieland. Bayous found too shallow to maneuver by sail, and those channels that were lined with trees, required oars for traveling.

When Grandpa Sanders died, Papa modified the *Early Rose*. He cut off the mast at the deck level and removed her fin from the bottom. He reworked the keel (removing the box designed to receive her fin keel) and installed a one-cylinder Palmer engine. More and more people are turning their sailboats into powerboats; it seems that very soon, sailboats will altogether disappear from the bayous. Papa was one of the last to make the conversion.

Papa is very proud of his powerboat. He boasts of her seaworthiness to anyone who will take the time to listen. He has escorted many a curious man below her decks to show them her sound construction, all the while boasting that its builder was a shipwright from Southampton. Everyone seems to agree with papa that his boat is a fine example of expert craftsmanship.

October 17, 1921

Once again it's time to sound her engine. Tomorrow we will make the ten mile trip up the bayou to the general store. We will be returning from Ole Doc Fursom's establishment with fresh provisions, and the excitement surrounding our departure for the winter will begin to escalate."Oh! boy!" This expresses the sentiment most often heard.

Doc Fursom will be anticipating our arrival. He has already renewed his inventory in preparation for the trapping season. This year, I'll be making the trip with Papa, Lee, and Brad to assist them in gathering the items on Mama's list and loading them aboard the *Early Rose*. Ole Doc usually blesses us with a bag of goodies after he and Papa finish conducting their business ("*Lagniappe!*" as my French neighbors would say).

Normally, I have to stay behind to help Mama finish with her necessary chores. I awakened extra early this morning; I helped Mama so much that she decided to let me go with Papa and the boys tomorrow. I haven't been to the general store since year before last. I love to look at all the things that Doc Fursom has for sale; I am quite sure I won't get the chance to see everything, but it will be fun trying.

October 18, 1921 (Early Morning)

Papa walked through the heavy dew that covered the front yard, crossed the dirt road that travels along the bayou, and boarded the *Early Rose*. Lifting the cover of the engine housing, he placed it against the front cabin wall to allow himself more room. With a spin of the huge flywheel, the one-cylinder engine sputtered. With the second spin of the flywheel, the engine sounded its familiar rhythm;

it's a rhythm that makes me giggle: *Puk-puk-puk-puk-puk-puk-puk-puk-puk-puk-puk-puk-puk-puk-puk-puk*, the engine reverberated.

Brad, Lee, and I had followed close behind Papa and hopped aboard; when he sounded the engine, we patiently awaited his orders as he allowed the motor to warm up. With a nod from Papa's head, Lee and Brad untied the bow and stern lines. Lee pushed the bow away from the wharf and Papa sped the engine; we were on our way to the general store. *Puk-puk-puk-puk-puk-puk-puk-puk-puk-puk-puk-puk-puk-puk-puk-puk-puk-puk*, sounded the engine, as we gazed along the shoreline looking toward our neighbors' houses for signs of early morning activity.

Most of the residents of the lower end of Bayou Du Large are English. We are commonly referred to as down-the-bayou people; most of us fish and trap for a living, making a garden to supplement the seafood and the game we consume.

A little farther up the bayou reside the Frenchmen; they generally own larger tracts of land. They make their livelihood primarily by farming; in the winter, they trap to supplement their income. Most of them don't fish for shrimp with seines as we do; they catch a few fish for the table, not for the market.

The "up-the-bayou people," north of where the general store is located, are a different class of people-- most are French. They generally own very large tracts of land, which are either under the plow, being grazed by cattle, or both. In addition to operating their farms, many own and operate businesses in Houma, a village about twenty miles upstream from where we live.

The more affluent "up-the-bayou people" don't have much to do with the "down-the-bayou people" (a division caused by wealth and religion I have heard Papa say). Though the Frenchmen who live below the general store are Catholic, they are also of a poorer class just as we are; consequently, they are much friendlier than their rich compatriots.

The native Indians (some descendants of the Houmas tribe and a few descendants of the Chitimachas) live among us "down-the-bayou people" and speak French (converted to Catholicism by Catholic missionaries in the late 1700s). They reside on very small tracts of land; they are loners, preferring to mind their own business and live in isolation. They live just as we do—hunting, fishing, farming, and trapping; they do whatever it takes to survive. They are usually friendly but reserved. I have had little contact with any of them.

All these differences don't matter very much to me. I am happy with the lifestyle we live, and I just want to be friendly with everyone. I can't understand the differences that religion and wealth make anyway; we are all created in the image of God—what else could possibly matter?

Traveling the ten miles upstream to the general store gives me plenty opportunity for waving to friends and neighbors. Almost everyone waves back at me, if I can get their attention. Most women already have dinner cooked, and they are either rocking in their favorite chairs or swinging on their front porch swings. Men are usually at work in their gardens during the cool hours of the morning, trying to beat the heat of the midday sun. I usually holler when I wave, "Hey! How are you all doing this morning?" I would shout.

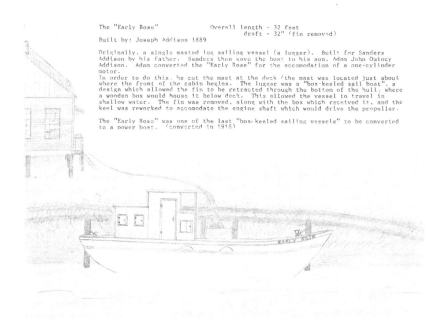

The "Early Rose"
Built by: Joseph Addison 1889

Overall length - 32 feet
draft - 32" (fin removed)

Originally, a single masted lug sailing vessel (a lugger). Built for Sanders Addison by his father. Sanders then gave the boat to his son, Adam John Quincy Addison. Adam converted the "Early Rose" for the accomodation of a one-cylinder motor.
In order to do this, he cut the mast at the deck (the mast was located just about where the front of the cabin begins. The lugger was a "box-keeled sail boat", a design which allowed the fin to be retracted through the bottom of the hull, where a wooden box would house it below deck. This allowed the vessel to travel in shallow water. The fin was removed, along with the box which received it, and the keel was reworked to accomodate the engine shaft which would drive the propeller.

The "Early Rose" was one of the last "box-keeled sailing vessels" to be converted to a power boat. (converted in 1918)

The noise of our engine usually drowns out any response, but a return wave is gratifying enough for me. I like standing on the bow; it provides the best vantage point for sending and receiving these neighborly greetings. I find it great fun. Lee and Brad are not nearly as enthusiastic as I am about sending out friendly waves; they just lay there, their back's resting against the boat's cabin, waving only to those who wave to them first.

I could see that we were approaching the dock site of Doc Fursom's store. Papa was already slowing down the engine as Lee and Brad took their positions with mooring lines in hand. Brad cast the stern line around a piling and secured the rope to a bit on our back deck. As the forward motion of the boat carried us close to the wharf, Lee cast the bowline around a pile and secured it to the front bit. Papa pulled on a special rope with a knot at its end and the motor stopped.

Ole Doc Fursom was rocking in his chair, smoking his pipe; while waiting for customers, this is his customary practice. To escape the sun's heat, he sits on whichever porch is shaded by his building. This being the morning, we found him sitting on the west side of the store, which overlooks the bayou.

Hopping from the boat onto the wharf, we made our way toward where Doc was seated; his pipe hung from his mouth, dropping below his chin. Cupping the bowl of his pipe in his right hand, he removed it from his mouth so he could speak.

"It's trapping time again, eh, Adam? I see you brought little Nora along with you this time," he seemed happy to say.

"Yes!" Papa answered. "She begged her mama to let her make the trip up the bayou with us. She worked extra hard for her until she finally relented, deciding to let her accompany us to your store," he added.

"She sure is growing up!" Doc commented.

I told Ole Doc that Papa says I am growing like the grass, and I scurried away from the two elders to take a peek inside. Lee and Brad were already looking around when I entered the store; they weren't saying anything, but they were staring very hard at the knives in the display case. It would not be unreasonable for my brothers to request new knives, since they will be put to good use skinning rats, minks and otters at the trapping camp; they won't dare ask Papa for new ones, though.

Papa walked into the store examining the contents of Mama's list. He began to call out the things that were recorded so Lee and Brad could carry the goods to the large checkout counter. It is there that Doc will prepare the bill, giving Papa the tally before the provisions can be taken to the wharf for loading.

On the large countertop, various items are prominently displayed. Catching my eye right away were the large jars of cookies, jelly beans, hard rock candy, and licorice. There is a coffee grinder and a balance scale near the cash register. A six-foot section of the counter supports a glass-shrouded knife case, which immediately drew Lee and Brad's attention the moment they entered the establishment.

While all the men were busy taking care of business, I decided to have a good look around the place. I was amazed by the number of goods on display; if I tried to write down everything I saw, it would take me a week to finish. Ole Doc must be a very rich man to have this large building stocked with so many things I deduced, as I continued to gaze in wonder at his store's vast inventory.

While Doc was preparing the bill, Papa was eyeing the knives in the display case. Lee and Brad were holding their breath in anticipation.

It appeared to me that everything Mama had requested on her list was waiting to be added to the invoice. Papa must be confident that we will have a good winter, seeing the huge pile of goods and supplies waiting to be checked out. There will be many trips to the boat to load all that stuff onboard.

Just as Doc Fursom was preparing to hand Papa a copy of the bill, Papa requested his assistance. Not only did Lee and Brad get new knives, but he got a new knife for himself also. Papa is partial to the Case knives; he prefers them over all the other brands.

Papa bought a new number 3 tub, he bought a pair of boots for Mama, and he bought three dozen new rat traps. Our old number 3 tub had rusted through last year; Papa had to whittle a few wooden pegs to stop the leaks so we could finish the season. I guess he figured it would be beyond repair this year. I know Mama did not ask Papa to buy her those boots, but it will be a wonderful surprise when he gives this new pair to her; last year, her boots were leaking and she nearly got frostbite. Though her damp boots made her suffer in the bitter cold, she never complained; she must love Papa very much. New rat traps mean that Papa intends to extend his trapping runs to cover more ground; this could give us a chance of being more productive than last year.

Papa got Mama a new washboard to go with her new tub; that will make washing clothes much easier than rubbing them together in the soapy wash water. We have a good scrubbing board at the house, but Mama didn't want to take it out to the trapping camp; now, she can take the one we have at home to the camp with us and leave this new one behind.

While I was daydreaming, Papa beckoned me to come to his side to see something. He told me to pick the color of the woolen cap and mittens I would like; I chose navy blue. I informed Papa that Alma's favorite color was brown, so we got her a pair of mittens and a hat also.

Papa got Lee and Brad each a new pair of boots. The broad smiles on their faces demonstrated the appreciation they had for Papa's generosity.

Papa brought us back to reality when he pointed out that we would all have to work extra hard this winter to be sure we will have enough money to pay for all these pleasant purchases. "That includes you, little Nora!" he teased.

"Yes, sir! I understand!" I quickly responded with a slight chuckle.

Papa bought some gunpowder for his double-barreled shotgun. He bought several brass casings, some primer caps, shot, and wadding material to load his own shells. Papa does not care for paper shells. He says they are not reliable; if they get wet, they swell and will not fit into the breach of his gun. If they do fit, once fired they are difficult to remove for reloading. Papa says the brass casings can be reloaded up to twenty times. If they begin to split, he throws them away. By loading his own shells, he can choose the load that best suits the game he is after—fine shot for rabbit and squirrel, medium shot for ducks and rails, and heavy shot for geese and deer.

"That will do us for this year!" Papa asserted.

"Are you sure, Adam?" Doc inquired. "It costs to live!" Doc consoled, trying to soften the blow of the bill's tally.

Bayou Dularge 1921

Farmer's Rows, Wagon Trails, Pasture Lands
General Store
Rural Homesteads
Flatboat with pushpole

"Yes, I am quite sure. This is more than I figured on buying," Papa offered with a tentative smile. Papa's eyes widened as he gazed briefly at the numbers. "Let's get all this stuff loaded aboard the *Early Rose* right away," he urged, trying to dispel the discomfort of this new burden of responsibility, which he knew was self-imposed.

Papa's bill would not be subject to payment immediately. The ticket will be held until the end of the winter. Next March, when we bring our furs up for sale, the bill will be squared away. Doc offers our furs to several buyers; the one who offers the best price for the entire lot, purchases the fur from him. Deducting the amount Papa owes to the general store, plus a 5 percent commission for selling our fur, Ole Doc takes his horse down the bayou to our house to pay us a visit. The amount of money remaining would determine if we had a good, fair, or poor winter.

Settle-up time is an anxious time; we always hold our breath hoping the news is good. Each year we work hard and do our best to earn all that we can; "the rest is in the Lord's hands," Mama always says. "Good or bad, we will take whatever the Lord sees fit to give us. It is He that gives the power to get wealth," Mama says, trying to instill courage in everyone and give us a lesson in faith at the same time.

Puk-puk-puk-puk-puk-puk-puk-puk-puk-puk-puk-puk-puk-puk, sounded the engine of the *Early Rose.* Lee cast off the bowline, then he ran to the back deck to give Brad a hand; they quickly transferred the stern line to the bit farthest from the dock. With the stern still moored to the pile of the wharf, Papa sped up the engine to swing the boat around. Once the bow was turned to the south, he eased off the throttle so the boys could take the loop of the stern line off the piling. With a well-timed jerk of the wrist, Brad loosed us from the dock as Lee hollered out, "Let's go!" and Papa put the motor in the corner (he sped up the engine). *Puk-puk-puk-puk-puk-puk-puk-puk-puk-puk-puk-puk-puk,* sounded the engine, as we sped fair tide down the bayou; we were heading for home posthaste.

On my way to the boat, Doc handed me a cloth sack with a string tied around its neck, so I couldn't see what was inside. Bending over so he could whisper in my ear, he said, "Now you share this with your brothers, little missy!" Grateful for the surprise, I hugged him around his neck before scampering aboard our boat. Once I was seated on the prow, I waved a hearty good-bye and thanked Mr. Fursom for the sack of goodies.

Now it was time to peek inside the sack. I allowed my brothers the first pick of the candy and cookies inside the cloth bag, and I returned to my seat on the bow to try a few of the treats myself. It was a nice gesture from Doc to give us this sack of sweet treats for our trip home, I thought. I will be sure to save some for Mama and Alma back home.

I was happy that Papa was able to get everything Mama requested on the list. She will be surprised with all the extras Papa is bringing home with us. Her new boots will keep her feet dry and warm this winter; she knew she needed those boots, but not wanting to burden Papa with this costly item, she refused to write it down. Papa got the boots anyway. I am glad I have such a loving and selfless family. Everyone seems to care more for the others than for themselves. I appreciate my family very much, and I love them all dearly.

On our way down the bayou, my best girlfriend, Mariah Lovett, ran out to the water's edge to greet us. She asked me when we would be leaving for the camp. I informed her that Papa said we would be leaving after church service this Sunday. She pledged to see me then. The rest of our trip was uneventful, since most of the residents were either eating dinner or taking a nap.

October 18, 1921 (A Time for Prayer)

After supper, Papa and Mama engaged in conversation about events gone by; the winters have been very cold these past few years. Last trapping season, the LaCoste family lost their little girl; she fell out of their pirogue into the freezing water. Attempts to warm her failed. She caught pneumonia and died in her mother's arms. It was a terrible tragedy.

The LaCoste family traps an area not far from our grounds. Jean LaCoste and Papa are close friends, and we visit each other often during the winter at each other's campsites. Last year was a rare exception; we were all too busy with our furs to exchange visits. We never left our campsite. We didn't learn of the terrible event until spring. Little Sabrina LaCoste (five years old) was buried on a high ridge near their camp; it was reported that the family could hardly finish the trapping season, sorely grieving over their loss. Marguerite LaCoste has not yet recovered from her daughter's sudden and tragic death.

Papa asked us to bow our heads for prayer: "We all know that God is good and His mercy endures forever. We thank Him for the many blessings He has bestowed upon us. We humbly ask for mercy for our dear friends, the LaCoste family, as they strive to overcome their grief over the loss of their little girl. Amen."

REFLECTIONS OF THE SUMMER STORM

Recalling the terrible storm that hit us in late July this year, Papa thanked God that no one perished as a result of the tempest. No one died, but Papa and several of the men had to mount their horses in search of the dead carcasses of the cattle that perished; they had to burn them to prevent disease. The storm tore off part of our roof, and our storage shed disappeared. Since our house is built atop large wooden piles, we escaped the flood waters. When the wind carried away part of our roof, we relocated to a back room to escape the driving rain. Words could never describe the relief we all felt when the storm subsided. There were many tense moments during the height of the ravaging deluge. It was three days before the grass began to reappear from beneath the mud and silt that was left when the flood waters receded. The grass would have been unrecognizable had it not been for the leafy formations, coated with mud and protruding through the ooze.

Many snakes came into the yard with the rising storm tide, and they left again when the water receded, but not all of them left. A large water moccasin decided he liked the shade of the house, and he was discovered coiled near one of our support piles. Papa picked up his hoe and chopped the snake's head clean off. Brad took the remainder of the slithery creature to the bayou and threw it to the crabs. Lee took a shovel and buried the head of the serpent deep in the ground to prevent the danger of anyone being hurt by its poisonous fangs.

The stench of rotting marsh and the slow dissipation of the mud deposits were the last evidence to be vanquished by the same forces that produced all the mess in the first place. The grass did not turn green again until heavy rains washed away the muddy crust from its leaves.

Within a month, most repairs to the damaged buildings had been completed. Neighbor working with neighbor, rebuilding all that had been undone by the storm, bringing the community closer together through the mutual sharing of their burdens. This is a good example of how the families of the lower bayou make the best of a bad situation.

Before our prayer time ended, we remembered our family members on Deer Island. Reports that Morgan City was struck by the worst of the storm made us concerned that Uncle Justin and Aunt Sarah and Felix and Gus had been in the center of harm's pathway. Their home is soundly constructed on the highest ground above sea level, but when nature unleashes her violent fury, nothing man can build is safe. Praying they have escaped all harm, we placed their well being in the Lord's hands.

October 19, 1921 (Friday Morning)

This morning we will be going up the road to Grandma and Grandpa White's to spend the day with Mama's family before leaving for the winter. Papa has instructed Lee and Brad to hitch the horse to the buckboard. As soon as they signal that they are ready, we will be leaving. Grandma Emily is preparing shrimp and okra gumbo, one of my favorite dishes. Dried shrimp, fresh tomato, green and white onion, and fresh picked okra, all blend together to create a flavor that is unmatched by any other combination. It is making my mouth water just thinking about the dish.

Lee hollered, "We're ready!" and we raced out the front door. Papa escorted Mama to the wagon and lifted her up to the passenger seat at the center of the carriage. Alma cried for help; Papa quickly bent over, grabbed her around her waist, and whirled her up to the seat beside Mama. Papa mounted the driver's seat; Brad, Lee, and I, jumped on the rear of the wagon. A slap of the reins and a giddyap, and we were ambling about from the side of the house to the roadway, and then up the bayou side wagon trail to Grandma's house.

Alma sang to her ragdoll as the boys and I swung our dangling legs forward and backward, keeping time with the horse's trot. *Smokey* is a dapple-gray gelding Papa acquired a few years ago when his owner passed away. The five-year-old is a gentle-natured horse, easy to handle; he is always eager to perform any chores. Everyone loves *Smokey*! I always enjoy a ride on the buckboard; anytime we go anywhere is a pleasurable experience.

The three mile trip up the road doesn't take long; before I knew it, Lee hopped off the wagon to tie the horse to the hitching post on the side of Grandma's house. While Papa was taking care to offload Mama and Alma, Brad and I raced to the front porch to announce our arrival.

One of my cousins, Andy, had already taken out his accordion; he began to bellow out a folk tune as the rest of my family entered the house behind us. Grandma White came into the sitting room, clapping her hands in tempo with Cousin Andy's foot stomping. Grandpa Matthew was sitting at the kitchen table, drinking a cup of fresh hot coffee.

Andy began to sing as he played, and Mama and Papa joined together in a dance. Alma and I tried our best to imitate their dance moves, while Lee and Brad poked fun at our efforts. When Cousin Susan entered the room, they suddenly got quiet and dignified.

Cousin Susan is one of the prettiest girls on the bayou. At fourteen, I have heard some refer to her as beautiful. When she came into the room, my brothers became strangely nervous. She grabbed my arm, and we walked to the back porch to chat awhile.

Grandma soon summoned everyone to the dinner table. The large pot on the woodstove was filled to the brim with the main course—shrimp okra gumbo.

"Grandma White's shrimp okra gumbo is my favorite dish!" I proclaimed, as others who were lined up behind me concurred with my statement, voicing their own accolades. A pot of fluffed rice, boiled potatoes, and some freshly brewed sassafras tea enhanced the joy of eating the main course.

The number of trips to the stove for second helpings attested to the approval rating for Grandma White's cooking. At the end of the meal, there was only enough left in the pot to serve an unexpected guest one plate; it was just enough to make someone wish for more.

As the custom goes, the grownups all retired for an afternoon nap. Alma followed Mama and Papa to bed. Andy, Lee, and Brad went to the bayou side to fish for crabs with hand lines. Susan and I returned to the back porch for more chitchat.

Late Afternoon

Cousin Andy and my two brothers caught two bushels of beautiful blue claws. It took them almost all afternoon to catch the fresh water crabs, but the praises they received from all the elders over their fine catch made them feel ten feet tall.

Papa and the boys went looking for driftwood to make a fire. Grandpa Matthew rigged up his huge black kettle on a specially made rack, which will secure it above the blaze. Before long, flames were tickling the bottom of the large cauldron.

The troubled water was blended with special ingredients, which had been tossed into the pot; the escaping vapors sent forth that unique aroma associated with boiling seafood. The crabs were thrown into the seething water, and the feast was near at hand.

The first bushel of boiled crabs was dipped out of the hot water and spread upon a large table that Grandpa kept in his backyard. While Grandpa and Papa tended to the second batch of crabs, the rest of us began to enjoy the sumptuous meal.

My favorite part of the crab is the claws; the dark meat inside is especially good. Lee enjoys the fat in the open backs and the eggs in the female crabs, when they have them. Everyone else says they like the whole thing. Mama is peeling crabs for Alma; my little sister has not mastered the process of removing the meat from the many compartments.

We had a lovely time together, especially Susan and I. Susan noted that the cool front that came through during the night had chased all the mosquitoes away. Though we found ourselves completing the meal under the light of the moon, the pestering creatures never made their usual appearance.

The atmosphere for telling a good story could not have been more perfect. The full moon, the absence of mosquitoes, the crackle of the diminishing fire, and a cool northerly breeze, set the stage for Grandpa and Papa to entertain us in the manner that we had grown accustomed to.

Grandpa White spoke first. "Most of you young folks never knew my father. Adam and Ida got to know him, but he died when most of you were in diapers. My father, Ezekiel White, was a stern man. He was a man who never smiled, even when someone tempted him to do so by telling him a joke. He felt that joke-telling was foolishness and should not be engaged in. Anyway, your great grandfather had an ornery bull he had named *Nicodemus*. He had raised that bull from a young calf, but the animal just never took a liking to

Papa. One day Ole Zek, as my father was affectionately called, went out in the pasture to check his fence lines. When he got to the rear fence line, the bull decided he would give Papa a little trouble.

"Now I wouldn't even have heard this story, if your great-grandmother hadn't seen it happen through her rear kitchen window.

"Anyway, that old bull charged after Papa with a vengeance. Ole Zek found himself in a pickle. He ran for a nearby tree. The problem was that there was a large briar patch that completely surrounded the tree. He ran in circles around that tree to avoid the bull's determined advances. That stubborn animal was meaning to mow him down.

"Worried that Papa might get hurt, Mama ran to the neighbor's house for help. The man of the house wasn't home, but his wife came to our house to witness the spectacle. Soon, a crowd of neighborhood women had gathered, nervously watching as the big Brahma Bull chased Ole Zek all over the field.

"The pasture had a few trees growing in it that afforded shade for the cattle. My father ran from one tree to the next, trying desperately to make it back to the house. I have no idea what made that bull so mad, but my mother said he was stomping his front hooves and shaking his head in a violent display of temper.

"Great-grandmother and the other women went to the corn-crib and fetched a basket of corn, which had not yet been shucked. Calling to the bull by name, my mother managed to coax *Nicodemus* to the feed trough.

"Dazzled by the experience and torn by the thorns of the briar patches, Ole Zek finally made it through the pasture gate to safety. When Mother approached him with the crowd of neighborhood wives beside her, he said, 'That bull is the most ornery creature of all of God's creation. Aside from me, that is!' and he let out in uproarious laughter.

"Not quite knowing how to respond, the group of women restrained their laughter for a while. When Ole Zek continued in bellowing laughter, pausing only briefly to say it was all right for them to laugh along with him, pandemonium broke out. Some of the ladies laughed so hard they forgot themselves, rolling on the ground in a display of uncontrolled hilarity.

"From that day forward, Papa Zek was a changed man. The bull and he were the best of friends afterward, and Papa became one of the bayou's leading pranksters before he died. In case you were wondering what became of *Nicodemus*, he died about a year after your great-grandpa."

Laughter is contagious, and for a period of time, it overwhelmed all of us. Everyone agreed that Grandpa Matthew's story was a very good one. It's strange that the mean streak left my great-grandpa and the bull at the same time, a bull he had raised from a calf; they must have known each other very well, I reasoned.

It was Papa's turn to speak: "My good friend, Toussant Theriot from up the bayou had a similar experience with his mule, *Johnny Crook*. He had purchased the animal the previous spring. *Johnny Crook* did not seem to mind pulling Toussant's plow, but he did not like pulling Toussant's wagon. Each time he hitched the mule to his tumbrel, the ornery creature would try to kick the floorboard off below the driver's seat.

"After a short deliberation, Toussant fashioned himself a sharp pole. No longer able to tolerate the mule's stubbornness, he voiced his displeasure right in the animal's face: '*Tetu tete de mule!*' he scolded in his native tongue. He called him a 'stubborn-headed mule!' Toussant showed the sharp point of the sick to his beast of burden and scolded him again: '*Tetu tete de mule!*' Making his intentions clear, he warned with his stick in his hand: 'This is for you if you don't behave!' After the second warning, he promptly nailed the makeshift pike to the floorboard of his wagon. With the sharp edge of the stick only two inches from the mule's rear end, he remounted the wagon and went on his merry way. I don't know if that mule understood French, but he must have known what that pike would feel like, because *Johnny Crook* never tried to kick the wagon again. That sharpened stick is still nailed to the floorboard, just in case the mule forgets himself."

That was another delightful story. Everyone applauded the two elders for their amusing tales. Mama informed Papa that she was getting tired; even the fire was spent, having burned down to ashes. Our horse was getting restless; the poor thing had been tied to the hitching post all day—he was fed and watered, of course.

Following the farewell hugs and kisses, Grandpa Matthew and Grandma Emily wished us well. "We hope you have a good trapping season and we will keep all of you in our prayers until you return home safely next spring," Grandma told us. "Be sure to give our regards to Justin and Sarah. Tell them it's about time for them to come and pay us a visit!" Grandpa bewailed, complaining about their long absence from Bayou Du Large.

"We'll see each other at the church service, Sunday!" Mama offered, as she mounted our buckboard with a little help from Papa. Alma was sound asleep in Mama's arms by the time we arrived back at the house. The day had been most enjoyable; it went by so quickly.

When I lay my head upon my pillow, I will have no trouble falling asleep. The visit with Mama's family has left me exhausted. Tomorrow is another day. Good night, Lord. Amen.

October 20, 1921 (Saturday Morning)

Saturday's sunrise found us up and eager. Papa and the boys are busy constructing a wooden cage, a holding pen to secure the piglets for our journey to the trapping camp. Mama and I are busy making last-minute checks to make sure nothing will be left behind when the men load everything aboard the *Early Rose.*

Mama is already wearing her new boots; I knew she would like them. When Papa gave them to her, she clutched him in her arms and thanked him. It was a touching scene watching my parents in a loving embrace.

Several times during the course of the day, Mama had to steal me away from my daydreaming. My attention has been focused on Uncle Justin, and Aunt Sarah and their two boys; I was thinking how happy I will be to see them again. I pondered the excitement surrounding last year's visit, and the fun I had with my two cousins, Felix and Gus.

Earlier, I was out at our trapping camp; using my mind's eye, I wondered how the structure would look since the storm hit the area. Once I used my imagination to survey the damage, I remembered the hustle and bustle of our last winter there; the hard work associated with processing the many fur-bearing animals, preparing them

for the moulds. Even though skinning, stretching, tacking, and drying the furs is hard work, I would not hope for anything to change.
Life together with my family there is always a wonderful experience.

Papa suggested to the boys that, since their chores were all done,
they should go along the bayou banks in search of bird eye peppers.
Papa requested they pick enough peppers to bring with us to the
trapping camp, and some extra for Uncle Justin at Deer Island. They
promised to do their best and took off, heading down the bayou.

I asked Papa if I could accompany the boys, but almost immediately, my little sister began to cry: she wanted to go too. Papa told
me I could go, as long as I promised to take Alma along with me and
that I would watch over her. I didn't really mind; I love my little sister; she doesn't have much to say to anyone who enjoys conversation
like I do; she would rather talk to her doll. That's just the way she is.

After a light dinner of leftover biscuits, Alma and I headed for
the pepper patch to try to catch up with the boys. The cool air and
the bright sunshine made our walk down the wagon path exhilarating. Alma and I hopped along our merry way singing, "Skip to my
Lou." My sister sang along with the zeal of a choirgirl; it didn't matter to me to whom she directed her affections; that ragdoll certainly
didn't care. I was enjoying her company, though I found myself competing with the doll for her attention to no avail.

By the time we caught up with my brothers, they had already
picked an abundance of the hot peppers. They had a stack of the cut
bushes heavily laden with the green and red-hot berries. The red berries are the hottest, but the green ones would add spice to any meal.
Mama uses these peppers throughout the year. We usually gather
enough to fill several jars. Mama heats a mixture of salt and vinegar;
she pours the boiling solution into the pepper-filled jars and they are
preserved for a very long time, saving them for future use.

Mama uses the spicy-hot bird eye peppers for cooking game,
especially deer and duck. I usually remove any pepper I find embedded in my portion of meat; if you bite into one by accident, it will
numb your taste buds. Papa loves the taste it gives the meat and he
eats the peppers. I have seen him spoon out a heaping measure over

his plate of beans and smack his lips until all is consumed. I always wait for smoke to come out of his mouth, or through his nose or ears.

When I was younger, I had witnessed Papa's obvious enjoyment of the fiery pellets. Thinking I would enjoy them equally, I made the mistake of trying one. I am glad I only dared to try a single one! What started out as a sensation of mild heat, developed into a fiery inferno by the time I was able to quench my mouth with several glasses of water. Even after three full glasses of water, the numbing pain did not completely go away. Since then, I have been very careful not to bite into one.

Mama had sent us to the pepper patch with two cloth sacks. One sack was for us, and the other one was for Aunt Sarah. We continued picking until both bags were nearly full. I had been to the pepper patch before, but this was my first time picking. The last few years, I came along to amuse myself, not to pick the hot berries.

I was about to learn another uncomfortable lesson about bird eye peppers. After several hours of picking, the juice from the peppers begins to burn your fingers. At first it was barely noticeable, but after a while, it was undeniable. Not only do your fingers start to burn, but each place on your body that your fingers brush up against starts to heat up.

By the time we got home, I was sorry I had wanted to pick the peppers with my brothers. I got tired of returning to the bayou-side wharf every fifteen minutes to try to get relief in the cool water of the stream. After several failed attempts, I just stayed there and dipped and dipped, drenching a rag with water and wringing it over the affected areas until the pain finally subsided.

I'm glad that Alma was totally engaged with her doll during our outing. The Lord only knows what tantrums she would be throwing had she made the same mistake that I did.

As for my two brothers, they didn't complain a bit; there was no hint of even a mild discomfort. Mama told me that their hands were tougher than mine since they were accustomed to performing more difficult tasks. That must have been the correct explanation because they seemed totally unaffected by the pepper juice.

We spent the remainder of the evening pickling the peppers. Mama was able to make twenty-four jars; there were twelve for Aunt Sarah and twelve for us. She praised our efforts, saying that we had picked the amount she was hoping for. I am always happy when I do something that pleases my parents.

October 21, 1921 (Sunday Morning)

Sunday church service begins at 9:00 a.m.; the bell sounds at a quarter till, but we will be arriving early this morning. Since the church is next door to our home, arriving on time is never a problem.

Our parish priest, Pastor Samuel, is a mild-mannered, soft-spoken minister; he is well liked in the community. Striving to transform his gospel messages into real-life experiences by applying biblical teachings to life on Bayou Du Large in 1921, his exhaustive commentary surrounding each chosen passage of Scripture makes every service a learning experience. I have never suffered from boredom during any of his sermons.

As usual, Papa will be greeted at the front door of the chapel by Pastor Samuel; since we are preparing to leave for the winter, he will request a special prayer from the congregation and the priest's blessing at the end of the service.

My great-grandfather, Joseph Addison, donated the land where the church is built. Several local residents of English descent pooled their resources and began construction on the structure in the spring of 1875. Work was completed on July 4, 1875.

In those early years, a priest would ride down the bayou on horseback from the village of Houma to conduct a service on Sunday afternoons. Later, a missionary priest was sent to live in our community. He was charged with the responsibility of addressing our spiritual needs, but he also began to teach the children how to read and write. Now the building is a church, a meeting hall, and a schoolhouse.

A parsonage was built at the rear of the church house in 1905. Pastor Samuel has been with us for the past five years. During school time, he has been like a father to me; he takes great care and patience to insure I learn my lessons well. Our priest is like a member of our family, and he is a frequent guest at mealtimes.

After everyone was seated in the pews, Pastor Samuel directed the members of the choir to begin singing the hymns that had been chosen for this morning. Before long, we were all joined in singing songs of adoration. The sermon was on the beatitudes. The presentation was direct, not sugar-coated. He exhorted that we should "deny our own selfish lusts, looking to another's wellbeing more than our own, lend strength to the weak, encouraging one another when life deals out its cruel blows, love one another as Christ has loved you!"

Before I realized it, communion had been administered and we were preparing to close with a hymn. Pastor Samuel announced that the Addison family would be leaving for our trapping camp immediately after the church service.

The pastor continued, "The Addisons desire your prayers and have asked for a special blessing before we dismiss this morning. Adam, Ida, Lee, Brad, Nora and Alma, would you come forward for prayer and a blessing?"

We walked up the isle to the front of the church and knelt down side by side. Pastor asked the congregation to bow their heads and make their petitions on behalf of the Addison family known to God, each in his own special way.

After a lengthy pause, the priest placed his hands on Papa's head and prayed, "May God go with you and may He bless and keep you. Amen." One by one, the priest prayed a like prayer, laying his hands on each of us as he did so.

The Anglican Church
On Bayou Dularge
Property donated by:
Patrick Adams
Established - 1875

WAGON PATH

When my turn came, Pastor Samuel laid his hands on my head and prayed. When he finished praying, I was overwhelmed by a sense of reassurance, as he left me to pray for my little sister next to me. Suddenly, I became confident that God would be with us no matter what circumstances arise. I thanked God for the peace and security the moment of solemn prayer had afforded me.

Little Alma was the last family member to receive the blessing, then the priest directed the congregation to sing "Rock of Ages"; he then dismissed the assembly.

My best girlfriends—Jenny Kraft, Alice LaCoste, and Mariah Lovett—stood outside the church near the bell, waiting for me to come and bid them a fond farewell; I had to wade through a sea of people to get to them. The greeting line extended from well inside the meeting hall to a point far outside the front doors. I paused to shake Pastor Samuel's hand and thanked him for his special prayer of blessing.

When I arrived at the bell, my girlfriends and I were quickly engulfed in laughter as we made various dares and pledges among ourselves over the things we would do or not do during our winter separation. Cousin Susan soon joined in our conversation; she gave me a hug and wished me well and said she would be looking forward to seeing me again next spring.

As the crowd dissipated, it was time to say our final good-byes. Jenny and Alice could not hold back their tears. Mariah, Susan, and I, struggled to keep from doing likewise. With one last hug for each of my friends, I began walking back to my house to join my family.

As I neared my home, I turned and shouted for all to hear. "I love you, Jenny, Alice, Mariah, and Cousin Susan. May God bless and keep each of you until we meet again next spring!"

I changed my clothes and was seated in Papa's rocking chair when the rest of my family returned home. Everyone seemed surprised that I had arrived there first; I was a bit surprised that they were back so late. "Get a move on!" I teased. "It's time to go!" I asserted. My earnest display of enthusiasm got everyone excited.

Within the next few hours, our animals will all be loaded aboard the *Early Rose*. Careful checks must be made to be sure nothing has been left undone. Once my brothers finish hauling the three barrels of rainwater from the cistern to our boat, Lee and Brad will unhitch our horse from the sled and *Smokey* will be put out to pasture. Our neighbor, Mr. Stanley Minor, has pledged to take care of our horse for us until we return from the trapping camp; he will make sure the animal has plenty of hay and drinking water during our absence.

Chapter Three

LET'S GO!

October 21, 1921 (Sunday afternoon)

"There was total exuberance!" That is how I would describe the atmosphere at the Addison house as we made last-minute preparations for boarding the *Early Rose*. The small vessel was sitting low in the water, having been loaded from stem to stern with supplies and winter provisions.

Mama, Alma, and I were already aboard, trying desperately to be patient while Papa barked out orders to my two brothers to make sure everything was done that he wanted done. Lee had just finished filling the three water barrels from our cistern, just in case the summer storm had damaged the cistern at the Plumb Bayou trapping camp (otherwise known as Camp Addison).

Brad is tending our horse; he stood hitched to our wooden sled, waiting to transport the barrels filled with rainwater from behind the house to the wharf. Papa constructed the sled for carrying heavy objects (too awkward to carry manually) with little effort, using our horse for locomotion. Once the sled is loaded, Lee will coax the horse by slapping his rear while Brad leads him by the reins to the dock.

"Let's get a move on!" I urged. "Sunlight is burning," I playfully warned. Soon the barrels were loaded aboard, and Brad and Lee placed them side by side along the front cabin wall. "That will do just fine," Papa commented.

Lee guided the horse and sled back to the side of the house where he loosed the harness and walked *Smokey* through the gate, cutting him loose in the pasture. "See you next spring ole boy," he pledged as the horse ambled off to graze.

Brad appeared on deck with the first of three piglets, which will be coming along for the ride. He had taken the young pig from our hog pen at the rear of the house and he was going to deposit him in the temporary holding pen purposely located at the rear of the cabin. Papa puts the pigs aft so our motor can drown out the sounds of their squealing during our long trip to the camp.

Our two goats, *Ninny* and *Nanny*, are both tied to the anchor bit at the bow of the boat. They are as still as a picture, except for their jaw movements. Chewing the cud is a normal activity for our pair of Nubian milk goats. Their floppy ears are black, and they have black markings on their legs, but the rest of their bodies are dark brown. If their ears would stand up, they could be mistaken for young deer Mama told me.

The two wooden crates that hold our chickens look like a confusion of feathers. Now and again, a head or a beak will appear, bobbing and weaving as they struggle to find a comfortable position, pecking at one another in the process.

All alone in his own cage is my pet rooster *George Washington*. He was the hardest to catch this morning; I guess it was due to the frantic crying of his hens as they were being snatched away from their roost before daylight. Papa had instructed the boys to gather up the chickens from the coop before the sun came up so they would be easily managed. *Ole George* escaped capture by flying over Brad's shoulder; he ran off hollering all over the yard and could not be overtaken.

Getting Ready:
Hauling Fresh Water To The "Early Rose"

George Washington decided to return to the coop to look for his beloved hens. Brad snuck up on him with a long-handled dip net and trapped him beneath the netting. After a short struggle, he finally settled down in his cage; he crows now and then to let his hens know that he is nearby. Mama brags that he is the best rooster she has ever had. "That rooster makes the hens run for the nest, even when they don't feel like it; with fifteen sweethearts, he stays busy!" Mama boasted. Besides doing his job, he is a very handsome bird sporting multicolored feathers.

Lee returned to the boat and reported that the sled was back behind the house; the horse has been released into Mr. Stanley's pasture, and the harness and bridle have been safely stowed away. "Good job, son!" Papa told him. It was obvious to me that Papa appreciated Lee's diligence.

Our neighbor has a large fenced pasture behind his house just as we do; he also has a barn and a store of winter feed to supplement our horse's diet while we are away. In exchange for his kindness, Papa brings Mr. Minor fresh pork every spring. When we return in early March, our piglets will be too heavy to carry; they will have feasted on marsh grass, roots, and animal carcasses all winter. When we return in the spring, the pigs will be fed a steady diet of pure corn to purge their intestinal tract. After a month of eating corn, they will be ready to slaughter, but that's another story.

October 21, 1921 Midafternoon)

Papa tied the doors open on the cabin. He lifted the motor cover and leaned it against the wall. Now, with the engine exposed, Papa could spin the large flywheel of our motor. The engine sounded, *Puk-puk-puk-puk*; then there was silence!

Once again, Papa spun the flywheel; this time, the engine sparked a smile on everyone's face with its continuous sounds. *Puk-puk-puk-puk-puk-puk-puk-puk-puk-puk-puk-puk-puk-puk-puk-puk-puk*, sounded the engine as it began to warm up for the journey. Papa returned the engine cover to its proper place. Alma began to clap her hands excitedly, putting her ragdoll down momentarily to do so. Then came the moment that we had been waiting for; Lee untied the bow and Brad untied the stern. Papa put some pep to the engine and, with a slight push away from the dock we were on our way at last. Papa announced that he felt we would make good time, since we were running downstream and fairing with the tide.

I ran to the bow of the boat and sat down beside our two goats. *Ninny* and *Nanny* both enjoy a good petting; as I stroked their heads gently, one at a time, I sang them merry songs. Turning my head back toward the cabin for a moment, I noticed Mama was smiling from ear to ear as she sat on a stool beside Papa.

Everyone is excited that we are finally underway; even the pigs began to squeal when they heard the engine sounding, though it was probably an expression of fear more than joy. From my vantage point on the front of our boat, I can barely hear their shrill cries. Lee and Brad have taken a seat on the water barrels and they are busy exchanging friendly chatter. I can't see Alma; ten-to-one, she is singing to her ragdoll on the bottom bunk in the cabin.

The light northern breeze is refreshing, but thankfully, the wind is not strong enough to trouble the open waters in the lakes we must cross on our journey to the camp. Loaded down as she is, the *Early*

Rose has only a few inches of freeboard; if we should encounter high waves crossing the lakes we might be in danger of losing something overboard.

I overheard Papa telling Mama that we should arrive at Plumb Bayou about two hours before dark; that would give us enough time to inspect the inside of the camp and do a little cleaning before the sun sets. Mama had expressed that she wanted to be sure there were no rats or snakes inside the camp before we bed down for the night. "Snakes and rats are difficult to see by candlelight!" Mama warned, as if Papa did not know that.

Mama is an industrious woman; this year, she taught me how to make candles. Papa purchased several ten-pound blocks of paraffin from Doc Fursom's General Store (each ten-pound block makes about four quarts of liquid wax). Mama had already prepared several wicks for the candle-making process (three heavy cotton yarn strands are braded together and soaked in a solution of water, salt, and boric acid overnight; the braided yarn is then cut to eighteen-inch lengths).

In an open kettle, Mama boils some water; one block at a time, Mama melts the paraffin in a second container, which she has submerged in the hot water bath. Once the paraffin wax is melted, Mama adds a measure of lard to the hot wax and blends it into the liquid (this helps to solidify the wax). Three at a time, we start dipping the braded yarn strings—these would become the candlewicks when the job is finished.

To weigh the braded yarn down for dipping, Mama has one-inch-diameter flat lead weights with holes drilled in the center. Each of the bottom wick ends is passed through a hole; a knot is tied to secure it to the bottom of each piece of lead. Mama makes three eight-inch candles at a time, so the tops of three wicks are tied to her dipping stick before being lowered into the melted wax. Nearby, Mama has a container of cool water she uses to quickly solidify the freshly dipped wicks.

The process is relatively simple: three weighted wicks are dipped into the melted wax and lard mixture; after a few seconds, the three soon-to-be candles are dipped into the cool water to harden (after the first dip the wick of each candle must be pulled straight to insure it remains centered in the waxen tube); after a few seconds, the three candles are patted dry and returned to be dipped again in the melted wax and lard mixture (dip in hot wax, dip in cool water, pat dry of water, dip in hot wax, dip in cool water, pat dry of water, dip in hot wax, dip in cool water, pat dry of water, this procedure is followed until the desired one-inch diameter candle is reached; this usually requires thirty to forty dips). The candles are then rolled on a clean, flat surface to finish the job. The wick is cut one-half inch above the top of each candle; a hot knife is used to cut away the lead, which is at the bottom of each candle. The job is done when Mama says it is done. It usually takes about six hours.

Mama makes ninety candles each fall—one for each day of our three-month stay at the trapping camp. She stores the eight-inch candles in old cigar boxes or some other convenient storage containers. Since kerosene lamps are our main source for light, we usually have more candles than needed.

Papa told us that since the weather was good, we would take the shortest route; if the weather had been poor, he would have chosen a much longer route, traveling through the various bayous to avoid the discomfort of stormy seas in the open waters of the lakes.

The short route, as described by Papa, is as follows: "From the dock at the front of our home, we travel eight miles down Bayou Du Large. We turn west through Old Pass into Mud Lake. After crossing the lake we steer northwest and traverse *Lake Mechant* (wicked lake). We then turn west southwest and navigate Blue Hammock Bayou, running its course into Four League Bay. Turning northwest, we will soon be able to see Mosquito Island off to our left and Carencro Bayou to our right. Steering due north, we will pass Mosquito Point out in the distance and begin to follow the east bank of Atchafalaya Bay. We will pass the mouth of Creole Bayou and continue to the next bayou along the northeastern shore of the bay. That will take us to the mouth of Plumb Bayou."

We untied from our wharf at 3:30 p.m., and Papa says we should arrive at the camp about an hour before it gets dark. The timing will depend on how rough the lakes are. So far, so good; Lake Mechant did not live up to its reputation of being a wicked lake; the lake is notorious for getting very rough very fast when the conditions are right.

Along the way, we encountered many pelicans (the Louisiana State bird). I saw seagulls, various species of cranes, herons, egrets, and countless varieties of ducks. I saw a few rails feeding on the mud-flats near the shoreline, but they fled into the marsh grasses as soon as we ventured too close to them. There were a few geese flying high overhead in their traditional "V" formation, but Papa says it isn't cold enough for them to have come this far south in the numbers we are accustomed to seeing here.

Ducks and geese are very plentiful near our trapping grounds. Many of those birds will end up in a pot on our stove this winter, helping to sustain us through the trapping season. The geese are so large that it only takes one to feed our entire family; Mama usually cooks sweet potatoes to balance the meal. It takes five ducks to equal the meat provided by one large Canadian goose, which can weigh as much as eight to ten pounds.

Mama is a very good cook. Anything she prepares in her favor-ite cast iron pot comes out tasting delicious. She cooks everything from alligator to venison; she even cooked a pot of young muskrat one winter. As I said, anything Mama cooks tastes very good; I espe-cially like the wild game.

The thought of Mama's cooking reminded me of the bird eye peppers we recently picked. When red, the peppers look similar to gooseberries to the inexperienced eye; they are smaller, but if placed among a handful of the sweet berries, an unsuspecting consumer of the gooseberries could easily be fooled.

I know all about this dirty little trick! Last fall, my brothers put a red bird eye pepper in a handful of ripe gooseberries they had picked for me. I popped the handful of tasty berries into my mouth without hesitation. I should have suspected something when they started making faces, trying hard to restrain their laughter as they waited for my reaction.

When my tongue was wetted by the juice from that single pep-per, I ran as fast as I could for the cistern near the side of our house. Lee and Brad laughed their fool heads off, but when Mama saw me wasting her precious cistern water to cool my tongue, she scolded them for their foolishness. Once the burning stopped, I must admit that it must have been a funny sight watching me make a mad dash for the cistern and hearing my cries for God's mercy until I finally got relief. I bet it will never happen to me again; it was a lesson well learned.

One of my favorite shore birds is the blue heron. The huge bird stands about four feet tall; it has a long neck, long legs, and long pointed bill. All these features enhance the bird's graceful appearance. I spotted about seven of the beautiful creatures on the way to Four League Bay.

Upon entering Four League Bay, we discovered that the wind had picked up and stirred up the waves. Since our course placed our bow directly into the wind, the two foot waves did not slow us down; Papa decided it was safe to make the crossing (Four League Bay becomes Atchafalaya Bay once you are north of South Point).

I untied the goats and moved them to the rear of the cabin since the spray from the waves was wetting the entire front deck of our boat. Everything on deck seemed secure enough to take the jolts from the waves as they pounded incessantly against the bow of the *Early Rose*.

Posing no real challenge to our well-constructed hull, our boat plowed through the troubled water at a steady clip; Papa didn't reduce the throttle one bit. "Steady as she goes," he hollered, as our engine consistently sounded its special tempo. *Puk-puk-puk-puk-puk-puk-puk-puk-puk-puk-puk-puk-puk-puk-puk-puk-puk*. The *Early Rose* proudly announced our determined progress, as we headed due north into a brisk wind and the choppy waters of the bay.

Trying to escape the spray from the waves over our bow, we all piled into our tiny cabin. Alma was asleep in the bottom bunk holding her ragdoll tightly in her arms. I jumped into the top bunk so I could continue to observe our passage. My brothers found a place on the floor near the engine housing to lie down as Mama and Papa chatted aimlessly over the sounds of our motor.

A half an hour or so after entering Four League Bay from Blue Hammock Bayou, we were passing South Point on our left side and entering Atchafalaya Bay. I could see the tree line prominently displayed on the horizon at the northeast corner of the bay. We will soon be on the lee side of the bay, and we will get relief from this rough water. That will be a pleasant experience. The bay was getting rougher by the minute; occasionally, the spray was entering the front cabin window, hitting Mama and Papa in the face. Papa said we were making it across the broad expanse of open water in the nick of time; our boat was pounding harder with each passing sea.

Mama suggested that we say a prayer: "Let us pray that our camp will be found intact when we arrive. Let us ask for God's mercy upon us, and also let us remember Uncle Justin and Aunt Sarah and their two boys in our prayers," Mama solemnly instructed.

We all bowed our heads in prayer in accordance with Mama's request. In addition to praying for the camp to be all right when we arrive, and the request for God's mercy upon all of our family, I also pleaded with God to help us get through this rough water. The northern sky is clouding up; there may be a cold front moving through tonight I thought.

Papa announced that there might be a cold front coming through soon after I pondered that very thing just a few minutes ago. Our camp is built on the west bank of Plumb Bayou on the point formed by a sharp bend to the left along the course of that stream. Joseph Addison, my great-grandfather, built the first camp in 1844; it remained intact until the Storm of 1904 destroyed the building. Papa's dad, Sanders Addison, was the second member of the family to build on this site; the Storm of 1909 destroyed the second camp. My Grandfather Sanders rebuilt it; this is the third time the camp was constructed, and we are hoping it lasts awhile.

My great-grandfather chose the site because it is the highest ground in the area. Long ago, Indians inhabited that very spot; for years, they deposited spent clam shells, animal bones, and broken pottery, forming what is commonly known as a midden. It provides a perfect foundation for the erection of a camp on the site. When Grandpa Sanders set the foundation piles for the third camp, he uprooted the broken and aged piles that were already there and replaced them with new ones. It was hard work, but with the help of his sons the task was quickly done; the new camp was constructed with both new and salvaged material. This camp site has been used every year for nearly seventy trapping seasons without fail.

This newest building (now eleven years old) stands six feet above the ground level at the top of the broad shell heap. The thick shell deposit prevents all but a few weeds from growing near or under the building. The clam shells also serve to keep the area clean and odor free.

Now, we were well into Atchafalaya Bay, having passed South Point (the north point of Point au Fer Island). To me, Atchafalaya Bay looks like the Gulf of Mexico; it is such a large expanse of water. In fact, it is the northern part of the Gulf, situated between Point au Fer Island and Marsh Island, which is farther west. I'll be happy when we reach the shoreline; this wide open water makes me nervous even though Papa didn't appear the least bit intimidated. I don't believe I ever saw my father nervous; Mama says he has nerves of steel.

Several porpoises were rolling in the bay. A few decided to travel alongside our boat, seeming to want to play with the boat's hull. These huge fish, swimming so close to the boat, make me feel that it would be dangerous to fall overboard. Heaven forbid what might happen if we should take on water and sink in this deep water; we are so far from shore.

I breathed a sigh of relief when Papa announced that we would soon be entering the mouth of Plumb Bayou. He pointed to a spot along the shoreline a few miles ahead. Half an hour later, we entered safe harbor, as we penetrated the shore of the bay by entering the bayou.

Plumb Bayou runs directly east for a mile or so before turning north and eventually back to the east again. Its course runs approximately five miles from the bay before entering into Plumb Lake at its easternmost end.

Our trapping grounds encompass a five-square-mile area, extending from the Atchafalaya River to the north side of Creole Bayou and from the west side of Plumb Lake back to Atchafalaya Bay. My family traps only a fraction of this vast tract of land.

Bounded by prairie on both sides, we traveled the first mile or so to the first north bend of the watercourse; another mile or so and we will be approaching the ridge where our camp site is located. The fresh water of the bayou is dark but clear. Plumb Island is clearly visible off in the distance.

Before reaching the camp, we will have penetrated the oak ridge known as Plumb Island. The scenery changes abruptly as we slowly reach the bend in the bayou, having followed its meandering course to get there. The trees growing on the high ground are oak, maple, gum, elm, ash, and a few other varieties that flourish atop the ridges of South Louisiana. From its mouth, the first couple of miles along the bayou is a picturesque view of golden prairie (perfect habitat for muskrat); once we penetrate the ridge, the changes are dramatic. Though densely forested, only the live oaks, the palmetto palms, and several varieties of evergreen undergrowth, retain their leaves; all the deciduous trees have already been stripped of their foliage by the northern breezes.

The camp was getting nearer. Having traveled north, then east through the island, I could see the second bend to the north straight ahead; just around that next corner is our campsite. "There it is!" I shouted. The sharp bend to the north was in plain view. Papa slowed the engine a bit. Lee hurried out the cabin and ran to the front of the boat taking the mooring line in his hand. Brad did likewise at the stern. Rounding the bend in the bayou, the pier that extended out from the left shoreline came into view. Papa slowed the engine to idle speed: *Puk-puk-puk-puk-puk-puk-puk-puk-puk-puk-puk-puk-puk-puk-puk-puk-puk*, the tireless engine sounded with diminished enthusiasm.

October 21, 1921 (Late Evening)

The tall trees were blocking out the late afternoon sunlight, making it seem later than it really was; their dark shadows shaded the campsite, as Papa stuck the bow against the left bank and sped up the engine to bring the stern of our boat around to the wharf. With the mooring lines secured, Papa pulled on the knotted rope to kill the motor. The cicadas and other night creatures were already announcing the late hour as we disembarked onto the dock.

As expected, the grass between the landing and the camp was over six feet tall. From our vantage point on the wharf, we could only be sure that the front of the camp was still standing. Papa ordered Lee and Brad to cut a trail straight for the front door of the cabin so we could get a closer look. Armed with long-handled cane knives, the boys made short work of the task. By the time Mama stepped off the boat, the pathway to the front door of the camp had been cleared.

"The camp is ready for inspection!" Brad proudly announced, making inviting motions with his hands.

"Come on, Mama, let's see what's inside!" Lee teased as he carefully opened the front door with a degree of caution, lacking the courage to be the first one to enter the dark room of the cabin.

"Good work, boys!" Mama praised. "Now let's take a look inside before it's too dark to see what's in there." With five candles in her hand, Mama entered the cabin first—something she usually does each fall. Striking a match against the cast iron stove, she lit the candles and placed them at strategic spots to improve her vision throughout the inside of the single room of the camp.

Meanwhile, outside in the yard, Papa struck a flint stone with his heavy knife, producing sparks over the freshly cut grass that Lee had piled beside the walking path. As the sparks fell gently upon the dry tender, the northerly breeze began to woo a flame; first called forth was a flicker, then a small fire, and finally a bold blaze.

Papa instructed me to continue feeding the flame with all the sticks and branches I could find. "Don't use any planks that may have been dislodged by the storm from the walkways or the cabin," he cautioned. "The smoke produced by the fire will keep mosquitoes away from our worksite. The fire will give us the light we need to finish with our immediate tasks," he informed us.

Papa instructed the boys to go inside to lend Mama a hand. They began moving the moss-stuffed mattresses around, checking for holes in the fabric, looking for signs of snakes or rats. When they were about to raise the final mattress, Mama could be heard hollering from outside the cabin.

"Shoo! Get out of my house you old nasty thing! Shoo! You get out of here right this very minute!" she raved. Mama appeared at the doorway with her broom, moving it swiftly this way and that, as a large snake slithered down the front steps and disappeared beneath the camp in hurried fashion. "And don't you come back here either!" Mama added in an authoritative tone. "I'll have Adam cut you in pieces!" she double-dared.

"Mama sure knows how to get rid of snakes, eh, Alma?" I quipped. My little sister merely shrugged her shoulders and smiled, completely oblivious to what had just taken place.

"There is not a single rat hole in any of the mattresses. This is the first time I can recall not having to spend time mending rat holes!" Mama proclaimed, clearly delighted by the pleasant, though totally unexpected discovery.

Papa said that he believes the large snake, which Mama so rudely removed from its summer home, is the reason there were no rat holes. Mama agreed with papa's deduction, making mention of how well-fed the serpent seemed to be—it was a very large snake. "The snake can return to the camp when we leave next spring," Mama teased, hoping the snake would heed her unusual invitation—not prematurely of course.

Our eyes had grown accustomed to the candlelight before we noticed it was totally dark outside. As Mama continued to sweep the floor of the camp, Papa began fashioning a torch using an old broom. He wound an old rag tightly around the stubble which used to be straw. Using some of the wire, which formerly bound the straw to the stick, he secured the rag tightly to the base of the broomstick. Walking over to one of the lit candles, he ignited the torch.

Papa had instructed Lee and Brad to find a handful of nails and a hammer so they could repair the roof. Three shingles had been blown away by the summer storm; this was minor damage considering the intensity of the tempest we had experienced back home. My two brothers promptly cut four shingles from a plank on our front walkway and stood ready for further instructions.

Papa lifted the torch toward the rooftop so the boys could see what they were doing. Lee and Brad climbed a ladder to the site of the damaged roof and quickly made the necessary repairs. "Good job, boys!" Papa proudly stated.

Alma and I continued to feed sticks and debris to the fire in the front yard. Papa stopped momentarily on his way back from the *Early Rose* to tell us we were doing a good job of keeping the fire going. I appreciated his kind gesture, and I redoubled my efforts to keep the blaze alive. I suddenly realized that Alma and I were a great help to the family by being diligent in our assigned task. The fire was one less thing that Papa and the boys had to worry about, leaving them free to accomplish the more important tasks.

Papa instructed Lee and Brad to remove the goats from the stern of the boat. *Ninny* and *Nanny* ran from the dock to the bank; they seemed to be glad they were once again on solid ground.

"Those goats won't stray very far. We'll leave the rest of the animals onboard the boat until tomorrow morning," Papa instructed. "You never know where those pigs and chickens will go in these unfamiliar surroundings," he added.

Lee recalled that last year one of our pigs was eaten by a gator; he remembered that we were lucky to find the other two when we returned from our visit to Deer Island.

"That is precisely the point, Lee!" Papa elaborated. "There is no reason for us to take any unnecessary chances. The remaining animals will be safe aboard the boat until morning. With the sunlight we will be able to keep a better eye on them."

Papa inspected the provisions on deck and went below to check the bilge. "Everything is all right, boys, let's go inside for the night," he cheerfully advised.

I asked Papa if he was sure our two goats would be safe during the night. Papa was reassuring, informing me that through all the years he has been trapping, he never lost a single goat. He told me they would probably sleep under the camp. With Papa's assurance, there was no need for me to worry anymore. I walked up to the two goats, hugged them around their necks, and told them good night.

We entered into the camp quickly, closing the door shut behind us to keep out the pesky mosquitoes. Our fire had died out for lack of encouragement. Mama had taken out a jar of pumpkin preserves and some leftover bread she had baked back at the house.

Papa advised us that we would be retiring early this evening. "We have a lot of work to do tomorrow," he warned. Encouraging us, he reminded all of us that the sooner we finish with our chores here, the sooner we will be leaving for Deer Island. We enjoyed a little small talk, as we consumed Mama's tasty snack, then we all climbed into the sack for some much-needed rest.

As I lay down, trying to go to sleep, I could not help worrying that there might be another snake somewhere in the camp. I know Mama gave the place a good going-over, but I remained frightened in spite of that awareness. What if that huge snake that Mama chased out the front door decides to return sometime during the night? What then? If you had seen the size of that detestable creature, you might better understand the reasons for my uneasy feeling. I began to wonder if it was my mattress that the snake was found under. I decided it would be better to pray than to worry. "Dear Lord, protect us from all harm. Have mercy on me and my family. Amen." Having put my trust in God, I decided to forget the snake. As soon as I did, I fell asleep.

October 22, 1921

The smell of burning wood and the aroma of fresh coffee brewing on the woodstove awakened me early this morning. Lee had gathered some driftwood from along the bayou bank, and Mama had the huge iron cooker getting hot from the newly introduced fuel in its belly.

Papa had taken water from one of the barrels stored on the deck of our boat so Mama could make the coffee; the cistern would have to be inspected before any water could be drawn from it. Even if the storm has left it undamaged, it would still have to be inspected inside in case some unsuspecting animal had tried to get a drink and fallen to its death by drowning; it has happened before.

Sunshine was entering the camp through the open shutters on the northeast side of the camp and through the front door, which faces almost directly east, welcoming inside the morning light and heat. Papa had the door and shutters tied in the open position so we could enjoy the sun's refreshing rays.

Mama said there was a chill in the air this morning. She told Papa that the temperature must have dropped below sixty degrees this morning before daybreak. Papa acknowledged that it was a bit colder, saying that the front we saw approaching as we crossed the bay must have come through; he said it must have been a weak one since it passed without any rain. "The winter months will soon be upon us!" Papa proclaimed, even though fall was not yet half over.

Ninny and *Nanny* strolled into the camp to have a look around. Just about the time *Ninny* began to nibble on one of the mattresses, Mama spotted them and chased them both out of the front door (the only door).

Brad cut *Ole George Washington* loose from his solitary confinement. Our rooster was so happy with his newfound freedom that he began to crow his fool head off. "Cock-a-doodle-doo!" Over and over, he repeated the sound. "Cock-a-doodle-doo!" Brad tried to mimic the loud display of the rooster's call, but *Ole George* knew his hens were listening; he ignored my brother's foolishness, sensing there was no real competition for his flock's affections.

Plumb Bayou
Trapping Camp

Lee released our fifteen barred-rock hens from the other two crates. Without fail, every one of those birds rushed over to greet their one true love. Observing the scene from the doorsteps of the camp, I found the activity very amusing. *George Washington* was strutting proudly among his hens, pausing briefly to crow awhile. This continued for quite some time—strutting awhile, then crowing awhile, strutting awhile, then crowing awhile. *Ole George* was proving he was all the rooster Mama is so quick to brag about.

The piglets remained penned up on the back deck of the boat until further cleanup of the yard could be completed. The condition of our hog pen was not yet certain. It will be inspected and repaired if necessary, before the young pigs can be released.

Meanwhile, our chickens were already busy pecking and scratching all around the place in search of lizards, roaches, worms, or any small creature they could find moving along the ground.

Papa asked Lee, Brad and I to join him in unloading the supplies from the *Early Rose*. Alma was still resting peacefully in her bed, hugging her ragdoll closely beside her. We immediately began hauling provisions from the boat to the camp's doorway so Mama could put them away.

After a short period of time, the doorway was almost totally blocked by a large number of items. Mama asked us to take a breakfast break so she could have time to catch up. We feasted on fresh hot biscuits while Mama continued to stow away everything we had hauled from the boat.

After breakfast, Mama instructed me to remain in the camp to lend her assistance in her laborious task. "The boys are capable of finishing the hauling without you," she stated. Mama was right; with my help, we were able to put away everything almost as fast as the boys could set things down on the floor. This was a great deal easier for Mama, I thought. Before long, all our provisions were neatly stored; the job was finished.

After another cup of coffee, Papa and the boys began cutting the grass around the camp. Soon the planked walkways were exposed to the sun, having been previously hidden from view by the tall grasses and brush. The walkway from the dock to the front door, the one that leads to the skinning racks and the drying shed, and the walkway that leads to the cistern and outhouse are now all in plain view. Soon the area in and around the hog pen will be cleared. "The men are making good progress," Mama observed, sharing her approval with me as she glanced out the door over my shoulder.

Lee informed Papa that he recovered two sections of walkway from the nearby marsh. They had been lifted up and floated away by the rising storm tide and deposited on the prairie grass when the water returned to the sea.

Papa was very happy with Lee's discovery: "That means less work for us to do, thanks to your keen eyes son. Good job, Lee!" Papa gleefully praised my brother's efforts.

I noticed that a large limb had been torn from the giant oak tree at the head of our trapping ditch. It fell dangerously close to Papa's dugout canoe, which was resting at the base of the tree. Just a few inches, that was all that separated the old canoe from utter destruction. If the limb had struck the boat, it is certain that it would have been severely damaged.

Papa and the boys tried to move the massive branch, but it was too heavy; they could not budge it from the spot where it fell. Papa said it would have to be sawed into pieces for firewood. "We'll cut it as Mama needs it," Papa instructed. "For now, the tree limb can remain where it is," he added.

There are three of these giant oak trees at our campsite. Our cabin is nestled within the triangle formed by the location of each of the massive trees. One is at the head of our trapping ditch, now minus one limb. Another oak is located at the front left side of the camp near the edge of the bayou. The third and largest of the three, is located at the right rear of the camp; it's just a few yards down the right side of Papa's trapping ditch, not very far from the tree where the canoe is resting.

Our largest tree was hit very hard by a terrible storm in 1904; that was the storm that took the entire camp away with it. The tempest managed to knock the tree down part of the way, but its massive branches touched the ground, preventing it from being uprooted. The tree now leans over papa's trapping ditch; it touches ground at the back left side of the camp. In appearance, it seems to be a giant canvas backdrop painted all over with dense green foliage extending beyond both sides of the rear of the camp by several yards. The grand old tree's resilience is prominently displayed, evidenced by the extent of upward reach the downed branches have attained in their quest for sunlight. The tree's expanding greenery attests to its stalwartness, demonstrating its robust recovery from the challenge for its life, announcing its victory over the marauding tempest with magnificent splendor.

This biggest of the trees is also my favorite. The branches that touched the ground to save its life make the tree easy to climb. The hump produced by a bend in one of the branches provides me with my favorite sitting spot. From that vantage point, I can spot Papa and the boys long before they arrive back at the camp, returning from their trapping runs. Able to see them at a great distance down the ditch, I have time to alert Mama of their soon arrival. I can also look over the vast prairie through which Papa's ditch travels. I have seen many animals from my special seat, catching a view of them without being noticed; that is if my little sister Alma doesn't start talking or singing to her ragdoll next to me at the time I spot one.

I overheard Papa telling Mama that our outhouse was missing; it was apparently a victim of this summer's storm. Misplaced marsh grass (turfs) and mud had filled the hole. Papa said he would dig a new hole and construct another little house to surround it: "For now, we will have to do like the wild animals do," he announced, trying to be funny.

Mama was not amused. She offered Papa a pair of stern-looking eyes, trying to show her displeasure over his jovial comments, but her sour look soon turned to laughter at the notion of such thinking. After all, Mama knew Papa was only joking. The new outhouse would soon be ready for use.

The roof over the skinning shed had been blown away. Papa speculates that if it could be found it might still be in one piece, since it was so cleanly removed from the building. Papa instructed the boys to go looking for it later during the day. "If we can't find the roof, I'll make a thatched roof with palmettos," he told them.

Papa set fire to a pile of cut grasses and brush, clearing the spot where he usually plants his precious mustard seeds. Every year since I was old enough to remember, Papa has planted a mustard patch; the leaves provide him with his favorite green vegetable. It seems to thrive in an area cleared by fire, being fed by the ash the flames leave behind. I can't say I share in Papa's love for the big green leaves of the mustard plants. I enjoy the taste of the dish, but I do grow tired of eating them as the winter months continue and the mustard plants continue to produce their greenery. Papa eats them all winter long and he complains when his plants quit producing.

The storm's waters had stripped some of the boards from the hog pen, leaving about half of them clinging to the slightly bent-over support posts, which outline its perimeter. Papa says that most of the wooden rails are wedged against a mangrove thicket, having only to be retrieved from where the flood waters left them.

I gathered some cut grass to use as nesting material for the laying boxes Papa has mounted on the support piles beneath the camp. I lined each of the twelve boxes with a soft cushion of grass so the hens could lay their eggs without breaking them. Mama says hens like privacy when they lay, so I took great care to mat down the grass to a level that would still provide concealment for most of their bodies.

One of the hens flew onto a nesting box I had not yet attended; after a brief inspection, she returned to the ground. Seeing no nesting material inside the hollow box, she must have rejected any notion of laying eggs for now. Mama says it always takes a few days for the hens to settle down; it will take time for them to grow accustomed to their new environment. As soon as they become familiar with their surroundings, they will begin laying eggs again.

Ole George Washington was strutting near the skinning shed. All but three of his fifteen hens were foraging around him. He was prancing about with his head lifted high; he was acting as though he owned the place. What a ham!

Our piglets were squealing in their holding pen on the boat. I gathered some of the freshly cut grass and brought it to them, thinking they might be hungry. They quieted down immediately as they consumed the grass in voracious fashion. I dipped a pale of water from the bayou, which they promptly spilled on the back deck. A second attempt to give them water met with the same fate. I decided to fetch more grass in an effort to satisfy their appetites.

Lee and Brad offloaded the three water barrels from the front deck of the *Early Rose*. They carefully rolled the heavy containers along the wooden walkway toward the camp. Papa instructed them to create a ramp using a couple of planks to facilitate the transfer of the large casks from the ground into the camp for safekeeping. Double teaming each wooden container, they soon had all three drums along the north wall near the woodstove where Mama had told the boys to place them.

The yard directly in front of the camp is solid ground (black jack clay covered over with clam shells). The area near the bayou around the outskirts of the midden is spongy marsh and prairie grasses standing in swamp water. (The shell midden covers an area of the oak ridge about one hundred yards square. The camp is nearly in the center of the clam shell deposits.) The marsh ground is of the same consistency as the surrounding prairie, which encircles the ridge; the surface is fairly solid, but below the thin crust, there is some root-laden peat and a few sinkholes. The farther away from the ridge you get, the softer the ground, and in some areas, there is nothing more than soft mud—very difficult to walk through; sometimes, especially in the winter at low tide, the mud is difficult to pole a canoe through when trying to access the traps.

There is a reason for all the wooden walkways. In order to prevent the rain-soaked ground from turning quickly into a muddy quagmire due to heavy traffic during our busy daily work schedule, the walkways prevent penetration during the many rainy spells we get each winter. Sometimes the skies remain overcast for days and the ground stays damp forever. With the walkways determining the path one takes to go to and from each site, our clothing and our yard remain relatively clean come rain or shine. There is a walkway from the camp to the boat dock, one to the cistern, the outhouse, the trapping ditch, the skinning shed, the drying racks, and one to the pig pen.

The *Early Rose* is looking like her regular self again. Her bulwarks were a foot below the wharf deck when we arrived late last evening. Now that she is unloaded, her decks are even with the top of the wharf; her prow lifted high on the shell bank due to a falling tide.

Papa asked me to get the wash-down bucket and splash water from the bayou on her decks to try to clean her up a bit. Before long, her decks were sparkling clean, being dried by the midafternoon sunlight; another chore is finished.

Papa said the piglets would have to remain onboard until tomorrow; by then, the pen will be repaired and ready to receive them.

Mama is making cornbread in the Dutch oven on the top of the stove. She hollered out the door that the food would soon be ready to eat. "It's time for a break!" she beckoned at the top of her voice.

Shortly after Mama announced that the food was ready to eat, another voice shouted excitedly: "The roof from the skinning shed has been located!" The voice came from Brad. He hollered from the thick brush on the north end of the ridge: "I found the roof intact a few hundred paces upstream from our campsite. It's not very far from the bayou, and it should not be very hard to retrieve from where I found the thing." That was good news.

"That is the best news I've heard today, Brad!" Papa exclaimed in a joyous tone. "Let's go in and get a taste of Mama's fresh corn-bread," he proposed.

By the time we finished eating, the shadows cast about the campground warned that the day was nearly spent, and darkness would soon be upon us. Though the night creatures were not yet sounding their familiar songs, Papa decided to give us the remainder of the day off. "Everyone did a good job today. I am delighted by each of your performances. Alma did her part by keeping her ragdoll busy and by helping Mama carry a few small items that had not yet been put away," Papa lauded. It was obvious to everyone that we had made good progress.

Papa and the boys discussed the condition of the skinning shed's roof. Brad told Papa that the roof was sound, missing only a few shingles which could be easily replaced. As they began making plans for recovering the roof tomorrow morning, I slipped out the door to go and sit on my favorite tree limb in the back of the camp.

Just as I was about to be seated, Alma came and took a seat beside me; she remained quiet as I looked to the northwest at the vast open prairie that borders Papa's trapping ditch. To my delightful surprise, there were two female deer having a drink of water, not fifty paces from where we were sitting. A large male deer appeared sud-denly; he was watching the two does as they lowered their heads to the water. He had a big set of antlers on his head—too far away for me to count the points of his rack.

I nudged Alma, making her a sign to keep quiet. I slowly but deliberately extended my arm to point to the three deer. When my little sister finally caught a glimpse of the beautiful animals, her eyes bulged with excitement, but she remained quiet.

The buck took a drink from the ditch and then he leaped into the thick brush, the two does following close behind. I don't believe they spotted us; the north wind was blowing our scent away from them. They just decided it was time to go I figured.

Papa, Mama, Lee, and Brad were all excited about our deer sighting. Mama boasted of how well she can cook fresh venison; none of us needed to be reminded of that. She has always been an excellent cook, especially when she cooks wild game. Lee wanted me to try to estimate the size of the horn rack. I had no idea; I just told him it looked big. Papa brought the discussion to a close saying, "Those deer will still be here when we return from Deer Island. Ida, at least one of those deer will end up in your cast iron pot," he pledged, with a broad smile across his face.

Darkness seemed to come quickly. We ate fig preserves and left over cornbread by candlelight. Papa outlined his strategy for attacking the work in the morning. He wants to tackle the hog pen repairs first so we can get the piglets off the back deck of our boat. Next on Papa's list was retrieving the roof of the skinning shed; he felt this would possibly be the hardest task we would face.

Mama interrupted Papa to remind him about the outhouse. That assertion was greeted with a great deal of giggling. Papa, trying to defend himself, began to offer an explanation. "Honey! Didn't anyone tell you that Lee found the old outhouse in the brush on the north side of my trapping ditch?"

"No one mentioned that to me!" Mama responded, seeming somewhat disturbed over someone's apparent oversight; Mama should have been informed.

"We decided to clean out our old hole and we placed the building in its same old location. We did not have to alter the walkway a bit," Papa boasted.

"I am glad to hear it, Adam! I have needed to use the facility since shortly after breakfast this morning. Now you can escort me to the building so I don't get snake bit," Mama chided.

Papa was embarrassed that no one told Mama about the outhouse being back in service; he pleaded with her for understanding. He got on his knees before her, begging her pardon and forgiveness. Everything was quiet, as we anxiously awaited Mama's response.

"I forgive you, Adam," Mama said tenderly. She extended her right hand; she lifted him up from his position on the floor and gave him a hug and a kiss. "Now, let's go!" she urged, pulling him behind her as she exited the front door of our camp in rapid fashion.

We all got a good laugh out of that event. Later, Papa told Lee and Brad that they needed to make a few shakes to replace the shingles missing from the skinning shed roof. He advised them to make a few more than we presently needed so we could have a few extra in store for future uses—that is always a good idea. Papa said there would certainly be a few trees downed or damaged by the summer storm and they could use the crosscut saw to cut a few logs. He suggested we carry a load of oak logs with us to Deer Island; with a little help from Felix and Gus, the boys can cut the short logs into shingles during our five-week visit with Uncle Justin and Aunt Sarah.

Mama asked Papa when he thought we might leave for Deer Island. Papa told her that if everything goes as smoothly tomorrow as it did today, we would be leaving early Wednesday morning. Excited by the prospect of leaving so soon, everyone began expressing their joy over the news.

Mama eventually called for some peace and quiet, saying it was time to blow out the candles and get some rest. Papa agreed; he walked around the camp blowing out all the candles. "Let's get some sleep!" he urged.

We exchanged our good night messages, but it was too late for Alma to participate; she laid beside me, sound asleep. I could not see her doll, but I am sure it was near her somewhere. I wondered when she would learn to put that doll away and leave it alone. I am sure that by seven years old I had stopped pretending to care for my doll as though it was a real baby. Time will tell, I guess!

As I lay awake in bed, I could not help thinking about Uncle Justin, Aunt Sarah, Cousin Gustave, and Cousin Felix. Are they in bed yet? Are they sitting around their kitchen table wondering about us like I am wondering about them? I wish I could be there with them right now. Weary of the quiet, I finally went off to sleep.

October 23, 1921 (Tuesday)

418

When I awakened this morning, the men were already moving the piglets into their holding pen. Papa was in the process of dismantling their temporary residence so he could use the wood elsewhere. Brad was busy administering bucket after bucket of water, splashing down the rear deck of the *Early Rose* to clean the mess the young pigs left behind.

There were fresh biscuits on the table, ready to eat. Alma was still oblivious to everything, including me; she's lying sound asleep with her doll. Mama was nowhere in sight. I ate a biscuit and drank a cup of coffee before heading outside to join in the family's activities. I inquired as to Mama's whereabouts.

Papa informed me that Mama had gone for a canoe ride. I could not believe she took off in the dugout by herself. "Mama told me to tell you to mind your sister, until she returns from her marsh excursion," Papa informed me.

"Yes, sir!" I promptly answered. "I'll be glad to do that for her."

The three piglets were happy to be enjoying their newfound freedom. They are already rooting in the ground contained inside the pen. At the rate they are foraging and tearing up the ground, it won't take long for them to turn their new home into a sloppy mess.

I returned to the cabin to keep an eye on Alma. When she awakens, I am sure she will notice that Mama is missing; it's the first thing I noticed when I got out of bed earlier.

Papa hollered that he and the boys were going to go after the missing roof just upstream from the campsite. They will be taking the boat to make the recovery easier. "We should be back in an hour or so," he told me.

"Okay!" I shouted back. "Alma and I will be fine," I pledged.

Puk-puk-puk-puk-puk-puk-puk-puk-puk-puk-puk-puk-puk-puk-puk-puk-puk... the motor sounded, awaking Alma in the process. By the time my little sister raced to the door, it was too late to say good-bye to Papa and the boys. Alma immediately began to focus on Mama's whereabouts. After I informed her that Mama went for a canoe ride, I was surprised by her calm reaction.

"She went all by herself?" Alma asked. "Why did she do that?" Alma again queried, puzzled by Mama's unexpected activity. I must admit that I too was surprised by her spontaneous swampland adventure.

"I guess it was because you and I are sleepyheads, and Mama didn't have anyone else to take along. Papa and the boys were busy repairing the hog pen earlier; now they are going to retrieve the skinning shed roof upstream from here." I shared.

This was the most conversation I had with Alma since only the Lord knows when. Trying to maintain her interest, I asked if she wanted a cup of coffee and a biscuit.

"That will be fine," Alma responded.

"When you finish eating, we will go sit on our favorite tree limb at the rear of the camp to see if Mama is on her way back from the marsh. What do you think about that?" I asked.

"That will be fine," Alma responded, with the calm of someone who was much older than she. I had expected tears, expressions of fear and anxiety, panic and tantrum-throwing, all of which could have been exhibited one at a time, or all at the same time. Little sister is growing up, I reasoned.

After breakfast, Alma and I strolled to the back of the camp. Alma had already lost herself by the time we were seated on the huge tree limb; she was caught up in the wonderment surrounding her ragdoll. The events of this morning proved without doubt that there is hope for my little sister. Someday she will break free of her childhood fantasy and come to live in the real world with the rest of us. I hope it happens soon. I do prefer two-way conversation; it's far more gratifying.

Ninny and *Nanny* were nibbling on the stubble grass left from our clearing efforts, only a few yards away from us. The two goats will have no trouble keeping the grass down for the rest of the winter (aside from the milk they give, this is an important benefit that they provide). Both of the yearling goats were bred this summer; their milk bags are already beginning to swell. Mama is looking forward to the day that they can be milked on a regular basis; goat's milk is useful for baking, and it also has a very good flavor.

Mama traded our old goats for these two youngsters this past spring; we used to own one male and two females. Mr. Geoffrey

Grayson, one of our neighbors, decided he liked our male goat and he offered the trade. In the deal was his promise to breed the two young goats for us, since we no longer had a buck. He has a relatively large herd of goats and sheep, and he wanted to add our male to his flock's gene pool. Mama and Papa both agreed that it was a good trade; *Ninny* and *Nanny* have many productive years ahead of them.

The gestation period for a goat is five months. Papa says that since they were bred in late July, their young goats should arrive sometime around Christmas. I can hardly wait!

"Here comes Mama!" Alma shouted, startling me from my daydreaming.

Sure enough, Mama was paddling herself up the trapping ditch like an old pro. She was moving through the water with little apparent effort—a sign of an experienced paddler. I wondered where she learned to paddle so well; maybe Papa taught her when she was younger. Alma and I strolled over to the head of the trapping ditch to greet her. Mama was smiling from ear to ear; she was in an especially good mood. "Did you enjoy yourself, Mama?" I asked in amusement, anxious to hear her response.

"It was great!" Mama answered with no hesitation. "It's going to be cold this winter. There are plenty ducks down from the north already. I saw large flocks of geese as they flew overhead. There might be a cold front headed this way," she predicted without much conviction—that was experience talking; I recognized that.

"Where is the *Early Rose*?" Mama asked.

"Papa and the boys are going to recover our skinning shed roof just upstream from here. They should not be very much longer," I informed her.

"Did you two eat breakfast?" Mama inquired.

"Yes, Mama! We both ate biscuits and washed them down with the fresh coffee you had on the stove," I replied, happy she had returned from her leisurely excursion through the prairie.

"Let's go take a seat inside and wait for the men to get back. I believe I will have one of those biscuits and drink a cup of coffee right now," Mama suggested. She was showing no signs of being the least bit weary from her canoe ride.

Before long, Papa was back with the roof of our skinning shed on the front deck of the *Early Rose*. He and the boys walked briskly to the camp for a much-needed break; they were sweating buckshot. After a brief pause for coffee and a biscuit, Papa urged everyone to join him at the wharf.

"I will need all the help I can get to put that roof back where it belongs," Papa informed us. We all lent a hand, and after a bit of simple engineering, Papa succeeded in using our combined efforts to raise the roof back on the shed where it came from. In a matter of minutes, Papa had secured the salvaged covering with nails and braces. He boasted that it would be stronger than it was before it was separated from the building by the storm's violent winds.

"That is that! We are all done with the most difficult task we had left. The hard work is now over!" Papa boasted, noticeably happy with the results.

Papa instructed the boys to use the lumber from the dismantled holding pen to replace the boards that had been robbed from one of our walkways to repair the roof on the camp the night of our arrival. They began work on that project right away.

Papa informed us that we were fast concluding all our necessary chores, and we would definitely be leaving for Deer Island in the morning.

I went beneath the camp to check the nesting boxes for eggs, but I didn't find a single one. They weren't even trying; there was not a single hen on the nest. Seeing our rooster foraging with his hens nearby, I shouted, "You need to get behind those female chickens *George Washington*. You better get to work!" I chided. "Mama needs some eggs!"

I walked over to the pigpen to see how the piglets were doing. I noticed their watering trough was nearly empty, so I decided to fetch some water from the bayou to refill it. The pigpen is twenty feet long and twenty feet wide. It is intended to hold the pigs long enough for them to settle down and grow accustomed to their new environment. One more day on the deck of our boat, and those poor animals would have gone crazy; they squealed and squealed until they had no strength to squeal anymore. I am glad they finally have space to roll around on the ground; a firm surface which they will soon change into mud; rolling their bodies in the mud is something pigs enjoy doing.

Once we leave for Deer Island, the pigs will eat all there is to eat in their holding pen. They will also run out of drinking water. Either one of these two factors will force the piglets to tunnel under the protective fencing in order to get out. They will then gain access to all the food and water their little hearts could dream of having.

"There! You won't be running out of water tonight!" I informed the young pigs, after filling the water trough with fresh water. They did not acknowledge my efforts; they were content to lie there motionless, basking in the late afternoon sunlight.

Papa and I went to sit on the big oak branch at the left rear of the camp; we were hoping to see the big buck again. We were soon joined by Mama and Alma; the four of us were sitting side by side on the huge branch anxiously hoping for any sign of a deer.

We heard the honking sound of an approaching flock of geese. Papa pointed to them as they flew overhead in perfect "V" formation. Papa surmised that they were probably heading for a roosting site near Plumb Lake; he had hunted for them there on many occasions. He also repeated something mama had told me this morning: "It is shaping up to be a cold winter," he reasoned aloud, seeming to be confident that his prediction would come to pass.

Papa explained, "I have seen an unusually high number of geese flying overhead today—more than yesterday. There are large number of ducks down also, but it is the large flocks of geese that tell the tale. They would not be this far south if it wasn't getting very cold up north, and that is a fact of nature," he deduced.

"We will eat geese this winter, eh, Adam?" Mama teased. "You can count on that, Ida!" Papa boasted. "If Lee and Brad can shoot straight," he teased.

That has never been a problem in the past, I recalled. Lee and Brad love the challenge of creeping for geese. Papa usually prepares a special load for goose hunting. Not liking to waste a single shell, he taught the boys to try to shoot when they can kill more than one bird with a single shot. Papa insists that they refrain from shooting too soon, cautioning them to get as close as they possibly can before discharging the shot. Geese are tough to kill; many times they must have their necks wrung after being shot to finish the job.

Papa allows the boys one gun, a double-barreled shotgun, when hunting for geese. The reason he sends both boys on a goose hunt with only one gun is the burden of carrying the big birds back to the boat after they have been killed. Weighing six to eight pounds each, a bounty of six or eight birds would be too heavy for one man to carry. The gun alone weighs about eight pounds and a single Canadian goose can weigh up to ten pounds.

Another large flock of geese appeared before us; they began to circle over the distant prairie. With each encircling pass, they flew lower and lower to the ground; finally they lighted and disappeared from view.

"It is time to beat the mosquitoes! Let's go inside the camp!" Papa urged. Arriving in the cabin, we found the boys sitting at the table talking about the good times they had with our cousins, Felix and Gus, last year. Joining them in conversation, we gathered around the table. We were all anxiously anticipating what lay ahead for us during our next few weeks on holiday.

Papa made it very clear that under the circumstances presented over the past four months, our camp had fared very well. He reminded us that we were last at the camp during the fig harvest. It's now the last week of October (that period of absence was normal for us; it's the summer storm that caused Papa's anxious concerns—understandably so). It has been about three months since the storm has passed; our tiny structure weathered the violent wind and rain and the high water it spawned; it was fighting for its very existence. The camp and its surrounding outbuildings endured the violent challenge from nature very well indeed. "We have much to be thankful for," Papa shared.

On that note, Papa requested that everyone bow their heads for a moment of prayer and thanksgiving; he then led us all in heartfelt prayer: "Dear Lord, we thank you for sparing us the grief of finding our camp in ruins. Thank you for extending your mercy to the

Addison family. We hope and pray that you did the same for our family members on Deer Island. Amen."

After a bit more small talk, Mama announced to everyone that she was getting sleepy. That assertion prompted Papa to order that all the lights be blown out and everyone should get some rest. "Tomorrow will be an exciting day for all of us. Now go to sleep!" Papa strongly advised. Amazingly, silence quickly prevailed throughout the camp; I could hear the mosquitoes buzzing at the windows and the frogs singing to their mates in the treetops outside. Now that is silence!

As I lay in my bed in the stillness of the night, I thought of Alice LaCoste and her family. I missed having them accompany us when we went to gather figs this year. I thought about the fig harvest. Every year the LaCoste family boards their boat, the *Miss Sabrina*, and they follow us to Plumb Bayou to pick figs during the last two week of June through the first week of July. This year was different; we went fig-picking alone.

During the last trapping season, Jean and Marguerite LaCoste lost a daughter. Sabrina was only five years old when she caught pneumonia and died. We have since shared our sympathy with the family; Alice LaCoste and I are the same age and we are the best of friends. Jean LaCoste Jr. and his younger brother Pierre are good buddies with Lee and Brad. Their only other daughter is Marie; she is twelve and a joy to behold. Still overcome with grief over their recent loss, Mr. Jean decided to skip the annual trip to Plumb Bayou with us this year; he told Papa he felt reasonably sure that they would be back at their trapping camp for the opening of this season. I hope they will have the courage to trap this winter; I look forward to seeing them.

It is always much more fun when you have at least one other family you can associate with during the times we spend away from home. Nearly half of each year is spent away from Bayou Du Large; a person can get awful lonely, even when surrounded by immediate family members. It's hard for me to explain, but I have experienced loneliness many times.

Every year, at the beginning of the last week of June, we come to Plumb Bayou to pick figs. My Great-grandfather Joseph planted twelve fig trees along the ridge that follows the left bank of the bayou, north of the trapping camp; planting the trees was part of his plan to demonstrate possession of this part of the estate. Upon the advice of legal counsel, he built the camp and planted the fig trees. Now over sixty years old, the fig trees are massive—thirty feet tall and at least twenty feet across; a full-grown man can climb in them.

Usually, the men and boys pick the figs and the women cook them and jar them for safekeeping. When Marguerite LaCoste is here with her family, we process well over one hundred quart mason jars of fig preserves; our goal is to fill at least eight cases of the prized dessert (each special wooden case holds twenty-four-quart jars). This June, even though Mama and the rest of us worked alone, we still managed to make one-hundred-twenty-four jars; that's five full cases plus five jars. (A little note on the process Mama follows to keep the figs fresh and safe to eat—once the mason jars are nearly full, Mama pours melted wax over the contents of each jar to seal out the air; once the caps are screwed on, the preserves will last for years provided the wax seals are not penetrated.)

We share at least two cases of our fig preserves with others—one case always goes to Aunt Sarah on Deer Island; we give some to family members and some to members of our church congregation. Mama and Mrs. LaCoste usually divide a case; the rest gets sold to cover our costs. Mama is in charge of fig production and distribution; she usually makes a few dollars by selling some to Doc Fursom. She then splits the proceeds with the LaCoste family. Even though Marguerite and her family weren't able to participate in this year's harvest, Mama made sure they got their share of the figs as well as the proceeds from the sale; isn't that the Christian thing to do? I reasoned.

From the twenty-first of June until the seventh of July, we pick and jar figs until the fruit disappear—the birds always get their fair share, which is appropriate. "God's creatures must be fed!" Mama always says. After two weeks of picking and jarring, we head back home, after securing the camp's shutters and the front door. "Lord, please give Alice and her family peace of mind so they can make it to their trapping camp this year," I solemnly pray; I really do miss their company.

Anxious over coming events, I tossed and turned until it was after midnight. Soon after I dozed off, a violent thunderstorm awakened everyone in the camp. Flashes of lightning lighted up the entire cabin, and the roaring thunder vibrated everything in the building. When the storm continued its rage, I lay back in my bed and prayed silently for deliverance from fear. Soon afterward, I drifted off into a deep sleep in spite of the flashes of lightening and the roars of violent thunder.

Chapter Four

ON TO DEER ISLAND!

October 24, 1921

Wednesday morning brought with it brilliant sunshine and a cold north wind. Mama and Papa are getting very good at predicting the weather; the temperature had fallen into the low fifties during the night. That violent thunderstorm was the introduction of a cold front as it passed through in its rush toward the gulf.

"What a splendid day for traveling," Mama announced in a joyful mood.

The heat from the stove was struggling to drive the chill from the air. Though the door and the shutters remained closed this morning, the north wind was howling through the many cracks in the wall and between the slats of the shutters.

There was no water on the floor from the brief but heavy downpour. That meant that the boys had done a good job repairing the roof the night we arrived. Papa praised the boys for their handiwork.

For some reason, Mama's hot biscuits tasted extra good this morning. Maybe it was the pleasant atmosphere created by the cold crisp air; maybe it was merely the joy of the moment; maybe the biscuits were just plain good. The coffee complimented our hearty breakfast.

Suddenly, Brad shared that no one had checked the cistern; he and Lee got up from the table and quickly ran out the door to the south side of the camp to take a look inside. Lee held the ladder while his brother peered over the top of the water tank to check for any signs of contamination.

I ran out to check the nests for eggs. *Ole George* was giving his customary wake-up call. We didn't need it, but his crowing seemed to make a good impression on the hens. One of the birds walked over to *George Washington* and gave him an affectionate gentle pecking all around his beak; what a ham he is!

I was not surprised to find the nests empty; I was just hoping I would find one egg before we left for Deer Island. It would have bolstered my confidence that I had prepared the nesting material properly. The truth is that I like to gather the eggs; it's one of my favorite chores. Oh well, it was Mama who wanted me to check the nests this last time before our departure; they will be laying eggs by the time we get back. One or two of the hens might even decide to set on the eggs; I might have baby chicks to play with before Christmas, I pondered. We will find out when we come back in December.

Brad reported that the cistern was clean and filled to the brim with water. He said the downspout was blocked by a heavy deposit of leaves and small twigs and branches, probably wedged there by the storm. The debris closed the entrance, preventing any animal from having a good look inside; it was not unusual for a raccoon, opossum, or snake to be found drowned in our water storage tank.

Brad said that he cleared all the debris from around the downspout and removed the cover to get a good view inside in the bright sunlight. He told everyone that the water was crystal clear and tasty; he said he could see the bottom of the tank. He told Papa that he replaced the cover and adjusted the downspout and that everything was all right.

Papa was happy over the good news and he was especially happy that the cistern was filled to the brim with water. We all knew how important that information was; water is one of those things that no one can do without. That is why we always bring three barrels full of fresh water out to the camp with us. If a branch had blown down in the storm and damaged the cistern or knocked it over, we would still have water.

"Excellent! We won't have to worry about water all winter long, even if it doesn't rain a drop," Papa asserted, breathing a sigh of relief.

Mama was wearing a colorful dress this morning; she looked elegant. My little sister Alma is clinging so close to her that she is beginning to annoy me. Mama never complains, but I do wish Alma would give her more free space so she can move about unrestrained. Maybe my little sister is remembering yesterday, when she awakened finding Mama was nowhere in sight; maybe that is what is making her feel so insecure. I don't recall acting the way she does when I was her age, although Mama says that Alma and I are like "two peas in a pod." If I was just like Alma back then, ever clinging to Mama's apron strings as she does, I think I owe my dear mother a sincere apology.

Papa and the boys inspected the parameters of the pigpen; they wanted to see if the piglets had tried to dig underneath the bottom rails. There was no sign of any attempt to escape from the confines of their pen. That is good news; the pen is serving its intended purpose.

The pigs have already eaten the grass stubble to the ground, uprooting most of them. The recent rainfall over the exposed soil, has been trampled into a muddy mess, but not yet a quagmire. Papa says in another day or two they could have the entire area of the pen torn up and sloppy. That's just the way pigs are it seems; they like wallowing in the mud.

It was about eight in the morning when Papa announced that it was time to start shutting up the camp. Everyone cheered the news and we all joined Mama in the process of securing the shutters and making sure everything that needed doing was done. The stove was emptied of all its fuel; any embers that remained were doused with water to dispel any risk of fire.

While we completed all our tasks, Papa started the engine on the *Early Rose*: *Puk-puk-puk-puk-puk-puk-puk-puk-puk-puk-puk-puk-puk-puk-puk-puk-puk . . .,* the motor announced our soon departure.

I gave *Nanny* and *Ninny* each a good-bye hug, and yelled a fond farewell to *Ole George Washington,* who was too busy to pay me any attention. "Keep an eye on the place for us while we're gone *George,* you old ham!" I hollered.

Mama, Alma, and I were the last to get aboard. Brad used a push pole to dislodge the bow from the shoreline. Easing the bow into the middle of the channel, Papa put some speed to the engine and we were on our way.

As we headed south around the point of the ridge, we startled a deer; the poor animal leaped into the bayou directly in front of us, so Papa slowed the engine to allow the deer to get across. Papa said it was a young doe; he said if it had been an older deer, it would have leaped into the brush for cover rather than making an attempt to cross the bayou. "An old deer would never have made that nearly fatal mistake!" Papa explained.

The wind was blowing steady from the north about twenty miles an hour; it was cold enough for a coat. Mama, Papa, and Alma were being shielded from the wind inside the cabin. Lee, Brad, and I had chosen to stay on the front deck, so we had to bundle up in our warm clothes.

I put on the new woolen hat and gloves that Papa had bought for me at Doc Fursom's store. They will keep me nice and comfortable this winter, especially if it gets as cold as Mama and Papa think it will.

When we exited the mouth of Plumb Bayou into Atchafalaya Bay, it was rough; the strong north wind had really troubled the water. The *Early Rose* was riding high in the water; the three-foot waves posed no real challenge, as we cut through the wave tops in open defiance. Papa turned her bow into the wind, and we charged straight ahead like a determined bull through a weak spot in a fence line.

Taking a northerly trek and following the shoreline about a hundred paces from the bank, we would soon pass the mouths of

Palmetto Bayou and Crooked Bayou on our journey to the mouth of the river.

Suddenly, a spray caught me square in the face. Lee and Brad saw when it happened and had a big laugh. I suppose it was funny; at least I am not afraid to melt like they are, staying in a safe dry place in the center of the deck leaning against the front wall of the cabin. I like it here on the bow where I won't miss anything; after all, I want to be the first to spot the mouth of Deer Island Bayou.

Papa kept the eastern shoreline in plain view as we entered the Atchafalaya River. Deer Bayou is harder to spot than the other bayous we passed; its mouth is obscured by the dense cypress forest that lines the eastern shore.

The mouth of Plumb Bayou is bounded by a vast expanse of prairie. Careful attention to the shoreline and knowing the approximate distance from the starting point, is all one needs to find the fifty-foot wide opening.

Both Palmetto and Crooked Bayous have oak-covered ridges along their banks; they are easy to see as they snake through the open prairie that surrounds them.

The Lower Atchafalaya River is bounded by dense cypress forest. An untrained, or careless eye, might never find the entrances to some of the river's tributaries. "There it is!" I proudly announced. "There is the mouth of Deer Island Bayou," I proclaimed, pointing as I shouted.

My brothers appeared astonished, with dumfounded looks on their faces; they could not believe I had been the first to see the entrance through the trees.

"Good job, Nora!" Papa lauded with an appreciative smile. I sincerely do not believe that Papa had spotted the mouth of the bayou before I pointed it out; I was proud I had seen it first.

Turning due east, Papa eased the *Early Rose* out of the grasp of the swift river currents of the mighty Atchafalaya. You could feel a noticeable difference in the way the boat was handling when we entered the calm waters of Deer Bayou. Papa is a good captain; everyone says it is so, and I believe them.

The dense cypress forest bordering the first mile or so of the stream is teeming with wildlife. As soon as we entered the channel, I saw a large flock of wood ducks take off; they were making a fast getaway.

At almost that very instant, I heard Papa yelling through the cabin window. "Look at the size of that flock of mallards!" He shared his observation excitedly, pointing to the right side of the bayou. There must have been at least fifty ducks taking off through the trees. As they got higher above the water and into the treetops, the sunlight reflected off the bright green heads and rust colored chests of the males of the species. It was a magnificent sight to behold. Even Lee and Brad stood up from their comfortable seats on the deck to get a prolonged look at the beautiful ducks until they eventually disappeared over the distant treetops.

The Atchafalaya River
Meets Deer Island Bayou
Clam shell banks and cypress
knees slow erosion

I saw several great blue herons feeding in the shallows of the bayou's edge; they were some distance away from us in the swamp, but not far from where we were passing. Many appeared unafraid;

they kept fishing in their favorite spots, failing to budge as we passed them by.

Great flocks of ibis scattered into the air, startled by the sound of our engine. In a few minutes, there were white ibis and black ibis everywhere around us. As we traveled further upstream, the birds settled right back down in the area from which we had chased them. Papa says they are feeding on crawfish and minnows in the shallow swamp waters.

I spotted a marsh hawk and its mate circling overhead; they were looking for a meal. Papa speculates that they are probably trying to ambush a pair of unsuspecting ducks. I would have never seen them if the fall weather had not denuded the deciduous cypress trees, leaving only the balls containing seed hanging precariously from their naked branches. In the spring and summer months, the forest almost totally obscures the sunlight; now that is a dense forest!

Other animals exposed by the absence of foliage are the gray squirrels and foxtail squirrels, which compete for the seeds contained in the round pods hanging from the bald cypress tree branches. The fragments from the cypress balls were falling like raindrops as the squirrels separated the hulls from their seeds. A few of the fast-moving tree-climbers were hauling the tasty morsels back to their nests, which could be easily spotted in the forks of a few distant trees. Some of the more bashful squirrels hid themselves behind the branches; others stood still, as though they were frozen solid. Some fled our presence seeming to be running for their lives; most continued doing what they were doing when we first happened upon them.

The overhead canopy, which began at the mouth of the bayou, will continue through the cypress swamp and through the ridge (the ridge is known as Deer Island). When it reaches the far side of Deer Island, it will disappear abruptly, as the bayou meanders through open prairie and leaves the forested ridge behind. Uncle Justin's place is located near the far end of the island.

Traveling through the cypress canopy will be starkly contrasted by the dense foliage from the branches of the giant oaks which will soon be twisting and towering over and around us; all but the faintest sunlight will be shielded from us as we travel toward our destination through the high ground of the ridge.

Lee and Brad pointed to a few snipes and woodcocks, as the bow of the *Early Rose* began to penetrate the high ground. Papa announced that we were on the final leg of our journey, as we left the cypress swamp in our wake.

Soon the stream was almost completely enclosed by the heavy forest around it; it's kind of unsettling. The arboreal canopy that shrouds the sun from our passageway creates an atmosphere that is near darkness in the daytime. The dense foliage of the sprawling live oaks forms an unnatural tunnel formed by timeless changes in the shapes of the trees which have spread their roots along the banks of Deer Bayou; they seem to beckon us to continue our journey into the heart of the island in a state of awe.

The lowest branches of the trees have shriveled and died long ago, perishing in their failed quest for sunlight. After years of competition and positioning, to the victors go the spoils. Massive limbs extend skyward, eighty to one hundred feet in the air, having conquered the darkness below them.

The majesty of the scene can scarcely be imagined by anyone who has not witnessed it for themselves. Everyone, except Alma, was canvassing this magnificent display of natural splendor, unable to escape the lure of its beauty and serenity.

The banks of the bayou and the grounds beyond are densely covered. Shooting skyward amidst the towering giant oaks are ash, gum, maple, elm, mulberry, cherry, chinaberry, and many other varieties of trees. The underbrush is crowded with palmetto palms. The green and red berries of the wild holly accent the scenery provided by the countless other growths of dense brush and diminutive trees. There are thickets of mangrove trees and countless seedlings and saplings competing for a little space in the rich alluvial soil of the ridge. There are vines everywhere! The large black-jack vines have grown up with the trees they cling to, dangling like giant serpents from the highest tree branches.

The clear blue sky, which existed before we entered the cavernous greenery, could only be seen through tiny openings in the overhead profusion. One could peer only a few feet into the woodland and brush on either side of the bayou's course as we drew closer and closer to Uncle Justin's place.

"It won't be long now!" Papa exclaimed.

Everyone began to cheer and sing, as the steady sounds of the engine reverberated within its stalwart enclosure, signaling our approach to anyone with ears.

An otter with his mate swam across our bow in rapid fashion, scampering into the thicket to escape our view. Birds were constantly moving, flying from one branch to the next in their vast sanctuary. Crows, sparrows, tiny finches, owls, egrets, blue jays, red birds, woodpeckers, mockingbirds, chick-a-dees, hawks, rails, diving ducks, wood ducks, and many other birds made their appearance as we continued traveling upstream through the heart of the forested ridge.

This is paradise! With the abundance of life, the richness of the environment, the peaceful atmosphere, how could anyone dare to ask for more than what God has seen fit to lend to this wonderful wilderness area? This place is truly amazing to behold.

As we traveled through the island's interior, I thought of Aunt Sarah. Last autumn, she told me that we had been their only visitors. Year before last, she said their only company had been a small group of fishermen who were seeking shelter during bad weather. They must get lonely more than anyone cares to admit; for visitors like us, the isolation is what we find most appealing—second only to the joy of sharing time with family we haven't seen for a while.

Uncle Justin is probably puffing on his pipe, seated in his favorite rocking chair on the front porch of the *big house*. I am sure that he and Aunt Sarah and the boys are excitedly anticipating our soon arrival. I can hardly wait to see them again.

Papa pointed to the poles sticking out of the water, spaced about fifty feet apart, with fishing lines tied to each; there was movement on a couple of them as we went by. Felix and Gus run those fish lines; maybe we will see them if they haven't already made today's pass. If they have already checked their lines, they must have loaded them with fresh bait; they seem to have hooked a few more fish since they were here last.

Lee and Brad joined me on the bow of the *Early Rose*, each of us straining to see around each new bend in the bayou as we snaked along through the course of the freshwater stream.

A large raccoon, looking like a masked bandit, was washing his food from atop a mudflat, which jutted out from the shoreline of the left bank ahead of us; he seemed unaffected by our passing, looking up only briefly as we went by him. It's a bit strange to me that so many wild animals care little about our presence; they almost seem to be tame. It is uncanny.

Alma suddenly appeared on deck; she was singing to her ragdoll with wild enthusiasm. How boring! I watched with curiosity, as I pondered when my little sister might grow tired of her childish antics with that doll. There are times when I have been tempted to hide the thing from her. I would not dare to throw it away; that decision could mean trouble for me from my parents, neither of which would like to endure the grief of hearing her cry. "*Pauvre bête!*" as our French neighbors might proclaim (an expression of sympathetic tolerance).

Lee and Brad were wondering if our engine could be heard from the landing where we will soon be docking our boat. Lee suggested that the way the sound of the motor bounces along the bayou beneath all the trees, we should be heard for a long distance; the crisp cold air will also enhance the noise we are making he muses.

Papa, seeing the anxious expressions on our faces, was wearing a massive grin. Papa is a good man; he is well-liked by everyone on Bayou Du Large. Mama says he is as strong as an ox, and he has the endurance of a plow mule; he can work the whole day through without breaking for dinner.

There have been countless times that my two brothers showed up at the dinner table without him; Papa tells them to go home and eat when they get hungry. When they return to the worksite, they say that Papa is always still hard at work, trying to finish whatever it is that he started.

Papa is a man that likes to get things done. If he is in the middle of doing something, there isn't much that can take him away from his work. Mama has a difficult time with him; she rarely succeeds in getting him to stop and rest awhile.

As we rounded a deep bend in the bayou, Lee startled me as he hollered, "I can see Uncle Justin's sailboat tied to the dock! Look! Aunt Sarah is waving at us from the wharf!"

Mama warned Alma to be careful not to fall overboard in the excitement. I grabbed her by the hand to ensure that she would remain safe until we tie up the boat.

Sure enough, the *Dreadnought* appeared in plain view as we rounded that latest bend in the bayou; there they all stood, waving vigorously to us as we approached the landing. I saw Uncle Justin, Aunt Sarah, and their two boys—Felix and Gus. As we drew nearer to the dock site, *Muskrat*, Uncle Justin's smaller boat, came into view; it was moored at the far side of the wharf, partially hidden from view by the larger vessel.

The excitement was reaching a fever pitch: "Yippee! Yippee! Yippee!" Unrestrained shouts could be heard from the *Early Rose*. Mama came out of the cabin to join in the exuberance on the bow of our boat, waving to our family members on the wharf as they awaited our mooring lines.

All the noise and commotion startled a big buck that had been drinking along the bank near the landing site as we approached. You could see movement in the brush, as he quickly hauled his tail away, startled by our unexpected activity.

Looking high in the treetops directly across from Uncle Justin's wharf, I spotted the eagle's nest atop the tallest cypress tree in the area. Uncle Justin says that tree is nearly 150 feet tall, and its crown is fifty feet across. The giant nest is about eight feet across; it is positioned directly in the center of the tree's massive head. I could not see any movement; the big birds must be hunting for something to eat, I speculated.

A few hundred yards north of Addison Landing (so named by my ancestors), Deer Bayou makes a sharp bend to the east and meanders through the remaining part of the ridge; it then travels through a vast expanse of open prairie. It's head is at Bayou Penchant about five miles upstream from here.

Papa throttled back to slow the engine, reaching the landing bow first with a slight bump. Brad and Lee tossed the bow and stern lines to Felix and Gus, as Papa pulled on the knotted rope to kill the engine. "Deer Island at last!" That expressed the sentiment we were all feeling when we finally arrived.

Our two families exchanged welcomes, hugs, and kisses; we did all this without leaving the front deck of our boat. We were happy to see one another again and everyone was going about the business of showing it; even Alma shared her joy with each and every one. She was clutching her doll, of course.

I could hear the gurgling sound of the bubbling stream, stirring up the water as it enters Deer Bayou near the front of our bow. We hurriedly disembarked; after receiving the okay from Papa, my brothers joined my cousins in a foot race to Aunt Sarah's house. Papa and the rest of us decided that it was time for a good stretch. Mama and Aunt Sarah were laughing and giggling over something I had not overheard; Papa and Uncle Justin discussed how each of them fared during the summer storm, sharing their experiences.

I listened intently as Uncle Justin shared that the storm waters never came close to their house, but the wind had been treacherous. He reported that several trees had lost their footing and had been blown to the ground by the ferocious winds. The *big house* sustained no damage at all; a few shingles loosened enough to let a little rain inside, but other than that there was no trouble.

Uncle Justin told Papa that during the worst part of the tempest everyone became afraid. He said the wind was howling like a woman grieving over the loss of her baby; it was a time for straight faces and a time for praying. It was time to plead with God for mercy, knowing we were desperately helpless.

As Uncle Justin continued to explain the ordeal they had endured, it was plain to see that they were very fortunate to have come through the storm so well. He told Papa that the *little house* sustained a direct hit from a heavy branch; he said it went through the roof like a javelin shot from a cannon. Part of the massive limb passed through the ceiling (which is really the floor of the second story) and lodged itself atop the ground level floor.

Uncle Justin mentioned that many birds died in the storm, having been battered and buffeted by the force of the angry winds; they were bashed against the tree trunks and the walls of our buildings. Uncle Justin said he had never experienced the loss of so many birds in a storm. That must have been some strong wind!

Aunt Sarah broke into the conversation to mention that God had spared them from harm. "The Lord knew that we were facing a very dangerous storm. There is no doubt that His mercy was upon us through it all," she proclaimed in a soft somber tone.

Papa told Uncle Justin and Aunt Sarah that we all had much to be thankful for, once he had related some of our own experiences during the storm. When he finished sharing our ordeal on Bayou Du Large this summer, we boarded the push skiff; it was tied to a tree at the head of the stream, which led to the homestead.

Once we were all seated, Uncle Justin stood at oars and rowed us slowly but steadily upstream against the fast moving water of the narrow stream. Forcing the oars forward from their pivot point while he stood upright, my uncle skillfully maneuvered his skiff. The circular motion created by his oaring strokes was fun to watch. Once the forward extension is completed, the oars are returned to their original position by first pushing them down and then following the body's motion toward the back; raising the oars when the downward motion is completed, they are then lowered back into the water for the next forward push. My uncle is very good at moving his oar skiff against the swift current.

The stream is about eight feet wide and three feet deep. The water is cold and crystal clear, sparkling in the filtered sunlight. For a time, the stream was my family's only source of drinking water. Coopers were hired to build three massive cisterns once construction on the two houses was completed. We still use the stream water, but there is rainwater collected in abundance for normal daily use. Having water tanks near to the kitchens of both houses is an added convenience that is well appreciated by the cooks; that is certain!

Pearly white clamshells contain the stream through its entire length. The shells add natural beauty to the stream, which flows from the fountainhead at the front of the *big house,* down the gentle slope of the ridge some three-fourths of a mile to Deer Island Bayou where our boat is moored. Uncle Justin says that over its course, the stream drops about four feet or more. The rise is not readily noticeable until you reach the summit of the hill (that is where the houses are) and look downstream.

There is an entire family of otters playing in a shallow pond formed by rainwater that is trapped in a low spot not twenty paces from where we are; there were at least five of them. Like many of the other animals we encountered, our presence did not seem to bother them; they continued with their playful antics. Otters are fun creatures to watch; playing is not an unusual activity of theirs. Papa catches a few in his muskrat traps each year; their hides are worth a great deal of money; I get no pleasure seeing the hides of those beautiful creatures stretched over a mould and drying in the sun.

The elders were steeped in conversation as I continued to scan the forest for other signs of life. There were a few squirrels dashing about along the ground; they were either playing or foraging for food. They certainly appeared to be in a playful mood; they were scampering around the base of the trees running up and down from the tree trunks to the ground and from the ground to the tree trunks again. It seemed like some cat and mouse game; they really looked like they were enjoying themselves, oblivious to our presence.

Upon our arrival at the *big house*, we stepped out of the boat. Aunt Sarah promptly announced that dinner was ready, and she and Uncle Justin invited us into the house for our first meal.

I paused at the front porch briefly to reacquaint myself with the tranquil sound of the troubled waters as they escape the fountainhead and rush down the slope through the stream. It has always been a delightful experience for me, even better than the raindrops falling on the rooftop during naptime. Oh, how I do love this place! "I thank you, dear Lord, for allowing me to be here again this fall. Amen." I felt like praying before joining my family inside for a wholesome meal.

When we arrived at the *big house*, the four boys were swinging from ropes suspended from the gigantic branches of the live oak that graces Uncle Justin's front yard. The trunk of that old tree is eight feet across; Uncle Justin says it is hundreds of years old. Its north side is covered by green fungus; the color of the fungus blending with the various shades of gray that color the bark makes the tree all the more handsome. There are many trees on Deer Island, which are close in stature, but none of the live oaks quite compare with the majesty of this one. I stand in awe of this gift from God every time I look at it.

"Felix, how are *Beauty* and *Patches*?" I asked, motioning for him to come near me.

Suddenly, Gus came up and stood before me; he could not hold back the surprise in spite of being warned by his older brother not to tell; he proclaimed in a raised voice, obviously excited to share: "*Beauty* and *Patches* are just fine, but we have two more horses now!"

No kidding! I was looking forward to riding *Patches* again this autumn," I shared, excited over the news.

Felix said, "Now you can have your pick. Your Uncle Justin bought a chestnut gelding named *Little John* and a golden palomino mare named *Peanut*. They are grazing near the barn as we speak. Do you want to go meet them Nora?"

"You bet!" I shouted. "We won't have to take turns like last year. Gus and Alma are younger, so they can ride double if they choose to ride with one of us," I posed.

Arriving at Uncle Justin's barn, I immediately spotted the new horses. Right away I could surmise why they call the gelding *Little*

John; he is a very large animal; his reddish brown coat is shining in the bright mid-day sun. *Peanut* the palomino has a golden coat with a cream colored mane and tail—such beautiful creatures they are!

"When can we go for a ride, Felix?" I asked, anxious to sit in the saddle again.

"We will have plenty time for horseback riding," Felix reminded me, after saying that we should get adult approval before taking the horses out of the pasture.

"You're right, Felix! I'll try to be more patient."

Lee and Brad were strangely silent, as we all walked back to the big house to join the rest of the family; our arrival was not a bit too soon.

Mama appeared at the front door to remind us that everyone else was seated at the dinner table, waiting patiently for us to join them. Assuming we hadn't left the front yard, Mama directed her statement to me. "You will have plenty time to daydream later; now you come inside and eat your dinner with the rest of us," she insisted in a no-nonsense tone. There was no need to let her think I could possibly have been doing anything but daydreaming (my favorite pastime).

"Okay, Mama!" I politely responded. When I finally got to my seat at the table with the rest of the family, I begged everyone's pardon; my entourage remained quietly innocent though they knew I had borne all the blame for our tardiness.

"Let's ask the Lord to bless our food," Uncle Justin suggested. We all bowed our heads as he led us in the blessing.

We dined on chicken stew, corn bread, flour bread, fresh smothered carrots, and squash custard. It was a meal fit for any king. We sat around the table for a couple of hours, doing more talking than eating, trying to catch up on all our current events and sharing our experiences with one another. After being separated for eleven months, there was plenty to talk about, that's for sure.

The *big house* is a beautiful home. There is a large front porch with a swing and several rocking chairs for those who wish to relax there. The front door is situated on the left side of the house. Passing through the front door, one enters the greeting room; at the left center of the greeting room is a single window facing south; from that same vantage point, if one continues to look straight ahead from the front door toward the rear of the house you would see an arched doorway leading into Aunt Sarah's sewing room. Once one enters the sewing room, there is a single window again facing south; looking toward the rear of the house, there is another door that exits onto the rear porch; the porch follows along the entire length of the kitchen. When the stove gets too hot in summer, Aunt Sarah can escape the heat by retreating to the adjacent breezeway provided by the porch. This is a description of the left side of the ground floor of the dwelling.

The "Big House"
Built by Joseph Addison
Completed July 27, 1842
Location: Deer Island

The description of the right side of the large home at the ground floor level follows: if one walks through the front door to the middle of the greeting room and looks to the right, he would see an arched doorway leading into the sitting room. The sitting room has two windows overlooking the front porch facing east and one window facing north, which provides a view of the pathway leading to Uncle

Justin's garden. If one enters the sitting room and goes to its middle, facing the back of the house, he would see an arched doorway leading to the dining room; the dining room has a single window facing north. If one enters the dining room and moves to its center from the sitting room, looking toward the back of the house, he would see an arched doorway leading to the kitchen. From the center of the dining room, if he looked left, he would see an arched doorway, which lends access to Aunt Sarah's sewing room. Both the sewing room and the kitchen have exits that lead to the rear porch. The kitchen has six windows: two facing north, two facing south, and two that face west. The window positions were designed to allow cross ventilation to try to ease the discomfort associated with cooking on a hot stove in the summer heat—any breeze is a welcome blessing. Easy access to the rear porch was designed with relief from the heat of the woodstove in mind.

The stairway leading to the second floor is located in the sewing room; it leads to a hallway that runs the entire width of the house, lending access to the four upstairs bedrooms; each bedroom has a dormer and a side-view window.

Uncle Justin and Aunt Sarah's bedroom is located at the front of the house (facing east) directly above the sitting room. Their dormer window facing east affords the best view of the fountainhead; their side view window faces north, providing a view of the *garden path* and the garden.

Felix and Gus have the bedroom directly behind their parent's room; it is located at the rear of the house (facing west) directly above the kitchen. Their dormer window faces west and lends them the view of the chicken coop, the outhouse, and the *beaten path*; their side window faces north and provides a view of the *garden path* and the garden.

The two other upstairs bedrooms are on the south side of the house, located above the greeting room and the sewing room. The front bedroom on the south side of the house has the second best view of the fountainhead through its dormer window, which faces east. This is the bedroom that Alma and I will share. The stairway leading to the second floor is located in the sewing room; it leads to a hallway that was designed with relief from the heat of the woodstove in mind. The side window of our bedroom faces south, and provides a good view of the *wagon path* that leads to the barn, the cattle pen, and the cemetery; it also provides the view to the out kitchen at the back of the *little house*.

Mama and Papa will share the south-side rear bedroom over the sewing room. Their dormer window faces west and provides a view of the chicken coop, the corn crib and the outhouse. Their side window faces south and provides a view of the pathway to the beehives, the *wagon path* that leads to the barn and cattle pen and to the family cemetery.

Lee and Brad will share the bedroom with their two cousins; Felix and Gus have two sets of double-level bunk beds in their room. They always have a good time; sometimes their rambunctious activity results in a scolding from the woman of the house, especially when everyone else is trying to get some sleep. "Boys will be boys!" That is the expression that Aunt Sarah is often heard to say after correcting the lively young men. "Boys will be boys!"

Offering protection to the large house from the scorching sun and stormy wind and rain is a vast canopy formed by six very large live oaks. The oak tree I described earlier is located near the east side of the head of the stream; its massive branches shade the fountainhead, the source of the stream leading to Deer Bayou. The five other giant oaks reach high above the roof of the house, shading nearly the entire structure for most of the day. Two are located along the northeast and northwest corners of the house. One is located west southwest of the rear of the house; the other two are located at the southwest and southeast corners of the house. They stand like guardian angels protecting the homestead from the occasional marauding forces of nature. There cannot be a more picturesque setting for a house anywhere.

Excusing myself from the table, I asked for permission to tour the *little house*. Aunt Sarah told me that would be fine with her, looking at Uncle Justin for his approval; he told me I could go right ahead, suggesting that I bring one of the boys with me. Gus was the first to volunteer, so he and I went together. The other three boys asked for permission to walk the *beaten path* to the Atchafalaya River; exiting the rear of the house, they scampered off down the quarter-mile pathway to the river.

"You two better be careful!" Uncle Justin cautioned. "No one's lived in the *little house* since your grandmother died," he warned.

Gus and I assured him that we would be careful and hurried out the back door, crossed the porch, and headed down the stream following the *landing path* that led to the front of the *little house*. The house is about one hundred paces from the fountainhead.

My great-grandfather, Joseph Addison, was a master carpenter. He was responsible for the construction of the only two houses on Deer Island. The fact that they have both stood the test of storm and time is a testimony of his expert craftsmanship.

In addition to his skills in homebuilding, he was also a shipwright. My great-grandfather built Uncle Justin's push skiff; he built the *Dreadnought*, Uncle Justin's sailboat. He built the *Muskrat*, a smaller sailboat more suitable for traveling the inside shallow streams and bayous. He built the *Early Rose*, originally a sailboat built for my grandfather, Sanders Addison; he passed it down to my father, Adam when he died.

All the vessels he built are still water tight and floating high. My great-grandfather also fashioned the two dugout canoes, which lay beached near the fountainhead. In addition to those two canoes, he also made the dugout that Papa uses at the trapping camp back at Plumb Bayou; it too, was originally handed down to my grandfather, Sanders Addison, and passed on to Papa when he died.

My grandfather, Sanders Addison, lived in the *little house* with his wife, Martha White, until the time of his death in 1916. My grandmother died one year later; no one has lived in the house since 1917, four years ago.

The *little house* is a story and a half. The attic has two small bedrooms accessed by a ladder on the front porch (there is a rear porch). Inside the house there is a large sitting room, a dining room, and one bedroom. The kitchen is located outside the house, not far from the rear porch. The out-kitchen has a roofed breezeway and a wall on its north side. The huge iron stove has a wall located directly behind it, that wall accommodates the stove vent and provides hanging space for the various kitchen implements. The other three sides of the out-kitchen are open to the weather, an obvious attempt to combat the heat generated by the stove; it was a great idea for the summer, but it must have been uncomfortable in the winter. I guess that is why they located the kitchen inside the *big house.*

The "Little House"
Built by Joseph Addison
Completed July 30, 1840
Location: Deer Island

As I inspected inside and around the house, I could not help wondering what it would be like to make my home here. Maybe someday it will be my turn to move in the house located only a hundred paces from my Uncle Justin and my Aunt Sarah; I'm sure I could learn to love it here on my family's estate.

Aunt Sarah must come here to sweep the house on a regular basis, I thought; the place was clean and tidy. The beds look freshly made and the linen smells clean and fresh. I wish my grandparents were still around to enjoy it.

Neither of the two houses ever saw paint. The durable lumber used in their construction has aged naturally over the years. The north side of both houses, like the north side of the oaks, has green fungus growing on the unprotected wood. Consequently, the houses blend into the scenery as though they were indigenous to the landscape; it is as though they always belonged here.

Shadows were announcing the sunset by the time Gus and I returned to the veranda of the *big house*. Lee, Brad, and Felix soon returned from their walk to the big bend in the river. After exchanging a bit of small talk, Aunt Sarah announced that supper was ready and we all went inside to join the grownups in the dining room. We sat down for a light meal as everyone continued to get reacquainted.

Before we arose from the table, I asked Uncle Justin, "Do you know anything about a Houmas Indian princess? Her name was Princess Callie! I've never heard anyone speak of her."

"Nora, how did you find out about her?" my uncle asked.

"Well, the truth is I just learned about her myself; there was an obscure sentence or two in Great-grandmother Josephine's diary. Though I've read the entire manuscript several times, I never noticed the short reference about her; I can't believe I missed seeing it for so long," I lamented.

"Did you know her Uncle Justin?" I asked with great apprehension.

"No, Nora, I did not know her; but Joseph, Josephine, Sanders, Pauline, and Elizabeth did meet her," Uncle Justin shared, whetting my appetite for information. "I'll share what I remember about what was told to me with you and the family during one of our nights of storytelling," he added.

"I will look forward to hearing everything you know," I told him.

"That should be interesting!" Mama exclaimed.

On that note, Mama carried Alma upstairs early, placing her gently in the bed we would later share. After a few hours of great conversation, the wick from the oil lamp was burning low; it was time to retire for the evening.

Before I laid my head on my pillow, I opened the shutters of my dormer window. I could see the turbulent waters of the stream glistening in the moonlight. The sound of endless gurgling drew my attention to the source of the stream, the fountainhead. The underground water is struggling for freedom, finding its way to the surface through a mountain of tightly packed clamshells, bubbling with enthusiasm as it scurries downstream, boldly proclaiming its recent independence. Sweet is the sound of the water's continuous victory. "May its voice never be silenced," I pray.

A gentle breeze from the northeast swept softly over my face through the open shutters as I lay down beside my little sister, Alma. The day is gone; the time well spent, as the night creatures compete with the babbling brook for my attention. I soon drifted off on a restful sea, where all my thoughts fled from my presence once again.

Chapter Five

AT UNCLE JUSTIN'S PLACE

October 25, 1921

Uncle Justin and Aunt Sarah have tenaciously adhered to the dreams of the founders of Deer Island. Though many of my family members have chosen to live elsewhere for various reasons, my aunt and uncle have chosen to live out the dream of the congressman who first recognized the potential that this remote site afforded as a veritable paradise.

Few people I know would choose to live in such a remote location. The isolation, the great distance from available supplies, the many inconveniences which accompany such a lifestyle, and countless other factors that deny one comforts that might otherwise be available has caused many of my family members to abandon the wholesome (understandably unique) ideals of my ancestors.

I am happy that Uncle Justin has had the determination to resist the alternatives that the outside world offers to weak-kneed conformists. I mean no disrespect to anyone; I believe it is a choice we all must make. As for myself, I would choose to live on Deer Island, if the choice was mine to make.

When Papa and Mama were married, both homes on the island were occupied. There is still a chance that Papa may decide to move into the *little house* someday. I know he is concerned with the education of his children; that's a valid concern for sure. No doubt there are many considerations that have prevented him from making the move. No matter what happens now, when I am old enough to decide for myself, I hope to fulfill my dream by moving to Deer Island; may God allow me the privilege of doing just that.

The nearest town from here is Morgan City. When Congressman Adams acquired this land, and my great-grandparents came here from England to establish this settlement, Morgan City was known as Brashear City. Shortly after the Civil War, a railway system owned by Mr. Charles Morgan, connected Brashear City with New Orleans; in honor of Mr. Morgan, the city was renamed. It is located about twenty miles up the Atchafalaya River from Deer Island Bayou.

Deer Island is located at the southwest corner of Terrebonne Parish, Louisiana. The Atchafalaya Bay is merely an extension of the Gulf of Mexico; the Lower Atchafalaya River forms the west and northwest boundary of the Adams estate. From the river eastward, below the first big bend in the Lower Atchafalaya, lies a vast cypress swamp. Farther inland, heading east from the river and adjoining the cypress swamp, is Deer Island, which is bounded by open prairie on the north, the east, and the southeast. Clamshell deposits and sandbars curtail erosion along the river and southern shoreline of the estate, ensuring the integrity of the island.

Also part of the Adams estate is Shell Island, named by Congressman Adams for its huge clamshell deposits. Shell Island is densely forested with evergreen trees and is bounded on all sides by shell reefs and clamshell heaps. It is located on the west side of the Lower Atchafalaya River. Shell Island Pass provides an outlet for the river, allowing it to flow into the bay; the pass separates the island from the mainland.

As for Deer Island, the Lower Atchafalaya River is the western boundary of the estate; the northwest portion begins below the big bend in the river and continues along its left descending shoreline to the bay. From the river eastward the five-square-mile tract is bounded by Creole Bayou. (Refer to the map of Terrebonne Parish, which outlines the boundaries of the Adams estate.)

Our homestead on Bayou Du Large constitutes the third element of the Adams estate. Our home and the Anglican Church are the only buildings constructed on the land that was acquired by Congressman Adams in 1835. My family is the only Addison family living at that site.

Uncle Justin killed eight ducks this morning; I don't recall hearing any shots fired. Long before any of us were out of bed, he walked to a favorite hunting hole of his (often referred to as a honey hole) located at the far side of the pecan orchard. I overheard him explain to Papa that the ducks were as thick as the hair on his head when he arrived at the spot just before sunrise. "I turned one shot loose on them!" he told Papa. "When the smoke cleared, eight birds lay floating on the water of the shallow pond, waiting to be gathered and carried home with me," he announced, boasting modestly.

The first thing that greeted me on the back porch was the eight-bird cluster of feathers hanging from their webbed feet from a nail on one of the support columns near one of the swings. Mama and Aunt Sarah were sipping a cup of coffee, paying no attention to the game tied beside them.

"Good morning, Nora," Aunt Sarah offered with a smile. "Did you sleep well?"

"Yes, Aunt Sarah," I responded. "I slept very well, thank you."

Aunt Sarah and Mama were planning the dinner meal. We will be feasting on the fresh game and a pot of sweet potatoes that Papa and Uncle Justin are digging from the garden. I decided to occupy the swing facing opposite from the one that the two elder women were sitting upon. After a few minutes of chatter, Mama suggested that we feather the birds and clean them for the roasting pot.

I followed Mama and Aunt Sarah around the back of the house to lend a hand cleaning the birds. Though I had little experience, I knew I could learn the correct technique by working alongside these two veterans as they plucked the ducks. In a short time, we had the eight wood ducks plucked and gutted. We kept the hearts, livers, and gizzards to enrich the thick brown gravy Aunt Sarah is accustomed to making. My aunt asked me to take the remains into the woods; she said that whatever the chickens don't eat will be consumed by the local wildlife.

The feathers, which were removed from the duck breasts, were stuffed into a large sack; they will be stored away until there are enough to stuff a pillow, mattress, or a cushion for one of the chairs.

Aunt Sarah instructed the boys to walk the *beaten path* to the river and search its banks for sassafras driftwood. Felix promptly grabbed a hatchet from the kitchen and handed Lee an empty flour sack. The two energetic young men hurried out the kitchen door and ran off, heading straight for the pathway that leads away from the northwest corner at the rear of the house. Their enthusiasm did not go unnoticed by the grownups. "You could swear they were going after a pot of gold!" Aunt Sarah commented, clearly amused by their quick departure.

The *beaten path* is the shortest distance from the *big house* to the river. The quarter-mile distance has been traveled so frequently through the years that it never grows over; thus it has been designated the "beaten path" to distinguish it from the other paths around the homestead.

My great-grandfather, Joseph Addison, built the two houses in such a way that they serve as a compass. The front doors of both homes exit onto porches that face east to catch the morning sun; the back porches of both homes face west. Any compass direction can be accurately determined by using a side or a corner of either house as a reference point.

Brad appeared at the back porch steps carrying a bucket over-flowing with sweet potatoes. I wondered where he had been all this time; he informed me that he had strolled to the garden with Papa and Uncle Justin to lend them a hand digging the potatoes.

While Brad was telling me about his early morning activity, Gus made his first appearance of the day. I told Brad and Gus that Felix and Lee had gone to the river to collect sassafras driftwood. I asked Mama and Aunt Sarah if we could join the older boys at the river.

With their approval, we headed out the kitchen door in a hurry; we wanted to get there before the two boys headed back to the house.

I had not given much thought about the whereabouts of my little sister. Gus and Alma are the same age, but Gus is far more adventurous than my young sister; of course having Felix for a big brother probably has a lot to do with his venturesome behavior. I am certain that Alma is still sound asleep upstairs.

Felix and Lee are the same age; they are both seventeen. My brother Brad is sixteen; he is a year older than me, plus an extra three months. Alma and Gus are both seven years old. In spite of our age differences, we are all good buddies. I have just as much fun with Felix and Gus as my two brothers have. Alma is the only outsider; she would rather spend her time entertaining herself with that goofy ragdoll. She doesn't care to be very far from Mama's scent, if you can understand what I mean.

By the time we met up with Felix and Lee, they had already found what they had been sent to gather. They had dragged a sassafras log from the water's edge to the top of the clamshell heap which lines the shore of the river. Felix had chipped a sack full of the aromatic tree fragments, and he was preparing to head back to deliver them to Aunt Sarah.

Felix began to extol the benefits that the deep bend in the river provides. "We get all the firewood we need!" he boasted. "Logs and branches, large and small, become lodged against the shoreline when the swift river currents force them into the shallows along the bank. If Gus and I would not come here every day to gather the driftwood, the bank would be cluttered with unsightly logjams, making the task far more difficult (having to untangle the branches before hauling them out). We use the resources provided by the river to keep the woodstove hot. At the same time, we keep the river bank clean and inviting," he concluded.

How good is that? I pondered. The river provides the family with all the wood they need so they don't have to cut down any of the beautiful trees that grace the island. I cannot forget to mention the added benefit of occasional sassafras logs (especially the root bark) so the family can enjoy a steady supply of wood chips for tea.

To make the tea, Aunt Sarah first boils the sassafras chips in water. The resulting liquid will be strained and enhanced by adding milk and sugar before serving to thirsty consumers. I enjoy the flavor of the special brew, as does everyone else I know. It is a good substitute for coffee if you run out of it, and it provides a different tasting beverage as an alternative to the "*café noir.*"

Brad carried the sack full of chips; Felix and Lee picked up what remained of the ten-foot sassafras log and headed up the *beaten path* with Gus and me trailing close behind them.

There are many sassafras trees on the island, but Uncle Justin and Aunt Sarah would never think of cutting one down for tea. Every year they gather leaves from the tree; they dry them and grind them into a light green powder. When Aunt Sarah makes a gumbo without okra, we use a spoon or two of the "file" (as the powdered sassafras is locally known) to thicken the gravy; it is a very tasty additive. Alma doesn't care for the greenish slime it tends to make when it is added to the watery dish; she's the only member of my family that detests the use of the native seasoning.

I suddenly realized that there was no need to rush back to the house. I asked Gus if he wanted to turn back toward the river to explore its banks for treasure. Gus was happy with the idea, so we decided to go treasure hunting together.

I enjoy exploring the sun-bleached clamshell bank. In the past, I have found many interesting things. I have found odd-shaped bones, broken pieces of Indian pottery, turtle shells, and many other items.

Gus and I began searching an area a few hundred feet north of the trail. Though we made a thorough search, our efforts did not produce any expressions like "Eureka!" We had no treasure to show off back home; nonetheless, I always find the hunt exciting.

Not the least bit discouraged, I told Gus that we better start heading back toward the *beaten path*. Looking up as we started back, I spotted a big doe with her fawn near the entrance to the trail; she and her young offspring were walking casually to the river's edge to get a drink of water. It was a magnificent sight to behold; we remained motionless, trying to avoid any sudden movement, which might frighten the wary creatures. The young deer had many white spots on its rear, and it was obviously in a playful mood, scampering all around its mother as she drank; occasionally it jumped into the air, kicking wildly in some sort of physical exercise.

Suddenly, the mother deer looked in our direction; Gus and I held our breath. To our amazement, instead of bolting into the brush, she lowered her head for another drink before walking off into the thicket. The fawn pranced and danced as it followed its mother, having never taken a single drink from the river. I guess mother's milk was all the refreshment that the youngster needed.

As the two deer disappeared from view, Gus explained why they seemed to be oblivious to our presence. He informed me that Uncle Justin rarely hunts this side of the island. "These are our pet deer," he teased.

It is certainly no secret that it was the abundance of deer on the island that inspired the name "Deer Island." The opportunity to observe these two wild creatures from such a close vantage point was awe-inspiring.

As we returned to the *big house*, smoke towered above the rooftop of Aunt Sarah's kitchen. Dinner was on the stove and the aroma of sassafras tea was in the air. Gus and I entered the kitchen from the back porch. The smell of pot roasting duck, sweet potatoes cooking in a sugary sauce, and freshly brewed sassafras tea, was the first thing that greeted us as we walked through the kitchen door. Mama and Aunt Sarah were busy kneading dough on a table near the hot stove; sweat was dripping from their brows, as they shared the labor required for preparing a good meal.

"Why don't you serve yourselves each a cup of fresh tea?" Aunt Sarah suggested. "The ladle is hanging by a nail on the wall near the stove," she informed me.

I grabbed two cups from a shelf near the stove, and using the ladle, I filled them to the brim with the special blend of sassafras, milk, and sugar. Handing Gus his cup, we headed for the front porch to see what Papa and Uncle Justin were doing.

Papa and Uncle Justin were discussing plans for harvesting the sweet potato crop. Uncle Justin told Papa the tubers should be harvested before the first frost and placed in the corn crib for safekeeping. I believe the plan is that we begin digging the potatoes very soon—maybe tomorrow.

Gus and I went out in the front yard to swing on the ropes hanging from the giant oak near the head of the stream. Just as I was about to take my first turn at riding the rope through the air, I spotted Alma on the front porch with her doll under her arm. She walked around the length of the porch, pausing occasionally to sit her doll on the top rail of the balustrade. She was acting in her usual way, pretending to be the doll's mother.

Curiously, the older boys were nowhere in sight. They were probably playing hide-and-seek, climbing trees, or exploring the island for wildlife. Though I had a notion to find them, I knew that dinner was nearly ready and they would soon be summoned to the dining table.

In the meantime, Gus and I enjoyed the vivacity of swaying back and forth beneath the ancient oak tree singing: "Lou-Lou, skip to ma Lou. Lou-Lou, skip to ma Lou. Lou-Lou, skip to ma Lou, skip to ma Lou, my darling" in perfect harmony.

Since Papa and Uncle Justin were discussing the sweet potato harvest instead of catching up on events of the last eleven months, I hope that means there will be storytelling on the front porch tonight. Once the family has exhausted their exchange of current events, Papa and my uncle will begin telling stories about family and friends that are meant to inform, as well as entertain us after supper.

Each night, one of the men will try to outdo the other with a presentation of some past event in the history of the island, a story about one of its founders and their ancestors or descendants, or a tale of some interesting event in the life of some friend or acquaintance of one or more of our family members.

After each man has shared one story, the family judges which was best. Storytelling continues every night during our entire stay on the island; it's my favorite pastime. A tally is kept of the times each man outdoes the other; at the end of our visitation, this year's winner is announced. The principle rule is that each story must be verifiable, either by a witness, or by tangible proof produced by the storyteller.

DEER ISLAND IN AUTUMN

Mama says that to date, the two men are just about dead even in the standings. Uncle Justin and Papa are both excellent storytellers.

Mama quietly summoned Papa and Uncle Justin to the dinner table before hollering out the front doorway. "Ya'll come and eat! Dinner is on the table!" she announced in her loudest voice.

Appearing out of nowhere, Felix, Lee and Brad stood at the foot of the front porch steps hollering at Gus and me. "The last one at the dinner table is a rotten egg!" Once the challenge was offered, they ran inside ahead of us.

I engaged in a foot race with Gus, beating him to the dinner table. The older boys chided him for losing to a "girl." At first, I felt sorry for Gus; I had beaten him fair and square. If I had lost the race, the fun making would have been directed my way. Realizing he would soon recover from this harmless kidding, I quickly dismissed any further notion of sympathy.

Aunt Sarah put an abrupt end to the foolishness by announcing that Uncle Justin was ready to ask God to bless our food. We all bowed our heads in reverence as he thanked the Lord for the hearty meal that we were about to consume.

The ducks and sweet potatoes were especially good; everyone was quick to compliment the cook. Aunt Sarah's culinary skills probably exceeded Mama's cooking, but I would not dare to risk hurting feelings by stating that aloud.

In her usual modest manner, Aunt Sarah said that the food was probably more satisfying to an empty stomach than it was a result of her cooking ability.

Mama affirmed everyone's accolades, saying that she considered Aunt Sarah to be the best cook she knew. I was glad that Mama was acknowledging what I had felt in my heart without having any part in saying it; honesty is indeed a virtue, I reasoned.

My Aunt Sarah is a good role model. She is an excellent cook, a good housekeeper, a caring wife, and a loving mother. She is slim and trim; in stature, she's a bit shorter than Mama. She is always neatly dressed, and she has a handsome face; she is not beautiful, but she has a dignified appearance. Her dresses sweep the floor as she walks, but her floors are always so clean that her clothes never appear soiled. Her voice is high-pitched and normally would not be intimidating, but when she means business, it is clearly evident. Her teeth are straight and untarnished, though they are rarely seen when she smiles. I hope that I grow up to be just like her.

After dinner and a bit of small talk, we all found our favorite resting place to take an afternoon nap. This short period of rest is a customary practice here on the island and at home on Bayou Du Large. It makes good sense to allow your food to settle before engaging in any activity.

It seems everything comes to a virtual standstill between one and two o'clock in the afternoon. Most of the chickens are on the nest; the rooster has long stopped his crowing; the milk cow is chewing the cud, laying beneath a tree in the shade; the three goats are doing the same. As I lay in my bed, I strained my ears, trying to hear a single bird singing anywhere around the place—not a sound. Peering through my bedroom window, everything seemed to be resting in peace. There was no motion detectable, except the motion that the wind was causing in the treetops—leaves rustling in the intermittent breezes and the drooping gray clusters of Spanish moss swaying in the wind.

And so we lay down to rest in the quiet of the day. Random breezes caress my face, left exposed from the covers of my bed, encouraging peaceful repose as all my thoughts escape me.

I slept longer than anyone else this day. By the time I stirred from my bed, the boys had gone fishing and the grownups were all congregated on the front porch sipping sassafras tea. Alma was swinging from the rope beneath the oak tree clinging to her doll as she sang some childhood song.

I grabbed a cup, filled it with tea, and joined Mama, Papa, Uncle Justin, and Aunt Sarah on the porch.

"Did you sleep well, Nora?" Aunt Sarah asked me.

"I slept like a log!" I answered, still a bit groggy from waking. The sun was now at the other side of the *big house*, making the front porch the coolest spot around. The wind was blowing from the southeast and we were enjoying its full effects.

"There may be a front coming through tonight," Uncle Justin suggested. "The wind seems to want to switch around to the west. See how it is slowly changing toward the south," he astutely observed. (He was right, of course, but the change was so subtle I never would have noticed that it had switched directions had he not pointed it out to me.)

"If the wind does go around to the west," Papa offered, "we may get a hard blow from the northwest in the next day or so."

Papa and Uncle Justin decided to go to the corncrib to prepare a place for the sweet potato harvest. When the boys get back from their fishing excursion, we will all be going to the garden to pick potatoes. My uncle wants to dig them up and put them away before the stormy weather gets here. Sometimes you have to act sooner than you had planned, especially when the unexpected can be anticipated. This action will prove to be a wise decision if the prediction for bad weather is correct.

I decided to enjoy a little time with Alma on one of the swings while waiting for the boys to return. I asked little sister if she wanted me to push her higher than she was swinging. When she agreed, wearing a big smile on her face, I positioned myself behind her and began to push her higher and higher. Before long, she was begging me to stop, though she did seem to be enjoying the thrill of the ride.

The boys returned with six large catfish lying in the bottoms of the two dugout canoes—three to the boat. They were still alive!

Aunt Sarah informed the boys that Uncle Justin wanted to dig the sweet potatoes as soon as they returned. She advised Felix to put the fish on a stringer and place them in the stream for safekeeping. "They will remain alive until we are ready to eat them," she assured him.

Felix and Lee immediately found a stick, tied a long piece of string to one end of it, and ran it through the gills and out the mouths of the six large catfish. Once they were all on the stringer, the boys carefully placed the fish into the stream, making sure they had enough slack between them to allow them to remain upright. Felix then tied the stringer to a nearby tree limb to make sure they wouldn't swim away.

That done, the boys went to the corncrib to meet Papa and Uncle Justin. I joined Mama and Aunt Sarah on the porch to await further instructions. We soon walked the *garden path* to assist in the potato harvest. After a brief period of instruction, we began digging the sweet potatoes. Alma stood nearby; yes, she was holding her doll!

By the time we were finished, the four one-hundred-foot rows yielded ten one-hundred-pound sacks of sweet potatoes for the corncrib. Once they were safely stored, Uncle Justin complimented everyone for their efforts. "Now, if the weather turns nasty and cold, I can rest assured that my potatoes won't be damaged by an early frost," he announced, breathing a sigh of relief. "Those potatoes will fetch a good price the next time we go to the mainland," he added.

Shadows were growing, announcing the coming sunset, as we gathered on the back porch for a sip of coffee or tea. Just as Papa and my uncle had suspected, the wind was beginning to switch to the west. The weather is moving in quicker than anyone thought. I was amazed by the accuracy of their prediction; wisdom that can only come from experience, I reasoned. Though digging all those potatoes was hard work, I am glad we helped to get the crop in before the bad weather arrived.

Mama praised Alma for being so good while we did our work in the garden. She would not have been much help otherwise, but she was worthy of the compliments she was receiving. Aunt Sarah hugged her and gave her a similar tribute, praising her for her proper behavior.

Felix and Gus will be going to Deer Bayou to check their bush traps for shrimp and soft-shell crabs in the morning. Felix invited me to go with my brothers when they leave tomorrow. Looking at Mama for approval, she gave me permission to accompany them. Excitement began to build within me as I pondered what the fishing trip would be like. It should be great fun!

I had never been asked to join the boys on a fishing trip before this year. I guess the general feeling was that I was too young to bring along. I was happy they had reevaluated their position, whatever it was; I'm glad they decided to ask me to go fishing with them.

Felix informed everyone that he had set twenty-four bush traps before returning home earlier today. A bush trap is made by tying several branches together at the base of their stems (usually willow or mangrove branches are used). The dense foliage provided by the branches is lowered into the water and secured to a pole with a piece of string. Freshwater shrimp and crabs, ready to shed, find safe haven amidst the dense foliage of the branches.

When running a bush trap, one positions a hand-held net to try to catch whatever is hiding inside the cluster of leaf-laden branches. As the trap is lifted slowly out of the water, the net acts as a safeguard against losing anything that may fall out prematurely. Once the trap is out of the water and positioned over a tub or wooden pail, it is shaken vigorously to remove the shrimp and crabs from the bush.

Felix explained to me how the traps are run several times before, but I neither witnessed nor participated in the operation myself. I will ask him to let me try to shake the traps at least one time for the experience. I'll wait to ask him when we start the run tomorrow; there is no need to risk rejection before we are close to the scene where all the action will take place.

We dined on cornbread and goat's milk for supper. Uncle Justin announced that he would lead off the storytelling competition tonight, since Papa had the privilege of doing so last year.

Everyone was bursting with excitement, each wondering aloud what he or she thought the first story might be about. Uncle Justin wasn't telling; he didn't offer the slightest clue. "You'll just have to wait for me to tell my story," he teased.

In an effort to stimulate us further, Papa and Uncle Justin began telling jokes and the tall tales that each had heard since last year. These funny accounts did not qualify as the kind of stories that would be shared from the rocking chairs on the front porch later this evening; they can be as wild as the imagination of the storyteller can dream up, without proof or verification of any kind.

During one of Papa's tall tales about a black panther, Lee grabbed me unexpectedly by the leg; my heart skipped a beat and the startling sensation sent shivers up and down my spine.

"I'll get you back, Lee Addison! Just you wait and see!" I pledged. "I will have my turn. I promise you that!" I warned, giving him a pair of eyes that let him know I meant business.

The weather was preparing to get nasty by the time we exited the front door of the *big house* to hear Uncle Justin tell the first story of the season. Light rain had already begun to fall and the wind was starting to blow rather briskly from the north; there was a noticeable chill in the air. Thunder accompanied by flashes of lightning portended what we were in store for during the course of the night—a strong cold front was fast approaching, and soon!

Amidst the threat of stormy weather, we young people gathered in a semicircle on the floor around the four grownups sitting in their favorite rocking chairs on the front porch. Papa and Uncle Justin were enjoying a good smoke on their pipes; Mama and Aunt Sarah were discussing tomorrow's menu. The thunder grew louder and louder with each tick of the clock. If Uncle Justin doesn't begin his story soon, we will be forced to go back inside to escape the strong winds and torrential rain, I somberly considered; that would spoil everything!

There was a bone-chilling cold being blown across the northeastern corner of the house. Fortunately, we were all seated just outside the front door near the southeastern corner of the building. The house was shielding us from the cold watery spray which had begun wetting the other side of the porch floor.

Uncle Justin began, "This past year, I was hunting for a deer near a small stream in the woods just north of here. As I followed the stream toward the northern boundary of the estate, the deer tracks and tree rubs looked promising. I decided to sit down on a fallen tree to wait and see if one would show himself. Earlier scouting trips had produced sightings of several bucks, including a nine-pointer—I saw it myself! I sat on that fallen log making no sound or movement, patiently waiting and hoping for a shot at one of those male deer. I waited for a long time without seeing anything but a few squirrels and rabbits running through the nearby brush. In the late afternoon, just as I was about to give up and go back home, I was about to get the biggest surprise of my life. All of a sudden, I began to hear a sound that was not familiar to me. It was a roaring sound, and it seemed to be getting closer and closer to where I was seated. Frankly, I began to get a bit worried. When the roaring stopped, I began questioning whether I had imagined the noise. I thought that I might have been confused by some other noise that may have sounded like a roar. After an extended silence, I began to regain my composure and the fear left me."

A sudden flash of lightning coupled with the deafening roar of thunder shook up everyone on the porch, sending Alma scurrying quickly into Mama's arms. Uncle Justin took another puff on his pipe, making it glow red in his tobacco bowl; he then continued to share his story.

"Thinking I might have imagined the noise I had heard, I calmed down and held my position on the fallen tree limb—then it happened! The nearby brush began to shake violently. First I heard a bloodcurdling roar, then all of a sudden, the unnerving sight of a bear charging toward me through the bushes was too much for me to handle. I ran so fast and furiously that I left my prized firearm behind me, lying on the ground next to the log where I was formerly seated. I admit I am a bit embarrassed by the way I handled myself, but at least I'm here to tell the story. Thank God!

"When I arrived back at the house without my rifle, it caused no small stir. Sarah was concerned that the bear might attack the chickens. It might maul our only milk cow. It may kill one of the pigs or goats during the night. Though I understood her anxiety, nothing could match the concern I had for my Kentucky Long Rifle. That gun had been in the family since Uncle Patrick purchased it for Grandfather Joseph Addison in 1840. The old muzzle-loader has been a proven weapon; it is extremely accurate. It has been used for deer hunting since before I can remember. When I was a young boy, my papa would load *Ole Long Tom*, as the gun was affectionately called, and send me into the woods after some meat. With only one shot for killing, I learned to be a good hunter at an early age. 'Don't take a shot unless you are sure you can hit what you are shooting at!' Papa would caution. As a result of this training, I've never lost a single deer; when I shoot at one, there it stays.

"Felix and Gus didn't know what to say to me. They seemed dumbfounded. I believe they were afraid they might make me angry if they began laughing at me, but I could see it in their faces. Inside, they were laughing at my cowardly reaction to the bear; I could understand their feelings. As I said, I was ashamed of the way I ran off without my gun.

"The next morning, we all decided to go look for my gun. Sarah accompanied the boys and me to the fallen tree where I had abandoned *Ole Long Tom*. As we neared the site, I prayed that we would find the gun intact. Felix carried the blunderbuss, loaded for bear; just in case! Sarah spotted my gun; it was lying on the ground on the opposite side of the branch, it was right where I had dropped it, just in front of where I had been seated. I must have held onto my rifle for a brief moment before losing it, as I hopped over the limb to make my escape.

"Gus wanted to investigate the other side of the log. There we found bear tracks, all over the area where I had been sitting. The log upon which I sat had multiple scratch marks from the bear's claws. We found the same claw marks on several trees near the site."

Uncle Justin took a brief time to ask if we could understand that his running away from that bear was probably the wisest thing he could have done. Everyone agreed that it was the right thing to do. He told us that his rifle survived the ordeal. He said that once he viewed the signs the bear had left behind, he was sure he had acted prudently.

"We haven't seen or heard any signs of that bear since that incident," Uncle Justin concluded.

The wind had intensified to an uncomfortable level. The continuous sound of thunder and frequent flashes of lightning had us rushing inside before any of us could begin to comment on the story. Felix lit an oil lamp on the dinner table; we gathered around, listening intently to the opinions of those who just heard Uncle Justin's story.

Papa asked the first question. "Justin, have you ever heard any accounts of bear on Deer Island before this incident?"

"No, Adam. This was my first experience with a bear on the island. I never heard anyone say that this has happened before now," Uncle Justin affirmed.

I asked Uncle Justin if he thought the bear might come back around the homestead, just to snoop around. He felt it would be foolish to try to predict what any wild animal might do or not do, especially a wild animal that he had no experience with; he was totally ignorant of the animal's habits. "We'll just have to wait and see!" He concluded his remarks with a concerned look on his face.

The weather was raging outside as we all made our way to the bedrooms. I was thankful that Uncle Justin had pane glass windows. The howling wind and the torrential rain of the norther were assaulting the north side of the house with a vengeance. Without the glass panes I am sure the wind-blown rain would be penetrating the shutters and finding the floor inside by now.

As I lay in my bed with Alma sound asleep beside me, I wondered where the bear might be in this horrible weather. I guess he is lying on the south side of some fallen tree or shielding himself in the dense thicket of the virgin forest which surrounds the homestead.

The heavy rainfall, the howling wind, the clap of thunder and the flashes of lightning just outside the closed shutters of my bedroom windows, and all the forces of nature being unleashed this night, have taken away the peaceful tranquility that would otherwise be provided by the environment surrounding the house.

There is no competition for the ears of the listener; the storm has demanded center stage. I drifted off to sleep amidst the temporary chaos, joining my sister in some other realm far away from the frightening spectacle outside my windows.

October 26, 1921

Morning brought sunshine back to the island. The wind was blowing briskly from the north at probably twenty miles per hour. By the time I made it down to the kitchen, Papa and Uncle Justin had just returned from Deer Bayou; they had gone to check on the boats, checking the bilge for excess water and making sure the moorings were secure.

The two men were happy to report that all was well. The *Dreadnought*, the *Muskrat*, and the *Early Rose* were unscathed by the severe weather last evening. It turns out that Papa and Uncle Justin, in anticipation of the hard blow, had secured all the hatches and windows on the three boats yesterday afternoon. "They are both dry and fit for traveling!" Uncle Justin proclaimed with pride.

The boys were gathered on the back porch swinging and enjoying conversation, as they ate some of Aunt Sarah's fresh hot biscuits. Partially shielded from the cold north wind, they were not dressed in the warm clothes I thought would be suited for this sudden drop in temperature. Papa said it was probably down to fifty degrees from yesterday's seventy degree weather; that's a drop of twenty degrees.

I had come downstairs wearing a light sweater, anticipating the temperature drop brought on by the strong norther. After all, if we are going to check the bush traps, I want to be dressed for the occasion; there is no sense in being cold and miserable; that would diminish the fun.

Mama suggested we wait to run the traps after dinner: "Maybe the wind will calm a bit by then." The other grownups agreed with Mama's judgment; we decided to follow their advice.

We ladies spent most of the morning huddled around the woodstove in the kitchen. Felix and Lee cleaned the fresh water catfish that had been kept alive on a stringer in the chilled waters of the stream since yesterday afternoon. I watched them fetch them out of the water; they were as lively as when they were first caught; I was surprised that they were so full of energy after being tied together for so long.

Papa and Uncle Justin were enjoying a smoke on the front porch when I found them. I asked them if they wanted a cup of fresh hot tea or coffee and they promptly said yes to my offer; they both asked for a cup of coffee. After delivering the hot beverage, I could tell they were involved in adult conversation, so I politely excused myself and headed back inside to join the women.

Aunt Sarah was preparing a seafood dish using the fish filets from the catfish and adding fresh tomatoes, onions, parsley, wild onion (a variety of domestic onion that makes a small bulb and a slender shoot that gets about a foot tall when it matures), bay leaves, ground peppercorn, and a little salt. The resulting fish and gravy will be applied to a pile of fresh boiled rice on each plate when served. The aroma from the tasty dish is making everyone hungry.

I tried joining the boys on the swings twice this morning; both times I tried, the cold made me uncomfortable, and I ran back into the kitchen where it was nice and warm. Alma and her ragdoll never moved from the dining room floor near the arch of the kitchen doorway. Little sister enjoys caring for her make-believe baby; she's a future mother in training, I figured.

After enjoying the succulent meal, we chatted awhile before retiring for our afternoon naps. The windows remained closed throughout the house to prevent the chill from creeping inside. Believe it or not, the heat rising from the woodstove in the kitchen was keeping the entire house at a comfortable temperature, especially upstairs. The wind had not diminished at all; with all the windows shut, I could not hear the gurgling sound from the fountainhead. Nevertheless, the rays from the midday sun were caressing my face, and the solemn quietude ushered me into a deep sleep very quickly.

When I awakened from my nap, the rest of the family was still enjoying peaceful repose. I went downstairs to the kitchen to help myself to a cup of sassafras tea from the pot simmering on the stove. Before I finished my first cup, Aunt Sarah joined me at the dining table.

"Did you sleep well?" I asked her; she looked a bit peaked.

"I slept just fine, Nora, but I do believe that this sudden change in the weather has caused my bones to ache a bit more than usual, that's all!" she said with an expression that showed her annoyance with the discomfort. As soon as she began to move around, the uncharacteristic stern look on her face turned again to a pleasant smile and she was her usual self again.

"Now, Nora, the weather has not improved since this morning. The wind is very strong and the temperature remains near fifty. I recommend that you and the boys wait until tomorrow to run those bush traps. What do you think?" she asked. "Don't you think tomorrow would be better?"

Trying not to appear too disappointed I responded with a smile. "I believe you are right, Aunt Sarah. It is still cold and breezy outside. If we leave the bushes in the water for another day, it could mean a better catch anyway," I said with a positive attitude.

"I wouldn't be surprised if there will be more in the traps if you leave them set another day," Aunt Sarah said, trying to encourage me. After all, it wasn't the end of the world; I must admit that I was looking forward to checking them this afternoon.

When the boys descended the stairway and entered the dining room, Aunt Sarah informed them of the change in plans. Everyone was in agreement; we'll check the bush traps in the morning.

Papa and Uncle Justin suggested we all take a stroll to Deer Bayou. "We can lounge around at the landing and enjoy the afternoon sunshine," he posed.

Having nothing more planned for the afternoon, we agreed it was a good idea, and we headed down the *landing path* to the bayou. As we walked past the *little house,* I could not help wondering if I might get a chance to live there someday. The well-constructed building would make a fine home for any family, I reasoned. The out-kitchen at the rear of the house is fully equipped and ready to be put into use. It would be great fun helping Mama do the cooking in an open-air kitchen, I thought silently to myself.

When we arrived at the dock site, I looked in the direction of the eagle's nest. One of the magnificent birds was basking in the radiant sunlight, occasionally spreading its wings and fanning the air with them. I was glad that the nest had not been damaged by the strong wind. The eagle's mate must be on a hunt, I surmised.

Uncle Justin began conversation by giving us the history of his prized possession, *Dreadnought.* He began to share with us. "Your great-grandfather, Joseph Addison, was a boat builder by trade. It was he who fashioned the hull, fitting her with her rigging and hardware. He built the sailboat to provide a comfortable means for traveling to and from the city. The city's name was changed from Brashear City to Morgan City shortly after the Civil War.

"The hull took two years to build. Her sails were made in New Orleans. It took six months to get them. On July 30, 1844, she was ready for her maiden voyage. This July she will have been afloat for seventy-seven years. She is as seaworthy today as the day she was launched.

"The keel was laid, the ribs were set, the planks were fastened to the hull's bottom, the decks were added and the cabin built; all this work was done on the bayou bank not far from here. Joseph enlisted the help of several men to get her into the water. Francois Marceaux, Frency for short, captain of the *Swamp Rat*, and his deckhand, Carey Trudeau, brought a dozen laborers from the mainland to accomplish the difficult task.

"Working very hard, the men slowly raised the entire vessel from the ground, having placed several freshly cut trees of uniform diameter beneath the hull to facilitate rolling the unnamed craft into the nearby water. Once the boat was lifted on its makeshift rollers, she was ready to be pushed gently downhill to its final resting place.

"The worst of the launching procedure now accomplished, it was time for a brief celebration. Great-grandmother Josephine had prepared a hearty meal for all the workers.

"While the men ate sumptuously, sitting at a large table in the front yard of the *big house*, Josephine entertained the weary souls by recounting her experiences during the voyage from Southampton to New Orleans. Since she had witnessed the construction of her husband's sailboat, and knowing that her husband had poured out his heart and soul, making sure the vessel would be expertly crafted, she boasted that she would have no fear when sailing aboard the magnificent vessel. As a result of her steadfast assurance that she would have nothing to fear aboard her husband's new craft, the boat was named *Dreadnought*, in fear of nothing.

"After the meal, the men mustered all their strength, gently rolling *Dreadnought* over the logs and into the waters of Deer Bayou at this very spot. A month later, after her planking below the waterline had swelled, the men helped Joseph set the two masts through the upper and lower decks, positioning them atop the solid brass plates which secured them to the massive keel. The arduous and delicate task took nearly an entire day to accomplish. When it was done, the vessel took on the splendor that can be seen in her today.

"Her foremast towers sixty-five feet above decks, the aft-mast stands five feet taller at seventy feet—the masts, jibs, and bowsprit are made of Siberian spruce, shipped from New England. It is the highest quality spruce in North America. The overall length of the vessel is seventy-three feet with a beam of twelve feet. The main cabin is positioned between the two masts. Its lower deck is six feet below the main deck, and it extends through the upper deck about thirty inches. The aft cabin is the cargo hold. It, too, has a deck six feet below the main deck. It rises above the main deck about eighteen inches.

"The *Dreadnought* is a box-keeled sailor; it has a retractable keel. Joseph got the idea for her design from Captain Frenchy's vessel, the *Swamp Rat.* The draft of the *Dreadnought,* with her fin lowered, is approximately ten feet without a heavy load of provisions. With the fin raised, the draft is reduced to about twenty-eight inches. With four oar stations, she can move through the shallows with little difficulty.

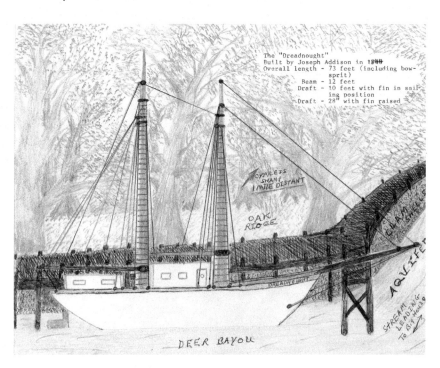

"The jib booms run aft of each mast pole, clearing the cabin roofs by about a foot. As you can see, there are countless ropes, each serving a special function. They run from various points on the bulwarks to the mast poles, from bowsprit to foremast, and from mast to mast.

"The engineering is fascinating. It makes one wonder who first figured out all that goes into building such a fine vessel. Each time I take her out, she makes me appreciate the skilled craftsmanship that went into her design. I often say a prayer of thanksgiving to the Lord for the boat and its builder," Uncle Justin concluded.

The history of *Dreadnought* is a fine story, everyone conceded. Papa said that he knew some of the boat's story, but he never grows tired of hearing it repeated. As for me, I always love sitting and listening intently to anyone who reminds me of my ancestors. I especially appreciate being informed about their accomplishments. These oral accounts seem to make them come alive again, even if it's only in my heart. Sometimes they become so real in my imagination, that it's almost as though I knew them personally.

Mama instructed Lee and Brad to get the wooden case that held Aunt Sarah's jars; there are two dozen filled with fig preserves, and six jars of pickled bird eye peppers, all stowed away in our cabin. Uncle Justin was ecstatic over the jars full of his favorite peppers and Aunt Sarah was equally excited over her jars of fig preserves; she told her two boys to lend a hand getting the valuable presents back to the house safely. "You boys better be very careful in the way you handle my case of jars; you can break them if you drop them!" she cautioned.

As we made our way slowly back to the *big house,* walking directly into the brisk north wind, a squirrel stopped abruptly about four feet off the ground clinging to the tree bark of a giant water oak. The nervy creature barked out its disapproval; apparently we had rudely interrupted his last minute foraging near the *landing path.* After giving us a good piece of his mind, he scampered off into the thicket after climbing down from the tree he had just swiftly abandoned. I could not understand the fearless determination of that furry little creature trying to stand his ground. The incident was very amusing.

When we passed the front of the *little house* the shadows of the trees were growing taller, announcing the coming sunset. As we strolled alongside the crystal clear waters of the spring, the songbirds were singing to us; they were bellowing their symphonic tunes that are so delightful to hear. Countless rabbits and squirrels fled our presence along the footpath, escaping into the thicket to avoid putting up with our riotous laughter, which to them must have sounded alarming.

Papa and Uncle Justin kept us in stitches with their humorously amusing jokes and tall tales. Even Mama and Aunt Sarah found themselves enthralled by uncontrolled spells of wild outbursts of laughter, much exaggerated by their sincere attempts to avoid such foolishness.

Papa reminded everyone that it would be his turn to tell a story on the veranda of the *big house* tonight. He proudly proclaimed that his story would outshine Uncle Justin's bear story that he had so admirably shared last evening in the midst of the terrible storm.

"We'll just have to wait and see about that!" Uncle Justin playfully taunted.

Immediately after supper, Papa and Uncle Justin went out to the front porch to enjoy a good smoke of tobacco. I trailed close behind them, asking Papa when he was going to share his story. Papa said he would take a little time to allow his food to digest before his storytelling would begin.

Felix, Lee, Gus, and Brad brought the peppers and preserves safely inside and came running out of the house, making a mad dash for the rope swings in the front yard. There was really nothing to rush for; there are four swings hanging from the branch of the giant oak. Finally, I realized they were trying to make sure that I wouldn't beat any of them to the base of the tree.

"I didn't have any inclination to swing anyway!" I yelled, as Alma appeared through the front door with her doll. She came and took a seat beside me on the front porch steps.

My favorite spot for sitting to listen to stories is at the head of the porch steps. I use the corner post, which supports the roof of the veranda, for a backrest. Since the grownups congregate near the front door in their respective rocking chairs, the vantage point from where I usually sit gives me the best chance for hearing every single word spoken by anyone on the porch.

Gus likes to sit at the top of the steps on the opposite side from me. Felix, Lee, and Brad usually lean against the balustrade with their backs after seating themselves on the floor. Alma has no customary practice; she moves about following her every whim, but she remains quiet and respectful of the person who is speaking.

The moon was rising over the horizon. The nighttime darkness was beginning to be dispelled by the light of the near-full circle shining in the eastern sky. The north wind had diminished; the brisk wind was replaced by slight intermittent breezes. This made the atmosphere on the front porch ideal for storytelling time.

Papa let out a hearty laugh in response to something Uncle Justin had told him. The sudden outburst awakened me from my daydreaming, but not in time for me to hear what my uncle said that Papa found so funny. The jovial way Papa was acting caused me to laugh along with him because I found his antics comical. Laughter is contagious! Everyone knows that!

The fountainhead emitted its varying tones. Its continuous gurgling served as the background music for the sounds of the night creatures. Northerly breezes now and again rustle the leaves, both in the trees and along the ground, adding to the natural symphony. What an atmosphere, I thought. The wonderful sounds of nature, the crisp cold air, and the bright light of a moon nearly full, set the stage for what was about to happen.

Papa called for everyone to come and gather around him. "Come and hear the story that will top last night's story of the bear!" He challenged his audience with the confidence of a master storyteller.

Mama and Aunt Sarah suddenly appeared in the front doorway dragging their rocking chairs behind them. The boys took their positions on the floor, leaning their backs against the railing. Alma sat between Gus and me on the front steps; we all listened carefully as Papa began to share his story.

Papa began, "It was two years ago this past May, when my good friend, Xavier Moise Moliere from Bayou Du Large, made an amazing discovery. The discovery was so fantastic that I seriously doubt that any of you will believe what I am about to reveal. Before I proceed any further, you must all promise that what you hear this night will remain a secret in your hearts until you are otherwise instructed. I have known about this for quite some time. Although there was nothing illegal about what transpired, I thought it best to keep it to myself until now. Xavier gave me permission to tell you this story with one condition. It must be kept a secret. Can all of you promise to keep this a secret?"

Everyone quickly agreed to remain silent about the matter; even Alma pledged to keep secret the story of Xavier's amazing discovery.

Papa continued, "The turtles were coming ashore to lay their eggs. May is the beginning of the season for this activity, as all of you well know (terrapins, otherwise known as diamondbacks, lay their eggs during the months of May and June each year). Xavier was working the coastline west of the mouth of Bayou Zero. He tied his oar skiff to a pile that he had driven near the shore several years ago. He carried his potato sacks over his shoulders and started searching for turtles. At first he had poor results, but after he had traveled a few hundred yards from where he started, he found his first diamondback turtle. 'That broke the ice!' he told me. As he continued west toward Oyster Bayou (about four miles distant) he picked up a turtle here and there. The further west he went, the more turtles he caught. In a few hours, he had two sacks full. He had to return to his boat to offload the catch.

"Aboard the boat he had a wooden holding pen with a lid on it to prevent any chance of escape. It was near midday when he dumped the two sacks into the box and secured the lid. He was doing so well that he decided to return to the site where he had stopped earlier to try to fill his sacks again. With sixteen diamondbacks in the crate, the day's catch was promising; sixteen more would be a near record for him.

"His ambitious plans for a record catch proved fruitful, and by six o'clock he had reached his quota of turtles. He was feeling good, but now he had to carry the two sacks of terrapins for nearly two miles to get back to his mooring site. The journey would be tiring and it was getting late.

"After the prosperous but hard day's work, he realized he had completely lost track of the time. The sun was setting when he entered Hell Hole Bay, and he had a long journey home from there. The day had been productive—he caught thirty-two turtles. If he would have had more daylight to burn, he would have caught many more, he told me. It had been a very good day!

"At least the tide would be in his favor for the long journey home. Standing at oars, he rowed steadily through Hell Hole Bayou and entered West Bay Junop. He skirted the northwest shoreline and crossed the open water of the bay into Cross Bayou. From there, he soon entered Little Bayou Du large for the final leg of his trip home. Since the tide was coming in, that was in his favor. He could row at a leisurely pace, taking his good time about it.

"Xavier had left the dock in front of his house before daybreak that morning. That was his usual custom when he was hunting for turtles. Now it was late, and he was growing weary from the long day's activity. His old age was finally beginning to take its toll on him. (In 1919, Xavier was sixty two years old.) A few years ago, a hard day at the seashore would have been more of an adventure than a chore.

"Now all of you are aware that there is a cemetery located on a small island we call 'Oak Ridge Island.' The oak trees on this tiny island can be easily seen from the west bank of Little Bayou Du Large. It's about a mile north of King Lake Cut—right after the bayou makes its sharp turn toward Grand Pass. The cemetery on the ridge has a dozen or so graves, most of which are storm victims from the 1909 Storm. The island is several hundred yards out from the shoreline and it is surrounded by open prairie."

Even my family from Deer Island knows where that cemetery is located, I thought to myself. It stands out in the prairie for everyone to notice; you would have to be blind not to have seen it. When someone mentions "Oak Ridge Cemetery," everyone from this region knows where it is, I quietly reasoned.

Papa continued, "It was totally dark. There was a new moon out. Only starlight was visible overhead, when Xavier rowed his push skiff past the cut that leads to New Route Bayou. As he was approaching the sharp bend in Bayou Dularge, something very strange suddenly caught his attention. He observed an eerie light hovering over the marshland, in close proximity to the graveyard. He had never witnessed such a sight. The light appeared greenish yellow. He had never seen those colors emitted by any lantern. Curious about what he was seeing, he rested his oars after the current had deposited his boat on a mudflat near the shoreline.

"Xavier strained his eyes to see if he could detect some human figure near the light source. Though he could see no shape or form near the light, the source of the light was moving about as though someone was carrying a lantern. He told me it was very strange.

"Old Xavier isn't afraid of anything! He tied his skiff to some brush along the bank, and he climbed ashore to have a closer look at the phenomena. Each time he felt he would soon be near the light, it moved away from him. After several attempts to catch up with the light failed, he deduced that the light might be beckoning him to follow. He continued to track it, even though it seemed to him to be beyond reason to do so.

"At first it seemed the light would bring him to the cemetery ridge, which is several hundred paces from shore. As he drew near to the ridge the light turned, leading him toward a smaller cluster of trees about a hundred yards from the gravesite.

"Xavier pursued the light source into the thicket of the obscure oak growth. Suddenly the light vanished. The small group of three live oaks was remote from the burial site by some distance. He said he had never seen this triangular cluster of oaks before; it was at the far side of the island, near its westernmost boundary. It had always been there, but it was hidden behind the larger growth of numerous oak trees on the eastern side of the ridge, he told me.

"Baffled by the experience, Xavier returned to his oar skiff and continued his long journey upstream. When he arrived at the Nicholas P. Moliere General Store at Grand Pass, he began unloading his catch. His bumbling at the dock site created enough noise to awaken the store's manager, Mr. Desire Dumond. He had just gone to bed after a long day of boiling shrimp for the drying platform—all the platform workers had retired to their small cabins nearby, long before Xavier arrived to offload his catch. Desire assisted Xavier in unloading the large catch of terrapins from his skiff to the holding pen which is located next to the shrimp-drying platform. The turtles would be held in the pen until the freight boat from the Bayou Terrebonne General Store comes and picks them up for transport to Morgan City.

"Once the turtles were offloaded, Xavier again boarded his skiff to complete the last few miles of his journey home. The incoming tide lent him welcome assistance for his six-mile push from the store-front to the wharf at his house.

"Xavier's brother, Nicholas Moliere, owns two general stores. He manages the larger of the two—Bayou Terrebonne General Store, located at the southernmost wagon trail along Terrebonne Bayou. The larger store has access to markets in Houma and Thibodeaux via horse-drawn wagon or motorboat. The store managed by Mr. Dumond at Grand Pass, is only accessible by water. It receives supplies from the larger store, but it conducts most of its trade with the Morgan City market.

"Both general stores sell dried shrimp, when they are available (seining for brown shrimp usually begins on the first of May and it usually ends by the end of June, seining for white shrimp usually begins in the middle of August and ends in late December). The shrimp drying platforms operate during both seasons. In the off-season, they make necessary repairs to the buildings and platforms.

"The general stores both sell turtles, primarily during the months of May and June, when fishermen hunt for them along the coast where they crawl ashore to bury their eggs. Both general stores sell oysters when it is cool enough to transport them to market (the oyster harvest ended at the end of April; it will begin again in September). The stores do a very good business.

"Each Wednesday, a freight boat is dispatched from the Bayou Terrebonne General Store to Grand Pass. It delivers fresh provision to be sold to the local fishermen. Once it offloads its provisions, it carries special crates aboard for transporting turtles and crabs(when they have them) to Morgan City. In the cool months, they transport oysters to the Morgan City seafood dock. During the seasons, if there are dried shrimp ready for market, the freight boat will deliver them also.

"On its return trip from Morgan City (usually the following day) it stops at Grand Pass to pick up dried shrimp, when in season; crabs, if they have any; oysters, when in season, and a few turtles, if they have them. Sometimes the freight boat tows a fish car back to Bayou Terrebonne from Morgan City (a fish car is a specially designed craft which has planks along its sides, which are purposely separated to allow water to pass through them. The aerated water keeps the fish alive until they can be sold at market—usually fresh water catfish). These items will be sent to markets in Houma and Thibodeaux by wagon or motorboat.

"Unlike his brother Nicholas, Xavier is a maverick. He's not satisfied with the mundane existence of standing behind a store counter, or sitting behind a desk in some office. He prefers it outdoors. He has deliberately chosen to live a simple life. Consequently, he is a man of little means. A bachelor can survive with very little income. I don't believe he ever plans to marry. At least, that is what he told me.

"Xavier arrived home in the wee hours of the morning. Exhausted from the day's activities, he fell asleep in his living room chair. During the course of his sleep, he had a dream. In his dream, he traveled back to the spot where the strange light disappeared. He saw a shovel and a pickax leaning against an oak tree. When he awakened from his dream, it was midmorning.

"Xavier knew that many people, in his lifetime, had reported seeing strange lights in the night-time darkness hovering over the vast expanses of open prairie throughout the marshy regions of South Louisiana. The French have a term for the phenomena: *Feu follet*. This can be interpreted as *strange fire* in English. It is a result of the spontaneous combustion of organic matter as it releases methane gas into the atmosphere and is ignited by some electrostatic charge (the phenomena resembles St. Elmo's fire, some experienced sailors have reported—the difference is only the color—St. Elmo's fire has a bluish color instead of greenish yellow). Previous reports he had heard were different than what he had seen; the light over the prairie appeared to those who had witnessed it to be stationary. The light they saw didn't move!

"Xavier sipped a cup of hot coffee and pondered his next move. Curiosity might have killed the cat, but his curiosity was turning into a mission of adventure—nothing ventured, nothing gained; so the old saying goes, he reasoned. Xavier walked to his shed, secured a shovel and pickax, boarded his oar skiff, and headed for the spot he had seen in his dream. The tide was heading in the right direction. It was moving south, returning to the sea. Oaring fair tide would make his long journey to the oak ridge easier in the heat of the midday sun. He would be there in about two hours, he estimated.

"Taking his good old time, Xavier wondered if he was beside himself; he was pursuing something he knew nothing about, as he continued to make steady progress heading downstream. An hour later, he passed the Grand Pass General Store. It wouldn't be long now, he reasoned. The anxious anticipation must have made him move his oars faster than he thought. He was making excellent time, shaving a half hour off his estimated time for reaching his destination. Xavier's heart began to race with excitement, as he wondered what he would find on that ridge.

"When he arrived at the big bend in Little Bayou Du Large, he grounded his skiff on a mudflat near the right bank and jumped ashore. He tied his boat to some nearby brush, took his shovel and pickax in hand, and headed for the ridge known as Oak Island with the stubborn determination of a mule.

"In the bright sunlight, Xavier could easily follow the tracks he had made through the prairie grasses a few hours earlier. Oak Island was straight ahead, the smaller group of oaks he had seen the night before were on the far side of the ridge and presently hidden from his view.

"Counting 350 paces, Xavier arrived at the cemetery. Beyond the ridge on Oak Island was the much smaller ridge with three large oaks. It was an additional hundred paces. The tiny ridge stood like an orphaned child, conspicuously separated from the much larger ridge where the cemetery is located."

Everyone acknowledged seeing Oak Island before. Papa always points it out to us as we pass it on our way to Last Island during the spring and fall months when we go seining for shrimp.

Papa continued with his story. "With digging implements in hand, Xavier made his way to the wayward island, the highlight of his overnight experience. When he arrived at the site and walked into the tiny island's interior, he noticed that there was a clearing within the triangle formed by the three large oaks.

"Without any explanation of his notion for digging at that spot, he began to penetrate the surface of the ground. First, he dug with his shovel. The many roots were hampering his efforts, so he switched to his pickax.

"Xavier dug frantically. After a few hours, the hole was at least four feet deep and had the approximate dimensions of an average coffin. He was beginning to think that he had gone mad, but he continued digging in spite of his reservations.

"By the end of the day, he was almost spent of all his strength. Tired and dismayed from the unsuccessful dig, he decided he would not have the strength to oar himself home. He walked over to Cemetery Ridge, cut himself a few palmettos, and made his shelter for the night.

"Thinking the light might reappear during the night, Xavier remained awake for part of the evening. Finally, sleep overwhelmed him; all his thoughts failed him until he awakened the next morning. The shrill calls of seagulls flying overhead disturbed his peaceful repose about an hour after sunrise.

"Determined to dig all the way to China if necessary, Xavier returned to the hole on the tiny oak ridge to continue his excavation. At this point, he told me, he felt he had nothing to lose. He was determined to play out his silly notion, even if at some point it would prove to be false.

"He dug and he dug, and then he dug some more. Down about eight feet below the surface of the ground, Xavier hit something solid with his shovel. He reasoned that no root from a live oak tree would be found at that depth. 'What could this possibly be?' he thought privately.

"Continuing to dig, he slowly uncovered the lid of a large chest. It was about four feet long and thirty inches wide. Xavier's heart began to race with excitement. 'What could there be inside this solid oak chest?' he wondered with amazement as he continued to expose more of the chest.

"The chest was fashioned with iron straps that held the wooden box securely shut. Front and center of the oak chest was a lock. Xavier took his pickax in his hand and struck the lock repeatedly. Again and again he struck the lock, until finally it broke loose.

"Taking a deep breath, Xavier paused briefly, trying to regain some degree of composure. Slowly, but deliberately, he bent over the wooden box, removed the broken lock, and opened the chest."

Papa paused to relight his pipe. We told him it was not fair to stop the story at such a critical point, just so he could enjoy the smoke from his pipe. Papa pretended not to hear our complaints and loud protests. Uncle Justin made everyone laugh, as he pretended to not be the least bit interested in the outcome of Papa's story. He lit up his pipe, imitating Papa's every move, paying close attention to every detail of his motions; he even tried mimicking Papa's facial expressions. After considerable entreaty, Papa finally agreed to continue with his story.

"Xavier's heart raced as he bent over to lift the lid up. Blood rushed to his head, making him weak-kneed as he pried open the heavy cover. What do you think was inside that chest?" Papa asked, getting the most from the suspense of that moment in his most interesting story.

"It was silver and gold!" Felix shouted.

"That is exactly what he found—a chest full of silver and gold coins. Xavier suddenly found himself staring into a chest filled to the brim with gold and silver coins from Spain. Not trusting his eyes, he plunged his hands into the bounty to be sure it wasn't an illusion. Then he sat down beside it for a long time, looking at the treasure in a state of awe.

"With little forethought, he filled his pockets full of coins and decided he would have to risk going back to the mainland to get flour and rice sacks to carry the loot home. Realizing possession of the coins may prompt unwanted curiosity in the eye of some beholder, he put the coins back in the chest and closed the lid. He gathered a few sticks and placed them across the hole, covering them with cut palmettos to camouflage the site of his recent activity.

"Intense anxiety persisted. He would not be able to rest until his coins were rescued from their grave and safely stored in some hideaway near his home. Xavier, usually a man of stoic countenance, was shivering like a frightened child. 'It's the worrying. That's what I wasn't accustomed to!' he told me. He knew he would have to move swiftly to ensure the safety of his discovery. He boarded his empty skiff, and he was determined to be back by sunset.

"He didn't want to draw any attention, so when he passed the drying platform at Grand Pass he looked up only long enough to wave to Mr. Dumond, who just happened to be watching him when he went by the store. The many platform workers were so busy with their activities, he felt reasonably sure no one had noticed when he passed them by. He decided it might be more prudent to wait until late night before returning. He was hoping the weary workers would be in their beds when he came back with his skiff traveling through the bayou right in front of them.

"On his way home, he stopped at several of his friend's houses and asked if they had any empty flour or rice sacks they could give him. He told everyone he was going to use them to beat the husks off some shrimp he was drying."

Mama recalled the day that Xavier stopped at our house. She gave him eight empty sacks that she was saving to make underwear for the family (a practice of many residents of the bayou). "I never found his request to be a strange one," Mama shared.

Papa informed her that those sacks were filled with silver and gold coins now. That announcement prompted smiles of amusement on everyone's face. "Papa, please go on with the story!" I pleaded.

"Under the cover of darkness, Xavier returned to the site of the treasure. He brought an oil lamp with him so he could see what he was doing. He separated the gold Spanish coins from the silver ones. There were seven sacks of doubloons, and twelve sacks of pieces of eight.

"By daybreak of the following morning, all the treasure had been transported to his home and hidden once again. What I find most amazing is that no one paid any attention to his secret activity. His plan was a complete success. He is the only man alive who knows where the loot is hidden. Now, Xavier is the wealthiest man I know!" Papa told us.

Everyone's mouth was gaping as Papa ended the story with the abrupt conclusion that Xavier is now a very rich man. I believe everyone wanted the story to continue; we were all captivated by the suspense of the subject matter. We were spellbound; none of us seemed to be able to break the silence.

After what seemed to be an eternity, Uncle Justin looked directly into Papa's eyes and asked in a somber tone. "Adam, is this a true story?"

"Honest Abe Justin!" Papa emphatically responded.

Everyone seemed to be skeptical; since no proof was advanced to support the tale, we all tried to laugh it off. Jokingly, we asked Papa to come clean and tell us he had made up the tall tale for our amusement (that is not an uncommon thing during storytelling, but the storyteller must either produce witnesses or some hard evidence to demonstrate that the story is true, or he must admit that it was merely a figment of the teller's imagination).

Aunt Sarah told Papa that the story sounded as though it really happened. Papa kept a straight face; he wasn't laughing. Mama was calling for a vote: "Who told the best story?" She posed the question to everyone on the porch.

The vote might have been a close one. Uncle Justin's true and verified story of the bear would have a distinct edge over Papa's unverified story of Xavier's treasure. Although Papa's story contained more intrigue and definitely stimulated everyone's imagination to a greater extent than Uncle Justin's story of the wild bear; the rules for storytelling would ultimately prevail, giving Uncle Justin a clear advantage.

Just as we were preparing to offer our votes, Papa asked us to wait a few minutes. He soon disappeared, entering the house; he could be heard ascending the stairs and walking toward his bedroom.

We asked Mama if she knew what he was up to; she said she didn't have the slightest idea. She did say that Papa was acting very strange. He is usually straightforward and not illusive.

Papa reappeared on the veranda, handing out six coins for our inspection—three doubloons of gold and three pieces of eight (Spanish silver currency). Words cannot possibly describe the outburst of excitement that prevailed among the porch-dwellers as we all gawked at the Spanish treasure.

Mama asked Papa why he had kept Xavier's discovery a secret for such a long time. "This happened two and a half years ago!" she reminded him. Papa told her that he was waiting for just the right time to share the story; everyone, including Mama, agreed that this was the right time.

Clearly, Papa won the first round of storytelling. Uncle Justin conceded that Papa's story was much more exciting than his story of the bear. Papa's story would stimulate all of us (especially us youngsters) to explore the possibility of finding buried treasure somewhere on Deer Island. It is no secret that Captain Laffite and his merry men spent a great deal of time on the estate during its early days; maybe he left a little something behind when he left for Campeche Island. Who knows? Wow! What a way to go to bed, I pondered. Think of it; there may be buried treasure somewhere on the Addison estate. I'm going to have a hard time falling asleep this night, I reasoned.

Papa said he felt like drinking a cup of good hot coffee. Felix volunteered to go fire up the woodstove to put a kettle of water on the boil.

Everyone of us, including the grownups, was excited over the possibility of finding hidden treasure; no one wanted to go to bed right away. "Some say Vincent Gambi and his men frequented lower Terrebonne Parish. Maybe it was he who buried the treasure near Oak Island Cemetery," Uncle Justin postulated. We spent the remainder of the evening talking about pirate's treasure, the spoils of war, and the possibility of there still being sunken ships, laden with treasure, lying undiscovered along Louisiana's coastline.

Papa informed us that there was more to his story, but he would save it for another night. Xavier's treasure will be a subject I will continue to mull over for a long time to come. I will be sure to remind Papa to continue his story in the not-too-distant future.

We continued our conversation until we all were sleepy-eyed; I'm sure a new day had already begun by the time we retired for the night. Alma was the usual exception; she went off to sleep long before Papa had finished his story. Mama carried my little sister up the stairway; I followed close behind her. Snuggling close to Alma as we lay in our bed together, my mind was busy, even though my body was growing weak.

As I lay there in the stillness of the night, with my mind's eye, I tried to imagine how Xavier must have felt when he opened the lid of that treasure chest. Euphoriant thoughts and a myriad of aspirations and possibilities waged a determined war against my attempts to go to sleep. I must have wrestled with my pillow for at least an hour before I lost myself. I slept like a dead person waiting to be somehow revived, oblivious to everything around me.

Chapter Six

LEND ME YOUR EARS!

October 27, 1921

About 10:00 a.m., my limp body crawled slowly out of bed after being rudely assaulted by cold water dripping down my face; the water was being squeezed from a rag just above me. My brother Lee had drenched a rag with cold water from the stream; he was getting a big laugh, as he watched my quick reaction to the cold touch of the liquid upon my face.

Mama heard me hollering all the way downstairs in the kitchen; she promptly wanted an explanation for what was going on in my bedroom.

"Everything's fine, Mama. I'm on my way downstairs right now!" I assured her.

"I'll get you later, Lee Addison, you can count on it!" I chided.

Recalling the invitation to accompany the boys on their fishing trip, I ran down to see what their newest plans were. Felix, Gus, Lee, and Brad had already eaten breakfast; and they were preparing to leave in the canoes. I grabbed a biscuit and ran out the front door bidding Papa and Uncle Justin a good morning, as I raced passed them on the front porch.

Gus volunteered to stay behind this trip to make room for me in Felix's boat. Lee and Brad tried desperately to keep up with us in the second canoe as we raced down the stream; we seemed to fly across the front of the *little house* on our way to Deer Island Bayou. I had no time to look behind me; my eyes were trained straight ahead. It's like sliding down slick mud from atop a large hillside. The swift current produced by the fountainhead, as it continuously spews a steady volume of water down the slope of the ridge, provides all the locomotion necessary for us to make a quick trip downstream to the landing.

Felix, an experienced canoeist, steered with his paddle, rarely making a stroke for forward propulsion. I looked behind briefly to see where my brothers were; to my surprise, they were directly behind us. When I returned to look in the forward position, I caught a quick glimpse of a large water snake just as the front of our canoe plowed over the top of it. I screamed, raising my hands expediently from the sides of our narrow craft.

Felix was laughing his fool head off; he was laughing so loud, I didn't need to turn around to hear him. I had to sit motionless for a while to regain my composure.

When we arrived at the landing site, we were moving through the water very fast. Felix performed a neat maneuver with his paddle to keep the bow of our dugout from hitting the side of *Dreadnought*, which was moored at the base of the stream. Placing his paddle into the water again, Felix maneuvered the boat around the stern of the *Early Rose*, and we headed downstream toward the Atchafalaya River.

Once again I craned my neck to see where my two brothers were. They remained right behind us as we sped downstream with the current, anxious to check the bush traps that had been set two days ago.

Felix pointed to the first pole as he slowed our boat down to a stop; he waited for Lee and Brad to pull alongside. He instructed the boys to watch carefully as he prepared to check the first trap, rising from the seated position to his knees. With his left hand, Felix positioned the net (sometimes referred to as a dip net) underwater, placing it beneath the bush trap to catch anything that might fall out prematurely; he slowly raised the tangle of branches out of the water and over a wooden bucket in our canoe. With his free hand, he shook the maze of leaf-laden branches frantically, forcing fifteen shrimp to fall into the pail and a single crab.

"Not bad for our first trap!" Felix proclaimed as he lowered the empty branches back into the water. He told my two brothers to continue downstream and to check every second trap. "You will be shaking the next one, Nora," Felix informed me.

Arriving at the next trap, Felix held the pole to steady the boat for my first attempt. I took the net in my right hand and placed it into the water slowly but deliberately. Making no sudden jerks, I raised the tight cluster of brush slowly out of the water, keeping the safety net in position to catch anything that might fall out before the trap can be shaken over the bucket.

Unexpectedly, a soft-shelled crab fell into my net before I was in a position to begin shaking. I put my net down and began to shake the bush trap as hard as I could, directly over the wooden pail; out came another soft-shell crab and a dozen shrimp.

"Yippee!" I declared. "Yippee!" I was proud that I was able to handle the trap so well. Felix asked me to settle down before my celebration resulted in turning the canoe over.

I raised my head just in time to see a funny sight. My brothers were checking their very first trap; when Brad shook the bush over their canoe, Lee jumped overboard. A water snake had entangled itself in the branches of the trap while trying to get a bite to eat; when the serpent fell into the boat, Lee abandoned Brad and escaped by jumping into the water. Brad could be seen trying desperately to push the snake out the boat with his paddle.

Brad hollered, kicked, and hit at the snake until it finally crawled over the side of his boat. Brad was so mad at Lee for leaving him alone with the snake that he wanted to leave him in the water. By this time, Lee was on the far bank waiting to be rescued. After a bit of encouragement from Felix, Brad paddled to the shore to pick up his wet brother.

"How many shrimp and crabs were in that trap?" Felix teasingly inquired.

Brad said there were five shrimp and two crabs. "That's not too bad for a trap with a snake in it, eh, Felix?" Brad proudly retorted.

With Lee back in his canoe, we resumed our activity. I yielded the honor of checking the rest of our traps to Felix. I told him that the snake incident had nothing to do with my decision, but I don't think I was very convincing. The tally at the end of our run was two dozen soft-shell crabs and a bucket full of fresh water shrimp. Lee and Brad had half as much as we had caught—a half a basket of shrimp and ten crabs. Felix said we had a good run; that was gratifying to me. We had enough to feed the family, that's for sure.

Lee, embarrassed by what had happened with the snake, begged us to keep the incident to ourselves. I quickly reminded him of the night he grabbed my leg, when Papa was telling us the story of the black panther. He apologized, telling me he was sorry he had scared me. I reminded him about sprinkling the cold water on my face to wake me up this morning. Again he pleaded with me, saying he was sorry. "I was merely trying to get you out of bed so you could come with us to check the traps," he insisted.

Wanting to torment him a little, I told him I would decide what I would do when we got back to the *big house*. I wanted to make him sweat a bit to teach him a lesson.

The grownups were ecstatic over the catch. Gus told me that I had done a good job; I didn't bother to tell him that I only shook one trap. I thanked him for letting me go on the fishing trip in his place; he said he didn't mind since he had participated in that activity countless times before with his brother. "I'm glad you had fun!" Gus told me, with a cheerful expression on his face.

Felix, Lee, and Brad took turns patting me on my back, congratulating me for not turning the boat over. At first I thought they were poking fun at me, but I realized that they were really praising me for a job well done. I felt good that my presence with the boys on their fishing excursion didn't spoil their fun; in fact, I believe they actually enjoyed bringing me along. After the incident with the snake, I don't believe I'll be going back with them this fall.

"How does a menu of deep fried soft-shell crabs and shrimp sound for our supper?" Aunt Sarah asked. "I'll make a deer vegetable soup to go along with the main course," she added.

Who could pass up a meal like that; I bet no one will be late at the dinner table! I decided to join Papa and Uncle Justin on the front porch to listen to their conversation.

When I sat down near the porch steps, I noticed that Uncle Justin was smoking the corncob pipe Papa had made for him. Papa rarely makes a pipe for anyone, but Uncle Justin is a special case; he and Papa are cousins, but they are also best buddies. Papa always carves the letter "A" on the bottom of his tobacco bowls. Uncle Justin is breaking in his new pipe; he has his old one in his top shirt pocket. He certainly seems to appreciate the gift; he's puffing away on it as he and Papa reminisce about days gone by.

Papa was telling Uncle Justin that muskrat pelts went for twenty cents last winter. He told him he was hoping to get a better price this winter because, at last year's price, we barely cleared up our bill at the general store. It had been a fair winter, but there could be plenty of room for improvement, Papa related.

Papa thinks the market might have been flooded last year; there were so many rats last winter that everyone we knew caught plenty of the little furry creatures; that drove the price down he figured. Uncle Justin is not a trapper, but he thought Papa's reasoning had merits. "Supply and demand!" Uncle Justin asserted. "Too much supply means there will be little demand!" he added.

Uncle Justin and his two sons seine for shrimp; they catch alligator turtles (using a pole with a hook fastened at one end—they watch for bubbles, feel with the pole, and set the hook in its flesh wherever they can catch him). They fish for catfish, buffalo fish, and carp for the Morgan City fish market. Uncle Justin plants a sizable garden; when the harvest is good, they bring part of their crop to the Bayou Boeuf General Store and trade their vegetables for other necessary commodities or desirable items on their "wish list."

Uncle Justin has a holding pen for the turtles he catches; it's similar to the one at the Grand Pass General Store. His turtle pen is located near the wharf at the landing. Part of the fenced enclosure is on the bayou bank to allow the creatures to sun themselves; the other part goes out into the bayou about twenty feet. He and his boys cut several small trees to make poles; leaving a one-inch space between them, they drive the pickets into the bayou bottom and the high ground encircling the pen. He says the pen has been more than adequate to keep the turtles healthy until there are enough of them to bring to market. "I never had a single turtle die," he proudly boasted.

Uncle Justin has a large "fish car" tied to a tree on the north side of the turtle pen. A fish car is a boat with watertight compartments at the bow and stern for buoyancy—the bottom of the craft is made in the usual fashion, but the sides between the watertight compartments have gaps in the planking (from below the waterline all the way to the top plank) to facilitate an ample supply of fresh water exchange; this keeps the enclosure aerated. This will keep the fish alive for extended periods while the fish car is waiting to be towed to market. Uncle Justin holds the fish in the fish car until he feels there are enough of them to justify a trip to the mainland; they always arrive at the market alive and well. "Since we have no ice, the fish must be delivered to the dock alive to get a fair price. The seafood merchants pack them in ice when they are delivered," Uncle Justin informed us.

I have heard Uncle Justin say that he and his family don't make a lot of money, but they do all right. He says they have never gone to bed hungry and they never really want for anything. They live a clean, honest, and simple life: "Life on Deer Island is genuinely good" is what he professes.

They raise Pekin ducks (easy to raise and fast to gain weight; good to eat) and Emden geese (excellent for meat and they lay about forty eggs a year). They raise goats and pigs; they keep at least one milk cow. They raise Plymouth Rock and Rhode Island Red chickens; last of all, they have plenty wild game to shoot for the table. With all these assets, one can easily see how they can be so self-sufficient.

Considering Uncle Justin's philosophy about life; he says if you have food, clothing, land, housing, and good health, what else could possibly be necessary to secure a good livelihood? I wonder! Certainly a loving family is the crown experience in life; if you have love for a foundation, everything else will take care of itself; that's the way I see it.

Mama appeared at the door to ask if I would like to help Aunt Sarah and her make bread. She knows I enjoy the time we spend in the kitchen together back home, especially at bread-making time. I love to knead the dough, and I've been doing it since I was Alma's age.

On the table in the kitchen near the stove, Aunt Sarah has prepared a mixture consisting of two cups of scalded goat's milk, one half cup of warm water, a cooking spoon of lard, a cooking spoon of sugar, a few dashes of salt, and dissolved yeast cake; into this mix, she just poured seven cups of flour.

While Aunt Sarah combines the ingredients in her large mixing bowl, Mama dusts the sides of the bowl with more flour so the dough doesn't stick. Once the ingredients are well-mixed, the dough ball is poured out onto the kneading board. Using the empty mixing bowl, Aunt Sarah covers the dough and lets it "rest" for about ten minutes—enough time to sip a cup of coffee or tea.

Now it's my turn! The first thing I do is glaze my hands with melted lard. Next, I double the ball of dough over on itself. Using the "heel" of my hands, I push at the ball lightly and quickly in an outward motion, pulling it toward me again with my fingertips. Repeating these two motions, turning the dough as I work it, I continue kneading until the surface of the dough becomes smooth and elastic. Usually, in about ten minutes, gas bubbles begin to form at the bottom of the ball of dough. When this happens, I check to see if the dough is light enough by placing the palm of my hand on it; if I can keep the palm of my hand against it for thirty seconds without it sticking, we are ready to move on to the next procedure. Aunt Sarah will take over from here; my job is done!

Aunt Sarah has greased the inside of her large mixing bowl, preparing to receive the dough ball from me. Once the ball of dough is placed in the greased bowl, it is turned so that the top of the ball is coated in grease. Next, Aunt Sarah covers the bowl with a damp cloth.

In about two hours, the dough will have doubled in bulk. In order to check to see if the dough has been allowed to rise adequately, Aunt Sarah presses her forefinger into the dough. If the dent that her finger makes remains when she draws it out, the dough is just right.

Next, Aunt Sarah divides the dough into two equal parts; then it's time to knead each part into a smooth ball. She covers the two parts, letting them "rest" for ten or fifteen minutes. Once rested, she folds and pulls each of the two parts into a loaf, placing each loaf on a greased pan. She covers the pan for about an hour, allowing the two loaves to double in bulk. It's now time to place the bread into the hot oven for baking.

It takes about an hour for the bread to bake. About ten or fifteen minutes before the bread is done, Aunt Sarah bastes the loaves with freshly churned butter to keep the crust soft. When done, the loaves are removed from the baking pans and placed on a cooling rack, covered to prevent the bread from hardening.

In addition to her bread, Aunt Sarah is preparing deer soup. Cut up pieces of salted deer meat are combined with several fresh garden vegetables and added to two gallons of water; she has the large pot of soup simmering on the top of her stove right now.

While we were busy in the kitchen, Papa and Uncle Justin were building a fire beneath the iron cauldron in the back of the house. The lard was already melting from the heat when I went outside to check on their progress.

Papa asked me to clean off the large table near the chicken coop, the same table that is used for processing the pigs when they lay them out to scrape their hides. I got a bucket of water from the stream and gave the tabletop a good scrubbing with a brush Aunt Sarah gave me. It wasn't very dirty; Uncle Justin said they haven't butchered a hog for months. A few chicken and bird droppings was all I found; that was quickly and easily removed.

The weather was perfect for any outdoor activity. The cloudless sky and mild northerly breeze will provide a comfortable atmosphere for our meal. Papa asked me to see if Mama had finished making the batter for the shrimp and crabs; it would soon be time to put the feast in the frying pot.

Mama had just finished the batter of eggs and goat's milk. She gave me one pan half full of batter and a second pan containing a blend of flour and cornmeal. I brought the two pans to the cooking site and placed them on the clean table.

The Out Kitchen Of
"The Little House"

Papa saw me coming; immediately, he put a handsome portion of peeled shrimp into the pan containing the egg and milk mixture; removing them from the liquid batter, he rolled them in the flour and cornmeal, thoroughly coating every one of them before transferring them to the hot grease in the iron pot.

Uncle Justin tended to the first batch while Papa returned to the table to prepare the next shrimp for frying. In no time, the seafood was nearly ready to eat. The same procedure used to batter and coat the shrimp was followed for the soft-shell crabs. I guess it took about an hour before all the frying was done.

Aunt Sarah sent the boys to gather pecans from the orchard so she can make some candy. They have been gone for at least a couple of hours; they should be returning soon. Pecan pralines! Man, that sounds good!

Papa and Uncle Justin were enjoying a good smoke of the pipe, waiting for Mama, Aunt Sarah, and the boys to join them at the table. They placed the fried seafood in two large roasting pots with covers on them. "Everything is ready to be served!" Papa announced.

I asked permission to check for eggs in the chicken coop. Aunt Sarah cautioned that there were four hens setting on the nest. "Any nest with more than a couple of eggs should not be disturbed. Some of the hens may have left their nest briefly to feed," she instructed. I was accustomed to picking eggs, but I don't blame her for wanting to be careful with her chickens; she raises many more chicks than we do. Aunt Sarah cooks chicken dishes often; that explains why she is so fond of her chickens.

I grabbed the egg basket and headed for the chicken house. "Watch out for my black rooster!" a voice shouted through the kitchen window; I had forgotten that Aunt Sarah's big black rooster is mean. I was glad he was nowhere around when I went to rob the nests of their eggs. Uncle Justin clipped off his spurs, but he still thinks he's got them. He has jumped the boys on several occasions, my aunt told me. Her *Rhode Island Red* rooster is mild natured compared to Aunt Sarah's black one; he still has his spurs because he never causes any trouble. The back rooster is the dominate bird, so the red rooster has to steal the affection of the hens when he feels he can get away with it. You would think that there would be no competition with so many hens that need servicing. That's nature I suppose; "survival of the fittest" is true even among the chickens.

When I entered the hen house, the four hens were on their nests(at least that's what I thought). Two exposed nests were full of eggs, so that meant that two of those four hens are laying fresh ones. I gathered the eggs from all the nests that had only a few, and I left the full nests alone. I decided not to disturb any of the hens, since I didn't know which ones were trying to set. Mama told me long ago that you should never disturb a chicken that's setting; if you do, she might abandon the eggs, leaving them to spoil in the nest.

Aunt Sarah is trying to raise as many young chicks as she can to lower the average age of her flock. She must have over fifty hens (Plymouth Rocks, Barred Rocks, and Rhode Island Reds), but she told me that a couple dozen of them needed to be culled and put in the pot. After two or three years, the laying habits of the older chickens begins to wane; there is no real benefit in keeping hens that have quit laying, so they will be the first ones in Aunt Sarah's stew. Once this next bunch of baby chicks become pullets, the older chickens will have to keep laying eggs if they want to try to keep their heads. They can't fool my aunt; she knows which of her hens have slaked off.

I picked fourteen eggs from the vacant nests and went to the stream to wash them before I returned to the kitchen. As soon as I placed the egg basket on the table, the boys appeared on the back porch with several sacks of pecans.

"Let's go eat!" Felix loudly suggested.

We joined the rest of the family at the outside dinner table. Now that everyone was present, Uncle Justin asked God to bless our food. Once the blessing was shared, we began to enjoy the feast that was set before us; everything was delicious. Aunt Sarah's bread was light and tasty, as usual. My Aunt can sure make good bread! Mama is a good baker, but sometimes her bread is less than perfect. We ate, and shared conversation until everyone was full.

After dining sumptuously, we cleaned up the mess. The boys cleaned off the table. Alma and I helped Mama and Aunt Sarah carry the leftovers to the kitchen. Papa and Uncle Justin covered the big iron pot to keep the grease clean; it would still be good for another frying. With everyone lending a helping hand, the chore was soon complete; it would soon be time for our nap.

Customarily, dinner is almost always the main meal of the day. Breakfast usually consists of biscuits, or leftover bread or cornbread. Supper is almost always a lighter meal, primarily leftovers from the noon meal.

After a little more conversation, we all retired to the bedrooms. It had been a very busy morning, filled with activity; I had no difficulty falling asleep.

October 27, 1921 (Midafternoon)

Alma and I must have been the last to get out of bed. The boys were nowhere to be found. I saw that Mama and Aunt Sarah were sitting on the back porch talking; we visited briefly with them before heading to the front porch to check on the men.

Papa and Uncle Justin were rocking in their chairs and discussing politics, a subject that doesn't interest me in the least way. I did hear my uncle say that he was glad that we are at peace with Germany; after eight years of Woodrow Wilson, it was time to give the Republicans a chance. They both believe Warren Harding will be a good president, even though neither of them voted for the man; after all, he was elected president of these United States. Who cares?

At some future time in my life, my attitude toward politics may change. Now that the nineteenth amendment has passed, the right of women to vote may stimulate interest. I've never heard the women in my family discuss the subject. The man being the head of the house is security enough for me; let the men make the decisions. That is the way I feel.

I took Alma by the hand, and we walked around the north side of the house. We walked to the head of the *garden path* and sat on a large fallen tree limb that had been hauled there after the storm. Alma began to sing to her doll; she never said a word to me. Many people have said that Alma and I look almost identical. I don't know if that is really true, but I do find that my little sister is a pretty girl.

Our long brown hair is straight and hangs about six inches below our shoulders. We both have brown eyes and dark eyebrows. Our complexions are fair; our teeth are white and straight like Aunt Sarah's. Our eyelashes are long and curved; our noses are ordinary and our lips are full. The only thing different about us is our height; I'm six inches taller than Alma is. I love my sister very much, and I'm not shy about telling her how I feel.

"I love you, Alma," I said tenderly, hoping to get some response.

"I love you too, Nora," Alma answered with a smile, as she reached over toward me and hugged me around my neck. "I like sitting here with you on this log," she added.

Alma had just uttered two complete sentences! I was flabbergasted. "Let's go pay Papa and Uncle Justin a visit," I suggested.

"Okay!" Alma replied, rising from her seat on the log and grasping me by the hand.

On our way back to the house, I noticed Uncle Justin's male goat peering over the fence which confined him and his three mates. He was standing on his hind legs, straining to see what we were doing. The big goat is black and white and he has long horns, which curve backward over the top of his head. His name is *Abe Lincoln*— named for his stubborn determination my uncle told me. "When that mule-headed goat makes up his mind to do something, he won't quit trying until he does what he has in his mind to do," Uncle Justin says of him.

He's not a mean goat, but he is stubborn. Every time Felix and Gus attempt to milk the nanny goats, *Abe* has to be tied to one of the posts along the fence; otherwise, he will wait until the milk pail is nearly full, and then he will dump it over; it never fails! No one can figure out why he does it. To keep good goat's milk from being wastefully spilled upon the ground, the ornery male has to be restrained with a rope around his neck.

All three of Uncle Justin's nanny goats are bred; they should be ready to deliver around Christmas, just as our two goats are scheduled to bare back at our camp. Last year, one of these goats had twins Felix told me; all of last year's young goats were bartered at the general store.

An unexpected consequence of having a poor corn crop a few years ago was that all of Uncle Justin's pigs have turned wild. When the corncrib became empty, there was not enough food for the pigs; most of the food went to the cow. Having little choice in the matter, Uncle Justin decided to turn them loose so they could find food for themselves. For a brief period, they would occasionally show themselves around the homestead, but in the course of time, they all but disappeared. "They have multiplied just as fast as the bad grass invades my garden," Uncle Justin says. "I had eight bred sows and three boars when I cut them loose about three years ago. Now I bet there are well over a hundred wild pigs running loose around the estate. We hunt for them just like we hunt for deer!" Uncle Justin told us.

Now that the boars are wild, and most of them weigh over four hundred pounds, they are animals that must be respected, especially if one of the creatures is sick or wounded. Uncle Justin said that Felix and Gus were on a hunt this summer; they walked up on one of the big boars unexpectedly. Felix had to rush his shot, and he only injured the beast. To his utter amazement, instead of running off into the brush to hide, the boar charged. Gus was standing there in shock with his twelve-gauge shotgun in his hand; he was panic-stricken. Felix quickly grabbed the gun from Gus's hand and fired a shot into the pig at close range. He killed that boar in the nick of time; it fell dead not more than three feet from where they were both standing. Both boys said they had never been more frightened in their lives; Gus says he still has nightmares over the incident.

When Alma and I returned to the front porch, Uncle Justin asked if we had seen the milk cow. I told him that I haven't seen her since yesterday: "I saw her foraging along the *wagon path* that leads to the cemetery last evening, just before we went in for supper," I shared with modest concern.

"She's probably eating in the pasture. I'll send the boys to check on her later," Uncle Justin stated.

Uncle Justin told us that his moderately brown Jersey cow miscarried this past spring. Once a year, he loads her aboard the *Dreadnought* and takes her to Morgan City; from there, he turns her out to pasture with a Brahma Bull, which belongs to one of his friends. He said he would be bringing her back to town after Christmas; he wanted to be sure she was totally well before she gets bred again.

Uncle Justin shared a brief history with us. "When Grandfather Joseph was alive, he started with a small herd of about ten cows and a single bull. As the cattle multiplied, he would butcher a calf or two during the cold winter months. In the spring, he would kill a cow and cure it in the smokehouse. The rest of the cattle would be culled periodically and portions of the herd were sold in Morgan City— some were bartered. The barn was being fully utilized back then, storing hay and grain for the animals and providing shelter for the oxen and mules as well as the cattle. During the Civil War, the oxen, mules, and cows were all donated to the Confederate cause and that was the end of his small cattle herd" Uncle Justin concluded. "After the war, Joseph was not interested in cattle anymore!" he added.

I guess I could understand why he felt that way, after being forced to endure the turmoil and grief that the war inflicted on his family. Uncle Justin told us that he made a sincere effort to rekindle his desire to begin a small herd himself—maybe three or four cows and a bull, he thought.

He began to explain what happened to spoil his dream, "A few years ago, I bought four cows and a Brahma bull. It was a difficult task just getting all the animals to the island without having to kill them first. That bull gave me so much trouble aboard *Dreadnought* that I was sorry I bought him. That was just the beginning! Over the nine months that I tried desperately to manage the creature, that half-crazy bull destroyed the chicken coop and he knocked down nearly every fence line on the estate. His final mistake came when he busted through the cemetery fence and trampled down several of the rose bushes at the gravesites. Unfortunate for the bull, his latest stunt happened in the cold of winter."

Uncle Justin continued, "The morning after the cemetery incident, beef quarters were dangling from the rafters of the smokehouse. That bull was tastier than he was crazy! After that, I sold all the cows but one. The trouble I go through to have this cow bred once a year cannot compare with the experience I had trying to manage that bull. That's the end of that story!"

Aunt Sarah hollered from the kitchen that the food was ready, and we went inside for our evening meal. Looking through the dining room window, I could see that the shadows were growing and darkness would soon be upon us. The boys had returned from the fruit orchard; they informed Aunt Sarah that the orange and grapefruit trees were loaded with fruit. They told her that we should be able to pick some of the fruit before we leave for Plumb Bayou; we usually leave on the morning of the twenty-ninth of November, a few days after Thanksgiving.

After supper, we all helped to clean the kitchen; we knew Mama and Aunt Sarah would want to relax a little while before we gather on the front porch for storytelling time. Papa and Uncle Justin went on the veranda to smoke their pipes while the two elder women of the family rested on one of the swings on the back porch. Alma and I briefly joined them on the porch, sitting on the swing opposite from where they were sitting. I heard a flock of geese honking as they flew high overhead, heading for their roosting site. This prompted Aunt Sarah's yard geese to try to communicate with the wild birds; that was an interesting exchange.

Felix invited Alma and me to join the boys; all of us youngsters ran frantically through the house, heading for the four swings hanging from the giant oak tree near the fountainhead. Four swings for six of us! I wondered how that would work; who would get to swing? Felix and Gus were true Southern gentlemen; Gus got behind Alma to give her a push, and Felix did the same for me. Before long, Alma and I were soaring through the air, higher and higher with each push. Alma and I were making our brothers jealous, as we were both flying through the air like we had never flown before. I know Brad and Lee were jealous; I could see envy written all over their faces.

We were having great fun; suddenly, Mama and Aunt Sarah exited the front door and sat down in their favorite rocking chairs. The stimulation of the moment was hard to subdue, but we all knew what was about to happen. Grabbing on the ropes to slow us down, Felix and Gus brought our swinging adventure to an abrupt end.

Uncle Justin, in his usual jovial manner, announced in a loud voice, "Is anyone ready to hear one of the best stories ever told?"

Eager to hear his presentation, we quickly arrived within hearing distance and took our seats on the veranda of the *big house*. It was storytelling time once again.

"This story I wager, will be a better story than the one Adam told about Xavier finding buried treasure. Come! Gather around me; lend me your ears!"

Uncle Justin's voice was loud and clear; that determined look on his face showed that he felt confident his story would be the best one yet. His story tonight would be the third story of the season; it seems the competition this year is going to be fierce.

Uncle Justin began, "I'm sure you all know that your great-great uncle, Congressman Patrick J. Adams, fought for America at the Battle of New Orleans in 1815. You probably also know that the congressman made many influential friends during the course of his short life, even presidents of the United States. My story is about one man that Patrick Adams befriended during the fight against the British that took place in New Orleans. The man was a Frenchman.

"This man had a reputation for being adventurous. He was renowned for being extremely wealthy and powerful. Many people feared him, but at least as many loved and respected him. He was a man of great influence. People would say that he kept his money in several 'banks' (not the traditional ones of course).

"Himself a Frenchman, this man had little use for the British marauders, as he called them. He distinguished himself at the Battle of New Orleans, where he won widespread recognition for his much-needed assistance. He fought side by side with Patrick Adams, helping General Andrew Jackson turn away the British forces from the city. He managed a small fleet of sailing vessels, and he knew Louisiana's coastal waters better than most men. These were only a few of the reasons why he was a valuable asset to the Americans.

"Patrick Adams continued his close relationship with this French gentleman after the war ended. He invited him to his home in New Orleans on a regular basis to discuss business, politics, and to reminisce about days gone by.

"The newly elected Congressman Adams informed his close friend that he intended to build a retirement home on a remote island near the mouth of the Atchafalaya River (the gentleman informed Patrick that he was very familiar with the site). Patrick asked him to visit the island once he began to develop the homestead.

"Shortly after Grandfather Joseph completed work on the *little house*, an unexpected visitor came to the site of the homestead. Joseph was working on his wharf (now Addison Landing) when a dory with several men aboard suddenly appeared. A smartly dressed gentleman climbed onto the wharf and identified himself as Captain Laffite. He said he was the captain of an armed merchant ship that was serving with the American Navy. He told Joseph that his vessel was on anchor in Atchafalaya Bay near the mouth of the river.

"Grandfather said there was something strangeabout the absence of uniforms on the captain and his men, but when the visitor began conversing about his relationship with the congressman, his suspicions waned.

"Joseph accepted the captain's invitation to visit his ship. He was so captivated with the moment that he forgot all about Josephine. He never told her he was leaving the island. He climbed aboard the dory with the captain and his ten oarsmen. Before long, the armed merchant ship was in plain view.

"As they neared the ship, Captain Laffite informed Joseph that he commanded five vessels like the one they were preparing to board. He said that each ship was armed with at least ten cannons. Each eighty-foot vessel has a displacement of four-hundred-fifty tons, and they carry a crew of eighty-five men. He told Joseph that each vessel carries square-rigged sails on the foremast and fore-and-aft mainsails. The square main topsails make the ships extremely versatile. The square sails drive the ships best in quartering winds and the fore-and-aft sails are effective when sailing to windward, the captain explained.

"Of course grandfather was always interested in learning details (like sail rigging as well as ship design) since he was a boat builder. He never passed on an opportunity to visit a vessel so he could closely examine its construction. Ships held a special place in Joseph's heart. It was one of the great passions in his life!

"Captain Laffite introduced Joseph to his crewmen and gave him a personal tour of his ship. He politely and patiently answered every question that grandfather posed to him regarding the hull's design.

"After enjoying conversation relating to the Battle of New Orleans and drinking several cups of black coffee together, Captain Laffite produced several charts and maps. Sorting through them, the captain placed one of the charts on the table before Joseph. Pointing to the spot where his ship was anchored on the chart, he asked grandfather to show him the approximate boundaries of the Adams estate. Dipping a quill pen in a nearby inkwell, Joseph carefully outlined the bounds of the five-square-mile estate.

"After thanking Joseph for his cooperation, Captain Laffite and grandfather began to engage in conversation about business. The captain said that his ship, *Osprey*, along with the four other ships in his fleet—*La Vengeance*, *La Diligent*, *Sophie*, and *Dorada*—engage in world-wide commerce. He said his ships deal with merchandise from all parts of the earth. The reason for the heavy armament is simple. Pirates have been raiding merchant ships along the gulf coast for a hundred years. Cannon fire is the only thing that discourages pirates from attacking and preying on my ships. He told Joseph that in all his years of sailing the seas, he had never lost a single ship to pirates. He was clearly boasting with exaggerated pride. He expressed a firm resolve to continue his good fortune, Grandfather later related. He explained that his allegiance was to America and that he and his men were perfectly willing to lay down their lives, should they be called upon to do it once again.

"Grandpa Joseph would vividly recall Captain Laffite's manner when asked, 'He was charming, hospitable, generous, and he had a patriotic spirit that is difficult to describe,' he would say of the Frenchman.

"To demonstrate his fondness for Joseph (of course he was aware that Joseph was Patrick Adams' nephew), he promised to send one of his ships back to Deer Island in a few days to deliver a few gifts. He said the presents would be a token of their new friendship. A week later, a crew from the *La Vengeance* showed up on the island. The crewmen built the out kitchen behind the *little house* and installed the heavy iron stove that remains there to this day. In addition to the stove, the men brought a cash or iron cookware—pots of every size, skillets large and small, various cooking utensils, an iron wood rack, and a large iron cauldron for use on an open fire.

"Just as quickly as they came to the island, they disappeared. Grandpa Joseph thought he would never see any of them again. Wanting to thank Captain Laffite for his generosity, Joseph prayed that some day he would return. Josephine was overwhelmed by the incident. She was moved to tears by the unexpected assistance from men she knew absolutely nothing about. Attempts by her husband to explain fell upon deaf ears: 'It's too bizarre a story for me to believe!' she told Joseph."

Everyone agreed that Uncle Justin's story was a good one. I wasn't sure where the out kitchen stove had come from, but now I know. Thinking the story was finished, I got up from the porch steps where I was seated.

"Where are you going, Nora?" Uncle Justin asked. "Take your seat. I haven't finished telling my story!" he quickly explained.

"In July of 1845, my father, Alexander Addison was only ten months old. My uncle John Quincy Addison would soon be three years old. Uncle Patrick had died three years earlier. On a sunny summer day, Captain Laffite appeared at the homestead with five dories and sixty of his men. He told Joseph that all five of his ships were on anchor in the bay, not far from the spot where he had anchored *Osprey* back in August of 1840.

"Captain Laffite began introducing his captains to Joseph as Josephine stood beside him speechless: 'First is my brother, Captain Pierre Laffite of the *La Vengeance*, next we have Captain Rene Pinchot of *La Diligent*, next is Captain Vincent Gambi of the *Sophie*, and finally, here is the last of my captains, this is Pierre Cadet of the *Dorada*.

"Joseph and Josephine recognized captain Laffite's brother. They had met before, but they had never asked him his name. When he showed up with the stove, he was friendly but focused. He performed the task he was asked to do and left. It was now making more sense to the young couple. The generosity was altogether linked to the close friendship that the brothers Laffite had with Congressman Adams. Regardless of why they were being treated so well, Joseph and Josephine were glad to be the recipients of the benefaction spawned by that bygone relationship.

"Laffite and his captains all wore beards with one exception, Captain Rene Pinchot. He was the only captain who did not speak English very well. He spoke French, but his English vocabulary was very limited. Though the absence of facial hair and his inability to converse in English made him look and sound conspicuous, it was the gold he wore around his neck and on his wrists and ears that caught the attention of our grandparents.

"Grandfather Joseph would later say of Captain Pinchot, 'With the amount of gold he was wearing everywhere that was visible on his person, Josephine and I could not help wondering just what the captain of *La Diligent* was scavenging—and from whom?' Captain Pinchot was affectionately referred to as 'Bozo' by the other captains (no one gave the reason for his nickname and no one asked). His charm and wit was alluring, and he quickly befriended Joseph and Josephine.

"Gambi and Cadet were burley gentlemen. Gambi had a distinctive scar across his right cheek from the base of his nose to his earlobe. Cadet was dark-complexioned, and his beard was braded into several strands. It made his appearance a bit queer. Neither of these two men was the sort that anyone would want to pick a fight with. Though they were stern-faced and serious men, they were polite and friendly and they enjoyed having good conversation.

"Captain Pierre Laffite, like his younger brother, was shorter in stature than the other captains. They both stood about five feet, ten inches tall. He and his brother were of medium build, and they dressed a bit smarter than the others. Pierre wore a single earring in his left earlobe. Upon his arrival, Joseph and Josephine were sure he was the man who had delivered the stove and helped in the construction of our out kitchen.

"Captain Laffite spoke French, Spanish, and English fluently. He seemed to be a very intelligent man, and according to the stories he told, he must have been a very good businessman. He certainly had earned the respect of all his men, including his captains. He told Joseph that he and his men had come to the island to pay tribute to the memory of his good friend, the Honorable Patrick J. Adams. He told Joseph that when he heard of the Congressman's passing, it was long after he had been buried.

"As a gesture of good will toward Patrick's heirs, Captain Laffite offered the services of himself and his men to clear timber from the land. He suggested that work begin by clearing the trees surrounding the congressman's gravesite to establish a family cemetery (not only was the good captain familiar with the area of the estate, it was clear that Uncle Patrick must have given him a copy of the plans for improving the homestead).

"Laffite and his captains and crewmen worked diligently for forty days. They steadily cut trees and uprooted stumps. Using two teams of oxen, they hauled the trees that would be good for boat construction to the landing. From there they would be floated downstream in rafts, destined to be loaded aboard the waiting ships in the bay.

"Before Laffite and his men were done, they had cleared the land for the family cemetery, the fenced pasture, the fruit orchard, the pecan orchard, and the garden, removing all the trees and their stumps in the process. It was a massive undertaking, but with the help of over four hundred men, the work was done expediently, serving our mutual interests. Laffite got his timber for his ships, and we got our open fields. It was a good trade for both parties.

"Laffite's men assisted Joseph in cutting and shaping the keel for his future sailboat, *Dreadnought*; a chore that proved to be a very difficult task. It took four men two days to finish the keel. While that work was going on, the rest of the men erected fences around each of the five clearings.

"Grandfather Joseph gave this description of Laffite's character. 'He was an accomplished sailor, a merchant, a soldier, he was an adventurer, a businessman, and most of all, he was a patriot.'

"Laffite told Joseph that some of the timber he had acquired by clearing the trees would be used to make necessary repairs of his fleet of ships. Most of the timber will be used in the construction of a new ship he has already named the *Gulf Warrior*. He said it would be his last ship, and the largest he ever sailed (One hundred fifty feet long, sporting twenty-two cannons and crewed by nearly two hundred men). 'The ship will be my retirement haven,' the aging captain told Grandfather.

"Joseph accepted an invitation to tour the fleet in the bay. Two of the ships (*Sophie* and *Dorada*) were armed with fourteen brass cannons, four more than the other three ships, which only had ten. Grandfather said of the fleet of ships: 'It was a magnificent sight to behold!' Grandfather loved ships. That's no surprise. He especially admired those that were well crafted.

"Laffite paid a very handsome sum of money to Joseph for the timber he cleared. I was told that it was a flour sack full of doubloons, which Joseph promptly had Senator Peltier deposit in a bank. Grandfather tried in vain to refuse the money, arguing that the labor involved in making the four clearing could not be valued in gold. The clearings were payment enough. Laffite insisted that to refuse the money would be an insult. That ended the discussion.

"Before their departure, Laffite and his band of merry men hosted a huge celebration between the giant oaks located between the *big house* and the *little house*. Flambeaus were lighted. The light was so bright that you could see a shirt button if someone dropped it on the ground, as darkness swallowed the surrounding forest.

"If you listen carefully, you can almost hear the sounds of accordions and violins. You can almost hear the gaiety of the celebration, the sound of dancing feet rustling through the dry leaves that cover the ground beneath the trees. The laughter accompanying the music being carried on the wings of intermittent breezes to destinations far, far away. Close your eyes and listen. Can you hear the sounds? Uncle Justin posed."

"Great-Grandmother Josephine was the only woman at the grand party. She remembered being treated with utmost respect by the motley band of 'gentlemen.' She recalled that the men danced with one another, cutting up and making merry as they drank wine from a battery of wooden casks. Grandmother Josephine said that although the celebration lasted until past midnight, there was not a single argument that resulted in fisticuffs.

"Laffite shouted from a position atop one of the wine barrels loudly proclaiming that this *soiree musical* is now ended! In a few minutes all was quiet, and all eyes were focused on Captain Laffite. He announced that he and his men would be setting sail for Campeche Island at first light. He spoke highly of Congressman Adams, his comrade in arms and dedicated friend. He pledged to continue his friendship with the Addison family. 'The descendants of Patrick Adams, especially those residing on Deer Island, will always have a special place in my heart' the gallant ship's captain asserted.

"Grandpa Joseph would later recall that he and Josephine were particularly moved by Laffite's sincere demonstration of the loyalty and devotion he held for his gone, but not forgotten, friend.

"Beckoning with his right hand, Laffite called for Joseph and Josephine to come toward the spot where he was standing. He presented them with a special gift, saying, 'As a token of my memories of the friendship I enjoyed with Congressman Patrick J. Adams, and as a token of my friendship toward both of you, his family, I hereby present you with this tribute.' Drawing a cutlass from the sheath he was wearing on his side that evening, he presented the weapon to Joseph.

"The hilt of the cutlass was made of solid gold and it bore this inscription—on one side it said, 'In memory of my comrade in arms, Patrick J. Adams, The Battle for New Orleans, January 8, 1815.' On the other side of the gold handle was inscribed, 'In memory of a Southern gentleman and beloved friend, the Honorable Patrick J. Adams, US Congressman, 1816–1842.' At the fore end of the hilt, where the handle meets the blade, the captain's name was inscribed, 'Jean Laffitte, 1845.' At the butt of the hilt the letters '*PL*' were inscribed. (These were believed to be the initials of Laffite's brother, but no one asked.)

"The following morning when Joseph and Josephine awakened, there was no evidence to indicate that Captain Laffite and his men had been there the previous night. Every discard from the celebration had been picked up, leaving only twelve empty wine casks standing upright near the front door of the *little house*. They were gone. They would never again return to Deer Island—at least not as far as we know. There is no family member I am aware of, that set eyes on Laffite or any of his men again," Uncle Justin guaranteed.

Everyone acknowledged that Uncle Justin's story was very interesting. It provoked much conversation, spawning countless unanswered questions about the character of the gallant adventurer who had befriended Patrick Adams. What uncommon loyalty would move a man to fulfill a commitment he made to his fallen comrade, acting for the benefit of his surviving family members? What strange business would engage Captain Laffite and five armed ships, with a crew of 425 men, men who instantly obeyed his every command?

While we all speculated over the answers to these and many other questions, Uncle Justin could see that our enthusiasm was beginning to build. He rose from his rocking chair and strolled toward the front door. Reaching the door, he turned back briefly to announce, "I'll be back shortly," before disappearing through the front entrance to the house.

In the bright moonlight, I could see that Aunt Sarah was acting a bit strange; she squirmed in her rocker and became uncharacteristically nervous. This sudden change in her demeanor caused me to deduce that she knew something about this story, but how could they have kept the secret for all these years?

A few minutes passed before Uncle Justin returned to the door; he stood in the doorway with his hands behind his back, refusing to reveal to us what he was hiding. A few seconds passed, and he began to laugh; he was taunting Papa.

"I do believe that I have your story of Xavier finding buried treasure beat there, Adam!" Uncle Justin confidently asserted, teasing Papa.

"We'll just have to wait and see about that!" Papa quickly retorted.

Uncle Justin continued to share the remainder of his story. "This past summer, when the storm put a heavy branch through the roof and ceiling of the *little house*, Aunt Sarah and I were going through Grandpa Sanders and Grandma Martha's personal belongings. Once

I had repaired the storm damage on the house, we decided to organize everything in the building. We went through all their personal effects and put them neatly away in several wooden chests that I had made for that purpose.

"The story I just shared with you is not a new one. Yes, it's true that this is the first time I shared it with you. My mother, your Great-aunt Elizabeth, was the first to share with me this story, but I didn't really believe her. I thought she was merely trying to amuse me with some tall tale (something she was accustomed to doing with me). Now I know with certainty that the story she told me was true!

"As I was stripping the linen from Sanders and Martha's bed, still cleaning house from the storm's intrusion, I felt something strange between the mattresses near the foot of the bed. I lifted up the top mattress, and there it was!"

Impatiently, we all asked with one accord, "There was what?"

"This!" he said, whipping out a cutlass with a golden handle for everyone to see. "I told you that I had your story beat Adam!" Uncle Justin proudly boasted.

My heart began to race as Papa strained to read the inscriptions in the moonlight. Felix ran inside, lit an oil lamp, and returned to the front porch to shed more light on the subject of our attention.

It was inscribed exactly as Uncle Justin described it. The only discrepancy between what he recounted to us and what was inscribed was the letter "J," the middle initial in Uncle Patrick's full name. His middle initial was not included in the description; it was a slight error in Uncle Justin's usually flawless memory. Another oddity everyone noticed was that the engraver spelled Laffite with two "T's" ("Laffitte"), a way of spelling his name of which none of us was accustomed.

Papa was impressed with the beautiful weapon. The contrast of the golden handle and the sterling silver blade made the cutlass a very handsome piece. It looked more like a very large piece of jewelry than a weapon.

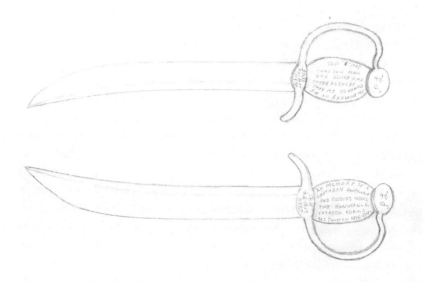

This Is The Cutlass Presented To The Family Of Patrick Adams As A Tribute To His
Memory. Note The P L At The Butt Of The Handle - Pauline Longère

The Handle Was Fashioned From Solid Gold
The Blade Was Sterling Silver

We took turns handling the short sword and admiring its beauty; it was heavy, and it was amazingly sharp.

In a sudden burst of inspiration, Papa realized that the man Uncle Justin constantly referred to as Captain Laffite has his first name inscribed on the handle. The captain who was in command of five armed merchant ships and 425 men was Jean Laffite.

"Isn't Jean Laffite the notorious pirate who plundered British and Spanish merchant ships throughout the Gulf of Mexico?" Papa asked excitedly.

Uncle Justin responded, "Yes, it is true that Jean Laffite was reported to be a pirate, but there are many who would argue the point. Many who knew Captain Laffite would offer that he lived in a time of confusion, a time when Spain, England, and France were fighting each other for the territories we now call the 'United States of America.' It could be argued that he was merely an opportunist, capitalizing on and exploiting the greed of other opportunists."

Uncle Justin's defense of Captain Jean Laffite's character was based on what he was told by our ancestors. Joseph and Josephine both knew the captain personally; they had time to acquaint themselves with the man who they say was always a true gentleman in their presence. My Great-grandmother Josephine, spoke of him with a very high regard to my Great-aunt Elizabeth and she related that to her son, Uncle Justin.

Getting back to the impact of Uncle Justin's story, Papa conceded without taking a vote. The possession of the cutlass, without a doubt, made his story the best of this season thus far.

"I don't see how I'll ever manage to top that story! The revelation that a pirate befriended our family and helped to develop much of what can still be seen today will be hard to outdo," Papa lamented.

Papa made it known that he was ecstatic over this new revelation; he said that this account will take its place as one more record, among many multitudes of the stories that constitute the Addison family's history.

The boys went crazy! I thought someone might get hurt as they wrestled each other in roughshod manner, rolling around on the floor, pretending to be embattled pirates fighting over the loot. Papa had to ask them to quiet down before the contest finally ended.

Mama and Aunt Sarah tried to console Papa; they told him that his story of Xavier's treasure was also a very good one and "Maybe the man who buried the treasure near Cemetery Island was the same character described in Uncle Justin's story, Jean Laffite," they begged him to consider. I guess we will never know the answer to that mystery everyone concluded.

"I can't wait to tell Xavier about Jean Laffite being a good friend of the family. He'll surely get a kick out of hearing that!" Papa exclaimed.

The grownups continued their conversation, speculating about the reasons that the notorious pirate, Jean Laffite (together with all his men and ships) was so keenly interested in the boundaries of the Adams estate. What about that uncanny demonstration of generosity? Could he afford to be so generous for other reasons, not so hard to imagine? Was he being forced to move his treasure further west along the Gulf Coast as a result of all his troubles in Barataria? Did he bury treasure somewhere on the estate? It would be a small matter for some of Laffite's men to be about the business of hiding treasure, while Joseph and Josephine were busy enjoying Captain Laffite's favor near the homestead. How many hoards of treasure might have been buried during their extended visit; what about afterward? Five square miles is a lot of territory! The vastness of uninhabited land, accessible by a number of bayous with ridges along parts of their banks, would provide any number of perfect places for hiding buried treasure. These are just a few of the points that were discussed.

As I lay in bed, these questions and countless others kept me tossing and turning. No matter how hard I tried, I could not escape the thought of someday finding buried treasure. I had romantic notions of discovering treasure near the trapping camp, or along Creole Bayou, or maybe along Palmetto Bayou, or Crooked Bayou. Was there hidden treasure beneath the shade trees where we all run, hide, and play horseshoes and many other games? It was overwhelming to consider; so much so that it was robbing me of some much-needed rest. Are there any unusual carvings on the trunks of any of the ancient oak trees or trees no one would suspect? What are the signs we should be searching for? What would they mean if we found any strange markings? The self-imposed anxiety over finding silver and gold was beginning to torment me.

I took several deep breaths and tried to focus on something else. What a wonderfully stimulating and adventurous story, I thought; the proof is in the emotional state it created within my conscious mind, aggravating the state I would like to be in now. I took a couple more deep breaths, and as I lay there quietly in my bed, I was suddenly aware that my body was being caressed by nature's appendages. The moon's light and the gentle breezes entering through my bedroom windows across my face, woo me into submission as I left the treasure behind me, and I traveled beyond the senses.

October 28, 1921 (Shortly after Midnight)

In the early hours of the morning, long before sunrise, there was a big commotion somewhere behind the *big house*. The domestic

518

animals were in a panic. Chickens were cackling, geese were honking, ducks were quacking, the milk cow was mooing just like cows do before stormy weather; the goats were bellowing unusual pleas for attention, crying frantically for help it seemed. I could hear a pig squealing in the distance.

There was something terribly wrong as the whole family convened in the dining room—all of us except Alma, that is. Uncle Justin lit an oil lamp and set it on the table. His trusty gun was hanging on the wall separating the dining room from the kitchen. Uncle Justin reached for *Ole Long Tom* and headed for the rear door which exited onto the back porch through the kitchen. He told everyone that he didn't want to risk making any unnecessary noise by exiting onto the back porch through Aunt Sarah's sewing room door; that door squeaks rather loudly since it is rarely opened. "It needs to have its hinges oiled," Mama whispered to me.

Before my uncle opened the kitchen door, he asked everyone to be still and to remain quiet while he went out to see what the disturbance was all about. I think he suspected what it might be by the expression he was wearing on his face. No one said a thing, but I do believe we were all thinking the same thing. There was an eerie quiet outside; all the animals had hushed. You could hear a pin drop.

Opening the door carefully, Uncle Justin exited the kitchen and disappeared as he left the back porch on a search and destroy mission. Though they were no longer cackling, I could see several chickens making a mad dash for the coop in the moonlight through the kitchen window. The coop door must have been accidently left open last evening (one of the last chores before sunset is to close the chicken coop door to protect them from minks or raccoons).

Was it a bobcat? Was it a timber wolf? Was it the bear that made Uncle Justin run so fast that he forgot his gun beside the tree he was sitting upon? A blast from *Ole Tom* rang out; its sound was like that of cannon, fired in the cool fall air.

We scrambled to the edge of the back porch. Papa instructed everyone to stay put until the all-clear sign was given by either he or Uncle Justin; he left us standing in anticipation, as he disappeared into the dense cover that shrouds the path to the beehives to find out what had happened.

The shot from the gun had startled all of us; even Papa jumped when the big muzzleloader sounded its discharge. Thank God that Uncle Justin keeps his gun ready; he didn't have to waste any time loading, time that could mean the difference between life and death for one of our family members or for one of the yard animals.

We could hear Papa's footsteps as he proceeded cautiously in the direction that the blast from the gun had sounded. The long silence and the sudden quiet calm was deafening; my heart began to beat rapidly with each passing moment. I could almost hear my heart as it thumped within my chest.

Finally, we heard voices some distance down the pathway that leads to the beehives. The all clear had not been given, so we continued to wait. It was a degree of relief just to hear Papa and Uncle Justin talking.

When they approached the house, Uncle Justin informed us that something had knocked over the beehives. He fired the shot as soon as he heard the familiar sound that has haunted him since his first encounter with the beast this past winter. He told us that it was definitely a bear. He shot over the animal's head intentionally to scare him off. Risking a kill shot without being able to clearly see the target area could cause greater problems.

"I don't want to go tracking a wounded bear!" he emphatically stated.

No one could blame him for making that statement, especially after what happened to him this past winter. A wounded bear would certainly be a dangerous adversary to face, particularly when the hunter has only one shot to do the job.

"I sincerely believe that the bear will come back; he's gotten a taste of honey. He won't be able to resist the temptation to come back for more!" Uncle Justin thoughtfully predicted. "For now, I believe the best thing we can do is to crawl back into our beds for the rest of the night."

I went directly upstairs to my bed and crawled beneath the covers where little Alma was resting peacefully, oblivious to what had just happened. She never budged during the entire ordeal. You would think the noise from *Long Tom* would have disturbed her, but apparently, it didn't. I quickly went off to sleep without giving the bear another thought.

October 28, 1921 (Midmorning)

It was 9:00 a.m. when I made it downstairs to the kitchen. Papa and Uncle Justin had already surveyed the damages caused by the bear earlier this morning. Of the six beehives, two were knocked over by the honey-loving creature. The bear had clearly robbed honey from the two disturbed hives; the fall to the ground had jarred both of them open, giving the bear easy access to the golden treasure inside.

There were bear tracks all over the back yard—around the chicken coop and goat pen, around the cistern and near the outhouse—there were tracks everywhere, it seemed.

After a thorough investigation, Papa and Uncle Justin concluded that the bear must have come from the north, following the west side of the garden fence. He continued south along the *garden path*, passing the goat pen and the chicken coop, pausing briefly to examine their contents (that explains why all the animals went into a frantic panic). Bear tracks surrounded both animal quarters, but none were found inside either of them. The bear apparently ambled around in the backyard, exploring everything as he traveled by, before heading down the path to the beehives where "Eureka!" The hungry bear finally found something irresistible—honey!

Papa and Uncle Justin are convinced that the bear will return to the beehives for more of the sweet treasure. They decided to leave the two hives that were knocked over where the bear had left them. The strategy behind this logic was to try to prevent further damage to the other hives and to let the fallen ones serve as bait for the sweet-toothed omnivore.

After a biscuit and a cup of piping hot coffee, having been completely informed about all that Papa and Uncle Justin had just explained to Mama and Aunt Sarah about the bear, I decided to go to the veranda where the two elder gentlemen were sitting in their favorite rockers enjoying a smoke of the pipe.

"Papa, what is an omnivore?" I asked as soon as I had the opportunity.

"An omnivore is an animal that eats just about anything," Papa replied.

"Could that diet include people?" I shyly asked, hoping the answer might be no.

"People are not part of the bear's usual diet, but a bear can be dangerous if he feels threatened by any human," Papa explained.

Uncle Justin was scratching his head; he was obviously disturbed by the entire matter. He said it was very unusual, almost unheard of, for a bear to be on the east side of the Atchafalaya River. Furthermore, he said that from the size of the tracks they had seen, the bear that knocked down the hives is a big one.

"We can't take this situation lightly," Uncle Justin sternly warned. "We know the bear will be back, but when?" he uttered with a puzzled look on his face.

"Everyone has been ordered to remain near the house until that bear has been dealt with," Papa instructed in a no-nonsense voice.

After much deliberation, Papa and Uncle Justin had concluded that the bear would return for the honey. When he does reappear, he will have to be shot and killed. Uncle Justin will have to creep into position and wait patiently for a clear shot. With a declining moon, the men are hoping the bear would return soon, so the visibility would be there to make the one shot count.

The boys were all chatting on the back porch; they were swinging, talking, and occasionally laughing. I decided to go upstairs to amuse myself. Alma was playing on the kitchen floor near Mama and Aunt Sarah when I rushed by them into the sewing room where the staircase is located.

I spent a great deal of my time looking out the windows in search of the furry creature that Papa had described to me. I've never seen a bear, but I'm certain I will be able to identify one, now that I know what the animal looks like. Everyone is a bit nervous over the incident, everyone but my little sister that is; I overheard Alma asking Mama, "Do bears eat ragdolls?" That figures!

In response to Alma's heartfelt concern for her ragdoll, Mama answered, "No, dear, I don't think bears like to eat ragdolls, but I would keep my eye on her, just in case!" Alma told Mama and Aunt Sarah that there was no mean bear that would ever sink his teeth into her ragdoll; that sentiment prompted a hearty chuckle from all present. Everyone silently was hoping that the crisis would soon be brought to a swift conclusion.

We shared a large pan of cornbread that Aunt Sarah had placed on the table; cornbread basted with a bit of honey butter spread all over the top is always a special treat. After dinner, we all retired for our customary naps. We rested amidst the peace and tranquility of a splendid fall afternoon on Deer Island. The temperature was in the high fifties, with a steady breeze coming from the northeast at about five to ten miles an hour. There was not a cloud to be seen; the skies were clear and blue.

As I lay down beside Alma, I could hear an owl calling to its mate in the distance. Before long, I couldn't hear its voice anymore. I was lost in a silent world.

October 28, 1921 (Afternoon)

The remainder of my day seemed to pass by quickly. After awaking from my afternoon nap, I found the boys; they were wrestling in the leaves under the giant oak tree near the fountainhead. Before long, they got up off the ground and began swinging from the tree, laughing at jokes I could not hear from the front porch. I overheard Gus challenging the other boys to a game of tag. They quickly dispersed, running in every direction, trying desperately not to be touched by Brad who was declared by Gus to be "it." Boys will be boys! I decided to go and see what the women of the family were doing.

I joined Alma on the swing, opposite from where Mama and Aunt Sarah were sitting, on the back porch. I asked if they knew where Papa and Uncle Justin were; Aunt Sarah said they were checking on the milk cow in the pasture near the barn. She said that they brought a gun with them in case the bear shows up while they are away from the house. "I have an ox horn, and I know how to blow it.

Should the need for the sounding of an alarm become necessary, I'll give a loud toot from my horn," Aunt Sarah told me.

"I hope the horses are okay, Aunt Sarah!" I stated, a bit nervous about how they fared during the crisis.

"I am sure they will be fine," my aunt assured me. "Knowing Justin, he will probably put the horses in their stalls and close the barn for added security," she added.

Mama and Aunt Sarah were busy cutting rice and flour sacks into large square patches so they could later be sewed together to make pillow cases, or covers for cushions or mattresses. The two women of the house make things basically in the same way. They use the cloth from the flour and rice sacks to save from having to buy material from the general stores. There is no end to what these two industrious women can do with cloth, needle, and thread.

Aunt Sarah and Mama were joking about the amount of feathers it takes to make a single mattress. She said that if someone would put all the ducks and geese that it takes to produce the feathers for a mattress in one place, they would no doubt have to fill an entire room from the floor to the ceiling. Mama argued that it would take two rooms full of the waterfowl to properly stuff an average-size mattress.

Who knows? One thing is for sure; it takes a whole lot of feathers to make a feather mattress. That's why most of our mattresses are stuffed full with cured Spanish moss—a subject for another story.

Feather mattresses are very hot to lie down upon during the summer months; they tend to wrap around half your body when you lay on them. It's for that reason that I much prefer the moss-filled mattresses.

My mother and my aunt both make beautiful quilts; they each have their own special patterns. Aunt Sarah likes square patches and a large variety of colors; she sews them together in random fashion. The resulting quilt is always unique and attractive. Mama uses a combination of diamond and square patches; she uses this combination of patches to make various designs in her patchwork quilts. Like Aunt Sarah, Mama likes to use patches with contrasting colors to enhance the appearance of her designs. If they competed for a prize,

I guess it would boil down to a matter of individual taste, not the quality of their needlework. I wouldn't want to be one of the judges!

Uncle Justin's first wife, Aunt Clara, was also good with a needle and thread. One of the comforters she made is still being used on Uncle Justin and Aunt Sarah's bed. Her clothes still hang neatly in a cedar robe in my upstairs bedroom. There is a beautiful hat, still in its original box, stored in a cedar chest along with two pairs of her shoes—size seven.

My Aunt Clara died of pneumonia during the Storm of 1909; I never got to meet her. She died right around the time I was born. I know Uncle Justin loved her very much. Though he doesn't like to speak of her very often, I have always heard him describe her as a charming, gentle-natured, devout wife. Mama told me that Aunt Sarah and Aunt Clara are very much alike; they are both tender-hearted women who care much more for their husbands than they would ever care for themselves—that is a heck of a tribute coming from Mama. I feel she is in the same special class as the other two Addison women. No doubt these characteristics in a wife would do me good to emulate; my husband will also be a lucky man, I mused.

October 28, 1921 (Early and Late Evening)

For supper, we dined on sweet potato fritters and fresh baked bread. By the time we rose from the table, it was dark outside. Uncle Justin recommended we forego storytelling and retire early. He told us he was hoping the bear would return during the night for a second taste of honey. He reminded us that the moon is in decline, and he needed all the light he could get to shoot and kill the animal so things can get back to normal around here.

I must admit that I was a little disappointed that there would be no story told this evening. Since I fully understood Uncle Justin's eagerness to rid the homestead of this uninvited guest, I would reluctantly retire early like everybody else.

Papa shared that All Saints' Day would soon be upon us; he said he didn't want to be fearful of a bear while paying a visit to the cemetery. He reminded us how dangerous it could be if the bear is not killed; a charging bear could easily snuff out someone's life with a single swipe of his claw, especially in an outburst of rage.

Sensing my disappointment that no story would be shared this evening, Uncle Justin came to the rescue!

"I know that we agreed to forego storytelling this evening, but since bear has been a subject of conversation this autumn, I decided to share with you an incident that Melvin Lacache (a close friend of the family) shared with Joseph and Josephine many years ago," Uncle Justin informed us, much to everyone's surprise.

"Let's hear it," Papa urged.

"One night, Raymond Lacache (Melvin's father) was making his customary evening visit to a friend of his family's house. Mr. Eugene Lejeune had been suffering from acute dysentery for a few weeks. The old man was seventy-five years old at the time.

"Both Mr. Lejeune and Melvin's papa were living on houseboats moored along the ridge that follows Bayou Chene. Eugene's home was about a hundred paces from Ray's dock site.

"Just about sunset, Ray left to attend to his good friend. He wanted to make sure that Mr. Lejeune was adequately fed, and he often kept company with him to help him cope with loneliness (Mr. Lejeune's wife had died a few years earlier).

"After a three-hour stay, Raymond told Eugene good night and headed for home. On his return trip, Melvin's papa heard a loud thump a few feet ahead of where he was walking. Something very large had suddenly fallen from a nearby tree. Straining his eyes to see in front of him, having only the light of the moon to show him the way, Raymond saw a large black bear ambling along the pathway between him and his houseboat. There was no roar. There were no signs of aggressive behavior. The bear just continued walking along, eventually disappearing into the deep woods of the Bayou Chene ridge.

"Since he had just performed a charitable act by caring for his friend, Melvin's papa always felt it was divine providence that had protected him from harm.

"That close encounter with a black bear was the subject of amusement for many years thereafter. Though this story might seem a bit strange, it really happened just the way I say it did," Uncle Justin shared. "The incident was recorded in Josephine's diary," he added.

"I guess bears and people can coexist after all," I told everyone.

"Nora, I am sure what you just said may be true, but I would much prefer that the bears kept their distance," Mama shared, no doubt concerned over recent events.

Everyone agreed that Uncle Justin was trying his best to bring the matter to a conclusion as soon as possible; we all wanted things to return to normal so we could resume our usual activities—horseback riding (weather permitting) exploring the island, going to the bend in the river in search of whatnots, picking pecans, canoeing down the stream to the landing to go fishing, and various other fun things we enjoy doing.

Aunt Sarah announced emphatically, "Let's go to bed! Tomorrow is just around the corner!" she correctly warned, knowing we would need to rest for what could be a very long night. On that note, we all headed upstairs.

I lay awake in my bed wide-eyed, unable to sleep. My little sister was singing a lullaby to her ragdoll while I reasoned silently. I prayed that the Lord would help us with our situation, not that I really wanted to see the bear killed. In fact, I wished that the creature would just return to where it came from; the problem with that is that we would never really know for certain that he actually left. What a dilemma!

I bet it was not yet ten on the clock when chaos broke out in the back of the *big house* once again. I could hardly believe that the bear would be so bold as to return this soon after being fired upon the night before.

I heard Uncle Justin quickly making his way downstairs; Papa was following him close behind. Fear gripped my heart, as goose bumps sent a tingling sensation throughout my entire body. I feared for Uncle Justin's safety. Feeling otherwise helpless, I realized that the only thing I could do was to pray: "Dear Lord, I ask you to protect my uncle from harm. He is going outside to face that bear to protect the rest of us from possible harm. Amen."

Suddenly everything came to a standstill. Again, the unexpected quiet was eerie. Time seemed suspended as I strained my ears to hear something, anything; all perception of a moment's passing was being exaggerated by the suspense. What is happening outside?

A lump came into my throat as I considered the courage it took for my uncle to brave the darkness in pursuit of that bear. The 45 caliber miniball will certainly take the animal down, provided the shot is well-placed; one shot is all he will get. I trembled as I contemplated what was about to take place.

The barrel of a gun exploded; Uncle Justin took a shot with his *Ole Long Tom.* I leaped from my bed, joining the rest of the family in a scramble to get downstairs. We all converged at the back door of the kitchen to discover what had just happened. Peering through the open doorway, we could see that Papa had Felix's twelve-gauge shotgun in his hands; he was standing near the cistern waiting for a signal from Uncle Justin.

Papa shouted, "Justin! Did you get him? Are you okay?"

Uncle Justin shared later that he was merely being cautious before answering. He said the bear was lying on the ground, but he was not yet sure the animal was dead? That explained the reason for his caution.

Papa, in a nervous tone, with voice mildly trembling, once again called out to my uncle, "Did you get the bear, Justin? Are you all right?" Papa's voice quavered as he spoke.

Finally Uncle Justin responded, having poked the lifeless body of the furry creature multiple times with the butt of his trusty rifle. "Yes, Adam, I killed him dead! Everything is okay!"

Felix lit a couple of the oil lamps in the kitchen and carried them out the house to light the pathway to the beehives. When we neared the site of the hives, we got our first look at the black bear; it was lying dead only a few feet from the animal's fatal honey trove. The crisis had ended, and we were all happy about that fact, but we were also curious about the size and the appearance of the omnivore. This would be an event that would be seared into everyone's memory, an experience that would be difficult to forget.

Uncle Justin ordered Felix and Brad to go for some rope that was stored in the corncrib. He estimated that the bear probably weighed between three and four hundred pounds. The plan is to tie the rope to the bear's legs and drag the animal to the smokehouse so it can be hoisted into the air by a pulley, which is attached to a large beam that protrudes out from the front gable of the structure. He will be suspended above the ground there and gutted; further processing will be done at first light in the morning. The temperature is now in the mid-fifties, so the animal will have to be skinned and salted early in the morning to preserve the meat.

Aunt Sarah says she can't wait to put a large piece of the fresh bear meat into one of her cast iron pots. She told us that she had eaten bear once before as a little girl; she recalled that the meat tasted very good. "It's different than any other meat I have eaten, but it was very good," she reiterated. "Just you wait and see!" she teased.

Though I am a bit skeptical about how good the bear meat will taste tomorrow, I am relieved that the animal is no longer a threat. When I returned to my bed, Alma was still in a deep sleep; once again, she somehow managed to sleep through the entire ordeal. After a few minutes of listening to the sounds emitted by the fountainhead, and feeling the cool touch of a light breeze from the east across my face, I joined my little sister; I was much too tired to dream about anything.

October 29, 1921

When I awakened this morning, the bear had already been dressed; its head lay severed on the ground near the smokehouse. Papa was busy scraping the hide so it could be salted and then tacked to the outside wall of the structure to cure.

The boys were assisting Uncle Justin in butchering the carcass. After consulting his wife, my uncle has decided to smoke part of the meat from the bear and salt the rest. Uncle Justin has promised to explain both methods of curing meat to me.

Aunt Sarah already has a bear roast cooking in one of the large pots on her stove; she told me that she was searing the meat (browning the meat). Once the roast is browned, she will put the covered iron pot into the oven to bake for several hours. She and Mama are busy in the kitchen, preparing the bread and side dishes that will compliment the main course. I have no idea what the meat will taste like, but if it tastes as good as it smells it will be delicious.

I got a lesson on preserving meat from Uncle Justin. "To dry cure deer meat, pork meat, and now bear meat, I use salt as a preservative. The carcass will be salted and hung to drain it of its fluids. Once this is done, it will be butchered (cut into steaks or roasts). Each piece of meat will be rubbed with salt before putting it into the storage container. A layer of salt is poured into the bottom of the crock jar, then a layer of meat. The process continues: a layer of salt, then a layer of meat, a layer of salt, then a layer of meat. When the last layer of meat is in the jar, another layer of salt is used to cover the meat before the lid is attached. Every five days, the meat is removed and the entire salting process is repeated for about a month, then the meat is placed in a cloth sack and hung by a tie string in a cool dry place until it is ready to be cooked."

Uncle Justin continued: "To preserve meat by smoking, I first rub salt on the carcass, then I hang the meat (usually quartered) to allow the fluids to drain. Next the meat is hung from special hooks inside the smokehouse. The fire pit, using oak for fuel, is ignited. Once the fire is established, a steady dose of damp fuel is added to produce a dense white smoke in the smokehouse. Once the temperature inside the structure reaches seventy degrees, it must be regulated (70–110 degrees) for the duration of the curing process, which usually takes four or five days. Once the meat is fully cured, it is stored in cloth sacks that are tied closed and hung by a string in a cool dry place until it is ready to be consumed."

Uncle Justin told Papa he was going to make a floor rug for the side of his bed out of the bear's hide. He says the furry mat of hair will keep his feet warm until he can put on his shoes. Papa jokingly asked, "What about Sarah's feet?" Uncle Justin's matter-of-fact reply was simple: "There is nothing to prevent her from getting out of bed on the same side that I do!"

As I gazed upon the stretched hide of the bear, nailed widespread to the smokehouse wall, I could not help feeling sorry for the creature whose only mistake was wandering into our homestead for a good taste of honey. Papa speculated that the animal probably crossed the river while clinging to a log during the summer storm. Uncle Justin quickly asserted that, if Papa was right, the bear isn't the same one he saw during this past winter.

In any case, this bear won't bother us anymore; now we can return to normal activities around here again. Oh, happy day! I am able to run free again; no more necessary confinement around the house for safety's sake. I hoped this afternoon someone would want to go with me down the *beaten path* to the river to hunt for beached treasure.

As I was about to be captivated by a daydream, Aunt Sarah stuck her head out the kitchen window and loudly announced that dinner was ready. Felix and Lee had already started the fire in the pit; they were in the process of adding dampened wood to the blaze to feed smoke to the smokehouse. Uncle Justin said that after our nap the smokehouse should be hot enough to introduce the bear meat for curing. For the present, the meat was still dangling from the beam protruding from the front gable of the smokehouse.

Having been summoned to the dinner table, we feasted on pot roasted bear. "Honey baked!" Aunt Sarah teased. We had fresh carrots, candied sweet potatoes, rice and gravy, and fresh hot bread. I have never tasted anything better; the meat was tender and juicy. The black bear had been turned from something to be feared to a delightful dish at the dinner table.

After our afternoon rest, Mama and Aunt Sarah plan to visit the fruit orchard to see if any of the citrus fruit have ripened sufficient to be eaten. There are lemon, lime, orange, and grapefruit trees in the orchard, but a visit by the boys earlier informed us that it was still a bit early to harvest the fruit. Felix and Gus harvested the peach and pear trees in August. The trees produced well; Aunt Sarah boasted that she had several dozen jars of peach and pear preserves put away. She told us she made muscadine jelly this summer. Uncle Justin is making a cask of wine from the purple grapes; they are now in the process of fermentation.

Papa has a cask of Uncle Justin's muscadine wine at our home on Bayou Du Large. He and Mama both enjoy a glass of wine now and again—never in access of course. I have tasted it; like my parents, I like the sweet-tasting wine. Uncle Justin insists that the older the wine gets, the better it tastes. I am sure he knows what he is talking about; he has several casks of muscadine wine stored in Aunt Sarah's pantry. He has a few that are over ten years old; he says he is saving them for when I get married—he was joking of course.

Papa and Uncle Justin have decided to set a few rabbit traps, hoping we can have stewed rabbit tomorrow. They know what they are doing; I suppose Mama and Aunt Sarah are already planning what to cook to compliment the *lapin cuire en civet* or rabbit slow-cooked in a stew.

I asked where the boys had gone, but to no avail; Alma and me decided to walk down the stream along the *landing path* with Mama and Aunt Sarah. About midway down the path, there is a large plank, which is used to access the path to the fruit orchard on the east side of the stream. The board is long and heavy, but it provides a strong bridge over the stream for "people crossing."

Arriving at the site of the crossing, without any help from the men, we teamed up to position the fourteen-foot long board in the correct spot so we could first raise and then shove the thing end-over-end across the ten-foot wide stream. We stood the plank up on one end near the shore and let it fall across the channel, hitting the far-side bank with a loud thump. Perfect! We did it on our first try!

Alma was afraid to walk the board, so Mama had to go back across the plank to carry her in her arms. At last, we were on our way to the orchard. Aunt Sarah told us that she and Uncle Justin and the boys planted several trees in the clearing over the years; they planted purple plum trees which ripen in late June or early July, persimmon trees which ripen in November and December, and a few pomegranate trees which ripen in late July and early August, most of these trees are old enough to bear fruit. She said many of them have been producing for about five years.

Mulberry trees and black cherry trees are native to Deer Island. Muscadine vines (also native to the island) line both sides of the footpath leading to the fruit orchard. The purple grapes played out by the end of August; Aunt Sara said the raccoons and the deer had their fill of the thick-skinned morsels of sweet pulp containing multiple seeds. Evidence of their presence was demonstrated by the raccoon droppings and the countless hoof prints the deer made on the ground at the base of the long line of vines. "Those wild animals must have had a feast!" I asserted. "It's a wonder they had enough grapes for you and Uncle Justin to harvest," I added.

Aunt Sarah assured us that the deer and the raccoons did not get all the grapes. "We got more than our share! We ate plenty, right off the vine, and I made several quart jars of jam. Uncle Justin had enough to make his usual cask of wine. Share and share alike! God feeds his animals, and at the same time, he provides enough for his offspring!" Aunt Sarah declared. "It's an amazing balance, isn't it?" my aunt posed, recognizing God's infinite mercy toward man and beast.

Aunt Sarah told us that the fruit orchard and the garden clearing are the largest of the four clearings on the island (the pasture for the cattle is the fifth clearing, but it produces nothing but grass for the horses and for the cow). The orchard clearing and the garden clearing are both three hundred feet wide and nearly a thousand feet long. The cemetery and the pecan orchard have clearings that measure about three-hundred feet by three-hundred feet. She said there are sixteen giant pecan trees growing in the pecan orchard.

When I think of what it must have looked like before all the trees and stumps were removed by Jean Laffite and his men, I can better appreciate what a massive undertaking it must have been. The evidence before me is awe inspiring considering all the labor that it took to clear the land; in stark contrast is the virgin forest that still remains around each clearing. It was an impressive accomplishment, to say the least.

The wooden fences that mark the outside parameters of each clearing are overgrown with blackberry vines. Though the blackberry season has passed, the partially denuded vines are so dense that one cannot see through them even though most of their leaves have fallen to the ground. This element of the landscape was intentional;

the vines actually make an effective functional barrier in at least two ways; on the one hand, the vines minimize access to the vulnerable fruit trees by the resident deer population. Secondly, the vines reduce the effects of the cold north winds on the citrus trees during the winter; they won't prevent damage from extended temperatures below freezing, but they do provide a degree of protection from the wind.

As we entered the orchard through the gate at the head of the pathway, the barren blackberry vines that have overgrown the parameter fencing were making me think of Aunt Sarah's blackberry jam. I know she has a stash of jars filled with the tasty dessert in her pantry; I intend to ask for some the next time we have biscuits for breakfast.

The citrus trees were laden with fruit; they obviously needed more time to ripen, just as the boys reported a few days ago. Aunt Sarah says they will be right for picking after the first frost of winter.

Some of the oriental persimmons were ripe enough to bring to the kitchen; a few days in the sun on the windowsill and they will be ripe enough to enjoy. They were approaching the right orange-yellow color, but they needed to soften up a bit more to pass Aunt Sarah's ripening test.

I love pomegranates; the orange-red fruit takes patience to eat, but the reward surpasses the effort it takes to extract the sweet pulp from the seeds. It is a fruit I really enjoy, even though it takes me about an hour to thoroughly enjoy one.

Equally requiring the patience of Job is the process of eating the muscadine. I didn't get to eat any of the purple grapes this year, but I learned at an early age the proper technique. The muscadine is a meaty grape with a thick outer skin. They are reddish-purple when ripe, and each grape has at least two seeds. The skin has a bitter taste; most people spit it out with the seeds. The proper way to eat a muscadine is as follows: first, pop one or more in your mouth and bite into the grape. Using your tongue, carefully remove the good insides from the thick outer skin (this automatically happens when you bite into the grape). Maneuver the hull of the grape with your tongue to the front of your mouth so it can be removed. Now, enjoy the meaty portion and spit out the seeds. It's not nearly as hard as it sounds. I can assure you that before long anyone can master the technique. Like the old saying goes, "Practice makes perfect!"

With a flour sack full of fruit, we headed out the gate, making sure we secured it behind us. When we approached the stream at the foot of the orchard pathway, we noticed the board we needed to cross was nowhere in sight. Had it somehow dislodged and floated downstream? That didn't seem likely; the board was above the water by at least a foot when we crossed over the stream earlier.

Just as we were trying to decide what we should do, we had the living daylights scared out of us. The four boys had crept up silently behind us, and they were yelling their fool heads off.

Aunt Sarah soon made it very clear that she didn't appreciate their foolishness. Mama, noticeably embarrassed by her reaction to the screams, was beet-red in her face. She threw the sack of fresh fruit so high into the air that she probably bruised the persimmons. The thought of damaging the fruit in the sack-filled projectile made her even redder in her face. I was worried her head might explode; I can't say I ever saw Mama in such a state before.

Apologetically, the boys said they were sorry for carrying out the silly prank and begged for forgiveness; they pledged to search and find the sack that had suddenly taken flight, and to gather any fruit that may have been thrown out by its sudden impact on the ground.

Not yet fully recovered from the startling event, Aunt Sarah again scolded the boys for planning such an assault on our sanity. It was clear that the boys realized that what they did was wrong, but they insisted that they had no intention of doing anything harmful.

The long board was promptly replaced to its proper position across the stream. The sack and the fruit were recovered and examined for any damage; the persimmons weren't bruised. It's a good thing they weren't fully ripe when we picked them.

As we walked up the *landing path* toward the *big house*, no one made a sound. Mama started giggling to herself, realizing what it must have looked like when she sent the sack of fruit flying through the air in a state of panic. Before long, she had all of us laughing.

Aunt Sarah said that when Mama jumped, she could have killed someone by hitting them with that sack full of fruit. She shared that

Mama's few moments of utter confusion prompted her to experience a few seconds of abject fear. "I lost control of my senses!" she confessed.

I was glad that the two older women had lightened up a bit over the incident. Although ultimately everyone had a good laugh, I don't believe the boys will test the limits of anyone's patience by trying anything like that again.

When we arrived at the front porch of the house, Uncle Justin and Papa were enjoying a smoke on their corncob pipes, rocking steadily in their favorite chairs. Mama could not wait to share the incident of the flying fruit sack. Making exaggerated faces and demonstrating how she hurled the sack into the air when the boys startled her, she quickly had everyone in stitches; she was making the two older gentlemen laugh so hard they were nearing the point of having tears in their eyes.

Alma and I joined the boys in the front yard. We played tag, and we took turns swinging from the giant oak tree, while waiting patiently for the announcement that supper was ready.

The sun had set by the time Aunt Sarah summoned everyone to the dinner table. We ate in the light of two oil lamps that were placed in the center of the long table. We ate leftovers from the noon meal; the pot-roasted bear was as good reheated as it was the first time around. Everyone expressed their interest in the story Papa would share with us on the front porch in just a few minutes. Speculation was growing about the contents. Would it be a continuation of Xavier's discovery? We will soon find out!

"Well, I don't know that I could ever top Justin's story about Jean Laffite being a personal friend of the family, but I'm certainly willing to try," Papa modestly proposed.

We all followed Papa from the dining room to our favorite positions on the veranda of the *big house*. The moon was in its declining stage, but it emitted enough light on the front porch for us to distinguish faces for identification.

I took my seat at the top of the front porch steps and leaned my back against the corner post. Papa and Uncle Justin fired up the bowls of their pipes. Puffing awhile, apparently to gather his thoughts, Papa announced that he was ready to begin.

Papa started his story: "Since the other night, when Uncle Justin revealed new information about our family's history, I have had quite a bit of time to search my memory. As past events came to mind, more things that I heard people say began to fit into the natural order of things. One particular story that was told by my father, Sanders Addison, fit particularly well into the other pieces of the puzzle, a puzzle that seems to be always expanding in size and scope (the puzzle is our family legacy of course).

"On April 3, 1861, Sanders Addison watched his father and two brothers leave for the mainland aboard the *Swamp Rat*. They were heading for training camps, preparing to fight for the Confederacy. Of the Addison family, only Sanders and Josephine remained on the island. Jennifer and Denise Lacache were invited to live with them in the *big house* until her husband, Melvin Lacache, and his three sons returned from the war.

"Sanders was seven years old at that time. Just as we are doing, my father enjoyed listening to the conversations of the elders of the family when they congregated on the front porch of the *big house*. Storytelling time on Deer Island has a very long history. It has become an important part of all of our lives.

"There is little doubt that Josephine must have desperately tried to maintain her composure when she shared stories with Sanders, the only one of her three sons who was around to hear them. She certainly did not want to appear overly distraught over the absence of Joseph and the two boys, knowing their fate was in the Lord's hands as they fought in a war that few southerners could understand.

"Sanders told me that he enjoyed the many stories his mother shared with him about days gone by—the couple's early days in England, stories of their journey across the great sea, the early days of establishing a settlement on Deer Island, and countless other stories.

"My father was an active participant in the story I am about to share. Uncle Justin may be familiar with parts of this story, but I am almost certain that this information will surprise even him.

"It was the month of July. The Addison men and the Lacache men had been gone for a little over three months. Sanders told me it was midafternoon on a sunny summer day, when an unexpected visitor came calling on the Addison family at the *big house*. Jennifer, Denise, Sanders, and his mother had little or no company since the war began.

"Like a sudden change in the weather, a flatboat appeared in the stream near the fountainhead. It was being poled by two well-dressed gentlemen. Seated in the flatboat were two other refined looking gentlemen. They were escorting a lady, a fashionably dressed lady.

"Josephine, surprised by the scene that was unfolding before her eyes, did not immediately recognize the fair maiden. When she approached the front porch, Sanders shouted, 'It's Pauline!' He meant no disrespect, he told me. He was just excited to see her.

"It had been only six months since her last visit. She celebrated Christmas with them the past year. None of the gentlemen who accompanied her to the island could speak English. Pauline instructed the Frenchmen to unload her chests from the flatboat. Sanders assisted the four men in their task.

"Josephine was ecstatic over the unexpected arrival of the woman she called 'sis.' Pauline had been invited by Joseph and Josephine to move to the island from Chacahoula, where she made her home, several times. (They had actually already given her the *little house*, but she preferred the independence that living alone had provided to her). It took the Civil War to make her consider making the move, but here she was!

"Josephine instructed the four men to put all Pauline's belongings in the *little house*. She informed the gentlemen that they could use the accommodations there for the duration of their stay on the island.

"Pauline moved into the *big house* with Sanders and the rest of the women. She was assigned the upstairs bedroom where Nora is sleeping tonight."

Papa paused to take a draw from his pipe, but the tobacco had cooled, and the fire was out. He struck a match and rekindled the flame over the bowl of his pipe; soon the desired effect had been achieved and smoke was being drawn into his mouth and exhaled once again. There must be something about a man and his pipe that I don't quite yet understand.

I could hardly believe what I was hearing; one of my favorite personalities from my great-grandmother's diary used to sleep in the same bed where Alma and I were now sleeping. My interest wildly stimulated, I urged Papa to continue his story.

Papa began: "My father told me that Ms. Longere was the most beautiful woman he had ever seen. He said she had a beautiful face, a beautiful smile, beautiful teeth, even her clothes and shoes were beautiful. In fact, he said that everything about her was beautiful, even her voice with her charming French accent. 'When she spoke, even the birds would stop to listen to her!' my father shared."

Having read Josephine's accounts of Pauline in her diary for myself, I knew Papa was not embellishing the story with nonsense; it seems everyone had the same perception of the special beauty this woman was blessed with. She was possibly the fairest maiden in all the Louisiana Territory.

Papa went on with his story: "An hour or so after Pauline arrived, the four Frenchmen appeared on the front porch of the *big house* with a pair of fiddles and a pair of accordions *pour la soiree musicale*. Pauline explained that they were preparing for an evening of music and dancing.

"There was music, singing, and dancing every evening during their week of visitation. Each and every night was an evening filled with gracefully enchanting merriment, my father told me.

"There was little doubt among the women present that the charming Ms. Longere had captured my father's heart. Though he was seven and she was forty-six, that made no difference to him. He was head over heels in love with the most beautiful woman in his world. I believe I am the only member of the family that my father shared this with.

"Until recently, there was part of this story that I always found difficult to believe. My father told me that she not only came to live on the island because of the war, but she brought along with her a special request. She asked to be buried near Uncle Patrick's grave. No one was surprised by her request, my father shared. Everyone knew she was the congressman's confidant.

"Here comes the surprise you have all been waiting for!" Papa teased, pausing again to take a draw from his pipe.

"What is the surprise?" I pleaded. "Please tell us!" I begged.

Papa continued, "What I found difficult to believe was who she told Joseph and Josephine she really was. Now that I know this part of the story, I don't find it so strange that Uncle Justin found the cutlass that my father had carefully hidden between the mattresses of his bed. It's all making since to me now. I can see the pieces of the puzzle beginning to fit neatly together. My father was secretly in love with Pauline Longere since he was seven years old.

"Let me add this important part to the family puzzle. We have all seen the cutlass, and we have seen the inscription 'PL' on the butt of the golden hilt. It is now becoming very clear to me that there was a much stronger bond between Uncle Patrick and Jean Laffite than we had previously thought. Now I am certain that what my father told me was the truth and nothing but the truth about Mademoiselle Longere."

Teasing us once again and prolonging the suspense, Papa paused for another puff on his pipe. I believe this is what I have heard some refer to as "a pregnant pause." Everyone was on the edge of their seat: "Who was she?" everyone asked. I begged him to continue.

"Did any of you ever wonder why her tomb was built next to Uncle Patrick's gravesite. It's as though she had somehow become a member of our family. Why does our memory of her seem to fit in with everything that is exciting about the history of our family's settlement here? She must have been someone special, not just some exceptional beauty that charmed a congressman. It all makes perfect sense to me now!

"Nora! I am certain you can remember the references that were made in your great-grandmother's diary about a fair maiden living in Chacahoula in a very nice home. Remember how she wrote in her record that she found it a bit queer that any woman would be so lavishly dressed at such a remote site. More specifically, she mentions in her diary that Mademoiselle Longere's lifestyle did not seem suitable for such a remote wilderness setting, especially since she had no visible means of support—no husband or boyfriend, only Uncle Patrick.

"In the truest sense, Ms. Longere was indeed a princess. Her father was wealthy beyond measure. It was he who built her the home at Chacahoula. He was the one furnishing her with all the fine clothing. It was her father that provided the means that enabled her to live such a gracious and carefree existence.

"Personally, I cannot imagine such a carefree existence. It is difficult to believe that the thing fairytales are made of could actually happen to anyone, especially someone that was much more than a friend of the family. She was someone Joseph, Josephine, Sanders, and several other members of our family knew in the first person.

"It was the cutlass that convinced me that my father was telling me the truth all those years. He had added no spice to the meat of the stories of Pauline that he shared with me. I will admit his stories seemed convincing, but I found them too fantastic to take very seriously at that time.

"All these years, the initials inscribed in the butt of the hilt of the cutlass were assumed to be those of Captain Laffite's brother, Pierre Laffite. I am telling everyone here tonight that those initials were not those of Laffite's brother. They were in fact the initials of his daughter—the initials 'PL,' signify a tribute to Pauline Laffite.

"In order to hide his daughter's identity for her own safety, Captain Laffite appointed Congressman Patrick J. Adams to be her legal guardian. Uncle Patrick assumed the role of Pauline's second father. He was her protector and advisor, responsible for her as though she was his own daughter. Now we know how she became Uncle Patrick's confidant.

"Ms. Longere was a princess. Her wild and free spirit could not be tamed by any man, though countless suitors must have tried in vain to woo her. Pauline had no needs. She was lacking for nothing. Her looks and her charm made her one of the most desirable women that any man ever set his eyes upon. What a unique person she must have been! My father was fascinated with her for his entire life, even after she died.

"All the pieces of the puzzle are now in place regarding the relationship between Pauline Longere (Pauline Laffite), Patrick J. Adams, Jean Laffite, Joseph and Josephine Addison, and my father, Sanders Addison. Pauline was an adopted member of our family, a surrogate sister to Josephine Addison and therefore a surrogate great-aunt to us all."

I had to wait awhile before making any comment. I fought back the tears, as I thought about the fair maiden I had so admired since I first read stories of her in my great-grandmother's diary. It is now more evident than ever that Pauline Laffite lived her fairytale life in a manner most people would never dream was possible. I was glad to discover that she was such a special person; I am glad the family honored her request to be buried near Uncle Patrick in the family cemetery on Deer Island.

I ran over and hugged Papa's neck. These new revelations about the woman I always wanted to emulate (a family hero of mine, if you will) are going to make my dreams all the more vivid; now, since I had the chance to visit awhile with the memory of my favorite princess, I find myself sitting on the front porch of the *big house* where, sometime in the distant past, Pauline may have seated herself. I found myself entranced in fascination.

Who could say where this story rated among the many others; the new revelations shared at storytelling time this fall have stirred the hearts of everyone in a way we had never experienced before. A vote was not taken this night; there will be time enough to cast votes later this fall. I do believe it will be a close race this year; who will win the honor of being the best storyteller for fall of 1921? For now, that is a question that is too close to call!

As I lay in bed this night, I could hear an owl calling to its mate in the distance. The moon was now directly over the house; I could see the light it cast upon the trees outside my bedroom window. The wind was breezing up a bit; there might be a cold front approaching I reasoned.

Before I succumbed to the gentle touch of nature across my face, I decided to pray: "Dear Lord, thank you for giving me such a wonderful, caring family. I especially want to thank you for Papa and my Uncle Justin, two of the best storytellers that ever lived. Sorry we had to kill the bear Lord! Amen." Once I finished praying, I heard one more hoot from the owl before all thoughts escaped me.

October 30, 1921

I awakened with the grownups this morning. I immediately went to the kitchen to pick up a fresh biscuit; the sun had barely begun to affect the eastern sky when I walked through the front door onto the porch. My biscuit was so hot that I had to hurry to a spot where I could put it down. I believe Papa and Uncle Justin were surprised that I was up so early; Alma and all the boys were still sound asleep upstairs.

Papa said that Mama and Aunt Sarah were busy cleaning the rabbits he and Uncle Justin had caught in the rabbit boxes they had set yesterday. "We checked the traps as soon as we could see this morning. Of the dozen boxes we set, we caught five rabbits," Papa told me. "That is pretty good, don't you think so, Nora?"

"That is more than enough for Aunt Sarah's dish. Now she can cook us one of her delicious rabbit stews," I answered.

Uncle Justin has a dozen specially-made wooden boxes. The rectangular boxes are each about thirty inches long; each box is designed with an eight-inch-by-eight-inch tunnel inside. The boxes have a closed end and an open end to facilitate entry without a way to exit. The front entrance has a trap door, which is set in the raised position above the opening. Three-fourths of the way inside is the trigger that tips the lever that holds the front door of the trap open. Once a curious rabbit enters the darkness of the hole in the box to investigate, it trips the lever; this allows the front door to close behind it. Once inside, there is no way to turn itself around; there is no way out. When a hunter sees the trap has been sprung, he opens the door and reaches inside, grabbing the rabbit by its hind legs; a quick blow to the back of the animal's neck and you have a rabbit ready to be cleaned for the pot. It's that simple; you don't have to shoot the animal. This saves shells that will be needed for taking other game not so easy to harvest.

I decided to check out the rabbit-cleaning activity that was ongoing near the cistern at the rear of the house. Mama and Aunt Sarah were sitting on one of the back porch swings; five cleaned rabbits were hanging by their feet suspended by a string that was nailed to one of the support beams. A pan full of hearts, livers, and kidneys that had already been washed and cleaned was set on the porch floor near the doorway to the kitchen.

"It looks like all the work has been done!" I exclaimed.

"All the work is nearly done," Aunt Sarah responded. "Now all I need to do is to cook us a good stew."

Mama asked me to bring the hide and the entrails out in the woods so the scavengers can eat the remains. I guess the opossum will eat what is left; maybe ravens will find the stuff. No matter! In a few days, I can return to the spot where I leave the discards and there will be nothing left. I have tried that experiment before; it takes no more than three days for everything to disappear, and that's a fact! Nothing gets wasted!

By the time I arrived back at the kitchen porch, clouds were moving into the area. Uncle Justin had told me earlier that there might be a cold front coming. I've had experience with weather predictions before; old people know how to read the signs; they can accurately predict the weather. We were all hoping that the front would hurry up and move through; All Saints' Day is the day after tomorrow. Too much of a rainy day might spoil our plans to visit the cemetery.

Papa and Uncle Justin are planning to sow mustard seed in the rows from which the sweet potatoes had recently been harvested. My uncle said Felix and the boys dressed the rows a day or two ago, and they are ready to receive the seeds. Nothing would be more perfect than to sow those seeds just before the rain from this cool front falls. I am sure that is what they are thinking also.

I asked the two elders if they would need any help. Papa told me that since the ground had already been worked, casting the seeds would be no chore at all; he said it would be nothing more than taking a morning stroll through the garden. I had seen the process of planting mustard before; you just broadcast the seed on the freshly cultivated ground and walk further down the row doing the same thing; the rain will do the rest.

"We have two chores for you, Nora!" Mama announced. "Since you seem so energetic this morning, I don't believe the chicken coop has been opened. Let the hens out and gather their eggs for Aunt Sarah. After you finish that task, milk one of the nanny goats if you don't mind. We'll be having fresh goat's milk to go with our corn-bread later. Uncle Justin made that request," she informed me. (Now Uncle Justin knows that milking one of the goats would be a challenge for me; I've never milked a goat.)

"When that is done, the rest of the day can be spent having fun with Alma and the boys," Mama added, trying to encourage me to finish my assigned tasks as quickly as I can possibly do them.

I gladly accepted the challenge; I wanted to please my uncle, but I looked forward to the fun even more. I wondered when the boys would drag themselves out of bed; Felix would help me milk the goat if he knew I was afraid to try out the new experience.

Remembering the cold water in my face episode that Lee had pulled on me, I was briefly tempted to respond in kind; I decided to allow the temptation to escape me, waiting for some other occasion before retaliation is administered. The timing for retribution must be just right, I reasoned. I decided to proceed with my assigned tasks.

As I walked around the south side of the *big house,* I observed a multitude of squirrels playing in the nearby oaks; they were scurrying from branch to branch and from tree to tree without ever coming to the ground. As I neared the chicken coop, the two roosters' calling was being muffled by the walls of the enclosure. Now that the coop doors are opened, they can cock-a-doodle-do until their heads fall off; their sudden freedom seemed to be received with great appreciation. They began strutting and crowing with unbounded energy, indicative of the invigoration of much younger birds. I hope their loud cock-a-doodle-doing will stir the residents of the bedroom upstairs.

I gathered about fifteen eggs and brought them to the kitchen. "I believe there are at least four of your hens that are setting on their nests," I informed my aunt, as I set the basket of eggs on the table.

"That's about right, Nora. When I last counted, that's the number I was aware of," Aunt Sarah told me. "I do hope one or two more hens will decide to set before the cold winter is upon us. It will be easier to save the baby chicks if they hatch soon," she added. "I believe we are down to less than fifty hens. We will need more this spring," she shared with modest concern.

I reported that the ducks and geese seemed to be doing well; I spotted a few of the duck hens with six or eight ducklings following each of them. I saw at least two dozen goslings foraging for food with their mother geese. There are two turkey hens setting on eggs on the north side of the chicken coop, and I saw a nest unattended with a dozen or so eggs in the nest. That turkey must have gone for food or water I figured.

Mama and Aunt Sarah were astounded by my report. It's not that they were surprised by the number of birds I reported to have seen; they were surprised that I had paid enough attention to have seen them at all. I must admit that if the boys had been awake, other activities may have robbed me of what the elder women perceived to be my sudden interest in the fowl population around the homestead. After coming to this conclusion, I realized that their astonishment was justifiable.

I decided to try milking the goat. I walked out the kitchen door and realized the goats were not in their pen. As I tried to approach one of the females, I realized I would need a rope to lead her to the milking pen. The small enclosure used to milk the cows and goats is adjoined to the corncrib; since tempting the animal to be milked with corn sometimes draws them near enough to coax them into the small enclosure, its location has proven to be quite effective.

Without warning, when my back was turned, the male goat sneaked up behind me and bit my shirttail. I wasn't expecting the tug in the first place, but turning to find the mischievous goat staring directly into my eyes startled me senseless. "You better watch out, *Abe Lincoln*. I'll ask Felix to put you back in your pen if you don't behave!" I scolded, hoping the warning would somehow temper the animal's propensity to play, especially when playing is the last thing you want to deal with, and he thinks that it's time to have fun.

From time to time, Uncle Justin gives his goats liberty to browse around the homestead. They help to control the weeds and briars that grow along the various pathways. The goats can't keep the paths perfectly clean, but between their browsing and the cattle grazing, they help to maintain the grounds around the place. What they don't remove, a man with a side blade in his hands will. Don't think that the domestic fowl can't keep much of the grass down; when they don't have corn or grain to eat, they have a voracious appetite for grass.

Before I could secure a rope, the sky seemed to break open. Rain began to fall from heaven in buckets. I made a mad dash for the porch, but it was too late. By the time I reached the kitchen door, Mama was already waiting with a towel for me to dry off.

"You were caught in the rain and you got soaking wet, didn't you, Nora?" Aunt Sarah teased.

"I was near the corncrib when the rain started to come down. I ran as fast as I could, but the rain was coming down so hard, that I got drenched before I could reach the shelter of the porch," I lamented. "That rain is ice-cold!" I told them. "Did Papa and Uncle Justin get the seeds planted?" I inquired.

Mama told me they got back from the garden in the nick of time; it turns out they made it back to the house only minutes before the weather broke.

As I dried myself with the towel, I saw no sign of the boys. It was hard to imagine they could still be asleep at this time of the morning; it must have been nine o'clock. The rain was pouring down; it looked so gloomy outside, I figured it might be an all-day affair. There was no longer any reason for anxious anticipation; what could we do that would be fun inside the house? It's beginning to look like a long day, void of any playful excitement. The trip I was hoping to make to the bend in the river would just have to wait, I sadly conceded.

I had to go upstairs to change into some dry clothes. The over-cast skies made the light dim inside the house. If it gets any darker, an oil lamp would need to be lit to improve vision, just to get around the house without stumbling over something. It was beginning to thunder.

After changing into some dry clothes, I strolled to the bedroom where the boys were to have a peek inside. Just when I thought I had seen all of their bodies covered from their feet to their necks, Lee bolted from behind the door making me scream in a panic. Once again, Lee had gotten the best of me.

Felix, Gus, and Brad were all in on the caper; they were all pretending to be asleep. It was a setup! Felix confessed that they all heard me coming up the stairs; he said the temptation to startle me was irresistible.

I was determined to get my brother back for his childish pranks, especially after this latest episode. I made up my mind, right then and there, that I would embarrass Lee as soon as a situation avails itself to me; fair is fair! If Lee can do this sort of thing to his beloved sister, then I can do likewise to my beloved older brother. I'll get him back!

The weather persisted for the duration of the morning. After eating rabbit stew and cornbread for dinner, some of us decided that it would be more enjoyable to watch the rainfall from the vantage point of the front porch rather than to take a nap. Protected from the windblown rain coming from the north, all of us youngsters decided to make the best of the situation without the need for an afternoon rest.

We shared jokes and told tall tales, entertaining ourselves while the rain splashed on the ground only a few feet from where we were seated. Thunder and lightning added to the cold dreary atmosphere that the stormy weather had spawned. I love a rainstorm; it soothes the senses. At least, that's the way it affects me.

Alma was singing "skip to ma Lou, ma darling" over and over to her ragdoll. If that wasn't enough stimulation for her, she began to dance with her imaginary friend all around the porch floor. That girl! She loves to live in her own special fantasy world; at least it seems to provide her with some degree of contentment, I reasoned.

About midafternoon, the weather relented; the sky seemed to clear up almost in an instant. No one took notice when it was happening, but now the change was undeniable. There was a strong wind coming from the north; it must have been blowing thirty miles an hour. The wind was blowing so hard that the leaves were being piled against the tree trunks in heaps.

Papa and Uncle Justin were seated in their rockers enjoying a smoke, while Mama and Aunt Sarah were enjoying a cup of coffee in the sitting room. The boys abandoned me while I went for a cup of coffee. I did not see them when they took off; one more of their silly pranks, I figured. Exiting the front door and expecting no response, I asked Alma where the boys went.

"They went that way!" she immediately responded while she pointed in the direction of the graveyard.

Uncertain that her first reply was genuine, I asked Alma a second time, "Alma, did they go down the *wagon path* to the cemetery?"

"That's where they headed!" she reiterated, pointing again toward the *wagon path* that leads to the cemetery.

I could not help wondering what the boys were up to; I asked Mama and Aunt Sarah if they knew anything about any plans I was not aware of, but they both told me they had absolutely no idea. I played around with Alma awhile, hoping the boys would return; I was still hoping someone would want to go exploring with me at the riverbank.

Time went by; the boys still had not returned and it was getting late. The shadows were beginning to shade the pathway leading to the cemetery. Without asking permission, I decided to go and search for the boys; I started by heading down the *wagon path*. I shouted back to Alma as I walked away from the house. "I'll be back shortly!" I pledged.

As I continued to walk, the boys were nowhere in sight. The songbirds were singing their peculiar melodies as I moved farther and farther from the *big house*. A host of animals greeted me along the way.

One of the nesting eagles flew overhead, the majestic bird had his wings outstretched; it was a magnificent sight. The bright white feathers on his head could be clearly seen through the treetops, as the diminishing sunlight reflected against its brilliant plumage.

A family of raccoons passed alongside me, apparently only mildly affected by my presence. Papa coon, Mama coon, and twin baby coons, crossed the path single file, only a few feet in front of me; they were heading in the direction of the stream. Seeming to be playing a game of "follow the leader," Papa coon was leading his family to their home for the night, or for a drink of water. He seemed deliberate in the path he had chosen; closer inspection revealed that he was following a well-used trail. Many animals in the wild are creatures of habit I have been told.

Hearing a rustling sound made by a sudden movement of leaves, not very far from where I was standing, caused me to yell, "Lee! Is that you?" I heard the rustle of leaves again. I walked in the direction of the noise, peering through the dense underbrush; it was an armadillo! I must admit that I was tense when I nervously approached the sound that the creature had made, much exaggerated by the dry leaves.

For no apparent reason, I decided to change course and head for the stream, taking the same general heading that the family of raccoons had taken just a few minutes before. Once I reached the stream, I would follow the *landing path* back to the house; the distance from the stream to the house would be shorter than trying to double back from the way I got here I figured. That was my plan anyway.

I walked about fifty paces and hollered, "Hey, boys! Where are you? It's Nora!" I got no response. Walking a little farther into the woods, still walking away from the *wagon path*, I hollered again, "Hey! Where are you boys? It's me, Nora!" Again, there was no response.

I continued to walk in the direction I thought would lead me to the stream, but somehow I must have lost my bearings. As time passed, I occasionally shouted; I was desperately trying to locate Felix, Gus, and my brothers, but to no avail.

The shadows cast by the trees blocking the sunlight were beginning to grow taller. It was getting dark much quicker than I had realized. The sudden awareness that I might actually be lost made me very nervous. At first, I resisted the notion that I had lost my way in the deep woods of the homestead; I continued to hope that I would soon encounter the pathway near the stream so I could rush back home before dark. After a while, it became clear to me that I was in trouble.

I strained my ears, desperately trying to hear the sound of rushing water coming from the stream; I never heard anything! I yelled again, "Felix! Where are you? It's Nora!" No one answered my frantic call.

I decided to sit on a log to think about the situation I got myself into; I was getting scared. Cicadas were calling each other from the treetops; darkness would soon limit my ability to see. What a mess I made of my afternoon, I thought; I should have stayed home with the grownups.

Suddenly, I heard a voice from right behind me, "What are you doing out here? It's getting late!"

It was my oldest brother, Lee. I almost jumped out of my skin when he asked me what I was doing out here so late in the afternoon. Felix, Brad, and Gus, stepped out from the bushes, laughing their fool heads off. It turns out that they had been shadowing me all along. They were having fun playing "cat and mouse," and I was definitely the mouse. They were following me to see what I would do; they all knew that I had gotten lost.

"You were lost, weren't you, Nora?" Gus asked me; he was somewhat apologetic, but far from feeling sorry for me.

"Yes!" I answered unashamedly. "I am not familiar with the woods like you guys are," I offered as my defense.

The truth is that, after I recovered from my embarrassment, I wasn't mad at them. I was so relieved to see them that I could have kissed every one of them, including my brother Lee. "The good Lord was punishing me for planning retribution for the stunts you pulled on me. I believe that's why this happened to me Lee Addison!" I surmised.

"Your plan backfired!" Lee scoffed. "You can't get the best of us!" Lee taunted further.

"I'm not so sure about that, Lee, the fall holiday here is far from over. There remains plenty time for me to play a good trick on all of you!" I mused, trying to get in the final jab. "We better hurry to the *big house* before we get a good scolding for being gone for so long."

On our way back to the house, Felix informed me that I had traveled in a wide circle, and I was actually heading toward the cemetery end of the *wagon path* when they surprised me. I was consoled, satisfied that I was going home in their company; Lord only knows how many hours I would have remained lost in the woods had they not showed up to assist me. How could I stay mad at anyone; I could still be sitting dumbfounded on that log, on the verge of despair. It's making me shiver just thinking about the predicament I could have been in.

The boys challenged me to a footrace; I was happy to oblige. Of course I came in last, but who cared. Mama was on the edge of the porch with her hands on her hips when we arrived back at the house. She scolded me for making her worry; I hadn't gotten permission to go and look for the boys. I only informed Alma of my intentions before I left.

Mama never realized how bad a predicament I would have created for myself (and everyone else for that matter) if the boys had not been playing one of their little games with me. I was not about to tell her either!

I informed Mama and Aunt Sarah that I was sincerely sorry for having disappeared from the house without their permission; I promised that it wouldn't happen again. After what I had just experienced, I had a deeper appreciation for the supervision provided by the adults who were responsible for me; a team of wild horses couldn't take me away from their careful oversight from now on. What I intended to be an innocent adventure could have turned into a time of trouble for everyone; it's much safer if the grownups are aware of what you are planning to do, I reasoned.

"That's why we have the various pathways cut through the woods," Aunt Sarah explained. "There are enough deep woods on this island for anyone to get lost, especially after dark," she warned.

After I had a good portion of "humble pie," I told my aunt that I understood what she meant; she was warning me that it can be dangerous out there! The episode with the black bear was suddenly vivid in my thinking; though it happened only a few days ago, I had already forgotten about it.

"The most important thing is that you are home safe," Mama told me.

"I can say amen to that!" I responded, bringing a smile to Aunt Sarah's face.

Aunt Sarah announced supper was ready. As usual, small talk was exchanged while we dined. We had a few laughs and enjoyed each other's company; excitement over the night's story was beginning to build.

In a momentary daydream (something I am becoming more and more accustomed to doing) I revisited my experience of being lost in the woods at dusk; I quickly shifted my thoughts to the event I was about to enjoy in the safety of the front porch.

What story could possibly raise more interest than the ones that have already been shared? This will be the fifth story of the fall season; it will be Uncle Justin's third attempt at thrilling his audience with some new revelation of a bygone event.

"Gather around! Lend me your ears!" Uncle Justin beckoned everyone to sit quietly and listen, while he struck a match, putting fire in the tobacco bowl of his corncob pipe.

Uncle Justin began, "I was going to wait until the last night of the season to share this story with all of you, but since the stories Adam and I have already shared stimulated us beyond what any of us thought was possible, I decided to move this one up on my schedule to try to continue the excitement we have been so privileged to enjoy thus far.

"The story I am about to tell might well cause more restless nights for some of you, especially those of you who will go to bed considering the possibilities presented by what I am about to share. In the light of the information we have already divulged this fall, this revelation will be a pleasant addition, spawning more imaginary adventures; a source for fantastic dreams, many of which might indeed come true, many of which are already true!"

What an introduction! I sensed that my uncle was setting the stage for another fantastic story.

Uncle Justin continued, "As you all know full well, one of the conditions for maintaining possession of land owned in Louisiana, the landholder must work the land and make improvements to it. In accordance with this stipulation, Congressman Patrick J. Adams meticulously drew up a schematic plan for the development of his newly acquired estate.

"Entrusting the responsibility for carrying out his plans to create a retirement haven to Great-grandfather Joseph, he left specific instructions about the order that he expected things should be completed. First on his list would be construction of the two houses. Next would be clearing the forest for a garden. Following that would be the clearing of trees for the pecan and fruit orchards. Last on the list was the establishment of trapping runs around the entire estate.

"As we have now determined through the sharing and discovery of events recounted over and over again by our oral history, Joseph was able to accomplish virtually all of the goals and plans that Patrick Adams had envisioned back in 1840. Of course, he had the unexpected help of over four hundred of Captain Jean Laffite's men. (This was a small detail that Patrick and Jean knew about, but failed to share with the Addisons until long after the congressman was laid to rest. Laffite's help was always part of the original plans for developing the estate. It was a monumental task that would not otherwise have been even remotely possible, without the manpower and resources that our privateer friend possessed.)

"Joseph enlisted the aid of a man who was familiar with trapping the prairie and marsh lands of the Atchafalaya River Basin, Melvin Lacache. Melvin and his family began trapping the estate, setting up their operation at Plumb Bayou, where the trapping camp is to this day. After a few years, Joseph built the first camp at the site and he began to learn how to trap alongside his good friend. The Addisons have been trappers for over seventy years now.

"My uncle, Sanders Addison (Nora's grandfather) began trapping around Plumb Bayou with his father as soon as he was old enough to walk, not long after the Civil War ended. At first, he trapped from Plumb Bayou to the western banks of Creole Bayou, which marks the eastern boundary of the estate. Eventually, he trapped more and more of the land, approaching the Deer Island ridge. This was quite a large area as you all know. The area he trapped included the marsh and prairie surrounding Palmetto Bayou and Crooked Bayou.

"Sanders became an excellent trapper, and he taught his three sons to be good trappers also. Adam and his two brothers were taught by one the best! They learned how to use the land to maintain possession of it, but they also learned to harvest the furry creatures that occupied the land and turn the sale of their furs into cash money, something that seems to be becoming more and more necessary these days.

"When Sanders Jr. and Arthur grew up, they both decided against continuing the lifestyle of their father. Adam is the only one of the three brothers who chose to continue trapping the Adams estate.

"As all of you know, the land along Plumb Bayou is high ground (it's actually a natural ridge that follows part of the bayou's course). Comparing it with the land along the other bayous that traverse the estate, the Plumb Bayou ridge is second only to the ridge along parts of Deer Island Bayou. Because there was high ground, Joseph planted numerous fig trees—long before the Civil War. I can't recall the year they were planted, but they are very old. Now they are so large that a grown man can climb their branches to gather their ripened fruit."

Uncle Justin paused to reignite the fire in his tobacco bowl, taunting and teasing his audience much like Papa had done. He took his good old time, prolonging the suspense for as long as practical. That was all part of the art of storytelling (keep the listeners spellbound, stimulate their deepest emotions). All good storytellers seem to possess this special gift.

Uncle Justin began again, "Now it is time to reveal the most exciting part of this story. This past June, I took the family to Plumb Bayou to spend a few days at the camp and to pick a few handfuls of figs. Adam and Ida had not come to the camp yet. It was a little early, and very few figs were ripe. We just went to enjoy ourselves and eat a few raw figs. I used to go to Plumb Bayou at the beginning of each summer with Aunt Clara until she died in the Storm of 1909. After that, I lost interest in the outing. Since I married Sarah in 1917, she and I and the boys have resumed the practice of a yearly excursion to the fig orchard.

"I believe it was the 10th of June last year, when we boarded *Dreadnought* and headed for the trapping camp. As expected, the massive trees were filled with green figs. There were very few ripe ones on the trees, but they had produced enough to satisfy our cravings for eating them right off the tree. On the third day of our visit, we were picking a few figs, moving from one tree to the next. When we got to about the fifth tree, Aunt Sarah noticed a hole in the ground near the base of the tree we were approaching. Closer inspection revealed that the parameter of the hole was lined by a rectangular-shaped oaken chest. From the looks of it, it had been covered with only a few inches of topsoil. Its lid had been unearthed and removed, but the bottom and sidewalls remained intact. Careful search was made for the lid to no avail. It was gone.

"I have been picking figs at Plumb Bayou since I was old enough to remember. In the light of all we have been sharing during storytelling time this season—the revelation of the family's close relationship with Jean Laffite, Xavier's discovery of buried treasure on a remote island near Little Bayou Du Large, Captain Laffite's keen interest in the boundaries of the Adams estate, strong ties between Jean and Patrick confirmed by revelations about Pauline Longere. I am convinced that the empty chest we discovered beneath the fig tree was once filled with treasure.

"Sarah and I got weak-kneed over the discovery. How many times do you think that members of the Addison family walked directly over the top of that chest, without the slightest suspicion that there might have been treasure somewhere nearby?

"Someone happened to be under that tree last year, whether planned or by accident we will never know. They unearthed the lid of the chest and broke the lock that had it fastened to the box, removing its contents. The chest was quite large. It was about the size of the chest Adam described in the story of Xavier's treasure. Can anyone of you imagine how much gold and silver and Lord knows what else was hidden in that chest?

"Speculation ran wild! Was it some unsuspecting fisherman, trying to get out of a heavy rainstorm, who may have sought shelter beneath the large canopy provided by the foliage of the giant fig tree? The rain may have exposed the lid, which he promptly removed to discover its contents. I guess we will be wondering about that for a long time to come."

Papa looked at Mama and in a no-nonsense voice said, "Ida! Go and get our clothes ready! Pack up the kids, we're leaving for the trapping camp immediately!"

Mama, seeing Papa rise from his chair as though he meant business, looked at him in utter amazement. "Are you serious, Adam?" she asked in a soft-spoken voice.

Papa returned to his rocking chair and sat down saying "I was just pulling your leg, Ida! The treasure is gone, no need to rush after something that's no longer there!"

"I hoped you were just kidding," Mama responded. "I certainly was unprepared for such an early departure. I wasn't ready to leave the island until after Thanksgiving," she interjected.

Everyone, including Mama, burst into laughter following Papa's playful antics. The grownups lingered on the porch awhile, exploring some of the infinite possibilities for finding buried treasure somewhere on the estate. I moseyed on upstairs to my bed as they continued to muse over finding pirate's loot; Alma followed close behind me, jumping into bed with me at the same time.

I became so enveloped in thought about gold and silver coins that I decided to try to block all of it from my mind; I focused my thoughts on *Ole George Washington* and his harem of hens back at the trapping camp. I wondered if our animals were lonely; were they getting enough food to eat? Did the pigs find their way out of their pen? I thought of *Ninny* and *Nanny*; I know those two spoiled goats are missing me!

In the quiet harmony of virtual solitude, I trained my ears on the babbling waters of the fountainhead and the sounds of all the night creatures that were singing outside my open bedroom windows. It was cold but not uncomfortable. I covered Alma and me with a light blanket. Owls were calling in the distance; the troubled waters of the fountainhead were rejoicing over their sudden freedom. In the diminishing light of the moon in decline, I watched the Spanish moss swaying from the branches of the massive oak that was just outside my window.

I managed to remember my Creator, amidst the splendor of His handiwork, before falling off to sleep. "Dear Lord, I thank you for my health. Thank you for giving me such a loving family. Thank you for the magnificence of all your creations. Thank you for everything. Amen. Good night, Lord!"

Chapter Seven

THE CEMETERY

October 31, 1921

We have been on Deer Island for a week now; the days have passed by quickly it seems, with all the excitement that the stories have generated. We are preparing to visit the gravesite tomorrow. All Saints' Day has special significance on Deer Island, especially since this is where all my ancestors are buried.

Uncle Justin's male goat, *Abe Lincoln*, got into the rice barrel this morning; it may prove to be a fatal mistake. My uncle told Felix to tie him to a tree in the backyard to prevent him from drinking any water. His belly is beginning to swell; the hope is that he didn't swallow enough of the grain to kill him. Uncle Justin said *Ole Abe* would be suffering from severe indigestion for a few days until he can adequately purge the swollen kernels. I hope he doesn't die as a result of his mischief; we've all grown fond of the ornery beast.

Thinking about the predicament that Uncle Justin's goat was in, I remembered a recent incident that happened to one of our neighbors on Bayou Du Large. His goat got into the rice barrel when no one was looking; when he got his fill, he went to a water trough and that's where he stayed. The poor animal's belly began to swell as the rice expanded, and eventually he smothered to death. I don't know how the female goats will get along, if *Ole Abe* should die; I'm sure they would be lonely without him, even though I am sure they wish he would leave them to themselves at times.

We will be gathering wildflowers today to make wreaths and nosegays; we will be placing them near the various grave markers in memorial tomorrow. With respect for our ancestors and the roles each has played in developing our heritage, we pay tribute to their memories once each year on All Saints' Day. We don't celebrate their death; we celebrate their lives, carrying on the family legacy.

I have visited the family cemetery every year that I can remember, but this year will be special. New revelations about my family's history has instilled new memories of those who have been laid to rest, bringing them "back to life" if you will, in my heart and in my mind.

Mama likes to start her bouquets with branches from the wild holly trees; the gray bark of the holly branch, the pale green of the holly leaves, and the bright red berries the wild holly produces at this time of the year, will produce contrasting colors that will enhance the beauty of the wildflowers that Mama will carefully weave into her arrangements.

The boys are busy milking the goats. With *Abe Lincoln* tied securely to a tree (not yet recovered from his swollen belly) their task will be an easy one today. Papa and Uncle Justin are enjoying a smoke on the front porch. Mama is helping Aunt Sarah in the kitchen; they are preparing a second dish of bear meat; they are stuffing a large roast from the bear's hind quarter with garlic cloves and bird-eye peppers. Alma and I are relaxing on the back porch swings; she's singing a lullaby to her doll.

Alma suddenly pointed to the milk cow; she was trying to explain something about the animal to her silent friend. It was gibberish and quite nonsensical. I asked my little sister if she wanted a biscuit from the kitchen; getting no response, I went to the kitchen for a cup of tea, and I fetched a fresh biscuit from a pan on the stove-top. Sweetening a cup of hot sassafras tea with a half spoon of sugar, I could tell it was too hot to drink, so I blew gently over the contents to cool the brew before tasting. Hot sassafras tea and fresh biscuits; it's a hearty breakfast.

To some, it may seem that preparing flowers to place them at the tombs of our family members would be a somber duty. Anyone who doesn't understand the special way my family deals with the departed might think it impossible to be happy while preparing for such a solemn occasion.

Our ancestors are no longer able to communicate with us; for that reason, they are sorely missed. Through the art of storytelling, they remain vividly present, albeit only in our minds and hearts. Because they are gone but not forgotten, I feel that I know all of them, even though I have never spoken to most of them in the first person. I don't find this strange at all; in fact, this conditional relationship that I have with my deceased relatives I find is extremely gratifying.

There is a degree of comfort associated with the knowledge that they rest in peace just over there, about a thousand or so paces down the *wagon path* that heads south and away from the houses. I find nothing gloomy about the way we treat death; it is certain to be a part of life's experience that will eventually come to every one of us. Each of us will have our turn to be carried through the deep woods to the cemetery clearing, never to return to either house again.

Death is one reality that we have learned to live with. I guess that's why we have become aware of the importance of appreciating the time we share together. A clear demonstration of the love we have for each other is the emphasis we place on storing up memories of one another, facilitated by a continuation of oral history handed down from generation to generation. When the day comes that one of us will no longer be able to contribute to our conversation in the first person, the memories we have of them will be present in their stead.

When Uncle Patrick died, the cemetery received a degree of public awareness due to the public service he provided, serving as a

Louisiana congressman for several years. You might say he was given a "proper burial" because of his status in the community; on the day of his interment, many dignitaries visited his gravesite. Since the family cemetery was created in 1842, no one has been denied a space for burial.

Over the years, my family has allowed strangers to be buried in our family cemetery. There have been victims of drowning; occasionally some who are too poor to afford the cost of interment elsewhere have asked to bury their family members here; there are now over twenty souls buried in the cemetery near our family members. Though we never knew them, their graves will be graced with flowers just the same; they have become a part of our lives here on Deer Island.

October 31, 1921 (Evening on the Front Porch Together)
The day seemed to go by swiftly amidst the constant sharing of fond memories of those who have gone before us. When nightfall came and supper was over, we gathered together on the veranda of the *big house*; it was storytelling time once again. This event would not be for competition; it would be a pre-memorial of sorts, a ceremony of remembrance (an example of continuing the oral tradition).

Uncle Justin and Papa shared their extensive knowledge of the colorful history of Addison family members, members who will be honored by all of us tomorrow. It is befitting that the stories began with memories of my great-great-uncle, Patrick J. Adams, Deer Island's founder and former owner. Papa and my uncle took turns expounding the political exploits of the former congressman and explaining how he felt about the prospects for fulfilling his magnificent plans for establishing a retirement haven on the remote island he named "Deer Island."

Uncle Justin seemed to know much more family history than Papa did. That is understandable; he has been a lifelong resident of the island; this gave him a distinct advantage. Living with his mother Elizabeth in the *little house* with Pauline Longere, and getting to know his grandparents, Joseph and Josephine before they all passed on, he was able, not only to listen, but also to participate in conversation on the front porch of the *big house* his entire life.

Speaking of the island's first settlers, Joseph and Josephine Addison, he recounted stories he was told about their lives in Southampton, England. He spoke of great-grandfather's life in the shipyard. He shared how the fear of Indians hampered any decision by Josephine to accept Uncle Patrick's invitation to move to America.

Of course I was very familiar with this portion of family history, having studied my great-grandmother's diary tirelessly since I was old enough to read.

Uncle Justin mentioned the fact that my great-uncle, John Quincy Addison, died heroically during the Battle for Chancellorsville on May 3, 1863. His brother, Alexander Patrick Addison (Uncle Justin's father) was severely wounded a week later, about fifteen miles from the Chancellorsville battlefield, on May 10, 1863. Alexander returned to Deer Island after the war, married Elizabeth Cotton, and had one child. He told us that his father died from complications due to his Civil War wound just a couple of years after he was born.

My great-uncle, John Quincy's body, was removed from the Vicksburg cemetery at the request of my great-grandfather and transported to Deer Island for burial in the family cemetery. Joseph had to enlist the help of members of the Louisiana State Senate who remembered Uncle Patrick; they assisted him in the fight to bring my uncle's body home to its final resting place (a necessary act for any degree of closure, I guess).

Papa spoke of his proud relic from the past, the *Early Rose*; it was the last vessel built by Joseph Addison. He boasts about the solid, durable construction of the hull to everyone who will listen.

Uncle Justin praised the craftsmanship of Joseph Addison by reminding everyone of another boat. He mentioned that not much had been said about the *Muskrat*, a boat my great-grandfather built to make traveling the inland bayous and streams easier. He shared that the boat remains in good shape; he was proud to say that it's been well-kept. He and his family use the smaller vessel to make trips to the trapping camp and excursions to the many inland bays in the area—mostly pleasure trips, local visits to the neighbors' camp boats, and fishing adventures. It's a versatile craft, and Uncle Justin is just as proud of it as Papa is with his historical craft.

Papa spoke highly of the Addison matriarchs. From Great-grandmother Josephine to the present day, Papa boasted that the Addison women have all had special attributes (commendable qualities). Great-grandmother Josephine, Great-aunt Elizabeth, Aunt Clara, and Ida have all been supportive of their husbands, industrious, diligent caretakers, lovingly tender as only a good woman can be. All the Addison women had one common feature; they are all blessed with very good looks.

Mama and Aunt Sarah giggled over that remark, but Uncle Justin was quick to defend my father's remarks. "I feel just like Adam does. All the Addison women are beautiful. They have all been good women!" he loudly proclaimed his mirrored assessment.

I could see my uncle was having a look at me and Alma after making his assertion. I just knew he was about to make another comment. "Yes, Nora, you and Alma will be carrying on those very same attributes. Beauty runs in the family!" he insisted. It was enough flattery to make a fifteen-year-old girl blush, and so I did.

Uncle Justin recalled how happy my grandfather, Sanders Addison, and my Grandmother Martha were to give us their house on Bayou Du Large; shortly after my father and mother were married, they moved into the *little house* on Deer Island. He told us that Grandmother Martha was a good housekeeper and she kept a neat house, but she was not shy to express relief that she didn't have to keep up the inside of the *big house*. "Cleaning that big house was a major task!" she often told Josephine and Elizabeth.

My uncle told us that Sanders and Martha loved the solitude of island living. Since their children were all raised, and since they were deeply in love, the time they spent here was filled with tender expressions of the feelings that they had for one another (walks down the different pathways of the homestead holding hands, sitting in their favorite chairs sipping coffee or tea and enjoying each other's company; they also kissed a lot, and they weren't bashful of who was watching). Uncle Justin said the time my grandparents had together here was the fulfillment of anyone's concept of what romance should be, and that's the way they acted until the very end of their lives.

If I ever get married, I hope my relationship with my lifelong partner will be as fulfilling as the relationship my uncle just described. I can only hope to be so happy with a man that hasn't showed himself to me yet. God knows!

Uncle Justin spoke of Sanders's love for duck hunting (he used to make his duck calls using the wild canes that can still be readily found around the homestead). He was an expert caller! Remembering one of their famous hunting trips they made together, Uncle Justin said that Sanders had killed fifteen birds and was already returning to the house before he had killed his first duck. When Sanders approached the duck blind he was in, he had a pile of black ducks (ring necks), widgeons, and wood ducks in the bottom of his canoe. "Why haven't you shot at anything?" Sanders playfully asked, with a broad smile across his face. Justin told him that every time a flock of birds flew by, he sounded his call and chased them away.

"They got spooked!" he told Sanders. Knowing full well what the problem was, Sanders gave the duck call he was using to Uncle Justin; he took the one he had been using and said, "Take my duck call in exchange for yours. The one you are using is obviously either worn out, or it is merely out of tune. I'll take it back to the house with me and check it over."

Uncle Justin told us that, sure enough, Sanders was right; the next flock that flew over his head returned for another pass, once they heard the sound of Sanders' duck call. In no time at all, he had killed the birds he wanted and returned to the house. He said that when he arrived at the front of the *little house*, Sanders waved at him from his front porch. "How did you make out with the call I gave you?" he asked. Uncle Justin said that it worked great. Sanders told him to keep the one he gave him; he had already made a new one for himself.

Uncle Justin said that Sanders was a crack shot. He had good vision, and he had an uncanny ability to identify birds at a great distance by carefully observing their flight characteristics. Using special calls to mimic the calls of each species of duck, Sanders would draw the unsuspecting waterfowl into the range of his gun. "A duck within the range of Sanders's gun was a duck in Martha's pot!" Uncle Justin lauded. "I don't ever recall seeing him miss anything he was shooting at," Uncle Justin told us.

Uncle Justin said that the difference in sound between his old duck call, and the one that Sanders gave to him, was not easy to discern; in fact, he insisted he could not tell the difference. There's one thing that I know for sure; the ducks knew the difference, and so did Sanders Addison! That man's ears were just as good as his eyes! Uncle Justin acknowledged.

Uncle Justin told another story about Grandpa Sanders that I had not heard before. He informed us that Sanders had the record for the largest deer killed on the island. It was a fourteen-point buck, and its weight was estimated to be 375 pounds or more. The best part of this story is where he shot the deer. "He shot it right from his front porch!" Uncle Justin explained, with a degree of amazement clearly written on his face.

Uncle Justin continued the story, after sharing that he too had planned to go hunting that frosty winter morning, "Sanders was sipping on a cup of hot coffee, sitting in his rocking chair, as I parted company with him on my way to my favorite deer hunting location. I can still see the steam vapors rising above his coffee cup as he sat on the *little house* porch. As was his customary practice on cold winter mornings, Sanders believed the hot brew would take the chill out of his old bones. He told me that just as he was preparing to leave (his plan was to try to walk up on a deer in the woods at the far side of the garden clearing) a huge buck suddenly appeared. He could see the massive rack of antlers penetrating the thicket on the east side of the stream, directly across from where he was seated. The fact that a deer would come that close to the house didn't surprise him. That was something quite ordinary. It happened all the time, as all of you well know. He told me it was the size of the magnificent animal that stole his breath away from him.

"One can scarcely imagine the excitement of that moment, but Sanders was an experienced hunter, and he was determined not to let this chance pass him by if he could help it," Uncle Justin shared.

"Now, let's continue with the story he shared with me when I returned from my unsuccessful hunt. Slowly but deliberately, Sanders said he raised his gun to his shoulder. The deer was looking straight at him. When the huge buck lowered his head for a drink from the stream, Sanders said he cut loose with his rifle. The shot hit him right behind the shoulder and the deer dropped dead where he had once stood. The antlers are stored in a wooden chest in the upstairs bedroom of the *little house*. They have been there for years," Uncle Justin told us.

Papa knew this story well, but he was happy Uncle Justin had shared it with us. He knew his dad was a skilled hunter; he just didn't like to brag too much about it.

Mama and Aunt Sarah took their turns; it was time for them to speak of the Addison men. They said that all the Addison men were good providers, and yes, they said they thought the Addison men were a handsome lot. Mama said that Papa was a loving man, a great deal more tender and sentimental than he tries to show. She told everyone that Adam was a perfect choice for her; plus, she said he's fun to live with! Aunt Sarah expressed similar sentiments about Uncle Justin. Neither of the two women raised a single point of criticism.

Eventually, all the stories had been exhausted, and we retired for the evening. As I lay in bed quietly, I mused over the memories that were shared on the veranda, this being the evening of All Saints' Day. I felt confident that the good and decent members of my family, a God-fearing family, had found their eternal resting place in heaven above. My family has always held the deep conviction that the most important thing in one's life is establishing and maintaining a close relationship with God as taught by the Holy Scripture. Though we support the Anglican Church through our giving, our confidence, our source of eternal security, rests in what our Savior did for us on the cross. Our faith is in Jesus Christ! It's not in our religion. I believe that is why we are at peace when one of us dies; we have that blessed assurance that we will go to heaven when we leave this earth.

My final prayer: "Thank you, Lord Jesus, for that blessed assurance, assurance only you have the power to give. Amen."

ALL SAINTS' DAY

November 1, 1921

Everyone was up early this morning. We gathered around the breakfast table as a family for the first time since our arrival at Uncle Justin's place. Breakfast is usually catch-as-catch-can, everyone with his own special plans to begin each day.

We dined on fried eggs and biscuits. The biscuits were glazed with fresh churned butter and were ready to be filled with either peach or plum jam that Aunt Sarah brought out of her cupboard. The biscuits were golden brown and flaky, easily separated to accommodate the honey butter and jam; they were totally irresistible. A whole pitcher of goat's milk disappeared during the consumption of the morning feast.

I am happy to record that *Ole Abe Lincoln* appears to be back to normal; he survived the rice barrel incident. No one is sure he learned his lesson, so Aunt Sarah said she would be more cautious with the grain stores in the future (not to imply that it was her carelessness that caused the problem; it was every bit the goat's fault).

Mama, Aunt Sarah, Alma, and I decided to relax awhile on the back porch swings. Felix, Gus, Lee, and Brad opted to go for a walk along the *beaten path*. Papa and Uncle Justin were back on the front porch rocking and smoking, rocking, and smoking.

There was a brisk north wind blowing; the Spanish moss was leaning against the wind, trying in vain to force its way back to the vertical position with only gravity to aid in its struggle. The sky was clear; it was void of any clouds. The fall weather was perfect for the day's planned activity.

The family cemetery is about a thousand paces from the south side of the *big house* where we are now seated. Uncle Justin and Papa will soon be harnessing the milk cow, hitching her to Uncle Justin's wooden sled (one just like ours but larger). The sled will be used to travel the distance to the gravesite carrying Mama, Aunt Sarah, me and Alma, and the boys, with all the wreaths and flower arrangements we women have prepared. Papa and Uncle Justin will have the task of walking beside the cow, steering her along the *wagon path*.

Uncle Justin's sled is much wider and longer than the one we have back home. His has two especially made removable seats, benches with back rests for the comfort of the riders. The girls will occupy the front seat, and the boys will take the second, aboard this "carriage without wheels." I especially enjoy watching the ground moving below us, as the skids slide along the smooth surface of the well-worn trail.

It was nine in the morning when we boarded the sled and began the slow-paced journey to the graveyard. The route to the cemetery was shrouded on every side by the dense forest and underbrush; the resulting natural throughway added an aesthetic quality to the sled ride.

The boys insisted on walking to the cemetery. They followed behind us in procession at a distance, having conversation that escaped my hearing. They are probably up to something; scheming their next prank, no doubt!

We have all dressed in our finest apparel. Mama and Aunt Sarah are wearing long gowns—Mama's is light blue and Aunt Sarah's is lime green. They have each donned a hat, splendidly adorned with fresh cut flowers for the occasion. Uncle Justin and Papa are wearing suits. Papa's is navy blue and Uncle Justin's is brown. Their bowties match their clothing and their starched white shirts contribute to their dignified appearance. The rest of us are not so smartly dressed, but we are wearing our Sunday clothes.

The journey to the gravesite took about thirty minutes. Upon our arrival, Uncle Justin opened the parameter gate that guards the site from wild intruders (not to mention the domestic kind). He and Papa then advanced the sled into the graveyard and came to a stop. Once we were inside the cemetery, the mood changed; there was an atmosphere of solemn tranquility that can only be experienced when visiting such a place.

The entire fenced parameter is grown over with blackberry vines, in appearance looking like a well-groomed brown hedgerow—not the least bit unappealing. The entanglement of vines is so dense that the eye cannot possibly penetrate the compacted row of briars to see what lurks behind them. The thorny thicket presents a formidable boundary that few animals bother to cross (except an occasional rabbit or squirrel).

Pink roses grace the site of each and every iron cross and tomb. Our family's graves are all housed in brick. As for the graves of those who have requested to be buried on the island, each of their plots is protected and appropriately marked; each one is outlined by bricks placed neatly on the ground's surface with an iron cross at the head of each grave. A pink floribunda has been planted at the head of each cross, just like the ones near our family plots.

Uncle Patrick's tomb is the most prominent site in the cemetery. His tomb is made of brick and he has a bronze plaque affixed to its front wall commemorating his service to his country. A brick walkway leads from the wrought iron gate to the foot of the tomb and circumvents it. A large cypress cross rises high above the brickwork of the tomb and is situated within the twelve-foot-by-twelve-foot iron enclosure near the head of the grave. In addition to the pink floribunda (originally planted from a cutting left at the site by Mademoiselle Pauline Longere when Uncle Patrick was buried) there are several others planted within the iron enclosure; it's a beautiful area and wonderful to behold, befitting my distinguished uncle, the former congressman, Patrick J. Adams.

The site of the huge cross always serves as a reminder of the supreme sacrifice my Savior made for me at Calvary, just outside the city gates of Jerusalem. The price He paid when He shed every drop of His blood for my sins offers me hope of eternal life through faith in his finished work. To God belongs the glory now and forevermore, amen.

Joining my Uncle Patrick in peaceful repose are my great-grandfather, Joseph Addison; my great-grandmother, Josephine Addison; my great-uncle, John Quincy Addison; my great-uncle, Alexander Addison; my great-aunt, Elizabeth Addison; my grandfather, Sanders Addison; my grandmother, Martha Addison; Pauline Longere, my Great-grandmother Josephine's surrogate sister (an adopted member of our family); and Clara Addison (Uncle Justin's first wife).

There are ten members of my family buried in the family graveyard. There are twenty-two other souls (four of which I am told were children) whose names we do not know; they have been buried here as well. The souls of all the faithful departed are long gone; their spirits returned to God that gave them. Now, only tributes to their memories remain in the lovely, but lonely solitude of the cemetery grounds.

The Tomb of the Owner and Founder
Of the Settlement on Deer Island

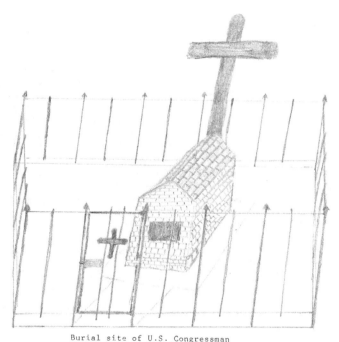

Burial site of U.S. Congressman
Patrick Adams
Born New Orleans July 4, 1791
Fought in the Battle of New Orleans Jan 8,1815
Elected to Congress 1816
Served as Congressman from Louisiana until he
died July 22, 1842
At the request of the
Louisiana delegation
President Zachary Taylor commissioned that a large cypress cross be
erected at his grave site along with a wrought iron fence and bronze
plaque commemorating his years of meritorious service to the Congress
of the United States of America.

My two great-uncles, John Quincy and Alexander Patrick, both have commemorative bronze plaques affixed to their tombs. Great-grandfather Joseph had them inscribed with information about their service to the Confederate States of America. John Quincy was killed at Chancellorsville and Alexander Patrick was severely wounded a week later, not far from the battlefield where his brother was killed.

There are three heroes in the Addison family buried in the island cemetery. Uncle Patrick served in the American Army against the English during the Battle for New Orleans in 1815. My two great-uncles served in the Confederacy during the Civil War. I do believe they are worthy of this special tribute; it will stand as a reminder that standing for a cause can be a costly endeavor, sometimes it can be fatal.

Ms. Longere is buried in a brick tomb directly behind the place where Uncle Patrick was laid to rest, just as she had requested. She died and was buried on July 1, 1900. She was eight-five years old; she never married. I guess life with the Addisons was gratifying enough for her. I've always been told she was a very happy sort, possessing a joyful spirit that she shared with everyone who had the pleasure of knowing her. I am sorry I never had the chance to be with her; she has always been one of my favorite personalities. That's why the recorded legend is so meaningful to me. I truly feel I know all the people I have visited here today. Their memories are alive and well, and now a matter of recorded family history.

I can easily envision, using my mind's eye and a little imagination, Pauline Longere in her fancy white dress, twirling her red velvet parasol in the brilliant sunlight, her long black hair waving freely in the breeze below her shoulders, her penetrating smile and deep brown eyes gazing innocently about, as all the men nearby gawk and become spellbound in her presence.

What a magnificent woman she must have been; she charmed the daylights out of everyone she encountered, including my Great-grandmother Josephine. Countless suitors must have been enchanted as they observed her singing French folk songs with her characteristic tantalizing demeanor. I cannot help but wish that I had been able to see her myself, even if it was for just a few minutes; I would have loved to have been able to sit and chat with her awhile.

We placed the flower arrangements and wreaths at all the gravesites and then we gathered together for a time of reflection and prayer (for the living) within the wrought iron fence, which marked the boundary that surrounds Uncle Patrick's tomb. As we stood on the brick walkway, the fragrance from the beautiful pink rose blossoms filled the air while Papa and Uncle Justin extolled the virtues of our deceased relatives.

Special mention was given about the many unknown souls who were put to rest near our family members. Prayerful petitions were made for all the living relatives of everyone buried in the island graveyard. Uncle Justin ended our visitation with a final prayer.

"Oh, Lord, we gather here today to pay homage to our deceased relatives and those we never knew. We thank you for providing us with this memorial ground for those who have gone before us. We know that after death there is judgment. We have long ago entrusted and commended them to your divine mercy, for they were yours before they were ours. We ask for your guidance in our lives. Help us to do what is pleasing in your sight. Help us to walk in accordance with the principles taught in your Word as we strive to trust and obey you. As your humble servants, we ask that you grant long life and good health to those of us who remain. We ask that you keep our family together and we thank you for the countless blessings you have bestowed upon us. We thank you for this wonderful day of remembrance, and the splendor of the sunshine you have graced us with for this our celebration of life with you. We praise the name of the Lord Jesus Christ to the glory of God our Father in heaven, amen."

Thus we paid tribute to our relatives who would forevermore link the Addison family heritage to the family cemetery on Deer Island. It has become an important part of the family legacy.

We returned to the *big house* to enjoy a day of leisure time together. The boys ran the fish lines and the bush traps and brought home a bounty of seafood. They filleted the fish, cleaned the crabs, and peeled the shrimp. Papa and Uncle Justin made quick work of the catch; they had the fried seafood served on the outside table by midafternoon.

We dined sumptuously on deep-fried seafood and fried sweet potato slices. We had taken no afternoon nap, so thoroughly exhausted from the day's activity, we retired early. Uncle Justin is planning a trip to Morgan City aboard his sailboat in a couple of days. Tomorrow we will begin preparing for the journey; I believe he plans to bring a few things to sell at the markets.

As I lay in bed thinking of today's highlights, I could hear owls calling to one another in the distance. The moonlight was dim as I gazed through my bedroom window. The brisk north wind that felt so invigorating when we awakened this morning has subsided. The many clusters of moss are hanging from the massive oak tree limbs vertically once again; there are no intermittent breezes to sway them from gravity's embrace.

I have been enjoying this fall visit to Deer Island immensely. The activities have been fun and the storytelling has been the best ever. I don't know what lays ahead for me this holiday season, but I promised myself I would make the best use I can of the time we have remaining. I like to trap with my family at the Plumb Bayou camp, but the visit to the island is the thing I most look forward to each year.

My little sister Alma has been sleeping for an hour. She was a sweetheart all day, but that was nothing unusual; Alma's a sweetheart every single day. She hasn't worn out her ragdoll yet; she has it tucked beneath her arm drawn tightly to her chest. I was feeling weary. My eyes were growing heavy; thoughts of my ancestors began to lead me away from myself, until suddenly, I was gone.

Chapter Eight

THE SAILBOAT RIDE

November 3, 1921

Activity on Deer Island has changed since Uncle Justin announced plans for taking his sailboat to Morgan City; he is determined to sell various items from the homestead, and he will be buying provision for the household with the proceeds.

Yesterday the boys were given the chore of trying to round up a few piglets for sale at the city market. They found a sow leading around her ten little piglets, but they had a difficult time gathering the stubborn litter. They left the irate mother pig with four of her offspring, but that didn't seem to appease the furious creature. The frustrating ordeal lasted nearly all day, culminating in the capture and transfer of six very unhappy piglets from the wild and open spaces of the homestead into a holding pen on the back deck of Uncle Justin's boat.

The endless squealing from the piglets brought the agitated sow all the way down the *landing path* to the wharf. Unable to free her young from the holding pen, she finally relented; she walked off through the deep woods, her four remaining piglets following close behind.

When I exited the front door this morning, I just missed Papa and Uncle Justin. They were heading downstream in the oar skiff when I noticed them; I made a quick dash from the porch to try to catch them. When I rushed down the *landing path* and got alongside the boat, Papa said it would be better to remain at the house to give Mama and Aunt Sarah a hand. "They need you more than we do right now sweetheart," Papa earnestly instructed.

I returned to the kitchen and offered my assistance. I helped Mama and Aunt Sarah wipe down the jars of fruit jams and preserves that my aunt intended to sell at the market. We placed the fruit-filled jars of desserts in wooden crates for careful shipment; a broken jar means money lost; it pays to be careful.

Alma assisted me in placing the jars in the special crates; we put a dozen in each box with moss shoved between the jars for safety. I carried the crates to the front porch so the boys could carry them to the boat landing later.

Aunt Sarah had numerous jars of pickled peppers, pickled okra, pickled squash, stewed tomatoes, and various preserves made with fruit grown on the island. She had jars of powdered sassafras leaves, jars full of whole sweet bay leaves, and a few crock jars of cooked wildlife—ducks, rabbits, and squirrels.

Alma tagged along with me, talking aimlessly to her ragdoll. As usual, though she was near me, she was in her own make-believe world. I spoke to her several times during the morning, but she only acknowledged she heard me say anything twice, answering in a faint voice, "Yes!" one time and "No!" another. That's not much of a conversation by any measure.

The boys are picking pecans. Aunt Sarah hopes to bring two or three twenty-five-pound sacks to market when we leave tomorrow.

Mama has assumed the role of cook today so Aunt Sarah can concentrate on what needs to be done before we leave for the city. She is preparing a chicken stew. I can smell the aroma of fresh bread baking in the oven. There is a pot full of sweet potatoes simmering in hot syrup.

Much like Mama does back home, Aunt Sarah is making a list of the items she needs from the mainland. She is reviewing the contents of the list to be sure she hasn't forgotten anything. She said Uncle Justin makes his own list.

By the time I finished my chores, it was late afternoon. Everyone had paused just long enough to eat lunch, and then we went back to work foregoing our traditional naptime—all of us except Alma, of course.

Papa and Uncle Justin were busy preparing the rigging for our journey to the city tomorrow. They pulled out the sails, checking them for tears in the sheets before attaching them to the various beams, cables and ropes in preparation for setting sail. Just before sunset, they arrived back at the *big house*.

Felix and the rest of the boys were proud to share that they had picked six twenty-five pound sacks of the tasty nuts; that was twice as many sacks as Aunt Sarah had hoped she would have to sell at the general store. Gus reported that there were more in the trees the wind had not blown to the ground. He also mentioned that the squirrels are having a feast; there must have been at least fifty of them foraging in the pecan tree tops.

"That's not such a bad thing," Aunt Sarah cited. "Pecan-fed squirrels are fat squirrels. It will take fewer of the little thieves to fill our bellies when we kill them for the pot," she thoughtfully heralded, making light of what some would say was a pesky nuisance. Practically speaking, I can see her point; pecan trees have to produce so we and the squirrels can eat. The squirrels have to eat so when they grow enough we can eat them; the process for getting there is mutually beneficial, at least until the end comes for the poor squirrel.

After the evening meal, we gathered on the porch to hear Papa tell the sixth story of the season. He announced that he and Uncle Justin had talked things over; they came to a mutual understanding about the new developments that have evolved as a direct result of the new discoveries that were revealed for the very first time this year. Surprisingly, Papa said there were two more fantastic events in our family's history that were uncovered this summer; he began to explain.

"In June of 1840, you may recall that Joseph and Josephine had visited a plantation home near the village we now call the city of Houma. On the journey from New Orleans to Brashear City overland, Uncle Patrick decided he would pay a visit to his good friends, William and Greta Henley, at their home, Sugarland Farms Plantation.

"The Henleys played host to Uncle Patrick, Joseph and Josephine during their overnight visit at their sugar plantation. Greta Henley and Josephine became friends, just as was recorded in the account of the visit in Josephine's diary.

"Before they departed on the following day, unknown to Joseph or Josephine, Greta Henley had two wooden crates stowed away atop Uncle Patrick's coach. Joseph and Josephine were not made aware of the gifts until they were being off-loaded onto Captain Francois Marceaux's sailboat, the *Swamp Rat*, at Brashear City (now Morgan City).

"At that time, Uncle Patrick informed Joseph and his wife the wooden crates contained presents from William and Greta Henley. He informed them of Greta's desire to keep the contents of the boxes a secret until the couple was moved into their new home, once it was built. The boxes were nailed shut to prevent anyone from peeking inside. He also cautioned that Greta insisted the two boxes be stored in a dry place (unintentionally giving a slight hint as to the contents).

"Have you ever wondered what became of those two boxes? What about their contents?" Papa inquired.

Of course everyone responded in the affirmative. "Yes, we want to know!"

"I have been curious over the whereabouts of the boxes ever since I first read about them in Great-grandmother Josephine's diary," I commented.

Papa continued to explain, "Tonight I will reveal to you what one of those boxes contained!

"When we first arrived on the island this fall, Uncle Justin explained that due to storm damage, he had to make necessary repairs to the *little house*. Roof damage had allowed the heavy rains to wet the inside of the house. He and Aunt Sarah had to go through Sanders and Martha's personal effects to check for damage and then to reorganize them. It was at this time that Uncle Justin discovered the cutlass with Uncle Patrick and Jean Laffite's names inscribed upon it.

"Uncle Justin did a fantastic job concealing the fact that he also discovered the two wooden crates that had been given to Joseph and Josephine by the Henleys. Justin will reveal the contents of the second crate as we near the end of storytelling for this season.

"The boxes are not ordinary crates. They were well crafted, having hinges, lock and key. The four corners were nailed shut using copper nails. If there is any doubt about how sentimental Great-grandmother Josephine was, let any suspicion be dispelled by the fact that the copper nails had been carefully removed and placed conspicuously inside the opened boxes for safekeeping."

Papa continued, "I must admit that my heart began to race when Uncle Justin gave me the opportunity to look inside one of the boxes that the Henleys had given to Joseph Addison. Taking the special key in my hand, I slowly but deliberately turned the key to unlock the box. I opened it and discovered a very large book had been kept inside. It was a family Bible."

Reading from a prepared statement, Papa began to recite what he had written: "Inside the cover of the book is a note to Joseph from William Harrison Henley. The note reads as follows: 'Dear Joseph, within the covers of this book you will find the Words of Almighty God. Searching these pages with an open and pure heart will lead you to the perfect knowledge of God's will for your life. In order to have a relationship with Him, you must learn who He is through a diligent study of His Word. Much like the contents of this letter will give you a better insight about my character, the contents of the Word of God will teach you of the character of God. I pray that your life's journey will lead you to a heavenly reward. As the head of your household, I entrust you with this gift. If you use it wisely, you will discover that the Bible is the best gift that one man can give to another. Kindest regards, William Harrison Henley.' Pardon me while I go inside to fetch the wooden box," Papa said, as he rose up from his rocking chair and went inside the house.

"What a marvelous gift!" everyone acclaimed. Based on what Mr. Henley wrote in the Bible's cover, everyone deduced that he must have had a special relationship with the Lord.

Now it would be my turn to see what Papa has already seen; in just a little while, Papa reappeared on the front porch carrying with him an exquisitely fashioned box. The wood was darkened by some sort of oily finish. The hinges were made of copper. There was a keyhole in the front center of the box. Papa reached into his pocket and handed me the key.

I opened the wooden crate and discovered a beautiful leather-bound Bible. It fit into the box perfectly. The box was twelve inches long, ten inches wide, and six inches thick. I opened the impressive decorative cover and witnessed for myself the note from William Harrison Henley to my great-grandfather. This was proof; it established the fact that this book was one of the two gifts that was given to the family from the Henleys so many years ago.

As I passed the book around for others to see, I asked Papa to give us at least a hint as to the contents of the other box. I knew that was an exercise in futility; he would never steal the element of surprise from Uncle Justin.

"You will just have to patiently wait for Uncle Justin to reveal that," Papa commented. "I don't know what the contents of the second box are. Remember, he gave me the privilege of opening the first box, not the second one," he added.

Uncle Justin shared that Papa had never asked to look inside the other crate; he said they agreed that they should each have a turn to reveal the contents to everyone. He said they both felt that was the only fair way they could handle the matter. "I have the privilege of choosing the time!" Uncle Justin proudly proclaimed.

"When everyone finds out what was in the crate meant for Josephine, all of you will better appreciate why I chose to wait until later to share the second latest discovery," Uncle Justin teased.

"I can't wait!" I anxiously announced.

As I lay in bed beside my little sister, I thought of the Holy Bible that Mr. Henley had given to my great-grandparents. I do believe that his gift has borne fruit, evidenced by my family's reliance on a personal relationship with the Savior, rather than trusting in some institution (otherwise known as religion) and trying to identify with those who blindly follow their approach to salvation. It is befitting that this story was the sixth of the season; after all, the Lord finished all His work in six days, and on the seventh day, He rested.

My family has always studied the Bible; I have a copy of my own. Like Mr. Henley, my father wrote a note to me on the inside page of its cover: "To my little girl Nora, find the Lord through a study of His word. If you diligently seek him, He will reveal Himself to you. Come to know Him and believe in Him, trust in Him. He is faithful and loving. His mercy endures forever. No matter what may happen in your life, learn this: 'Go to God whenever you need an answer to any question, no matter how difficult you think it might be, go to God when you have a problem, go to Him when you need to talk to someone.' I present this gift with all my love, Papa."

God, I thank you for your Word; thank you for the love you showed to us through the Henleys' generous gift. The Bible has been a source of inspiration that has helped my family beyond any measure. It has provided us with the straight path, a path that gives hope and assurance of eternal life through faith in your Son, Jesus Christ. Amen. Good night, Lord.

November 4, 1921

Morning brought with it a flurry of activity at the Addison homestead. The boys have been lending their assistance to Papa and Uncle Justin; they have steadily transported items from the *big house* down the *landing path* to the sailboat. The bustling activity continued until lunchtime.

The wooden crates containing the six piglets, the crates of fruit-filled jars, the sacks of pecans, and a crate containing a number of large turtles, have been placed on the deck of the boat. Several large fresh water catfish from the fish car have been transferred to a holding tank onboard, and now await transport to the city. The fish were the last item to be hauled aboard; now we are prepared to leave the dock and head for the mainland.

Aunt Sarah was going over her list with Mama at the kitchen table while I sipped a hot cup of sassafras tea. She began to enumerate: "Kerosene, lamp wicks, two lamp globes, gunpowder, flour, sugar, rice, coffee beans, fabric for new clothes, Felix wants a knife, Gus wants rock candy. The boys want new sewing needles and twine for making fishing lines, mending our nets and seines, and making new ones (two needles for netting and one for hanging the seine lines). They also need a few fish hooks. I hope I haven't forgotten anything," she told Mama, searching her memory for any unintentional omission.

"What about jars to replace the ones you are sending to market?" Mama asked.

"Indeed, we will need new jars!" Aunt Sarah responded, glad the oversight was revealed. She immediately recorded the number of jars she needed on her ever-expanding list. The Addison family knows all about the expanding list; if one is not frugal, the list can be far longer than the pocket book can stand. It's easy to do, but much harder to undo. I think it is better to keep the list as short as possible.

Aunt Sarah baked some ginger cookies and several loaves of bread to bring with us on our overnight excursion to Morgan City. We ate a light luncheon, and then we boarded the oar skiff and the two dugout canoes and headed downstream a little faster than the swift moving water could carry us. Alma and I rode in the oar skiff with the grownups. The boys split up into two couples; Felix and Brad took one canoe, and Lee and Gus climbed into the other.

The canoes went ahead of us, racing downstream. Uncle Justin stood at oars, steering us away from the banks of the channel, traveling down to the landing at a more leisurely pace.

The plan is to use the motor powered *Early Rose* to tow the sailboat to the mouth of Deer Bayou. Papa will moor his boat there to a few nearby trees; then he and the boys will join us aboard the *Dreadnought* for the sailboat ride up the Atchafalaya River to the city. Papa and Uncle Justin say that this plan will save about two hours of daylight (the amount of time it would normally take to oar the larger vessel to the river from Addison Landing).

Papa boarded the *Early Rose* and gave a spin of the flywheel. The engine began to sound its familiar tune: *Puk-puk-puk-puk-puk-puk-puk-puk-puk-puk-puk-puk-puk*, sputter then stop. Another spin of the flywheel, then *Puk-puk-puk-puk-puk-puk-puk-puk-puk-puk-puk-puk-puk*, sounded the little one-cylinder engine. With tow lines secured, Papa's smaller vessel began leading the large sailboat to the mouth of Deer Bayou. Uncle Justin instructed Felix to man the rudder of *Dreadnought* to assist in the steerage of his vessel.

Papa slowly maneuvered the sailboat into the center of the channel; once the two boats were midstream, he put the engine in the corner and the increase in the forward motion of the two vessels was readily noticeable. I could feel a significant tug on the tow lines when they suddenly went taut.

The towering masts of my uncle's boat seemed destined to be struck by the overhead branches as we passed through the arboreal tunnel that shrouded the portion of the bayou that traversed the island ridges. I believe the aft-mast towers sixty-five feet above the decks of the boat. Uncle Justin assured us that there was no danger of hitting any branches that form the canopy above us, having passed through the channel many times at both high and low tide. "We should clear the lowest of the branches by at least ten feet," he told us.

I took the time to tell Uncle Justin and Aunt Sarah how much I appreciated their hospitality. I told them I was having the time of my life and that there was no place on earth I'd rather be than to be on Deer Island with my family.

Uncle Justin told me that he and Aunt Sarah, and the boys, always look forward to our arrival on the island each fall. He told me how much he and his family enjoy our company and expressed how glad he was that we were enjoying our stay.

I told my uncle that Grandfather White wanted us to tell him that it has been far too long since he and his family paid a visit to Bayou Du Large. He wants us to invite you to come and spend a few days with them: "They will be glad to see you," my grandfather told me to tell you.

Uncle Justin paused to glance in my aunt's direction to read her facial expressions after the invitation. Seeing she obviously approved of the idea, Uncle Justin said they might meet us at Plumb Bayou at the end of the trapping season and follow us to our home. He told me that *Dreadnought* would need a tow through Mud Lake, and then up Bayou Du Large, because of the shallow waters. He said that he would talk it over with Papa, and take advantage of the invitation if he agrees.

"That would be great!" I excitedly announced. I recommended they come a week before the trapping season ends to spend some time with us there at the Plumb Bayou camp. "I'm sure Felix and Gus would enjoy that!" I posed.

"We just might take your advice, Nora," Uncle Justin said, wearing a big smile on his face and making Aunt Sarah giggle.

Maybe it was the good conversation, but before I realized what was happening, we were nearing the Atchafalaya River. Without noticing it, we had traveled through the cypress swamp west of Deer Island, and Papa was slowing our forward motion down to a crawl.

Felix and Gus scrambled to the front of the sailboat to untie the tow lines so Papa could properly steer his boat against the clamshell deposits that lined the left descending bank of the bayou. Lee and Brad helped in the process of loosening the lines and untying the ropes. Once free, Papa nosed the bow of the *Early Rose* against the left bank of Deer Bayou. Lee and Brad, carrying one mooring line each ashore, tied the vessel securely to two cypress trees.

Once we were all aboard Uncle Justin's sailboat, Felix and Gus went into action. First they went below deck to lower the keel from its raised position inside the box and they locked it into the extended position below the bottom of the hull. Next, they began to unfurl the sails in the order that they were told. In a short time, we experienced the sudden jolt prompted by the wind-filled sails. The modest southeast wind propelled us forward against the river currents as it expanded the giant canvass of the mainsails. I suddenly became aware of the power of the wind being harnessed by the sails as we began to move swiftly upriver from the mouth of the bayou.

This being my first sailboat ride up the Atchafalaya River, I must say I was fascinated by the experience. I don't pretend to understand how a sailboat can move upstream against such a swift ravaging current, but my Uncle Justin sure knows how to make it happen.

Mama and Aunt Sarah remained inside the main cabin, located between the two masts; Alma was already asleep in one of the lower bunk beds, clutching her doll with both of her hands as though she feared that someone might steal the thing. I decided it would be more fun to watch Uncle Justin sail his craft from the steering station near the stern of the boat.

The boys assisted Uncle Justin by keeping a sharp lookout for fallen trees floating downriver and any other obstructions that might damage the hull of our boat. Sometimes, water-soaked logs will submerge in the swift water, making them hard or impossible to detect; many times when they are spotted, it's far too late to maneuver around them. All you can do is hope they don't do much harm when they hit. Uncle Justin says there have been cases when a submerged log, or some other obstacle, hit and penetrated the hull of a boat and the vessel went down to the bottom; I hope that doesn't happen to us. God forbid!

This is my first trip to Morgan City. In spite of the dangers posed by traveling the river, my confidence in my uncle's sailing ability has kept me from being fearful. After all, at the end of this journey, the big city awaits us. I have a feeling we have much excitement in store for us.

What a great adventure I am having; I have never been on a sailboat this big under sail before. I've played around on small boats with a few of my friends, rigging makeshift sails to push poles that have been haphazardly secured to the skiffs to catch the wind. Sometimes we succeeded, but most of the time, we failed. It was fun, but not very efficient; we always wound up either paddling or poling our way back home. I've played on smaller sailboats that were tied to their owner's wharf, and I've played on Uncle Justin's sailboat many times in the past, but this is my first true sailing voyage.

The relative quiet of the ride is exhilarating. Moving through the waters of the river without the annoying sound of a motor is more pristine. At the very least, the absence of noise allows for conversation without the need for screaming and shouting at one another to be heard. I can even hear the splashing sound made by the pelicans as they dive for fish thirty or forty yards away.

The weather is beginning to change; it's beginning to get cloudy. The wind is blowing much harder than it did when we started upriver and it has shifted more to the southwest. Since the wind picked up, we are moving faster, much faster than I ever thought possible. I do believe that *Dreadnought*, under full sail, is moving faster against the current than our motor vessel's propeller could manage.

While Lee, Brad, and Gus continued to watch for river obstructions, Felix pulled a harmonica out of his pocket and began playing folk tunes. Before long, we all joined in song as he played. We had a great time singing and laughing at Felix's half-crazed gestures.

The seventy-five-year-old sailboat was proving to me that its name was well-chosen. The splendid craft moves gracefully along in fearless pursuit of its destination. Guided by the skilled captain, the passengers aboard *Dreadnought* have nothing to fear; the vessel is living up to my wildest expectations. Great-grandmother Josephine could not have chosen a more appropriate name for this fine-sailing vessel.

I remained on deck throughout the trip up the river. Overcast skies brought darkness early; it was dark by the time we moored the boat to the fish market dock at Morgan City. There was a roar of thunder sounding from the north as the boys began taking down the sails, wrapping them and then securing them with their tie ropes.

THE ATCHAFALAYA MEETS MORGAN CITY 1921

Plans are to spend the night aboard Uncle Justin's boat, and conduct our business in the morning. After Uncle Justin sells all the goods he brought from the island, he and Aunt Sarah will go shopping for fresh provisions and other necessary and incidental items at the general store. Mama says this store is three times the size of Doc Fursom's store on Bayou Du Large. I can't wait to get inside and have a look around.

Shortly after the boat was secured to the large piles at the seafood dock, the weather began its furious assault on the city. The clouds burst; gale-force winds and driving rain pelted the top and sides of the cabin structure. The extreme forces of the storm pounded the boat against the side of the dock. Papa, Uncle Justin, and the boys worked frantically to finish securing the sails, forced to endure the nasty and unexpected onslaught.

Soaking wet, the men entered the lamp-lit cabin obviously shaken. Lightning bolts and deafening thunder preceded our crew's sudden appearance through the main cabin door. The chilled rainwater, which soaked their clothing had them all shivering.

Aunt Sarah and Mama assisted the men, giving them towels to dry off and handing them dry clothing; they were trying to get them warm as soon as possible. The men took turns, changing behind a couple of towels Aunt Sarah had stretched across the back corner of the cabin.

Uncle Justin told us that we were fortunate to have arrived at the dock site when we did. If the boat had not been securely tied when the weather broke, we might have found ourselves in a great deal of trouble. He said the wind was blowing so hard from the north that it was difficult to secure the sails. He was glad to have the assistance he got from all the other men.

Putting our fears to rest, he informed us that all was secure and so far nothing had been damaged by the storm. The wind was howling outside the cabin and the rain was beating hard against the north side of the boat. It looked like we were in for a long and stressful night.

Aunt Sarah produced the ginger cookies and the fresh bread she had baked earlier this morning. "There are a few jars of preserves that are opened. You can use them for spread on the bread, if anyone wants some," Aunt Sarah informed everyone.

By the time we finished eating, the rain had slacked; the wind continued to howl, as the strong norther made its way toward the Gulf of Mexico. The temperature inside the cabin began falling; it created an uncomfortable chill in the air. The changes in the atmosphere caused the windows to fog up from the excess moisture.

Aunt Sarah said she would let the oil lamp remain lit during the night to try to keep the cabin warm. She also announced the sleeping arrangements.

On each side the front cabin there is a set of bunk beds; each bed can accommodate two people. Mama and Papa have chosen the top bed on the right side of the cabin (the starboard side); Alma and I will occupy the one below them near the floor. Aunt Sarah and Uncle Justin will occupy the top bed on the left side bunk (the port side); Brad and Gus will sleep below them in the bottom bed near the floor. Felix and Lee will spend the night on two small mattresses that have been laid out on the floor.

After a little small talk, we hit the sack. "I hope everyone has pleasant dreams!" Papa wished aloud, as the howling wind brought tranquility and sleepy eyes to the listeners.

November 5, 1921

The strong cold front reduced the temperature by at least twenty-five degrees. The pleasant seventy-degree weather of yesterday has been replaced by crisp cold air and clear blue skies; there was bright sunshine and the gauge on the cabin wall read forty-three degrees. That is quite a change!

The aroma of hot sassafras tea stirred me from my bottom bunk bed. Alma and I were the last to rise; I shook her to make sure she was awake when I got out of bed. The men were nowhere in sight. Mama and Aunt Sarah were enjoying pleasant conversation and sipping a cup of the hot brew.

"Well, good morning. Wake up, you sleepyheads!" Aunt Sarah teased.

"Good morning!" Alma and I responded at exactly the same time. "Where are all the men?" I asked.

"They're out on deck. They are awaiting the proprietor of the seafood market," Aunt Sarah told me.

"It's cold outside!" Mama announced. "You and Alma will have to dress in warm clothes today," she instructed.

"Yes, Mama, we'll dress in warm clothes," I responded. "I hope we bought some!" I added.

Entering the cabin, Uncle Justin informed us that the seafood market would soon be open for business. "Adam and the boys will call the buyer to our boat as soon as he arrives," he told us.

Aunt Sarah was telling Mama she was hoping for a good price when we heard a knock on the cabin door. It was the fish buyer. Uncle Justin introduced Mr. Gordon Foret to everyone and offered him a cup of hot tea.

"I would be delighted" Mr. Foret said, pleased to accept my uncle's offer of Southern hospitality.

Mr. Foret said he was interested in all the goods that Uncle Justin and Aunt Sarah had to sell. He asked them to take a few minutes and give him a price on everything from the fish to the pecans. He said he was well aware of the quality of goods that the Addisons bring to town; he wanted to make a deal for the whole lot.

Uncle Justin informed Mr. Foret that the proprietor of the general store, Mr. Jenkins, was anticipating six large turtles; the turtles have been promised to him.

Mr. Foret said he and Mr. Jenkins were good friends; he offered to unload the turtles at his dock and hold them for the owner of the general store, if that was agreeable.

Having thoroughly enjoyed the cup of hot beverage, Mr. Foret asked Aunt Sarah what it was that he had just tasted. She informed him that it was sassafras tea, blended with fresh goat's milk and a little sugar.

"It was most excellent! I enjoyed it!" Mr. Foret commented. "Now I will leave for a while to allow you time to work up a price for all your goods," he said, before walking out the cabin door and heading for his store.

"It would be most convenient to sell everything we have at one place," Uncle Justin told Aunt Sarah.

They sat down beside each other at the dinner table and carefully went over the list of items they had for sale. It took them a long time to arrive at a figure they thought would be fair to both parties. Uncle Justin wrote a figure down on a piece of paper and showed it to Aunt Sarah before leaving the cabin to find Mr. Foret. In a few minutes, he was back in the cabin with a funny grin on his face.

"What happened?" Aunt Sarah inquired, seeming a bit apprehensive.

"Everything is sold! Mr. Foret is having his workers help Adam and the boys unload everything right now!" Uncle Justin happily announced.

When Papa came in for a cup of tea, my uncle informed him that he and Sarah were happy with the settlement; in fact, Mr. Foret gave him a better price for the goods than he had asked.

As soon as the boys finish unloading, we will be going to the general store; it is located just a couple of buildings downstream from where the boat is moored. Mr. Foret has given his permission to leave the boat at his dock until we are ready to leave.

Unloading took a couple of hours; it was nearly 11:00 a.m. when we were finally able to disembark and head for the prominent two-story building, the Morgan City General Store.

Morgan City streets were alive with activity. When we crossed the fence at the top of the levee, using the specially designed steps, we entered a world I had never seen the likes of before. There were horse-drawn carriages of every conceivable description and several Model T Ford motorcars traveling about. I was awestricken!

In front of the general store was parked a delivery wagon with the store's name printed on its sideboards. A steady flow of customers were entering and exiting the front doorway.

The first thing I noticed when we entered the store was the height of the ceiling; it must have been twenty feet high. There was a distinctive smell in the air; I don't know if it was the smell of the bare wood walls, floors, and ceiling, or if it was the combined odors from the contents of the massive building. It wasn't an offensive smell; it was merely a smell I was not familiar with.

The women were modestly dressed, but they all donned some sort of covering for their heads. Every woman I encountered was either wearing a hat, bonnet, or scarf. They were all friendly and personable; they didn't seem disturbed by the fact that none of the Addison women had anything but hair over the top of their heads.

I saw that my little sister was clinging tightly to Mama's hand, so I used the opportunity to ask permission to have a look around the store. Mama said it would be all right as long as I didn't leave the store without them; she was only being cautious, because the store was so large it might be possible for someone to get lost.

The general store must have contained anything a woman or a man could want to possess; they even sold eyeglasses! I took the grand tour without a guide; I walked over every inch of the place with wide eyes, leaving nothing unseen.

The boys were cutting up, hiding from each other, ducking around the corners of shelves, running about. I kept waiting for Mama, or one of the other grownups, to embarrass them with a public scolding, but they got away with their playful antics, at least as far as I know.

By the time I got back downstairs from the second story, Uncle Justin was preparing to check out the goods he was about to purchase from the store (settle-up time). I noticed he bought some beef jerky, a bag of sugar cookies, and other assorted treats. The store owner, Mr. Jenkins, deducted the value of the six large alligator turtles from the bill, and my uncle paid the balance.

The boys assisted the store attendants in loading the large pile of goods onto the delivery wagon that was waiting outside the store. Once loaded, the goods would be transported to the stair-crossing at the riverside of the fish market where our boat was moored.

I don't know where all the time went, but after conducting the business at the fish market and then shopping for provisions at the Morgan City General Store, it was already two in the afternoon before we started carrying goods over the levee fence to load them on the sailboat.

Once everything was securely aboard, Uncle Justin ordered the bow to be untied and the stern line loosened so the large sailing vessel could swing around in the swift river current. Once the bow came around and pointed south, the stern line was loosed from the large pile at the dock. With my uncle at the helm, the sails were unfurled and with a sudden jolt, the brisk north wind filled the canvas and propelled us downstream faster than the fast moving waters of the mighty Atchafalaya River. The wind must have been blowing at twenty miles an hour as we raced downriver at a steady clip.

"We're going to set a record for the fastest trip home if this wind persists!" Uncle Justin posed, having a broad smile on his face. "With the force of the strong north wind behind us and with the swift current moving below us, we just might make it to the homestead before dark!" Uncle Justin earnestly predicted.

It was an eerie experience for me to watch the activity of the water as we traveled along. The waters seemed angry and violent! I observed the turbulence (eddies, whirlpools and undercurrents). I could not help but pray that no one would fall overboard. In spite of my apprehensions, our trusty vessel was having no difficulty defying the river's menacing threats.

The evening shadows were growing when we reached the mouth of Deer Bayou. The *Early Rose* was patiently waiting there to be boarded for the journey back to Addison Landing. Reducing sail, Uncle Justin maneuvered his boat near the stern of Papa's boat so Lee and Brad could jump aboard from the bowsprit.

While Papa, Lee, and Brad were preparing our motorboat for the tow home, Uncle Justin had Felix and Gus go below deck to raise the keel back into its special holding box within the hull for traveling the shallow water of the bayou.

With all the sails furled and the towlines secured, the engine sounded, and Papa began to tow Uncle Justin's boat up Deer Bayou toward the homestead. We disturbed countless flocks of waterfowl, as they were attempting to roost in the cypress swamp along both sides of the waterway. The thickly shrouded tunnel overhead took virtually all the remaining daylight away from the water's surface, as we traveled slowly through the heart of the ridge.

It's a good thing that Papa has excellent eyes; by the time we reached the dock site to moor the boats, there was only the light of the stars to assist his vision.

Uncle Justin suggested we spend the night aboard the boat. Though it was true that it was too late to unload the store-bought goods and too dark to oar upstream, I think he just wanted to spend another night on his boat. No one objected; there was plenty enough food on board to have supper, and that was all we needed.

Aunt Sarah lit an oil lamp and we settled down for the evening. I asked Felix to play us a few tunes on his harmonica, and he gladly did so; the rest of the evening was spent enjoying song and merriment together.

As I lay in my bottom bunk bed below Mama and Papa, I was thinking of my favorite spot on the front steps of the *big house,* leaning my back against the large support column. There would be no storytelling tonight; I had sincerely hoped we would have gotten back from the city in time to hear Uncle Justin's next story. It was not meant to be. I relived the sailboat ride to Morgan City; it was an adventure I thoroughly enjoyed. Before I drifted off into another land, I took the time to thank God for our safe return home.

November 6, 1921

At the crack of dawn, Uncle Justin awakened everyone. The wind had completely diminished during the night, and the still calm and heavy fog made it cold and damp outside the cabin. Aunt Sarah predicted we would soon get our first frost of the season.

Papa agreed with my aunt's prediction. "It seems winter will soon be upon us. Cold might come early this year!" he announced, expressing his own feelings about the seasonal changes we were experiencing.

We loaded some of the newly purchased provisions aboard the push skiff for transport upstream to the *big house*. The boys carried what they could in the canoes, and we all made the slow journey toward the fountainhead.

The men spent most of the morning hauling goods from the landing to the front porch of the house. From there, the women put the goods away in the cupboard, pantry, and other storage places.

Pausing for a biscuit and a cup of hot coffee, Uncle Justin asked me how I liked the trip to the city. I praised him for his sailing skill, but that wasn't what he wanted to hear.

When I began to praise the seaworthiness of his craft, acknowledging the comfort and convenience of traveling on such a large vessel; when I began expressing my delight over the experience of hearing the wind biting at the canvas of the hoisted sails and feeling the power created by that natural union; when I told him I found the trip aboard *Dreadnought* exhilarating and pleasurable, he smiled, sensing my deep appreciation and admiration for his sailboat.

"Joseph Addison knew what he was doing when he designed and built this sailboat," Uncle Justin boasted.

Mama and Aunt Sarah told me that my impressions of Uncle Justin's prized possession had made his day. I had no trouble understanding the pride the men feel about the sailboats that Joseph Addison had built for them so many years ago. It is something we can all be proud of, I reasoned.

Uncle Justin and Papa settled down in their rockers for a smoke just before dinner. They were steeped in conversation about the prospects for a good trapping season. Mama and Aunt Sarah were scrambling to prepare the noon meal in between all the other chores that needed doing.

We will be dining on pot-roasted bear meat, baked sweet potatoes with a pan of cornbread on the side; that will stick to our ribs! Alma must have found a place to lie down and fall asleep; she's nowhere in sight. She'll present herself when the dinner bell rings I figured.

After dinner, Mama and Aunt Sarah went upstairs for a much-deserved rest. Alma fell asleep on one of the back porch swings. The boys ran out the back kitchen door and headed for the river. I didn't feel like tagging along with them; they hadn't asked me to go with them, not that it really mattered.

I chose to join the men on the front porch to listen to the latest topic of their conversation, but they had other ideas. Uncle Justin and Papa were fashioning a hammock from a remnant of seine netting which Mr. Jenkins had given them at the Morgan City General Store. It was Mr. Jenkins who suggested it would be just right for a hanging bed.

At each end of the makeshift bed, Uncle Justin weaved a stick through the netting. The eight-foot length of netting was secured to the two sticks with some of Felix's fishing twine. Next he tied a rope, one for each of the four corners of the newly fashioned stick supports (which acted like spreaders and support beams), so he could hang the netting by suspending it between two trees.

With the bed now finished, he and Papa strolled off the porch in search of the right trees. A few paces northeast of the fountainhead, they spotted two ash trees about twelve feet apart. Once the bed was tied to the trees, it was time to try it out. Offering Papa the first lay in the bed, Uncle Justin moved aside.

Papa insisted that Justin take the first lay in the hammock. The bed was suspended about four feet above the ground. I could hear Papa laughing as he wondered how his buddy would climb into his hanging bed. "How are you planning to get into that thing, Justin?" Papa was teasing him of course.

Sure enough, Uncle Justin's first attempt to mount the bed proved to be a hilarious failure. He lunged forward, trying to position himself lengthwise in the netting only to overshoot his intended mark, falling to the ground on the far side of the dangling contraption.

Papa and I were both in stitches after witnessing his failure.

Clearly determined not to give up, Uncle Justin made several attempts before he finally mounted the bed successfully. He lay there perfectly still, looking like an ear of fresh corn waiting to be removed from its shucks.

Not satisfied that he had mastered the technique of mounting his hammock, he clumsily dismounted and jumped back in; he did this over and over until he was able to land correctly every time. Dismounting the bed for about the fourth time, Uncle Justin asked Papa to give it a try.

To our amazement, Papa mounted the hammock the very first time he tried. He must have been paying very close attention when my uncle made his several attempts at success I surmised.

"Oh shucks, Adam! You must have used one of these things before!" Uncle Justin decried.

Papa was honest; he informed Uncle Justin that he used to enjoy the comfort of sleeping in a hammock many years ago, but he hadn't jumped into one for quite some time. Having displayed his agility (for his personal satisfaction), Papa dismounted from the hanging netting and yielded its comforts to Justin.

Papa told Uncle Justin to go ahead and enjoy his new hanging bed. "I'm going to sleep in a real bed!" Papa teased, disappearing through the front door, heading upstairs to take a nap next to Mama.

I watched amusingly as my Uncle Justin hopped into his bag of netting and tried desperately to get comfortable. After a few minutes of restlessness, he jumped out of his disagreeable nest and decided to join his wife upstairs in his customary bed.

I seized the opportunity to try the vacated shroud of netting on for size. Though I was able to climb into the net on my first attempt, it took some time for me to gain confidence enough to relax. As I lay there suspended between the two trees, I envisioned Uncle Justin's smiling face; a good and gentle-natured man, he is much like my father. He likes to play practical jokes, especially on the younger members of the family. He is constantly trying to draw a smile or a laugh out of you; he's good at it.

Whenever he calls me pumpkin, he does it in a way that makes smiling irresistible. One would have to see his facial expressions to appreciate why it is so; he can be a clown when he wants to mimic one—something he often does.

When my uncle is in a playful mood, he sometimes changes our names. He calls Alma "tea cake," he calls Aunt Sarah "Say," he calls Felix "Fee," he calls Gustave "goose," he calls Mama, "I," he calls Lee "Lee Lee," he calls Brad "Button," he calls Papa "Addie." With so many nicknames, it makes me wonder why he didn't call his goat "Abe" instead of "Abe Lincoln."

Whenever Uncle Justin uses one of our nicknames, there is a playful antic associated with it that is intended to generate laughter. For this reason, and many others, he is my favorite uncle. His story-telling and hearty conviviality, keeps us entertained during our fall visits to the island.

His face is always clean-shaven—Aunt Sarah sees to that. At six feet tall, he towers above his wife. He's a slim man with just a hint of a potbelly. His ears are rather large, a characteristic of all the Addison men. His brown hair is graying around the edges with a spatter of white on top. His brow is furrowed and the hair above his eyes is dark brown.

Uncle Justin loves good conversation. He enjoys listening to a good story, and he enjoys telling them himself. The first love in his life is Aunt Sarah, next is conversation; his third love is definitely smoking his pipe while relaxing in his favorite rocking chair on the front porch of the *big house*. I love the aroma of burning pipe tobacco. When the two elder gentlemen are smoking, I try to position myself so I can smell the aroma without inhaling the smoke.

This time of reflection reminds me of the important part that my Uncle Justin plays in my life; I don't care to imagine how life would be without having him around.

Turning my thoughts toward the activity of the boys this afternoon, I know they are busy scouring the banks of the river. I noticed they were each carrying a slingshot when they ran swiftly out the kitchen door. In seconds, they disappeared down the *beaten path*. I hope they find something worth keeping.

Mama and Aunt Sarah will be shelling peas after they get up from their naps. I'll probably join them on the back porch to assist them with the chore. I enjoy shelling peas.

As I pondered all these things, gentle northern breezes coaxed me beyond reason, and I succumbed to the beckoning call of senselessness.

November 6, 1921 (It's Midafternoon)

The first thing I remember seeing when I came back from dreamland was Alma's face; she broke my deep sleep with a song she was loudly singing to her ragdoll (something uncharacteristic for her). She definitely intended to rob me of my time of subliminal bliss.

Peering through the netting that formed the bed beneath me, I could see that Papa and Uncle Justin were already back in their rocking chairs; with one foot each producing locomotion, and one leg each draped over the left arm of their chairs, and with feet dangling in mid air, they obviously have been rejuvenated since they awakened from their afternoon nap. Their pipes were cupped in their right hands, using their right knees for a rest; there was a hint of smoke rising into the porch air; their mouths were moving, of course, as their left forearms lay atop the armrests of their rocking furniture. Naptime was over! I must have overslept!

I asked Alma if she wanted to swing awhile. Nodding her head in the affirmative, we strolled beneath the giant oak near the fountainhead and sat ourselves on the dangling planks. Suspended by long ropes hanging from the oak tree's massive branches, we soared through the air in pendulum fashion with varying degrees of reach. Alma could swing nearly as high as I could; she must be growing stronger, I reasoned. Last fall she wasn't able to keep up with me, but soon she will be doing everything I can do; maybe she will be better than I am at whatever she does. I hope she has gotten faster than I am in a foot race; maybe she will beat the boys, whenever we are challenged by them I hoped.

This first night back from the "big city" found us dining on fresh field peas, carrots, rice, and pan-fried bear meat. This was the third time any of us had tasted the meat from this honey-loving omnivore. Though coarse and stringy in texture, it is very tasty. It is as good as any meat, tame or wild, that I have ever eaten—the honey must not have had time to affect the taste of the meat; there was nothing sweet about it. I am sure I can attribute the taste sensations to the excellent cook who prepared the dish—Aunt Sarah! One of the best cooks anywhere! Ask anyone who has tasted her food!

Tonight will be a time for storytelling on the veranda of the *big house* once again. Uncle Justin has given no hints as to the topic he has chosen; I'm wondering what the subject will entail. Well, it won't be very long before I find out. This will be the seventh story of this fall season.

LIFE'S NOT ALWAYS A BED OF ROSES

We lingered at the table after supper. Uncle Justin recalled the sudden violence we experienced as the cold front unleashed its energy against us at the dock in Morgan City. He shared that the norther came upon us like a marauding juggernaut attempting to destroy us to satisfy its sacrificial cravings. "God was merciful!" Uncle Justin acknowledged in reverential tones. "He held back the curtain until the proper stage was set. Thank God that He has authority over all the powers that be. His mercy was upon us."

Uncle Justin has had experience with violent weather before. His somber reflection of this recent encounter lends a hint of the seriousness of his past weather-related adventures. Everyone had expressed their appreciation to the Lord Almighty for sparing us from any harm from the big storm this summer. I guess the mood was set for what my uncle was about to share.

We all accompanied him to the front porch and took our favorite seats. Uncle Justin did something queer; he didn't light his pipe. I noticed Papa had left his pipe in his pocket also, as my uncle began to speak.

"To this point, all the stories Adam and I have shared with you have been adventurous, exciting, and even historical. Many of the stories have yielded new revelations about our family heritage. Some have stimulated our imaginations and have kindled new and exciting impressions of many persons we never had a chance to talk to in the first person. Some of the stories have been fantastic—without exaggeration. Sadly, there are other kinds of stories that need to be shared. Tonight's story is neither exciting nor glamorous, but it is a valid part of the Addison family legacy.

"Life is filled with experiences. There are events that bring joy, happiness, satisfaction, anxiety, fear, anguish, tears, remorse, and sometimes even despair. Tonight will be a story of family tragedy.

"It was late in the summer of 1909. Aunt Clara and I were living alone in the *big house*. We laid my mother, Elizabeth Addison, to rest earlier that same year.

"Sanders and his wife, Martha, were living in the *little house*. They had come to live on the island after giving their home on Bayou Du Large to Adam and Ida for a wedding present back in 1904.

"We had an unusually hot summer that year ,1909. We experienced a period of drought during the better part of July and August. Our crops did not manage very well due to the combination of heat and extremely dry conditions.

"Finally, the rain came. It rained continuously for an entire week. That's how it happens sometimes. When you want it to rain, it doesn't. When it does rain and you need it, it rains far too much. So it goes with life it seems.

"After the seven-day soaking, the sun returned to scorch the earth for three straight weeks, another drought seemed to be in the making. The crops failed!" Uncle Justin lamented.

"1909 was a year of heartaches for the Addisons. In particular, the Addisons who were living on Deer Island were experiencing a time of want and a time of loss. Elizabeth's death was weighing heavy on our hearts; she was being sorely missed. The failed crops left us short of many food items. We had to replant late in the season and we had to pray for a harvest that would take weeks to produce something—anything. For many days, we had only potatoes to eat. We had run out of ammunition and powder for our guns, and there was no money to buy anymore. It was a year of struggle, but not a time for despair. There would be a new crop maturing in a month or two, and we clung to the hope of a good fall harvest.

"One late afternoon, the clouds began racing inland. They seemed to glide over the treetops, heavy with moisture from the gulf. Their dark colors portended rain and we had a few light showers during the night.

"For the next couple of days, the skies remained overcast. Something did not seem right. Sanders and I exchanged thoughts of concern, as we rocked here together on the front porch. The yard animals were restless. The cows were lowing, emitting deep bellowing sounds in an uncharacteristic manner. They seemed to be aware of something that we suspected, but weren't quite sure of. What could it be?

"Seagulls began demanding our attention, making their shrill calls from high above the treetops as they flew overhead, heading north. Our cautious observations led us to believe that there was severe weather brewing out in the gulf. Just how bad a storm it would be, we had no way of knowing. We would have to wait and see.

"I remember asking Sanders if he thought we should prepare for a big blow, but he seemed to not be overly concerned. I told him I would walk the *landing path* to see if *Dreadnought* and *Muskrat* were well-moored, just in case. I told him I did not want to have to worry about the boats after nightfall.

"When I reached the landing, I closed the cabin doors on the big boat, and I secured shut all deck ports and windows. I secured both vessels with additional mooring lines, tying ropes to a couple of the large trees nearby for added safety.

"Late that afternoon, as I observed the western sky, I saw something I had seen before. From the viewpoint of the back porch, the western sky was colored with tones of gray, yellow, and green clouds. Once, before a great storm, I had seen this eerie portrait in the sky.

"This observation, combined with the other signs we had witnessed, had me convinced that we were getting ready to be hit by a strong storm. I informed my wife Clara of my concerns, and we walked over to the *little house* to discuss the matter with Sanders and Martha.

"I shared my feelings with my aunt and uncle. I told them I had gone to the landing and the two sailboats were as secure as I could make them, having added additional mooring lines: 'I believe we are prepared for the worst if the weather intensifies into a storm during the night. I would rather be safe than sorry,' I told them.

"Sanders continued to weigh everything I told him, as he puffed on his pipe in his sitting room. After a few moments of silence, he instructed Martha to begin shutting up the house. He told her they would be spending the night with Clara and me in the *big house*.

"After closing up the house, we went to the out kitchen to secure everything that might fly through the air in a strong wind.

"Clara and Martha went ahead of us to the *big house* to get out extra candles and fill all the lamps with kerosene. Meanwhile, Sanders and I secured everything in the yard. We checked the chicken coop doors and tied them shut. We did the same to the doors on the corn-crib, outhouses, and the smokehouse. The barn had a breezeway, and we knew the doors were tied in the open position. We felt that would be good enough. We brought extra firewood inside the kitchen— enough wood and kindling to burn in the stove for three days.

"The last thing Sanders and I did was to drag the two dugout canoes from the banks of the stream. We tied the oar skiff in such a way that it would remain afloat in the center of the stream. It was far too heavy for us to drag ashore. The plan was to monitor the amount of water the rain deposits in the hull and bail it out if necessary to keep it from sinking—frankly, we didn't think that would be a problem. We drug the two canoes with all the paddles and oars underneath the house to prevent damage that might be caused by falling tree limbs.

"After supper, we sat together right here on the veranda. Our conversation was centered on our past experiences with storms. When the rains failed to materialize and the winds remained near normal, we wondered if we had over reacted. We could hear thunder from squalls in the distance, but none were affecting us as yet.

"We must have talked until midnight. I believe the nervousness created by our anxious concerns kept us awake much longer than we anticipated. When our eyes grew heavy, we pulled our rocking chairs inside and we closed the front door, bolting it shut—something we rarely do.

"We had all the windows closed and all the shutters bolted shut. The house was closed up tight in preparation for the anticipated storm. Time would tell if we had done all this in vain. I felt we had taken every conceivable precaution and I had absolutely no trouble falling asleep.

"I was first to arise the next morning. I put some wood in the stove to bake some biscuits and to make a fresh pot of coffee. It was raining heavily outside, but the wind was not violent. Rain was falling straight down from the sky as the trees just stood there, practically unaffected. Where were the heavy winds?

"The biscuits were beginning to brown when Clara, Sanders, and Martha entered the kitchen. Soon after, we ate breakfast and discussed the unusual weather. I asked Sanders what he made of the situation. He told me the absence of heavy winds was peculiar and he didn't know what was going on. We decided to go onto the back porch for a closer look.

"The rain was falling so hard that the chicken coop appeared as a faint shadow in the distance; it was barely visible. Like a white sheet, the heavy rain obscured the *little house* completely; it's only one hundred paces from where we stood on the back porch. The two cisterns were the only objects clearly visible and they were both only a few feet from the back of the house.

"The humidity was so high that it was uncomfortably cold standing beneath the shelter of the porch. We each took a swing and decided to light up our tobacco pipes for a good smoke. We used the swings for a while, having to raise our voices to be heard, but the dampness in the air sent us back into the house before we could finish our smoke.

"Clara and Martha were going about their business as though nothing was amiss. They were busy discussing things that ladies enjoy talking about. There was not a hint of worry detectable in their voices. I was happy to see their minds were at ease.

"The rain continued to fall in torrential fashion. Conspicuously absent, were the strong winds that are usually associated with any dangerous weather conditions. We found that very strange.

"Early afternoon found Sanders and I sitting on the veranda. Clara and Martha were both upstairs taking themselves a nap. We were steeped in conversation about the long hot summer and this year's disastrous crop failure.

"I was in the middle of preparation for a second planting in mid-September. This heavy rainfall could interfere with the plans I had. There was still a great deal of work that needed to be done; a dry spell would be needed to accomplish the task.

"Gradually the winds began to build. At first, the change was hardly noticeable. After all, occasional gusts were not anything out of the ordinary during any rainstorm. In less than one hour, the winds had strengthened to a level that was clearly discernible. Strong wind from the east and southeast began to blow rain onto the front porch, forcing us to vacate our seats and run inside, pulling our rockers through the front door behind us.

"By midafternoon, the wind was howling. The deluge persisted, and the combination of rain and wind caused the roof to leak in many places. We scrambled upstairs and moved the bedding to the lee-side of the house to try to keep it dry.

"We could feel the wind's assault against the house. Pressure was building against the walls of our dwelling. Rainwater was finding its way inside, as darkness enveloped us prematurely.

"Clara lit a couple lamps. She placed one on the kitchen table, and the other on the dinner table where we were seated. The roaring wind and pounding rain forced us to yell at each other in order to be heard. The terrible storm was bearing down upon us in relentless fury. There was no safe haven and no way to escape the effects of this onslaught. Recognizing the gravity of the situation, Sanders led us in heartfelt prayer.

"After a three-hour assault, an eerie calm fell upon the home-stead. Concerned about the state of the two sailboats, I decided that I should take advantage of the lull and make a quick trip to the land-ing to evaluate the damages; at least I could be sure they remained properly moored. It was about six-thirty in the evening. The sky seemed clear overhead. There was enough light remaining in the day for me to hurry down the stream and loosen the mooring lines if they needed to be adjusted. There would be plenty time to make it back to the house before dark.

"Clara is the only person who raised any objection to my idea. She pleaded with me to wait until morning to check on the boats. By then, she felt the entire ordeal might be over. She was deeply con-cerned that the storm might start again before I was able to return. She said I might get lost or hurt. Maybe something bad might hap-pen to me.

"I tried to reassure her by saying I wasn't going to take the oar skiff downstream. I would run down the *landing path* instead. I told her I would not take any chances, and I would be back shortly.

"With that tiny bit of reassurance, Clara tentatively smiled; she seemed to accept my intended plan. She merely told me to be careful. I kissed her tenderly on her lips and told her I would soon return for a loving embrace. 'Don't worry! God will watch over me,' I told her, as I left her standing right here on the front porch of the *big house*.

"When I neared Deer Bayou, I was surprised to see the tide had risen so high. Water was overflowing the banks by several feet. I was in waist-deep water, and I still had not reached the dock. I proceeded cautiously, using the trees along the path for support. I could no longer judge where the edge of the bayou was. I certainly did not want to fall into the deep water. The swift undercurrents below the surface might suck me downstream and carry me 'who knows where.' Fearfully, I thought if that happened I might drown.

"I could see that both boats were listing on the side of the wharfs where their mooring lines had been tied too tight. I would have to somehow reach the docks and loosen the lines. I knew if I didn't, there was a possibility that one or both of the vessels might take on enough water to sink.

"Slowly, but deliberately, I made my way through chest-deep water to reach the wharf. The current in the bayou was treacherous. I proceeded to the bulwarks of *Dreadnought* and climbed aboard. I was getting a chill. My clothing was soaked and the water was cold. I was determined to hurry and get the job finished as soon as possible. I had to cut the lines. They were too tight to unfasten from the piles. Having extra rope aboard, I was able to re-tie the vessel high enough on the huge piles to allow movement both up and down as the tide would determine. I followed the same procedure on the *Muskrat* and my job was done. Thank God the pilings of the wharf were six or eight feet above the water level. I was confident the adjustments I made to the ropes had made the moorings safe and secure.

"Once everything was adjusted and the boats were floating level once again, I climbed back out of the boat and carefully made my way toward the *landing path*. This endeavor was dangerous because the current was moving so fast I had to grab from one exposed piling to the other to keep myself from being swept away. Finally, I reached the *landing path* that was now five feet underwater. I found myself clinging desperately to anything I could grasp with either hand. I slowly made the journey uphill to shallower and shallower water. When the water was only to my knees, I noticed that darkness was fast approaching. I remember thinking that I better make it back to high ground before all daylight escaped me. It was dangerous enough without any additional hindrance or obstacle.

"I reached the high ground in the nick of time. Not only had darkness fallen, but the storm began an assault from the north and northwest. This was the opposite direction from which its initial attack began several hours earlier. In a very short time, I began to feel the effects of the violence and ferocity of the raging tempest.

"I was about halfway back to the house when I first heard the faint cries of Clara, her voice was being carried toward me by the strong winds. At first, I thought I was only imagining her cries, but as I drew nearer and nearer to the *big house*, I could hear her mournful pleas more clearly.

"The sound of her voice still haunts me: 'Justin! Justin! Where are you?' she cried at the top of her voice. 'Justin! Where are you?' There was the sound of panic in her voice as she continued to scream: 'Justin! Justin! Justin!' Over and over she shouted at the top of her voice.

"I struggled against the wind and rain to get to my beloved wife. The wind was now blowing so hard that the rain peppered me like the shot from a scatter gun. I had to shield my face as I leaned forward to walk against the powerful forces that were trying to throw me backward.

"Clara had run out of the house to come find me. When I reached her, she clutched me in a tight embrace. She told me she could not bear to think something had happened to me. She was blaming herself for my predicament: 'I should not have allowed you to leave the house,' she bewailed.

"Realizing the love she was sharing with me was selfless and genuine, I regretted my decision to go and check on the boats. Clara was clinging tightly to me as though she was desperately happy that I was still alive.

"I kissed her and told her that I loved her. We broke free from our embrace and proceeded to struggle against the cold wind-driven rain, slowly making our way to the house.

"The front porch was now the lee-side of the house. I could see Sanders and Martha peering into the darkness, each holding a lamp in hand. The two light sources assisted me in finding the house amidst the blinding rain.

"When we arrived back at the house, we immediately toweled off and changed into dry clothing. We nestled around the woodstove and sipped on several cups of hot coffee, trying to drive the chill from our bones.

"Now I was beginning to question the wisdom of my decision to leave Clara to check on the boats for a different reason. After a few minutes near the heat of the stove, I was all right. The chill had departed from me. My wife Clara was struggling. I hugged her tightly, trying desperately to help her stop shivering. I could see that her hair was still damp, so I toweled it dry. After two cups of hot coffee, she didn't care for anymore. Aunt Martha fixed her some tea.

"I began to worry when I realized she could not quit shivering. Her lips appeared swollen, and she was beginning to turn blue. I coaxed her into drinking a cup of hot tea, but she could barely get it down. We became so perplexed with caring for Clara that we nearly forgot that the storm was still unleashing its fury outside.

"In a mournful state, I lamented, 'If only I hadn't decided to go check the boats,' I cried. I couldn't hold back my tears. The situation was one of helpless desperation.

"Clara looked at me with penetrating eyes and said in a feeble voice: 'It's not your fault, Justin, you did what you had to do, you did the right thing. I should have entrusted your care and safety to Almighty God. How foolish I was to doubt Him. What good could I have done if something had happened to you? It was a foolish thing for me to do!' she insisted.

"I kissed her gently on her forehead and asked her to save her strength. I threw our bedding on the floor near the stove, and I laid myself down beside her, embracing her around her wrappings, trying to drive the cold from her convulsing body.

"I pleaded with God to keep her well. Martha and Sanders threw their bedding next to ours on the floor near the stove. By now, nearly the entire house was wet inside. Some of the shingles had been blown from the roof and the rain was coming inside in liberal doses. In fact, the kitchen was the only dry spot left in the house.

"I don't remember exactly when, but sometime during the night we fell asleep. When morning came, Clara was no longer with us. She lay there peacefully beside me. There was an angelic look about her. Her face seemed to have a special glow about it. I wept bitterly as I embraced her, knowing I had lost everything that was dear to me. I cannot describe to you the pain I felt.

"Sanders and Martha tried to be strong for my benefit, but they mourned and cried as much as I did. The violence of the storm had ended, but the effects of the storm would last for the rest of my life. I wrapped my dear Clara in a clean white sheet. There was a drizzling rain outside. I instructed Sanders and Martha to remain in the house. There was no reason to risk anyone else getting sick.

"Holding a shovel in one hand and carrying dear Clara over my shoulder, I walked through the rain down the *wagon path* to the cemetery, and laid my dearly beloved wife in her final resting place.

"As I dug her grave, I remembered the words that she spoke to me as we embraced during the storm near the stream: 'I could not bear to think that something had happened to you, Justin. I should not have allowed you to leave the house.' Oh! How those words did haunt me. I had to stop digging several times to cry. I laid her to rest that day, commending her soul to God. It was the hardest thing I have ever been forced to endure.

"So ends the story of tragedy during the storm of 1909. Aunt Clara now rests in the family cemetery, a victim of the storm's violent fury: 'Rest in peace, Clara.' Amen."

There was not a dry eye on the porch. Mama and Aunt Sarah had to go inside. They were crying uncontrollably. I don't believe Alma understood it all, but when she saw everyone else crying, she began to cry also. The boys were all sobbing near the balustrade.

I began to lose control of my emotions when I witnessed Papa and Uncle Justin sobbing openly before me. I had never seen grown men cry this way before. They placed their hands over their eyes and sobbed, weeping for the loving, caring, selfless matron, my uncle's first wife, Clara Addison. She loved Uncle Justin more than her own life.

As I lay in bed, I thought of the love Aunt Clara had for her husband. That is why the event was so tragic I reasoned; that storm stole her love from my uncle. This story of tragedy has been my first experience of sharing in the grief and pain associated with the untimely death of one of my family members. It has been a painful lesson, another side of life's unexpected adventures and one that has been difficult to digest.

It was nearly impossible for me to dispel the thoughts of the dramatic scenes portrayed in Uncle Justin's story. Eventually, I abandoned all unpleasant feelings; I began another journey, which lost me in consciousness.

Chapter Nine

THANKSGIVING: GETTING READY!

November 21, 1921 (Bedtime Comes Early)

Tomorrow is the day before Thanksgiving. There will be no time for storytelling tonight; the chickens are not yet settled on their roosts, and we are already in bed for the evening.

There is a new moon out; its location between the earth and the sun has stolen its luster. The temperature is in the upper thirties; we may have our first frost in the morning. Aunt Sarah warned that tomorrow would be a day of preparation, and there will be much work to be done. Heeding her admonition, we were expected to get a good night's sleep: "I'll tolerate no foolishness!" she ordered in her high-pitched voice; after supper was done, we scurried upstairs in respectful obedience to her plea.

As I lay in my bed, I tried desperately to fall asleep. There was no moonlight for inspiration, but there were two owls talking and carrying on with each other in the distant treetops. In the crisp cold fresh air, their hooting sounded like it was emanating from my window sill—that might be slightly exaggerated. The condition I find necessary to succumb to oblivion is complete silence; it takes peace and quiet to allow me to fall asleep before I am ready. Even nature is not cooperating. If the owls stop hooting, there will be the gurgling sound of the fountainhead. I was exasperated; I could not rid myself of the restlessness I was being forced to endure.

I began to think about how quickly our holiday on Deer Island was coming to an end; we will soon be leaving for the trapping camp at Plumb Bayou. We have been at Uncle Justin's place for twenty-eight days; we have one week left. Papa told us we would be leaving next Tuesday after the noon meal.

I wish fall would never end, but it always does. *Ninny* and *Nanny* will soon be delivering their young; we should be there for when that happens. Our rooster, *George Washington*, probably has his hens with all their nests full of eggs by now. The piglets have probably doubled their weight, dining on the rich marsh vegetation around the campsite—that's if the alligators are dormant and not interested in fresh pork meat.

Finally, my feathered friends quit hooting. It's time to say good night, Lord. I pray we have a wonderful Thanksgiving Day celebration this season; I want to thank you for your many blessing. Have mercy on my family and me. Amen.

November 22, 1921

The first frost of the season blanketed the ground before sunrise this morning; Aunt Sarah ushered everyone out of bed at five thirty. While waiting for the biscuits, I decided to go outside so I could make the frozen grass crunch beneath my feet.

Papa and Uncle Justin were swinging on the back porch, smoking their pipes between sips of hot coffee. Papa asked me if I was losing my mind walking over the iced ground in the chilling moisture of the predawn air. With that hint of a mild scolding, I returned to the comfort of the warm kitchen and waited for my aunt's biscuits to come out of the oven.

Mama had instructed me not to disturb Alma when I got out of bed this morning. There's no need to have her up early, she told me last night.

The boys were having a yawning contest at the dinner table; it was contagious. After watching them open their mouths as wide as they could numerous times, I involuntarily began to yawn myself. Isn't that a strange thing? I wasn't sleepy and I didn't feel like doing it, but I was yawning tit-for-tat with the rest of them.

After breakfast, Papa, Uncle Justin and the boys walked out into the back yard; my uncle had a gun in his hand when he exited the kitchen door. They are heading for the holding pen behind the chicken coop to shoot the fatted hog; she's had a steady diet of corn for nearly three weeks.

The day after we used the sled to visit the cemetery, the men put a special wooden enclosure atop the solid-planked skid and trapped a hog in the pen so they could give it a good purge. She's been a bit gruff, but a steady diet of corn has kept its disposition agreeable. She's gained quite a bit of weight; it's amazing what corn can do.

Uncle Justin uses this portable holding pen to catch a hog whenever he wants one; since most of them are running wild around the homestead, he uses this device instead of running all over trying to catch one with a rope, which is no small task. The entrance to the pen has a trap door; the enclosure is baited with corn or discarded vegetables (not suitable for the table). When the pig smells the food, the temptation to eat the bait overcomes its fear to enter through the only opening in the pen. When it nears the food, a string securing the door in the open position is tripped, and the trapdoor is closed behind it. It is an effective tactic; I've seen it work before.

There is a good reason for setting the hog trap atop the sled. The hogs around the homestead are very heavy—some weigh as much as five hundred pounds. Catching them in this way affords an easy way to carry the hog to the slaughtering table, using a cow for locomotion.

The hog in the pen is not much shy of five hundred pounds, Uncle Justin told me. She was caught the same day that the trap was set. The females are much better tasting than the boars; the males, especially the big ones, have a strong taste he told me.

I was startled by the discharge of the gun behind the chicken coop; the loud blast sent a chill down my spine. It was a deafening sound, amplified for my hearing by the cold quiet morning air.

The shutters on the rear kitchen window were opened, so I ran to take a look from a distance; I had absolutely no interest in witnessing the gory scene from a closer vantage point. I knew that immediately after the shot rang out, a sharp knife would be used to slit the pig's throat to bleed it. I could see the boys gathered in a circle around the older men who were busy collecting the blood from the fresh neck wound.

The huge hog lay on its side motionless; it was a morbid scene. The notion suddenly struck me that I was glad I was not a man; I was more than happy that this task was their responsibility and not mine. I tried desperately to rid myself of the unpleasant feeling I was experiencing as I stood there staring out the window.

Reluctantly, I followed Mama and Aunt Sarah out the kitchen door as they headed for the butchering table (a table used for many purposes, including eating). We cleared the top of the huge table of leaves and other debris, preparing it to receive the carcass. It was soon evident that the chickens had been paying regular visits to the top of the table and the two benches—one that followed each side. Mama instructed me to fetch a pale of water from the stream so the surfaces could be thoroughly scrubbed.

The iron cauldron had been filled with water yesterday evening; a steady blaze from the fire beneath it is tickling the bottom of the large kettle and the water is already boiling. The boys have a stockpile of wood they had gathered from the river bank nearby to continue to fuel the fire.

Rear Of "The Big House"
Kitchen, Porch, Cisterns,
Chicken House, Out House, Wood Storage Shed,
Cauldron, Table, Wagon Path To Cemetary (This Side Of House)

Using the cow to move the carcass-laden sled to the side of the table, the hog lay there on its side waiting to be lifted into place. Felix and Lee arrived with several burlap sacks from the corncrib; some of them were spread on the freshly scrubbed surface. The pig was dead and would soon be in position to be processed; the water was on the boil and ready for dipping. It's time for a short break; the hard work is about to begin, a process the local Frenchmen call a *boucherie* (it's a kind of celebration of the slaughter of a pig, the preparation and dressing of the meat, the preserving of the residual pork and the festivity that follows, culminating in a wonderful meal, which always includes fried pork rinds).

As we watched the flames of the fire embrace the cauldron, we all drank a cup of sassafras tea and talked about the massive size of the pig we were about to assault with scraping knives and butcher blades. Using a stone, Aunt Sarah sharpened her best carving knives to a razor's edge. I could not help being impressed by her diligence; what a hard-working woman she is! She never stops! Though she is small in stature, she has a very healthy body. She has a heart of gold;

I'm glad she married my uncle. If anyone could fill the void left by Aunt Clara's untimely death, Aunt Sarah has certainly filled the bill.

Papa instructed me to fetch a pail of water from the cistern and get the ladle from the kitchen; he wants to be sure there is fresh drinking water available near the worksite.

The water in the open kettle is scalding hot. Sacks have been placed on the carcass of the hog, covering it completely. Using a long-handled pot to dip out the hot water from the cauldron, the boiling water is poured slowly onto the sacks. As water is taken from the pot, more water is added and allowed to boil. Once the sacks are steaming, and saturated with the boiling water, one sack at a time is removed so the hide can be scraped. More hot water is applied as needed. Special sharp knives are used to scrape the hair from the skin (some people use cane knives to scrape the hides); it's kind of like shaving, Uncle Justin says.

Papa and Uncle Justin took turns performing this arduous task until one entire side was done, the carcass was then flipped over; the process of steaming the hide, preparing it for scraping, and then scraping the hair from the skin, began all over again until all the hair was removed.

Once the hide has been scraped, the head is severed; the breastbone is split with an ax. A knife is sent down the length of the belly; the entrails are removed and placed aside for safekeeping. The legs are chopped off at the first joint using a meat cleaver. The skin and fat is cut away from the meat.

By this time, all the water has been removed from the hot cauldron. The fire has been continuously fed fresh fuel. The skin and fat has been cut into pieces and thrown into the pot. The result is the formation of two useful products.

The hog fat is rendered into oil. It is dipped out in its liquefied state and placed in large crock jars where it will cool and resolidify. This lard will be used for weeks to come in Aunt Sarah's kitchen for cooking and frying other foods.

Once the oil has been removed, the remaining crispy treats are placed into a clean wooden box and salted to taste. Once they are cool enough, they are consumed with mouth-watering enthusiasm.

Of the two by-products, the most important one is the lard. Properly stored, it will remain useful for weeks to come. The second product, though there were several pounds of it, will most likely be consumed in a couple of days—fried pork rinds are that good! If these two products were the only benefit derived from butchering a hog, the time and effort expended would be well worthwhile to me, as long as I'm not the one who has to kill and clean the animal. That does seem a bit selfish I reasoned; nonetheless, that's the way I feel.

I like the smaller pieces of the fried pork skins best. When warm, they almost melt in your mouth. Aunt Sarah puts just the right amount of salt on them to enhance their special flavor.

More water is now being added to the cauldron; this time it will be filled only to one-third of its capacity. With only its eyes removed, the head, feet, and other less desirable parts of the hog, are put on the boil together with some of Aunt Sarah's special seasoning: salt, fresh parsley, green onions, white onions, celery, ground peppercorns, and chopped fresh peppers.

The carcass is quartered and hung from a tree limb to dry in the cold air. With a temperature in the thirties, it has been a comfortable day for hog butchering. The excess blood will be allowed to drain from the dangling quarters. If the weather was colder, it would be allowed to hang for a day or two before being cut up and salted-down in crock jars, just like the bear meat was. Since the temperature is a little too warm, the meat will be processed sooner; this will have little effect on the quality of the meat though hanging it for a longer period is preferred by most.

Mama and Aunt Sarah are busy cleaning the hog gut, turning it inside out for careful scraping. They have to be careful to avoid tearing the thin casing; a small forked stick is used to turn the gut inside out. The pig's stomach is also cleaned and scraped for later use. (It will probably be stuffed with pork dressing and baked in the oven.)

The pig gut can be sliced into pieces and cooked as chitterlings or they can be stuffed with meats and various seasonings, cooked then served as sausage. Aunt Sarah plans to stuff the stomach with pork bits and spices, rice, potatoes, and fresh seasoning. It will be sewed shut, using needle and thread, after it has been filled with stuffing; it will be roasted and then sliced for serving at the dinner table.

The heart, kidneys, and many remaining interesting parts have been cut into small pieces; they are now being cooked with the head and the feet of the disappearing hog in the iron cauldron.

Once all the parts have been thoroughly cooked, they are removed and cut into smaller pieces. All meat is removed from the skull and legs. Once all the boned meat and internal organs have been finely chopped and mixed with a bit more seasoning to taste, it is put back into the pot and cooked a little longer. When the fresh seasoning is well blended into the mixture and cooked to my aunt's liking, then the resulting concoction is poured into pans and allowed to congeal. Once the mixture has cooled, the "hog's head cheese" is sliced into portions and eaten. Boy! That stuff is good!

The work of processing the hog now finished, we all sat down at the outside table (freshly scrubbed and clean once again). We feasted sumptuously on fried pork skins and "hogs head cheese." Uncle Justin complimented everyone for a job well done. Aunt Sarah added a sincere "amen" to my uncle's accolade.

After lounging around for a while, Aunt Sarah instructed Felix and Gus to fetch the three Peking ducks; she had been corn-feeding them for the past two weeks. "Tame ducks for supper tonight!" Aunt Sarah announced, as the boys showed up with the three birds, carrying them by the feet as the poor creatures loudly voiced their displeasure.

Reaching for the duck's necks, one at a time, she promptly wrung their heads off, dropping them to the ground so they could flop around awhile. When they stopped moving, Mama and Aunt Sarah started plucking. Once the feathers were removed, Felix and Lee assumed the task of cleaning the birds for the pot, saving the hearts, gizzards, and livers, of course.

I decided to walk back to the house for a cup of tea or coffee. My little sister was resting peacefully on one of the swings. She was lying down, clutching her ragdoll tightly in her arms, motionless. I thought she was asleep, but as I stood over her she opened her eyes.

"You're playing opossum, aren't you, Alma?" I teased.

Alma reached up and grabbed me around my neck and she whispered in my ear: "I love you, Nora."

"I love you too, Alma," I told her. As I sat down to chat with her awhile, Mama asked me to lend a hand cutting fresh seasoning for tonight's supper and tomorrow's dressings and gravies.

The daytime hours were quickly winding to a close. I don't know exactly what time it was when we finished our work in the back, but it must have been at least five o'clock when I started helping to cut up the seasoning.

The men were given the remainder of the afternoon off. Papa and Uncle Justin went for a fishing trip in the oar skiff. The boys went in the opposite direction, heading down the *beaten path* toward the river; vowing to return with treasure, they quickly disappeared from view.

Aunt Sarah never raised an eyebrow over the boy's frivolous boasting. She commented that she had heard that nonsense many times before; with all their high expectations, there is still nothing to show for their endless attempts at searching the bend in the river. "One day they will learn that there is no treasure to be found on those clam shell deposits along the river bank," my aunt emphatically stated.

I guess after all the years of looking and not finding, it has made my aunt overly pessimistic about their chances. Privately, I was hoping they would make a significant discovery in order to bring back an air of excitement that has prevailed thus far during our entire stay here this fall.

Once all the seasoning was cut, Mama told me I could relax for the remainder of the day; she and my aunt would carry on with the rest of the kitchen chores. Alma wanted to walk to the pecan orchard to see the squirrels running through the trees. Mama said it would be all right but warned us to watch the time. "You don't want to be caught in the woods after it gets dark," she correctly cautioned.

Soon after dismissing me, Mama and Aunt Sarah went upstairs for a short nap. The ducks were in the oven, and the other dishes were simmering on the stove; they were merely taking advantage of the temporary solitude.

Alma and I headed out the front door of the *big house*; we hurried down the front porch steps and raced toward the northeast path that would lead us to the pecan orchard.

By this time, the pecan harvest was all but finished. The boys had visited the orchard several times in the past few weeks. During the short time we've been here, they have gathered well over a hundred pounds of the oily nuts; some were sold in Morgan City and other sacks are stored in Aunt Sarah's pantry. The last report from the boys was that there were only enough pecans left to feed a few squirrels; the frequent cold blasts have probably denuded the trees by now, I reasoned.

Alma and I strolled along the orchard pathway singing merry tunes and enjoying one another's company. There were a large number of crows calling to each other from the treetops along the well-worn trail, as we continued toward the clearing.

A very large snake slithered quickly across the walking path only a few feet ahead of us; it was apparently trying to avoid us since it was moving so fast. I was glad that my little sister was busy looking up at the crows. If she had seen the massive serpent, there is no doubt in my mind that I would still be trying to catch up with her to try to calm her down. It probably would have resulted in a foot race back to the house.

When we arrived at the pecan orchard clearing, we began looking for any nuts the boys and the foraging squirrels may have missed. Without warning, I felt something tugging at the back of my clothing. It couldn't have been Alma! I knew that for sure; she was in front of me looking for nuts. For a few seconds, I felt really scared; a myriad of silly notions crossed my mind.

It was *Abe Lincoln*, Uncle Justin's mischievous goat. I must have jumped two feet off the ground when he butted me gently with his head. He looked like he was laughing at me, until I realized he was chewing the cud.

"Why did you scare me like that *Abe*!" I scolded.

Alma had seen the whole incident; seeing the goat had gotten the best of me, she burst out in laughter. My little sister was laughing so hard she fell on the ground, dropping her doll in the process, as she laughed and laughed uncontrollably.

It didn't take long for me to see the humor that Alma was enthusiastically enjoying at my expense. I quickly regained my senses and burst into a fit of contagious hilarity myself.

"I forgive you *Abe Lincoln*!" I told the goat. "That ornery creature must really like us," I told Alma. He had to go through a lot of trouble to follow us all the way over here just to play with us," I added.

Alma agreed with my deduction. We decided to quit looking for nuts, and we played with the goat instead. He seemed to enjoy our attention; he allowed us to stroke him on the head and pet him across his back while he just stood there.

I could hear the sound of rails cackling in the prairie grasses beyond the orchard clearing to our east. Only a thin line of trees separate us from the open prairie on the north and east sides of the clearing. The wooded ridge has a dense forest growing all over it, but one only need walk about fifty paces through the thicket and the prairie would be clearly visible. Rails are plentiful here, just as they are around our trapping camp; they make a good gumbo. They are tender and have a mild taste when comparing them to other waterfowl I have eaten.

There were many cat squirrels (gray squirrels) feeding in the pecan trees; with few pecans to forage, they might have just been playing. Those threatened by our presence would freeze, remaining motionless until they felt they had eluded us. That too, seemed to me like a game they were playing. Once in a while, we would see movement in their tails as they carefully watched us watching them. When the timid ones saw an opportunity to escape, they would scamper off as fast as their feet could carry them, desperately searching for another tree while trying to put distance between us. I don't recall seeing a single fox squirrel (red squirrel); they must have moved out when the pecans were depleted, I reasoned.

As I was enjoying the splendor of nature, I paused for a moment to reflect on the past. Ever since I was old enough to read, I have enjoyed the accounts recorded in my Great-grandmother Josephine's diary. I must admit that my interest in my family's history has gone beyond mere fascination; one might conclude that I have become obsessed with the legacy of the Addison family. For me, Deer Island is the centerpiece of everything related to the Addisons; here lay the roots of my heritage. The intrinsic value of the island is greatly exaggerated, because this is the place where my ancestors settled, lived, died, and it is here that many of them have been buried.

The aesthetic value of the island is impossible to measure. An estate consisting of five square miles of wilderness, bounded and crossed by the mighty Atchafalaya River, that is accessed by numerous streams and bayous; miles of virgin swampland and a remote, densely forested ridge, combine to enhance the beauty of the open prairie, which surrounds the eastern portion of the homestead: wildlife abounds, love abounds, peace abounds. How can one evaluate anything that Almighty God has done here (with a few modifications by my predecessors of course)? I say it can't be done!

Reading about my great-grandmother's experiences lends a romantic quality to this place; this unique distinction makes the island virtually incomparable to any other place on earth. From her writings, I learned of the inner struggles she faced; a tangle of emotions that almost prevented Joseph Addison from coming to this land in the first place. I experienced the excitement of the overland journey from New Orleans to Brashear City, traveling the entire distance by horse-drawn carriage. Her recorded legend introduced me to many of the interesting people they befriended along the way here (Mr. Cortez, the produce vendor; Albert Huie, Uncle Patrick's coachman; Greta and William Henley, owners of Sugarland Farms Plantation; Francois Marceaux and Carey Trudeau, the captain and deckhand of the *Swamp Rat*: Mademoiselle Pauline Longere, Uncle Patrick's ward).

The Addison legacy is my legacy. I will do everything I can to fulfill my important role, not only as a member of the Addison family, but the custodian of the past and future adventures that life presents to me. I will continue to document my experiences, intending to expand the family history. God help me to record as much information as possible, so that even the memories of my elders will never perish in the minds of their offspring—at least for those who care to read about it. I pray someday I will be able to call Deer Island my home.

Alma stole me away from my daydream by tugging at my clothing. Thinking it was only the goat, I ignored the distraction for a while. When little sister persisted, I noticed the shadows were growing; it was time to walk back to the house.

"We must get home before dark, Alma," I warned.

Walking hand in hand, Alma and I slowly made our way home. We arrived back at the kitchen before supper was served, having followed Mama's instructions besides.

I informed my aunt that the squirrels were getting the last of the pecans; all we found were the broken shells that had already been robbed of the nut they were designed to preserve. Like Aunt Sarah always says, "The animals need to eat just like we do!"

The goat followed us all the way home; he was on the back porch looking through the kitchen door. Mama told me to run him off the porch; she said it was for his own good. I understood the sentiment, remembering the episode with the rice barrel. Mama told me that if the goat gets into the habit of climbing onto the porch, it's one step closer to trying to get inside; that could mean trouble for him and for us.

As I was instructed to do, I went out the kitchen door and gently coaxed the animal off the porch. As soon as I turned my back, the stubborn goat came back on the porch behind me. Seeing the trouble I was having, Aunt Sarah appeared at the door. In her usual shrill voice, she hollered at the ornery creature, "You get off my porch right this minute *Abe Lincoln*, and I mean right this minute. I mean business!" she sternly urged.

The animal must understand the language my aunt speaks; he knew she meant business. The goat walked off the porch and did not return again; he did not want to test Aunt Sarah's will.

"That goat knows who he can mess with!" Mama stated, chuckling as she spoke.

I certainly could not question the truth of that statement. It was clear to me that the animal knew who had all the authority around here.

On our way back to the house this evening, Alma and I paused by the fountainhead for a drink of ice cold water from the spring. I dipped a hollowed gourd into the water, penetrating its bubbly surface, capturing some of its thirst-quenching benefits. We had to sip it down slowly to prevent our teeth from hurting due to contact with the icy-cold liquid.

The water in the spring has a special taste; Papa says it is because of its mineral content. All that matters is that the water is good and safe to drink; it's cold and refreshing. This is just another example of the unique things we do when we visit the island. The very thought that our vacation is nearing its end, is making me lonely to return already. How is that possible since we haven't left yet? It's strange how attached one can get to a place.

Papa and Uncle Justin boasted that they caught several large catfish; they deposited the fish directly in the fish car when they returned from their fishing excursion. "We have six large fish for the Morgan City seafood market," Uncle Justin happily reported. "Catfish are bringing a good price this year," he told us.

Papa said they encountered a large alligator near the wharf, very close to the fish car. Uncle Justin mentioned the gator was probably more interested in the turtles in the holding pen than the fish. Who knows? The gator might have just been passing by, heading for some other happy hunting ground, Papa speculated. They estimated the reptile to be about twelve feet long. "He was as wide as one of our canoes!" Uncle Justin told us. Papa said he was a "humdinger!"

After supper, everyone expressed how tired they were from the day's activity. Felix and the boys found a nice wooden pail floating near the riverbank. Boasting it was in perfect condition, Felix proceeded to go get the bucket so we could all get a look at it. The boys were proud of their find, and a wooden pail is something that comes in very handy around the homestead. Aunt Sarah congratulated the boys on their utilitarian discovery. "That bucket will be put to good use," she said with an appreciative smile.

Felix was first to reach the veranda. By the time I made it to the front of the house, he was playing "Dixie" on his harmonica. Alma was dancing with her doll and Papa and Uncle Justin were singing the words to the song.

> I wish I was in de land of cotton,
> Old times der am not forgotten
> Look away! Look away! Look away! Dixie land!
> In Dixie land what I was born in'
> Early on one frosty mornin',
> Look away! Look away! Look away! Dixie land!

I joined in the joyful singing of the tune, knowing it honored the memories of my two great uncles. Written by Daniel Decatur Emmett in 1859, "Dixie" was adopted as the song of the Southern Confederacy. Each fall we celebrate the memory of those who sacrificed and died during the War Between the States.

> Ole missus marry 'Will-de-weaber';
> Willum was a gay deceaber;
> Look away! Look away! Look away! Dixie Land!
> But when he put his arm around her,
> He smiled as fierce as a forty-pounder;
> Look away! Look away! Look away! Dixie Land!
> Den I wish I was in Dixie! Hooray! Hooray!
> In Dixie Land we'll take our stand, to live
> An' die in Dixie.
> Away! Away! Away down South in Dixie
> Away! Away! Away down South in Dixie!

After singing all five stanzas of Mr. Emmett's beloved poem, repeating the chorus after each six lines of verse, Papa began the evening of storytelling. "Everyone gather around and settle down," Papa instructed.

"This being the eve of Thanksgiving Day, I thought it would be appropriate to focus our attention on a few of the many blessings, which Almighty God has bestowed upon this family.

"Tomorrow will be the eighty-first celebration of Thanksgiving on Deer Island. The Addison name was brought to Louisiana by Great-grandfather Joseph Addison when he accepted the invitation extended to him and his wife by our distinguished ancestor, Congressman Patrick J. Adams. The *little house* completed, Joseph immediately went to work constructing the *big house* when the first Thanksgiving was celebrated here on the island.

"In addition to the two houses he was commissioned by Great-uncle Patrick to build, Joseph was already making plans for the construction of his own sailing vessel.

"Stimulated by the challenges that lay before him, Joseph pursued Uncle Patrick's dream of founding the settlement on Deer Island with boundless determination. Uncle Patrick's dream became Joseph's dream, and today we can see the results of his efforts, the accomplishments of a man with a purpose.

"We all need a dream and a purpose. Our ancestors found purpose in the fulfillment of their dreams. May we endeavor to do the same thing. Let us never forget the importance of acknowledging God in our lives. It is Almighty God who has afforded us the opportunity to be caretakers of His handiwork. Our Lord and Savior, Jesus Christ, must be at the center of any earnest expression of thanksgiving to God the Father. To God only wise be the glory through Jesus Christ forever. Amen."

Everyone being in agreement with my father's comments, in unison every voice said, "Amen!"

Uncle Justin began to speak, "Great-grandmother Josephine's diary includes records of our ancestors from both the Adams family and the Addison family. The records indicate that both of our lines of ancestors were willing to answer the call to duty when it goes out. Though there is no account of any of those distant ancestors paying the ultimate price, dying for the cause they were defending, many of them meritoriously performed their duty.

"On the eve of this great day of celebration, I felt this night would be an appropriate time to remember three of our family members who gave of themselves on the field of battle during the Civil War.

"Joseph and two of his sons served in the Confederate Army. John Quincy and Alexander Patrick fought together in several battles. Sanders was a young boy when war broke out. He remained at home, and he was a source of great comfort to his mother during the conflict.

"Great-grandfather Joseph fought alongside his best friend and neighbor from Bayou Shaver, Melvin Lacache. Melvin and three of his sons served with Confederate forces. Melvin returned home unscathed just as Joseph did, but he lost two of his three sons in battle.

"Joseph Addison and Melvin Lacache left Brashear City by rail for military training at Camp Moore on April 3, 1861. John Quincy Addison, Alexander Patrick Addison, Terry Lacache, Terrence Lacache, and Troy Lacache, were all sent by rail to New Orleans on the same day to receive military training at Camp Roman.

"After military training at Camp Moore, Joseph and Melvin were dispatched to Vicksburg. They only remained there a short time before receiving orders to join the Eighteenth Louisiana Regiment under General Alfred Mouton. The two men fought in battles at Lafourche Crossing and Irish Bend.

"The Confederate forces rid the Lower Teche Region and the Atchafalaya River Basin of Union troops through a plan of attack orchestrated by Major General Richard Taylor. Under the command of Confederate Generals Mouton, Green, and Major, the entire operation was a success (Major General Richard Taylor was the son-in-law of Confederate President Jefferson Davis).

"Once the areas from Irish Bend along the Teche to Lafourche Crossing were secured, Joseph and Melvin were honorably discharged from military service on June 25, 1863—this was only a few weeks before Alexander was sent home.

"John Quincy and Alexander Patrick were first deployed to Corinth, Mississippi. They were sent there under the command of

Colonel Alfred Mouton to defend the railroad terminal there. That railroad was a vital supply route from the Trans-Mississippi region to the Confederate armies in the east. After a small skirmish at Corinth, they were sent to Shiloh together, again under Mouton's command. Mouton was wounded at Shiloh, and when that battle ended, John and Alex returned to Corinth under the command of General Van Dorn.

"After the Battle of Corinth, John Quincy and Alexander were dispatched to Gettysburg, where they were assigned to General Hill's division under the command of General Robert E. Lee. General Hill was wounded at the Battle of Chancellorsville and John Quincy was killed on the last day of that battle, May 3, 1863.

"My father, Alexander Patrick Addison, was wounded seven days later in a skirmish about fifteen miles from the battlefield where John Quincy was killed—it was not very far from Chancellorsville. After being sent to a hospital to recover from wounds he received in battle, my father was honorably discharged from military service. As you all know, he died from complications due to his war wound shortly after he and Aunt Elizabeth bore their only son—me.

"Though they are not family members, I believe we should remember the Lacache boys: Terrence Lacache died in battle at Cemetery Hill, Troy Lacache was killed in battle at Big Round Top, Terry survived the war, but was wounded in battle at Chattanooga, and honorably discharged from military service.

"Let it always be remembered that Joseph Addison and his two sons, John Quincy Addison and Alexander Patrick Addison served the Confederate States of America with dignity and honor. When all was lost, their new allegiance was to the United States of America with honor and dignity."

After Uncle Justin ended his solemn tribute to the Addison family members who heeded the call to service, carrying on a tradition established by both the Adams family and the Addison family going back over two hundred years, I must admit I was proud of my heritage. As I lay in bed pondering the family's rich history, I felt a great sense of satisfaction, and a new sense of responsibility.

Though no one is pressuring me to do so, I intend to carry on the traditions of my forefathers. It may be that I should begin my own legend of recorded family history for posterity's sake. How many times have I wished that my Great-grandmother Josephine had continued her diary; I believe she was healthy enough to write until the day she died.

I had to add another quilt to my bedding tonight. The cold chill across my face tells me that we will have an early winter this year. I tried to keep still beneath the heavy covers to take advantage of the warm spot beneath my prostrate body. Before long, weary from the day's workload, I drifted off into a place where nothing at all exists save quiet bodies unaware that anyone else can see them there.

Chapter Ten

THANKSGIVING DAY

November 23, 1921

I awakened early today, and the first thing I did was speak a solemn greeting to the Lord, even before the sun had a chance to do so: "God bless my family and may He bless this day, and a good morning to you, Lord!" Those were the words I prayed the moment I opened my eyes.

Arriving downstairs, I was surprised to see that the only person still in bed was Alma. The chill inside the huge house made me very happy that Mama and Aunt Sarah had the woodstove hot; the warmth it was providing was a welcome sensation.

There would be no time for making breakfast this morning. With the extensive menu planned for today's feast, the stove will remain hot until the noon meal is served. I grabbed a handful of fried pork skins and poured myself a cup of sassafras tea. I could see the boys were enjoying conversation on the back porch. Lee and Felix occupied one swing, and Gus and Brad were swinging in the other.

I decided to join Papa and Uncle Justin on the front porch, where they were still awaiting the morning sun; as yet, there was no clear evidence of its appearance. Frost covered the ground around the homestead for the second consecutive morning. I overheard Papa and Uncle Justin discussing the effects of cold versus mild winters. Papa says the grade of furs is better when the winters are cold; the fur is thicker. I figure it's how nature protects the furry creatures from the icy weather.

Papa says in warm weather, not only is the muskrat fur a poorer grade, but there are other problems that present themselves. In addition to alligators remaining active far longer than usual, in warm weather the rats are more difficult to trap; they don't move around as much. With plenty water and food available, they remain in the close proximity of their mounds. This condition means many more hours of walking the marsh, working harder for less money. The conclusion of the matter is that cold winters are much more productive for trappers.

In an instant, crimson and mauve streaks, painted by the hand of God, appeared over the horizon. Sunlight reflecting off early morning clouds created a spellbinding scene, as Uncle Justin's rooster sounded the alarm in the backyard. "Cock-a-doodle-do-cock-a-doodle-do!" The curtain began rising on another day, as the brilliant orange disk sneaks a peek at my gleaming face.

"It's about time you come out from your hiding place!" I yelled at the sun. "I can see you trying to sneak a peek at us from behind the ridge! Come out so we can have a look at you!" I ordered.

Amused by my personal conversation with the sun, my uncle asked me if I thought the sun was listening to my demands; it took me only seconds to respond: "Sure he heard me. Look! He's halfway up already!"

That prompted a bit of laughter from my elders, but it was short-lived. They immediately returned to their conversation. "That's some girl you have, Adam!" I heard Uncle Justin comment, as I headed for the kitchen to see if I could be of any help.

I asked the women of the house if I could be of any assistance. They told me I was free to do anything I'd like. "Good! Can I go down to the river to look for treasure?"

Mama said it would be all right as long as I could convince at least one of the boys to go with me. Gus volunteered, so after I informed my mom that I had a companion, we headed down the *beaten path* toward the big bend in the river.

As we exited the porch, we passed near the remainder of the hog carcass hanging from a nail on one of the porch's support beams. The men will apply more salt to the outside of the large portions of meat-laden bone to extract more of the blood; once this is done, the meat will be packed away in salt barrels for safekeeping.

As Gus and I scampered along the path to the river, Felix, Lee, and Brad, whizzed by us; they were trying to get to the riverbank first. There wasn't much chance of us spoiling their efforts; it really didn't matter to me who got there first. That wasn't really true; I was merely trying to convince myself that it didn't matter. After all, it was my idea.

There was an eerie haze over the river when we arrived. The difference between the water temperature of the river and the cold morning air was causing the light fog over the water. It looked as though the water was smoking.

Driftwood lined the shore for as far as the eye could see. The recent cold front had forced the water level down a bit, leaving the floating relics high and dry. Felix and Lee dragged several nice logs to higher ground so later they could be hauled back home and cut for firewood.

Lee offered a challenge. "Let's split up and see who can find something worthwhile first! Felix and I will head south downstream. Nora, you, Gus, and Brad head north scouring the bank upstream."

"Agreed"! I blurted out, accepting the challenge willingly, determined to outdo my brother.

I was amazed by the amount of firewood the river had temporarily deposited along its shore. No doubt, when the tide returns to normal, the wood that could have been used for fuel will disappear into Atchafalaya Bay and head for Cuba via the Gulf of Mexico.

As Gus, Brad, and I approached the northernmost boundary of the estate, I noticed a peculiar-looking log floating near the shore at the approximate center of the bend in the river. The closer we came to the conspicuous log, the more strange it appeared. Closer inspection revealed that it was a capsized dugout canoe. None of us could believe what we were seeing. What could have happened here? What happened to the man who owns this finely crafted canoe? Is it for a white man, or for an Indian? We thought of all these things while we stood knee-deep in the water staring at the strange discovery in a state of utter amazement.

I instructed Brad and Gus to wait at the site while I ran downstream to get the older boys. I've never been so excited in my life. What will Aunt Sarah have to say about my discovery? What will the boys say when they see the boat for their first time; it appeared to be in perfect condition.

I turned briefly to caution Brad and Gus not to venture out from shore. "Don't go in the water until I return with help!"

I ran so far so fast that I had to sit down a spell to catch my breath. Just as I was preparing to take off downstream again, I spotted Lee and Felix; they were heading my way thank goodness.

"Come quickly!" I shouted, motioning them toward me with my arms. I don't believe they heard me above the sounds of the river as its waters whisked by me in the shallows of the huge cove just offshore from where I was standing.

I yelled once again, motioning with my extended arms. "Come quickly! We have made a great discovery!" I screamed at the top of my voice.

Finally, Lee looked up from the clamshell bank and saw me waiving my arms. They began to hightail it in my direction. I hoped they didn't misunderstand, thinking something might be wrong with one or both of the other boys. That notion could have prompted them to run at such a fast pace; I was just glad they were coming!

"What's wrong?" Felix asked, noticeably concerned about what was going on with the other boys.

"Nothing's wrong! I found an abandoned dugout canoe!" I informed Felix, as Lee stood beside him dumbfounded.

"You found what?" Lee asked. "Where is it?" he impatiently quizzed.

"Follow me!" I proudly suggested. "You guys aren't going to believe what I've found!"

Nearing exhaustion from all the running and excitement, I was glad when we reached the discovery site. Brad and Gus were standing there stoically, awaiting our arrival.

Felix waded into the water, testing as he went, with a long stick for any sudden drop-off of the river bottom; Lee and Brad followed close behind, while Gus and I waited patiently on shore. The boys were successful in turning the boat upright; they then proceeded to empty the water out of the canoe.

As Felix and the boys floated the boat to shore through the clutter of debris, I could hear them sharing their excitement with one another. Lee exclaimed, "What a great boat!" That expression became even more evident as the canoe was finally dragged ashore.

"Papa won't believe his eyes when he sees this canoe!" Brad predicted.

"It's an Indian canoe!" Felix shouted.

"What makes you so sure?" I inquired, curious about its origins.

Felix confidently gave the rest of us his opinion. "There are two reasons why I am certain that this is an Indian canoe. Number one, there are no seats in this dugout, Indians paddle kneeling down. Number two, there are markings carved into the front and back of this canoe, no white man would take the time to carve these startling images on his canoe," he stated with surety.

That seemed to me to be an astute evaluation of what we had found. Felix has me convinced that the canoe belonged to some Indian. There remains the mystery of how such a fine boat wound up against the riverbank.

Felix and the boys tried to figure out the best way we could carry the water-soaked canoe to the *big house*; they knew it was not going to be an easy task. I would have been happy to find a wooden pail! Lord, I hoped no one had to die for me to get my hands on this finely crafted prize! Could its owner have drowned in the river? That's something we may never know, I pondered.

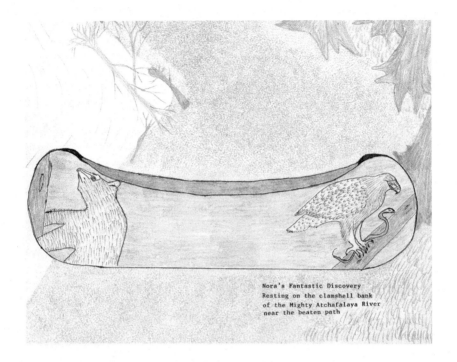

Nora's Fantastic Discovery
Resting on the clamshell bank
of the Mighty Atchafalaya River
near the beaten path

Felix sent Lee after some rope while the rest of us admired the workmanship and beauty of the Indian canoe. The outside of the boat was as smooth as glass, except where the images had been meticulously carved; one side was the mirror image of the other. Both sides at the front of the canoe had the image of a great bird grasping a serpent in its talons. Each side of the back of the boat had a great bear, standing upright clawing a tree, as though he was marking his territory.

"It's a beautiful canoe, Nora!" Felix blurted out, ecstatic over the discovery.

Felix searched the riverbank for two strong branches to slide under the boat so it could be carried home without damage, dragging the canoe along the ground would certainly mar the smooth bottom.

Lee returned with the rope, and Felix used it to secure the canoe to the two branches; one was tied near the front, the other tied near the rear. Felix took one side of the front branch and instructed Gus and I to double-team the other side of the front branch. Lee took one side of the rear branch and Brad took the other end of the rear branch.

Felix instructed everyone to lift the boat at the same time. "Everybody must raise the canoe up together!"

I was amazed by the ease we managed to carry the heavy boat. Working together as a team, the task was easily done.

Lee said that no one saw him when he went for the rope, just in case Nora wants to surprise everyone back at the house with the magnificent discovery.

"I'm glad you weren't seen Lee. Are you sure that no one, not even Alma, saw you?" I asked.

"I am almost positive that no one saw me take the rope from the side of the smokehouse," Lee assured me.

"This is the discovery of a lifetime!" I reasoned with the boys. "I want to make the day of this discovery a day to remember. It's Thanksgiving Day 1921, a day we will remember for the rest of our lives. Let's do our best to make sure the grownups never forget this day!" Everyone agreed wholeheartedly with my plan.

We decided to let the boat down at the rear of the chicken coop, shielding it from view from the kitchen windows on the west side of the house.

Scouting the territory, Lee and Felix walked around the north side of the house to see where the adults were. Not a soul was on either porch. Peering through the dining room window, they saw that all the grownups were seated around the dinner table steeped in conversation.

We raised the canoe once again, and headed along the north side of the house, keeping low to avoid being seen. When we made it to the fountainhead, Felix and Lee untied the boat from the branches we used to transport it from the river and placed the boat on the ground with part of the front end in the water of the stream. We positioned it in a way that it could be easily seen from the veranda of the *big house*.

My plan for surprising everyone was working; we had done everything without being detected. Just as we started walking toward the house, giggling with excitement over our plan, Alma appeared on the front porch. I motioned for her to come near me, trying to get her away from the house so I could explain what was going on with the canoe.

Right away, curiosity prompted a question from my little sister: "Where did you get that Indian canoe?"

"I found it at the big bend in the river," I explained. "I want to surprise the grownups. Don't say anything," I pleaded.

Alma quickly responded. "Okay!"

We agreed to enter the house from the rear porch, pretending we had just returned from the river. Felix had suggested that everyone act discouraged, as though we hadn't found anything. As we were coached by Felix, we entered the kitchen through the porch door and joined our parents at the dinner table.

"Dinner is not quite ready!" Aunt Sarah told us, seeing our expressions were less than joyous and not knowing why. "Did you find any of Laffite's treasure buried somewhere along the riverbank?" my aunt asked.

Searching my soul for a witty answer, which would not be a lie, I said, "No, Aunt Sarah! We found no gold or silver today!" I asserted with true conviction, having no sense of guilt since I told no lie.

Trying her best to console us, Aunt Sarah said, "Maybe next time!" She was trying to keep us from being discouraged.

"After literally hundreds of trips to the river (whether the search was for wood for fuel, or the search was for treasure for fun) the wooden pail that Felix and Lee found the other day has been the most valuable discovery thus far," Uncle Justin remarked.

"You kids don't get discouraged," Papa told us, trying to inspire us to continue trying. "You never know what might turn up along the bank of a river as powerful as the Atchafalaya," he added.

We went back outside and sat in a row, dangling our feet over the edge of the back porch floor. "They don't expect a thing," Lee whispered.

"Wait until they take their customary seats on the veranda," Brad teased.

"I wonder, how long will it take for them to see the canoe once they arrive on the front porch?" Gus quietly asked.

We walked out into the back yard to distance ourselves from the house so we would not be overheard. Lee figured they would remain inside until after dinner; maybe they will wait until after naptime. Felix is inclined to agree with Lee's speculation; the afternoon nap is customary.

"If we don't want to spoil the surprise, we'll just have to be patient," I cautioned.

In a sudden act of panic, I asked, "Where's Alma?"

"She stayed inside with Mama and Papa," Brad bewailed.

"Dinner is served! Come and get it!" This was the call heralded from the kitchen door.

We scrambled into the house, taking our seats at the dinner table. Even though we were all famished and ready to eat, all eyes were on Alma, searching for any indication that might reveal whether she betrayed our confidence or not.

Slowly, Alma touched her right index finger against her lips; she had kept her word. The grownups still knew nothing about the fantastic discovery; our plan was working. I smiled in approval to let my sister know I appreciated her cooperation.

Mama and Aunt Sarah had decorated the dinner table. There was a white sheet spread over the surface, and there were place settings before each and every one of us. There were so many vessels containing different dishes that one could hardly see the tablecloth at the center of the table.

"What a bountiful sight to behold!" Papa boasted.

Uncle Justin led us in a prayer of thanksgiving, and we began to consume the feast. The menu was announced by the cook. "We've got fresh pork roast soaking in my special gravy. We've got baked chicken with browned onion gravy. We have pan fried pork sausage. We stuffed the pork stomach with rice dressing made with bits of pork meat and the livers, hearts, and gizzards from the chickens and the ducks. We have fresh baked bread. For dessert, we have sweet potato and pumpkin pies. Top it all off with more goat's milk than we can drink."

Mama and Aunt Sarah had good reason to be proud of their cooking skills. We fully intended to show our appreciation by consuming a portion of each and every thing on that table. Mama interrupted our aggressive assault on the many dishes before us to announce that we still had hogshead cheese and fried pork rinds.

Knowing it would be impossible to finish the multicourse meal that was on the dinner table, Aunt Sarah teased us by thanking Mama for reminding everyone about the leftovers from yesterday's meal. Everyone considered the announcement to be a holiday joke.

I can't recall ever having a bigger or a better assortment of prepared food set before me. It's no small wonder that Mama and Aunt Sarah have been steadily working in the kitchen for eight hours; they began firing the stove at 4:00 a.m., and we sat down to eat a little after twelve o'clock noon.

"This meal is a real blessing," Gus announced, sincerely enjoying the food. "Amen!" was the word next heard. Everyone voiced their agreement with Gus's statement, saying how good the food was and also how blessed we were to have this bountiful table set before us.

Everyone took a turn praising the cooks for the delicious food they had worked so hard to prepare. Alma joined in by praising the two matrons for their hard work.

Felix shared how much he was enjoying our visit to the island; he said we lifted his spirits. He told us that it gets lonely on Deer Island with little or no company during our absence. He lamented over the sorrow he was certain to experience when we leave for the trapping camp next week.

I shared with the family that I felt the same way that Felix did about our leaving. I surprised everyone (at least to some degree) by suggesting that I would like to move into the *little house* and live on the island permanently.

There was a strange silence after I made that remark. I looked toward Papa to see his reaction to my comments, but he just kept right on eating. Mama told me not to lose hope, saying that no one knows what the future may hold. She advised me to be patient, and she left the idea of moving to the island in God's hands. "If it is meant to be, it will be," she consoled. Putting things in God's hands is always a comfortable feeling, I reasoned; at least no one spoke against the idea, that counts for something.

Dinner lasted much longer than usual; not necessarily because we ate more food, but more as a result of the fact that we were enjoying good conversation. Since the meal was the focal point of the day's celebration, no one wanted it to end. I was so involved in the enjoyment of the moment, I nearly forgot about my fantastic discovery and the surprise we had planned for the grownups in the front yard.

Wouldn't you know that right after I was contemplating how they might react when they see the Indian dugout canoe, Mama announced that she was going upstairs to take a good long nap; that was both expected and quite understandable. Her enthusiasm over the prospects for a restful sleep prompted the rest of the grownups to say they would do the same.

The surprise would just have to wait. Aunt Sarah removed her apron and hung it on a nail on the kitchen wall. As she turned back into the dining room, she paused to recommend that we go upstairs for a nap as well. Since this is a holiday, she gave us the option to make the choice and headed into the sewing room to access the stairs leading to her bedroom.

"Have a good rest!" I told her.

Alma was upstairs already; she had opted to take a nap before the rest of us rose from the table. The boys and I ran out the front door to swing beneath the giant oak, not far from our special surprise.

Our planning and patience has paid off; Alma kept our secret quiet. When the adults awaken from their naps, they'll get the surprise of their lives. What a day this is shaping up to be; the greatest Thanksgiving Day celebration of my life.

The more I gazed at the Indian canoe, the more I began to appreciate the value of the discovery. Not only was it the most beautiful canoe I had ever seen, but it was in perfect condition.

No matter what the fate of its owner, it would most certainly have found its way into the Gulf of Mexico if it would have not been discovered floundering in the shallows of the great bend in the river. Not knowing its origin, it cannot be returned, I reasoned.

We took turns swinging each other as high as we could and we enjoyed the pleasure of good conversation. The exhilaration we were lavishing was dampened when Gus inadvertently brought up the fact that we would soon be leaving the island.

"Well! If we don't leave! We can't come back!" I exclaimed, purposefully interjecting nonsense into our temporary grieving process.

The digestion of those choice words made all the boys scratch their heads (that was the affect I intended). I wasn't quite sure what I meant by that series of remarks myself. I certainly did not expect them to understand what I meant to say.

It must have been near 4:00 p.m. when we heard voices nearing the front porch door from inside the house. We all giggled with joyful expectation.

Papa and Uncle Justin came outside first, taking their seats on their favorite rockers and packing fresh tobacco in the bowls of their corncob pipes. Before they could strike a match to them, Mama and Aunt Sarah appeared, exiting the doorway backward, pulling their rocking chairs into position next to their husbands. The stage was set; conditions were perfect. The culmination of all the suspense was nearing an end.

Before she sat down in her comfortable chair, Mama looked in my direction. As she panned the horizon, she spotted the new attraction in the front yard. "Adam, Justin, Sarah, look at that canoe!" she cried out, overwhelmed by the unexpected sight.

Scrambling off the porch, everyone congregated around the canoe, staring at it inquisitively. Uncle Justin was the first to utter a sound.

"Where did this come from?" Uncle Justin asked in an abnormally loud voice.

It was my honor to explain. "Uncle Justin, I found this canoe floundering in the shallows of the great bend in the Atchafalaya, near the northern boundary of the estate. It was swamped, leaning on its side partially submerged because the current had wedged it under a mass of debris. At first sight, it looked like a peculiar log in the distance. Closer inspection revealed it was a boat. With the help of all the boys, we raised the canoe to an upright state and bailed the water until it could be floated ashore. Lee secured some rope and Felix used two strong pieces of driftwood to make a makeshift carriage for transporting the heavy, water-soaked canoe to the spot where it is sitting now. We have waited all this time to surprise all of you with this fantastic discovery."

Uncle Justin was spellbound; he didn't say a word. Papa's mouth was gaped, as he walked around the fountainhead to take a look at the craft from another vantage point.

"Come have a look at this, Justin!" Papa beckoned.

The two curious men squatted near the canoe to get a closer look at the markings carved on both sides of the front and back of the boat.

"I don't believe a white man would have taken the time to do this intricate carving. What do you think, Justin?" Papa asked, seeking his opinion.

Before Uncle Justin could give a response to Papa's question, Felix blurted out, "Look, Pa! There are no seats!"

Uncle Justin asked Felix to pull the canoe out from the stream for a closer inspection. Slowly, meticulously, the two grown men examined ever square inch of the beautiful craft.

Uncle Justin paused to gather his thoughts and he then looked me straight in the face and said, "Well, Nora! Maybe you didn't find any of Laffite's treasure, but you did find something very valuable. This was truly a fantastic discovery! It is in excellent condition and amazingly beautiful with its detailed carvings. This handsome boat will be useful for countless years to come. You found it! It's yours to do with as you please!" he concluded.

I wasn't really prepared to hear that; I never expected to keep the canoe for myself. I thought I might leave it here with my family members on Deer Island. Now that it has officially been given to me, I'm most sure it will be put to good use.

Papa began to share his feelings about the boat. "Nora, your beautiful canoe will be used for entertainment purposes only. We won't be using it to trap or to hunt for alligators. You and your brothers and little sister can use it to have fun. It's your boat," he concluded.

As we enjoyed the novelty of the find, Alma finally appeared on the veranda of the *big house*. With her doll in hand, she sat down on the front steps, not the least bit interested in what the rest of us were doing. That girl! I wished she would come and join us in the "real world."

I asked Uncle Justin to speculate about who he thought could have been the owner of the canoe and what he thought might have become of him. He told me that he and Papa would consider the matter during the course of the remainder of the afternoon. They will discuss their conceptions of the truth at storytelling time tonight. In the meantime, he suggested we go for a canoe ride. That prompted renewed excitement and we decided to give the boat a try.

Felix offered to assist me with my new canoe. We launched the boat; Felix, Gus, and I got aboard and began racing downstream with Felix paddling in the rear. "Here's a paddle!" Felix shouted. "There's no better time for you to learn than now! I'll show you how it's done!" he promised with a determined look on his face.

Lee and Brad were following close behind in one of Uncle Justin's canoes when we reached the landing and made the sharp maneuver to the east to prevent hitting the wharf. Having sped our way downstream with the aid of the already fast moving current, by the time we got to Deer Bayou, we were moving at breakneck speed; at least that's the way I felt. We narrowly escaped a collision with the dock.

Felix hollered for me to put my paddle into the water on the left side of the boat and leave it there. Just as I was about to brace myself for the crash against the bow of the *Dreadnought*, the front of our canoe, aided by the paddling maneuver Felix had ordered, turned us out and away from the monstrous hull of the big sailboat.

As I was breathing a sigh of relief, Felix hollered, "She handles very well. She floats higher and moves quicker through the water than our canoes!"

We spent the rest of the daylight hours racing up and down Deer Bayou; we had so much fun! The Indian canoe was no fair match for the bulkier dugout my great-grandfather had made. After countless victories over my two brothers, I asked Felix to swap boats with them, to let them experience the fun we were having with the new boat. We paddled against the bank near the eagle's nest and exchanged canoes.

I had never been this close to the massive confusion of sticks and branches that is the eagle's nest. From this vantage point, I could see the bottom of the nest in the towering height of the massive cypress tree, but there was no possibility of seeing what was inside.

Drawing my attention away from the awe inspiring home of the eagles, we resumed the boat races up and down the bayou. After being defeated by my brothers several times, Felix exclaimed, "The proof is in the pudding! There is no doubt that Nora's Indian canoe is superior to our canoes!"

We arrived back at the fountainhead just as the sun was disappearing over the river. We dragged the canoes onto the shore and then we went straight to the kitchen where the grownups were preparing to have supper. Papa and Uncle Justin set out the plates as Mama and Aunt Sarah heated what they thought would satisfy our appetites for the nighttime meal.

"We have enough food cooked to last through the noon meal tomorrow," Aunt Sarah told us. "Thanks to the cold weather, our leftovers shouldn't spoil," she was happy to relate.

"Good!" Uncle Justin shouted. "You two lovely ladies deserve a break from the kitchen!" he ordered. "Tomorrow, Adam and I plan to take you two sweet women on a fishing trip!" he raved.

Uncle Justin's loving invitation caught Mama and Aunt Sarah by surprise; I saw both of them blushing, something that doesn't happen very often. They looked at each other in a dumbfounded way, unable to say anything it seemed. There was a time of silence at the supper table.

Finally Aunt Sarah spoke, "Going fishing will be a wonderful experience Justin, but you will have to take the fish off my line for me if you want me to enjoy myself."

"Sugar dumpling, I'll not only take the fish off your line for you, but I'll bait the hook for you as well!" Uncle Justin playfully announced.

Not wanting to appear outdone by Uncle Justin's sudden display of charm, Papa said, "I'll do the same for you, Ida!"

"It's a date then!" Mama responded.

These displays of affection made the evening meal that much more enjoyable; when people love each other this should be a common occurrence. I can only hope that if the Lord sees fit for me to marry, that my spousal relationship will equal theirs; true love is a wonderful thing to see.

Felix and Lee boasted to Papa and Uncle Justin about the smooth traveling provided by the Indian canoe; it glides through the water rather than plowing through it, they said. They bragged that the canoe's rounded bottom and sharp prow and stern design make the boat extremely maneuverable. They said my Indian canoe was superior to those our great-grandfather made.

Papa and Uncle Justin vowed to give the boat a try in the morning. Aunt Sarah promised she would never again scoff at the notion of finding treasure along the riverbank. "After this discovery, heaven only knows what will be the next interesting treasure found at the bend in the river."

We understood their surprise, just as we understood their skepticism before our new discovery. Now, searching for treasure will be more exciting than ever. Though it is hard to imagine anything that would surpass the discovery of the Indian canoe in fascination, it will be fun to try nonetheless; now we know that our efforts may sometimes be rewarded.

Uncle Justin said that the conversation was good, but it was time to eat before the supper gets cold. He said a prayer of blessing, and we enjoyed the meal while indulging in more conversation and loving fellowship. As we remained at the table for a lengthy stay, I thought about how glad I was that the grownups were planning a day of fun and relaxation tomorrow. Mama and Aunt Sarah have earned a break from the heat of the woodstove and from the many other necessary activities associated with keeping up such a massive house.

The two matrons have daily activities filled with mundane tasks, especially since there are so many of us. Aside from cooking responsibilities, they must wash clothes using a tub and scrub board and then hang them out to dry (putting them out, taking them in). Next, they have to fold them or hang them to neatly put them away; that chore alone would drive most women to frustration, lending support for the old adage, "Man works from sun to sun, but woman's work is never done!" How true that is! Yes, they have earned a break.

That night, we had much good conversation about the food and festivities which highlighted our eighty-first Thanksgiving Day celebration on Deer Island. My fantastic discovery will be forever remembered on this blessed day, November 23, 1921.

Out on the veranda, Papa and Uncle Justin shared their views regarding my "fantastic discovery," as my uncle has dubbed it.

Uncle Justin began by applauding the skilled craftsmanship exhibited by the manner the boat was painstakingly fashioned. He said that the maker of this canoe must have been a proud and honorable man to have taken so much care in creating this floating masterpiece. He praised the maker's artistic ability, referring to the lifelike images carved front and back and mirrored on both sides of the craft.

Papa speculated that the owner of the canoe was perhaps a great warrior; a man of great distinction among his people. Like the image of the eagle, he was probably an expert hunter, a good provider for his family. Like the image of the bear, he may have staunchly defended his territory, warning intruders that he was always prepared to stand and fight when necessary; he was even prepared to die in the defense of what was rightfully his.

Uncle Justin said that like the eagle, the bear, and the human, we all have one common enemy. This enemy can never be adequately thwarted by force; it can never be defeated in battle. Though one would be the master of his environment, this enemy can never be vanquished. That common enemy is death.

Papa said that whether the owner of the canoe drowned in the Atchafalaya River by accident, or if perchance his people set him adrift on the river in some Indian burial rite, the consensus of opinion is that he is now dead.

Uncle Justin told us that no Indian would be so negligent that he would lose his only mode of transportation, especially a canoe as splendid as this one.

I was indeed saddened by the notion that the Indian who owned my canoe is now dead. He must have been a great warrior, maybe even a chief, I reasoned.

Suddenly, I remembered Princess Callie; she would have more insight about the owner of the canoe. Even though I have asked my uncle to share with me what he knows about the fair maiden, thus far there has been no mention of her. He did promise to tell all during storytelling time before we leave for our trapping camp. I can't wait!

As I lay in my bed beside my sister Alma, I envisioned a group of Indian warriors paying tribute to their fallen brother. I watched as they sent him adrift in the swift currents of the great waters, allowing nature to reclaim his spirit, somewhere upstream from the great bend in the river. I could not see his face, but I could see his form resting at the bottom of his most prized possession. In his hands, tightly grasped, are his bow and his hunting knife. His arms were crossed over his chest. His bow, clasped by his left hand, guarded the right side of his deerskin clad torso; his knife, clasped in his right hand, guarded the left side of his body. Later, the great Indian warrior released his canoe so that I could find it.

Nestled below a spread and three heavy quilts, the cold air enters my bedroom window; I felt it brushing softly against my face and gently ushering me into another realm; suddenly, I forgot what I was thinking.

November 25, 1921 (Storytelling Time)

At last, the evening has come! Uncle Justin informed me that he would share all he knows about Princess Callie tonight. After the discovery of my Indian canoe, the information shared might help me understand a bit more about our Native American neighbors; I'm sure my uncle's narrative will be exhaustive. His stories are always carefully thought out before he delivers them; this is one of the qualities that all good storytellers have in common.

As supper ended, Uncle Justin announced that it was time to share another story; a story that many of us probably know little or nothing about. I could see that assertion stimulated everyone's interest.

After everyone was seated in their favorite spots on the porch, it was time to listen.

Uncle Justin began, "This summer, Nora stumbled upon a little known passage in Great-grandmother Josephine's diary. A princess came to Deer Island, accompanied by her father, shortly after the war ended. At Nora's request, tonight I will share all I know about a young woman who made quite an impression on our ancestors. A woman who may still be alive today!" he posed.

"Everything I share with you I learned from listening to those who actually met her—Joseph, Josephine, Sanders, Elizabeth, and Pauline."

Uncle Justin continued, "Josephine received this young woman's portrait as a gift from William Henley in 1865. This was before I was born. Once Josephine studied the image, she clearly had a desire to meet her. She told everyone!

"I believe it was around 1870 when Joseph, Josephine, and Pauline decided to leave the island in search of Princess Callie. Sanders, was seventeen at the time. I was not quite two years old. Josephine instructed him to stay at home to mind me.

"Princess Callie was living with other tribal members of the Houmas tribe at a village located at Tigerville, a settlement easily accessible by sailboat from here.

"Josephine told me that after arriving at the site without being announced, several braves met them at the boat landing and asked Joseph what he wanted. After expressing a desire to meet Princess Callie, the three visitors were escorted to the center of the encampment. First to greet them was the tribal Chieftain. Once he understood that Joseph and company wanted to meet his daughter, he immediately summoned her to where they were standing.

"Josephine related to me her first impressions of the fair maiden. 'Her portrait did not do her justice. She was dressed in her native attire and every bit as pretty as I had imagined,' she shared.

"After an hour or so of exchanging pleasantries, the chieftain called for one of his braves. He instructed him to gather up a few items and bring them back to him. While awaiting the brave's return, Joseph and the Indian chieftain smoked a bit of tobacco.

"Callie spoke French, but she understood a little English, so she and Pauline struck up a conversation straightway. Not wanting to be impolite to Josephine, Princess Callie paused after a few sentences. This allowed Pauline to interpret for her. The discussion was cordial and filled with gaiety.

"When the chieftain's servant returned, Josephine was given a wickerwork basket. It was a colorful item with blue and red and brown images painted all around the open container. The basket was filled to the brim with pouches of herbal medicines.

"I remember what happened to that basket. For years it was used to gather eggs. One day the basket was accidently left on the back porch of the *big house*. One of our goats found the basket appetizing and he ate it until it was hardly recognizable. I believe Joseph burned what little remained."

Uncle Justin went on. "Pauline was given a pair of moccasins made from deer hide and a rug made from the hide of a huge black bear. Princess Callie presented Josephine and Pauline beaded necklaces strung with gar fish scales dyed with extracts from the native indigo plants. Each of the scales was colored either dark blue, or a grayish purplish blue.

"The Houmas Indian chieftain presented Joseph with a ceremonial peace pipe, a hunting bow made from ash (a tree common to this area whose properties of elasticity make it suitable for making strong resilient hunting bows) and a quiver full of arrows whose tips were fitted with the boney stingers found on the common stingray (each arrow is split at one end to receive the barbed stinger that has been filed so it can be strongly secured by wrapping the arrow's end with horse hair. This was the preferred tip used by the local tribesmen)."

Uncle Justin continued, "Nora, since you asked me to tax my memory for anything I could share about Princess Callie, I decided to search through Joseph and Josephine's personal effects to see what I might find. Guess what I found?" he asked.

"What did you find?" I asked with wild anticipation.

Reaching for his pocket, Uncle Justin produced the two necklaces he had earlier described in his oratory. I know my face turned red from all the excitement as I reached forward and took the beautiful items into my hands.

Pausing to reignite the fire in his pipe, Uncle Justin smiled. I looked at Papa and he had the same smile; I had seen this subtle tactic used by both men before. Uncle Justin was not finished. As predicted, my uncle raised himself slowly from his rocker and went inside, closing the screen door behind him. He said he was going in for more pipe tobacco. Mama, Papa, and Aunt Sarah were all grinning. All the boys sat quietly, waiting to see what would happen next.

Though only a few minutes passed, it seemed like hours before the door was opened again. Uncle Justin was obviously hiding something behind his back. "What's that behind you back?" I quizzed.

I could not believe my eyes! I knew there was more to the Princess Callie story!

"Here is the ceremonial peace pipe the Houmas chieftain gave to your Great-grandfather Joseph," he informed me.

"Did anyone share with you the Houmas chieftain's name?" I asked.

"Somehow I knew you would eventually ask me that question Nora. His name was Chief Kalamos. Princess Callie's name does not start with the letter C, but it begins with the letter K. The spelling is a derivation of her father's name," Uncle Justin noted.

"Chief Kalamos and Princess Kallie visited the island only once. By this time, the chieftain was old and feeble. He and his daughter arrived in a dugout canoe. It was a very large canoe I was told. Six braves accompanied them to the front porch of the *big house.*

"Justin, Sanders (now old enough to smoke) and Chief Kalamos smoked tobacco from these very same rocking chairs. Josephine, Elizabeth, Pauline, and Kallie spent several hours together. Princess Kallie spoke in French, and Pauline interpreted so the rest of the women could understand. Kallie expressed concern that her father's health was beginning to fail. The uncertainty about what lay ahead was disconcerting to her.

"After spending much of the afternoon together, the chief summoned his braves and they escorted the two tribal leaders to their canoe. Joseph and the chief shook hands and parted in friendship.

Sanders had befriended the six braves and they exchanged fond good-byes. Josephine, Elizabeth, and Pauline took turns hugging the princess, each kissing her on her cheek before bidding her farewell.

"The Addison family continued to wave until the visiting party of Houmas Indians disappeared around the bend in Deer Bayou, as they headed north for the mainland.

"From what I have been told, the consensus among the women was that Kallie rivaled Pauline in beauty and elegance (Grandpa Sanders did not agree with their assessment, having a strong bias on behalf of Pauline coming from his heart). It is true that Pauline believed that Kallie was a suitable rival (though there was never a beauty contest)."

"What a wonderful story, Uncle Justin!" I interjected.

"That's not all, Nora!" Uncle Justin shouted. "In 1875, Princess Kallie fulfilled her destiny, becoming the first female chieftain in three generations. She was only twenty-five years old when she assumed the position her father once held," he concluded.

I was spellbound!

In a sudden display of feigned jealousy, Lee stood up from where he was seated and promptly asked, "What about the hunting bow and the quiver full of arrows?"

"I knew I had forgotten something!" Uncle Justin teased, disappearing one again through the screen door of the front porch.

Soon Uncle Justin reappeared carrying all the items that were asked about. "I believe the only one to use this bow was Grandpa Sanders. I believe he killed a deer with it," Uncle Justin shared.

"Lee, you get the bow and Brad gets the quiver full of arrows," Uncle Justin instructed.

It was obvious his intention was that they share in its potential as a hunting bow. He told the boys that with a little patience they might find it a useful weapon for killing deer. The boys were just as excited about the bow and arrows as I was over getting a look at the peace pipe and receiving the necklaces as a gift from Uncle Justin; I gave one of the two necklaces to Alma of course. Placing the necklace around her neck made a broad smile appear.

The Indian jewelry was quite beautiful; their color had not faded at all; it's hard to believe that ordinary fish scales could be made into such an elegant piece of costume jewelry.

Felix and Gus had patiently waited their turn; they told Lee and Brad to wait on the porch for a few more minutes while the grownups went inside for a night cap. I stayed to see what the commotion was all about while Alma voluntarily headed for bed.

Felix and Gus suddenly appeared with each a bow and quivers of arrows in hand, challenging my two brothers to a contest in the morning. Of course, Lee and Brad accepted the challenge, pledging to give them a contest on the morrow. I can't wait to see them all in action; competition is nearly always a good thing.

Princess
Callie

Tigerville
1865

As I entered the house, bringing up the rear, I was met by Aunt Sarah; she handed me a piece of paper. It was a portrait of Princess Callie, the one given to Josephine back in 1865. It depicts aspects of village life at her home in Tigerville. "Something to stimulate your dreams little missy!" she told me.

I hugged my aunt and thanked her for the gift and then I rushed upstairs to join Alma in bed.

As I lay in bed to rest for the evening, two owls traded their usual calls. I could not extinguish the vision of the Indian princess from my mind. After a stretch of time I could not measure, the owls stopped calling in the distance.

Chapter Eleven

GETTING READY TO LEAVE

November 27, 1921

Papa has already announced that we would be leaving for our trapping camp tomorrow after dinner. Our time spent on the island this fall seemed to vanish into thin air. As I reflect on our visit here, I am sure the many exciting experiences we have shared contributed to this phenomenon; time seems to flash forward, making days seem like minutes. Though the number of days we spent together on the island is the same as it has always been, it's been the shortest, most inspiring, most action-packed adventure I have ever had. A veritable treasure chest of memories will leave the island with me when I go. My body will leave for the trapping camp, but my heart will remain with my family here; what a delightful fall season this has been.

Storytelling time this fall has been the best ever. New information about my family and their acquaintances will provide me with countless hours of reflection during the coming year. I am hopeful that this food for thought will make the time away from the island pass faster than it has before; eleven months is a very long time, especially when one is starving for inspiration I reasoned.

Back at the trapping camp as well as at our home on Bayou Du Large, Papa does occasionally tell us stories to entertain us; it usually happens after supper or when we are forced to remain inside due to inclement weather. He is a good storyteller, but he usually saves the best ones to share with all of us during the fall season at the island.

Storytelling has become a friendly competition between Papa and Uncle Justin. We all come away excited and inspired by their efforts; they put their hearts and souls into each story. The fact that their stories must be true and verifiable, makes the time spent listening all the more enjoyable and suspenseful.

Papa and Uncle Justin take great care to tell their stories accurately; each story must be verified by one or more eye witnesses, or physical evidence must be produced. This year's examples of proof would be the cutlass, the coins that Papa produced to support his story of Xavier's discovery; there was coalescent evidence such as the "P L" on the butt of the cutlass which both supported and blended honestly into the story of Pauline Longere and her father, Jean Laffite, as that story was told to Papa and Grandfather Sanders.

My "fantastic discovery" will serve to remind me of all the wonderful events of this season, the fall season of 1921. Each time I look at my Indian canoe, I will no doubt long to be here; but patience, and the grace of Almighty God, will see me here next fall. The interim period will become meaningless if I don't record current events in my legend for future readers to enjoy. My future will always be associated with the past, it seems; I have no clue what life has in store for me, but I can choose never to forget what has already been. It's my destiny.

Maybe we will find a treasure chest someday; one that has not yet been opened. Considering the close association between Uncle Patrick and some of the Baratarians, the possibility of finding loot is not as far-fetched as it may have once seemed. If we find enough treasure, Papa and Mama can move to Deer Island, and we can move into the *little house* and live happily ever after; that would be a fulfillment of my dreams. Time will tell! You can bet I'll be there to listen when it does. God willing!

I was the last to rise this morning. When I came downstairs, Mama and Aunt Sarah were busy in the kitchen; Alma was on the back porch singing to her doll. My little sister has never beaten me downstairs after a period of restful repose, whether it is morning or after the noon day nap; it just doesn't happen! I must have been in a mild coma, intoxicated by my wonderful experiences this fall. Mama told me that all the men went fishing right after Papa announced we would be leaving tomorrow; he and the others grabbed each a cane pole from the pantry and stormed out the kitchen door, making a dash for the canoes.

"The fishermen are having a contest!" Aunt Sarah announced. "They took all three canoes, dividing themselves into three teams. Adam and Justin took your Indian canoe. Felix and Brad took one canoe, and Lee and Gus took the other. You missed all the commotion over which team would catch the biggest or the most fish Nora. You should have seen them!" Aunt Sarah shared, obviously amused by the incident.

"What's on the stove?" I asked.

"We're having fresh mustard greens and a pot of rabbit stew made with fresh picked turnips. Felix checked the rabbit traps early this morning. He and Lee skinned and dressed the three critters for the pot before they left for the fishing excursion," Mama informed me.

Those two women can make anything taste good, I thought as I exited the kitchen door to join my sister on one of the porch swings. Before I could sit down, Mama asked me to fetch a pail of water from the stream. "Okay, Mom," I shouted, as I quickly ran for the stream with the pail hanging from my arm.

Mama is a loving person. Though she is not quite as industrious as my aunt, "she's a heck of a woman," I have heard Papa frequently say of her. It must be a tough job being the mother of four children and a good wife. Mama never complains; she has worked tirelessly at Papa's side, keeping us fed, making sure our clothes are always mended; she nurses us when one of us falls sick. Her love and devotion to her family has been commendable.

The other night, Uncle Justin shared the story of the selfless love and devotion that his first wife Clara had for him, even as she lay dying on the kitchen floor. I took notice when Mama and Aunt Sarah began crying uncontrollably. I believe the reason for their tears was that they could identify with Clara's feelings. Maybe if faced with the same situation, both Mama and Aunt Sarah would have reacted in the very same way, having more concern for the well-being of their spouses than for themselves. How noble can love between a man and a woman be; what devotion? I pondered.

"Here you are, Mama," I announced, as I presented her with a pail full of fresh cold water from the stream and placed it on the table in the kitchen.

"Thank you, Nora," Mama affectionately mentioned as I rushed back out the kitchen door.

The weather was beautiful outside. It has warmed up a little since Thanksgiving, but I'm certain it is still in the fifties. There is not a cloud in the sky. This has been a relatively dry fall compared with last year. During our entire visit here, it has only rained three times; all three downpours were initiated by cold fronts moving through the area. The brisk north winds quickly blew the grounds around the homestead dry—no muddy shoes. Since one of the strictest rules for horseback riding is that the ground be absolutely dry, we have had the joy of this privilege more times than we had last year. Having four horses instead of two made it even more fun; we all participated.

I asked Alma if she wanted to follow me to the fountainhead for a drink of cold water; fetching the pail for Mama suddenly had me thirsty.

As my sister dipped the gourd into the water near the fountainhead for a drink, the troubled water reminded me of the agitated water boiling in the huge cauldron when we butchered the hog. The boiling water in the cauldron was being tormented by the heat from the heavy coals and fire below and through the cast iron kettle, assaulting and challenging its very existence while consuming it in the process; this forced some of the liquid to escape its tormentor's grasp in the form of invisible gas. It vanished into thin air. So is the water at the fountainhead, but this time, the tormentor is underground pressure. Feeling the tight grasp of its tormentor, some of the water escapes in the form of exploding bubbles, which release their contents into the air. The remaining liberated prisoners run furiously downstream, fleeing the site at their captor's weakest point. Unlike the troubled waters in the hot cauldron, these waters, though troubled, are cold and refreshing.

After taking my turn with the hollow gourd, Alma and I went for a walk. Alma wanted to find the milk cow. She said she had seen her from the back porch earlier; it was browsing along the path that leads to the cemetery. I hollered at Mama, "Alma and I are going to take a walk on the *wagon path* to look for Uncle Justin's cow!"

Mama stuck her head out the kitchen door, saying, "All right! You girls be careful! Nora, you mind you sister and don't leave the pathway. I don't want you two to get lost in the woods," she cautioned.

"Okay, Mama! We won't be very long, and we'll be careful not to get lost," I assured her as we headed south toward the cemetery.

About midway from the house to the graveyard, Alma and I startled a very large buck; he had a huge set of antlers, but he took off so fast into the dense forest that we barely got a look at him. "What are you so excited about?" Alma asked.

"Alma! The attention you give to that doll has robbed you of everything that is exciting about our visit to Uncle Justin's place," I mildly scolded.

I wasn't trying to be harsh; I was merely trying to reason with my sister awhile. By raising my voice, I knew I had her ear, even if it was just for a few moments. "You have to strike while the iron is hot!" just as the saying goes.

Unfortunately, my words must have fallen on deaf ears; Alma just shrugged her shoulders and said, "I love my ragdoll." That certainly was not a fresh revelation.

Exasperated over my failure to stimulate my little sister's senses, I was forced to modify my plan for meaningful conversation with my apathetic pal. Facing the reality that only the passing of the years would change her state of mind, I sought to be her friend and companion, giving time its chance to work the wonders in her that I was obviously incapable of bringing about.

To my surprise, we were already nearing the clearing that marks the family burial site; the entranceway was straight ahead. I had not realized the distance we had traveled. The sun was shining brilliantly over the open space, inviting us to enter the confines of the graveyard.

I asked Alma if she would mind making a short visit to the graves of our ancestors. Getting no response, I assumed her silence meant yes; she wanted to walk around the clearing. I opened the gate and we strolled through, shutting it behind us. It was then that I got the response I had waited for; I guess I hadn't waited long enough. "I don't mind, Nora, let's visit the graves," Alma suggested, as though it was her bright idea.

The pink floribundas were blooming profusely. The copious presence of their flowers brought a cheerful atmosphere to what would otherwise be a somber place—a place of bricks, crosses, and tombstones. The rose bushes planted near every grave, afford quiet dignity to the ordinary appearance of tombs in a graveyard. I am glad that Great-grandfather Joseph planted the rose stem left by Pauline Longere at Uncle Patrick's gravesite the day of his burial. Knowing the history behind the rose bushes makes me appreciate the tradition of taking a cutting from that first bush and planting it near every plot in the cemetery (family member or not).

We paused at Aunt Clara's tomb. It must have been difficult for Uncle Justin to walk way out here through the rain, having only the Lord and a shovel as companions, to bury the woman whose love for him could only be exceeded by the Lord Himself. It is fitting that the Lord was with Uncle Justin when he laid his wife here to rest. God understood his pain and grief, and it was He who gave him the strength he needed to do what had to be done. "Thank you for your help in time of trouble, Lord. Amen."

I broke a stem from the rose bush near Aunt Clara's tomb; it had nine blooms on it when I handed it to my little sister. Next, we walked to the tomb of Pauline Longere; she has always had a special place in my heart. The princess from Chacahoula is alive in my mind's eye as well as in my heart; I'm sure I will think of her often this coming year, especially while I am enjoying Great-grandmother Josephine's diary. I read it all the time.

Alma spotted the cow near the closed gate of the cemetery. "Let's go pet her," she pleaded.

After pulling the cemetery gate shut behind us, we petted the gentle creature awhile before starting back to the house. In a matter of minutes, I discovered the reason the cow had gotten loose; the pasture gate must have been left open. I hadn't noticed it on our way here. I decided to try to coax the animal into its pen. Alma and I worked together; positioning the cow between us, we escorted her through the gate. After accomplishing this easier-than-I-thought task, we shut the pasture gate, securing it with a rope before we continued our walk home. Looking over the confines of the grounds set aside for grazing, seeing the lush grasses growing everywhere, I wondered why Uncle Justine's milk cow saw the need to escape; maybe it's true: "The grass always looks greener on the other side."

On the journey back to the house, Alma commented on the sweet fragrance emitted by the many blooms that were clinging to the single stem of pink roses she was holding in her hand. "Hummingbirds must love these flowers," she volunteered.

I could hardly believe my ears. Alma was initiating conversation that had absolutely nothing to do with her ragdoll. "There is hope for you yet, Alma!" I proclaimed excitedly. Of course she did not understand the nature of my proclamation; she immediately handed me the stem of roses so she could hold her ragdoll with both of her hands. At least it was a good thought, I reasoned to myself; I refused to be discouraged by Alma's lack of apparent receptivity.

The men had returned from their fishing trip by the time we arrived back at the *big house*. I informed Uncle Justin about the big buck we startled on our way to the cemetery.

"That buck is one of our pet deer," Uncle Justin explained. "We never hunt the west or south sides of the island. There are plenty enough deer on the north and east sides of the ridge for us to shoot."

Felix was explaining that even though Papa and Uncle Justin had caught the biggest fish; on average, both teams of boys had caught more fish than they had. "We should declare the winner by the total weight of each stringer," he respectively demanded.

Uncle Justin conceded that Felix's suggestion was a fair one; they all hurried to their boats to establish the undisputed winner of the fishing contest. Using the oar from his push skiff as a balance beam, Uncle Justin placed one end of the oar over Brad's shoulder and the other end over Gus's shoulder.

He tied a piece of rope to two wooden pails and suspended them over the oar. One bucket hung from each side of the oar suspended by a common rope. "The bucket with the most weight in it will send the other one skyward," Uncle Justin proposed. "Now let's find out which team has won the day."

Papa and Uncle Justin placed their catch over one of the buckets (they were too large to fit inside). The first bucket was held steady until the second bucket was filled. Lee and Gus were the two old men's first challengers. Skyward went the losing bucket. "Next!" Uncle Justin confidently challenged.

Felix and Brad placed their catch into the bucket vacated by the losing team. To Uncle Justin and Papa's surprise, skyward went their bucket.

"The winners, fair and square, Felix and Brad Addison have won the fishing contest!" Aunt Sarah announced in a loud, shrill voice.

"Now that we have settled that matter, let's go inside and eat dinner before it gets cold," Mama urged.

At the dinner table, Uncle Justin could not stop bragging about the Indian canoe. He feels that its superior performance in the water is due mainly to the way the boat is shaped. In addition to its other fine attributes, my uncle says the canoe is very stable, even with two full-grown men aboard.

I didn't think it was possible, but the continuous praises that my Indian canoe was prompting caused me to feel all the more ecstatic over my discovery. I will miss those adventures along the big bend in the river, I thought quietly.

I could not help myself; suddenly, I blurted out, "I can't wait until next October!" My bark had no bite, and momentarily I felt helpless; while preparing to explain the sudden expression of my inner most feelings within hearing distance of my startled listeners, I found myself uncharacteristically speechless.

"I don't know what I'm going to do with you, little missy," Mama gently scolded. "We haven't even packed to leave the island yet and you're already acting like a homesick child," she added.

There was no doubt in my mind that I was merely expressing everyone's true feelings; we were all somewhat gloomy because we knew the holiday would soon be over once again. This is the general mood every year the day before we leave, but this year seems to be worse for everyone.

After dinner, I asked Felix and Gus if they would escort me one last time to the bend in the river; it would be my last chance for this season. Mama had no objections and the boys liked the idea.

As the grownups left the dining room to go upstairs for their afternoon naps, Alma decided to go with them; the rest of us headed for the *beaten path*. The customary footrace was no close contest; the older boys arrived at the riverside long before Gus and I. I was last once again.

I wanted to make the best of my last view of the river. Uncle Justin says that at the widest part of the great bend where I found my canoe, the river is approximately fifteen hundred feet across. Fifteen hundred feet! What a monster this river is, I thought. Its whitecaps and eddies are readily noticeable, and not very far from the shoreline.

A huge uprooted tree just floated by me. It would be more accurate to say that it raced by me in the swift moving waters of the river. I watched the massive obstacle as it continued its journey to the Gulf; it occasionally disappeared, as the powerful undertow dragged it below the surface temporarily. This is one reason why the river can be dangerous to navigate, especially during the spring floods my uncle told me.

The noises made by the river are intriguing. I closed my eyes to take in the full effect of water struggling to find peace that will never come. This is a river that is alive, I thought. To still its waters would be tantamount to stealing its breath away; it would soon die. "Roll on!" I shouted. "Roll on, you mighty river, as you give and take away many lives along with you to the sea!" It's the natural order of things, I reasoned. God has made it so.

I must have lost track of time. When I noticed the boys were gone, I decided to take my time as I slowly returned to the house from the splendor provided by the river. I wanted to make this day last forever; it's strange that I was the last to awaken this morning. I wasted at least three hours asleep, I lamented.

The boys were swinging on the back porch when I got back to the house. They insisted that they hollered at me several times, begging me to return to the house with them.

"You just ignored us. It's like we weren't even there Nora!" Lee told me.

I've had these midday trances before; I get lost in the moment, oblivious to anything going on around me. It's queer the way I am sometimes. Maybe I'm not as dissimilar from my little sister as I consider myself to be; her obsession with her ragdoll is not very different from what Lee just expressed about me. It might not be such a bad thing; it's the product of a creative mind, a writer's mind, I reasoned.

Lee reiterated, "You looked as though you were in some sort of trance, Nora!"

"Maybe I was, Lee! Maybe I was in a trance!" I responded, not the least bit annoyed by his astute observation. He was merely telling the truth.

The grownups are planning a trip to the fruit orchard this afternoon; I overheard Mama talking to Aunt Sarah in the kitchen. My aunt was telling Mama that the frosty mornings we experienced around Thanksgiving should have raised the sugar content in the citrus fruit. We'll be taking several baskets of grapefruit, oranges, lemons, and limes with us to the trapping camp when we leave tomorrow.

The grownups boarded the push skiff and brought Alma with them; they were making final preparations for the trip to the orchard, loading several empty baskets into the boat. Felix, Gus, and I boarded my Indian canoe. Lee and Brad followed in one of the other canoes. We raced to the site of the *orchard path* ahead of the oar skiff. Arriving there first, we pulled our boats ashore and waited for the rest of the party of fruit pickers to pull up behind us.

The citrus trees were loaded down; some of their branches were threatening to break from their heavy burden of ripened fruit. In no time, we had picked a dozen full baskets of assorted fruit—oranges, lemons, grapefruit, and limes.

Uncle Justin suggested that the boys transport six bushels of citrus fruit downstream and stow them away aboard the *Early Rose*. The other six bushels will go to the house for his family to enjoy.

There are so many citrus fruit in the orchard that Uncle Justin says he will bring most of them to the city to sell them at the general store. He told Aunt Sarah that there will be enough fruit in a few weeks to make a trip to Morgan City. It is always good news when you can produce more than your family can eat; the money the bumper crop will bring will be put to good use.

Uncle Justin and company headed back upstream with six bushels of fresh picked fruit. Following my uncle's recommendation, we young kids made a dash for the landing to offload the citrus fruit on our boat. When we arrived at the dock, all of us got out of the boats and stretched our legs. After a brief stretch, we all took a seat—some along the wharf, and others on the bulwarks of our converted sailboat.

Felix and Lee quickly loaded the six baskets into the cabin of our boat. Afterward, the boys wanted to go for a paddle in Deer Bayou. Felix challenged Lee to a race. "One man to the canoe!" he insisted. Lee accepted the challenge, and they were soon off to the races. "The first one back from the point of the first curve in the bayou wins!" Felix yelled, as he pointed to the spot.

I was surprised to see Papa show up at the landing in the oar skiff. "Who wants a ride?" he offered. Gus jumped aboard the skiff before Papa could come along to tie the boat to the wharf. Gus was so eager to enjoy the ride that he and Papa continued on into the middle of the bayou and headed downstream with the slow-moving tide.

Apparently disturbed by all the activity, I detected motion in the eagle's nest. Suddenly, one of the great birds hopped out the nest and perched on a nearby limb. It seemed as though he wanted to keep a sharp eye on us, but when he spread his wings out and left them that way, I realized he was merely sunning himself. With a seven-and-a-half-foot wingspan, looking at the eagle with his wings out was an impressive sight to behold. I could see the white feathers on the crown of his head clearly in the sunlight. What a spectacle; this was the best sighting of an eagle I had ever witnessed. Just as I was wondering about the majestic bird's mate, I saw it perched on the nest's edge at the far side; I guess it was curious about what the male was looking at in the distance. I wondered if there could be any young ones in the nest. Careful observation yielded no positive conclusion one way or the other.

Of course, I knew there would not be any young ones in the nest; it's too early! Uncle Justin says the eagles don't arrive here until September each year. I can't really be sure which of the birds was a male; other than a slight difference in weight (a pound or so) the male and female eagle are not distinguishable (the male being the smaller of the two).

Uncle Justin told me that the magnificent birds begin nest restoration in October and they begin to lay their eggs in early winter (typically during the two weeks between December 25 and January 7). Incubation takes thirty-five days, and the fledglings are out of the nest by the end of February.

In May, these eagles will migrate north to escape the heat of summer. Uncle Justin has been told they may fly as far north as Canada. Uncle Justin says it has taken years of observation for him to understand their habits. I find all this information most interesting; I am always delighted to learn more about nature.

Felix beat Lee in the first race, and Brad was the next to challenge him in a canoe race. Once again, Felix prevailed. I guess that even though the Indian canoe is superior to the other dugouts, the man behind the paddle makes some of the difference. Both my brothers lost in my canoe.

Deer Island Bayou
Near Eagle's Nest

Papa and Gustave go for
a ride in Uncle Justin's
"push skiff"
(carries 4 passengers)
(comfortably)

When Papa returned in the oar skiff after giving Gus a ride, the boat races had ended. The shadows in the bayou made it clear it would soon be dark, so we all headed upstream following closely behind Papa and Gus in the push skiff. We slowly made our way toward the fountainhead at the head of the clear water stream.

As darkness enveloped the homestead, Papa lit two oil lamps on the dinner table. The moon was growing; the first quarter would provide enough light for the last night of storytelling. The temperature outside remained in the mid-fifties—not too hot and not too cold. The setting for the night will be perfect, I surmised.

We dined on bread, fig preserves, and goat's milk. As we were enjoying our last supper of the season together, I suddenly realized that Papa would be revealing the contents of the second wooden box that was given to Joseph and Josephine by the Henleys. I had nearly forgotten that this would be the subject for the last story of the season.

As I relished in the excitement of the soon-coming revelation, discouragement knocked at my door. The stark reality that time was flying was disconcerting. I can't stop the clock! Our last day on the island is coming to an abrupt end. We'll be gone for nearly eleven months! Woe is me!

Excited about the contents of the second box and at the same time saddened by the realization that in a matter of a few hours we will be leaving this island paradise, I found myself torn between two powerful tugs at my emotional stability. I felt I would be soon torn asunder by these opposite feelings.

My heart is here and my body must leave; what a dilemma!

I dare not reveal the inner turmoil I am struggling to control. The last time I allowed an outburst of my true feelings prompted a scolding by my mother. It's better to suffer silently, I reasoned. I believe the inquisitive glances Mama has been sending my way, shows she is cognizant of my inner agitation; she is no doubt praying I will maintain control of myself. I took a few deep breaths to try to dispel my uncomfortable state.

When everyone settled down in their favorite places on the veranda of the *big house*, Uncle Justin said he had an announcement to make. "I just wanted to take this time to say how much Sarah and I and the boys enjoyed your visit with us this autumn. While you are away from us, taking care of business, you will all be on our minds and in our hearts. I won't speak for everyone. Each of my family members can take their turn sharing how they feel, but as for me personally, I want you to know you will be sorely missed. Like little Nora, I'm really looking forward to next year."

Aunt Sarah wanted to speak next. "The weeks we spend together, before the cold weather sets in, are precious to me. During the course of the year, it is the fall that I look forward to the most, more than any other season or holiday. I hope that my efforts here have made you all comfortable and that you have found your stay with us as enjoyable as I have. I'll miss all of you dearly, but Lord willing, we will have this opportunity again next year."

Felix stood up and spoke next. "This is the best autumn I ever had, and I look forward to more of the same next year." I believe he was crying when he finished.

Gus was next. "I did not know exactly what to say. I do know this. When you leave it will be very lonesome here without you. There will be no one here to say good night to, and no one to tell good morning. I will miss all of you, that's for sure." Well, here was another boy with tears running down his cheeks; it was quite moving.

Papa and Mama expressed their sincere gratitude for the splendid hospitality and the warm welcome. Papa said that these qualities of Southern hospitality always make our stay here most enjoyable. Speaking for all of us, Papa thanked Uncle Justin and his family for their expressions of love, kindness, and extreme generosity. "As with you, so it will be with us. Though we will part for many months, you will all be on our minds and in our hearts. Nora, our legend keeper and the guardian of our history, will make sure of that," Papa said in a quivering voice.

I was not surprised that everyone was anguishing over our departure. Somehow it lends me a degree of comfort, knowing we all feel the same way. This seems to me to be a good example of how it must feel when someone loses a wife, a husband, or a child. It's a part of life that must be difficult to bear.

These exchanges between our family members provide the glue that binds the Addison family together. Love is the strong sentiment that keeps us longing for more time with each other; it is the substance that has nurtured a family heritage that has continued for eighty-one years, a legacy that is destined to continue for many years to come. Sharing our feelings with each other is the key to our past and the door to our future, as the Addison family legacy continues to be built on a sure foundation—love for God and love for one another.

"Is anyone interested in the final story of the season?" Papa asked, teasing his captive audience.

Everyone shouted, "Let's hear it!"

Papa began, "As all of you know, Great-grandmother kept a diary from 1836 to 1865. In her recorded legend, she wrote about events that took place in her life from the time of her wedding through the time of her arrival here on Deer Island. She continued to record events through the years starting with the establishment of the homestead and ending shortly after the Civil War ended, including a brief history of the aftermath of that conflict.

"My daughter has cherished her great-grandmother's diary since she was old enough to read. I would venture to say that the intrinsic value she has found within the pages of that diary far exceeds the value of her 'fantastic discovery' this autumn, on Thanksgiving Day; how appropriate it was for this to happen to the young women we have entrusted with the responsibility of continuing the Addison family legacy for generations to come.

"We all could say that we found it strange that Josephine's careful record of events stopped abruptly shortly after the Civil War ended. It has remained a mystery, leaving Nora and the rest of us, suspended in time. The events that transpired over the years since the war seem to have vanished over time, since no one thought they were important enough to write down; what a failure to communicate that would be, especially to those of us who would really like to know.

"From Joseph and Josephine there sprang forth a family legacy and family traditions that have spanned all these years. The nucleus of a loving family, the establishment of the homestead; the establishment of an Anglican church on Bayou Du Large. Things we can be proud of for generations. Where are the accounts of all these important events?

"I have it from a reliable source that the end of the Civil War did not mark the end of Josephine's record as all of us thought. In fact, she recorded every important event of any significance until the week of her death in the latter part of July 1905.

"Within the pages of her recorded legend is a veritable treasure chest of family history. So rich in descriptive experiences is the diary that we will be able to share its preserved memories for countless autumns to come. The stories she has recorded for us are some of the most intriguing and thought provoking accounts I have ever read.

"I will not take time this last night of our season together to read a story from Josephine's diary. I will, however, share the last entry she recorded shortly before her death. This entry was intended to be her farewell address to the generations of Addisons that would come after her.

"Let it be known to my family and to the whole world that Joseph and Josephine Addison pursued a dream and they lived it. My husband and I shared a full and rich life together, and with God's help, we accomplished every single one of our goals. Though death may separate us for a season, let this legend serve to keep Joseph and me alive in the hearts and in the minds of all who care to read it. This is the record of the life and times of Joseph and Josephine Addison from the time of our marriage to the time of our departure from among you. I close with this final admonition: 'Love one another as God has loved you, be content with what you have, don't ever be afraid to share your feelings with one another, set an example you need not be ashamed of, pursue your dreams and strive to live them out; happiness is fleeting, enjoy it when it comes.' I thank God for sending Joseph into my life. It was Joseph who taught me these life-long principals. Always remember that Uncle Patrick was the catalyst that made the entire homestead possible. God used him to bring us here; he will remain a cornerstone of the Addison family legacy. My faith in God has sealed my destiny. Through a diligent study of Scripture, I have grown in the knowledge of God. Jesus has become my Lord and Savior, now and forever, amen. My recorded legend contains my testimony; it is my final gift to all of you. Farewell!"

"So the record ended on July 25, 1905, just two days prior to her death," Papa concluded.

"Did you find great-grandmother's diary, Papa?" I asked with tears flowing down my cheeks.

"No, Nora; I did not," Papa responded.

Seeing the disappointed expression on my face, Uncle Justin asked me to remain patient. "I'll be right back," he said, as he disappeared into the house. When he returned to the front porch, he handed me the second box.

Uncle Justin instructed me to open the box. I looked at Papa who said, "Open the box, Nora!"

My heart was racing; I could not get the lid open. "I almost forgot," Uncle Justin teased. "Here's the key!"

I could feel the blood rushing to my head as I placed the key into the hole at the front center of the chest. Inside the chest was a large leather-bound book. Carefully removing the massive document from the box, I opened the front cover. In the light of the moon I read the transcription.

> To dearest Josephine, please accept this diary as a present
> from me to you. As you record events in this legend, remember
> you will always be
> welcome at Sugarland Farms Plantation.
> With kindest regards, Greta Henley

Uncle Justin announced that he had something important to tell me. "Nora, there is no one in the family more intent on keeping abreast of all there is to know about the Addison family. With that in mind, after consulting with everyone in the family, on behalf of all of us, I present you with 'The Life and Times of Joseph and Josephine Addison,' a comprehensive record of our entire family history from 1836 to 1905.

"You will discover that your great-grandmother transcribed her earlier diary into this legend so everything would be contained in a single volume. You will discover that she was true to her philosophy about living your dreams to their fullest. You will discover that her final entry is recorded in the last available space on the very last page of her diary. There are over two thousand pages in this exhaustive history of the Addison family. It is hereby entrusted to your care."

I did not know what to say. I just cried and cried and cried. I have never been so happy in my entire life, and yet I was crying uncontrollably. I clutched the heavy volume tightly to my chest.

"All Laffite's gold and silver could not equal or compare with the treasure you have just presented to me. This I will cherish for as long as I live," I pledged as teardrops continued to run their course down the sides of my cheeks.

Uncle Justin wasn't quite finished with his surprises; it turns out that Pauline was not the only princess written about in Grandmother Addison's diary. The oldest of three daughters, Princess Kallie, the daughter of a Houmas chieftain, was introduced to me by Uncle Justin during storytelling time as he promised; now I can read about her relationship with my family for myself in great grandmother's extensive record.

"Aunt Sarah gave you the original sketch of her portrait that was presented to your great grandmother by William Harrison Henley on Thanksgiving Day, 1865. Well, Nora, that is not the end of her story," Uncle Justin told me. "Now I believe Adam has something he would like to share."

Papa began, "There is little disagreement among us, that this autumn has been a special one. Storytelling time, I'm sure you will all concur, has been nothing less than sensational. Nora's fantastic discovery, the gifts Joseph and Josephine received from Chief Kalamos being presented for all of us to see. These things have brought attention to our native peoples, the Chitimacha and the Houmas Indians.

"Nora, if you recall, Uncle Justine shared with you just after we arrived that there was the possibility that Princess Kallie is still alive. I have something to support that assertion.

"I purposely waited to share the following information so I could compete with Uncle Justin's story about the short relationship between members of our family and the Houmas chieftain and his daughter."

Papa continued, "Princess Kallie informed me that although she is still recognized as chieftain of the Houmas Nation, her people have dispersed all over the parish, particularly along bayou banks in the south. Splinter groups have settled in places like *Mauvais Bois* (bad woods) Goat Island, Bayou Sale and Dulac to name a few."

Astonished by what I had just heard, I interrupted Papa and asked him, "Have you spoken to her, Papa?"

"Allow me to continue," Papa urged.

"Princess Kallie lives on Jean Charles Island with about a hundred of her fellow Houmas Indians. She's seventy-one years old and in fair health.

"She shared that many of her people have married outside their race—French and English settlers. 'It's a sign that times are changing. No longer do we wonder from hunting grounds to hunting grounds in search of food. We buy our food from local general stores, or we barter for what we need,' she shared.

"It seems that Jean Charles Island residents have taken to seining for shrimp and culling for oysters at low tide, since these two commodities are always in demand.

"Inquiring about the Addison family, the local mail delivery man told her that members of the Addison family were living on Bayou Du Large. Curious about how we have fared as a family over the years, prompted her to write us a letter. She hopes we will visit her island sometime this spring. She has learned to speak English very well, thanks to a Catholic missionary priest that visits the island on a regular basis.

"Since Princess Kallie's letter had a return address, I wrote her back, accepting her invitation to visit her sometime in the month of April.

"I know this decision will be received with hearty approval, so it is a plan we can look forward to following through. I am told we can reach the island by motor vessel. Now that the *Early Rose* has been converted, we can easily navigate any inland waters that it may be necessary for us to travel.

"What do you think about that Nora? I am certain you and the Houmas princess will have much to talk about. If Justin and Sarah, Felix and Gus, wish to join us, there's plenty enough room on board the *Early Rose* to accommodate us all. We might spend a few days on Jean Charles Island if we aren't much of a burden on the people there. What do you all think about this idea?"

Felix spoke first, pleading with his parents to join us on our adventure. "I believe it would be a wonderful experience; mingling with the native Indians will make us appreciate what they have endured over the past thirty-five years. I wonder if Princess Kallie has retained any of her beauty and charm," he added with a smile.

Uncle Justin looked at Sarah to try to judge her reaction; her smiling face was all he needed to make the announcement. "We haven't seen Matthew and Emily White for a few years now; it's high time for us to leave the island for an extended vacation. We will make our rounds along Bayou Du Large to visit old friends. When Adam decides to make the trip to Jean Charles Island, we'll be aboard when the engine starts," he told us.

"By the way, I have the letter right here!" Papa told everyone; reaching into his pocket, he promptly showed the letter Princess Kallie had written to the Addison family.

"I knew the story was true, Papa, but producing evidence is one of the rules for storytelling," I shared.

"I have more proof, Nora!" Papa said. "Along with the letter, a portrait (by the same artist) of the fair maiden, now a Houmas chieftain, was included. It was dated 1875. The same year Chief Kalamos died," he concluded.

"Where is it?" we all asked in unison.

"It's right here for all to see!" Papa said as he proudly displayed the stunning image.

"Isn't she fascinating? I wish I could have met her, Uncle Justin," I responded.

"Josephine said the exact same thing all those many years ago," Uncle Justin shared with a wink of his eye.

"I believe you are holding back on me, Uncle Justin," I speculated.

"With your inquisitive mind, Nora, I am certain that by next autumn, once you've had the chance to read more of Josephine's diary, you will be able to host storytelling time with all the information you gather about Princess Kallie and her relationship with the Addison family," Uncle Justin told me.

Everyone was happy for me. Alma came over to where I was seated and hugged me tightly around my neck. "I love you, Nora," she whispered in my ear.

"I love you too, Alma, my dear little sister," I told her as we continued to embrace on the front steps near the corner support post of the veranda of the *big house.*

As I lay me down to sleep for the last time during our autumn visit, I imagine the aged princess; is she living in a thatched hut or is she in a wooden structure? Does any evidence of her former beauty remain? Is she still the fascinating woman she once was? I can't wait to see her! I found myself completely exhausted. New revelations tonight have overwhelmed me. I fought off the urge to escape my thoughts, but I lost the battle quickly.

Chapter Twelve

AT THE TRAPPING CAMP

November 28, 1921

With all the help I could muster, my Indian canoe was placed safely onboard; it was positioned diagonally across the front deck, nestled between the bulwarks, the left front corner of the cabin, and the front mooring bit near the bow. With my "fantastic discovery" safely loaded on deck, Papa was preparing to start up the one cylinder engine of the *Early Rose*. With the motor housing removed, and the sliding door opened for the exhaust fumes to escape the interior of the cabin, Papa kicked back against the motor housing and made a spin on the large flywheel. The engine sounded: *Puk-puk-puk-puk-puk-puk-puk*, sputter, silence. Another spin of the flywheel and the perky sounds of the Palmer engine filled the afternoon air: *Puk-puk-puk-puk-puk-puk-puk-puk-puk-puk-puk-puk-puk-puk-puk...*

My brothers cast off the bow and stern lines as we all waved our hands and arms frantically in a good-bye gesture. Soon we were traveling slowly downstream, heading for the mouth of Deer Bayou.

The sounds of the engine must have irritated the eagles; they were on the nest when we boarded this morning; I could see them clearly in the mid-day sun. They flew overhead with wings spread, casting shadows on the deck of the *Early Rose,* as we moved through the water below them.

Alma is sitting inside the canoe singing to her ragdoll. The boys and I rushed to the stern of the boat to say our final good-byes.

"Take care of yourselves!" Felix hollered.

"See you next autumn!" Brad yelled.

Screaming at the top of my lungs, hoping they would hear me, I shouted, "I love you, guys!" We disappeared from view as we rounded the bend in the bayou and entered the canopy of the deep woods.

Puk-puk-puk-puk-puk-puk-puk-puk-puk-puk-puk-puk-puk... sounded the engine as we traveled through the arboreal tunnel, which would lead us to the Atchafalaya River.

I pondered a few things as I returned to the bow to take my favorite seat on our boat. This is a new day, I thought to myself· we are heading in a different direction. Life can be grand! Who ca⌐ hope to know one's future when even the events of a single day are ⌐ uncertain; it must be normal to wish for the best. Uncle Justin's st⌐ of tragedy will forever remind me that sometimes life can be hars' know that God will be there for me in any event, especially if I ⌐ strength and consolation during fiery trials; He will always b⌐ source for comfort.

Once we entered Atchafalaya Bay, I looked north one la⌐ to get a final glimpse at the island paradise I have come to kn⌐ love. *Puk-puk-puk-puk-puk-puk-puk-puk-puk-puk-puk-pu⌐* the sound of the engine kept distracting me, as Deer Islar⌐ peared behind our wake and Four League Bay appeared ov⌐ of the *Early Rose.*

A stiff north wind was stirring up the bay as we got f⌐ the shoreline; we were heading southeast from the mouth⌐ The seas were growing bigger and bigger as we passed ⌐ Crooked Bayou. Papa said the northers would soon be '⌐ way through on a regular basis.

There were many seagulls flying overhead, heading inland. This is a sign of bad weather to come; the Gulf of Mexico must be stirring up I thought, as I envisioned waves breaking against the sandy beach of *Isles Dernier* in a roaring fury many miles southeast of here.

During the summer, my family seines for shrimp behind the barrier islands; that's too far in the future to consider now, since trapping season is about to begin. I do love to comb the beaches when the weather gets too rough to work for shrimp. I scour the beaches for seashells, sand dollars, and interesting things that wash up on shore, especially after stormy episodes.

Trapping will begin on December 1, and it will continue until the end of February next year; then it will be settle up time with Doc Fursom at the general store. Once our pelts are tendered, we'll return home to plant a spring garden. It will be time to share all of my exciting experiences with my girlfriends—Jenny Kraft, Alice LaCoste, and Mariah Lovett.

All my girlfriends are with their families at their trapping grounds by now. Jenny's father traps Big Carrion Crow Bayou; Alice Kraft's father traps Carrion Crow lake and Biscuit Bayou. Mariah's family works the Copasaw. Since every year we are the first to leave Bayou Du Large for our trapping grounds, my girlfriends always accuse me of giving them trapping fever. It's just another way of saying that our departure makes them get anxious and excited about leaving for the winter, a tradition most people I know look forward to doing.

Though they would never admit it, I sometimes get the sense that my girlfriends are a bit envious of our annual trek to Deer Island; can't say I blame them. Maybe someday Papa will allow each of my girlfriends to take a turn sharing the experience with us. I'm sure Uncle Justin won't mind; it would be a great opportunity for Felix and Gus to meet a few nice girls.

As I was in the middle of a daydream, my eye caught the mouth Palmetto Bayou as we passed it by. The next bayou we come to will Plumb Bayou, our ultimate destination for this short voyage. The *Rose* will remain dormant there for three whole months. Papa may run the engine a few times, but the boat rarely moves away from the dock at our trapping camp during the winter.

Palmetto Bayou is one of Papa's favorite places to hunt for gators. The waterway snakes its way through the vast prairielands of the Adams estate. Along the banks of that bayou, and in the prairie ponds that dot the area, are some of the best breeding grounds for the big-mouthed carnivores. There are numerous alligator nests; many are visible from the deck of a boat as it travels along its course.

Alligators make their nests and lay their eggs in late June, or early July. The female bites the marsh grasses in a large circle; she heaps up the material forming an oblong-shaped nest about two feet tall. When the time is right, she enters her makeshift den to lay her eggs. By September 1, all the eggs have hatched and the young must begin to fend for themselves.

Last winter Papa, Lee, and Brad were running muskrat traps in the marshlands along Palmetto Bayou. Brad was moving his trapping lines, and he happened upon a shallow pond that had a huge alligator lying on its bottom; it was clearly visible. The cold temperatures had him in a state of slumber. He hailed Lee and Papa and told them what he had found. Upon arriving at the spot, Papa suggested they leave the creature alone until the next day; there was nothing they could do without the proper gear. Papa told the boys the animal wasn't going anywhere in the bitter cold.

There was excitement at the camp that night (I remember it well). There was little debate about the gator's size; the best estimate was twelve to fourteen feet long. Early next morning, well before daylight, I heard the engine sound, as Papa and the boys headed for Palmetto Bayou.

When the day was nearing its end, Papa and the boys arrived back at the camp; the front deck was loaded with muskrat. Behind the pile of furry creatures was the massive body of the gator they had seen the day before. We all joined in the task of carrying the muskrats to the skinning shed, making room for the offloading of the huge reptile.

Once the creature was dragged onto the dock, its size could be measured; it was fourteen feet, three inches long. Papa told Mama that he had used his trusty pole (a long pole with a huge hook secured at one end) to draw the big animal close enough to the shoreline of the pond for Lee to get a clean shot. Papa was proud to relate what happened. "Lee shot him right between the eyes at the top of the skull. Your eldest son hit the soft spot on his very first try. The gator barely had time to react to my assault when it was killed."

Mama marveled at the girth of the creature's body; she was accustomed to seeing many a large alligator, but this was the largest one she had ever seen; I remember grabbing hold of the rope to assist Papa and the boys in dragging the gator along the walkway leading to the skinning table. When its mouth was stretched open, the snout reached from the planked walkway to above my knee; now that's a big alligator!

Once the hide was separated from its carcass, Papa and the boys towed his remains into the bay where the crabs and shrimp could feast until its form disappeared into their digestive tracts. This was the usual manner for disposing of the denuded carcasses, the difference in this case was the fact that the body was so heavy that it had to be towed rather than carried on deck.

As colder weather ensues, most gators will resort to shallow pools surrounded by prairie where they will hibernate, remaining submerged for the winter, and coming up for air only briefly from time to time. Papa says during cold winters, heavy ice can prevent the creatures from surfacing; on rare occasions, some of them suffocate (they drown). It's strange to me how their bodies slow down as the temperature of the water drops. The weather has been consistently below fifty degrees since shortly after we left home in late October. We've had at least two days of morning frost while visiting Deer Island. Though still active for now, it won't be long before the gators will seemingly disappear; they will remain in their winter homes until spring. Hallelujah for that!

We entered the mouth of Plumb Bayou about twenty minutes ago; we're rounding the point, and we will soon be at our winter home. The sky is getting cloudy, and there is a dark line of them coming from the northwest; there will probably be a cold front moving through tonight. I am glad we will make it to the camp before bad weather sets in and makes life unpleasant.

When we approached the camp wharf, Papa slowed the engine; the boys took their positions at the bow and stern as we prepared to moor. Papa nosed the bow into the shallows near the bank of Plumb Bayou and sped up the engine to swing the stern around closer to the dock. Once the mooring lines were secured, Papa pulled on the knotted rope that would silence the motor. Our ears were now trained on the sounds of lonesome goats calling nearby.

Both *Ninny* and *Nanny* hurried to greet us on the wharf. I walked up to them and hugged them around their necks. In my own version of "goat talk," I asked, "Were you lonesome for us?"

When I gazed up, I spotted *George Washington* foraging for food, surrounded by his ever loving hens near the pigpen. The piglets were nowhere in sight; it was obvious they had escaped from their holding pen just as we had planned. Papa says the young pigs will probably show up later, once they hear our voices around the camp.

Lee entered the camp and tied the shutters in the open position to encourage a bit of cross ventilation to freshen the air inside. There were no surprises this time; no snake to shoo out the doorway. Mama immediately put firewood in the stove to heat water for a pot of fresh coffee.

The first thing we unloaded was my Indian canoe. We all pitched in to carry it from the wharf to Papa's trapping ditch. That will be its new home, at least for now. Next, Brad, Lee, Papa, and I began unloading the provisions that Aunt Sarah and Uncle Justin gave us to carry home. There were jars of jelly and preserves of various kinds; we unloaded the six bushel baskets full of citrus fruit; we had a cask of salted bear meat. There were several jars of honey, and three different kinds of pickled hot peppers, preserved in Aunt Sarah's cider vinegar.

Uncle Justin presented Papa with a new duck call as we were leaving this afternoon. It will no doubt be soon put to good use; Papa is already practicing with a few calls from his seat on the steps of the camp. Though I didn't get to hunt with my cousins this autumn, I'm sure Papa will teach me to duck hunt this winter.

With everything offloaded and stowed away, Papa told us we could spend the remainder of the afternoon relaxing. It was already getting late and the cicadas were making the noisy sounds we are accustomed to hearing before the sun sets. We have two full days to prepare for trapping season. With almost everything that needs doing done, we will have plenty free time between chores tomorrow and the day after.

I took the wooden chest containing my great-grandmother's diary, and placed it under my bed. I hanged the key that unlocks the box on a nail on the wall, high enough that Alma can't reach it. I wasn't doing it for selfish reasons; it was only a precaution to prevent someone too young to appreciate its value from accidently damaging it.

Papa took his first sip of hot coffee as he looked across the front yard of the camp and admired his pride and joy, the *Early Rose*. "Did you see how well she rode over the seas in the bay today Ida?" he quizzed. There was a degree of vainglory evident in his question.

Knowing what Papa wanted to hear, Mama responded, "She performed like the well-built boat that she is Adam." She wasn't pandering him; she was telling the truth.

"That Indian canoe of Nora's has to be one of the most beautiful canoes to be found anywhere. There can't be any that could be more skillfully crafted, not to mention the intricate carving of the eagles and bears," Papa pondered in an elevated voice so he could be sure Mama could hear him.

"Yes, Adam, Nora's 'fantastic discovery' was truly fantastic," Mama told Papa.

Brad and Lee were lounging around on the ground near the front of the camp reminiscing about our recent adventure, as my parents continued to enjoy conversation on the steps of the camp. Alma and I decided to walk the planked walkway that led to the cistern and the outhouse. We continued around the back of the camp to sit on our favorite oak limb overlooking the prairie near Papa's trapping ditch.

When my little sister and I took a seat on the large oak limb, we immediately spotted three doe and a buck drinking from Papa's ditch. They weren't a hundred yards behind the camp. I managed to point them out to Alma before they disappeared into the thicket.

Conspicuously absent was Alma's ragdoll. I was not about to ask her where she laid it down. Could this be the beginning of a transformation in Alma's character? I hoped so!

As we sat together on the storm-twisted oak that bent over and touched the ground to thwart its attacker's plans for uprooting it, I began to communicate with my little sister in a meaningful way. It didn't take long for me to discover that Alma had been paying much closer attention to all that has been going on around her than I ever suspected or dreamed.

Alma began to comment on the Thanksgiving Day celebration back at Uncle Justin's place. She told me she enjoyed all the good food we had to eat. She told me that she thought my Indian canoe was the most beautiful boat she had ever seen.

I hugged her dearly as though she was awakening from some dangerous prolonged unconscious state, as though I was relieved that she was suddenly showing signs of recovery and lending me great expectations for her future wellbeing.

"I love you, Alma!" I told her, excited by the change in her disposition I had just experienced.

"I love you too, Nora!" my little sister responded as she pointed to the sky. "Look, Nora! Look at all those geese! See how many there are!"

"Yes, Alma, there are many geese in that flight. Cold weather is coming soon, and the geese and ducks are coming down south before it. They are coming to escape the colder temperatures up north," I explained.

Continuing to amaze me, Alma quizzed, "Do you think Lee and Brad will kill any of those geese for us to eat?"

"That is almost certain, Alma. I would not be a bit surprised if Papa sends those brothers of ours on a goose hunt tomorrow morning," I speculated, trying to keep my little sister's mouth moving.

"Do you really think so, Nora?" Alma wondered.

"There is only one way to find out," I told her. "You'll have to go ask Papa," I suggested, further testing the possibility of a transformation. Alma would never have gone to Papa with a question about any subject before now.

"That is what I'll do then! I'm going to ask Papa if he will let Lee and Brad go hunting for geese in the morning," she proudly stated. She promptly arose from her seat near me and headed for the front of the camp.

Not long after she disappeared around the cistern, she returned to inform me that we would be having roasted goose for supper tomorrow night. She was so excited to tell me what Papa had told her that she was getting me excited. She was learning to communicate her feelings, a definite Addison trait.

I am glad Papa paid attention to her unusual request. I must remember to tell him just how much it meant to his youngest daughter.

"Aunt Clara loved Uncle Justin so much that she could not bear the thought of living without him. That's why she risked her life during the storm. She had to find out what had happened to him. She was no longer caring for herself. She found herself living only for him. Isn't that a beautiful kind of love, Alma?" I was continuing to stimulate my little sister's mind, probing further to see if she was paying attention to what I was saying.

"Why did Aunt Clara have to die?" Alma bewailed.

"Well, Alma, there are many things in life that are difficult to understand. I don't know why Aunt Clara had to die. It makes me sad every time I think about it. It seems so unfair. Since I'm lost trying to discover the reason for the tragedy, I choose to focus on the positive things, things that I do know about. Aunt Clara's actions on that fatal day demonstrated that she was a woman of impeccable character. She set a good example for those of us who would follow after her. I can only pray that I could exhibit the strength and character she did as I grow into womanhood."

I continued to try to explain. "I believe that one of the lessons we learn in life is that we must be able to look at difficult things in a positive vain. We must try, as best we can, to grow and learn from all our experiences—good or bad. These trials cause us to exercise our feelings. Sharing our deepest and most personal emotions, in a loving and meaningful manner, serves to draw us into a powerful bond. In this way, love will always keep the family together, through thick or thin."

I continued to explain. "Just as the excitement of some new discovery, or the listening to an amusing story for the first time, stimulates us in one way or another, so it is when we discover that we have lost something or someone that was dear to us. The edges of despair, experienced by those who have lost a loved one, should be diminished through the moral support and uplifting encouragement of friends or family members. All of these times of sharing serve to bring us closer together; they help us to better understand one another. Sharing from heart-to-heart is what makes a family whole and complete.

"You and I are going to be best friends, Alma. We will be able to share our true feelings with each other for as long as we live, and my hope is that our time together will be long and mutually fulfilling. Now let's make our way inside the camp before the mosquitoes get us," I strongly suggested.

On our way back to the front of the camp, I posed a question to my little sister: "Do you want me to share our Great-grandmother Josephine's diary with you, Alma?"

"I would love for you to read to me from our great-grandmother's diary. Maybe you can help me learn how to read better," Alma lauded, gleefully accepting my proposal.

"You bet I can! I'll be happy to help you learn to read better!" I eagerly accepted Alma's sudden desire to read and learn everything she can. I hope I can do a good job, but her desire to learn is a very good start; there is little doubt about that.

When we entered the house, darkness enveloped the surrounding prairie; Mama had the inside of the camp brightly lit by the glow of two oil lamps resting on the dining table.

It was strangely quiet around the table as we supped on fresh biscuits and fruit preserves. This will take some getting used to, not having additional faces around us. There was a distinct air of loneliness at the Addison trapping camp at Plumb Bayou. Breaking the deafening silence, Alma loosed her tongue. She began acting like a tightly wound spring that had been suddenly released to perform some task of noisemaking. Her endless chatter soon had everyone witnessing the event spellbound.

Mama, in an effort to try to slow her down, said, "Now, Alma, if you expect to have conversation with another person, you will have to stop talking once in awhile so someone else can say something. If you keep this pace up while expressing your thoughts, you may well lose your voice," she cautioned.

Papa laughed at the notion that his shy, passive, and quiet little girl had finally discovered what her tongue was made for. Papa's uninhibited laughter prompted the rest of us to do likewise. It was just the shot in the arm we needed to break the spell of impending loneliness that was looming only minutes ago.

"I have a good idea!" Papa ventured. He was noticeably excited that Alma suddenly could talk.

"What is it, Papa?" everyone wanted to know.

"Let's each take a turn sharing our feelings about this autumn's visit at Uncle Justin's place. Everyone should try to limit him or herself; try to choose one fascinating experience that you feel has made the most lasting impression on you. I will begin the evening of sharing with my own personal reflections. I'll try to set the example for the rest of you to follow. Alma, we'll finish the night with your account of your biggest event during our visit," Papa instructed us, explaining his desired format for the evening discussion. Naturally, everyone agreed.

Papa was first to speak. "The thing that impressed me most about our visit is the way that storytelling on the veranda of the *big house* brings us closer together as a family. Yes, many of the stories are meant for entertainment, but they are tales of actual experiences. I firmly believe that we are a better family because of our time-honored tradition of sharing both the wild and exciting events and those that are tragic and sorrowful. These stories present family members, friends, and acquaintances in an honest and forthright fashion. It is my heartfelt desire that, as members of this household, you would consider everything you hear carefully, then subject what you hear to shared reasoning. In this way, you will get the most from each shared experience or event. Dare to dream! Dare to explore new thoughts! Dare to communicate what you feel inside, for everyone's sake! Each and every one of you is an important part of the whole family, but if you don't contribute by sharing what is within you, our family will suffer for it. Communicate!"

We exchanged a few comments over Papa's remarks, and then it was Mama's turn to speak. "When Uncle Justin shared the tragic events of the 1909 Storm with us, it made me examine feelings I have deep within myself, feelings I don't ordinarily share with any of you. As he told us of his tragic loss, I could feel his anguish and pain. It was being conveyed to us as he relived the particulars surrounding the event. As I later reflected on what he shared, I began to have a deeper appreciation of the love Aunt Clara exhibited for her husband. I recognized something about her that I truly feel for all of you. I believe if I would be challenged with a similar crisis, and if one of you would be facing a perilous situation, I would act in the same way Aunt Clara did that day. I want all of you to know that this is how much I love each and every one of you."

Mama arose from where she was seated and walked over to Papa and gave him an affectionate hug. When she left him to return to her seat, I saw Papa wiping the tears from his eyes; it was a touching scene.

Papa made a comment. "Can you see how much clearer we can understand each other, especially when we express our true feelings unashamedly. I love all of you!"

Now, it was Lee's turn to speak. "Felix and I spent many hours together, having conversation and sharing how we each felt about things. The most common thing we shared was our deep appreciation for those who have gone before us, and the recognition that we have been blessed with the best parents anyone could hope for. Felix shared that his paternal father died of the fever in 1915. He shared that when his mother married Uncle Justin that he and Gus went to live with them on Deer Island. He was twelve years old. He told me that, from the very beginning, Uncle Justin treated the two brothers as though they were his own sons. I could not help feeling privileged to know that I am part of a family that is willing to share and also to demonstrate how important we are to one another. I thank God for teaching our family how to love each other in such a pure and simple way. I thank God for my family. Amen."

Mama told Lee that his was a touching account, and that we were all happy he shared it with us.

It was Brad's turn to have our ears. "I am very happy that we have a special meeting place, a place where each autumn we come together as a family and revel and reflect upon the historic events in our family's past, and at the same time adding new pages of history to our family legacy. Storytelling time is my favorite experience during our stay at Uncle Justin's place. I hope that someday I will become as good a storyteller as Papa or Uncle Justin. I would love to be able to captivate the minds and the hearts of listeners in the way they are so capable of doing. The story of the cutlass; its connection to Pauline Longere. Their connection with Mr. Laffite and Patrick Adams. These stories will remain with me for the remainder of my life. Uncle Patrick's political career and his involvement in the Battle of New Orleans, reminds me that many of our family members had very uncommon experiences, and I'm sure the possibility exists that many members will continue to do so. This all serves to keep our expectation for a full and complete life, a goal within reach for anyone who dares to dream and to conduct his life in the pursuit of that dream. I thank God for my colorful heritage. Amen."

Papa commented about how true it is that we have been blessed by an extraordinary heritage. Mama applauded everyone's evaluation of our visit saying she was proud of the comments that reflect sensitivity and perceptual wisdom, and she was amazed that they were expressed so articulately.

Now it was my turn to speak and no one was surprised when I began to expound on the life of the "Princess from Chacahoula," Mademoiselle Pauline Longere. I began with "This year's new revelations about Pauline's relationship with our family and Mr. Laffite, as well as the effects she had on certain members of our family, will serve to further my nostalgic appreciation for her existence. Now, more than ever before, I believe she was the most charming, the most beautiful, and the most talented woman to ever grace the Louisiana

Territory. As long as I live, I will ever admire her characterization as portrayed in the recorded legend of Great-grandmother Josephine's diary. I look forward with great anticipation, to reading further accounts of Mademoiselle Longere, as I begin to explore the massive volume of Josephine's writings. Lest I forget I must say the prospects for meeting Princess Kallie, a woman said to rival Pauline in beauty and charm, this coming spring is filling me with joyful anticipation. I know we will become best friends in the end. I can't wait to read about her in Josephine's extended record. I thank God that great-grandmother took the time to record for all of us 'The Life and Times of Joseph and Josephine Addison,' Amen."

Everyone acknowledged that they weren't surprised by the contents of my presentation. Papa said that he knew I valued the family history more than the Indian canoe.

I confessed that I had almost forgotten about my "fantastic discovery." Because they knew me well, they found the oversight understandable.

"Alma, it's your turn to share with us," Papa encouraged.

Alma began, "I enjoyed the fresh air, the comfort of Aunt Sarah's bed, the hoot of the owls outside my bedroom window at night as I was preparing to fall asleep. I enjoyed looking at the chickens, the ducks, the geese, the turkeys, the goats, the pigs, the cow, the wild animals of the forest, and the eagles. I learned a great deal about cooking and mixing seasonings to make the food taste better. Most of all, I enjoyed holding Nora's hand and taking walks together around the homestead. I loved the fragrance of the roses she picked for me at Aunt Clara's grave. I want you all to know how special my sister is to me. I will never forget the fun I had at Uncle Justin's place this autumn. I would like to thank God for it. Amen."

When little sister finished, I rushed over to her and gave her a fond embrace. I told her that I loved her very much and that I was excited about her new awakening.

"Nora, have you seen my ragdoll?" she asked.

"No, Alma; I haven't," I told her. With a stern look on her face she looked me in the eye and said, "I must have forgotten it at Uncle Justin's."

"Maybe so," I softly informed her. The truth is that I remember seeing Alma singing to her doll while she sat in my Indian canoe on the deck of the *Early Rose* as we were leaving the wharf at Uncle Justin's place. I dare not remind her about it. If this is her time to come alive and be part of reality with the rest of us, I was not prepared to do anything that would spoil the progress of that transformation. I am ecstatic that my sister has begun to take an active role in conversation. Now our communication will be meaningful. What a rousing interest she has demonstrated! What new personality she has exhibited tonight! I could not be more excited!

Thinking the night of sharing was over, I started to get up from the table when a familiar voice uttered, "Papa, you never told us what became of Mr. Xavier Moliere and his pirate's loot. Can you tell us what happened after he left Bayou Du Large?" Alma was beside herself; she has turned into an eager beaver.

Papa was surprised by the request from his youngest child, but after a brief consultation with the rest of us, he decided to finish the night with the end of that story.

Papa began: "The story of Xavier's treasure brought much excitement to those who heard it this autumn. When I was at Doc Fursom's for provisions this fall, while the rest of you were ogling the things he had for sale in his store, he handed me a letter from Xavier addressed to Adam Addison in care of Fursom's General Store. I read the letter and never told anyone about it, including Mama. I was saving its contents for an appropriate time. I thought of using it for one of my stories this year. If you recall, I did acknowledge that there was more to the story than I had revealed that night.

"In brief, this is the rest of the story. Xavier moved to New Orleans; he bought himself a mansion in the Garden District. The Audubon Zoo is within walking distance of his house. He purchased a 1919 Packard Twin Six, a 6.9 liter Tourer, at a cost of thirty-seven hundred dollars.

"Xavier's home is built in the Victorian style, and it is an antebellum home, which simply means it was built prior to the Civil War. The home is located on St. Charles Avenue, definitely a place for the affluent. You might say he is doing very well with the proceeds from his unexpected discovery.

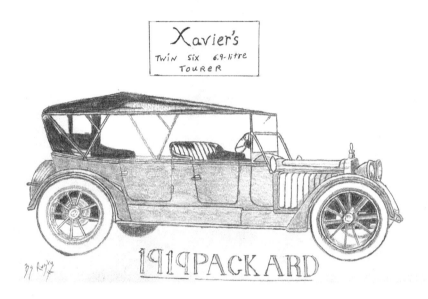

"In his letter, he informed me that he bought a building that was in a state of disrepair on Conti Street. He is remodeling the building and has plans to open a Creole Restaurant. The placard for the establishment will read:

Moliere's French and Spanish
Creole Restaurant
Turtle Dishes are our specialty!

"He told me he hired a local chef, Antoine Fauchet, to run the establishment when it opens. He plans to sit back and enjoy his wife and new home.

"You heard me right. Mr. Xavier is married. He met a Spanish Creole maiden on a pleasure trip to Baton Rouge aboard a steamboat. She is fifty-two years old with no children, her husband died of rheumatic fever in 1912. At the time of her marriage to Xavier, she had been a widow for nine years. Her name is Helena Maria Hidalgo.

"Mr. Xavier told me in his letter that he gave his house and land and his oar skiff to his niece, Denise Ann Moliere. She is planning to marry a boy from the bayou, his name is Charlton Moise, he is a fisherman that most everybody knows.

"And now everyone knows what happened to Mr. Xavier Moliere after he found buried treasure near Cemetery Island, located about three hundred yards west of the big bend in Little Bayou Du Large. He took the loot and moved to New Orleans, never to return to the bayou where he was raised.

"Xavier extended an open invitation to visit him in the big city whenever we would like to go. He wrote in his letter that he would be willing to come get us, so we could vacation with him sometime; the end!"

Papa had one more surprise. "By the way, Nora, Uncle Justin informed me that he discovered a daguerreotype of Pauline Longere dated 1839 among your favorite princess's personal effects while he was cleaning up the *little house* after this summer's storm," Papa shared.

"Because of the extensive number of new revelations we shared during storytelling time this autumn, we both decided to wait until next year to present it to you," he added.

"Have you seen it, Papa?" I asked.

"No, I haven't, Nora. Justin and I felt it would be a bigger surprise if we waited to see her for the first time together," he concluded.

"After visiting Princess Kallie next spring and with the anticipation of seeing what Pauline Longere looked like, there will be plenty food for thought. Lord willing, our next visit to Deer Island in autumn of 1922 will possibly be as fascinating as it was this year," I told Papa.

"The Lord knows; the Lord knows!"

Papa announced that it was time for bed. Alma seemed reluctant to follow the suggestion; she was the last to leave her spot at the table. Finally, she rushed to her bed as Mama blew out the lamps.

As I lay silently in my bed, pondering all that was shared at the table this evening, I heard an owl calling to its mate somewhere across the prairie. Though the shutters were all closed, the stiffening north wind found its way through the cracks to gently caress my face, reminding me that outside the camp, life goes on; it stops for no one even though we sometimes wish that it would.

I stayed awake to play host to the many memories that presented themselves to me, one at a time, until I began to lose sight of the images portrayed within my mind and the owl stopped calling loud enough for me to hear him.

(So ends the saga of Deer Island in Autumn in 1921. This concludes volume two, "Carrying on the Legacy." I wonder what next year will hold for the Addison Family.)

Epilogue

Note: The following excerpt was taken from the diary of my Aunt, Nora Addison. Recorded the day before her death; it would be her final entry.

ALMA JOSEPHINE MAXWELL

August 13, 1990

"I did manage to write a third volume of 'Deer Island in Autumn,' entitled 'Deer Island in Autumn (the untold story) The Addison Family: Reconstruction to 1924.' The text was exhaustive and complete but as yet has not been published. I am planning to examine my notes and try to consolidate the most interesting events into a manageable size for future publication. The Lord's will be done. Amen.

"My family recently celebrated the one-hundred-fiftieth anniversary of the founding of Deer Island. Sadly, the last of the island residents left for the mainland ten years ago. All that remains on the island is the family cemetery. The buildings have long been destroyed by violent storms and neglect.

"Although Uncle Justin, Aunt Sarah, Felix and Gustave, Mama and Papa, Lee, Brad, and my little sister Alma, have all been laid to rest in the family cemetery, they remain alive in the hearts and minds of everyone who has had the privilege to either read, or hear the stories of 'The Life and Times of the Addison Family.'

"This entry will complete the third volume of my family's recorded history—the third comprehensive diary. I intend to give these three books to my sister Alma's grand daughter who is now twenty-five years old. I hope these records will inspire her to carry on what my great-grandmother started in 1836.

"Now, at eighty-four years old, I find little left to write. It is time for another to put pen to paper so others can enjoy the contents as I have for these many years. I followed my course to the end. Like my great-grandmother, I have written over two thousand pages. My Great-aunt Elizabeth did not record near as much as I did. When Uncle Justin died, he left his mother's diary to me.

"Rhapsodies were prompted by the discovery and subsequent digestion of the food for thought provided by the steady menu of episodes recorded and bequeathed to me by Josephine and Elizabeth Addison. Josephine, the first Addison matron to arrive in America, painted vivid pictures of life and living during a bygone era spanning a period of seventy years. From uncertain beginnings, to the achievement of goals and the fulfillment of dreams, she and Aunt Elizabeth established a family legacy. Their record of events along the way, present us with a tangible reality—albeit through the mind's eye of the sentimental—which produces a perpetual bond between the living and their ancestors, for posterity's sake.

"Now I must bid you good night as a cascade of memories compete for my attention. As I lay me down to rest, I pray someone will be watching, for I know not whether this will be the end of me. God willing, I pray not. Amen."

"My great aunt, Nora Addison, was buried near her favorite princess, "The Princess of Chacahoula," Mademoiselle Pauline Longere, at the family cemetery on Deer Island; may she rest in peace. Her extensive record of the Addison family 1916–1990 remains the family's most prized possession. If a fourth diary is to be set forth, I have been charged by Nora to facilitate it."

—Alma Josephine Maxwell

The end of volume two.

Introduction to
Deer Island in Autumn
Volume Three
Deer Island in Autumn
The Addison Family:
Reconstruction
to 1924

January 1, 1924

Volume Two: "Carrying on the Legacy" ended after the Addisons from Bayou Du Large visited with family members living on Deer Island in autumn of 1921. Over the past three years, I have learned much from my great- grandmother's second diary, as well as the diary left to me by my Great-aunt Elizabeth. Taking up where the first diary ended, I recorded interesting passages from the records of my two ancestral matriarchs to form a third Volume in the Deer Island trilogy. The story continues to share the lives of my family members on the island from Reconstruction (the aftermath of the Civil War in Louisiana) through 1905, when Josephine was laid to rest in the family cemetery there, and continuing to the present year, autumn of 1924. I believe that the contents of this third book will be every bit as enjoyable to the reader as they have been in the first two books. I invite you to experience the Life and Times of the Addison family one more time.

—Nora Addison

About the Author

I was born in Baton Rouge, Louisiana in 1949; when I was three we moved to Houma, Louisiana, a city located in Terrebonne Parish. I attended parochial school for twelve years under the tutelage of the

Carmelite nuns and Brothers of the Sacred Heart; strict discipline and high academic standards ensured that I would receive a good education.

I attended college at Louisiana Polytechnic Institute in Ruston, Louisiana, for two years; I made it through my freshman year okay, but lack of discipline caused me to flounder during my sophomore year. My GPA dropped significantly; that marked the end of my college career.

After college, much like Forest Gump says, "I've worn lots of shoes."

My wife Patricia and I reside in a house not far from my mother's ancestral home, on the lower end of Bayou Du Large. My mother was a descendant of the founder of the village of Theriot (my community) Michel Eloi Theriot; he established a settlement here in the mid-1800s. My wife's mother was a descendant of those who originally settled Deer Island around this same time period; many of their family members are buried in the cemetery there. I found the roots to these two beginnings very fascinating, so I decided to write "Deer Island in Autumn," which has elements of both.

CPSIA information can be obtained at www.ICGtesting.com
Printed in the USA
BVOW05s1656180716

455934BV00068B/432/P